GUTTERIDGE / *Lily's Story*

Lily's Story

A Novel

By
Don Gutteridge

Note for Librarians: A cataloguing record for this book is available from Library and Archives Canada at www.collectionscanada.ca/amicus/index-e.html

ISBN – 978-1-77084-388-2 (Pbk.)
ISBN - 978-0-9916798-9-8 (ebook)

Printed in Canada
♻
on recycled paper
FIRST CHOICE BOOKS

firstchoicebooks.ca
Victoria, BC

10 9 8 7 6 5 4 3

For my Aunt and Uncle
Betty and Bob Gutteridge
of Point Edward

In loving memory

BOOK ONE

St. Vitus Dance

1

Moore Township, 1845

Something stirred in the darkness ahead. It made no sound, as yet. But it was present, and alive, or coming alive: she always knew. She did. The breath from a fawn's cough could tease her skin – like this ripple of shaded wind against her cheek – long before her ear caught the sound and recorded it. Lil was glad once again to be in the comfort of the trees' canopy. It was cozy here, like the cabin with Papa's fire blazing out of icy logs, when Mama was not in her bed. Lil wasn't afraid of the dark. Mama sometimes shivered in the dark at night, the rare night when Papa "was off" and Lil was beckoned to press her thighs and chest and swan's belly against her mother's clenched form. She dreamt she was a moth spinning a cocoon of silver words about them both, full of charms to drive the gremlins from Mama's eyes, while outside, heard only by her, the snow sang to the wind and no one in the world was lonely.

It was never lonesome in the bush. Here things bulged and endured in the dappled undergrowth – ferns and worts and fungi and mosses, and, in the few random spots freckled by sun, surprised violets. They made their voices known. Lil could hear them already though she was moving with short quick steps towards the deepest cove of the back bush, the place forbidden by Mama, the home of the almost-sound that vibrated the air with furred bat-wings and no eyes. She stopped. Beyond, a branch stretched, umbilical and biding. Ferns sighed in currents only they could feel. A thrush untangled his song: pastel and longing. Lil set her face against the tiny drafts of air raised by her own body-heat. A snakeskin combed the grass; she heard a birdwing flex and fold, a deermouse scuttle and freeze, a caterpillar dissecting a resistant leaf. The sound had stopped.

You stay away from the Indians, you hear? Mama said so every day. Mama hated Indians. They were the cause of everything. They took whiskey; they went crazy and hurt people; they never did a lick of work; they went off hunting god-knows-where in the back bush, taking good men with them, so's the trees didn't get cut. And them squaws, Mama would say in a special voice, her eyes getting fiery and pure, why they

3

– she'd look at Lil and stop, and the passion would ebb from her face. Well, they're wicked, Lil, they take whiskey and – dance and do bad things with men... Lil would be trembling with anticipation at seeing her mother's pale flesh puff out with some kind of necessity beyond self-preservation. Lil wanted to ask, not about the bad things, but about the dancing. Though she never did. It was after one of these bouts that Mama often took to her bed.

But Lil knew where they stayed. Many nights, curled in the straw of her loft, she heard the drumbeats come across the tree-tops from miles away and settle into their clearing as if they had been aimed there. They were not like her heartbeat, back and forth, nor like the sprightly songs Mama sang in her other language when she was "feeling better" and sitting before her spinning wheel in the bright sun of the garden she had helped to clear. It was a pounding, repetitive music that set her heart ajar, that made her dream of strange creatures who preferred breathing in the dark, that made her long to know what words would be sung to such cadence, what dances would find their feet in such grooved frenzies. She wanted to see these women, how they moved in the firelight that twisted above the black roof of the bush, what their eyes did when they danced in their smoky, burnished, mosquito-driven dark.

An axe rang against a tree-trunk, clear as a church bell. *Papa's back*. Lil recognized the signature of his chopping: two vicious slashes, the second slightly more terrifying than the first, followed by two diminished, tentative 'chunks'. Maybe Mama would hear it and leave her bed. He was in the North Field. That was good. He'd only "gone off" as far as the Frenchman's. Sometimes one of the Frenchman's boys came back with him and helped Papa. Lil hated them, all three of them. They watched her all the time with the edges of their eyes. And Papa would shout at her to go away. Sometimes though he brought Thérese back. Lil liked Thérese though she talked crooked and had an ugly belly that poked out in front of her like an old melon. Thérese cooked soup, made bread in the mornings, and laughed. She was happy.

Thérese showed Lil how to skip. She put a small tin instrument to her mouth and made music. She laughed when Lil hopped and jigged, and then Papa came along and took her by the hand and swung her about in the midst of the music, and laughed from the back of his throat. "Well, my Lady Fair Child, so you can dance, eh? We'll have to take her down to London to see the Queen, won't we, Thérese?"

Thérese got pains in her ugly belly, though, and had to go back to the Frenchman's.

"She's dead," Papa said, that evening, standing in the open doorway, his hands helpless. "The babe, too."

"All for the best," Mama whispered from her bed. "Whose was it?"

"Luc's I guess. The eldest." Papa did not see Lil at his knee peering up with the question "What's dead?" on her lips. "*God damn them all, may they rot in hell*," he hissed in a voice that came from nowhere inside him Lil had ever known.

Papa was back. Every day he swore he would "kill that damn Frenchman", but all the same he went over there. Though Mama didn't mind too much. It was the Indians she hated. Whenever Papa "went off" in that direction – through the East Field to the back bush, where Lil was at this very second – Mama got mean. So Lil would look for berries along the edges of the cleared area, and when she got back Mama would be in her own bed in the curtained-off area to the right of the fire, her body folded on the straw pallet, rigid as a pin.

For a moment Lil thought she ought to go over to the North Field. The place where the Indians were was forbidden. The strange sound she thought she had heard had stopped, or never been. Papa might be in a good mood. She listened carefully to the desperate repetition of Papa's axe against the grained flesh of the tree. He was at one of the hardwoods again. She would not go. Though she wanted so to dance for him again, the way Thérèse had showed her, to have Papa laugh and say "Lady Fair Child, may I have the pleasure of the next dance?"

Suddenly the axe-blows ceased. Lil held her breath. Then she heard the thunderous, sustained shriek of disbelief and betrayal as the two-hundred-year-old walnut came crashing through the forest to stun the ground with its abrupt goodbye. Lil sat for a while in the sun-lit beaver meadow below the creek and listened to the tree's dying reverberate through the earth.

She hated him. He trapped rabbits in the east corner, their strung-up bodies stiffened by the night air, the warmest morning could not thaw them. He nailed the head of the dear-with-no-eyes above the fireplace, where it stared down at them pretending to see like Old Samuels, the blind Indian who sometimes sat in the sun in the dooryard, telling stories to the Frenchman's boys and twitching his white head about from person to person as if it could perceive the smiles and nods of an audience. She hated Papa. He made Thérèse "be dead".

Lil laughed. A butterfly, yellow as honey, was tilting the breeze on one wing, then the other, before a thistle rescued it. When Lil stretched out a finger, it gratefully accepted the offer. She could feel the wind's ripple flow down the golden sails of its wings, shudder through its stiff rigging and hum against her fingertips. Then she saw its ugly mouth-parts, scissoring and askew. A hand pounced. The sails exploded. She was about to regret something when the premonition of the sound came again. From the grove just beyond the clearing. This time she felt it. She *knew*.

There were two sounds. The strongest was a tearing, pent-up sensation she felt somewhere in her groin, forcing its way upwards towards her throat, an inchoate cry of pain in which anguish and joy were equally mixed, as if something precious was fighting to be liberated and lost, welcomed and regretted. Lil's stomach twisted with the urgency of her need as she waited for its full articulation to reach her ears. At which point she felt the presence of the second voice, in her lungs and swelling through her heart and up behind her eyes where she often measured the echoes of Thérèse's music – a cry not nearly so loud or anxious as the first but somehow stronger, not yet formed but ripe with confidence and possibility.

Lil's bones rang like tuning forks. Something alive and dangerous lay in the forbidden place where the Indians dwelt, where they drummed and sang. Tremors of pure fright shook her body. She was scared; she was alive; she wanted to dance; she wanted to know where Thérèse lived. She stepped into the gloom ahead. She saw before she heard.

The tableau that materialized in front of her could not have lasted more than a few seconds, yet was vivid and detailed, illuminated as it was by that curious half-glow which thrives in the underbrush, relishes its kinship with the mushroom dark, and is more defining to the eye in tune with its motives than the most glaring sunlight.

Though the images came almost as one, Lil picked out the doe's eyes, fear afloat in them; a dishevelled mane of black hair electric around them; then a mouth, attached to nothing but the tongue whose cry it seemed desperate to swallow. The shriek from that disembodied instrument struck the pine-boles behind Lil at the very instant she felt its incredible agony burst up through her own throat and enter the air. In the increasing light, Lil saw the stems of a woman's breasts aimed upward and knew she was witnessing someone or something "going dead". Her instinct now was to run, to save something precious and violable inside her from annihilation. Instead, she watched the woman's hands thrash, independent of each other, against the unresisting air, and waited for the next, the final, cry.

Then Lil saw that the eyes, hair, tongue, hands and nipples were connected to a single body, were even curiously coordinated to some mysterious purpose. The bronze skin, utterly vulnerable to the air, told her she was seeing, for the first time, an Indian woman in her own place. She was lying on her back, braced now on her elbows, her legs flung or pulled wide, in a sort of protected hollow in the brush that looked as if it had been prepared for this chance event in some way. Even before the next wrenching cry came out of her, Lil herself heard the second voice and gazed, in horror and delight, as a tiny head, like a water-logged walnut, battered against the woman's opening, timing its own assaults with the latter's convulsive flinching, till at last its gleaming skull burst forth in a halo of blood whose petals spun at Lil's feet, whose medallions dripped from the slow leafage. Behind the blood-slick head a brown vermiform trunk thrashed and strove, till its dormant extremities kicked clear. As the babe slid onto the carpet of the forest floor, the little head twisted sunward, then turned to reveal a miniature face with eyes that looked straight at Lil.

They were as black as Thérese's.

2

1

Mama was in her bed again. She went there quite a lot now. Yesterday she had smiled at Lil and said, "Well, little one, it's time we went down to see this North Field of ours." Pale and tine, occasionally clutching at Lil's shoulder, she picked her way past the charred stumps of last year's slash-and-burn, careful to avoid the ripening wheat of the older East Field, and coming at last out of the shadow of the huge pines to a point where she could see, at a glance, the five acres of cleared land to be called forever after the North Field. The odour of ash and singed wood and languishing smoke struck their nostrils. Mama breathed it in, like an elixir. In the distance Papa turned, stood still, and then waved. "Pick some raspberries this side of the creek," she said to Lil. "I'll make a pie."

There was no pie. The berries had shrivelled a month before and Mama had one of her coughing spells. Papa as usual took some day-old soup in to her. Lil listened, as she always did, to catch the slightest whisper of a word between them. There was none. Though Papa stayed a long while, until the haze of evening grew like a moss along the sills and Mama's breathing became regular again, heavy with exhaustion.

This morning he "went off". "Gotta have meat for that soup," he used to say to Lil, taking down his gun and putting on the buckskin he'd gotten from Old Samuels. Lately he just went off. "Probably," Mama said, her voice shaking with effort, "with that Acorn fellow." Acorn, one of Old Samuels' nephews, never came near the house, sometimes standing for hours (Lil had seen him at the edge of the East Field) just waiting, before slipping back into the bush.

But Lil was 'a help' now. She was seven. If Papa set the pot on the irons and started the fire, she could cut the turnips up and toss them in, and stir the soup with its tiny rabbit bones disconnected and afloat. Papa had made a lovely stone oven at one side of the fireplace, and Lil would take the sourdough prepared by Maman LaRouche, and doing exactly what she had been shown, make bread for Papa's supper. Next spring Papa was going to get them a pig. Already he'd built a pen for it against the east wall.

"Plenty pigs in the bush," Old Samuels would chortle. "Only White Mens builds him a house and grows him food." Then he would shake his head in mock bewilderment at the folly of his hosts. Nonetheless, he would wait with the patience of his seventy-odd years till Lil or Papa reached into the stew and offered a respectfully large morsel. Mama didn't like the way Old Samuels came into the main room without announcing his arrival. Sometimes Lil would be working over the fire, humming one of Mama's songs, and when she turned, Old Samuels would be no more than five feet behind her, the black pennies where his eyes should have been giving nothing away. "You gonna be a good cook, like the Frenchman's woman."

Occasionally he would stay all day, sitting on his knees to the left of the fire where he could detect any cool draft from the curtained doorway, saying nothing. Sometimes he would talk to Lil, raising his thin voice just enough to include Mama, willing or no, in the one-way conversation. Old Samuels told long stories, most of which began, "Wasn't like that here in the olden days" and ended "and that's the truth, and I know 'cause I seen it, I seen it before these eyes of mine withered up on me." When Papa made the slightest demurral, he'd say, "Besides, blind men don't lie."

"He's got the manners of a ghost," Mama used to say, but not once did she ask him to leave.

"How does he get here if he can't see?" Lil asked Papa. "He says he's lived here so long he knows every bush and beetle in the territory," Papa said. And it seemed to be true, as Lil would watch him enter their land at the far corner of the East Field just past the Brown Creek (that went, they said, all the way to the Indian camp in the back bush), and then thread his way through the maze of stumps and ash-heaps, never once stepping on the haphazard swirls of wheat between.

"Redmen smells his way in the bush," he told Lil. "Don't need eyes. Redmen sniffs the air currents like the white-tail." He demonstrated. "Raspberry jam," he announced, "from the Frenchman's woman."

"Yes," said Lil, duly amazed.

Last week, though, after the Frenchman and his three eldest – Luc, Jean-Pierre and Anatole – had finished piling and burning the last log in the North Field, and after some firewater had been consumed by all, Lil saw Old Samuels weave his way towards the back bush, teetering and righting himself as he went. At the corner of the East Field, he paused. The sounds of the men parting in the other direction diminished and died. Old Samuels appeared to look towards the east. Then a small brown boy slipped from the bush and touched Old Samuels' hand. He shook it off. The boy turned. Old Samuels followed, exactly two paces behind until the woods reclaimed them.

"Your Papa got a nose for the wind," he said whenever Papa went off with Acorn or Sounder. "Hunting's no good here now. Not like the olden days. They go all the way to Chatham, I guess, to find any bucks this time of year."

Lil wanted to know more about Chatham but Mama began coughing and she had to take the soup in. When she got back, she saw it was no use: Old Samuels had lit up his pipe, stuffed with aromatic tobacco. "White Mens' tobacco no good," he would say. "Not like the olden days." But when he got smoking, he didn't talk.

Lil may not have known much about Chatham yet, or any other town – Port Sarnia, Sandwich, London – but she was seven and she had travelled some miles into the bush with Papa when he trapped in the winter; she had seen the other farms along the line north of them. She could read the blazes on the trees and find the faint paths through the bush that would open suddenly upon sun-lit beaver meadows, some of them as big as the East Field. Beyond the Millar's farm she had seen the 'road' that was said to meander all the way to Port Sarnia, and from there to London hundreds and thousands of miles to the east. She knew too that a great river swept by them no more than half-a-day's walk from their own doorstep.

Someday Papa would take her with him.

"Yes, little-blond-one-with-doe's-feet, your Papa he likes Chatham very much. Not like it used to be. I was there a long time ago when the Yankees come across and my brothers all died in the field there by the antler river. All changed now. Full of niggers now."

Lil knew it was futile to ask but did so anyway. Old Samuels surprised her. "Black men", he said. "Come from where the Yankees live. Niggers is afraid of the Yankees. The Yankees takes their land, their houses, their women. They run away, a thousand days journey, all the way to Chatham."

"Do the white people there help them?"

Old Samuels paused. Then he began to laugh. Since he was blind, Lil was used to watching, not his blank eyes, but his mouth and nostrils. The laughter started with a trembling of the latter, spread to the wrinkling corners of the lips and shook without mercy the flaps of flesh below his chin.

Lil waited.

"Niggers run away. Ojibwa and Attawandaron just stands around and wonders what'll happen next. Once we get some place, we don't like to leave."

Lil wasn't sure what he meant, but she found herself laughing along with him. "Make me laugh, little one. Good for the rheumatism."

2

Lil was not prepared for the Frenchman's place. The customary procedure for the homesteader in the new territory was to clear room for his cabin near the front 'line' of the property, then proceed in a systematic fashion to open up 'fields' to the north, east and south. When at last Lil was allowed to accompany Anatole back to his place to fetch some garden greens for Mama, she was surprised to find their house somewhere near the centre of several haphazard 'fields' of no determinate shape. Several nut trees had been left standing, in random wonder, amidst the fledgling wheat and enthusiastic if undisciplined vegetable garden. All trees were to be cut down: that was the unspoken code here, one of the unarticulated motives that drove the homesteaders to the mutual service and support they required to survive.

The Frenchman's cabin had begun life as a log structure of the typical rectangular design, but time, weather, whim and exigency had added their intentions to the original. Rooms of planks and split logs – packed with mortar and straw – jutted out, sagged, or lay half-built and dazed where the Frenchman's imagination or optimism had failed him. No windows looked in or out. Against the east wall, roughly speaking, a lean-to of sorts had been erected wherein the ox-team of Bessie and Bert found little comfort at day's end among the resident pigs and visiting barred rocks.

Much of the cooking and indeed family life took place outside the murky interior of the homestead. LaRouche, using the trade he had abandoned for farming after the war against the States, had built a fine stone oven-and-fireplace protected from the rain by a canvas affair rigged out of army tenting, deer-hides and one old sail salvaged, according to its owner, from the Battle of Put-In Bay. Here Madame LaRouche – referred to as Maman by her brood of eleven and as Fluffy by her husband in undisguised admiration for her three hundred pounds of flesh, sturdiness and good health – presided over hearth and oven with a temper that alternated between wheezing cheeriness and tongue-biting pique.

Lil could not for an instant take her eyes off Maman. She watched in awe as Maman punched and tormented the sourdough as if she were beating the belly of an obdurate husband, her great breasts rolling and protesting beneath the homespun smock she wore night and day. Lil shuddered whenever Maman's hand, operating on its own, would shoot out or back to stun the cheek of anyone who ventured too close or dared too much. Later, she would see that same child comfortably housed in Maman's lap, drifting into secure sleep.

In return for offerings from Papa's hunting expeditions, Maman LaRouche made much of the staple food during the times when Mama was in bed. Preserves, jams, greens from her garden in season, salt-port and 'bully beef' from the venison Papa brought home. While the Frenchman himself did not hunt – having given up guns following his service – he usually went along on the shorter excursions to supply encouragement, unsolicited advice, and refreshments from his still in the bush. The older boys did not share their father's pacifism.

Often, then, Lil was left alone with Maman and her youngest children, all boys except for Madeleine who was just six and now the only girl. Maman soon took Lil "under wing". She was teaching her to cook and spin and sew – all of which Lil had a talent for though not as much persistence and application as Maman would have hoped. But then Lil was not French. Often Maman sang while she worked – wistful melodies in her Norman tongue that seemed more sweetly fragile because they sailed towards serenity out of such an unnavigable bulk. Although Maman did not tell conventional stories, she had opinions on everyone and everything.

"Those Millars," she said with the usual hushed stridency reserved for such remarks, "they're gonna be trouble, wait and see. Scotch, the both of 'em. Give me the Irish any day, even your kind."

For good measure, Lil smiled back.

"An' you keep away from that Ol' Sams," she said daily in another more sinister tone. "That carrot of his may be shrivelled up but it's still got juice in the root. You mind them hands too, little chickadee; believe-you-me, Maman knows all about them kind of paws."

Lil of course paid little direct attention to any of this, but she nodded and queried and did all she could to get Maman going.

"A pretty, fair thing like you oughta get away from this place as soon as you can. That's Maman's advice. Go to the city. Go to Chatham or Sandwich. They're real nice places. Lots of people."

Then Maman would be launched on a description of her brief but dazzling courtship with Corporal LaRouche of Malden, of the clapboard house they lived in, the dances they went to, the clothes they wore, the times they had before the Yankees came and the world collapsed. "I said to Gaston, I'll go with you to the bush, I'll have your babies, I'll clean your shit, but I'm not about to die out there without a priest at my side, prayin' in my ear and rubbin' my head with holy oil an' smoothin' my slide into Heaven."

Lil swallowed her gooseberry tart.

"I told him I don't care if he has to hop to Sandwich on one snowshoe in a blizzard – a promise is a promise." Maman surprised the pastry dough with a sucker-punch to the gut.

"What's a priest?" Lil ventured, at last.

A priest, it turned out, was a kind of preacher. Papa didn't like preachers. Once, last summer, when Lil had been on her own in the withered garden near the 'line', watching the black ants ooze in and out of their honeycomb, she heard the crack of a twig along the Frenchman's path. She looked up in time to see before her a large florid man dressed all in black. He was still puffing from the exertion of his trek through the bush. His blue eyes bounced like agates in his puffed face before they came to temporary rest on the rims of his cheeks. His smile was as broad as his belly.

"Good afternoon, little elf." The sound boomed, echoed, receded.

Lil stared.

"I am a man of God."

"I've come all the way from London."

"Just to see you."

"Do you know who God is, little one?"

"Would you kindly tell your pa that the Methodist man is here."

Lil did not have to tell Papa. He had heard, even in the North Field, and had come striding past the cabin towards them. Lil knew enough to run. She heard Papa's voice raised the way it was when he cursed Bert and Bessie or a stubborn ironwood. His axe flashed in the sun. However, the preacher was already scuttling like a duck into the safety of the Lord's bush.

Lil wanted to ask Papa who God was.

Mama did not hate preachers as much. Sometimes, after being in her bed for several days, when some colour had come back into her eyes, she would reach under the little bed Papa had built especially for her and pull out the large, dark book she called the Bible. Lil watched, poised and alert, as Mama's fingers made the pages, thin as bee's wings, flutter and settle.

"There are the words God gave us."

"Read me some of them, Mama."

"Not today, my sweet. Mama's just a bit too tired. Tomorrow."

"Promise?"

"Promise."

Then, seeing the look in her child's eye, she would close the book and in a reedy quaver begin to sing the spinning song, which reached Lil's ear in this form:

> Hi diddle dum, hi diddle dare-o
> Hi diddly iddly, hi diddle air-o
> Hi diddle diddly, hi diddle um

At first Lil would hum along, then gradually pick up the exotic, tongue-tumbling syllables one at a time, like stitches, giving to them whatever meaning the emotions of the moment allowed.

3

Papa was not back. Lil had been able to find enough small logs to keep the fire alive overnight though it was not banked properly, the cabin became suffocating in the late August heat. She made some tea, warmed up the soup and went into Mama's room.

Mama spilled most of the soup. Lil held her hand to guide the tin cup to her lips. Mama closed her eyes.

The morning outside was beautiful. The sun, sensing the loss of its powers, steeped the windless air over the fields. High in the pines and arching elms, cicadas announced noon.

When Lil came in, Mama was sitting in the rocker Papa had fashioned for her out of cedar. She gave Lil a wan smile and said: "Would you help Mama with her hair?" As her mother watched her in tender, wordless encouragement, Lil managed to heat a kettle of water and get it foaming with some of the soap Maman said she bought off the pedlar Papa had chased away. Mama leaned over, her brow at rest on the arm of the chair, her long hair caressing the floor. For a moment she seemed to be asleep, but when Lil began to pour the soft warm water over her, letting it fall gently back into the kettle, she murmured and her hand reached out to squeeze some part of Lil's. How beautiful Mama's hair was, its former glory regained as she lay back in the rocker and let the afternoon sun kindle and hearten and scatter praise where it would, and Lil took her mother's bone-brush and stroked and stroked, and Mama's eyes brightened before entering some dream where beauty was still possible. A long time after she said, "Let's have tea, little one."

Lil, excited, got out the china pot and the two tiny tea-cups with their matching blue saucers, stirred the slumbering fire and prepared tea just as she remembered Mama doing it. She even fetched the last of the little blueberry cakes Maman LaRouche had given them. But best of all Mama began to talk – in brief whispered phrases, the pauses like hours or seasons between them.

"The place we come from, your Papa and me, is a long ways across the biggest ocean in the world. We were married there. We were very happy. But it wasn't a happy land. The priests and the preachers didn't get along. The crops failed, many times. We were hungry. Papa got angry and decided to leave. You were already tucked inside my belly. We went on a sailing ship three times bigger than this house. We packed everything we owned into two trunks they put in the hold."

The odour of hot ash and decay hung in the humid air outside the cabin and in the room itself, as if a whole summer's burning was spreading like fungus in the thickening heat. Blue-bottles buzzed, unappeased.

"I figured we'd die on that ship, but we didn't. We made it because we loved one another, we wanted happiness or death. Then after we got onto another ship, a smaller one, we sailed along the big lake just south of here, and a storm struck us down. The boat come apart in the waves near the long point. Dozens of people drowned. Papa and me were in the only boat that got to shore. We lost everything but our lives. Even the tools Papa bought for us in Quebec."

The room darkened steeply, the sun was eclipsed by the high horizon of the trees. Gently Lil unwound Mama's fingers from the blue tea-cup, hearing her deep, anxious breathing. How Lil wished that Old Samuels would slip in unnoticed, and be in the mood to tell a long story. Mama could just rock there and listen and smile.

"Before the White Mens come, this was a magic place," he would say, that ambiguous twinkle ever at the edge of his voice. "The gods of the Mohawk and the gods of the Huron fought their great battles here among the spirits of my own people, the Attawandaron. In them days, the bears were as big as hickory trees." Pause: for the power of that image to take root. "When the foreign gods left, they took all of the Hurons and most of my brothers with them. But the souls of my ancestors stayed right here where they been for a thousand generations. Attawandaron don't run; they hang round, like Old Samuels and Sounder and Acorn. Even when them silly Ojibwa sells this land they don't own to the White Mens, Old Samuels just laugh. And smoke his pipe – with White Mens' tobacco stolen from our gods who gave it as a gift to all men."

Old Samuels did not come. The smoke of early evening drifted in, adhered. Lil decided to let the fire go out; the air was already too warm. Leaving her mother asleep in the chair, Lil started up the ladder to the loft.

"Lil. Don't go up. Sleep with Mama tonight."

Barely able to contain her excitement, Lil scrambled back down and then helped her mother towards her curtained-off cubicle. Her arms were thin as willow, the flesh draped over the bones. Lil slipped out of her cotton dress and under the sheet with Mama.

"Open this, please," Mama said. In her hand, in the fading light, Lil could see a small box made of aromatic, in-laid woods. It was the most beautiful object she had ever seen. With her nimble fingers she tripped the slim gold latch, and the lid opened.

Mama held out a cameo pendant with a silver chain that shimmered in the gloaming. Fortuitously the last log in the fire burst into brief and final flame, and Lil was able to see that there was, beneath the cameo's glaze, the merest sketch of a woman's head: two or three quick but telling strokes. With a start, Lil recognized her own eyes.

"Lily. Your grandmother."

Mama's eyes filled with tears. She reached into the box again. "I saved this, out of the storm." She held up a gold chain on the end of which dangled a slender cross no more than half an inch long. Instinctively Lil leaned forward and the crucifix settled on her throat as if it had always expected to be there.

Then Mama fell back against her pillow. She crooked her left arm and Lil, as she had seen Maman LaRouche's little ones do so often, slid into the embrace and held herself there as if the world would leave if she blinked.

Lil had left the curtain open. In the dark, the embers of the fire glowed, blood-red, and succumbed without a murmur. The night-air, remembering that it was almost September, turned as chill and sharp as the sabre-shaped moon guiding it. The season's heat and smoke and ash rose with it: distilled, crystalline, translated.

When Lil woke, the sun was already above the tree-line, sifting through the east window and toasting her feet. She had been kept warm throughout the night by the final, fierce heat of her mother's will. Beside her now, that flesh lay as cold as the ice that clenched the streams of mid-December.

3

1

Sometimes Lil tried hard to remember Mama exactly as she was before she took to her bed and left. It wasn't easy. In summer, the wheat in the East Field turned golden brown under the lazing sun. The LaRouche boys came over to help them cut and thresh it. Lil sat in the shade of the big maple near the house and let the kernels whisper through her fingers like Indian beads. Papa smiled. Luc and Jean-Pierre watched her as they worked. When she turned her own gaze back on them, they looked away sharply. Lil felt something fresh, unruly and alien surge up through her chest: she wondered at it but gave it no name or image. In the fall, the trees that were not pine gave forth their second bloom – brighter and more prodigal than the green gifts of April: like a rush of blood against the sudden foreboding of cold. The leaves swam – dizzying, breathless – and drowned in pools of their own composition. For a while even the bush relented a little: the eye could meander now, reconnoitre, improvise, surprise the sun here and there in hollows of snow, loiter among shape and shadow where the winter light married the dark configurations of trees. In the winter you breathed out more than in.

They put Mama's body – carefully wrapped in a white sheet of the softest cotton from Maman LaRouche's cedar chest – in the ground on a slight knoll where the East Field was about to join the North one. Jean-Pierre and Anatole dug the hole; Maman sent everyone out of the house while she dressed Mama's body. Papa and the French-man and Luc sat in the lean-to shed sipping from a jug, murmuring occasionally in low voices, but mostly staring straight ahead into the bush. Once Lil thought she heard her mother's name spoken – 'Kathleen' – like a sort of unintentional exhalation of breath, but she wasn't sure. The best part was when Maman surrounded her with her generous arms, clapped her close and fast, and crooned some soothing French lament just for her. After a time she was able to cry.

Old Samuels came with his nephews Sounder and Acorn and, to Lil's astonishment, a tribe of wives and children who stayed well behind them with heads down, though still resplendent in their skins, secret furs and black-and white featherage. The

Millars and even the two new families from the North section came also. Lil had never before seen so many people gathered in one place. She held Papa's hand tightly, and he squeezed back, hurting her, gently. Her heart reared through its sadness.

Mr. Millar stepped forward, opened a black book, read some words from it that the wind caught with ease and carried off. Maman suddenly burst into sobs which she made no effort to staunch. They rose and fell drowning the Bible words of Mr. Millar, vanquishing the wind-sound in the pines, and Lil knew even then that Maman LaRouche was weeping for them all.

Old Samuels began to hum from somewhere deep in his body, letting the music of it find its own course and pace. The gravesite became quiet; the wind shrank. Old Samuels' mouth opened and the music of his lamentation found syllables and eerie repetitions that might have been words though no one present had ever heard the language they had borrowed. His blank eyes like death's pennies began to shuffle in time with the rising/falling cadences of his song. He turned his ancient face upward, and the syllables rolled in his mouth as in water, muted and infinitely mysterious. His whole frame tensed, expectant, as if he had been asking some question over and over. He turned and looked towards Papa and Lil. He smiled as only a man without eyes can smile: with every feature of his face. In English he said: "The gods are listening; that is all we can ask."

Many times, of course, during that long winter when Papa was away trapping or hunting, Lil asked who God was, thinking of Mama lying unattended in that cold oven under the snow. But Maman used the question to get herself started on her obsessive musing about priests and the promises of faithless husbands. Papa, who was always too tired to talk after his journeys, would just grunt in an almost hurting tone, "Go ask that Millar, he knows all about everythin'." Then he would be off.

"Off to Chatham," Old Samuels would shake his head sadly. "Plenty bad people in Chatham, for sure." Or when Papa sometimes pointedly picked up his gun, leather pouches and haversack, and said to Lil, "Better tell them lady deer to stay back in the bush, darlin', your Papa's comin'," Old Samuels would whisper after him, "Your Papa's gone to Chatham to hunt *bucks*," and chortle.

On the subject of God, though, Old Samuels was eager and loquacious. "White Mens has the silliest ideas about the gods. It takes us Indians a day to stop laughin' when we hear about it. For sure. First they say there's only one god. If that's true then the white god must fight with himself. Anybody with ears and eyes" (he'd always pause here for a tiny ironic smile) "knows about the god in the thundercloud whose voice speaks blackly to the quiet gods in the lake and the summer creeks. And the god of the gentle winds has no love for the god of the blizzard that tears the trees in half and buries the earth. Anybody knows there's the good gods and the wicked gods, the guardian spirits and the demons that lurk everywhere. We must listen to the good gods to keep them on our side: they will help those who listen for them. Remember that, little one. But we must also help the gods. Sometimes the demons are too strong and the good gods go into hiding. That is a sad time for the world."

When Lil mentioned that Maman LaRouche told her that Mama was in heaven, Old Samuels chuckled bitterly. "That woman talks silliness. I tell her I come to her funeral and dance on her grave, and she throws a pot at me. Me, a man with no eyes. The gods made her miss, for sure."

"What about heaven?"

"Your Mama, who was the dearest White Womens in this world, is not in heaven, little dancing one. That Millar, he tells me heaven is a pretty house with beads and ornaments on it up over the moon and the stars. That is silliness. The good gods would not build their house up there, they live here in the green world and in the stars themselves. Your Mama's body is under the earth, but the guardian gods have taken her spirit with them. Wherever they are, she will be also. If your eyes and ears are listening to the good gods, you will hear her voice among theirs. In that way she will always be near you. You must not listen to the silliness of that Millar."

"How do you know the good gods'll speak to me?"

"Ah, that is easy. Because you sing their song, and you dance, and you are happy even when you're sad. And you make Old Samuels happy."

"I can't dance," said Lil.

Old Samuels paused to light his pipe. Lil thought he was finished talking for the day. "But you can. I hear dancing in your voice; every day."

Lil did not like to be teased. For a while she sulked and hated Old Samuels. She waited in the woods by the gravesite for a demon to whisper something outrageous to her. The old man took no notice. He stayed his usual time and without saying goodbye made his way across the field towards his great-nephew at the edge of the bush.

One night, alone in her loft, Lil woke to the harvest moon igniting the straw at her feet. She caught herself humming:

> Hi diddle dum, hi diddle dare-o
> Hi diddly iddly, hi diddle air-o
> Hi diddle diddly, hi diddle um

Soon she felt the presence of a second part in flawless harmony with her own. She stopped. Her mother's voice continued, as elfin and crystal as the moon's.

Lil was often alone. But then she had been as long as she could remember, even when Mama was here. She was not lonely though. She could sit beside her father while he chopped wood or cursed after Bert and Bessie – for hours without the need to speak. Often she hummed, sang songs or made them up as she watched whatever rhythmic, repetitive scenes were being played out before her. By herself in the fields she would lie on her back and dream the clouds into shapes of her wishing, or follow, minute by minute, the extravagant exit of the sun as it boiled and dissolved or tossed itself on the antlered tree-line and uttered its blood. The few acres that demarcated her world pulsated with sights, sounds, smells; with minute dramas of birth, struggle and demise. And now there were the guardians and the demons to listen for, the good gods in their hiding to be touched and revealed.

"This bush don't go on forever," Old Samuels said that spring, sensing restlessness in the girl. "Half a day's walk towards the sunset and you'll come to the River of Light that's been flowin' there since the last time the wild gods stirred the earth like a soup and started it over again. Two days walk towards the North Star where that river begins and there's the Freshwater Sea of the Hurons, bigger than the lakes on the moon. Someday you'll get to see them. For sure."

I already have, thought Lil. She had been dreaming of water ever since the first snow had widened the woods in October. In the midst of the bush, beyond the last blazed trail, she would suddenly see before her a stretch of blue, unrippled water, without edges or end, clear as cadmium and silent as if waiting for the wind to be invented or a sun to come birthing out of it. Then a crow would caw and the snow-bound trees pop back into view. In the early spring the bubbling of Brown Creek below the East Field would unexpectedly become magnified as if it were a torrent ripping out the throat of a narrows, roaring triumph and terror until Lil stopped her ears, knowing somehow that she had transgressed, that the demons had indeed inherited part of the earth.

"You're like Old Samuels, little one. Sometimes you know."

"I'll ask the guardian to bring back your eyes," Lil said.

"So I can see all the wickedness and all the silliness again? It's not like olden times any more. Two days walk south of here and they say you'll come to roads chopped through the bush, and White Mens drives his wagons on roads made of dead trees, and Chatham is bigger than ten Ojibwa villages and the niggers prowls at night with eyes as white as a cat's."

"Why does Papa go there?"

"I like your Papa. He's a good White Mens. He gave me my name: Old Samuels. I tell him my name is *Uhessemau*, he says 'I can't say that so I'll just call you Old Samuels, all right?' I like the name Old Samuels, so I keep it. Redmen don't fuss about names; we have many names before we die. If I die with Old Samuels, well that's okay with me." The old man puffed on his pipe and thought about the many names he had lived through.

Lily was only half-surprised , then, when Papa appeared that evening at dusk, his haversack full of store-bought bacon and sausages, and said: "Start packin', little one, we're goin' up to Port Sarnia to watch the ceremonies."

2

It was Indian summer. The leaves had turned but not fallen. No wind disturbed their shining in a sun that blazed with more hope than heat. Along the forest track, purged of summer's mosquitoes, autumnal shadows stretched and stilled, preserved in light. Air in the lungs was claret, flensing. Lil breathed and strode. Papa measured his own practiced stride to hers; she floated in his grateful wake. She was holding his hand as surely as if they were touching.

They had left home while the sun was still a promise in the east, and the path linking the four farms to the north was sullen with shadow. Lil had never been north of Millar's farm; Lil had never seen the River. In the absence of birdsong this day, her heart fluttered and drummed. The beaten path, so familiar to their feet, disappeared. The sun had risen but not above the tree-line; there was just enough light to see the blazes, newly slashed, that marked the bush-trail ahead. They were going north, through nowhere to somewhere. At last.

Just as the sun bested the tree-line far to their right, they were joined by Old Samuel's nephews – *Metagomin* or Acorn, and *Pwau-na-shig* or Sounder. They slipped behind Lil without a word. Only when they stopped much later for a drink from a shallow spring and a brief rest did she notice that they were not in their hunting attire. Their red and blue sashes against the white calico of their *capots* were dazzling, even amongst the maples and elms. Like Papa they carried haversacks stuffed with supplies. Sounder, as usual, grinned broadly at Lil, giving her a glimpse of the merriment that must have once quickened the eyes of Old Samuel himself. Acorn, according to his custom, nodded at Lil without changing the impassive, set features of his face. Lil stared at the grimace of the black squirrel peering out of the fur on Acorn's shoulder.

To Papa they spoke in Pottawatomie, the speech (according to Old Samuels) their parents had adopted when to utter Attawandaron or Petun meant death. No one was alive now who remembered those sweet/sharp sounds. Lil thought sadly of her mother's lullaby tongue. Sounder was chattering away to Papa like a jay in the soprano range. Already Lil could pick out some words; the pitch of rising excitement was plain. She detected "presents" (several times), "white soldier", "big river" and "village". Papa replied laconically, half listening as he did with Lil. But he was happy. His large hands cradled the back of his head, his eyes glowed with something remembered and anticipated. Lil found herself beside him. She put her hand on his knee.

Sounder had switched to English. "Little-maiden-with-the-goldenrod-hair is a brave walker, no?"

The ghost of a hand bent over hers…

"Big white general only give presents to squaws with black hair. White generals plenty fussy 'bout presents."

…brushed and settled.

"Sounder like all squaws; give presents to everybody." His eyes danced at the thought. "Even Acorn," he laughed, and did a little jig around his unimpressed cousin. The squirrel seemed curious.

"Ready to move?" Papa said, in Acorn's direction.

Some time after noon, they turned north-west, still following the blazed trail. To the west lay the River. Lil strained to hear its voice. The bush was awesomely silent. The odd crow, unmated, cawed in complaint; a bear crumpled the dry brush nearby, seeking the late berries, the crab-apple windfalls, a sour-cherry unravaged by headlong flocks. Unobserved, squirrels broke open the chestnut, hazel, beech, walnut, acorn. In the pines, steadily diminishing now, chickadees tumbled out of tune. More and more, there were large natural clearings – beaver meadows or sandy patches where the hundred-foot oaks and pines had given in to be replaced by clans of cherry, crab and snow-apple which, though silent and satiate now, in the spring must have emblazoned the bush with immaculate flame.

Mostly, though, they heard their own footfalls in sunny glade or pillared gloom. Sounder, impatient with Papa's considered pace, scooted off into the semi-dark and popped up in front of them with a red squirrel in his hand kicking out the last of its life.

"For supper," he explained, setting off again, guided by his own compass.

They came not to the River but to a genuine road, a fifteen-foot swath cut through the bush, the stumps pulled out and smoothed over with sand. Across the myriad streams trickling west towards the river, bridges of demi-logs had been crudely constructed. Lil realized that a horse and cart could travel here. No vehicle approached. They followed the road due north until the sun began to tilt sharply to their left. It will sink soon, right in the River, Lil thought.

"Are we near the water?" she said, no longer able to keep this feeling to herself. How she wished she were Sounder, able to dance sideways and chatter jay-like to any tree that would listen.

Papa increased his pace. Acorn muttered his disapproval. After a while Sounder said quietly to Lil: "River of Light is just through the trees there; we been following it; but no path, even for a brave walker."

Lil looked longingly through the trees to her left but saw only black irregular columns fluted by the sun behind them. Her disappointment was interrupted by Sounder's exclamation.

"Here's the farms."

Never had Lil seen such an expanse of open space unimpeded by trees. To the east of the road the bush had been, in typical pioneer fashion, denuded of all timber, all brush. Not even a windbreak separated one farm from another. The stumps of the slain trees had been piled lengthwise to create makeshift fences demarcating fields, properties, gardens, dooryards. At first such angularity seemed alien to Lil, even painful to look at. But the sight of cabins, several of them the largest buildings she had ever seen, ranged neatly back from the road in neighbourly view of one another, was overwhelming. She barely noticed that the sun was fading quickly, the dusk rising from the newly ploughed fields already burgeoning with fall wheat, its fern-green haze lending the last of its light to this miraculous community.

The others were apparently impervious to miracles for they had moved well ahead of her and were stopped, waiting for her, in front of the third cabin, the smoke from its fieldstone chimney lingering and friendly in the motionless air. It was only when Lil came up to them that she glanced away from the farms to the west again and discovered that the bush had, for a stretch of two or three hundred yards, been cleared all the way down to what could only be called the River.

"This way," Papa commanded as she stood staring into the scarlet, gouged eye of the sun.

Mrs. Partridge was really very kind to her. She bathed Lil's blistered feet in soda water, rubbed them with ewe's grease, and put into her moccasins little pads of the softest cotton in the world. "Store-bought at Cameron's," she said with restrained pride, "up to Port Sarnia." After the meal of quail roasted in a genuine iron stove, potatoes, squash, corn-bread with molasses, tart apple-pie and mugs of warm goat's milk, the men slouched together by the fire, lit up their pipes, and conversed partly in English and partly in Pottawatomie. They were soon joined by two sturdy neighbours with buffed red cheeks and flaming hair. Mrs. Partridge and her two elder daughters sat near the stove in the kitchen, one carding wool, the other preparing to 'full' several man-sized macintoshes. Lil had many questions to ask but no sentences in which to express them. She listened, though, her eye never leaving the printed calico dresses of the elder daughters and the rounded, urgent flesh so restless beneath them.

The Partridges had a small shed where you went to relieve yourself. Lil left the door ajar; the moon poured its amber warmth through the wedge in the tree-line. Lil did not go back to the cabin right away; she walked past it and straight onto the moon's carpet. She heard the River just ahead in the darkness behind the beam of light. Strange sand-grasses caressed her bare legs. She came to the edge. The voice of the River filled her ears. On either side of the brilliant filament she could see only a blackness deeper and more resonant than the darkest sky in January. The weight of the moon was a feather on its face. It roared with the hoarse breath of a stag plunging through blood-soaked snow towards absolute cold. In it, Lil thought she detected longing, anticipation, and the joyous ache of seeking what always lay a handspan ahead. Under the circling stars, Lil listened for the language it used, but it was no tongue she had ever heard.

From her cot near the board wall that separated the sleeping area from the main room, Lil tried to catch the meaning of the scattered words spoken by the men.

"Them surveyors was through here again last week, Michael."

"I heard," said Papa's voice, barely recognizable.

"Rumours floatin' about, up an' down the line. Talk of makin' this here territory a county, they say."

"White fella draws lines in the bush," said Sounder, making no attempt to disguise his disdain for the irremediable folly of the intruders.

Lil dozed. Dreamed of water bigger than counties, borderless and infinitely serene.

"It's all right, I reckon they're all asleep by now."

"Went to the meetin' down at Chatham. Things is gettin' worse, we hear tell. Some new law comin' in over there about returnin' the poor devils. All legal-like, too."

"Sun-in-bitch Yankees," Sounder added.

"Over a hundred come across since August. We're lookin' for a new route, Harry. Them raiders is gettin' smarter by the hour. New houses, too. Reckon things could get real bad by summer."

"The committee can count on us."

"Damn right. None of us forgets what it was like to be a Highlander under George's boot. What do you want us to do?"

"Sun-in-bitch English!"

Lil was swimming, her hair fanned out like a parasol in the blue wind.

Once again they rose and were well on their way before sunrise. But this time Lil knew more about what lay ahead. From various overheard conversations at the Partridges she learned that the village of Port Sarnia sat less than two hours walk along River Road to the north; and that one was not to be surprised by periodic farms in lee of the road, though the spread of a dozen at what the locals called Bloomfield was the largest group below the Port itself. Here and there slash-roads were cut eastward through the woods so that one could imagine not merely strips of humanity but blocks or successive waves challenging the hidden heart at the centre of the territory, known only to the natives and the hibernating bears said to rule there unmolested. At the end of River Road the bush would relent and they would come to a huge clearing where the river eased into a wide bay, the site of the new town, and behind it to the south and east the Ojibwa, or Chippewa, Reserve where several thousand Indians lived in scattered equanimity. What they were heading towards, what Sounder couldn't stop dancing about, was the arrival of the government ship for the annual dispersal of the presents given in exchange for lands of which the aboriginal owners had already been dispossessed. And Lil watched it all come about amidst the wonder of being eight.

3

Just moments before Lil and the others emerged from the bush into the misty dawn-light, the steamer *Hastings* weighed anchor and slipped from its overnight mooring in the bay towards the river bank below the town. Major John Richardson, of literary and military fame, who had joined the official expedition at Windsor on October 9, 1948, has left a vivid account of those gift-giving ceremonies at the Reserves on Walpole Island and at Port Sarnia. The weather was flawless: the sky unscarred by cloud, the sun brilliant as a rubbed coin, the wind at ease in the sea-grasses along the shoreline. As if the whole enterprise had been choreographed beforehand, dozens of parties of Indians, large and small, materialized from the forest of their Reserve at various spots along the two-mile curve that formed a parallel to the natural bend of the bay. Most walked, single file, the women and children behind; some, more resplendent, rode the motley ponies bred on the Island. At some undetectable signal, the Government contingent marched down a single plank to the shore – a sort of colour guard dazzling in blue and red and white, breaking off and standing crisply at attention while a larger platoon of regulars from the Canadian Rifles wheeled southerly just ahead of the navvies freighted with the Queen's largesse. At the same moment five dignified Indians, obviously chiefs, moved towards the colour guard, stopped dead-still, and waited. Major Richardson, wan and aged beyond his years but impeccably turned out, stepped forward with Captain Rooke. While Her Majesty's gifts were being carefully laid out in predetermined rows, neatly bound in fleece-white blankets tied at the four corners, White Man and Indian exchanged formal greetings, then sat down nearby at the doorway to a huge skin tent that had magically arisen – the officers awkwardly, the chiefs elegantly – and passed the ceremonial pipe. Major Richardson was seen to talk animatedly in Ojibwa to several of the chiefs whose smiles were all-encompassing. Meanwhile the more-than-one-thousand natives who had now reached the plain began to pick up their presents.

The bundles were not marked in any way, but each individual or group knew, from custom and tradition, which kind of bundle was intended, and deserved. There was no rush, no confusion even though the scattered actions of the numerous families and several tribes appeared to be random. Bundles were carried off to the edges of the plain where most families had set up their cooking apparatus and blankets for the events of the day ahead. Fires sprang up, smoke lifted and hung, cards and dice gathered attention, fresh calico was paraded, Cavendish proffered and puffed; babies complained and were content. The Great White Mother had wafted her attention and grace across the world-sea and blessed them with this day.

Only one element seemed out of place on a morning described by Richardson as having 'all of the softness of mellowed autumn.' One of the chiefs, a wrinkled and scarred veteran of the Battle of the Thames who had stood beside Tecumseh as the Yankee bullets ruptured the great man's heart, did not smile, did not sit, did not sip peace with his brothers, did not take the gifts offered, did not bend his gaze away from the badges and brass before him. He was *Shaw-wah-wan-noo*, the Shawnee or Southener, the only one of his race known to inhabit these tragic grounds so long after those cataclysmic events. Richardson, at an age when romanticizing is either foolish or profound, says that this man 'notwithstanding five and thirty years had elapsed since Tecumseh's fall, during which he had mixed much with the whites, suffered not a word of English to come from his lips. He looked the dignified Indian and the conscious warrior, whom no intercourse with the white man could rob of his native independence of character'.

Lil was dizzy. She had to sit down near the fire-pit and close her eyes. Never had she seen such an open space, so many variegated objects in that space, and so much colour and motion freed from necessity. The Indians' regalia took two forms: the outlandish harlequin suits of many of the younger Chippewa – complete with scarlet sashes, blue leggings, black and white ostrich feathers, and an English-made beaver hat; and the traditional deerskins, rabbit furs and eagle feathers of the older males and of most of the Pottawatomies. At first Lil could look only at the natives, since, when she had stepped out of the bush that morning, the plain was dotted with them. Only later did she venture forth behind the slow-paced Acorn towards the bay and the ceremonial party. Here she saw the soldiers she had heard about only vaguely from the tales of the Frenchman who had been in the War. Their scarlet uniforms caught the mid-morning sun, imprisoning it; the bright steel and gilt of the swords flashed and darted at any who dared look their way. Never had she seen men – uniformly attired – prance in step, swing their arms unnaturally high in unison, let their motion be driven by the panicked hammering of drums. She saw too the sleek rifles carried by some of them and the bayonets thin as a wish-bone: these weapons, she knew, were not for hunting.

About noon-time Lil found enough courage to go down to the River. The paddle-wheel steamer blocked her view. From its iron stack clots of soot shot periodically upwards, smudging the sky. Several men were tossing whole logs into a square stove-like affair; the flame inside blew white and venomous. Suddenly a man in a blotched uniform gave a shout; a metallic thing whined, the wooden sides of the boat shivered, something almost-animal shrieked as if mortally wounded, and, beating frantically at the calm water, lurched northward along the bayshore towards the townsite.

After a while, Lil opened her eyes. The River was now hers. She could see the other side, but the trees over there were faded and shapeless, so vast was the blue torrent pouring past them. To the south she could trace its surge for miles as it swept through the bush with power and disdain. This was no creek, however magnified in imagination. No shadow touched its translucent face save that of the welcome herring-gull or fish-hawk; it was forever open to the sun and the stars; there was an eternal earth-light in that blue tidal twisting – even in the depths. It was the enemy of darkness. It diminished whatever it touched. It rejoiced in its flowing.

To the north, beyond this brief inlet, the near-bank bent slightly west, and Lil strained to see through the autumn haze the place where the Freshwater Sea of the Hurons fed its own waters into the River. She felt its mammoth presence behind the mist. I will be back. I will see you. I will.

In the direction the boat had gone Lil saw the outlines of what she knew was a genuine town. Like Chatham. Perhaps there were even black people with charred faces and cavernous eyes. From here she could see only the white splotches that were cottages, not cabins. Tendrils of the purest smoke rose from their stone chimneys. Somewhere amongst them was Cameron's store. For the first time she was aware of her sack-cloth chemise, her improvised leggings, her straggling reddish-blond hair unadorned by flower or feather. She sat down by the fire-pit, in the midst of laughter and joyous commotion, and wept.

She did not hear Acorn squat beside her. When she had stopped crying, she became aware of his presence, and noticed he had been holding out his hand towards her.

"For you, little fawn," he said, averting his eyes.

It was a gift. A buckskin jacket with intricate configurations of beading that might have been inspired by the Big Dipper or the Pleiades.

Papa spent a lot of time talking with the officers and other white men from the boat and the town. Many times he laughed, out loud. Sometimes his eyes would cloud over the way they did when he talked about Mama. Twice his gaze had searched Lil out among the comings and goings, looked relieved, and then twinkled. Sounder hopped and skittered, chattered and horse-traded, threw the dice and snoozed beside her in the afternoon grass.

"I'll give you a half-dollar for it, ancient one." The officer held the piece up to the sun as if it were a jewel or a talisman. The old Pottawatomie chief followed its flight, tempted. His hands unconsciously rubbed the black walnut warclub they had polished with their affection these many years since the wars ended.

"This club belong to my father," he said, more to himself than to the pot-bellied Canadian before him.

"Two half-dollars, then."

The old one looked momentarily puzzled, then hurt. Finally he said, "One half-dollar," letting the officer reach across and draw the club from its accustomed grip.

Papa was about to step forward when something in the Indian's expression made him pause. Papa watched him put the silver coin into his pouch without examining it, and turn towards the river. Lil saw the look on Papa's face; it was the one he used just before he swung the hatchet at the beaver or muskrat not drowned by the trap.

"Sun-in-bitch Canadian," said Sounder behind them. Then, after a decent interval: "They start dancing now."

The dancers were not human. Against the squandered tangerine sun they were silhouettes freed from gravity, embodiment, the etching of light. They moved to the will of the drum only. You could see the dancers' feet strike the ground like the skin of a living tom-tom, like the heartbeat of the hunted, like the music bones make when breaking. The air above the performers shook with their cries. They danced towards enchantment, expiation, communion – but the sun flattened and gave out behind them. The drum ceased.

Lil's heart was like a sparrow's. She skipped across the field, letting it flit and sail at will. She squeezed her eyes shut and dared the earth. She reached their spot, unscathed.

"We've been asked over to the Reserve," Papa said, ignoring her exhilaration. As they packed up their few belongings, Lil turned for a final look at her River. No doubt she observed the last image recorded by Major Richardson as the *Hastings* swung round in the bay to head south: the old Pottawatomie seated on the river-bank, unmoving, his single eagle's feather brittle against the horizon. The Major waves. The figure remains still. The Major, remembering Tecumseh and the mist of blood along the Thames, waves again. It is too dark to see whether the shadow has responded.

4

The Indians' homes were scattered across the fifteen square miles of their allotted territory. The wigwams were grouped in threes and fours as family size or friendship dictated. The area that Lil, Papa, Sounder and Acorn were led to was probably the largest of such communities with six ample bark-and-skin wigwams arranged in a rough circle with some cleared space behind each dwelling for the gardens, still swollen with late pumpkins, squash and marrow. This was the home of the Pottawatomie clan, whose fathers had taken in the dispossessed Attawandaron and then themselves been driven off their lands.

Small fires were lit in the wigwams and a large one in the circle among them. The night closed in, quick and black. No stars, no moon. Each fire held its adherents captive; food was heated, shared, consumed; brave talk floated over the pipe-smoke, languished and was revived. Lil dozed against a shoulder. She was dreaming. Her fingers detached themselves from her hands, and without her consent began to tap upon her belly, filling it with distant music.

She opened her eyes, squinting through the smoke-haze. The air quivered. There were tom-toms singing out of the dark spots – not the steady war-dance of the daylight hours but the wild, a-rhythmic, celebratory beat of the all-conquering. This time everyone was dancing, it seemed, whenever the moment called for it. Lil caught the frayed outlines of men, women, children twisted into grotesque forms by the uncertain flames, made insubstantial by the sculpturing smoke, lifted to momentary frenzy by the intoxicant drum.

Lil rose, drawn into the melee, and felt her feet take off, seeking out the cadence, finding it with astonished ease, letting her body sail over them, swing free, the heart launched like a swallow at dawn.

Dizzy, coughing, and exhausted from the physical effort of the past two days, Lil groped her way to one of the wigwams. She crept to the rear of it and retched into the ragweed. Chills ran up and down the length of her body, though she could still feel the sweat pouring off her chin. A few feet away she heard a sort of mellow grunt. As her eyes grew used to the dark, she saw, in the weeds, the outlines of what could have been several bodies – unclothed, fastened together, it seemed, like a pair of earthworms after a sudden rain, sweat like a mucous bonding them to some mutual appetite. Lil took little notice. She felt the night-air cooling her. She was glad she had danced. She had never felt anything so wonderful. Not even the sound of her River.

She crawled back into the firelight. Papa was nowhere to be seen. Nor Acorn. Sounder had gone into one of the wigwams right after their arrival. She was alone, and very tired. She would find a blanket and sleep – anywhere. Out there, the dancing was diminishing as the participants retired, mostly in twos, to a wigwam or to some sheltered place behind the circle out-of-earshot.

A strange feeling came over Lil. Her eyes came wide open. All fatigue magically drained from her.

A huge shadow passed between her and the nearest fire. Someone was beside her, still and silent. No words were exchanged. After a while a small group of Pottawatomies came out of the next wigwam. From their laughter Lil guessed they had been drinking some of the whiskey brought in by two or three of the Chippewas from the town. They appeared to be members of a single family – a somewhat pudgy mother and father, some grown sons and a slender girl on the brink of puberty. As they gathered near the central fire, the news spread and several dozen others stopped to watch what was about to happen. Two of the girl's brothers or cousins stood, one on either side of her, gently lowering her to her knees. The girl showed no sign of fear; her face was, if anything, radiant with sweat and reflected flame, her eyes alert to every movement around her. The tom-tom had stopped. At a signal from the girl's father it started up again, subdued and throbbing. Stepping towards the kneeling girl, he placed a garland of some sort on her head. She looked up and out – straight at Lil. Her eyes had devoured last night's moon.

The father, responding to the increased tempo of the drum, began a long incantatory song in Pottawatomie. Lil could catch none of the words, but she knew it was a joyous chant, full of affection and hope.

"She has changed her name, little dancer." It was the voice of Southener, the Shawnee, seated beside her. "Her name was White Blossom. Tonight she's no longer White Blossom. She is Seed-of-the-Snow-Apple. It has been proclaimed before all of the tribe. Now she must strive to live up to the name bestowed upon her."

Not once did Southener look over at her. He said nothing else, as the ceremony ended and the fires grew smoky and fickle. But Lil knew all she had to do was let her head droop onto a waiting shoulder. And she did.

All the fires were out when Lil woke with a strange feeling inside her even stronger than before. Her friend had placed a blanket over her and rolled another one as a pillow for her head. She got up and, as if impelled by some force both familiar and inscrutable, stepped straight into the darkness behind the circle of dwellings. A slice of moon, as it sailed through ragged cloud, was glinting streaks of light – enough for Lil to be able to pick her way past the vines and overripe melons into the pitch of the bush itself. If she were following a sound she was not conscious of hearing it; and nothing could be seen ahead but the denser shadow of the tree-trunks themselves.

Lil stopped, in a bit of a clearing. Overhead the moon popped out like a glass eye in a jelly jar. A bat brushed its bachelor wing against the sky. In the nearest pine, a Massassauga stuttered against bark. Owl's eye flicked shut.

Lil was already watching them. The Indian girl, the one named *Petta-song* (Rising Sun) who had led Sounder into her wigwam, was tipped over backwards on the ground. Her hair, unbraided, parroted the lolling motion of her face lathered with moon-sweat. Papa was kneeling between her bare legs like the Frenchman when he prayed, though he wore no clothes. Papa's hands were gripping her breasts as if they were axe-handles, and his whole body was bunched and aimed at hers as it was when he had marked a pine-tree for chopping. With each blow *Petta-song* whimpered and Papa sighed, until at last the girl flung both legs at the moon and let out a shriek that shook the melons out of their sleep and roused the embering campfires, that sounded like some virgin giving birth to a god. To which news the axeman responded with the seasoned groan of a man bearing the word of his own demise.

4

1

From her sanctuary in the loft Lil could see – through the new glass window Papa had installed in honour of her eleventh birthday – the stars, the quarter moon, the black rampart of trees, and the outlines of a genuine road to the west, now that they were officially a county. Behind her the deer-mice pretended to skulk and cower, the swallows dozed with their new brood under the eaves. Very clearly Lil saw the two figures detach themselves from the road and walk purposefully towards the cabin. They walked like no farmer Lil had ever seen. Just as they knocked, doffed their hats and entered, the candlelight caught their red hair, slick lapels, polished boots.

As soon as Lil heard them speak she knew they were Scotch. She was very good at voices. One spoke smoothly, the other with a sort of hitch or kink somewhere in every sentence.

"Yes, thank you very much, but just a thimbleful if you don't mind: good for the gout my doctor says."

A gurgle of whiskey escaping.

"I'll join you as well. I-er-haven't got the gout, but of course I'm anticipatin' it."

They both laughed.

"Bein' a gentleman who gets out and around, you'll know all about the new county and the marvelous – could I say miraculous – improvements it's bringin' its citizens, whatever their race or beliefs."

"Or, uh, colour," added Kinky.

"Citizenship in Her Majesty's kingdom is colour-blind, I thank the Good Lord."

"To Her Majesty!"

"What sorta changes do you have in mind for me?" Papa asked, evenly.

"Well now, they aren't really, they don't exactly apply to you, specifically or –"

"What my cousin is sayin' is that we are merely servants, appendages of the council who in turn must carry out the laws duly passed by the Legislative Assembly to which – may I remind you – we all sent the Honourable Mr. MacLachlan."

"We got snowed in," said Papa.

"Precisely why the new road is bein' expedited."

"No citizen will be disenfranchised by a...by the weather."

"What laws?"

"You'll recall that the survey of '43, lamentable though it was, served us well enough, but a new one has been made necessary by certain *irregularities* discovered in the original."

"They had, after all, only the, ah, crudest of instruments and the Indians, we are told, ah, pulled up the markers as fast as they could be laid."

"Done, I'm assured, in all innocence."

"This ain't my land, then?"

"Dear sir, please, uh, please –"

"– don't leap to such dire conclusions. We're here on a mission of mercy, as it were. To be blunt, and to allay any apprehension on your part, let me say straightway that I have been authorized by the duly elected council of Lambton County to inform you that several small errors were made, back in '43, in the lot alignments along this particular strip of Moore Township."

"Very small errors, I assure you."

Papa's chair emitted a sudden groan.

"Infinitesimal."

"Tell me the truth."

After a pause, Smoothie said: "Your property is too far east, sir. That is why the road out there runs so far from your cabin-line. Your farm should front almost on the road."

"Five yards from it accordin' to the, ah, lawful survey."

"But that still leaves more than thirty yards –"

"Thirty-three to be precise. Ninety-nine feet, three inches."

"More than half my East Field!"

"That's correct."

"What does this mean?"

"Calm yourself, sir."

"In technical terms it means that you do not own a half of your East Field. And, correspondingly, you own a hundred feet of land to the west –"

"Covered in bush!"

"There's no need for, uh, that sort of tone."

"Donald is right. You'll have every opportunity to buy that improved field. No plans exist for a second line of farms behind this in the immediate future. We're movin' south with the new road, and the crossroad will continue from Millar's farm to the east."

"I'd say you have four – even five – years to buy that field."

"What with?" Papa's question went unanswered.

There was a long silence broken only by the pouring of a single glass of whiskey.

"There is, I'm afraid, one more point to be made."

"A very wee one," Kinky said.

"But pertinent. Accordin' to your contract you were to make a specific number of improvements within ten years, excludin' your first winter here."

"Very reasonable demands, I'm told."

"I've met them, every one of 'em."

"In a sense, yes."

"A moral sense, you might say."

"But with the technical loss of your East Field, you have, uh, technically –" Smoothie's smoothness began to fail him.

"You'll need, sir, to clear another ten acres."

"But not by fall. That's why we've been sent here. The council is quite willin' to accept either solution: the immediate purchase of the cleared field –"

"On reasonable terms you may, uh, be certain."

"Or the clearing of ten acres by a year from September."

"No one wants to see you lose this farm or be cheated of the, uh, fruits of your labour. All of us are here to build a better country than the one we've known, in a spirit of, uh, co-operation."

"And love and harmony, free from prejudice."

"And republicanism."

"I ain't got the cash. You know that. So does MacLachlan. I'd need cash to get help to clear a new field. I owe everybody in the district – time and dollars. I got no sons, you know. I got no wife."

Papa drank. "I'm no goddam *squatter*, you know!"

The Scotch gentlemen's fancy clothes brushed restlessly against the coarse deal of the chairs.

"Perhaps the Lord will help you, sir."

"God damn the Lord!"

Gasps, scraping of chairs, rustle of coats, quick double-steps to the doorway.

A little distantly and in a quiet voice that came from a different, darker part of the soul, Smoothie said: "We both know where you can get cash, anytime you want it. Your comings an' doings have not gone unobserved. Good night, sir."

Papa did not reply. Lil could not see below, but she heard his laboured breathing. As the night visitors passed by her birthday window and turned onto the path towards the county's road, she heard their parting comments.

"The man's a – a republican!"

"He's a fuckin' Irishman, that's what he is!"

In the darkness below her, Papa was sobbing. Lil was frightened. A cold rage constricted her throat. Bee-bee, the deer-mouse, was edging expectantly up her arm. She swung her other fist at him, savagely. He fled, untouched. She should go down to Papa. He had no son. He had no wife. On the beam above, she saw Bee-bee, puzzled and hurt. She didn't go down.

2

By that summer of 1851, while the hand-axe still challenged each oak and ash, and the crops surprised themselves by flourishing, the machinery that would soon transform the countenance of Lambton was already in motion. Road-gangs of disenchanted rustics and dispossessed natives hacked their way east to London and south to Wallaceburg. Surveyors with their sextants and their unbounded faith in Euclid – their chiseling eye straightening bog and bend – roamed the back bush like Queen's spies on the most precious of missions. To the east and south, barely out of earshot, the first locomotives soon would chuff and clang through morning mists undisturbed since the granite and peat and leafage rose triumphant from the steaming glaciers. Crows, more ancient than the myths that impelled them, shook the soot from their evening wings and stared. Eagles along the Erie cliffs followed the spiral of smoke and steam, unable to break its code. The politicos in Port Sarnia, dreaming their mercantilist dream, strained to hear the chorus.

In the midsummer heat with only a smock on, the sudden lustiness of a cooling breeze felt good on the calves, arms, neck, the stretch of inner thigh. And if you crouched down and looked out at a certain level, the wind seemed to be coaxing ripples out of the wheat as it rolled, resisted and sighed into acquiescence. Lil watched the waves, like the shadows of hands, settle and reach, settle and reach for some far shore beyond the forest's edge. In the twilight the wheat shone, blue as flax.

"Your Papa now, he's gone and surprised us all," Maman LaRouche said, showing Lil how to pick the potato bug off his perch and squeeze him between thumb and forefinger just enough to split his seam. "Everybody 'round here says 'he'll run off to the bush for sure now', or 'cain't run a farm without a woman and a crop of kids' an' so forth an' so on. Your Papa now, he ain't no ordinary Joe. *Ow!*" One of the victims had bitten back. "Goddam *maudit* bugs! I don't know why anybody'd want to hang 'round this hell-hole. I tell you, little flower, I ain't dyin' out here all by myself. I sure ain't. If that *calice* pot-belly's got to skate on his ass all the way to – Here now, you go ahead an' try it, *ma petite*."

Papa had indeed disappointed them all, especially the Millars with their thirty cleared acres, their crossroad and their planked facade, white-washed and all. Following the trip to Port Sarnia, Papa had thrown himself into work. The North and East Fields were both fully cultivated; there was a vegetable garden guarded against the wild pigs by a split-rail fence, a small shed for housing the oxen when they were visiting, and, surprise of surprises, a root cellar on the north side of the house. Papa took special care with this. He and the elder LaRouche boys spent several days digging a cavernous hole in the ground. Lil was curious, being only nine then, about what lay in or below the earth, and when she wasn't helping Maman with the meals, she peered across their broad, bare, sweating backs wherein the muscles churned like trapped weasels, and watched the pit grow larger and darker. Soon, however, a roof and plank walls covered it, and a little set of stairs appeared behind a fresh door. Lil was the first to try them out. They led down to a platform of sorts, and when you turned right you saw a cave with shelves across it and an earthen floor below where the canning and the potatoes and turnips would find a cozy berth, summer and winter. Lil felt the dampness exuded by the violated ground and the slats of sunlight caroming through the planking of the east wall.

Old Samuels attended the launching of the 'new room', politely refusing the proffered drink, feeling the marvel of the deal planks and the cold metal eyes of the spikes that secured them. But he refused to enter the cellar itself.

"Bad spirits in there," he muttered theatrically.

"In here, ya' means," said Gaston LaRouche, shaking the jug and winking at the others.

"White Mens always tries to fix up Nature," he persevered, searching the planking with his fingers for those icy arrowheads.

Nonetheless, Papa continued to be away a great deal of the time. Fewer were the occasions when he returned with a deer or a bear to share among the neighbours. Some mornings Sounder and Acorn would be standing before the dead fire when Lil came down, guns in their hands, peering around in puzzlement. "Your Papa not hunt today?" Sounder would say. "Got too many venisons already, I guess."

"Off to Chatham if you ask me," Maman would announce, asked or not. "That place is full of darkies, I hear tell. A decent body can't walk the streets." But despite any disapproval, she would invariably send little Marcel along to check the pig and help out with the chopping.

Sometimes when Papa came home from Chatham he would be tired but whistling, his eyes aglow. Other times he would be very sad, you couldn't talk to him for hours or look him straight in the eye. "It's a hell of a world out there, little one. We're better off right here."

Once she saw a letter on the table. "Can you read, Papa?" He looked stung, as if she'd struck him with an axe-handle. "Uh huh. A little." "Can you write?" "Not too good." "Can you teach me?" He looked at her, confused, as if seeing someone else in her place. "You'll get to read, an' write too. Real soon. When you're a little older." Lil sensed it would be some time yet. But the thought of it, the mere promise, was enough.

"Little White-Women's smart," Old Samuels said, "up here," pointing to a spot just above the shutters of his eyes. "And here," he added, indicating his ears. He meant of course that she had picked up, from him and his chattering nephew, quite a bit of the Pottawatomie tongue. At first she would carry on full conversations only with Sounder, grilling him constantly for new words. Finally Old Samuels took over her 'education', correcting much of the folly prompted by his nephew, and delighting in the increasingly extended exchanges with this waif, this orphan of the forests.

"There's hope, maybe, for White Mens," he would say to his ancestors when she had mastered some grammatical intricacy he felt to be untransferable to the simple mind of the intruders. In the darkest, deepest winter-dens of his mind, he could hear the blurred echoes of his mother's Attawandaron, and the regret would be so overwhelming he would have to get up and leave the cabin quickly lest he weep in front of the child.

Papa, it seemed, had overheard Maman's advice, for in the winter that Lil was nine he brought home with him, one day, a woman. Lil knew who she was, for she had at last seen the squatter's camp in the back bush, not nearly so far away as she had imagined and much dirtier and sadder than she'd ever expected. No wonder Old Samuels liked to spend his day along 'the line'. Squalling papooses, yapping dogs, quarrelling squaws amid the smelly, humid habitation of makeshift wigwams that possessed none of the redeeming dignities she had witnessed at Port Sarnia. Among the squaws was a pretty young woman with eyes like polished chestnuts, whose sinewy beauty was already softening towards sumptuousness. Her name was *Penaseweushig*, or Birdsky, and she brought with her a four-or-five-year-old son of somewhat mixed blood (his hair was brown and curly), the incidental offspring of some heated, casual lust between the girl and any one of a dozen drifters happy to oblige and vanish. Birdsky, being herself a Chippewa, gave him the name *Waupoore* or Rabbit. From Birdsky and Rabbit, Lil, among other things, learned to speak yet another tongue. The first time they came they stayed only a couple of months, until the snows melted – when mother and child simply disappeared one morning. Papa said nothing. He never said anything about Birdsky to Lil. Indeed, even though they could converse haltingly in English or fluently in Ojibwa, they talked little, in the manner of the Indians themselves. Birdsky was very kind. She did much of the cooking and cleaning, deferring to Lil whenever necessary. When she returned with Papa later that summer, she pitched in with Lil and Maman to harvest the potatoes and turnips, and helped Maman 'do down' her pickles and jams. Maman clucked a great deal about Birdsky's presence and moderate dexterity, but was kind to her, and, Lil began to suspect, genuinely fond of her company. In December one of her relatives from the camp came by and she went off with him. They didn't see her until that spring. Papa was away and when he got back he looked immediately for her, but said nothing to Lil, nor could she read anything in his face. He's getting to be like Old Samuels on one of his taciturn days, she thought.

Lil slept in the loft. She had slept there as long as she could remember anything. Rabbit was put in the small bed that Mama had used before she passed on. That bothered Lil for a while. But she liked Rabbit: he laughed at her antics, he believed everything she told him, and he kept the prowling Luc off-guard and at bay. Papa and Birdsky shared the big bed almost below her.

She never tried, through the flimsy partition, to watch what they did at night. The image of that drama was still vivid in her mind and her dreams. She could not help hearing though. And the sounds became, willy nilly, attached to parts of the pictures flashing before her in the resilient darkness between gable and eave. Not once did Birdsky ever cry full-out, either in anguish or jubilation. Her hushed thrashings were pitted with mewling, aborted sighs, ambiguous gasps, and the hiss of air through teeth desperate for release. Papa's heavy plunging was accomplished with a grim silence that was broken, near the end, only by a staccato wheeze of relief accompanied on rare occasions by a lurching, crippled soprano cry that never took flight fully into pleasure or despair.

The first winter Lil cried herself to sleep most nights, though she had no idea why. She was happy that Papa had someone to hold and whisper to. She liked to watch

Rabbit molding his myth-creatures out of blue clay from the dug cellar. She knew that being adult meant coming together like that in pleasure and pain. Still, she cried, as quietly as she could.

By the second winter, some things had changed. She felt strange stirrings in her own body that summer, as if invisible limbs were stretching in preparation. On her chest she watched in consternation and satisfaction as her breasts swelled around the blossom-heads she'd always known. Her leg-bones ached with growth. Luc's eyes fastened like beads on hooks to the bumps on her chest as she whirled and gambolled at the edges of his wretchedness. After, she would feel sorry, contrite, and furious at her own innocence, her inability to read what lay inside Luc's manic glance, what feelings shot uninvited through her own increasingly alien flesh. That winter as she lay above Papa and Birdsky, she took their smothered, muted, ambivalent passion and made her own translations in all the languages she had learned till now. Perhaps in the weird adult world they inhabited they were as happy as she, though not once did they hear the open descant of her joy when the lovers in her dreams, however vaguely, meshed and grew harmonic.

Lil was watching the bees in the basswood near the house. Birdsky's mama was sick so she and Rabbit were gone for a while. Lil was annoyed that Old Samuels had not come around for days and days. She was alone. Maman had asked her to stay over, but she was ashamed to be too near Luc. Here she wasn't really lonely, but with the chores done, she was a little bored. The bees, however, were up to something. They were gathered into a single, swarming blob that rolled and oozed, then miraculously began to lift itself into the air. It staggered, gained momentum and rose against the sky. Lil followed the swarm with her eyes, and was about to move after it to see where the new home might be when she heard a twig crack behind her.

A bear? No, the tread was too light, too cautious. Curious, she turned to the treeline in front of the cabin, saw nothing, and waited. She was about to set off after the homing swarm when, quite distinctly, she heard a human sigh – the exhalation of someone either utterly exhausted or stunned by despair. She scanned the underbrush, more than curious now. Nothing moved. No more sounds.

"Who's there?"

Silence. Breathing, then, constricted but deep. A man's. A large man's.

"You hurt in there? You want me to come in after you?"

Panic, very clear – to the left, behind the wild raspberries picked clean by the starlings. Lil walked in that direction. She was not afraid, though the fixed intensity of her stare might have suggested so.

"I won't hurt you. I'm Lil. See, I'm just a girl."

She heard the body turn over. It was down, in the twitch-grass, and struggling without energy to rise. Lil moved quickly through the raspberries into the afternoon shadow of the tree-line. The figure had collapsed face-down, its head in the shade, its shoulders and body in the sunny grass. The body was motionless except for the steep breathing.

No sign of injury or wounds; no blood. The man, for so he definitely was, was clothed in rags, mere strips of cloth that might have been a shirt and trousers. No shoes at all; the feet were blistered and scarred. And the man was incredibly dirty; he must have slept in ploughed fields. Through the holes in his shirt Lil saw what appeared to be further scars on the back, like livid vipers twisted in some foul congregation.

The entire body began to tremble, the way a child's lower lip might just before it bursts into tears. For the first time Lil was a bit scared. Maybe he had some terrible disease, cholera or something. She saw the sweat bead and quiver on his almost bare shoulders. Holding her own breath, she gently touched his arm to bid him turn over. "Please, sir, let me help you."

"I'se past help," came the voice, fatigued yet vivid and deep. Wearily, one limb at a time, the man rolled over in the grass. He was not dirty. He was black.

3

"His name's Solomon Johnson," Papa explained. "He run away from us soon as we touched shore." Papa shook his head slowly. "Wouldn't believe he was in Canada; he thought we was attemptin' to trick him." He was talking more to himself than to Lil, who sat rigid beside him. She was certain of this when he muttered, "Poor bugger…"

Lil filled his mug with coffee from the dipper. Papa had not told her much that afternoon when he came home to find the black man in his bed being tended to by Lil. But it was more than she had ever heard before about what he had been doing on all those 'hunting' trips. Papa and some men from the township had rowed Mr. Johnson across the River in the moonless dark. He was 'a slave' Papa said, to be pitied, but here, once he got safe to Chatham, he would be free forever. Right now some bad men were chasing him, trying to take him back to his chains. Lil tried to imagine chains that could bind a human limb; all she could picture was the teeth on the muskrat trap, like a skeleton's smile.

After talking a long time with the black man, Papa helped him to his feet and led him outside and around the cabin to the root cellar. Lil followed, certain from Papa's movements that he wished her to. They descended the little steps. Papa held up his hand. They stopped. Then he reached down and pulled the platform that served as a floor up on its hidden hinges. Without hesitating the black man stepped into what appeared to be a black pit. He disappeared. Lil shuddered. Suddenly the flare of a match shot across the darkness. The flickering, homey light of a candle revealed before them a miniature bedroom about five-by-six by six-feet high. A pallet with blankets served as a bed. There was a stool and a sort of bench to hold the candle or other necessities.

The black man looked up at them, exposing his huge, sad eyes. Then he smiled the wildest smile Lil had ever seen. "How c'n I thank yo'all?" he said.

"Lil here will bring you your food. You can stay up here long's nobody comes 'round. You need somethin', you just tap on this here wall," Papa said, demonstrating.

"If'n you doan mind, suh, I prefers to stay down here. Down here I feels safe."

Papa didn't reply. He turned to leave. "I got a sturdy lock on this shed door," he said. "Lil's gonna lock it every time she brings you what you need. Nobody'll get in here.

You'll be safe here. I gotta go to Chatham, to the Committee. Won't be more than a day or so. We'll work out a safe route once we know where those bastards are or when they're gonna go back where they belong."

"I'se gon' stay right here, mistuh Cor'cran, suh. I'se gon' be all right now. I be no more trouble, no suh."

"I'll be back in two or three days. You just keep your hopes up, Mr. Solomon Johnson. My Lil here will take good care of you."

The black man peered past the candle at his temporary abode.

"Jus' like home," he said.

Papa showed Lil how to put the key in the lock and open it. In an hour the sun would be draped and dying on the western tree-line. It would be dark down there, not like the shadowed, shifting, motley dark of the woods under the stars, but the opaque, impenetrable pitch of the rabbit's den, day or night, with only the intermittent trembling of the ground above to mark the predator's advance.

"You'all got dat lock on now?"

Lil was charged with excitement. Never had anything so interesting happened to her before. She felt trusted. She wanted to throw her arms around Papa and kiss him like a grown-up. She wanted to make him coffee and sit with him near the fire and listen to him tell all the stories she knew were stored up inside his head, stories of the strange country he and Mama had fled, the brothers and sisters and cousins she knew he must have there still, all of them with faces and lives and tales to be told in front of fires. She wanted to learn more about the black men they rowed over the River, and what this slavery was, about who these Yankees were, and why some of them, like the bastards chasing Solomon, were so bad. Lil realized, with a deep sigh, that she wasn't even sure what 'bad' really was, though both Mama and Maman had used the word liberally. And she had a feeling – preparing some cold beef, greens and biscuits for Solomon's supper and watching Papa walk toward the trail that led south – that she was about to find out a lot more about it.

Papa reached the road, visible through the trees from this angle, but instead of wheeling left he paused and looked up the line as if he were waiting for someone to catch up. Even from this distance Lil saw the tell-tale sag of the shoulders, the large bearded slouch to the right – the jauntiness, the intensity of purpose which this afternoon had sharpened his glance and given an edge to every action, was gone. Just like that.

Lil recognized the voices hailing Papa long before the figures emerged as silhouettes against the fading light. This time, though, the Scotch cousins were accompanied by a third man who – despite his powerful, squarish slope – trod a respectful distance behind his betters. An official of some kind, Lil thought. Old Smoothie linked his arm with Papa's, and together the entourage continued at a ruminative pace towards Chatham.

I'll never tell anyone he's down there, thought Lil. Ever.

Two days passed with no signs of Papa. Lil rehearsed how she would talk and what she would say when Old Samuels or one of the LaRouche boys came over. No one showed up. The sun shone. The bees settled nicely in their new hive. Lil and Solomon had the homestead to themselves.

The first two or three times that Lil brought around his food, Solomon said nothing except "Who's dat?" at the first rattle of the key in the lock and "Thank yuh Miz Lil, ma'am," his eyes downcast or averted.

"Why don't you eat up here? The sun's comin' through."

Solomon, below, devoured his food noisily.

"I can fetch a chair from the house, with a back on it."

The tin plate with the spoon undeployed appeared through the trap-door. "Thank yuh Miz Lil, ma'am."

"Did you like the pickles, Solomon? Maman and me made them last fall. Maman's been all the way to Chatham. A long while back."

A hand, seemingly detached, reached up and pulled the trap-door down like a mouth snapping shut. Reluctantly Lil gathered the utensils and with difficulty locked the outside door. She could feel him straining to hear the comfort of its click.

"Tell me what it's like in the United States."

"Well, Miz Lil," Solomon replied, finishing the last of the dills from his noon dinner and settling back a little on Papa's chair. "Yuh wouldn' wanna go dere, no ma'am. It's an ebbel place, a wicked, wicked place – 'da debbel hisself doan go dere, no how."

"Is that why you left?"

"Cain't talk 'bout dat, Miz Lil. Jus' cain't." He looked at the cellar floor.

"It's nice in Chatham. Maman says they got brick houses there. And board sidewalks. And schools for little children."

"Sound's if'n yuh been dere yuhself."

"And, Maman says, plenty of dark people like you."

"Long's they ain't no slaveholders dere, Ol' Solomon be happy."

Lil was so used to asking many questions and getting few answers that she barely noticed that as the afternoon eased westward and Solomon showed no inclination to escape, she was doing more talking than she ever had (except when Rabbit avidly trailed her every word and move around the farm, and that didn't count, though it helped). It appeared that Solomon was a good listener. Every once in a while in mid-sentence she would toss a glance in his direction only to find him alert and gazing wondrously at her as no one before ever had. Ever. Even his habitual sadness and the animal jumpiness seemed to abate, at least to Lil's satisfaction.

So she told him about all the things she knew that were interesting and that he might need to know when he got his freedom down in Chatham. He got a royal earful about the LaRouche's and the war against the Yankees, about Old Samuels and his miraculous all-day pipe; about a baby being born in the green undergrowth just like that, with blood splattered so far it looked like red-trillium day; about the quilting bee at Maman's last summer when the Frenchman drank too much hooch and dressed up like a priest in one of Maman's black slips and scared Maman and the ladies out of their wits so she was barely able to hit him on the head with the skillet, ruining a whole pan of perch; and of course she told him about the trip to the Reserve, and he paid particular attention, she warranted, when she described the odd behaviour of the Southener and the sad behaviour of the old Pottawatomie, though she brightened up her tale by ending with the antics of Sounder and a brief demonstration of the dancing she herself had participated in by special invitation.

"Now you tell me a story," she said with a gentle urgency.

"Solomon jus' like to listen, Miz Lil, ma'am. I'se accustomed ta jus' listenin'. A body get used to it, he do." She thought she caught the vestige of a twinkle in his eye.

"But how am I to get to know a person if they don't tell about themselves," Lil said.

"Nothin' ta tell. My life ahead of me, missy. Got nothin' behind me 'tall. My Mama tell me ta say 'Satan, get thee behind me!', an' I reckon I'se 'bout to do jus' dat."

"But you was born. You had a mama and a papa. You lived somewheres."

"Had no papa, no ma'am; had me a wonderful mama, but no papa ebber come round us. No suh."

Lil was puzzled, but Solomon failed to elaborate.

"Why'd your mama give you a funny name like Solomon?" she said.

"T'ain't funny 'tall," he said. "Come right from da Bible. Doan yo'all know da Lord's Book in dese parts? What kinda place I come to?"

"What kind of place did you *come* from?"

"Hertford County, Norf Carolina, nigh Murfreesboro," he said as if responding to an interrogator. "Work fer Mastah Cartwright dere. In da fields. I'se his slave, all da time."

Lil ached to know more but prompt as she would she could get little more out of him. Indeed all the sadness and original suspicion poured back into his face and demeanour as soon as Lil switched from telling to querying.

Lil was tired of telling. "I told you everythin' interestin' I can think about Canada. An' you don't tell me nothin' about yourself. You think that's fair?"

Outside, thirty feet back in the bush, branches cracked and broke underfoot. Solomon had the trap-door half way up when Lil said: "It's just the wild pigs."

"Yuh sho' of dat?"

"I'm sure."

"Better be hunkerin' down anyways. Your Papa be 'long real soon, I 'spect." But he sat down again in the chair.

"Are you never gonna tell about yourself, Solomon?"

He looked up, directly at her. "Most things I gots ta tell's awful sad, little missus."

"Then tell only the good parts," Lil said.

Solomon paused as if considering the import of that remark.

"Like I done," Lil said.

Later that day after a shared but quiet supper, Lil reached over to pick up the plate and mug. Solomon's left hand lay on the stool beside them. Lil let the petal of her right hand whisper to the ebony one. Solomon jerked his entire body back as if he'd been lashed. The plate and cup clattered on the platform.

When Lil recovered from the shock, she said "Are you hurtin' there, Sol?"

Solomon could not reply. He was trembling head to toe: a cottontail before the weasel struck blood.

"I'll let you be," Lil said.

As she turned the key in the lock, she heard him squeezing into his ground-hole.

On the third morning he took his breakfast only after Lil had retreated. But at noon with the bright midsummer sun lancing into the upper cell and setting the dust adazzle, she found him seated in Papa's chair looking sad but recovered. She stood watch as he went into the woods to relieve himself. On the way back he scuttled like a crab across the twenty feet of open space, not knowing whether to look ahead or behind or everywhere at once. Lil wanted to leave the slatted door ajar to catch as much as possible of the noon sun but she closed it as soon as he hurried past her. He sat down – embarrassed, ashamed, seething with irresolvable passions. Sweat sizzled on his brow until he got his desperate breathing under control. Lil did not leave. Nor did Solomon retreat to his burrow.

After a while he ate. Lil had brought her own dinner with her. They ate together. The tea was cold but refreshing in the heat. When the huge black man lifted the mug to his lips and tossed his head back, he seemed to drown the room with his presence – his substance and shadow, the dark roots of his birthground. In contrast, Lil's porcelain arms seemed to float free from their trim body like swan's wings over a carbon pond. Lil's hair was for a moment indistinguishable from the sun's.

"Where's your wife?" Lil heard herself say.

Solomon looked up in disbelief. Terror and wonder passed simultaneously over his face. Lil could see plainly that he wanted to tell her the story of his wife and their grief, that he was overwhelmed with the need to confide and the need, at last, to trust someone enough to share with him the full horror and inhumanity of his ordeal. But he did not. It would be many years later before Lil would understand why he didn't, when she herself would withhold full knowledge from the innocents before her.

Solomon held his gaze steadily on Lil. Tears washed out of his doe's eyes, but did nothing to erase the indelible pain and the memory of pain. The anguish harboured and held back in all two hundred pounds of red flesh and white bone was released into the beleaguered face, the stunned eyes for whom, ever after, laughter would be a form of betrayal.

There was no need to tell. Solomon's pain was enough. Lil looked straight through it and saw in a single second, in one terrible tableau, the entire narrative of his travail. Whether she fell into a trance and dreamed it whole or whether Solomon himself entered that dream to relate his story in the wordless epigrams of that state, she never knew. She only knew what she saw, and would never forget. She saw Solomon's master, that worthy of Hertford County, glorying in his notoriety as a 'nigger-breaker', daunted by the very presence of a young man named Solomon whose stamina and moral courage were a threat to a whole way of life, to God's ordained ordering. She saw him stripped and lashed a hundred times, roped to stanchions like a steer, his skin flayed to make him utter cries that never came, till the master himself slashed his head open with his cane, breaking it even though it was a gift from his daughter, and when he could not break the black man's spirit, he had him measured by the smith for fetters that tore open his flesh till scab healed over ruptured scab, scars multiplied over scars, and out of desperation, despair, longing for some kind of ending, he fled into the woods, dragging his chain with him, and found some unexpected measure of contentment among the foraging mammals and the morning birds who sang as sweet in hunger as in plenty. She felt the shock of his betrayal at the hands of a coloured man who didn't need the ten dollars, and wasn't present when the gang of white boys trailed him through the swampland and just before the dogs got him put a bullet through his thigh and dragged him, hounds lapping up the spoor of blood behind him, back to his master, who, chagrined, sent him off to the auction block to be sold to the killing grounds of New Orleans, but landed instead in Memphis, Tennessee, where he suffered two years of ordinary slavery; no beatings, no starvation, just minute to minute humiliation, labour dawn-to-dusk, nights of muscle-ache, mosquitoes, sexual gropings paralyzed by fatigue, brutalized by congestion, contiguity and the absence of hope. She felt the momentary joy of their union when Solomon gathered Mary to him and together they struggled to keep their love private and aimed, somehow, towards a farther day, until one morning in March he was hauled away without warning to the slave-pen in mid-town to be groomed for auction. Filled with a rage and terror beyond even his own imagining he battered his way through the roof of the cell and dragging his chains with him leaped from the roof into the featureless dark below. He was running as he struck the ground, straight back to his master's, which saved him of course because the guards did not even put the hounds' noses in that direction. So Solomon in the mist of the dawn slipped into a blacksmith's shop at the edge of town, stole a rasp (he later returned through his benefactors) and filed off his chains. He found Mary – beaten a hundred times with the elm paddle – ready to run anywhere, to Canada, to Heaven, to the tender fires of Hell itself. She saw then in rapid sequence the six-week's trek to the North, a hundred and thirty miles through swamp and bush, the bloodhounds giving up after a week, Mary having to be carried much of the way, food running out, the swamps disgorging mosquitoes and adders, the bounty hunters alerted, watching all exit points as owls wait so knowing in the dark, until at last with spring dawning on the Ohio they crossed into Cairo and were found dazed and despairing in a field by a white man who said, 'Come with me.' And so, as Lil saw, they were fed, rested, and pointed to the next village up the line, the string of safe houses that would eventually, past the North Star itself, end in a sanctuary known only as Canada. Between each town, though, lay the bush of southern Ohio and Illinois, and when the night skies clouded over, North was elusive, they staggered off-course, slept by day in caves or hollow logs, sometimes daring to follow the sun, coming to the edge of an unknown village (Sparta? Centralia?) dozing in its own hearth-smoke, so peaceful, so welcoming as domestic voices carried into the sunrise. Many times they sat on a hill looking down for hours on end, too terrified to knock on the first door, too starved to head back into the bush, till at last Solomon would walk up to the kindest-looking white gentleman he could find and say, 'I'se lookin' fer mas' so-and-so livin' on such-and-such street,' and wait, heart hammering for the response that spelled life or death. More than a dozen times was this scene re-enacted, and each time Solomon's voice failed him worse than the previous time till it was often only the look in his eye that prompted the reply, 'You a runaway? Come with me.' Until that day in Centralia when, exhausted after getting lost and heading as far west as the Mississippi River, threading their way back by starlight, living and eating and sleeping like animals, they collapsed at the doorstep of their safe house. To find two children there who seemed kind and well accustomed to such occurrences, giving them food and salves for their scrapes and bites and telling them to rest until their Papa returned. Lil shuddered as she saw the boy slip out of the house, the reward notice in his hand while the girl sat on her pink bedspread and wept. Then Mary's screams, as if she were being dragged into Hell still alive, woke Solomon but by the time he got to the window Mary was already being carried by a posse of bounty-men towards the railroad station where she was bound, gagged and slung aboard a south-bound train like a piece of stray baggage. Solomon, out of instinct, was into the bush in a minute, lost his pursuers easily and arrived at the station in time to see the train pull out in a cloud of soot that took ten minutes to settle into the silence at the centre of Solomon's heart. He took little notice of the man who found him there and arranged to have him put aboard a cattle-car on the Illinois Central headed that night for Chicago. They were very kind to him there, consoling, holding out the bitter promise of freedom only two or three days away. It was decided to send Solomon by the lesser-used northern route via rail through Schoolcraft, Lansing, almost to Port Huron before which town he was smuggled off, numb and submissive as if he were placing his body gratefully into the hands of a caring undertaker, and led through the forest to a secret point on the St. Clair River and thence rowed across to the liberated shore he greeted with dismay and a terror unadulterated by fear, memory or hopelessness. Dashing straight into the bush as if it were composed not of separate trees but a monolithic weld of blackness, he gave himself up to the dark at the heart of the world.

As Lil was leaving, she snapped the lock shut but did not loop it through the hasp on the door-frame.

4

Lil, thinking it was Papa, was half-way across the dooryard towards the road before she stopped to stare at the pedlar. It was not Lame Peter, from the north.

"'Afternoon!" he called jauntily, tying the donkey's halter-rope to a nearby birch and ambling towards her.

Lil waited, uncertain. He was a wiry man, all legs and arms with a long neck and a tiny bobbing head that made him look a bit like a tom-turkey combing gravel for tidbits. His blue trousers, scarlet shirt and smudged yellow bandana shone in the hot, high sun. A cherry-wood case, or valise, dangled from two fingers of his right hand.

When he saw that Lil was not about to move, he stopped a few feet away and set the case down.

"A mighty fine Ju-ly afternoon it is, young lady."

Lil waited, feeling she should say something normal.

"You the lady of the house?" he asked with a smile that was all teeth. She saw that though his skin was leathery and his brown beard unkempt, he was not an old man at all. The eyes were as black and lively as two tadpoles. They looked through her and beyond, taking in, in a single cast, the cabin, garden and distant fields.

"Yes," said Lil finally.

"Mama home?"

"Mama's up there," said Lil waving in the general direction of the mounded gravesite.

"Mighty sorry to hear that."

"Died 'bout four years back."

"The Lord's will. So be it." After a pause he grinned with his enthusiastic teeth and said, "You sure appear to be a young lady could look after her Papa, all right."

Lil looked at the ground.

"Papa home?" he asked, bending down to his case.

She was about to say 'no' when something made her tell an outright lie. "He's over to the Frenchman's, just past the North Field there, a-helpin' with a stump, he said. Be back home any minute. I was just fixin' some coffee for him."

The pedlar didn't even glance up. "Name's Jones," he said. "Spartan Jones." He was fidgeting with the clasp on his case.

"You're not regular," Lil said. She'd caught a strange twang in the accent; it wasn't one she could place right off, but it was definitely foreign.

"Nope. Come up from the south. Chatham way. Bobby and me tramped over the bush trail to the new road. Fresh territory, eh?"

Lil glanced over at Bobby who was chomping contentedly at the twitch-grass near the edge of the woods. "You a Yankee?"

"Yessiree," he laughed. "Same as half this here province is Yankee. My Pa come over after the war. Been here ever since."

"Windsor?"

"Nearby. Say now, I got here, just for a pretty young lady of the house like yourself, a whole box-ful of tiny wonders: needles and coloured thread, and baubles and bar-rettes."

"I couldn't look at them unless Papa was here," Lil said. "Besides, we ain't got cash for that kind of foolishness," she added in her best Madame LaRouche tone.

"But you ain't seen it yet," he said, lifting the lid on his treasure trove. "Can't hurt nothin' just to have a peek at it, can it now?"

Lil looked hard at his face. He was smiling, the beads of his eyes danced and held her but gave nothing away. He was not much taller than Lil. The donkey brayed and the pots on his back tinkled.

"Why don't we go inside out of this here heat, and just have a quick peek at the goodies? If your Papa comes back, then maybe he'll buy you a barrette to tie up all that pretty yellow hair you're sportin' for the boys, I expect."

Lil wondered what was in the cherry-wood case.

"If'n your Papa don't come back, I gotta move on anyways. Gotta be in Corunna by dark. Bobby don't take to night travellin', he don't."

Lil turned and the pedlar picked up his wares and followed her. They didn't go into the cabin.

"You can set it on this," Lil said, pointing to one of the stools she always placed along the south-west corner during the day – partly in sun, partly in shade. If he were disappointed, the pedlar didn't show it. Under Lil's tense gaze, he put the case on a stool and flung it open with a theatrical wave of his arm. Lil saw how nimble, how strong he must be under that loose blouse.

"There you are, lass! Tools for the industrious, cosmetics for the hopeful, temptations for the bold!" he said with another over-rehearsed flourish. His eyes did a Cajun two-step.

Lil did stare, despite her vows. She saw a silver locket with a link chain so delicate she could feel it like a feather on her throat exposed by the upsweep of her barretted tresses.

"Jumpin' Judas but it's hot here!" said the pedlar, mopping his brow. "Got a cool cup of water inside?"

Lil came out of her reverie quickly enough to skip around the corner and return with a dipper full of water from the bucket she always kept in the shade of the cabin's west wall.

"Fresh outta the spring, 'bout an hour ago," she said.

For a second he looked hard at her, not changing his ever-friendly expression but focussing it in a slightly different way. It was as if the temperature had dropped a degree or so. Noisily and with obvious relish he drank from the dipper and then splashed the remainder of the water over his face. His beard went limp. Lil saw the scar just below the cheek at the line of the beard, like a stretched maggot.

"I hav'ta go now. Hate to leave off conversin' with a young lady as pretty as you, all grown-up an' lookin' after her Papa and, I'll bet, fendin' off the boys 'round here – but Bobby's gettin' anxious."

"Thank you for comin'" Lil heard her grown-up voice say.

He was only three steps away from Lil when he turned very casually and said, off-hand, "Will you let me give you a present, lass?"

"Papa wouldn't –"

"Just a trifle. Got me some bolt ends of cloth on Bobby there, no good to me now. I reckon, though, they'd make a pretty scarf or two. In the hands of a young lady that could sew," he added, with a wink as big as a rooster's swallowing corn.

Lil waited for the pedlar to leave. He stayed where he was, unsure of himself for the first time since his arrival. Lil noticed that he was staring over her right shoulder towards the north-west corner of the house. Could he see the root-cellar shed from that angle? Why would he want to? She knew she must not glance in that direction. She had to get him to leave. Without the slightest suspicion.

"Perhaps Papa wouldn't mind, if they're real small pieces," Lil said, starting towards Bobby.

"Trifles," the pedlar grinned. "But on you –"

Lil was ahead of him, half-skipping towards the donkey whose indifference seemed absolute. The pedlar came at a bow-legged trot close behind. Lil stopped a few feet from Bobby, leaving ample room for the pedlar to sidle up to the beast and display his special wares. Lil was closest to the cabin, and she was fleet of foot.

"I reckon the scarlet would go nicest against that lily-white skin of yours, girl," he said, flipping the swatch of cloth from its pouch and letting it alight across Lil's shoulder only partly covered by the sack-cloth smock she wore all summer. His voice seemed suddenly to have dropped an octave, and it was full of razors. Lil was already bent to flee when his left hand grabbed her wrist and wrenched it with such unexpected force that Lil felt herself twist and collapse into the weeds, her skirt flung up over her thighs.

"No use a-cryin' out, ya sweet little bitch, nobody's gonna hear ya. Your pa's a long ways from here, and besides, you're about to get the surprise of yer life if I ain't mistaken, an' if I am, then we'll both enjoy ourselves."

Lil did not cry out, though she was sure her arm was broken. She was simply stunned for the moment, unable to grasp the import of what had just happened or comprehend the flow of opprobrium from the pedlar.

"Quit squirmin', ya little snake, I'll bust yer other arm. Now let's see what we got 'neath all this cotton."

He was tearing at her underwear and trying at the same time to get his braces over his elbows – hopelessly contradictory moments that gave Lil time to re-establish her breathing and feel the impact of her terror. "Fuckin' nigger-lovin' hoo-ers, the lot of ya! You let them darkies taste that pink twat of yers, eh? *Eh?*" The underpants came apart with a shriek of their own, jerking Lil forward and up, a motion which she merely continued with accelerated determination, and with either the deepest of instincts or mere good fortune, she rammed her head like a ballpeen on his pope's nose.

With an explosion of wind resembling a death-rattle he folded, and fell into the grass. Lil was up in a wince and headed on a line towards the cabin where, under the big bed, a loaded fowling piece was kept at the ready. Clutching his wounded parts, the pedlar came after her in a sort of wobbly turkey-trot, his lust consumed temporarily by rage. Lil would have made it easily to the gun and shot the pedlar dead without compunction, had she not stumbled and fallen no more than a dozen feet from the cabin. When she tried to get up, she cried out – once, sharply – and toppled back to the grass. Her right ankle was sprained, and this time the pain swept unfettered through her whole body.

The pedlar, seeing this, slowed his agonizing pace. When he came to Lil, she was whimpering and shuffling backwards towards the house. He laughed, watching her pathetic retreat for several moments with grim satisfaction. Suddenly Lil stopped. She sat up as best she could, biting her lip to hold back the breakers of pain rolling up the back of her throat. She stared up at her tormentor.

He was taken aback by this unexpected response, sensing a loss of piquancy to his revenge, but the fire in his groin had little abated. "I'll soon have ya whimperin' again," he seethed, pulling his braces, somewhat belatedly, all the way off. "A bit of buckle across the arse'll do it all right," he muttered while Lil remained motionless. He came around behind her, his back to the cabin, expecting her to squirm away or at least cover herself. She did neither. She remained bolt-upright, swallowing her pain, forcing her eyes open.

"I'm gonna whip yer butt an' then feed it somethin' it'll never forget."

Lil braced herself against an invisible wall of air. The pedlar's braces came down randomly like a loose flail, metal slicing into her shoulders and arms, leather burning two diagonal strips across her back. The pain was just about to register from the first blow when she heard the whistle of leather drawn back for the second. It never came. Lil heard another sound and turned in time to see the water bucket bounce back from the pedlar's head with a crunch of flesh, maple and angle-iron. The pedlar's eyes popped skyward, his tongue flopped out of the gasp his mouth made, and he pitched forward onto the dooryard in a tangle of blood and grass.

"I'se killed him! I'se killed a white man!" Solomon was in a sorry state. He was pacing in circles, trying not to see the motionless body with its head caved in, sprawled in plain daylight at the cabin door.

"Nobody saw, nobody saw nothin'," Lil kept saying, trying to catch the whirligig of his hand and stay on her one good foot. When she touched him, he stopped moving as if lightning had singled him out. He collapsed on the stool, staring away from the corpse towards the bush now deepening with late-day shadow.

"I jus' hears ya call out, jus' like… an' I comes runnin' through dat door an' I sees de man with de whips an' I jus' go crazy. Doan even 'member pickin' up dat bucket, I doan." He shook his head, then stared again at the bush beyond. "Yo hurt, littl' un?"

"No," Lil said. "He didn't hurt me none." The stout flour-bag cotton of her smock had absorbed some of the lashing, though the buckles had left two stinging but superficial cuts. Her arm was sore but undamaged, and though her ankle was swelling, she found she could hobble satisfactorily.

"Well, I'se sho' glad he dead, if'n I have to go hang an' to hell for it. Guess I was wishin' to do dat to somebody fo' a long time now. A long, long time," he said.

"Papa'll be home soon, everything'll be fine," Lil said without much conviction, trying to stop her body from shaking head-to-toe and make her voice do what it was told.

Solomon heard her teeth start to chatter. From the bush something warm and sable was singing to him. "You best lock me up in de shed, missy. You best lock me in dere good."

Leaning on his arm, Lil led him to the shed. Holding onto his hand a second longer than necessary, she watched him ease down into whatever comfort darkness afforded him. "Everything'll be all right," she said, suppressing the quiver in her tongue, "I promise."

"Jus' bolt up dat door," he said. "Please, Miz Lil, ma'am."

Reluctantly Lil – overcome by a second wave of shakes – closed the door to the cellar. As she clicked the lock into place she noted that both the hinges had been knocked more than half-way out of their moorings. In his frenzy to save her, the black man, thinking the door locked, had hurled his body almost through it. She pushed the screws back into place.

If he wants to go, Lil thought, nothing will keep him there.

She knew exactly what she ought to do. Papa often got home just before dark. The sun was just about to sink below the tree-line, which left about two hours of hazy daylight. Lil ought to act the full measure of her eleven years and drag that man's body into the brush. She ought to throw dirt on the blood and mess to hide it. She ought to bring the donkey to the empty hut reserved for Bert and Bessie. She ought to fetch the fowling gun and have it ready for use. She ought to be able to stop the treachery of her own body which would not cease its shivering.

She did none of these. She hobbled, hopped and crawled into the undergrowth where the new South Field would be someday soon, and hid herself. She closed her eyes tight enough to squeeze even the dreams out. But the image persisted of the pedlar prone in their dooryard in the stiffening afternoon breeze, the eyes jammed shut, the blood oozed from his clamped jaw like an adder's tongue skinned and raw in the dust. Around her, shadows strengthened, the haze lost heart, the whippoorwill's cry was inconsolable. Owl unshuttered the moons of his eyes.

Papa would not be home. She knew it. She thought she knew why. She couldn't stay here. There was just enough light left for her to see the outline of the cabin. From that direction came a sudden intermittent moaning. Terrified, she strained through the dusk to see a corner of the cellar shed on the north side of the cabin. The moan grew louder, but it wasn't coming from the cellar. Lil turned in time to see the dead man raise his head a few inches off the ground, groaning piteously all the while. In a moment he propped himself up to his elbows so that he could peer anxiously, inquisitively, about him. He appeared to be trying to think. Lil never moved a hair. The pedlar flopped to the left; Lil was about to cry out but he was just turning over so that he could sit up and get his bearings. Then he did a strange thing. He put two fingers to his lips and whistled softly. To Lil's surprise, Bobby, pulling free from his loose tether, stepped leisurely over to the pedlar, now evidently returned from the dead. The pedlar pulled on the halter, Bobby sank shakily to his knees, and his gravely injured master with a scuff and rattle of pans rolled onto his loyal back. Then donkey and burden moved into the near-dark where the north-road lay. They turned neither north nor south, however; instead they continued due west, probably following the ancient deer-trail that wound its way eventually to the River.

Lil waited until the mosquitoes had become unbearable before she inched her way, the wrenched ankle still tender, to the cabin. She no longer shook. She was, rather, consumed by a dread that was worse than any feeling she had felt before: a silent, impending apprehension that would not name itself. The image she carried across the clearing at that moment was a strange one: Maman LaRouche's pudgy-strong grip ripping turnips out of the stunned ground, her sickle slicing green from root before the plant could gasp, as Maman's sturdy foot, surging forward, buried itself cosily in the unresisting gash.

5

All that night Lil sat at the table facing the window and door on the south side, the fowling piece lying before her, cocked and expectant. When she had first entered the house, she had rapped in code on the far wall and heard, after a while, the mutually reassuring response from Solomon somewhere below. Determined to remain awake to face whatever grim retributors might appear, Lil – fast asleep – dreamed she was awake, and very brave.

What woke her was the sound of horses. She recalled that peculiar atonal drumming from the races that day on the Reserve. Never had such sounds penetrated this far into the bush. With a start she came fully awake. The gun jumped too but held its peace. Though muffled by the heavy foliage and the heat haze above it, the pounding was nonetheless deafening as it moved towards the spot occupied by Lil. Forgetting the weapon, she ran to the door and flung it open. In the disfiguring light of the false-dawn, Lil saw three mounted creatures, two of them already in the dooryard, the third frozen behind them in the opening before the road. The horses snorted and jangled – bloated and blurred and sweating. Lil felt the pent-up power in them as the wave of their heat washed over her.

The two men dismounted with a certain practised grace. Behind them, unsuccessfully camouflaged by the brush, Lil noted the third arrival: still mounted, the swath of bloody bandages on his head beaming like a Turk's turban across the clearing.

"Mornin', ma'am," said the taller of the two in a strange accent, mellifluous as honey on green apples. "Beggin'-your-pardon for disturbin' you this early in the day, but we're-all here on pressin' business."

The other one nodded but said nothing, glancing nervously around.

"What's your business with us," Lil said, trying to shake the sleep out of her voice. She wished she'd brought the gun with her.

"Your Papa and me's made a certain transaction, ma'am."

"What kind of...transaction?" Shorty was edging towards the north-east corner of the cabin, holding his hat in his hand, nodding and trying to look casual.

The tall one brought out a leather purse; Lil heard the clink of coins inside. Her heart froze.

"My job is to bring you this here payment in return for certain goods you have in hand."

"This ain't a store," Lil said. Shorty had slipped around the corner.

The tall one put the purse into Lil's hand and as he did so grasped her gently but firmly by the wrist. "No need to get riled up, missy. We ain't in the habit of hurtin' decent folk. Beauregard and me are businessmen, that's all."

Lil was about to attempt a knee to the groin when Shorty's voice pierced the dead-quite of the pre-dawn. "The son-of-a-bitch's gone! He's flown the coop!" Breathless, he reappeared from the rear of the cabin.

"You sure?" snapped his partner, tightening his grip.

"Goddam right. The door's busted half off. They had him holed up like a polecat back there, but he's done beat it to the bush!"

"You let him out, gal?"

"Fuck no, I tell ya, Sherm, the door's lyin' in pieces. That big buck just blew outta there!"

"Cut the cursin'," Sherm said, more calmly. He loosened his hold on Lil's arm. "No call for that. Either your Daddy's cooked up this little treachery or that nigger's lit out on his own. Either way, we're gonna get him." He pulled the purse from their mutual grip. "You won't have need of this no more."

"We goin' into the bush after the nigger?"

"Yes, we are. Tell that pedlar to vamoose. We don't need him no more." He turned to Lil. She saw in the growing light that he had the kindly face of a father but one that could change, with little warning, to that fierce, inexplicable parental anger she had suffered in her own childhood. "You tell your Daddy to stay out of our way. Nobody's out for revenge so long's we get our hands on the nigger. Good mornin' to you."

They mounted and cantered as far as their enswaddled accomplice. Sherm spoke sharply to him, and Bobby wheeled and loped southward, towards Chatham. They watched him for fully ten minutes, then circled and headed north in the direction they assumed Solomon had fled after brushing aside the hingeless door.

It must have been mid-morning when Papa came home. Lil had returned to her vigil at the table, the gun an inch away but untouched. She was no longer scared. Her ankle no longer hurt. The dread which had so possessed her had finally divulged it names, and her soul longed for some relief beyond dreaming.

Lil didn't know how long Papa had been standing in the doorway when at last she looked up and saw him there. He turned his face away wearily and slumped on the stool before the spent fire. His flesh appeared to be too heavy for his bones.

"He got away," Lil said.

"They hurt you any?" he asked, rising and taking the hunting rifle from its place, not looking at Lil.

"None."

"An' that pedlar?" His sudden stare burned through her.

"Solomon, he run him off. Then he went, too."

Bullets clicked coldly in Papa's pouch.

"I turned my ankle just a bit."

"Keep an eye out," Papa said. "I'll be back."

After him, in a voice that made her skull-bones hum, Lil shouted *Why? Why? Why?* Papa of course did not hear. He had turned south. Towards Chatham.

It was dusk when he came home once again. Lil had dreamed of something farther than death. She opened her eyes to catch Papa's face bending towards hers. It was sad; she saw her Mama in it.

"I'm sorry, princess. We're gonna have to leave this place."

5

1

Seven days later they were packed and ready to go. Papa of course had planned to get away at dawn, but he hadn't counted on the goodbyes that needed to be said. Maman surprised everyone by not weeping openly. Instead she braved a smile for Lil, hugging her fiercely as if she might transfer to those sapling limbs some of the bruised strength from her own decades of travail. She may have seen in the sad, trudging reluctance of departure some sign of her own leave-taking, so close at hand. The Frenchman and his boys touched their caps and mumbled *au voir* with exaggerated politeness, except for Luc whose heart was irreparably broken and shamed itself with silent, unconcealed tears.

Lil knew it was pointless to ask Papa why they had to leave, but she was certain it was due to more than their troubles with the Scotsmen and the pedlar. Papa would not give up the homestead, would not abandon Mama's grave to the winds and seasons, would not tear his little girl away from the only life, the only world, the only people she had ever known – not for a mere Scotsman or a pedlar with a cracked head. Somehow – she did not know how – it had more to do with Solomon and the look Papa gave her when she woke to find him staring from the doorway, the shed door in back of them protesting as it swung on one precarious hinge.

"We're goin' to live near Port Sarnia," was all he said, "with your Aunt Bridie."

Who was news to Lil. From Mama she had gleaned a little now and then about her relatives – enough to conclude that Papa came from a large family, her own being mostly dead, but never had she put a name on any of them though it was obvious she sometimes wished to. Instead she told stories only about long-gone relatives, all of whom apparently were squires or beauties or gawains of the first order. Mama's stories were like her songs – a kind of lullaby. Bridie was no lullaby. She was a real, living aunt with a name as durable as a fieldstone. Lil wanted to ask about an uncle for Bridie but restrained herself.

"I wrote her a letter a while back," he said some days later, seeing Lil seated near the ripening wheat of the East Field and staring across its tender, involuntary undulations towards the red-blue granite on which one of Old Samuels' nephews had chipped the name 'Kathleen'. "Chester and her been wantin' us to come up there ever since your Mama passed on."

Chester? Lil came out of her brown study.

"Land's mostly cleared up there. We'll help 'em out at first. Then get our own place." Lil wanted so badly to believe the enthusiasm now in his voice. She wanted to ask about Chester but held back, hoping for more.

"We'll bring your Mama up there, too; some day," he added with effort, his hands trying to be light and consoling on her shoulders.

Mama wasn't *up there*, Lil knew, but could find no words to help Papa understand. She's here – in these trees, the wheat, the undug stones, in the birdsong enticing shadows towards dawn, in the wind that lives in these special places only, in that part of the sky she shared with us and that brings such joy to the guardian gods. Lil's quiet weeping made Papa's hands shake, and he turned back to the cabin, confused. Lil licked her own tears with her tongue, savouring them.

It was a regular road now running abreast of the line of a dozen farms north of theirs. The new neighbours, above Millar's, came out to watch them leave: whole families lined up at the edge of their land and waved curiously, tentatively, uncertain of the meaning of what they were witnessing. When Lil and Papa passed the last farm – with only its doorway cleared, and stumps and tree branches smoking behind the un-chinked log hut (where the new road abruptly became the old slashed trail again) – Lil did one of the things she promised herself she would not do on this day: she glanced back. Standing in the middle of the road a hundred feet behind them were the unmistakable silhouettes of Old Samuels and his favourite nephews. A few days before all three had materialized one morning, unannounced, and stayed the entire day, helping Papa with some of the packing and dismantling but never once mentioning the fact of their leaving. Sounder chattered and laughed, Acorn smiled with his soft eyes, and Old Samuels puffed his pipe and talked exclusively to Lil in Pottawatomie. "White Mens always coming and going," he said several times, unprompted, "Attawandaron stays." Once he added, not without charity, "'Course, White Mens still young, got a lot to learn before this world ends." At dusk they left, saying no formal goodbyes but carrying Papa's old sow in their arms as graciously as they could manage. Lil knew she wouldn't see them again.

Even now it was only their darker shadows in the constant early morning that she saw as she peered back over her shoulder. Acorn was as still as his name; Sounder was hopping and gesticulating beside Old Samuels as if describing for him exactly what he was seeing and feeling, like a honey-bee's dance of direction; Old Samuels had his face aimed at Lil's diminishing figure, his posture giving nothing away of sadness or hope, resignation or complaint, certain only that he did not need his eyes to see what was happening under them nor many other things life had reputedly reserved for the sighted.

Lil then broke her second vow. Fortunately Papa, who was now several strides ahead of her, didn't hear.

They followed the well-tramped trail north for several hours. The sun warmed them with its mid-day welcome. Wild Phlox and amber columbine nodded jauntily from the verges. In the pines, tanagers and siskins tumbled and iridesced. A fox snake yawned his whole length in the heat kept cozy by the trail.

They were travelling light, of course. Papa had a backpack with food and overnight utensils, a water bottle, rifle and hatchet. In a harness neatly rigged by Acorn, Lil carried two blankets and some goodies secretly slipped to her at the last moment by Maman. In the beaded pouch given her by Sounder and belted to her waist, she had carefully placed Mama's cameo pendant, the gold cross, and the rabbit's foot Old Samuels had rubbed almost smooth in thirty years of not worrying. There was no need for anything more: they had packed their few belongings – clothing, trappings, utensils, tools – in two large wooden cases about the size of a child's coffin. Luc, in a rush of altruism, had promised to hitch Bert and Bessie up to Mr. Millar's cart as soon as they were free from their summer stumping, and deliver the trunks to Port Sarnia.

So it was only the weight of the day itself that bore heavily on them as they trudged step by step away from all they had become a part of. Indeed whenever the little eddy of excitement (which Lil had been suppressing all morning) bubbled up on its own, she felt an acute sense of having betrayed something secret and previous. I will hate Bridie, I will, was her less-than-satisfactory antidote.

There would have been no eddy of anticipation if Lil had known it would be sixty years before her feet again touched this ground – now so sacred, so indistinguishable from herself. And she would learn, only much later, that before the coming winter was out Maman LaRouche would, only partly against her will, succumb to the engorged, mutinous thing fattening itself inside her. And Monsieur, who had seen death routinely in the War and on the stark faces of babes ravaged by cholera and worse, would not recognize it in the pleading eyes of his wife until she herself begged for the priest. Then, as he had so often vowed, LaRouche strapped on his snowshoes and headed north for Port Sarnia through the maze of deer-trails he thought he knew well. Confused and exhausted he stumbled into the Partridges at Corunna three days later. Partridge suggested a horse, which the weeping, grateful man accepted before he realized that while he had fed and groomed horses for Colonel Baby during the War, he had never actually gotten around to riding one. The priests at St. Joseph's naturally assumed that it was LaRouche himself who required the last rites, and it was almost an hour before the matter was straightened out and Father McAllister tucked the babbling man into the cutter beside him and started on the return journey. At Partridges a Chippewa lad was attached to the entourage to guide them to the interior of the township. However, when they reached Millar's corner at nightfall, the old man was dreaming that he and Mathilde – his Mattie, his Fluffy – were whirling at the centre of the governor's reel under the candelabras of the demi-royal salon as the fiddles and drums applauded their bravado, their *panache*, and Mattie's eyes glowed like chestnuts set in the sweetest, deepest cherrywood flesh. The hubbub of the sleigh's arrival at the cabin woke the dreamer too abruptly and, not quite realizing the transition that had taken place, he flung his partner wide, skipped intricately to his place in the 'set' – to wondrous applause – and keeled over in the snow, half-in and half-out of the cutter. His leg snapped like a cornstalk.

Madame was dead. She had died with as much dignity as the engulfing pain and the absence of God would allow. The ground was frozen during this coldest of winters. LaRouche, in his grief and his own pain, announced that she would be buried properly in sanctified ground at St. Joseph's in Port Sarnia. Father McAllister, doing what he could, returned there the next day with some doubts about the wisdom of God's suffering so many of the French to come unto Him. Meanwhile the boys were despatched to Brown Creek to cut ice. Luc paused long enough to stare piteously at the McGee girl who had arrived with her family that fall to occupy the forsaken farm and who, before donning winter garb, could do little to disguise the wayward curing of her flesh. Maman's body, wrapped in the linen shroud she had brought with her from Sandwich, was packed in ice in the ox-shed, where it remained until spring.

Despite the most professional ministrations of an itinerant quack, LaRouche's leg did not set properly. He suffered constant pain which made it impossible for him to grieve the loss of his life's mate as he should. By March and the first signs of break-up, it was clear that gangrene had set in. Millar sent his eldest boy for a legitimate doctor from Port Sarnia. When he arrived a week later, frost-bitten and muddy, he pronounced gangrene and offered either amputation (in the town, of course, after a jaunt across the spring 'roads') or opium. LaRouche cursed him in English and *joual*, and had him escorted to Millar's corner.

The old man's cries ceased the spring nights, silencing the whipoorwills and bobwhites, piercing the deepest, fatigue-driven sleep of his neighbours for a mile around. He was saved from the final agonies of a gangrenous death when, in the midst of the first warm rain of the season, he contracted tetanus, which pursued him faster than the green venom in his leg. Propped on his bed near the pure-glass window, he watched the last of the snows disintegrate in the rain, exposing as they did the maidenhair mist of his autumn wheat. Over in the ox-shed the last of the ice-blocks was melting.

LaRouche rose in his bed like an unrepentant Job, foam and blood boiling through his seized jaws, his leg right up to his spent loins burning as if someone by mistake had dropped it into a campfire and forgot to apologize. With his last breath he attempted to hurl maledictions at the God who claimed responsibility for all this, to fling at chaos one perfect curse, one jarring repudiation of the sham and hypocrisy he had acquiesced in: coward that he was he would spit in God's face.

His sons drew back in the room at the horror they saw, bracing themselves. Madeleine plugged her ears. Nothing came. The eyes bulged with speech, the clamped jaws ground and held, blooded spittle shot out in garbled strings staining Maman's quilt.

LaRouche died sitting up in seething silence. Outside, the rains continued their soft benediction.

As luck would have it, a Methodist man on his quarterly circuit happened to be in the area scouting converts. At the boys' behest he presided over the double interment, offering comfort to the dead and the surviving. Later on, proper headstones were erected. They rested not more than forty feet from the granite one of their neighbour.

There were now two routes to Port Sarnia. The sort of lumber trail they were now on led north-east to where it met the main road running south-east from the town towards Enniskillen, the undisturbed heart of the Lambton bush. Twenty miles to the west, hugging the River, a trunk road – parts of it already planked – took the circuit rider and carpetbagger all the way to Wallaceburg and thence to Chatham. A number of Indian trails – blazed only – would take them to this latter marvel of the age. Sometime during the mid-afternoon, Papa veered left into the bush, leaving the sun above them.

2

Neither father nor daughter was aware that the frenetic surveying and road-building through the undeveloped townships of Plympton, Enniskillen and Brooke was prompted in part by recent upheavals in Europe and their cataclysmic fallout. In half-a-dozen countries upstart peasants and workers and a few middle-class dreamers had decided – without consulting their betters – to make a home of the lands they had laboured on for generations. They failed. And even as Lil bent to pick a sprig of columbine clinging to a patch of sun-lit grass, the suppressors were wreaking their revenge in the ritual rapine and domestic terrorism indigenous to the race. Thousands more were being added daily to the earth's dispossessed. In Ireland, encouraged by some whimsy of the wind or season, potato blight deposited its indelible pennies on the summer's crop, and hunger happily joined the avengers. Starved and hopeless, a hundred thousand Irish crammed themselves into stinking cargo-ships and sailed for the world's end where, some of them believed, a plot of arable ground lay undespoiled by human intercourse. One contemporary report describes their plight in these terms: "From Grosse Isle, the great charnel-pit of victimized humanity, up to Port Sarnia and all along the borders of our magnificent river; upon the shores of Lake Ontario and Lake Erie – wherever the tide of emigration has extended – are to be found the final resting places of the sons and daughters of Erin; one unbroken chain of graves where repose fathers and mothers, sisters and brothers, in one commingled heap without a tear bedewing the soil or a stone marking the spot."

Lil was annoyed with herself, but she couldn't seem to help it. She was slowing them down. Her head began to spin, probably from too much sun earlier on the open road. She lingered behind a bit to vomit secretly in the underbrush, but Papa's hand was soon on her arm. He wiped her mouth with his flannel hanky. He gave her the last of the water. He sat down and in the healing shade they rested a while. Lil was thirsty so Papa went off in search of a good spring. He took a long time. When they started up again, moving carefully from blaze to blaze under Papa's practiced eye, they stopped every half-hour or so. They rested and drank the cool spring-water. Lil felt better but very weak. When she rose to signal she was ready to go, Papa touched her shoulder with one finger, and sat down. Just before supper she shamed herself utterly by drifting off to sleep.

When she woke she saw that Papa had built a small fire and in the only pot he had brought had boiled some tea, which made their dried beef and biscuits taste much better.

"Why don't you have one of Maman's cookies?" Papa said.

Lil did.

As a result of Lil's pokiness, a trek of four hours or so took much longer. The shadows around them thickened and grew aggressive. So did the mosquitoes. Papa paused to examine a configuration of blazes on a huge hickory tree.

"The river road's only a half-mile away," Papa said, not to himself as he often did, but to Lil. "It's too late an' we're too tired to walk the other five miles up to the Partridges," he continued. "We'll make camp right here on the high ground."

Lil was sure she could hear the River tuning up for its nightsong.

With his swift, sharp hatchet Papa cut down several saplings, bent them into a frame and covered it with cedar boughs. The lean-to was just big enough for two, with a sturdy elm-bole to rest your back against. More boughs were spread on the ground to serve as a bed when they were ready for sleep. But not just yet. In the opening of the lean-to, Papa built three small fires ringed by stones, two of which he smudged with damp evergreens, leaving the middle one to flicker brightly below the steaming coffee. Papa and Lil were scrunched inside with the blanket over their shoulders, the cozy smoke keeping the mosquitoes at bay, and Maman's raspberry tarts sweetening on their tongues. Papa's left arm was raised and Lil snuggled in against him, relishing the smokiness of his rough shirt. Lil was about to slide down into sleep when she realized that Papa was talking.

"Bridie was the eldest. Eighteen and a local beauty. To us, she was a second mother. Then one day, just like that, Pa announces she is gonna be married up with an older man, a crony of his. Bridie says *no* in that sweet, iron-willed way she had. There was a terrible row, I can tell you. Ma hid in the stairwell cupboard. Next day without sayin' good-day-to-you or by-your-leave, she's gone. 'She'll come back,' I said to Ma, 'she loves us.' 'Let the harridan be and be damned!' Pa rants and raves for three days, 'She's no kin of mine.' 'But sure an' she's off in a ditch or a bog somewhere, injured an' callin' out for our help,' Ma says whenever she can stop her cryin'. Pa says nothin'. The case is closed. He refuses to say her name an' forbids us to. She's drummed out of the tribe. Dead."

Papa lit his pipe. A mosquito was biting Lil's neck but she was not about to slap it. For a few moments Papa breathed through his pipe.

"I felt terrible," he said in a lower, different kind of voice. "I felt she'd abandoned me. When you're only twelve, somethin' like that seems like a betrayal. You put all your trust in one person an' then, like that, it's gone."

The mosquito perished in its own blood. Papa drew the blanket around Lil's head. She snuggled close again, gripping his left hand with both of hers.

"It was two years later, Ma was quite sick, an' this letter arrives addressed to her. We all recognize Birdie's writing. She was a beautiful writer. She taught me to read, as best she could. So I read the letter, after Pa had headed for one of his meetins', of course. Bridie was in a place called Toronto, Upper Canada. She was well. She was goin' off to a town somewheres in the bush to work as a domestic and as a tutor to some little boy. She didn't name the town. She said we wasn't to bother tryin' to find out, she loved all of us dearly but she just had to do things this way as it was the only way for her. When I grew up, I knew what she meant. Back then, I hated her even more."

The moon slipped out from behind one of the high, breezy clouds – feigning interest in the world's affairs.

"When your Mama an' me come out here some years later, we made no attempt at findin' her. As you're gonna see soon, this is a big country. But nobody ever put one over on Bridie, not even Pa with all his political shenanigans and bluster. Just after you was born we got a letter hand-delivered from Port Sarnia. From Bridie. She welcomed us to the county an' said we was welcome in her house anytime. We always intended to go up there but your Mama was never well enough. We thought it best, for a while, not to get your hopes up. Then things just went on as they often do, an' nothin' ever really gets done. Some important things just don't get done, 'cause we go on as we are, day after day."

He poked at the smudges, scattering the swarms.

"'Course that'll all be rectified soon. You're gonna see your Aunt Bridie and Uncle Chester at last, you are." Papa gave her an extra squeeze. And the little boy? She thought.

"Yes, my precious, you're gonna have the time of your life up there. We'll help out Aunt and Uncle for a while, then we'll buy ourselves a chunk of that cleared land with the cash we get for the homestead, an' before you know it we'll have a white clapboard house to live in. We'll only be a mile from the town, too, with stores and mills and meetin' halls. First thing I'm gonna do is take you into town to Cameron's emporium and buy you your first store-bought dress – calico or lawn or kendall, take your pick, you'll be as pretty as a butterfly in a flax field in August."

Papa squeezed again. Lil gripped his hand to let him know she was still awake. The main fire was in its mellow, amber phase.

"Naturally your Aunt Bridie, bein' an' educated woman herself, will want you to have some proper schoolin'. They've got a school in Port Sarnia where anybody can go to learn readin' and other things. You're gonna grow into a genuine young lady, I reckon: there'll be no stoppin' you once you reach that town."

Are there lots of Scotsmen there? Lil wanted to ask.

Papa took his arm from her shoulder, shook the fire vigorously until the flames jumped again, and then reached into his pack. In his hands he held something small and leather. A book.

"I don't want your Aunt Bridie thinkin' your Mama an' me didn't bring you up properly," he said, as Lil for the first time looked directly up into his face where the flame-induced shadows fluttered irresolutely. "This here's a New Testament, a Bible. It was a gift, long ago, from my mother. I wrote an inscription to you in the front cover. My spellin's not too good so I had Mr. Millar write down the actual words. Someday real soon you'll be able to read it, an' the Bible, too. I want you to keep it an' treasure it, no matter what happens to you in this awful, tryin' world."

Papa had to stop to clear his throat. Lil reached out and took the Testament, its covers carrying the warmth of Papa's hands into hers.

"I'll tell you what it says, for now," he went on. Once again he cleared his throat like an actor before an entrance. "To my dearest princess, the Lady Fairchild, from your Papa who loves you forever."

Lil tucked the precious object into her secret pouch, and slipped drowsily into the care of Papa's arms. Tiny tremors shook her, gently, to sleep.

She dreamt that Mama and Papa were seated on a scarlet sofa before a roaring fire: Papa was talking and talking, and Mama – curled beside him – listened with love.

The sun, well above the tree-tops, woke Lil with a start. She was not in the least surprised, however, to look over and see that she was alone.

3

Papa had left her the food, water and utensils. And a note. On folded, thick, yellow-white paper. Lil did not open it. *I can't read. I can't read.* But another voice said: you're grown up now; the new road is a twenty-minute walk across a blazed trail; there will be travellers on that road; they will help. Mrs. Partridge is five miles up that road; she will remember. Everyone in Port Sarnia will know who Bridie is. I have nothing to fear. Papa loves me; he expects me to go to my Aunt Bridie.

But then maybe he's gone off to scout the new road? Besides good folk, there are pedlars and bounty-hunters to beware of. It would be terrible if I wandered off and Papa came back to find me gone. He'd be so worried, he'd be so disappointed in me. I must stay here till he comes for me. That's why he left the food and water. He thinks I'm sick. He loves me. It says so in this little book, it's written there, forever.

When she finished the last of the water, Lil began to worry. It was past five o'clock. Papa was not coming. (It would be much later before Lil would learn that the abolitionist man – who had rowed Papa to safety across the River and who was to return before dawn to lead her north to Port Sarnia – had got caught in a whirlpool on his way back, ran aground and lay unconscious for half a day before he awoke to find his leg broken in three places.) He expected her to get to that road and find the Partridges. Still feeling dizzy and very weak (what was wrong with her? she thought), Lil gathered her belongings and looked westward for the next blaze. The shadows were massing even now, and it was not easy to pick out the year-old slashes from trunk to trunk or the modest impressions left on the trail by its mocassined patrons. An hour or so later Lil admitted reluctantly that she was lost. She was not scared of being alone in the woods; she never had been. The mosquitoes were bad but she had matches, she could make a camp of sorts. What concerned her was that she didn't know where she was. Nor would she be able to find her bearings in a terrain bereft of familiar landmarks. Desperately she tried to keep to the westward by the sun but it disappeared, even as a hovering light, for minutes at a time in the closed canopy one hundred and fifty feet overhead.

When she stumbled into a beaver meadow, she looked up and saw in despair that it was now fully night-time. The stars winked invitations at her. Then she saw the dipper – the Silver Gourd – shining clear in its northern berth. She turned due left into the mosquito-fed darkness. Ten minutes later she emerged from the dense forest onto the roadway. The fresh planking hummed beneath her feet. Inside she hummed too and did a little jig. She looked northward up the forty-foot width of the highway. She was exhausted. A sort of numbness was starting to spread up the calves of her legs. She couldn't make it to the Partridges. She really couldn't.

She was also very thirsty. She knew she shouldn't sleep without drinking. Then she remembered: this was the River Road. To her left she saw that the bush was thin and intermittent, smallish pines in a sandy soil that glittered in the starlight. She listened, forcing her breath in. Though the night was still, her River poured its restless, endless energy onward. What a wonderful sound, Lil thought aloud. Slowly but with more certainty than she had felt all day, Lil eased her way through the pine grove towards the beckoning music of the great waterway. There would be some breeze there, and open space: she could sleep undisturbed in the sandy bank. In the morning everything would be all right. Papa would be proud of her.

Just as the muted roar of the River was beginning to build in her ears, Lil came to a tiny feeder stream. Bending, she scooped the fresh, chill water to her face, drinking and cleansing simultaneously. The breeze off the water ahead was cool on her cheeks. She could see the moon plainly through the last trees between her and her goal. She was about to step out onto the sandy bank when she froze. The first warning she had of danger was the waver of firelight above the shoreline; then came the smell of burnt meat; then the voices; and their unmistakable accents.

In the shimmering glow around her, Lil saw that she was standing, still hidden by the pines, slightly above a sort of cove where the stream entered the River, a gravelly indentation really that formed a beach four or five feet below the main line of the bank. A pit-fire was in full bloom; two figures were seated on stumps, roasting something that might have been rabbit. A longish bundle of something lay rumpled in the shadows behind them. On the point formed by the cove, tied to a boulder, a row-boat rocked and complained.

"Goddammit, I figure we oughta haul his black arse across while the gettin's good."

"I'm hungry. So are you."

"Hungry for two thousand dollars, I am."

"Besides, I don't like that moon. It's gonna cloud over afore midnight. Eat."

"This shit's all burnt."

"Suits you then, don't it."

Without realizing it Lil had backed off so that she was fully shielded by a tall pine. Neither man was looking in her direction; they faced the south-west where the moon sat, unclouded. Something icy and alien gripped her. She could not flee; she could not even close her eyes. Hence, she was the first to see the rumpled bundle flinch, stretch, and assemble itself. Solomon was sitting up, his hands bound behind him with rope. Another rope dangled loosely from an ankle. Somehow he had worked his legs free. Without once taking his eyes off the backs of his captors, he rose to his full height without the slightest sound and edged towards the boat fifteen feet away.

"Sometimes, Sherm, you talk to me's if I was no better'n that nigger."

Sherm let the opportunity pass.

"Matter-of-fact, think I'll feed some of this here charcoal shit to him right now. Cain't have him lookin' too lean an' all, can we?" Beau turned. "Christ! He's after the boat."

Both men jumped instantly, but Solomon was already there. He placed one foot over the gunwale, the other on the rock next to the painter, and gave a tremendous shove. Lil could hear the whoosh of air leave his lungs as he did so. The painter rope popped free and the boat shot out into the swift current. Solomon fell face-down into the aft section with a clatter of wood and bone. Unruddered, the boat spun slowly – caught in a momentary eddy.

"What the fuck you doin', you stupid nigger! You cain't row that thing with your hands tied up. Come on back here!"

"We'll get him downstream," Sherm said, already heading back for his gun. "If not, he'll end up on the other side. They always do."

But Beau wasn't listening. "Oh *Jesus! Jesus!*" he screamed as if his soul had been seared. "He's goin' over!"

Solomon was standing upright; his powerful six-foot frame burned black against the pre-harvest moon behind him. He was standing on one of the thwarts staring down into the current that was just catching the boat and swinging it, it seemed, southward to safety, and freedom. But Solomon leaped high and northward, as if his fugitive eye lay still upon the gourd of the North Star. His figure, abandoned by the boat, arced across the horizon and entered the welcoming water face-first. The eddy of bubbles, which was all that marked his exit, was soon swept away.

"I never seen the like o' that, *never*. Did ya see the stupid fucker, Sherm. Jumps right in there an' takes our two thousand bucks with him. I tell ya, I'll never figure out a nigger if I live a hundred years."

Sherm was throwing water on the fire and gathering their things together. "We better get lookin' for another boat. This ain't exactly friendly territory, you know."

Beau continued to stare out over the foaming torrent, wild with the weight of the glacial seas behind it, and yelled to that portion of the universe he could see: "Why'd ya go an' do that, ya stupid, ignorant son-of-a-bitch?"

"*Why?*"

No echo came back.

"Maybe we can get the body," Sherm said.

4

Long after the bounty-hunters had left – their fire doused, the sky clouded over and menacing, the wind rushing to keep up with the river's urgency – Lil stood where she was and wrestled with the dark angels of her imagination. Once again she saw Solomon hunted through the unending nights, fleeing further and further into the forest. Later in her life she would know that he fled not because he feared capture or bondage or humiliation – these he had known and borne already – but because he needed to find, in these woods, a nightmare more horrific than his own, to stare it straight in the eye, and whisper oblivion to it.

How welcome those waters must have felt, she thought, how sweet the tender descent, how soft the bottom-sands sifted and cleansed by centuries of seeking, how loving the icy currents that would let the flesh float unrotted from the bones that would drift, inch by hour, seaward over time – they eyes in the blanched, purged skull titled forever towards light.

Lil knew she must get to Corunna as soon as possible at whatever cost. She had no idea how much time she had spent staring out at the River. The night wind was up; the sky was covered and threatening. She was shivering with fright or, worse, fever. She couldn't feel her feet against the road as she turned north, stumbling in the dark on jagged boards, patches of logs and branches. Then the rain came, lashing and cold, blending with the blood running down her calves

She fell. She rolled onto her side, partly screened by some underbrush, numb and shivering, peering curiously at the silver imbedded in her right hand. Her eyes closed. No dream forestalled her slow falling away.

Even though she had not yet opened her eyes, Lil was awake. She was warm. Her shivering had subsided. She was propped up against something soft and inviting. A wooly shawl curled affectionately over her shoulders. She had slept. Someone had found her and brought her to a warm, safe place. Nearby a dampened fire radiated heat and welcome. *Papa!* She opened her eyes and looked over at the crouched figure across from her.

"Ah, the little one wakes up."

"Have you seen Papa?" she asked, faintly, in Pottawatomie.

Southener, his kindly eyes scrutinizing her, said: "I made you drink the tamarack tea; I am sorry if I hurt you. You were shaking with the swamp fever."

Lil felt too weak to move, but Southener noted her anxious glances about the campsite, which was deep in one of the pine groves.

"They are safe, little one," he smiled, his skin as rough as hickory bark, his sable hair flecked with gray and tied behind with a leather barrette, his gnarled warrior's hands too large now for the uses to which they were put and turning restlessly in upon themselves. "I found them near you when I picked you up, soaking and hot, on that pitiful roadway." He reached down and produced Lil's drenched pack and the pouch with the sacred treasures of her life in it.

"Thank you," Lil whispered, keeping to his language.

"You're young and very strong," he said, stirring the fire a little to give more light to their conversation. "Already the fever is gone. By morning you'll be ready to go north."

Did he know?

"When I started to dry out your things after the rain stopped, I found this map," he said unfolding for her Papa's letter which she could not read. "It will tell you where to go."

So Papa had not left her a note after all. Lil tried to think of what that meant, but she could not think at all, she was drifting into sleep again, relieved even to feel the jagged pain in her right hand. When her eyes once more opened, the glow of false-dawn was visible through the pines overhead. Southener was awake, watching her as if she were some sort of wooden idol whose very presence would bring the news he was waiting for. He was beside her, with steaming tea at the ready. As she sipped at its fragrance, Southener washed the cuts on her legs with a piece of flannel and then stuck some tiny leaves on each of them. The stinging was not unpleasant.

"As soon as the sun comes up, I must leave you. There's meat in your pack; eat it if you can. You're safe here. When you feel like walking, the road is directly east of us; the morning sun over the tree-line will take you right there."

"I remember you, Southener," Lil said. "I'm much bigger now."

"You were the best dancer," Southener said. "I watched you all day. You let the elves loose in your legs. You let the trolls decide for themselves. Now your tongue tells the true story."

"Old Samuels taught me," Lil said, wide awake now, every nerve alert.

"You have made me happy in my age," he went on in a hushed tone that Lil had already come to recognize and revere, perfectly aware that both of them were, in a special sense, listeners. "I am almost at the end of my exile. I have little use any more for the magic amulet that has shielded me from my enemies and rescued me from my own folly many-a-time." From a pouch at his waist he drew a pebble of blood-red jasper that glowed even in the dull dawn-light, that pulsed as if quick with hope and memory, whose indistinct oval had been rubbed over generations to resemble – if you looked long and rightly enough – the vibrant, plasmic bubble of a baby's heart. Southener let it lie in his open palm, let it breathe the fire's flame for a while.

"This will bring you luck all your days," he said. "Not happiness, as you already know, for they do not wear the same colour. It will make your life a good one, with enough joy to keep you from despair, enough hurt to keep you loving. It will help you find a home, here and in the hereafter. It has helped me do all these things, fivefold. I am nearing the end of a journey that's bigger than I am. I received this magic stone on a sacred ground, long known as such by generation upon generation of tribes who have dwelt in these woods and waters and passed on, as we all do. I ask only two things in return. The days of its guardianship are almost over; there is little magic left in the forests and the streams, older now than our legends; the locomotives of the white man's soul are on their way. You will hear them soon. So, when you have no more use for the stone's powers, I ask that you return it to the sacred grove whence it came, to the gods of that place who lent their spirit to it. I have looked at the map your Papa left, and I know when the proper time comes, you will be close to it. There is no way of marking such a place on a map, for the penitent must feel its presence before he can see it. You will know when you are standing on it, though, because it resides beneath the protecting branches of a giant hickory on a knoll just where the forest begins, and when you look west and north you will be able to see, at the commencement of summer, the joining of the Lake and the River set perfectly on a line to the North Star, whom we call the Eye of Wendigo."

Lil was watching the miniature heart, absorbing light like blood.

"Secondly, I am nearing my own end. My people have been scattered like chaff before the flail. There is no home for us to rest our souls in. Save one. North of the town your father has chosen for you lies the military reserve, a boggy swampland no one, not even the rapacious whites, will ever want. Above the main bay, just past the point where lake and river meet, is a small cove among the sand dunes, and here, unobserved among the grasses and snakeweed, is an ancient Indian cemetery which bears the remains of hundreds of souls who could find no burial place with their own people. It's a graveyard for wanderers, for the lost, and for the permanently dispossessed. If the military knew it was there they would perhaps allow the spirits to remain undisturbed, but certainly they would let no new dead be interred there. So it is that we few remaining outcasts must have our corpses carried there in the dark and secretly and unceremonially buried in that consecrated earth. My request to you is to keep that ground holy in your mind, protect it with your life, and once in a while honour it with your presence and prayers. If you see a freshly-turned mound among the milkweed and rustling poplar, know that I lie under it, wanting, like all of us, to be remembered."

With that he placed the talisman in Lil's left hand and rolled her fingers gently over it. Some part of its potency must have been immediately transferred for when Southener looked up to check the wonder in Lil's face, she was blissfully asleep.

The instructions the map gave were sharp and ineluctable. Lil was good at drawing and pictures. With her pendant, crucifix, rabbit's foot, Testament and Southener's amulet tucked lovingly in their leather sachet, Lil began the long walk north moments after sunrise.

She did not stop at the Partridges nor acknowledge, if she saw it, the wave of greeting and farewell anxiously offered. She walked steadily, purposefully, and to any one of the startled onlookers in the booming hamlet of Froomfield below the Reserve, almost serenely. "She's in a daze or a reverie," was one unsolicited opinion. "Nobody passes through *this* town and ignores our windmill," was another. If Lil saw or heard the creaking, anomalous replica of its Dutch cousin that intercepted the north-west blows from the Lake, she gave no sign.

Through the Reserve, six miles long, the road meandered and rested, but the wisp of a figure of a girl kept its pace – noticed and unaccosted – sights set on what a map held out. Just before noon, with the sun in full stretch, Lil walked into her first town.

In her head Papa's map hovered like a detached palm-print, a legacy in code. Her boots, worn thin, cracked on the town's singular macadam. Lil was tempted neither left nor right. It was possible that she did not see Cameron's Emporium with its checker-glass windows a-glitter with frill and frumpery; did not smell the dust and wheeze from Blaikie's Foundry, home to the famous Blaikie Patent Steam Engine; did not sniff at the delectables from two bakeries nor the acrid smarting of Hall's tannery in the weighted, standing heat of summer; did not hear the torturing of wood nor the grinding of ill-matched gears in Flintoft's steam-mill; did not respond to her own reflection in the coppery mirror of Durand's pond where the little walking-bridge crossed the canal from Perch Creek, nor laugh at the gleeful whoop and water-slap of near-naked youths emancipated by summer; did not cross herself or say a grateful prayer on passing the seven chapels dedicated – each in its own fervent, unecumenical manner – to the indivisibility of the Divine Spirit; did not smile, in passing, at Crampton's "Double-N-One" tavern for wayfaring tipplers who, if they stood on their heads, could discern the sign INN as it was meant to appear to the sober and upright. Indeed, no-less-than-three respectable ladies and one irrespectable gentleman nodded to her out of concern or curiosity, and received no decipherable recognition of their magnanimity.

As Lil left the last of the ordered pathways, her eyes set upon the red-pine forest to the west of the Errol Road, the one o'clock factory whistle at Blaikie's shrilled and beck-oned, and out in the blue bays of Lake Huron just beyond the pine-ridge the steamer *Ben Franklin* hooted cheerily and democratically as it pointed itself north to the fresh-water oceans of the Cree and Ojibwa. A mile up this high road Lil noticed the break in the forest wall. For the first time in many hours her heart jumped in its stirrups. The map was real. She could read. Something vital with a future waited for her at the end of this lane. Although her exhausted feet made no distinctive shift in their cadence, Lil was sure she was skipping. A melody disarranged itself in her head and sailed like a loose trapeze.

At the end of the lane, set in two pockets of cleared pine, lay the farms. Small one to the left with a log hut and sheds; large one to the right with the whitewashed, split-log house and the sideboard barns and the emerald grapevines and the pond with Sunday-white geese on it.

For a while she just stood at the point where the lane branched into paths, waiting for something to happen. Some large creature let out a muffled sneeze; hens, unseen, clicked pebbles into their craws; a sow wallowed, setting off a sequence of squeals and oozing. Above the stone chimney on the white-washed cottage, a bubble of pale smoke lifted in expectation, then stalled. Above it a red-tailed squirrel hung and craned, feigning patience.

At the last moment Lil remembered to knock on the firmly latched, blue-trimmed door set in the exact centre of the facing wall. She felt the shadow of the overhanging eave cool her cheek. She pulled tightly the bridle on her heart, and waited.

The door was pulled inward slowly, guardedly. Lil saw the strong woman's-hand, red from the sun, gripping the sash before the face and figure were disclosed.

"Yes?"

"Aunt Bridie?"

"An' who might you be, if I may ask?"

"I'm…Lil."

"What do you want here, girl? State your business or leave a body in peace."

"Papa sent me."

The hand dropped from the sash, the door sagged fully open, untended.

Sensing the bewilderment in the woman's face, Lil's heart sank. She fought against the faintness and vertigo as best she could, but it felt as if her bones had melted outright in a treacherous sun. As she slumped onto the doorstep, she was certain she heard herself say, "I'm Lily. Lily Fairchild."

6

1

Saturday was Lily's favourite day. Summer and winter, spring and fall, Saturday was the day of deliverance. Even though the late June sun had lifted barely half a brow over the forest rim in the distant east, Lily felt liberated; and she conveyed her mounting sense of excitement to Benjamin, the Walpole 'paint' who jogged happily over the rough road towards the village. Soon-to-be an official town, Lily recalled. A Saturday in June was particularly magical.

Although Aunt Bridie had rejected Uncle Chester's plea for a genuine birthday cake – "You'll spoil the child silly, you old coot" – she had baked strawberry tarts special for the occasion and even wrapped the newly-made linen blouse and plain calico skirt in tissue as if it were a real surprise. Uncle Chester clapped when she opened it; Auntie gave him one of her quartering glances but said nothing. Later as they sat outside on wicker chairs in the dooryard perfumed with wild hedgeroses, with the gloaming of the solstice settling as softly as ash about them, Bachelor Bill walked over, and through his shy grin – made more prominent by the absence of all but two mismatching front teeth – presented Lily with a blue hair ribbon that might have been made of silk. "Ma bought it for Violet way back, but she don't wear it," he explained. Lily kissed him on the cheek, which either frightened or scandalized him so much he could not be per-suaded to play the mouth-organ that never left the back pocket of his overalls. When he had gone, Auntie mumbled about such "fool things" as hair ribbons, so Lily, though tempted by the encouragement in Uncle's eye, hid the gift away with her other precious things. Several weeks after her arrival, so long ago now, she had thought she ought to reveal to Auntie the sacred objects in her treasure-pouch, but even then something told her to hold back, that a lady as angular and impressive as Aunt Bridie would not likely be overawed by a talisman or even one of God's Testaments. So they remained secreted in her room to be taken out on those few occasions when she had felt unhappy here, and even then with no sense of why she would be overwhelmed suddenly with a sadness for things once prized and irretrievable.

Which was not often. And certainly never on Saturdays. She reined in Benjamin as they neared Exmouth Street, the edge of the vast, cleared plain that was soon to be an official town, a county seat. It was a new split-log road and very rough. She peeked anxiously back at her cargo of eggs and fresh raspberries – so neatly packed in the little boxwood containers Uncle Chester tacked together with such guarded delicacy. Auntie had given him part of the barn for a workshop, which he shared uncomplainingly with Sultana the Guernsey and this good-natured Indian pony. Indeed, even before Lily's coming Uncle had fashioned the market-wagon with its double-leather springs and straw padding and custom compartments for Auntie's eggs and seasonal specialties.

Lily had no reason in this world to be sad – ever. She loved her Aunt and Uncle. She was loved by them. Auntie, her flame-red hair so earnestly harnessed during the day, would come to Lily in her own bed with its feather tick, her hair loose and haphazard, her ice-blue eyes weakened by fatigue, and bending over her bless Lily's cheek with a dry, well-meant kiss. "Thank your maker for makin' you and givin' you such a day," she would invariably whisper before snuffing the candle. It was the only religious sentiment ever known to have passed her lips. Auntie did not, it seemed, believe in "all this churchin'" and what-is-more preferred not to debate the point. Uncle Chester, if he held an opinion on the subject, did not offer it. Auntie taught Lily everything about "how to get along in this world", taking the girl with her into the fields where, in the rich humus of the cleared pine-woods, they grew vegetables of every tint and texture. Not wheat like the farmers in the townships east along the London Road or north along the Errol Road, who had to haul their crop to the grist mills where they "left half their profits" and had to count on England's wars in Russia and elsewhere to bump up the price or let it come crashing down. "Turnips are slow-growin' but they eat easy and winter over," Auntie said more than once during a back-bending weeding of the strawberries or a hoeing of the potatoes. Auntie's skin never tanned, as Lily's did if she persisted, so she always wore a bonnet that framed her sharp features like a sapper's helmet and a linen shawl that came down over her wrists and was fastened with a workmanlike pewter clasp. In the August humidity sweat poured down her legs, staining the tops of her guardsman's boots, but not once would she pause to mop her brow, swinging the hoe or rake or turnip-knife with dogged efficiency. Lily, wanting to cry out sometimes at her rebellious muscles, swallowed her aches and grew strong.

These vegetables, and the eggs from their hundred Rhode Islands, were taken to town each Saturday where they found a ready market. Although most of the villagers had gardens of their own, the three hotels and five-boarding houses that served the numerous bachelor workers busy in the new factories and on the right-of-way clearance out to Enniskillen – along with the stopover sailors and passengers – needed a ceaseless supply of eggs and vegetables in season. Aunt Bridie had been the first to seize this opportunity, and though she had periodic competition from the farmer's market and several other hopeful entrepreneurs, her reliability, home-delivery service, and unfailingly superior produce had won her – despite the suspicion with which she was viewed by the respectable burghers of the fledgling county seat – a steady and profitable business. "Well," said Mrs. Salter, the lay preacher's ample wife, "I'll give the Devil her due, she's a real worker, that woman." "Take care of the pennies an' the pounds'll take care of themselves," Auntie told Lily that day three summers ago when she had taken her along for the first time to "learn the business" and "see for yourself how the other-half lives."

"Your Auntie's the smartest woman in this township," Uncle Chester said, helping her stake the beans that second summer. "She knows how to keep the bugs off these plants better'n anybody else for miles around; learned it from a book she did, back in the London days. Then she sees this pine-bush when we first come lookin' up here, an' she says here's the best spot for what we want but I says it's a mile from town an' no-where near the cleared lots on the London Road, but she says the soil'll be better here, and of course she was right, includin' that sandy stretch towards the lakeside where the berries grow big as plums, an' includin' the pine itself which we sold the first year and every year since – never burnt a log, we didn't."

Uncle Chester had lost his rhythm and a section of the bean plants crashed stupidly to the ground. "Mind you now, it was cuttin' them pines that give me the crick in my back, so's I ain't been too good at weedin' an' heavy work ever since, which along with my fluctuatin' ticker don't make me the hardiest farmer." The bean-bush, surprised, tripped again.

"Then your Auntie decides to go in for eggs, so we buys the hens an' I build the two coops and we're in business." Lil looked at the east field next to Bachelor Bill's make-shift barn where their only field-crop – feed corn – was greening in the sun. "Yessir, it's your Auntie's got the head for business." And the hands to straighten this crooked wood and the will to make soft things stiffen and yield.

The sun was fully up when Benjamin went past the London Road crossing and kept southerly on Front Street at a brisk trot. To her right, Lily could see the cobalt of the St. Clair River, its beauty only slightly dimmed by familiarity. She had not yet seen the Lake, though every day steamers left the bay for distant points north, and its un-touched beaches lay less than a mile through the pines behind her house – the muffled thunder of its breakers audible below the wind on stormy nights in April or November. Auntie did not appreciate young girls "traipsin' off". "Nothin' to see up there but a lot of water," she'd add, though Uncle's look said otherwise.

Past the London Road lay the town itself, boasting more than a thousand souls. Al-ready a second main-street back from the River was filling up with clapboard and split-log houses and shops and a second tannery. She liked its name: Christina, which made her think of a copper necklace tinkling in a breeze. Benjamin, unaided, drew driver and cart straight down Front Street to the Western Hotel opposite the Ferry Dock, no more than half a mile from the site of the last gift-giving ceremony. She always started with the hotels since their staffs were up at dawn and happy to have her wide-awake greeting. Then she did the boarding-houses on the five east-west intersecting streets that stretched, houseless, into cleared land for more than a mile. To Lily this section looked like a graveyard for trees. By then it was usually after seven and she moved on to the fifteen or twenty scattered homes on the route – abodes of the well-to-do who, though they could afford gardens and gardeners, preferred to be observed dispensing cash for their produce.

As she pulled up to the St. Clair Inn, Lily thought fleetingly of those early days when she had huddled under a shawl clinging to a straight-backed Aunt Bridie, afraid of things that even months before would not have fazed her. But she had suddenly become Lily Ramsbottom and strange people stared out at her and spoke at her in eccentric urban accents. Even so, she helped by handing Auntie the right boxes, rearranging those left in the cart, and feeding, watering and soothing Benjamin excessively. And she kept her ears and a sly eye open…

"Good morning, Bridie," said Mrs. McWhinney, the clothier's wife, in an off-hand way from her watch at the rose bush. "Just take them right through the shed there and leave them on the right side of the bench by the sink, that's a good dear," she added, addressing her Sunday school class at the C. of E.

Auntie set the eggs and case of cabbages raucously on a table by the shed door. "No need to stir, Maggie," she called out, "I'll collect next time."

Maggie inadvertently cut the throat of a prize rose.

"Morning, Miz Ramsbottom," said the Reverend McHarg's missus from the back door of the red-fronted brick manse, her voice carrying to the far pews.

"Three dozen today, Clara?"

"Who's the little bundle you brung with you?" Pince-nez poking around Auntie, glinting towards the cart on the street.

"Got some late raspberries I think the youngster'd like. Like to see 'em?"

"I'll come out and have a look, I will," burbled Mrs. McHarg, tying up the strings of her mottled bonnet and brushing past a startled Aunt Bridie, who recovered in time to insert her body between the pince-nez and the cowering shawl on the cart-seat.

"Oh what a dear little orphling! Where *did* you pick such a precious thing up?"

Auntie reached into the cart, drew out a quart of enticing berries, and said evenly: "These are free, for my best customer."

Mrs. McHarg, as a Presbyterian inured to temptation, faltered long enough to take the offering in both hands, but quickly regained the offensive. "A foundling?" she asked with the tip of her Calvinist nose.

Auntie touched the reins smartly and Benjamin lurched forward. Looking straight ahead she said, "My daughter," and was already moving too resolutely for any sort of riposte to be heard. There was none – though a berry-box may have cracked open as it struck the ground.

"My gracious, you're early! Barely got my bonnet on! But ain't you a sight for sore eyes; an' you brung the wee one along for company. How's my Lily Blossom doin' today? Cat got your tongue?" Mrs. Salter was constitutionally cheerful despite her husband being a Methodist lay preacher who could, according to Auntie "rant and roll with the best of them hell-an-damnationers."

"Heard a box of your berries went bad on you last week," Auntie said from the side porch of the St. Clair Inn. "Here's an extra two boxes of the best. Guaranteed."

The good lady blushed. "Goodness me, but it's that big-mouth girl of mine blabbin' an' exaggeratin' all over town. I'll take the switch to her, I reckon." She also took the berries.

Vines of ivy and other exotica climbed about a third of the way up the walls of the stone cottage belonging to the Misses Baines-Powell, plump Caroline and fat Charlotte. The sign in front of their shiny oak door announced "Baines-Powell: Musical Instruction, By Arrangement." Auntie tried to explain what that meant. Only one of the instructresses ever came to the back door, though not always the same one. The other one hovered in the draped shadows of the sitting room about five feet behind.

"Found a slug in my cabbage," said Miss Charlotte, peering past Auntie at Lily – who was holding a rack of berry-boxes – as if there were some direct but unnamable connection between slugs and girl-helpers of questionable kin.

"Boil them like I told you?" Aunt Bridie said.

"Of course. Made no difference. Ugly thing popped out onto Miss Baines-Powell's plate an' she almost 'et it, *didn't you dear?*"

Muffled assent from within.

"Get a rollin' boil, Charlotte, an' keep at it for five to seven minutes. Nothin' else can be done."

"Hard to get satisfactory service these days, *isn't it dear?*" Caroline, recovered from her fright, agreed.

Auntie took three boxes of berries from the rack and set them beside the eggs on the porch step. "Almost forgot the carrots. Lily, dash out an' fetch the regular order of carrots, will you, dear?"

"You hear about the new delivery service startin' up next week?" Charlotte said. Caroline apparently had heard all about it and thought it a grand idea and high time, too.

Aunt Bridie waited for Lily to come up. "There you are, Charlotte. That'll be ninety-six cents. Any changes for next week? The corn'll be in most likely."

Charlotte gave Auntie the money and stood watching them leave. Lily always lingered behind a bit, ears pricked.

"Scruffy little ragamuffin, ain't she?"

"You think with the prices she charges a person she'd be able to put a decent dress on the little wretch."

"Might even be pretty, don't you think, Lottie?"

"It'd take some srubbin', I'm afraid."

Auntie always walked steadily forward; she was not a lingerer. Once she turned and said, "Don't let those two old maids go puttin' a lot of tom-fool notions in your head."

2

The Templeton house was special. There was about it an immediate and palpable magic that never left even after three years of weekly stops. (The first day she saw it, a voice as strong as Old Samuels' said: "Someday you're going to live here.") It was the most attractive, though by no means the most ostentatious, house in town. It wasn't even brick, but the siding was lovingly lapped and painted a shade of blue that resembled the river just as the ice leaves it in March. In spring and summer – even into fall – the gardens here flourished, rejuvenated, and bedazzled. Never had Lily seen such exotic, such wholly domestic, flora: delphinium, giant poppies, sunflowers, peonies, arboured roses, and marigolds and lilies with the tang of marsh still in them. In the winter the snow blossomed in its own way, keeping an echo of former lushness absolute. Mrs. Alice Templeton almost always intercepted them at the side door. Trim, silver-haired, neatly attired, smiling at you with both eyes, she invariably asked them to come into the little den. Sometimes even Maurice Templeton, the prominent lawyer, was there snoozing into a gray volume on his lap. Sometimes if it were raining or exceptionally cold, Auntie would accept, and Lily would slip in behind her and feast upon the book-lined walls, the porcelain figurines and wispy-blue chinaware tempting her from an adjoining sanctum. The odour of pipe-tobacco malingered and stirred the memory.

"Do come in, for Pete's sake, Bridie Ramsbottom," Mrs. Templeton would say. "You think we hadn't known one another for ten years."

"Well, then, just for a minute. The girl's a bit chilled, I daresay. But we can't stay long."

The girl was frozen through, and aflame with curiosity. On a lucky day there was Ceylon tea and tarts, and talk.

"Got a schedule to keep," Auntie would say, warming her fingers on the tea-cup. They always stopped here last. "Don't tell Mrs. Templeton, though," Aunt Bridie would say as they drove off. "We'd never get away from the old gabbler. Never did hear anyone like to carry on so and fritter away so much time. Besides, your uncle'd wear his shoes to bed if we left him alone too long."

"Your brother's daughter, you say? I can certainly see your eyes there, no question about that."

"She's had no upbringin', mind you, but she's a good worker."

"Another cake, Lily?"

"No ma'am. Thank you."

"Go ahead, you look like it'd do you good."

Lily glanced at Aunt Bridie. "No, thank you, ma'am."

"Say, Bridie, my girls are both at boarding school in London, as you know, and I've never thrown away any of their dresses or slips, or God knows, there's a pile of bonnets up there in a trunk –"

Auntie rose to her full height. "Thank you for the tea, missus, but we really must be gettin' along with our deliveries. Drink up," she said to Lily.

"But it's still blowin' out there. I haven't paid you yet."

"Next time," she replied; they were already at the door. Suddenly Lily wondered why Luc had never delivered Papa's trunk.

Against the flailing of the snow on their faces, Auntie said: "They're all the same, Lily. You remember that. Never leave off interferin' with people's lives, they don't."

Lily was not sure. "Waste not, want not," was her aunt's oft-repeated warning. Ought a body, then, to merely bury such dresses and bonnets – some of them as flagrant and impertinent and wonderfully hopeful as a summer's bravest delphinium radiating enough blue to carry you through a winter?

And long hard winters they were. The numbing repetitiveness of the planting, weeding and harvesting was exchanged for the dark, indoor tasks between seasons. Aunt Bridie made quilts out of cast-off rags she collected each September on her rounds. "That's a nice job you done, missus, cuttin' down the dress for the girl, looks real good on her, don't it, Lottie?" Auntie soon discovered that Lily's fingers were more nimble than her own, and was delighted to have the girl help her at every spare moment when she wasn't involved with the chores in the barn and coops, with the preparation of the cuttings and seed for the spring, with her share of cooking, regular sewing and repairs, or candle-making (for sale along with the quilts), and even chopping wood when Uncle Chester's back "played its trump card" as it did more often of late. Lily found the fine needlework as fatiguing as hoeing lettuce; but she loved the harlequin swatches – their eccentric shapes and the unpredictable figures they assumed as her fingers played with them on the table, as if she were arranging Mrs. Templeton's flowers: poppies on yellow iris, asters on gladioli – composing something beautiful that no one, not even the flowers themselves, had dreamed into being. From some lady in London, however, Auntie had learned two basic patterns which she scrupulously alternated so that by April – eyes strained and fingers paralyzed by monotony – they had produced eight quilts that would bring ready cash to tide them over the lean spring months and even buy them each a pair of leather boots fresh from McWhinney's Haberdashery. (Uncle Chester drove into town with Lily proudly in tow; Auntie would not "set foot in that Tory's den". Nevertheless, she drew several silver coins from the butter-box under her bed, and sent the shoppers on their way.)

By the third summer – after her fourteenth birthday – Lily Ramsbottom was making half of the deliveries herself. More and more, Aunt Bridie was leaving the egg-and-vegetable side of the business to Lily while she herself drummed up further trade in the expanding sections back of Christina Street, peddled her candles and quilts, or scouted the competition's prices at the Saturday market beside the St. Clair Inn. As far as Lily could tell, her Aunt was never tempted by the garish displays of finery in the shops along Front Street.

"Tell me, Lily dear, what Church is your Aunt raisin' you in?" asked Mrs. McHarg, sweetly, for her husband's sake.

"The green peppers're good today, ma'am. Crisp as ice."

"You *are* attendin' a Church of some kind, aren't you?"

"No, ma'am." Lily felt her eyes drop, a flush of red staining her cheeks.

"You poor, poor thing, you." The woman's voice trembled with delicious shock. "An' why not?" she ventured.

"We work on Sundays," Lily said, looking up proudly.

Mrs. McHarg was speechless. Lily was already giving Benjamin a hug when she heard faintly from the back doorway: "That woman oughta be hanged!" Then: "Lily, you tell that so-called Aunt of yours not to bother comin' round here again!"

Lily did no such thing.

"Carrie, come an' see, quick! Lily's on her own!"

Miss Caroline stayed in her place. "Where's the old bat?" she whispered.

"Nowheres in sight. Down with the gout, I hope."

Lily came up to Miss Charlotte with the order.

"*Aren't we all grown-up now?* She's got a bonnet on, ain't that grand?" Carrie thought so.

"There's be change from that quarter," Miss Charlotte said, peering up the street.

"I'm on my own," Lily said with the correct change already in hand.

"We hear you and your Auntie labour on the Sabbath, don't we dear?"

"Will there be any special order for next week?"

"Such a scandal, an' this pretty little thing caught up in it. What's to be done, dear? Do you suppose we can carry on givin' out good cash for the Devil's work? No wonder them cabbages is full of slugs no amount of boilin'll kill off!"

"Same order for next week?"

"Just don't see how we can carry on an' call ourselves decent folk, I don't. You agree completely, don't you, Carrie?"

Lily walked carefully to her cart.

"Can't get over how pretty she is, can *you*, dear?"

Lily loved the boarding houses, especially the rambling clapboard one on Lochiel Street run by Char Hazelberry. If she wished, which was often, Lily got right inside the cozy kitchens where aproned servants cooked and scrubbed and gabbled; where some of the working men – dilatory, hungover or recuperative – lingered about to tease the landlady. When Lily appeared puzzled by the oddity of the landlady's name, Badger McCovey whispered breezily in her ear: "Short for Charity, but she ain't got none, get it?", and Walleye Watson, his good peeper next to hers, said, "It's the way she cooks the food!" and burbled so rapturously his veined hand slipped down and across Lily's bottom. He tried to wink, with absurd results, and she laughed with the rest of the room.

"Hi, toots, gonna take me to the shindig, Saird'y?"

"What mine d'you stash all that silver in, eh?"

"I get first dance, promise?"

"Not me, I'll take the last one, eh Lily gal?"

"Don't you pay them geezers no mind," Char would say, taking Lily under wing as usual. She'd cock her head towards the scullery crew, wink and say in her stage whisper, "Most of them's well past it anyways! They couldn't raise dust in a hen-house."

"Leavin' so soon, sweetie? Ya ain't give Badger his nighty-night kiss."

"You take off them diapers of your'n," roared Char to her audience, "an' you might just get yourself a live one!"

Lily usually left Char's place feeling faintly wicked, cheered, welcomed, guilty – and humming all the way to Exmouth.

Once, Char pinned a purple iceland poppy in Lily's hair and in front of the girls – Betsy of the shimmering ringlets and apple-cheeked Winnie with her sudden belly –

and several of the men called her "the sweetest strawberry blonde in the county". Lily kept the compliment intact until Benjamin made the turn off the Errol Road towards the farm, where she held it up till the wind blew the waferous petals far and wide. At Christmas Char let her take just a wee sip of dry sherry and gave her a beery hug, almost as if she were her mother.

Mrs. Templeton was in her front garden among the zinnias. She waved at Lily, pulled her gloves and apron off, and called out: "Take the things all way round to the back yard, would you dear? I'll be there in a jiffy." And she hopped to her front porch and headed through the house.

Lily carried the last order of the day to the back of the blue cottage – under the rose arbour in primary bloom and into the meadow of the Templeton's dooryard. She was delighted to see the cedar table covered with a linen cloth and set for tea. The missus must be planning a garden party, she thought. And by the looks of the fancy cakes and scones and the silver tea-set, the company expected must be from the hoity-toity. Mrs. Templeton popped from her shed, brushing back her unbonneted hair, and swept across the lawn to Lily.

"Well, young lady, don't just stand there lookin', *sit down*."

Mrs. Templeton showed Lily the proper way to pour tea and how to hold a scone with three digits and some dignity. She smiled sideways and whispered, "Wouldn't want to upset the good ladies of the town, now would we?" She took Lily's arm and escorted her about the English gardens, explaining carefully how one nursed and groomed such unruly beauty, prompting Lily to talk – even a little – about the wild blossoms of the townships.

"Well, Lily my sweet," she said with a sigh, "you must go now. Bridie will soon be frettin'." She tied Lily's bonnet snugly below her chin. "I just hope your Auntie knows what a prize she's got."

Lily blushed. Aunt Bridie, she knew, would not approve of such "spoilin'" that could "turn a girls head" in a direction which would eventually – one had to assume – prove regrettable.

As Lily was leaving, Mrs. Templeton turned suddenly and called after her, "Oh, Lily!" She had a note in her hand. "I almost forgot to tell you. Maurice and I are holdin' a campaign meeting here in a week, we'll need a lot of extras, delivered early in the mornin' if that's all right."

"Yes, ma'am." Lily's eyes were fastened on the fluttering note.

"There's so many things I wrote them all down for you and your Aunt. Here, take this along with you."

Lily took the note, turned and was almost under the rose arbour when Mrs. Templeton said, a bit too quickly, "Oh Lily, would you mind dear, checkin' that note to see if I put down eight bunches of carrots or not?"

Lily froze. She felt the confiding coziness of the morning ebb away.

"Just take a quick glance at the list, love." Mrs. Templeton seemed to squeeze the sentence out.

Lily looked straight back at the anxious stare. "I can't," she said tonelessly.

"Well then, it's high time we did something about it!"

Lily desperately wanted to be present when Aunt Bridie and Mrs. Templeton had their *tête à tête* over her attending the common school in town. A letter in an envelope had been delivered right to their door by a suborned errand-boy. Auntie read it, her brow pincering, her lips half-saying the words. "Some nerve!" was her only comment. But next morning she and Auntie scoured the house and, to Lily's amazement, a pewter tea-service materialized from the steamer-trunk to be set upon a crocheted tablecloth of ancient but unblemished vintage. Then she and Uncle Chester – only one of them protesting – were banished to the barn.

"I'll show you what I been workin' on, Lily love," Uncle Chester said, running his hands through his sandy mop as he always did when he was nervous or excited. "It's for you. I been thinkin' about it all winter."

With a regretful glance backwards Lily followed him into the barn. In the stall now converted into a workshop, Uncle Chester showed her his "latest contraption". It was a wooden 'flat' for berries that would hold six quarts; it had a screened top ("to keep off the flies") with a handle on it for easy carrying and a device that held the boxes in place and could be unlocked by sliding a lever along a piece of doweling. "You can swing it over your head like a skippin' rope," he beamed, "an' nothin'll come loose!"

Lily tried it out. The sliding lever jammed.

"Just needs a bit of sandin'" he blushed. "You go for a walk if you like. I'll just whittle away here."

"I'll check the water in the coops," Lily said. "That'll be a big help," she added, admiring the bulky device. "It really will." She could feel Uncle Chester's eyes upon her as she walked away from him. They were loving eyes, she was certain.

Aunt Bridie was a good reader. Uncle Chester said so many times. But there were no books in sight. Lily did see her aunt reading, though, for each week she picked up at the St. Clair Inn the weekly issued of *The Canadian Observer* and brought it home. Auntie took special pains to read it on the Sabbath. Uncle Chester would peek at it occasionally but would say to Lily, "It's full of radical ranting, girl, an' bad politics that'll come to no good end." He would then sigh with the feigned resignation he used whenever Auntie's behavior was beyond him. "It's beyond me why she takes in that stuff. 'Course, you gotta remember where she come from."

Lily couldn't remember what she didn't know. Auntie would not talk, ever, about the old country. Uncle Chester would, after a slug or two from his cache in Benjamin's stall, ramble of about the Ramsbottom tribe in Lancashire, his innumerable interchangeable cousins whom he had never met, having been alas born in the colonies the only child of a shipwright attached to the military command during the Simcoe regime and who, along with his wife, died inconveniently of cholera. The Ramsbottoms, however legendary, were not blood.

"Don't ask," Auntie would say, seeing the tilt of Lily's chin. "The Old Country's old, it's only good for forgettin'." Or, outdoors with a modest sweep of her hand: "This is where it's real. The Old Country was for livin' in; this one's for thrivin' in." Then, in a rare mellow mood she might peer up from her quilting and say, "Some day I'll tell you all about your folk. Especially your grandmother. You've got a right to know."

Once, startled by her own boldness, Lily asked: "Who was my mother?"

Aunt Bridie answered – not without a touch of sadness in her voice, "I don't know, child."

Seeing how "down" Lily was after this disappointment, Uncle Chester – risking all – slipped into his bedroom, opened the trunk with a squeal that arched Auntie's eyebrows, and returned with a large leather-bound book. "I'll just read her the story parts," he said in Aunt Bridie's direction. "It's her right, you know," he added vehemently though his voice didn't quit quavering until Samson had pushed both columns aside and brought the wicked temple down upon himself. The next winter he grew bolder and brought forth a calf-covered novel called *The Last of the Mohicans*, from which he read aloud to Lily all through that dark, cold season – his voice sonorous and comforting and quickened by the images and passions released by the words on the page. He insisted that Lily curl upon his lap on the wing-backed chair he bought from Cameron's with his "own money". "Waste and rubbish," Auntie warned, and never once was she tempted by its cushioned luxury. Last winter, though, when *The Deerslayer* made his debut, Lily did not sit on Uncle's knee. She perched on the ample arm of the chair and watched his lips transform the letters. She would say some of the words over to herself, and Uncle, delighted, would repeat a sentence, point to a word and when she guessed right, smile and pat her arm affectionately.

"See, Bridie love, the young lady can read. Smart as a whip, she is."

Aunt Bridie, who appeared not to be listening, snapped, "Don't be turnin' her head, you old fool. She can't read. Soon as I get some time, soon as everybody around here pulls their weight, I'm gonna teach the child to read properly."

"Don't blame the girl," he said petulantly. "After all, she's had no upbringin' to speak of."

"An' never *will* with the likes of you around her." The reading was over for that evening.

When Lily came in, Mrs. Templeton was adjusting her Sunday hat and looking quite pleased with herself. "Thanks for the tea, Bridie. You really must let me return the hospitality soon."

In her working smock Lily felt smudged and unworthy, but Mrs. Templeton kissed her warmly on the cheek, smiled and turned towards Auntie.

Bridie, in her gray-and-blue gingham, smoothed her skirt and said to Lily: "It's all fixed. You'll start in at the Common School first thing next Monday."

Lily turned her shining face to Mrs. Templeton. "Don't thank me, young lady. Thank your Aunt; she's givin' up the best helper she's got."

Bridie wanted to be severe but couldn't manage it.

Auntie, of course, had argued for starting in September when the new term began. After all, only one week remained in the current school year. "This way," Mrs. Templeton had insisted, "she can try it out, introduce herself to Miss Pringle, and get set up for the fall term." What she really meant was that it would be cruel to let a girl of Lily's temperament wait in anticipation over a whole summer.

"Only if Chester'll help out with the weedin'," Aunt Bridie had countered. Fortunately Uncle's trick back took a turn for the better, and dressed in a brown-and-tan gingham especially cut down by Auntie and with a lunch-pail in tow, Lily set off for Port Sarnia.

The Monday-morning sun had risen full of hope, then retreated. An east wind brought dark clouds prophesying thunder, and worse. The rain gusted and slashed sideways at Lily, who was torn between sheltering in the bush by the road or being late for school. Mrs. Templeton had made the arrangements. She was expected. Using her thin broadcloth shawl as deftly as she could, Lily manoeuvred her way through the squalls and mud into the open streets of the town. She was soaked through to the skin. Even her petticoat, improvised from a plain calico skirt, was sodden. Her boots were wet and plastered with grime that splashed up to her ankles and soiled the hem of her dress. Lily gritted her teeth and wedged her right cheek into the rain.

When she got to the schoolhouse on George Street, the rain had stopped; the sun was making a comeback. No children skipped or cavorted in the grounds. Lily paused at the door about to knock when a large boy with a pimple on his nose opened it, and called back: "It's the new girl, Miss Pringle! Looks like she's fallen in Durand's Pond!"

A gale of laughter greeted Lily as she entered the room, her shawl dripping. Standing at the front behind a table, Miss Pringle – frightfully tall, angular, eyes overly brilliant like a starved cat's – slammed her fuller down. "Behave yourselves, class," she shouted an octave above normal. "Remember, you're young ladies and gentlemen."

The ragtaggles and strays among the motley group of ages and sexes were not taken in: ladies-and-gentlemen-to-be went to the Grammar School on Christina Street. When the hubbub had died of its own weight, Miss Pringle said, "Please hang your *cloak* on the nail to your right, and take a seat. Class, say hello to our new pupil, Miss Lily Ramsbottom."

The surname had barely left Miss Pringle's lips when three or four unsynchronized snorts were emitted, followed by several inferior female imitations. "That's enough!" screamed Miss Pringle. "We don't make fun of people's names," she informed the tiny and timid among her troop, "no matter how odd they may be."

Lily sat down at an empty spot on the bench that held three other girls who might have been her age. Her gingham, still sopping, clung to her and shivered. The dark-haired girl next to her edged away.

"Have you attended school elsewhere?" Miss Pringle asked sweetly, not leaving her post.

"No, ma'am. This is my first time."

Miss Pringle paused, her gasp communicated instantly to the class. Lily felt the humidity and reek of the almost windowless room. She watched the teacher's eyes, and tried to breathe.

"Then what on earth are you doing sitting with the Fourth Book?" she snapped with more satisfaction than the situation warranted. Her ruler pointed left like a claw. "You'll have to sit with the First Book, then, won't you?"

Lily saw the empty place at the end of the back-left bench beside an oversize boy who swivelled and beamed at her. Lily hesitated.

"There's a Reading Primer waiting for you," Miss Pringle said, indicating the gray-backed tome on the desk, her voice honeyed again.

Lily went round the perimeter of the spectators and eased into the appointed place. Her fingers touched the worn cover, rubbed threadbare by a generation of Grammar School children down the road. She looked up and waited.

"My God!" screeched Miss Pringle, hitting descant. The class reeled as one and swung to the point of Miss Pringle's glare. Lily flushed. She reached up and tried to smooth her damp hair back. "Stop! Don't do that!" wailed Miss Pringle, and twenty-three necks craned, irreparably scandalized. "You can't sit there, just *sit* there…like that!" she spluttered, unconsciously lifting her hands towards her own well-harnessed bosom.

Beside her, not unkindly, the boy in Book One whispered: "Your bubs are peekin'."

"Well?" Aunt Bridie asked as she washed the dirt off her hands under the new pump beside the sink.

"I don't wanna learn how to read," Lily said. "Ever."

"Don't you fret about it, child. Not much learnin' goes on in them schools anyway." She was looking at Lily now. "Come September, we'll teach you to read proper." Then as if that were not enough, she said, "We're not gonna spend all our life chewin' dirt. Just remember that."

Uncle Chester, fresh from his stall, was all for driving into town and taking his buggy-whip to Miss Pringle. Of course Lily related few of the details, but when she went off to the hen-house, she heard him holler, "I know all about that hard-titted old bitch, I've a good mind to teach her a thing or two she won't soon forget!"

"Eunice Pringle is not old," Aunt Bridie said calmly, and all the steam was gone from Uncle's whistle.

3

The summer of Lily's fifteenth year was not, as she feared, uneventful. Aunt Bridie seemed more obsessed than ever with expanding production and business. Bachelor Bill, content to let his wheat ripen unaided, was brought over to help with the incredible weeding, picking and preparations for marketing. Auntie herself "gave in" and opened a stall at the farmer's market on Saturday mornings during the growing season, giving over the house-to-house sales to Lily, who now looked after the money-side of the operation as well. Uncle's back seemed baukier than usual, but his new devices for storing and delivering the produce were, even Bridie had to admit, "helpful for a change." In mid-July she astonished Uncle by announcing that she was going off for a few days to cook for the road-clearance workers who had set up a tent city near the

Reserve. Rumours in the incorporated town suggested that some of the clearing was in anticipation of the railway coming, but no confirmation was available.

"Your Auntie ain't worked for nobody, cookin' or cleanin', since her days in Toronto. She don't believe in it. Got her pride, that woman." Lily nodded. "'Cept of course when she come to work for me at the shop in London, but then her main job was tutorin' little Bertie." He grinned only as he did after a couple of "snorts", winked with one-and-a-half eyes, and said: "I had to marry her to get any house-cleanin' done!"

"We need the money," was all Auntie would say. "I'm gonna hire a man to cut pine again. Those trees are doin' nothin' for us just growin' there. They're a cash crop like anything else. Besides, we're gonna try for another two acres next year."

Aunt Bridie was so exhausted when she came home from her three-day stint at the camp that she went straight to bed and slept right through Bachelor Bill's Saturday serenade. Lily was even persuaded to do a jig. The two men sipped from Bill's flask and followed every graceful line of the dancer's leg.

"Why don't you ever bring Violet over?" Lily asked, flushed and sweating. "I could teach her to dance."

"Oh, she don't dance none," Bachelor Bill said in his drawl that was as lethargic as his music was sprightly. "She's a bit tetched in the head, you know. Been like that since she were a babe. No sir, she don't like to come outta the house at all."

Uncle Chester asked Lily if she'd like to try a "wee drop", and was so persistent that Lily made a great show of tilting the flask against her teeth, wincing and gasping in feigned pleasure. They seemed satisfied with her performance. To deflect their further hopes she called for a hornpipe and flung her body into the music's coil. Uncle watched with his sad bloodhound's look, and Lily thought back to that first summer when she had been given her own bedroom, wondering even then why they had built a cottage with *two* bedrooms and a hallway down the middle, and recalling, even as she spun towards a shaky climax, Uncle's words to her less than a month ago: "She was a wonderful tutor, you know, she loved my Bertie like he was her own, she looked after both of us real good, an' she loved to read that boy story after story, an' him only nine years old. It was awful, Lily, one day he was playin' an' laughin' and readin' back stories to your Auntie, an' the next mornin' he just puffs up, turns blue and dies on us. Your Auntie, she ain't read a book since, not a one."

The two men applauded zealously as Lily came to a stop in the middle of the room. She was facing the window over the sink. The last filament of Bachelor Bill's music still quavered in the coal-oil light. A face was staring back at Lily through the glass: the eyes widened by music, intrepidly innocent, carnal in their longing. For a second Lily thought she was looking at herself.

Then Violet let out the whirring, wordless cry she used for delight or despair, and vanished into the night.

It was August. Auntie was off to the camp once more "just to help out a little." At Uncle Chester's insistence, Auntie consented to put their savings in the Bank of Upper Canada in Port Sarnia. At the beginning of the month the hired hand appeared to cut timber and be otherwise useful around the place. Uncle Chester was made to give up his workshop wherein a pallet and table were installed for the new arrival. Uncle's back "did a dip" and he was laid up with lumbago for several days. Lily did the chores by herself. She might have tried to be a little resentful but then watching the hired hand proved to be adequate compensation.

Based on past experience, Lily expected him to be old, grizzled, and down-on-his-luck. Instead, Cam was twenty, as sleek and muscled and firm-jawed as a muskellunge, with an open smile and black Scotch-eyes that were curious, cheering and bold. "A bit too bold if you ask me," said Auntie, too exhausted to eat her supper. "But he's a good worker, for what you're payin' him," Uncle protested from his makeshift bed. He was quickly skewered into silence, and sulked for the remainder of the evening.

To Aunt Bridie Cam was painfully polite and deferential: "Which section of trees ought to come down next, mum?" And he certainly was a good worker. In ninety-degree heat he stripped to his waist, confronted the four-foot girth of a pine, and slung his executioner's axe. Sweat raced in rivulets down the small of his back, staining his trousers to the thighs. Positioning herself perfectly from row to row among the beans, Lily was able to keep a close watch on his performance for her Aunt.

The feelings Lily was experiencing were new, and puzzling. She knew what animals suffered to procreate and what men and women, for inscrutable reasons, accomplished in their midnight chambers. That such acts might be imbued with the most exquisite configuration of emotion, titillation and imagining had not occurred to her outside the vague intimations of her dreams. Until now. Her legs, made sturdy with labouring, went to jelly, and she found herself having to squat on her knees while her heart yearned outward towards bursting and her mind swelled with images of Cam's arms like axe-handles grappling her, bending her till she dissolved and floated through them.

When he spoke to her at lunch or after supper as he lay in the hay-patch scrutinizing her feeding of the hens, she lost her breath, and his eyes would twinkle with accomplishment. Always he was polite, solicitous: "Can I help you with that, Lily?" "Looks too heavy for you, that pail." But his glance clung to her, and she wondered frantically if he too could see them, if even the extra band of muslim Auntie insisted she tie around them were not enough to bridle them.

"That young man's got to go," Aunt Bridie said near month's end. "He never stops leerin' at Lily."

"But the girl's fifteen," said Chester. "She's bound to attract the boys."

There was more puzzlement than pique in Bridie's glare.

"I'll stay out of his way, Auntie."

"He's a real good worker, woman. You know how bad my back's been lately."

"I know how bad your medicine's been," she shot back. Then full of weariness she said, "All right. He stays. But just till the next section's done. Then out he goes, bag and baggage."

As if he had overheard the threat, Cam took his glistening biceps and shoulders to the farthest corner of the timber stand, out of sight and harm's way. He ate his lunch in the woods. At supper he wore a clean shirt and got Auntie talking about her business, the scandal of the Family Compact banks, and even radical politics. She was amazed to learn that one so young and handicapped by muscle could understand the imperatives of George Brown's 'true grit' policies. Lily, naturally, had expected such genius from the outset. Uncle Chester swung between envy and relief.

September came. The muggy weather remained. So did Cam. Aunt Bridie went off to cook "for the last time, I swear by all the snakes in Scotland!" Lily was now hurt because Cam made no attempt to break his vows to Auntie. He stayed in the bush after supper until twilight. Lily heard the punch of his axe against the yielding pine. Auntie would be coming home for sure next day. I'll have to go to him, Lily thought. And why not? Something inevitable and foregone has already happened; it's only the working out that's left.

Leaving Uncle Chester slumped in a stupor, Lily slipped out into the gloaming. It was a perfect night. Even Bachelor Bill had gone off to town in his buggy. They would be alone under a consenting moon. With no particular stratagem in mind Lily walked through the haze towards the barn. A sound, like the cry of a bird struck by talons, came from Lily's left. She stopped. Now it was a soft mewling. Old Bill's tabby sprouting kittens again? Lily sidled through the beanstalks and came up behind the Indian corn that bordered on Bachelor Bill's property. His log barn was visible. Lily knew there were no animals behind that barn. The hair on her neck rose; she closed her eyes, but it made no difference: the images before her were inerasable.

Violet was half-sitting with her back against the wall, her loose dress ripped open to expose her sac-like breasts, which Cam was pulling at with the stems of his fingers as if he were stretching dough, while Violet's own hands were busy in Cam's lap coaxing his flabby thing as they would the Guernsey's nozzle. Even at this distance, Lily could feel all the hurt and excruciating joy in Violet's unfettered wail of sexual release – with no word to mitigate its coarse, untongued violation of the night-air.

"Shut up, ya goddam fuckin' bitch! Shut the hell up!" He slapped her so hard her head snapped back and hit the boards behind her. Then he was shoving his instrument into his trousers and stomping away into the dark. Violet's sobs pursued him, mongoloid and discordant. But, at the first nicker of Bachelor Bill's pony in the lane, she stopped, touched her breasts tenderly where Cam's hands had fed themselves, pulled her dress together, and scuttled towards the unlit cabin.

Lily stood in the corn, letting the mosquitoes have their way. Above her the jib of the quartering moon luffed, and went out.

5

If it hadn't been for Bachelor Bill, they would have had no warning at all.

"Three of 'em, city-biddies," he said to Auntie at the doorstep, thrilled and appalled. "All dolled up for christenin' by the look of it." And he winked mysteriously towards Lily. "An' they already made the turn, I reckon."

Aunt Bridie never panicked, especially on Saturday afternoons in September with the weather clement and the week's marketing done. "If God hadn't been Presbyterian," she would say, "he'd've made his Sabbath on Sair'day afternoons so's all of us could rest together." Nonetheless, she went indoors at a trot, signaling for Lily to follow.

"It's the ladies aid for sure," she mumbled. Wordlessly they hurried about "straightening up" the living area. Auntie covered the table, set it for tea and seeing that Lily had automatically stirred the ashes from the dinner-time fire, smiled shortly and put the kettle on. She turned to Lily. "This is about you, you can be sure."

No doubt they were coming to drag her away to Miss Pringle's school. Well, they'd need a block and tackle, and some good chain.

"Go an' see that Uncle of yours is safe in his stall," Aunt Bridie said, putting an apron over her Saturday housedress but otherwise making no further personal concessions to the visitors. Lily's heart sank. "Oh, don't start poutin' before you're pricked", snapped Auntie. "I want you in here for this, I do."

Lily raced back to the barn, scattering a conference or two of hens en route. Uncle Chester was in his shop, now fully restored to him since Cam's sudden departure. Uncle had not bothered even to remove the pallet, finding it a more convenient spot to rest between stints at the workbench. Uncle Chester was resting.

The "delegation", as Auntie called them afterwards, had arrived: the mistresses McHarg, Salter and McWhinney – in convoy, the minister's wife leading.

"I think we oughta get right to the point," said Mrs. McWhinney with mercantilist efficiency, draining her cup and licking the sugar off the edges.

"We're grateful for the tea an' all," said Josephine Salter. "Them little tarts with the crunchy centre was *superb*; could you let me have the recipe sometime?"

"The point," said the Reverend McHarg's ambassadress, "is Lily." Lily watched the mobile ball-bearings of her eyes. Auntie poured Mrs. McWhinney another cup of tea. "The point is the baptism of this innocent, abused child."

"We know how good you been to her an' all," added Josephine hastily, though the accused seemed busy with estimating Mrs. McWhinney's capacity for sugar. "Nobody can take that away from you. You been a wonderful momma to this dear little foundlin' here. Just the other night I says to Mr. Salter –"

"What Josie's sayin', Bridie, is that it may be all right for you to reject your Maker, to live out here in a state of sin and run the risk of eternal damnation –"

"Go ahead an' take it," Aunt Bridie said to the C. of E. with her eye on the last of the walnut tarts. "Sorry, Clara, you was sayin'?"

"She was talkin' about the fires of Hell, she was," said Mrs. Salter, warming to her husband's favourite theme.

"You're a bright woman, Bridie. Nobody denies you that. You work hard an' you keep your own counsel. Well an' good. But we're talkin' here about the immortal soul of an innocent. Now we all might come from different churches, an' we have our set-to's from time to time, but we all agree on this – the girl deserves a chance to save her own soul."

"It don't even matter who baptizes her," added Mrs. Salter with Methodist charity. "It's just gotta be done, that's all."

Mrs. McWhinney agreed on behalf of the Church of England but her assent was muffled by walnut tart. No one had looked directly at Lily during this entire conversation though she was occasionally appropriated by flutters of a finger or a glancing nod. Lily was trying to catch her Aunt's eye but Bridie was now seated with her back straight, watching each of the speakers with intense interest.

"Do you intend to toss a coin?" she asked.

"Bridie, this is serious. We're just askin' you to think about the girl, about her future."

"In Heaven or Port Sarnia?"

The sudden edge to Aunt Bridie's voice silenced the bumptious Mrs. Salter and the satiated Mrs. McWhinney. They hadn't expected it to come to this. Mrs. McHarg, being Orange, had more ancient claim on self-righteousness.

"Both," she said.

Mrs. McWhinney coughed, a portion of crust caught in her throat.

Aunt Bridie leaned forward, occupying the silence. At last she looked over at Lily, who could not read the emotions held in check by that awesome will. "Well then," she said. "We'll let *the girl* decide. Lily, dear, what do you say?"

Lily, concluding it was time to find out once and for all who this God was, answered, "Yes."

It was agreed that Lily Ramsbottom's religious education would begin a week Sunday with an interview with the Reverend McHarg himself. In his study, in the Manse – for the purpose of determining the status of the girl's 'natural' inclinations to religious sentiment, after which she would be placed, for a time, exclusively in the hands of Mrs. McHarg for special tutoring before being released to the general influence of Sunday School and Service.

On the Saturday before the scheduled interview, a parcel arrived from McWhinney's haberdashery addressed to "Miss Lily Ramsbottom." It was one of the new-fangled corsets worn by ladies of good standing and generous figure. Auntie said gruffly, "We don't take charity in this house," but Uncle Chester, buoyed by a nap in his stall, said, "The gift is for the lass, woman, not you," and Auntie cut back with, "Go back to your bottle an' button up." But she didn't order the trembling delivery boy to return the goods, and he left at a gallop.

Lily was overwhelmed. Somehow she had been able to read her name on the parcel before a word had been spoken. She stared at the penciled block letters pretending to say each of them over in order. Maybe I *am* Lily Ramsbottom, she thought.

Naturally the corset was a disaster though not a disappointment. The springs and whalebones and stiff cloth converged mightily to push the bosom upward and athwart, but Lily's breasts were small and intractable, preferring their own propensities. And where the instrument was meant to chastise any amplitude of buttock, it swung freely, devoid of purpose. "We'll send it back," Lily said. "Not at all," said Aunt Bridie. "We'll just put it away till the time is ripe. After all, the lady meant well." Auntie put the contraption safely away in her room, but Lily kept the brown paper package with the writing on it.

So, attired in her furbished gingham rendered decent by the addition of a muslim camisole and proper slip, Lily stepped down from the cart in front of the imposing red-brick Manse where one of God's spokesmen awaited. Uncle Chester held her hand, squeezed it, and tried to say something, but couldn't. Lily watched the rig move west down George Street and stop in front of the Anglican Church whose spire glinted above the horizon. Uncle Chester got out and, a bit like a thief entering a shop, went in.

"Come in, come in, my child!" boomed the Reverend Mr. Clarion McHarg, swivelling in his desk chair and waving the deaf housekeeper away.

Lily obeyed. The woman had taken her shawl somewhere. She peered across the dimly-lit room embroidered with walnut and cherrywood and leather-skinned tomes of impressive dimension.

"Sit," said the Reverend pointing to a padded, armless chair perched on a scatter-rug a few feet from the littered secretary. "My, don't we look pretty, today," he added, finishing up a sentence and blotting it. Adjusted now to the poor light, Lily saw that his features were all crags and cliffs and deep coombs, with eyebrows that bunched and released parenthetically – a pair of singed caterpillars. Despite the eager teeth of his smile, his eyes burned through you, like gallstones. The only thing soft about the man that was visible were his plump fingers, which lay during the first part of their conversation as motionless as raw sausages.

The gallstones at last took her in. He had just remembered who she was. "You're the…young lady from the township my wife was telling me about?"

"Yes, your reverence."

While he was casting about for a suitable exordium, his stare consumed her, at a gulp.

"I ain't been baptized," Lily ventured.

"*Haven't* been," he said automatically.

"Yes, sir. Auntie says I ain't had a proper upbringin'."

"Do you know what being baptized in the Lord means?"

"No, sir."

"Well, then, let's find out, shall we, how much you *do* know." The caterpillars hunched forward. "First of all, why don't you remove that bonnet and give those pretty tresses some air?"

Lily obeyed.

"Much better. God will be pleased, I'm sure, to have you join His congregation of the Saved."

"Yes," Lily said. "I come here to find out about him."

"What do you know about Him now?"

"Can I talk to him?"

The good Reverend smiled as if charmed by the naiveté of such a remark. "You may *pray* to Him."

"What's that?" Lily wanted to hear it from the source.

My word, the corruption of some of these country folks was complete! "You get down on your knees, close your eyes, and tell God about your sins and ask Him to offer you strength and succor."

"What's sin?"

The Reverend stared at Lily as if trying to catch her out at some trick. "You don't know?"

"No, sir."

"Well, I can see that Mrs. McHarg has some tough cloth to cut here."

"Can I talk to God, like this, like we are?" Lily said.

"Of course not," he snapped. "The Lord will answer your prayers if and when He decides. Our role is to try to be good, and obedient, and free from sin."

"When he does talk back to me, will it be in English?"

The caterpillars jumped, even the sausages began to quiver. "Are you being blasphemous, child?"

"What's blasphemous, sir?"

"God speaks to each man in his own tongue; He hears, sees and knows everything."

"Uncle Chester says that his Bible says that God talks in Hebrew."

"Damnation to Uncle Chester!"

Lily looked at the floor, unable to contend with the fiery fusillade.

"Excuse me, child. You see why we must all pray."

Lily didn't. She straightened up, charily. "Would God, if I prayed to him real hard, talk to me in Pottawatomie?"

The caterpillars popped close to the butterfly stage; the sausages sizzled. "Who put you up to this, eh? That heathen aunt of yours?" He had both of her shoulders in his grip.

"No, sir. I just thought if your god can talk in every tongue, then he could if he wants talk to me in Pottawatomie. Or Chippewa or Attawan —"

"Cease this sacrilege! *Now!*"

Lily quaked before the upheaval of the Reverend McHarg's notorious temper. She pressed the tears back into her head where they smouldered, unattended. His pulpy hands had now slipped down so that they were squeezing her exposed forearms. Suddenly he let go of her as if she were quarantined. He sat down again, gathering the frayed ends of his composure. Lily didn't move. He seemed surprised, even discomfited, by the fact that she had not dashed out in disarray. He felt her presence in his room – the Lord's anteroom, as it were – as something indefinably dangerous, something darkly feminine, and intricately tempting.

"Mrs. Beecroft will show you out," he said at last. When she reached the study door, though, he shouted in a desperate whisper, "Whatever becomes of you, miss, just remember this: *God is not a Pottawatomie!*"

As best she could, Lily told Aunt Bridie what had trespassed at the Manse. Auntie listened with interest, not once interrupting. Then she said, "You may've had no upbringin' an' little educatin', but you're as smart as a June bug in July!" She scanned Lily's face as if realizing for the first time that this was her brother's flesh and blood, that they did indeed share lineament and lineage.

"God's not there," Lily said. "I know it."

Auntie's face clouded. "Just remember one thing, though. If you turn away from all the churchin' these folk 'round here can't do without, they'll never ever forgive you. You'll have to pay for that little luxury all your life."

"But you –"

"Yes, I did it, I know. As far as I'm concerned, the god they pray to was invented by landlords and greengrocers. An' now that I look at you, I see somethin' in your face, somethin' from that mad father of yours or the wild bush you was let roam in –" She didn't finish, as if on principle she'd already said too much. Then: "Well, don't just stand there with your legs in a knot, get that frumpery off, we got corn to shuck!"

When they were again working side by side, Lily said, "Will you teach me how to read?"

"Yes, honey, real soon. That's a solemn promise." And she tore at the stubborn shocks in a frenzy.

6

Aunt Bridie was off to cook at the camp "for the last time between now and kingdom come." As many of the workers brought their families to be with them and moved to more permanent quarters, Bridie's business followed them. Already she was plotting the use of the new acres cleared, cut and sold by Cam before he left, not even taking his last week's pay. Two sets of orders were left with her subordinates: Lily was to bake two dozen pumpkin pies for a special Thanksgiving celebration at the camp, courtesy of the soon-to-be-announced candidate for mayor of the newly incorporated town: Maurice Templeton, Esquire. "I'm trustin' you to do as I've showed you; somethin' big could come outta this," Auntie said. Secondly, Uncle Chester was to give the north coop a thorough scrubbing and white-washing as several hens had recently died from some mysterious cause.

Lily was delighted; but Uncle Chester's back went on leave. Lately Auntie had been more than usually stern and grumpy, snapping at her and Uncle Chester with little or no provocation. At night her deep snoring rattled the kitchen pots and often drove Uncle to the barn. Most of her wrath was directed towards him, though Lily failed to see why. Seldom would he talk back, and even then the rebellion always collapsed after a single strike. Sometimes he would look over at Lily, aggrieved and helpless, as if to say, "See, this is what it's really like." Once in September when Cam was still occupying his sanctuary, Uncle Chester, unaware he was being observed by Lily from her bed, picked up Auntie's pince-nez – which she used to read *The Observer* and "do the books with" – and hid them under the mattress. Aunt Bridie searched high and low for them, more than routinely disturbed that she had been so careless as to mislay them. Uncle Chester meantime made a great fuss about helping her locate them: "Thought they might've fallen off in the fruit cellar when you was labellin' the jars, but not so, I'm afraid," he said solicitously. "Not like you to be so careless with your valuables." Three days later when the spectacles turned up magically between two butter-boxes on the kitchen shelf, Aunt Bridie gave Uncle Chester the oddest look, then went about her business.

Uncle Chester, grumbling about his lumbago, went off to the north chicken coop, tools in hand. Lily went to the pumpkin patch and started the laborious task of loading the ripest ones into the barrow and pushing it through the loose soil to the dooryard. On the very first load Lily saw she had been too ambitious: the wheel buried itself in the ground, and when Lily got angry with it, it lurched sideways and sent the pumpkins thumping overboard. Uncle Chester was suddenly beside her. "I'll help you with that," he said. "Damn woman oughta know better'n to make you push a thing like this. There's times I think she just forgets you're a girl...a young lady," he said, puffing and huffing a huge pumpkin into the barrow.

"Be careful of your heart, now," Lily said, but she was happy to have help. Together they managed to get three loads of the unwieldy fruit safely to a pile beside the stoop.

"There now, my lass, you can go on with your woman's work," said Uncle Chester.

Lily leaned over and kissed him on the cheek. "Maybe I can get this done an' come help with the coop."

He sighed: "That's a dog's work," and trudged off.

Lily hummed to herself as she split and removed the pulp from the pumpkins. Beside her were three large kettles and just inside the door several dozen tin plates delivered by pony-cart from Mrs. Templeton. She felt useful and content, and let the Indian summer cast its blessings abroad.

Lily felt the strange eyes upon her long before she looked up. Violet was watching her from among the sunflowers, their stiffened stalks askew, their heads puffed and blasted, their ebony eyes bulging with seed. She was motionless except for her bare toes which wiggled happily among the withered jaundice of abandoned petals.

"Would you like to help?" Lily said.

Violet whirled to flee. "It's all right," Lily said. "Nobody's home but me."

Violet inched forward. "You could roll that big pumpkin over to me," Lily said. Violet sat down, wholly relaxed now, on the dirt path, her fleshy thighs exposed almost to her hips. She made a sound, heavy and laboured like a horse wheezing through the pain of the heaves.

Lily blinked hard: she was certain that Violet had just spoken to her, that through the distortion of the girl's cleft palate and wayward tongue, she clearly detected the words "I watch".

"You want to watch?" Lily said.

Violet's eyes lit up. "Ahh waajjh, ahh waajjh," she said over and over, contorting the vowels even more in her excitement. "Lily work, Lily work," she said in her way, and laughed.

So Violet watched in fascination as Lily's fingers went about their practiced tasks. The sun warmed them equally. The afternoon rung its gentle changes. Lily found herself humming one of her mother's Gaelic airs. When she paused for breath, the melody continued, an octave lower, in perfect pitch and cadence, and with no loss of the lamentatious joy that originally suffused it. Lily laboured while Violet sang.

Lily had strained and prepared the pulp and placed the kettles in the cool of the back shed. She would have to build a hot, sustaining fire in the stove when the day cooled off some. They would eat a cold supper. Lily was tired and covered with the sticky effluent of pumpkin, and feeling a bit empty inside because as soon as Bachelor Bill's cart squeaked around the bend, Violet had leaped up and frantically dashed across to the log hut, using the coops and her barn as camouflage. Moments after her brother entered the house, she heard him shouting, followed by two loud smacks, and then Violet's familiar wail.

She was also wondering where Uncle had been for the whole day. After getting a good fire started, she set out to fetch him home. The first place she looked was the barn. He wasn't in his workshop; nor were there any signs that he had been there. Puzzled, she walked over to the north coop from which no noise save the clucking of hens had come since mid-morning. When she opened the door, she was greeted by a spray of feathers and dust; when it settled in the fading light, she saw Uncle Chester. He lay sprawled on his elbows and ankles, his clay jug overturned and empty beside him. He was awake, but his eyes were half-lidded as if he were just waking or about to drop off. His face glowed as if he had been sunburned. The place was a mess, and Uncle Chester lay fully in it; bits of cast-off straw and chicken droppings and hen-pecked dirt and disembowelled seed-husks and the spilled semen of Springer, the ageless cockerel.

"Uncle?"

"Ah, is it you, Lily? You see what she's done now, you see what she's driven us to?"

"Come on, Uncle. Your supper's ready."

"You're the loyal one, though. Chester can always count on his little Lily." She had him by the arm, and he made a half-hearted effort to get up. "You wouldn't drive a man to this, would you, my sweet?"

He was up, but when she let go, his eyes rolled and he slumped back into the muck. "Where'd the room go?" he said, trying to laugh through his coughing jag. When she got him up again, he leaned his bulk against her and they both toppled. "What're we on, a whirligig? Jesus, let me off. Oh, sorry. Pardon my French," he spluttered. "It's all her fault, you know. The whole shitty mess."

Lily was able to wrap one of his arms around her shoulder and with great difficulty manoeuvre him out of the coop and onto the path that led to the house. The odours of whiskey and offal contended in the evening air.

"You always thought she was so damn smart, didn't you, pickin' this spot out. Well, you're old enough now to be told the truth," he said, guiding his slurs. The revelation was interrupted when he had to stop and retch into the last of the cucumbers.

"I'll put some tea on," Lily said.

"Always thought she was so damn smart, she did. Picked this hell-hole in a pine-bush 'cause it was next to the army reserve. They're gonna build a fort an' barracks right there, she says, an' we'll be right next to them. Some fort, eh? Nothin' but pine trees an' always will be! Some smart, eh?"

"The fire's already goin'," Lily said, trying to change shoulders. Uncle's limbs flopped joylessly over her.

"She was good to little Bertie, I'll give her her due there," he said. "Then Bertie went an' died on us."

They were at the house. Uncle Chester dropped to his knees and vomited copiously on the flagstones, spraying Lily in the process. Then he looked up at her as if he had just wakened from a messy dream and was wondering where he was: "Your Auntie's a good woman," he said softly. "An' don't you ever forget it."

"I'll get out the tub," Lily said. "I'll bring your robe out. You can just sit right here." Lily hurried inside, got Uncle Chester a cup of clear tea, which he spilled over his shirt, and then proceeded to prepare a bath for him. Using the extra kettles from the Templetons, she boiled enough water to almost fill the shiny metal tub Uncle had bought last winter to help "straighten out" his unreliable backbone. Auntie had objected, resorting to reason, then anger, then ridicule but eventually giving in, her fingers almost paralytic as she counted out the silver coins from her locked cash-box. Not once had she used it, nor had Lily – both of them continuing to wash at the outside pump in the sheltering dusk or once-a-week with a pail and warm water and soap in the dank kitchen.

Lily went out to Uncle Chester with a flannel sheet, and after managing to slurp half-a-cup of tea, he wobbled to his feet and let Lily pull off his reeking shirt and trousers under cover. Somehow, with Lily keeping the sheet in place, he succeeded in removing his undervest and linens. Through the sheet Lily could see how thin his arms and legs had become in the last year or so, and how ludicrous his unhobbled belly looked as it jiggled and sighed against his knees. He held her hand like a little boy as he stepped into the tub, cupping his private parts in an automatic gesture. But Lily had already turned away, leaving the warm steamy room and walking wearily to the well-pump through the cloudless afterglow of twilight. Her arm ached as she primed and pumped, and her skin recoiled at the icy touch of the water. Nonetheless, she stripped naked and scoured herself with lye-soap, letting it sting and purge. The chill air, free of mosquitoes, soon dried her, and she slipped her nightshirt on over the gooseflesh. Suddenly she felt famished, and very thirsty. She felt the moon's weight on her back as she headed for the house.

Uncle Chester was out of the tub, sitting in his wingback chair with the flannel 'towel' wrapped around him, toga-like. He was clean, but the fatigue and strain of the day's excess was etched into his face. He's an old man, thought Lily. He forced a sheepish smile.

"What would I do without you, Lily?" he said wanly.

"I'll get some bread and cheese for us," Lily said. She didn't know why but she added, "Auntie won't be back till tomorrow night."

"Come here an' sit beside your old uncle," Chester said, avoiding the lamplight over the sink. "Like you used to."

Lily hesitated, but sensing the pall of irreconcilable sadness over him, she padded across the room and sat gingerly on the left arm of the chair. Uncle took her hand in his as he used to after he had read to her or told her one of his fantastic tales about the lawless Ramsbottoms of Lancashire.

"Sometimes, Lily my lass, I think you're the only reason I carry on. Just the thought of you smilin' at me in the mornin's, or dancin' for me in this room, or puttin' your hand in mine like you're doin' now..." His voice trailed off. He squeezed her hand tight, closing his puffed eyes. The maple-wood in the firebox crackled. The lamplight wavered. Lily felt very very sad. She squeezed Uncle's hand. She couldn't think what else to do. Exhaustion was about to claim her. She was at the furred edge of a dream. Something male and insistent was trying to shape her right breast to its own liking. The left one cried out in its loneliness. A throaty version of her own voice was chanting: *Cam, Cam.*

Uncle Chester, looking straight ahead, was kneading her breast with his left hand while the right one slithered unmolested up the wedge of her thighs. "Oh please, Lily, please…" he canted softly, like a plea from the near-dead. For a second Lily was paralyzed – not with fear but with the blind panic of indecision. The compulsion of this whispering in her ears – rising and falling across the whole spectrum of despair – left her unable to act or cry out or plead. Uncle's fingers moved up to her belly where they caressed and marvelled as they would upon the pink sheen of a newborn. At last, dawning on some instinct as old as the species itself, Lily said calmly but directly into his ear: "Please don't do this…*Papa!*"

Uncle Chester jerked back, tilted and fell out of his chair. He put his face in his hands, and in a moment he was wailing uncontrollably into them.

Lily was over by the stove. Uncle's sobs stabbed into her back, begging absolution. After a while they subsided. She could hear him struggling to his feet.

"Lily…lass…you won't..you won't tell –"

"Sit down. I'll get you your supper," she said, shoving another faggot into the fire, and remarking in awe how much of her Aunt's tongue she had already made her own.

7

Much had happened to the world since 1855. The boom of the mid-fifties gave way to the bust of 'fifty-seven and 'fifty-eight. In the wake of the depression few if any in Lambton County prepared themselves for the imminent publication of Darwin's *On the Origin of the Species* and if they had, would have been conveniently outraged by its apostasy while simultaneously appropriating it to explain – despite temporary recessions – the inevitability of progress, North American style. The word itself was in the air and in the seasons, on the tongues of Tory and Reformer alike, and its principal articulation was in the pounding of spikes and chug of the locomotive. The Great Western Railway had hammered its cross-ties through the startled forests of Kent all the way to Chatham and Windsor, eclipsing villages and fathering towns, its patronymy as ineluctable as a mutant gene in biological ascendancy. Mr. Brydges, the celebrated British railroad architect, had already dreamt a horizontal line through the primeval maze between London and Port Sarnia. Unbeknownst to the good burghers of either town, the Grand Trunk had already hatched a nefarious scheme to drive a second line, slightly north, from Stratford to the military reserve at the junction of Lake and River, denoted on the official maps as Point Edward though known locally as "the ordnance lands" or "the rapids" or just plain "Slocum's fishery". At the stroke of an architect's pen, the hamlets of Forest and Thedford were declared to have a future. The future also looked brighter for John A. Macdonald (later Sir John) who, having purchased a leasehold on said lands, carried off what may have been the first Canadian *flip* (as the quick turnover is now known in high finance).

Important as these latter developments were, the most pressing concern for the Lambtonians of 1858 was the poor weather and the resultant general crop failure. It rained all spring, followed by weeks of summer drought. Every imaginable variety of blight and vegetable pestilence – taking their cue from Darwin – took full advantage of the situation and ravaged those inferior species in need of extinction. Whilst some of the cereal crops fared reasonably well, Aunt Bridie's garden plot suffered most cruelly. They watched it mildew in the wet and wither in the desiccating heat, while slugs and mites and chiggers and rusts flourished, as if somehow they deserved such happenstance. In August, some paralytic bacterium swept through one of the coops; the corpses had to be burned, like stubble.

For a time Uncle Chester even forgot about his weak ticker and bad back, and pitched in to salvage part of the potato crop and most of the hardy turnip. Lily flailed at bugs, pinched worms and popped caterpillars till exhaustion overtook her each night that summer, even though she could feel in every fatigued muscle of her body the surge of the inevitable: their business was in ruins.

"We'll start over again next spring," Auntie said after each disaster. "That's why we got cash in the bank." In desperation she would mention the recent survey of the pine-bush and swamps of the ordnance grounds, and Uncle Chester would sigh knowingly.

But there was more to it than the accidents of weather. Unable to keep up any deliveries except for a few eggs to the old customers, Auntie had been compelled, as other farmers had been tempted, to sell what produce her garden did yield to jobbers, who collected it at the farm gate with their great wagons and took it off to the expanding markets in town and to the wharfs where lake-steamers whisked it daily to the hostels of Detroit and Cleveland. Within months the stock-cars and hoppers of the Great Western would be shunting produce between towns within hours, not days. The ear of large-scale cash cropping had been inaugurated.

"We'll lick them," Aunt Bridie said. "We'll get by. We always have, haven't we, Chester?" Uncle had succumbed to sleep.

One stroke of good fortune was that Bachelor Bill, with his own farm in disarray, had abandoned it and become more or less their hired man. Without him they could not have managed to salvage anything of that summer. On the twenty-first of June he brought over a bottle of mulberry wine and they all toasted Lily's eighteenth birthday. There was no coming out, however, unless you counted waltzing with your Uncle in the kitchen.

After Uncle and Bachelor Bill had poured oil on the chickens and set them ablaze – the stench of their feathers and diseased flesh befouling the twilight air – Lily went into the house where Aunt Bridie sat at the table with her chin in her hands. She was ashen; the perpetual glint in her eyes was glazed with fatigue and disappointment; and something much worse. Lily saw immediately what it was: Auntie, with her intrinsic strength and constitutional optimism, could face up to any temporary calamity, indeed even to the despair and seeming hopelessness of the near-future; she would suffer any physical pain, any mental anguish and take any risks offered by Fate so long as there was hope of some kind – however faint – that she could escape the one thing in life she feared the most: being consigned to the drudgery of a labour which merely repeats itself in days, in weeks, in years – and gains for its victims merely a form of survival wherein the whole scope of one's being, one's reaching out, one's caring is defined by a debilitating and inescapable regimen. Even the meaning of seasons would be lost. In the pleading of those eyes Lily saw the fear of a life lived without a future tense; she got her first clear look at what it was to be a woman in such times. She felt her heart lurch with inexpressible tenderness, unfocussed rage, and a boundless empathy with the oppressed.

Aunt Bridie looked up. She spoke. "The worst of it, Lily, the very worst of it is somethin' I've dreaded like the plague itself: you'll have to go out to service."

Lily could think of nothing to say.

"We'll need the cash. I got plans to rearrange this place, I have. Next spring. When things get better. But we'll have to have money."

By now Lily had found a voice to reply. "Who wants me?" she said.

"I dread to tell you," Auntie said. "Lord knows what'll become of you in that town."

Lily tried as best she could to look concerned.

"But she'll pay well, no doubt, Mrs. Templeton will."

Lily burst into tears – of mixed origin.

2

Lily hardly ever cried. She never had. It was nothing to be particularly proud of nor ashamed of; it was just the way she was. "Weepin' just messes up what you should be seein'" Old Samuels would say with special relish. "With me, it don't matter." But she never saw him cry, sad as he might become telling one of his stories of the disapora of the Attawandarons and the demise of their ancient tongue. Sitting in her new room, couched for the first time in her life with luxury, she examined her tiny chest of accumulated treasures – the rabbit's foot, pendant, crucifix, Testament, the jasper talisman – and simply wept. Later when she was able to stop and present a decent, grateful face to the wonderful Templetons, she realized how utterly fatigued she had been on her arrival here at the end of September. From pre-dawn till deep dusk, they had all toiled in the devastated fields to salvage what they could of the harvest, to garner seed and cuttings for a doubtful spring, to pickle and can and store what they could to tide them over the winter and, most important for Aunt Bridie, to conserve their depleted supply of cash. By ten o'clock each night, barely able to stuff some cold mutton and sourdough bread into them, they collapsed into a drugged and dreamless sleep. In such circumstances conversation seemed not only redundant but threatening. Relying as she did on day-dreams and the spontaneous hum of music inside her, Lily soon found herself laboring without the solace of fancy or song.

It was, then, almost a week before she was able to leave this pink and papered boudoir – young Pamela's room before she left for school – and join her new family. Mrs. Templeton came in several times a day to talk to her, listen to her incoherent weeping with patience and near-understanding, and divert her with household talk or a display of Pamela's "old" frocks for which she assumed Lily would be a "perfect match". Gradually the numbness of the mental and physical fatigue wore off, and Lily felt the re-emergence of the self she was most familiar with. She fell asleep in the feather tick with the talisman in her clutch, and that night she dreamed of a fine-boned young man with loose, sandy hair and a careless moustache and a radium stare that held her in its power till he dissolved in an ambiguous mist.

"You're certainly not goin' to be a servant in my house!" Mrs. Templeton exclaimed when Lily appeared on a Saturday morning attired in her own housedress and a maid's apron she had found in the upstairs hall closet. "Gracious, what *would* Bridie think of me, then?"

She marched Lily back up the carpeted stairs to Pamela's bedroom and with commendable briskness re-attired her for her new role. Pulling Lily in front of a long mirror on the inside of the door of the black-walnut wardrobe, she said with satisfaction, "*There*, now. What do you think?"

Lily was sure what Aunt Bridie would think. Since no mirror ever graced Auntie's house – "Greatest time-waster and corrupter of good intentions ever devised" she huffed – Lily had little experience in physical self-assessment. On occasion she had peered at her rippled face in the goose-pond and watched fascinated as that other visage – fay, unmoored, incomplete – yearned back at her from the intensity of its own medium. Once when no one was around, she tried to discover in the pond's mirror the whole, sudden shape of her body – with its new breasts, widening hips, furred vee – but she could not catch it all at once, only partial, curved tableaux or quick configurations that pleased without purpose. Lily's reverie that day had been terminated by the lunge and honk of Booster the gander, who had a fetish for the exposed flesh of foolish humans.

"Well, what do you think?"

"The dress is beautiful," Lily said. "But how can I work with these petticoats on?"

"The dress is not beautiful, pet, *you* are." She beamed like Pygmalion surprised by Galatea. "It's high time you realized that. Walk around for me. That's it. See, you have no idea how graceful you really are. Bridie tried to take it out of you, no doubt, bein' a closet-Presbyterian an' all, turnin' you into some sort of darkie slave out there, puttin' calluses on your hands an' lettin' the sun burn an' freckle that glorious Irish skin of yours."

Lily was abashed. She felt she ought to defend Aunt Bridie but couldn't find ready words to do so. Mrs. Templeton was not looking for commentary.

"She ought to be ashamed, though of course I know she ain't – hasn't – got any. My, my," she sighed stepping back, "you're goin' to wow the gentlemen, you are. There's no helpin' that."

"How can I work for you like *this*?" Lily said, unable to prevent her mirror-image from bouncing back to her.

"I got Iris to do the housework, pet," she explained, "an' Bonnie comes in to serve an' scull at parties. But I do my own cooking an' you'll be a big help to me. Other times, like now, I want you to be my 'companion', to sit with me at teas, to talk to me when you feel like it, an' to let me make a lady out of you."

Lily looked dubious.

"I'll send your wages to Bridie every month," she said, picking up one of Pamela's cloth-and-china dolls and fondling it.

Lily did not smile on cue, as Pamela did, but she appeared resigned. Aunt Bridie was counting on her. "Will you teach me to read?"

"Of course, pet," said Mrs. Templeton, suddenly as serious as Lily. "Why do you think I arranged your rescue?"

They began with recipes, just the two of them working in the kitchen. Mrs. Templeton was amazingly patient. She sounded out the recipe words slowly and repetitiously with Lily at her shoulder. They would say them together, Lily's rich alto voice melding with the older woman's strained soprano.

"And I thought my Janie was the smart one," Mrs. Templeton said. "She should've been a boy, Maurice always said when she done – did – her sums. But you, *you* take the cake."

After the second week Lily was reading the familiar recipes haltingly to Mrs. Templeton who matched her actions to Lily's words. She felt like Old Samuels must have when his sight darkened and he discovered a fresh way of seeing that had been a hidden part of him all along.

"Remember now, pet, read them words clear, 'cause I'm doin' exactly what you say. If the pie wins a prize, then we'll know you can read!" she giggled with a twinkle as silver as her hair.

Towards the end of October Mrs. Templeton would sit with Lily before a blazing fire in the parlour – surrounded by daguerreotypes of her daughters and husband ("We'll get you done soon, pet, when all the bloom in you is through workin'") – and read from *The Arabian Nights*, a book that Auntie would have found scandalous not because of its racy tales but rather for its utter "silliness". Lily began to 'read' parts of these stories aloud, easy sections carefully picked out by Mrs. Templeton and abetted by repetition and memory. One evening she was allowed to take the book to her room where she struggled once again through the early paragraphs of Aladdin and his magic lamp. There was some imperative in this story that drove her to try and decipher the huge, exotic words, to grasp at the central thread of events whose import she sensed but could not pin down. Suddenly the aura of meaning faded and went out like the genie himself. In frustration and disappointment she threw the book across the room and sat shaking for five minutes before she hurried over in panic to see if she had damaged it. Only her pride was bruised.

Even his Worship the Mayor got into the game. He would call Lily into his den, detonate a cigar, wave her to a plump chair, and begin to read aloud from one of his legal tomes. "Know what *that* word means, Lily?" he'd say with mock-sternness, rolling off his tongue some arcane polysyllable. Lily would shake her head. "Neither does Judge Maitland!" he'd rumble. "And I doubt if the dolt who thought it up does either!" Then he'd go dead-serious again. "But that's the law, Lily dear. Men have been hanged on it!" Lily soon realized that his was a game he had played with both his daughters before they left for school in London and marriage in Toronto. And some of the words she did remember.

Lily found herself doing little work. The calluses on her hands shrivelled and dropped off. Bonnet and parasol soon whitened her skin. The freckles remained as permanent record of a different past. Lily even went to Church – the Anglican one – with the Templetons, though no word was ever said about baptism or question raised about her not taking communion. The Church of England seemed to be quite catholic and commodious. Lily watched, listened, and learned. After Church she would be given the pony-and-surrey and allowed to drive out to visit her Aunt and Uncle. Chester was always overjoyed to see her, though he would sometimes embarrass Lily and Bridie – for different reasons – by bursting into tears without proper notice. Aunt Bridie's assessment of Lily's gradual transformation to ladyhood was not discernible in her talk or her manner. She continued to refer to Lily's "work" and as the girl prepared to leave each Sunday, she would grasp her hand and say, "Thanks, lass. You're a good girl."

Most of Lily's 'work' consisted of being at Mrs. Templeton's side during her frequent 'At Homes', given in deference to her role as the wife of the new mayor. "Sweet but dreadfully quiet," Lily overheard one of the dowagers remark to one of the duchesses. "Might be pretty, in time, though Lord knows where she comes from." Because of previous experience with them during her days as an egg-lady, Lily had little trouble dealing with the women at tea. The surprise and challenge came from the gentlemen and grandees who frequented the bi-weekly political 'socials' (salons was a word not infrequently heard) held by his Worship. As hostesses, Lily and Mrs. Templeton engineered the distribution of food and drink by the servants co-opted for the evening, and were expected to provide casual divertissement for those gentlemen who found the strain of political discussion too hard on a thinning intellect.

The political topics of that month in 1858 were about the coming of the Great Western and the machinations of its rival, the Grand Trunk. Much bitterness, not fully assuaged by the good brandy and home-made chocolates, was educed over the shabby treatment of the town's noblest citizen, Malcolm "Coon" Cameron, whose moderate reformers had been outflanked by the chicanery of the Clear Grits who had recently abandoned "Coon" and his gang to the uncertain mercies of the new liberal-conservative party taking shape under John A. Macdonald. Lily was thus exposed to the intemperate talk of radicals as well as the lamentations of old-compact Tories and the hollow bellicosities of the local Orangemen – for though his Worship would soon depart Port Sarnia and later join the coalition as a repentant reformer, his hospitality was so lethal that the warring factions in town not only answered all invitations to attend, but often broke protocol by appearing unannounced. The result was a series of spirited and spirituous soirees which furthered Lily's education in ways that might have surprised the participants.

Regardless of party affiliation or ideological bent, Lily learned that there were four elements common to a politician's life: food, liquor, gossip and sex. Indeed, she soon became adept at identifying parliamentary loyalties not by the swagger and fire of the rhetoric but by the method through which the fourth element was realized. The very first evening she attended one of these salons – radiant in Pamela's 'best', her hair brushed to perfection, her eyes alight with curiosity and undirected intelligence – Lily was standing suitably aloof from a heated exchange about the abomination of separate school rights, intent on following the swing of the argument, when she felt a broad, fingerless appendage slink its way across the stretched silk at her lower back.

"Don't let those Orangemen put ideas into your pretty head," whispered the owner of the errant hand into her left ear. Lily turned to see Dr. Michaelmas, the ardent Reformer, smiling behind his trimmed moustaches.

"It's not my head concerns me at the moment," Lily said, slipping to one side and casting him an ambivalent smile. Without a doubt, she concluded, you could tell a Reformer because they were all sly touch, accidental nudge, a fleshy press in tight corners. She assumed they believed too passionately in the causes of justice and individual liberty to take full-frontal advantage of maids or vulnerable lady's companions. The Old Tories, on the other hand, because of their advanced infirmities or belief in divine right, where the boldest. Judge Maitland, for example, stalked her in the den on the pretext of discussing recipes and tried to pinch her bum through two layers of crinoline. "My God, you're a little beauty," he drooled, aiming a claw at the exposed pink of her bosom, his lust positively aquiline. Lily knew she could scream for help, but instead she curled up her fingers and delivered a muted rebuff to the old scarecrow's lower abdomen – not hard enough to cripple his intent outright yet insistent enough to make him wheeze, double, clutch his ringing bells, and hobble towards the parlour. She watched him trying to straighten his stride as he headed for the brandy. "Got your limp again?" said McWhinney, the clothier. "Touch of the gout," whistled his Honour. At the close of the evening Lily came up to the startled jurist and said, "Here's the recipes you asked for. Mrs. Templeton helped me write them out for you."

The radicals, or Clear Grits as they styled themselves, so loved the buzz of their own perorations that they made their passes at her in verbal terms only: innuendo, *double entendre*, a *sotto voce* vulgarism when desire overwhelmed – though she had little doubt that, were their sundry propositions to be accepted, they might have flashed the genuine metal. However, they soon discovered that this waif "from the sticks" was unconscionably swift at rejoinder and not as accustomed to "holding her peace" as a real lady would be.

"Women'll never play a role in politics," declared Andrew Plympton, sitting member for Kent. Lily had been nodding politely to his insatiable sermonizing for almost twenty minutes. "You ask them to talk and they gossip; you ask them to act and they dither. Politics is a tough, hard grind to hold your nose to. Women," he said, lowering his voice and leering into her bodice, "are not *up to it*, their house is *divided*, they're a *soft touch*, if you get what I mean."

"Like this?" Lily said, squeezing a forefinger with unimpeachable naiveté into the pudge of his protruding belly. His blush bordered on *rouge*.

"That orphling brat of Templeton's got a wicked tongue in her head," he told a consoling judge later. "She needs to be taken in hand." But of course they had already tried that.

Not once had she been accosted by any of the Orangemen. They were either uninterested in anything but the eradication of popery or were put off by the gold cross she wore on these occasions.

Lily's rebuffs and inventive parries did not escape the notice of Alice Templeton. "You're learning fast and well," she said with undisguised admiration.

"Are they all like that?"

"Most of them, I'm afraid. It's the climate."

Lily laughed but then said soberly, "Why do we put up with it?"

Mrs. Templeton sighed deeply enough to accommodate the feelings of most of her sex. "There's an awful lot more we have to put with," she said.

Not me, Lily thought. There must be another way.

3

When Mrs. Templeton heard that Lily had never seen the Lake, she was shocked, and set about to remedy the situation. Lily politely refused her offer of a cruise on the *Michigan* or one of the other steamers now plying the water routes on a regular basis.

"You mean you wish to walk down there and just look at it?" she said, swivelling on the piano bench to face Lily.

"Yes, that's all."

"But, pet, why didn't you do so when you lived at Bridie's? The sand beach is no more than half-a-mile through the pinery back of your place. You mean to say in all the years you lived there you never once saw the Lake?"

"Auntie was strict about that," Lily said defensively. "She was always worried about the fishermen. Besides, she never liked me just traipsin' off on my own. Could you blame her?"

"Not at all," said Mrs. Templeton, closing the sheet music. "Goodness knows a number of the town girls've been accosted by the riff raff down there cuttin' brush for the railway. Fishermen, I hear tell, are even worse." Her tone was less-than-serious.

"May I go, then?"

"Of course, pet. I'm teasin' a bit. You just follow Front Street until it turns into the train the Slocum people sometimes use to get down to the fishery. Just before it comes out at the swamp below the beach, veer right – you'll see an Indian trail that'll take you over the dunes to Canatara beach. Of course, you could also walk up the coast past the fisherman's shanties, but I wouldn't advise it."

"I'll go right now, if I may?"

"Well, all right. But I *was* tunin' up here to start your dancin' lessons," she said. "We mustn't wait too long. Never know when a big fancy-ball might be upcomin'."

Though it had been seven years since she had walked through thick brush, Lily felt quite at home on the fishery trail with the pines flaring overhead, the undergrowth spare and cushioned – inhabited mainly by shadows and sudden gusts of brilliant light where the sun fitfully penetrated. This trail was worn and clear. Ten minutes or so into it, she heard the shouts of the men with their nets along the river bank sweeping for pickerel. Just ahead the woods brightened, so Lily, her instincts surprisingly sharp, peered to the right and spotted the crossed-blaze – perhaps ten years or more in age – that signaled a Pottawatomie trail. She entered its welcoming shadow and with mounting excitement moved from mark to mark towards the sound of waves breaking in the near distance. She was scanning the trunks at eye-level when she found herself abruptly in the full glare of early afternoon sun. The roaring of the waves was much louder, but when she looked ahead expecting to see the Lake, she saw only a series of sand-dunes about twelve feet in height.

Lily took off her shoes and stockings, dashed barefoot through the hot sand, fell scampering up the nearest dune, got up – her palms burning, her legs scything until she stood on top and caught her first glimpse of the Freshwater Sea of the Hurons. What she saw initially was a single colour – blue – stretching to the north and west so far that it became indistinguishable from the sky. The sun's light and the sun's heat were lost in a greater immensity: the vast, tense energy of water on the move – homeward. When Lily was able to pull her gaze from the vanishing point directly to the north-west – the very spot where Arcturus would find his reflection that night – she saw and heard at last the reach and yearn of the wavelets on the shore. Their sound was the intermittent, quiescent breath of a hibernating bear. Below the brassy surface that lay so placidly across the whole of her vision, Lily could feel the pulse of a cobalt heart whose energies charged the secret and vital and imperishable parts of the earth's anatomy. There was here, *she knew*, the sign of some pilgrimage whose spirit she shared.

Then, a girl again, she dashed across the crystalline beach and splashed and paddled and strutted and planted her footprints in the permeable sands. It was Indian summer: the air was warm and thin as new wine, the water icy, the sand purging. She did not care to leave.

When she did, she mounted the highest dune north from the trail and looked back towards the townsite. The houses of Port Sarnia were not yet visible. But she could see – where the Lake poured into the chasm of the St. Clair only half-a-mile across – the shanties in which Slocum's people kept their nets and cleaned their catch. The northwest breeze blew the stench of dead fish inland. Between the edge of the pinery and the River lay a quarter-mile of swamps full of disheveled cattails and yellowing milkweed. Could they ever build a railroad over that? To the far south-west Lily saw also the palisades of Fort Gratiot, the Stars and Stripes saluting self-importantly above it. Overhead, herring gulls whirled and rehearsed their mating dance.

As she was about to start looking for the blazed trail, Lily noted that to the north the sand-dunes were thicker, reaching far back into some brush composed of runt alders and hawthorn. Something drew her that way, away from the marked trail. The dunes gradually diminished, as if at one time they had been waves whose reward for such brave and ceaseless repetition had been the blessing of silication. At the last of these unfulfilled crests lay a small, rolling field dotted with dwarf trees. The pinery enclosed it on the three remaining sides. Though there was nothing visible to the unpractised eye to suggest that something unnatural lay here concealed, Lily sensed immediately that she was in a graveyard. The breeze did not penetrate this far but Lily felt the eddies and parabolas of moving, sentient beings occupying space. She stepped carefully ahead. The grave plots were not clearly evident, the knot-grass and hoarhound and sand-burs slightly smaller and less robust than those at the edges of each site. Moreover, the ground had sunk almost imperceptibly, marking the modest dimensions of these nether abodes.

After a while, Lily spotted the new grave; its sand was piled two inches above ground to accommodate the natural sinking later on; clusters of grass had been replanted to root and flourish and camouflage in the coming spring. Winter would soon provide its own disguise.

You are here at last, Lily thought. You came under cover of dark and they laid you to rest among the other nameless wanderers and refugees, the outcasts and pariahs and survivors of genocide, the renegades, and the prophets like you, Southener. I haven't forgotten the jasper heart. Already it has brought me more luck that I ever hoped for. I wish I could tell you about it. And I won't forget the vows. Somehow I'll find the sacred place in these woods and return the magic to it. I'll come here every time I can, and honour your grave. Surely here, with swamps and dunes all around, you'll be safe. No one would ever want this land for anything. No one but me will ever know you're here.

Suddenly she thought of her mother's headstone, alone in an unfrequented corner of some stranger's field, the script of her name chipped out by Sounder so crudely no one would recall whose soul sought refuge below it. I must go back there. *I will.*

"Lily, pet, you're back at last," said an excited Mrs. Templeton.

"I hope you weren't worried," Lily said, embarrassed by the state of her attire.

"Heavens no, I just couldn't wait to tell you. It's all been settled. The new station'll be ready in a week and the first train is comin' in on the nineteenth. There'll be a dinner and a ball."

"Are we invited?" Lily said.

"Invited? We're givin' it! And you got exactly two weeks to learn how to dance!"

4

A few minutes after the appointed hour, the crowd, gathered on either side of the cleared cut that cradled the tracks, heard the first sound of a locomotive in Lambton. Two thousand necks craned south-eastward where the rails, a mere three hundred yards away, curved past the town's edge and sank into the gloam of bushland. Nothing was seen but a glint of cold sun on the shine of iron. The dignitaries, more than a hundred of them, pulled their coats tightly over their chests and felt the crushing obligation of having to appear moderately disinterested.

The sound – when it came – was low, ferric, iron-on-iron, gaining volume and pitch as its mechanical, pistoning repetitions consumed miles and scattered wildlife helter-skelter through the shuddering swamps and fernshaws. Trunk and bole and root quivered like tuning forks in its wake. Its thunder drowned forest-sounds unchallenged since the ice laid down its alluvial silence. Mouse and mole abandoned hollows in the earth eons-old and fled, dizzy and blind, through the slicing light. Unable to recognize its own voice, a trumpeter swan went mad in its music. In unison, the engine shrieked steam.

The onlookers responded to the steam-whistle as one: a raucous, antiphonal cheer went up from the town choir. It had barely subsided when the first smoke was spotted above the bush, occasioning another cheer which was instantly answered by a blast of steam louder than the first and carrying in its cry the intimations of an irreversible momentum, a manic potency, a hungering for the future on any terms. It was at once a whoop of self-congratulatory joy and a uvular lament for losses not yet discerned. The worshippers at trackside watched the chuffing puffs of woodsmoke smite the air with the force of a behemoth's breath. Moments later the charred stack itself appeared to float out of the bush before the entire juggernaut hove into full view and, at speeds only dreamt of, roared past their applause and braked towards a stop at the platform where the pooh-bahs dropped all pretense of impassion.

The locomotive itself was the principal source of wonder and mock terror: with #52 painted in gold letters across its fern-green skin and alongside its name: *Prospero*. It pounded into the station on four gigantic driving wheels – its sleek cow-catcher bobbing on the smaller bogie-wheels; its open tender plugged with stovewood and swaying behind it like a dervish; its brass headlamp that could embellish sunlight and intimidate darkness with Cyclopean aplomb; its three passenger-cars lurching and hopping to every flinch of locomotive energy. In the unglazed window of the cab, a dwarf of a man was slowly being raised in the grip of a lever bigger than a grenadier's broadsword. Before the station – an imposing, pseudo-gothic structure of stone, red brick and elm – young *Prospero* skidded to a halt with a hiss and a screech that stunned the parishioners: a keening skirl of a cry like that of a disembowelled recruit at Culloden. The Great Western Railway had arrived.

Lily did learn to dance in the two weeks before the event-of-the century. As Mrs. Templeton never tired of saying, "The girl's a natural!" Natural or not it took some practice to even begin to disentangle the intricacies of the quadrille, galop, valse, polka and inevitable lancers. While Mrs. Templeton played a suitable tune on the piano, his Worship would act as Lily's partner, then hop to one side and quickly demonstrate what the other couples of the quadrille would be up to – often forgetting where he was or two-stepping inadvertently into the galop. One of the three would invariably begin to laugh, setting the other two off and deflecting the learning process by several rods. In the waltz, or *valse* as it was then called, his Worship was superb, guiding Lily and his wayward paunch around the parlour in mutual three-quarter delight. Lily could not help humming, though it was apparently a form of impoliteness.

"Let your *feet* feel the music," Mrs. Templeton said, pouncing on the keys.

"But she is, sweet, she is; her whole body is," puffed the Mayor, sensing the triphammer pulse of the tune through Lily's right hand and the small of her back, and marveling at the weightless power of her presence. She will do well, this one, he thought. Suddenly, he loved his wife more than ever, and that night surprised her with his need and its slow, caring aftermath.

When the train had come to a full and panting stop, it debouched onto the freshly planked platform several squads of V.I.P.'s – some genuine, many self-appointed. The forward platoon consisted of Sir Oliver Steele, vice-president of the Great Western, with Lady Marigold Steele, and the Mayor of London trailed by four councilors and their wives. Then with a scandalously blonde, unattached female anchored to his right arm came a scandalously handsome figure-of-a-man soon identified as the notorious roue of London and Toronto, Stanley R. Dowling, known abroad as 'Mad-Cap'. Not only had be debauched a succession of willing virgins, but it was rumoured he had been drummed out of the militia. For reasons no respectable person could understand or commend, he had, from obscure origins, made his way up in the world and in a society whose standards were obviously rotting at the core. He was said to have been made a director of the Great Western and to have speculated recklessly on local railway ventures that left *him* rich and the *towns* bankrupt. Of course, one had to make allowances for rumour. And success.

Lily was looking at Lady Steele as the official party slow-marched towards his Worship's group, behind which the lady folk of the town were expectantly assembled. Lady Steele was several decades younger than her beknighted husband, with fresh-scrubbed skin and sloe eyes bearing a look of distant, wry amusement and something netherward wanting to be plumbed and disclosed. Dowling, Lily noted, smiling publicly at his tow-haired poppet but cast sidelong glances at Lady Steele, who absorbed them, unreturned. He himself, it was clear, would be lord of any demesne he chose to occupy: with his jet-black hair, browns and side-whiskers; eyes bitumous and smouldering; chin masculine in jut and intent; carriage regal and never without purpose; the flesh full, grateful for the good things life had nurtured it with, with just a hint of puffiness and sag that would later plague his middle years. For now, he was a man in his prime, with poise and presence. His dowry: the future.

As his Worship shook hands with the worthies from London and Toronto, the band struck up a martial air and the crow, crushing in around the train and dignitaries, applauded wildly. If they had any doubts about the intrusion of railways into their lives, they did not express them on this occasion. As the formal introductions and exchange of greetings were taking place, Lily looked anxiously at the throng of faces about her. Just as they were turning to pass through the station to their carriage, she spotted them. Uncle Chester grinned and waved excessively; Aunt Bridie, apparently, did not see her.

A dinner was served at six o'clock for the more than one hundred and fifty well-wishers and their guests. All were men. In 1858 and for some years to come, the wives and darlings of celebrities did not grace the tables of such public colloquies. Hence, the 'intelligence' emanating from the event had to be derived from second-hand sources. Fortunately the ladies of the town had access to a number of impeccable, though not coincident, accounts of what transpired. Since this was the largest dinner ever held in Port Sarnia, the only room big enough to accommodate the guests and their appetites was in the Orange Lodge near the St. Clair Inn. Thus it was that Mrs. Josephine Salter, whose kitchen was called upon to cater the meal, was able to store up enough gossip to feed her habit for a year; likewise, at a lower level, for Char Hazelberry whose own kitchen provided the tarts and trifle, and who luckily was required to bring along her best girls, Betsy and Winnie, to aid in the service thereof and in the dissemination of news thereafter.

No less than eighteen toasts were proposed and replied to – with claret for the elect and water for the saved. His Worship led the way with one to the Queen Herself, followed rapidly by those to the president of the Great Western, his board of directors, his English backers and the British Parliament. A toast was even offered to the President of the United States of America and responded to at length by the Mayor of Port Huron, Michigan, whose country also had a stake in these enterprises. According to the report in *The Observer* his American Worship emphasized that two things were held in common by both peoples – republicans and monarchists – a tradition of fair play and justice as well as an unshakeable belief in progress, a progress rendered visible and demarcated by the march of iron through the untracked wastes of the continent. Indeed, he concluded, the password of both great nations was identical: *onward*. The applause was deafening. Lily heard it, sitting in her room – with Bonnie and Mrs. Templeton fussing over her with pins and thread, and thinking only of Aunt Bridie there at the station in the midst of such commotion: staring at nothing.

The ball, in the concourse of the new station, began at nine in the evening and through its twenty-two dances endured until almost three in the morning. The town band of Goderich, who had come down by steamer in the afternoon, provided a passable imitation of its betters at Osgoode in Toronto. The gentlemen of Port Sarnia – attired in the severe, black formality of that period – offered a striking contrast to the uninhibited exfoliation of the wives and young ladies. All agreed that it was a heaven-blessed sight to see against the drab umbers of late autumn such butterfly hues as danced in the gowns, coifs and cheeks of the weaker sex. The only exceptions, on the stronger side, were a handful of elder townsmen who had dusted off their faded militia uniforms from the time of the rebellion, and five young rakes from London, three of them in the scarlet-gold-and-white of the British regular and the other two in the blue tunics of the new militia unit just formed in Middlesex. Needless to say, their military vigour and courtly manners did not go unappreciated by at least half of those assembled.

Mrs. Templeton, flush with excitement and her first sip of French champagne, her lashes aflutter under the sizzling gas-jets, taxied up to Lily and said, "It's filled already, pet. They saw you in the promenade and near trampled me to death to sign up." She was waving Lily's dance-card which she herself had two-thirds filled out – before their grand entrance – with local worthies and beaux and, as she called them, "regrettable necessaries". "Including", she now added, "several of the nicest catches from London."

Lily, too, had been keeping her eyes and ears open. She watched Lady Marigold in earnest conversation with Sir Oliver, and nearby Mad-Cap Dowling was chatting animatedly with one of the smooth-cheeked young soldiers and pouring assent into the upturned gaze of his blonde *devotee*, but managing all the same to cast little semaphores of affection towards the dark lady. She in turn would incline her ringlets slightly in his direction, lending him part of a damask cheek and the pip of one of her sloe-eyes. It was during such an exchange that Lily noticed for the first time one of the two militiamen standing beside Dowling. Next to the regulars and to Dowling himself, the young corporal certainly seemed non-descript: he was of medium height, his hair a sandy tint in the uncertain light, the face oval, beardless but for a thin moustache, fine-boned, housing two eyes that darted about, she thought fancifully, like curious bluebirds avid for the high air. She could see him straining to fill out the tunic, to accommodate its formal projection of power, but there was a restlessness in the very way he stood with his weight on one foot and his hands fretting for a place to light. When he turned in her direction, Lily saw the force of his glance, felt a vulnerable masculinity upon her, and realized with a start that she had been staring at him for no less than five minutes. He gave her a polite across-the-room smile and rejoined the conversation at hand. No matter. The cause was already won. That strange sense of knowing-for-sure, of seeing the thing-before-its-shadow – which she had given up as a lost jewel of her childhood – came back with a rush of blood to her cheeks and a thumping of her heart in its bower. *I will share my life with this man; he will love me as no other.*

The band from Goderich had just struck up a quadrille.

"Here comes your first admirer," said Mrs. Templeton. Gratefully Lily let herself be swept into the square by his Worship. Her beloved was not among the set.

Once the dancing actually began, Lily found herself completely engaged in it. She couldn't think when there was music in her, she could only feel, and mime that feeling with her feet and arms and the bow of her body in the will of the dance – as if, hobbled by cadence, her spirit could soar. She galloped and polka-ed and waltzed and qua-drilled. Her black-suited partners – so cordial, so deferential in their requests – became faceless extensions of her own need to make shapes in the smoky night-air, to bend them to the same obedience gripping her. Between dances, however, where couples chattered, sipped champagne, nibbled sandwiches for solace, or dampened their fan-tasies in the public loos – Lily felt anxious and drained. With only two dances left, her beloved had not by chance appeared in the same set nor was he, as Fate ought to have allowed, one of her partners. Delicately she asked Mrs. Templeton if she knew the names of any of the military gentlemen from London. "Oh yes, pet. Mr. Carleton and Mr. James are both lieutenants in the fuseliers." "Oh." "The others I don't know." "Oh." "Though one of them, mind you – I can't recall which right off – did ask for a place on your card." Lily's hopes slipped a notch. The waltz in the middle group had been taken by the militiaman she had earlier seen beside her lover, and she had been too shy to ask him any question – even his name after she'd forgotten it – despite the fact that they were dancing together, that he pulled her cheek close to his own sweaty one, and that he averred she was the prettiest girl in the room, etc. That's that, then, she thought.

She looked up from her card to see just who "Mr. Marshall" might be when he said, not a foot from her, "I believe I have the honour of this dance. My name is Tom Marshall. I'm from London."

The penultimate dance was the fast-paced *lancers* with eight couples pacing through the military complexity of its steps and manoeuvres and musical stratagems. There was little opportunity to converse – even if Lily had been able to think of anything to say, though she ruefully noted that one couple – obviously lovers – managed a series of looks and touching that were more eloquent than any *tête-à-tête*. Nonetheless, she felt Tom's arms momentarily about her waist, her hand clasped in his, and confirmed her premonition of his vulnerable strength, his erratic energy, his need for collaboration. She placed her face naked before his gaze, released to him for scrutiny and care a locked part of herself through the dance as far as it might flow. He smiled at her when they were apart and possessed her with his grasp when they sashayed or twirled in linked curves. He wafted words to her and she nodded as if they were real.

When the lancers ended, he ferried her towards the table where the punch was wilting in the heat. Now they would talk and it would begin. He placed a crystal goblet in her hands. She drank thirstily.

"Lily, you're the best dancer of the lot. Surely you can't be from Port Sarnia," he said with a twinkle.

She was about to reply when his eye was caught by some movement to their left. "Damn," he muttered to himself. "Would you please excuse me, Miss Ramsbottom; I'm wanted by my party. It's been a pleasure meeting you. I hope we'll meet again."

We will, Lily thought. She thanked him and watched him walk over to the Dowling group. Lady Marigold and her husband had joined them. When the music started for the last dance, a Strauss waltz, she saw His Nibs take the withered fingertips of the judge's wife; then Dowling put his arm about the waist of the dark lady and they strolled with utmost ease to wait for the music to stir and legitimate their illicit lusts. So engrossed was Lily in this minor melodrama that she almost missed seeing Corporal Marshall provide a military escort for Miss Platinum to stage-centre where, the second the music began, he clasped her pliant bodice and pulled the bullets of her breast against the blue shield of his own.

You will come back, Tom Marshall. I know.

I hope.

Lily was in a deep, daylight sleep – following a night of restless dreams and near-dreams – when she was awakened by Mrs. Templeton gently shaking her hand. She blinked at the invading light. "What's wrong?" she said.

"It's your Auntie," Mrs. Templeton said.

Lily saw Aunt Bridie hovering behind Mrs. Templeton, her face ashen.

"Are you all right, Auntie?"

"Yes, love. It's your Uncle Chester." Her voice was close to breaking. "His heart give out," she said.

8

1

The year was born in hope. For the County's farmers, after the 'black frost' of 1859, there was not much else left. In the days before welfare and government subsidies, those who tilled the soil were left with charred blossom, shrivelled root and wizened leafage to mock them through the hot summer of 'fifty-nine with little chance that they could afford even to buy seed for next year's planting and some chance in the back townships that they might starve or chew their way through a winter of turnip, chicory and hazelnut. But then it must be remembered that death was more common, more random and variegated in those days. Typhus, cholera and diphtheria trimmed the infant population with regular and reliable horror, and struck down among the adults those who were weakening, unwary or conspicuously wanton. Moreover, the high cost of progress – of living up to the County's adopted motto, *ongoing* – appeared to be routinely accepted by the populace. Certainly the 440 shipping disasters listed for 1859, at a cost of $668,565.00 and 105 lives, offered no deterrent to the expansion of water commerce – the taming of the Great Lakes – nor did it in any wise discourage excursionists and pleasure-seekers from boarding hundreds of cruiser-craft and heading out 'into the blue'. In September 1860 the excursion boat *Lady Elgin* went down with a loss of 287 lives. The disasters on the new, often jerry-built, railroads, though not as calamitous, were as frequent and as cavalier. Notwithstanding, the Great Western moved more than 800,000 passengers per annum in Upper Canada in these years. And the Grand Trunk had designs of its own on the landscape. Elsewhere, bridges were being dreamed and flung across the St. Lawrence at Quebec and at Lewiston, swing ferries wobbled and broke in the St. Clair rapids, canals deepened and widened – each leap forward taking its routine toll in killed and maimed, the latter being cast upon the public charity, to be pitied as freaks or shunned as exiles in their own land.

One of the more curious cataclysms occurred in the backwater township of Enniskillen, where a recently arrived homesteader, in desperate search for water to keep his stock and kin alive through the drought, dug straight into the earth and struck, not a spring, but a suppurating ooze of molasses-like 'goo' which no amount of packing could staunch. Naturally he abandoned the place for more healthful terrain. Though the significance of the latter event would not be appreciated for several more years, and only then by the prescient and the daring, few politically aware citizens of the County missed the import of John Brown's aborted uprising at Harper's Ferry in the fall of 1859: to the Tories it signified the folly of all rebellious acts however noble their cause; to the Reformers it was a painful reminder that the passion to be free, though universal and irrepressible, was – like love itself – rarely a direct, simple, unadulterated affair.

But the following spring of 1860 seemed blessed by that same Providence whose hand was ever on the tiller and the throttle. Sun and rain collaborated so that the wheat throve and the fruit trees blossomed on cue. Even Aunt Bridie began once again to entertain the notion of a future. She had become resigned to the fact that all of their efforts had now to be put into maintaining a few cash crops to be sold, at outrageously low prices, at the farm gate. Nonetheless, she persevered through two long winters with her quilting despite the onset of arthritis, which she mocked as "a little twinge or two to remind me I'm gettin' old an' to keep me honest." Much of their precious cash had to be used for them merely to survive the ravages of the black frost, but as Auntie often said, "We're holdin' our own with our heads up, lass, don't ever forget that." But Lily sensed a new hollowness to Auntie's aphorisms, a whisper of world-weariness in them. Many times before the glorious spring of 'sixty, in the daylight dark of the cottage as they sat sewing with Uncle Chester snoring anonymously in his wicker, Lily glimpsed the panic in her Aunt's smile, and found it so painful, so terrifying that she had to look away, ashamed and aching. She knew that Auntie Bridie could not live long without hope: her resignation – so deeply a part of her Celtic heritage and uncontaminated by Christianity – was in her only a temporary manifestation designed to help her endure momentary, even prolonged, setbacks. But it was not constitutional: she would die rather than succumb to the orthodox debilitations of her pioneering sisters.

With Uncle Chester now an invalid, there was no talk of Lily's going back into service even though that expedient would have helped them a great deal. Someone had to nurse poor Uncle Chester, night and day, summer and winter. His heart attack had been real, and he was fortunate enough to have the doctor arrive from town too late to be of immediate assistance, and thus managed to survive. For several months he lay on Lily's bed (she now slept on a cot in the kitchen) barely able to flick his eyes at her in appreciation as she fed him with a spoon, emptied his festering bedpan, bathed his bleached flesh, or 'read' to him the few stories from Mrs. Templeton's *Arabian Nights* she had been able to memorize. By the spring of 1859 he was able to whisper "Thank you" in a hoarse guttural, like a wraith calling from some shallow part of purgatory.

"I don't pray much, Lily, as you know," Bridie said. "But if I did, I'd ask my maker to take Chester back. Nobody oughta suffer like that."

Lily knew which of those two was suffering the most. Uncle's eyes welled with tears of constant gratitude; they opened up at her with the unaffected love of a puppy; they had regained a kind of innocence. However, early in the summer of 'fifty-nine, even as the black frost's legacy deepened, Chester murmured, moved, sat up, smiled, and became impossible. Aunt Bridie stared at him as if he had, for a second and more unforgivable time, betrayed her. But she did her duty. They bought him a wicker chair with feather pillows and wheels so that he could sit by the stove or on the flagstones in the sun or be ferried about on short excursions through the garden and woodlot. His gratitude alas was not continuous nor his appreciation perfect. He whined and wheedled, threw tantrums and dinner plates, cried like a baby and grumbled like an octogenarian, and generally wallowed in self-pity.

"I should've gone, like *that*," he'd say, failing to make his fingers snap, "the world'd be a better place without old Chester in it." Auntie would sever him with a stare, then relent and say without conviction, "But you'll be up an' walkin' soon. Is there anythin' special Lily can fix you for supper?"

"Well, rhubarb tart'd be nice, but I expect it's too late for that." It invariably was, and he then had to be mollified with whatever second-best offer could be effected.

If it hadn't been for Bachelor Bill, the farm itself would have collapsed. When his wheat crop was wiped out by the black frost, he came to Aunt Bridie and asked her to buy his fields, leaving him only his shanty and garden, and to let him work as her hired hand for his food and a dribble of cash. Sniffing the scent of a future on the wind, Bridie went into town that very day and removed most of her life's savings from the Bank of Upper Canada and doubled her land holdings when everyone else was retrenching or going under. Of course, a second killer frost and they would have lost everything.

The hope that Aunt Bridie nurtured through the brutal winter of ice storms and blizzards and murderous thaws – auguries of disaster all of them – bordered on the hysterical. Lily took to spiking Uncle Chester's *Ayer's Cherry Pectoral* with some of his own hooch (discovered when they dismantled the north coop) just so he would sleep through the grating January afternoons. Several times at night Lily heard her Aunt crying alone in her room: not the sort of weeping women use to release or publish their sundry griefs, but the half-repressed anguish that is one part rage and two parts despair. The next morning she would be bright with forced cheerfulness as she pulled on her macintosh and headed back to the woodlot to help Bill with the cutting. "That's pine's cash in the bank!"

More and more, also, Auntie seemed to be placing her hopes on the sounds not only of their own axes but those now ringing through the pinery that lay between their fields and the waters to the north and west. The long-rumoured arrival of the second and most ambitious of the great railway octopuses, was happening. And less than half-a-mile from them.

"I told you, didn't I, Chester, they'd build somethin' big on that property. That's why we moved way out here in the first place, Lily. Mayn't be soldiers over there, but there's gonna be trains," she said wistfully, "an' people, too. We're gonna have neighbours, lass, a real town of our own to belong to. Didn't I say so, Chester?"

Chester was asleep, dreaming perhaps of an unscorched carpenter's shop and a boy name Bertie – his Cherry Pectoral clutched in his hands like a rosary.

2

July was sweltering. Aunt Bridie, Bachelor Bill and Lily sweated and slaved in the fields. Lily burned, freckled, peeled and then burned anew. Uncle Chester took his first baby steps, tottered and sprained his wrist, after which he too sweated and whined. About the middle of the month, Violet ran off. Work was halted so that a search could begin. Lily went to the pond first because Violet had been peering into its coppery mirror on several recent occasions, near daybreak. Only Booster and his harem were there, looking on in bemusement. Throughout the afternoon they combed the pinery, and Auntie even walked as far as the oak ridge and Little Lake to the north-east, pausing as she crossed the freshly-laid imprint of the Grand Trunk to contemplate the future. But it was Lily who found her sitting in a daze in a field near the railway worker's shanties down by the construction site for the new wharf and station. It was dusk, and Violet must have become alarmed enough to start crying. When Lily arrived, Violet was sobbing incoherently; even Lily could make out no word. She put her arm about the wretched girl and half-carried her home. Auntie intercepted them near the house and together they took Violet into the tallow-lit gloom of the log hut. Bachelor Bill, sitting with his head buried in his hands, looked up with mixed rage and relief, but said nothing. He glared at Lily as she stroked Violet's hair and rubbed her neck and shoulders till the sobbing stopped. Auntie left to answer Uncle Chester's piteous calls for aid, but Lily stayed, murmuring softly into the girl's ear and watching Bachelor Bill. Finally she rose and with reluctance left the house. Outside she paused, waiting for the explosion within and deciding that somehow she would intervene. Aunt Bridie was suddenly beside her. Together, they listened in the dark.

From the hut came the unmistakable sound of Bachelor Bill's harmonica: thin strains of an old-country air, reedy and elegiac. The women went home.

Lily decided to have a look at this railroad in which Auntie had placed so much of her faith. For a year she had listened to its saws, axes, hammers and curses of work-in-progress, but she had no desire to see the results. Towards November of 'fifty-nine, Auntie would walk over there every day she could and watch the ties straighten the landscape, foot by foot, amazed that such delicate calligraphy had printed its message from here to London and beyond, they were told, to the edge of the ocean itself. During the search for Violet, Lily had glimpsed in the dark the havoc wrought here, and felt an irresistible urge to return in the daylight.

Nothing could have prepared her for such a sight. A few hundred yards north of their woodlot the destruction began. Lily had imagined a neat swath cut through the bush; there was no bush left. Every pine within a mile's radius of the wharf-site, on the River just below the Lake, had been hacked down haphazardly as if some deranged troglodyte had avenged himself for some fancied slight. The areas near the right-of-way were efficiently trim, but the so-called townsite was a wasteland of split trunks, charred branches and smouldering needles. After a fashion Lily could see all the way to the River's edge; she could see how the main-line curled in from the north-east across the ballasted swamps and aligned itself with boundaries formed by the water. The sprawling, unpainted wharfs and freight-sheds were three-quarters completed, and to the south at the periphery of the remaining stand of trees Lily spied the brick station-and-hotel towering three stories above the shoreline, the roof slates reflecting the sun and the several dozen glazed windows beaming 'progress' across a clearing that, it seemed, must inevitably yield houses and people to inhabit them. But why would they come here? Why would they want to? For now, only a handful of workers' shanties, which had served the fisherman before them, gave any promise of domesticity. Below her Lily watched the ripple of muscle and sweat as the navvies raised their hammers and drove their spikes into wood like nails into the cross-struts of a coffin.

Though she was curious, Lily didn't approach the station-hotel. Something told her she would see the inside of it soon enough. Instead she walked down across the tracks to the point where the Lake and River joined, and stared out at the self-sustaining, generous beauty of the blue waters flowing out of the north-sky itself and condescending to the south. She glanced anxiously over at the scrub bush and dunes along the lakeshore, noting with relief that progress had by-passed the sleeping graves of the lost. You are safe, Southener, she thought. Satisfied, Lily turned to go and as she did she found herself looking back across the mangled plain for the first time. Smoke from the foundries was visible to the south, but her eye caught something more impending. About half-way across the curving rim of the tree-line she saw rising above the pines, a towering hardwood – its branches unfolding, outreaching – magnificent in is solitary grandeur. The troglodyte's mad slashing had stopped less than twenty feet from its aboriginal root.

As Lily picked her way through the wreckage towards home, the immense depression settling over her was partially relieved by the thought of this lone survivor, by the belief that not all the magic in the world had flown.

"She's gone again," said Aunt Bridie sternly when Lily entered the garden.

This time they did not find her. Not that evening nor the next morning. At noon several men on horseback rode up the lane and stopped in front of the shanty. Bachelor Bill was with them. Lily and Auntie hurried over, leaving Uncle Chester to fend for himself. When they arrived, Bachelor Bill, distraught, said to them: "They say she's crazy an' they have to take her away, an' they just picks her up an' she's bleedin' and squallin' an' her eyes is beggin' me, an' they just up an' cart her off to London, they're gonna lock her up, Bridie, they're gonna lock her up somewheres."

Aunt Bridie took control, and got the whole story. But nothing could be done, they said. Three or four of the railway workmen had pulled Violet into a field where they raped her repeatedly, and then left her there bleeding and babbling in her alien speech. The incident had been witnessed by a minor official of the Grand Trunk who was inspecting one of the fancy new rooms on the third floor of the hotel. He couldn't exactly see who the men were from such a distance, and didn't report the incident till the next morning because he saw the girl get up on her own and wander towards Sarnia, and naturally he reckoned that it wasn't really rape after all. As it turned out, no one was ever charged with the crime. No reliable witnesses could be found. Violet, her terror and pain locked forever inside her, "went crazy", and the constable and the magistrate decided she would be better off "getting proper treatment". Bachelor Bill was inconsolable. Aunt Bridie ranted against all officialdom and seethed and grew grim. Lily felt quite alone, bereft of something of immense and irreplaceable value. She got a taste of what despair would be like.

3

Some time towards dawn Lily was awakened by a blaze of lightning, followed soon by a crack of thunder that sounded as if Adam had pulled his own ribs apart. Then the rain came, slashing at the dry woods and vulnerable gardens. Soon it relented, easing off to a steady, sustaining downpour. When she arose with the sun, the air would be sweet with growth, the leafage radiant, the earth slaked and grateful. She turned back towards sleep, towards the hurting dream – anything to avoid such a day.

When she did get up, hearing Auntie stir restlessly in her room, she sat on the cot for a long while letting the infant light brush over her, quicksilvering her skin. She reached into the applewood box below the cot and drew out the leather pouch. The jasper talisman felt cold in her cupped palms. She pressed it tightly, squeezing her eyes shut, and begging the wordless, driven thoughts in her mind to seek some shape, some release, some reconciliation. It occurred to her that she might be praying. The talisman grew warm, incarnadine, then pulsed – like the first flexing thrum of an embryo's ventricle.

"Are you up, dear?"

"Yes, Auntie. You stay put a while. It's a bit wet for weedin' right off."

She heard the creak and shuffle of her Aunt rigging her body for the day ahead.

Lily glanced up from her hoeing. Aunt Bridie was waving from the yard, something white and fluttering in her hand. When Lily came up to her, she saw that the stranger was only Silas, the butcher's idiot son.

"He's brung a note from Alice Templeton," said Aunt Bridie evenly. "Do you want me to read it?"

"Please."

In a somewhat overly formal and halting manner, Bridie read: "Dear Lily: You are cordially invited to attend the official luncheon for His Royal Highness, Albert Edward, Prince of Wales, to be held at the Grand Trunk Hotel at twelve noon, September 13, 1860. Please say you'll come. Affectionately, Alice Templeton."

Aunt Bridie looked at Lily expectantly. "The writin's funny," she said to fill the silence. Silas nodded.

"Tell her, thanks. But no."

"You want me to write that?"

"Yes."

"Lily, love, I think you oughta go."

Silas agreed.

"What else *is* there?" Aunt Bridie said with feeling.

"We got weedin' to do," Lily said, and started for the potato patch.

Silas came back two hours later, having missed the turn-off and gone part-way to Errol before beating a meandering retreat. Again Aunt Bridie read the note aloud.

Uncle Chester, who despite his 'sprained' wrist was walking now with two canes, came out to listen.

"This is even queerer than the last one," Aunt Bridie said. "It says: 'Lily dearest: there will be a military escort from London.' Now what's that supposed to mean?"

"It means he's the Prince of Wales," Chester said. "The heir to the throne."

"The *English* throne," Bridie snapped. Silas sided with her.

"Now don't start again, woman, with them radical ideas. I got a bum ticker, you know."

"An' how could the world ever forget it?"

"Tell her *yes*," Lily said to the startled trio.

9

1

The visit of Queen Victoria's firstborn son to Her Majesty's dominions in August and September of 1860 was the biggest public event of that year and until confederation seven years later the most 'historic' occasion in the fledgling existence of British North America. The Yankees, busily preparing to dissolve their shotgun marriage with the South, had to be shown what it was like for a people to freely love a monarch and to accept with grace the authority of the ties that bind, etc. No fewer than four books were published to consecrate the events of the pretender's 'progress' (one of them in Boston, no less) and newspapers everywhere devoted their column-inches to tracking each royal manoeuvre and recording the public's response. Even the Prince's dance cards were faithfully reproduced as if they were imperishable poems.

Hence it is that the hour-by-hour sweep of H.R.H. through the County of Lambton on 13 September 1860 has been exhaustively delineated and willed to posterity. The Royal Party and a regiment of well-wishers and hopefuls boarded the Great Western in London at 9:00 a.m. (the Prince's special car, however, belonged to the Grand Trunk: the rival railways had declared a truce to demonstrate their unshakeable faith in the Empire). At 11:00 a.m. they touched down in Sarnia where H.R.H. stepped from his mobile drawing room – flanked by railway moguls, hastily promoted lieutenant-colonels, and the young scion's guardian, the unflappable Duke of Newcastle – onto a scarlet carpet variously reported to be either one hundred or three hundred yards in length (the latter being a local estimate). More than five thousand were said to be gathered around the Great Western depot and wharf – almost the County's total population. The succession of toasts and responses which followed – in their quest for eloquence – managed to put out the schedule by almost an hour. The only speech worth the space given to it was that of Chief Kan-was-ga-shi (Great Bear of the North), one of the several hundred Ojibwas who had come down from the wilds of Manitoulin for the occasion:

Brother, Great Brother – the sky is beautiful. It was the wish of the Great Spirit that we should meet in this place. I hope the sky will continue to look fine, to give happiness to both the whites and to the Indians. You see the Indians who are around you. It is their earnest desire that you will always remember them.

It is not recorded whether any of those assembled caught the ironies either in the words themselves or the situation in which they were delivered.

After presenting the chiefs with silver medallions, the Prince led a cavalcade of carriages, mounted citizenry and rearguard foot-soldiers from the less opulent parts of town to the magnificent station-hotel of the Grand Trunk near the wharf of the new townsite already being referred to as Point Edward. Therein, an hour late, the pooh-bahs received their luncheon and basked in the reflected glory and unabashed good humour of the young and future king. With no coaching whatsoever the Prince proposed a toast to the "Prosperity of the Grand Trunk Railway." Its regional vice-president, Dunbar Cruickshank, seated beside Mad-Cap Dowling (now called somewhat ambiguously 'Cap' Dowling), responded with unforced enthusiasm.

After the meal H.R.H. and a very select group of dignitaries boarded the Grand Truck steamer the *Michigan* and sailed up the River and onto the Lake. By 3:30 p.m. the Royal Cortege was back at the Great Western depot and entrained for London where the Prince gave a levee that same evening which outshone even the shameless extravagance of the one given at Toronto's Osgoode Hall two nights earlier. The entire episode – emblazoned forever in local annals – had lasted a mere four-and-a-half hours.

2

When the royal train pulled into the station, Lily was standing beside Mrs. Templeton just behind the Mayor and his officials. She had a clear view of the Prince as he approached them gingerly across the red carpet, his chaperone at his elbow, both of them aglitter in military regalia. The next rank brought the railroad bosses – the one who had replaced Sir Oliver (dead of a mysterious stroke) and the fiercely ambitious Dunbar Cruickshank looking not a day over thirty-five. Next came a wider and less orderly phalanx of minor factoti and politicians, including one of the newest vice-presidents of the Grand Trunk, Cap Dowling, at whose elbow, Lily was not perturbed to see, ambled the dark lady out of her widow's weeds just for the occasion. Fanned out behind were several scarlet-coated regular officers and blue-clad militiamen, including the young man Lily had waltzed with. Tom was not among them.

Only Lily's affection for the Templetons and her deep sense of gratitude towards them gave her the courage to continue smiling and pretending to be moved by the ritual references to her beauty and charm. Certainly Mrs. Templeton had done her best with a sow's ear. It was Aunt Bridie who'd insisted she come into stay with her benefactress for a full week before the event: "You'll have to get used to city ways all over," she said.

"Won't be easy gettin' them feet of yours into shoes again." Mrs. Templeton had sent two strapping farm-lads out to Bridie's place "to help out", but they returned crestfallen an hour later. Lily's outfit had been made by Mrs. Templeton's dressmaker "from the ground up this time", with the addition even of a parasol, white gloves and linen hand-kerchiefs. "My word, Lily, what a figure you've got! Not even the farm can spoil you, though it's tryin'," said Mrs. Templeton, tears pressing against her lids as her fingers unconsciously brushed the calluses embossed on the girl's hands. Lily tolerated all the fuss, tried to be joyful when his Worship whirled her about the parlour to the thump of the piano "for old times' sake." She knew how much they missed their daughters. From the maid she learned that both daughters had promised to come down from Toronto for the Prince's visit but at the last minute received invitations, through their prominent husbands, to attend the Royal Ball at Osgoode. Despite her own personal anxiety about the coming event, Lily felt and responded as best she could to the special obligation placed upon her.

"I don't think you'll see madam stay in this town much longer," Bonnie candied to Lily one day. But she would say no more.

Why didn't you come, Tom? Lily thought, listening to the last of the toasts. She was as puzzled as she was hurt. The talisman had pulsed as she had held it; its augury was as clear as a proclamation. How had she mis-read it?

"Great news, pet! I just knew the Prince had an' eye on you! We've been invited aboard the *Michigan*! And –" Mrs. Templeton lowered her voice theatrically, "that old snoop of a Duke ain't comin'."

But Lily knew whom the royal glance had favoured whenever discretion permit-ted. Seated two chairs from her at the woman's table, the dark lady occupied her own special kind of throne.

3

Alice Templeton and Lily sat apart from the others on scarlet-striped deck chairs letting the warm September breeze ruffle their tea and parasols, and watching the guests preen and promenade before the princely presence. The ladies coasted by like bevies of exotic sea-birds looking for land. The men gathered for serious gossip around a ring of cigars. The Prince himself had changed into a smart blue tunic of only faintly military charac-ter with gilded epaulettes and splendid brass buttons. He stood in his proud accoutre-ments on the foredeck of the ship for all the world like a Viking commander daring the horizon to drop away or a Nelson staring down the two-eyed French. Surreptitiously he munched on a cookie as the conversation of Cap Dowling and his party of monopo-lizers drifted insubstantially around him. Undaunted, the young ladies, loosed from chaperones and made valiant by their fletched and crinolined finery, tacked and jibbed past the Commodore in hope that he might cast a mariner's eye upon an unguarded throat, a careless ankle, a shameless *coup d'oeil*. The Prince hove to his duty.

Ahead of them Lily could see only a vague horizon of mixed blue – sky and water – as if out here the elements were permitted to blend their irreconcilable properties, the ordinary bonds of space being temporarily forfeit. Behind them and to the west the vee of the shoreline grew faint. Lily began to feel queasy. She quit staring out at the water and turned back to catch Mrs. Booth-Pickering's bitter denunciation of the Dowlings of this world. Lily noted that said apostate was engaged in an animated monologue with His Highness. A few feet away Lady Marigold – her luxuriant sensuality limned by a white hat and dress – observed her lover's gestures with cunning impassivity, with the patience of instinct and chastening experience. While the debutantes and duennas fought against the debilitating sea-breeze by clutching hats to head, manning bumber-shoots, and wheeling astern whenever it was propitious, Lady Marigold removed her hat and hair-pins and let the wind have its way. Lily remarked with some satisfaction that the Prince took every opportunity to glance over at the bereaved widow, though she gave no signal to either man.

Dowling suddenly turned away from the Royal Guest and came over to the Templeton clique. "His Highness has had a long day," he proclaimed. He's going to take a nap in his quarters."

No one would have been terribly surprised if Cap had trailed His Eminence and joined him in his nap, but he did not. The Prince moved alone towards the cabin deck with the stiff grace of an aging monarch who relies more and more on his tunic and brass to carry the burden of *noblesse oblige*. There was a flutter and rearranging of plumage among the ladies, fresh cigars and configurations appeared amongst the men, and the ship – almost beyond landfall – circled and headed south-east towards civilization. A low mist had come up, blurring the horizon on all sides; the afternoon sun glowed carmine, shimmered and bled into the mist, eerie and menstrual.

Lily was waiting to see if Lady Marigold would make her move when someone touched her sleeve and she turned round to find the Prince's valet: "His Highness would like to see you in his suite," he said as if announcing supper.

It took a few seconds for the import of the message to reach Lily. When it did, she glanced about, saw that the Templetons were engaged, and followed the valet's trails to the royal rooms. Actually the captain's quarters had been hastily re-tailored in Detroit to fit the Royal Personage. When the man-servant opened the little varnished door with the brass knobs, Lily entered what would normally have served the skipper as office and sitting room. A large desk, a brocade settee and purplish Queen Anne chair struck Lily's eye immediately. The Prince was not at home.

"This way, miss," the valet said, using his usher's voice.

Lily stepped through the opened door and entered a small chamber. The Prince was seated on an undersized, embroidered chair before an escritoire beneath the porthole. Smoky light poured in through it and fell diagonally across a twin to the Prince's chair, across an oval Oriental rug on which Samurai contended with a specie of giant in defence of several robust, semi-clothed virgins, and over a vermillion-and-white scrolled quilt which made no pretense of hiding the silk sheets beneath it. This was, incontestably, a bedroom.

Set up on the escritoire was a table cloth on which had been placed a silver bucket sprouting a bottle of champagne and two crystal glasses that would sing at the merest hint of a fingernail. A black cigar, cut but unlit, lurked in a gold ashtray.

"Please, come in," said the Prince rising and extending his hand with careless elegance towards the unoccupied chair. "It's Lily, is it not?"

Lily was so struck with the English orotundity of his voice – at once formal and casual, distant and ingratiating, a voice that would deliver speeches-from-the-throne as if they were Elizabethan sonnets – she did not immediately reply. "Yes, Your Highness," she said. Then: "Lily Fairchild."

The Prince looked puzzled for a moment. "Please, sit down. Let me take your gloves and hat."

Lily sat on the edge of the chair. When she peeled off her elbow-length gloves, she tried to keep her palms down. In removing her hat she pulled out not only the hat-pin but the barrette that held her hair in check. It tumbled forward. She heard the royal breath indrawn. She didn't look up again until he said, "Will you join me in a glass of champagne?"

"Yes, please, Your –"

"Call me Albert," he said. "My mother does."

Lily laughed. "I don't think I could," she said.

"Please forgive my informality," he said, referring, Lily assumed, to the fact that he had removed his tunic, vest, collar and ties, and was seated in evident comfort in his trousers and open shirt. "Uniforms, I'm afraid, offer more pleasure to the adulating crowds than to the objects of their worship."

Lily smiled, quite aware that this was a quip used on many an occasion – in part to disguise the shyness, perhaps even uncertainty, she was sure she detected in his demeanour when she herself grew brave enough to look directly at him. He was popping the champagne cork with practised aplomb, but when he came to pour it, Lily saw his hand shake a little.

"Damn!" he said when the bubbly hopped over the escritoire and down one of its legs – fizzing and exuberant. He was about to say he was sorry for the *damn* when Lily's giggle cut him off. He grinned boyishly, then stared at her, puzzled but powerfully attracted.

"What do we toast?" Lily said.

"Well, that Dowling fellow told me they're going to name the village where the station is after me: Point Edward. In my honour."

"Some honour," Lily said, lifting her glass.

He hesitated, gazed at her, then released his mirth, spilling champagne on his shirt. "Some honour, indeed. *Some* village: a hostelry that would make a Montparnasse madam blush and a row of rundown navvy's huts."

"And it's not even your name," Lily said.

He laughed again. "To Point Albert, then!" he said merrily.

They clinked glasses, marvelling that each struck the self-same note – high and sweetly diminuendo. The Prince, a bit hastily perhaps, filled the glasses again. Lily got up and took a step towards the door.

"Please don't go," he said. "I just wanted to talk," he added. "Really."

Lily paused, her back still to him – the sunburnt, freckled skin of her neck, the undisguised calluses on her palms reminding him that she was no mere chatelaine. "I get so sick of all that polite chatter, all that hypocritical handshaking and endless palaver about the weather and the crops and the engines of progress, and –"

"Are you gonna help me?" Lily said jauntily.

"And here I am, only...twenty," he lied.

Lily took a step backwards and the Prince, using all eighteen and three quarters of his years to maintain his composure, moved up and began to unhook her dress. "Thank you," she said when he had finished. She drew her arms out of the liberated sleeves, then let the vast folds descend gratefully over the layered crinolines. "Help me get these cages off," she laughed, and joining in the game, he hoisted them over her head and let them clatter to the floor where they rolled away like lopsided tankards.

"I hope you don't mind the informality, Your Highness," she said. "Back home, this is the way we dress, proper." And she sat down again clad in her full-length muslin slip, stockings and camisole that might have been mistaken for a simple housedress in the less cosmopolitan confines of the province.

The Prince tried to take in all of this blemished beauty – the burned-flaxen hair irreconciled to ringlets, the rough-tender hands, the freckled buff of cheek, her flecked hazel-green eyes, the timidity and jut of each movement, the unawakened wonder of poised womanhood – but he was eighteen not twenty, and he lit up another cigar.

"Shall I open the window?" he offered.

"No, please. Smoke don't bother me none. I like it." It wasn't pipe-smoke in a wigwam, but it would do.

He puffed and temporized, casting sideways glances in her direction, like a puritan at a peep show. Lily finished her champagne. She poured herself a third glass, emptying the bottle. Just as well, the ice had wilted. The second that the valet had touched her arm she had known what was expected of her. She had followed him in full knowledge. She put down her empty glass, rose, and pulled the cigar from between the Prince's teeth. She dropped it in its gold groove, the live end white-hot. She grasped the young man's hands in her own, surprised at their fleshiness. He raised up, then watched her back over to the bed, sit for a second, then stretch languidly across the comforter. Her shoes struck the floor with a do-or-die ring.

Lily closed her eyes. Yes, she thought, it's time to act, to make something happen, *anything*. She heard the rustle and clink of His Highness at the extreme edge of dishabillement. She reached down and drew her slip, then her camisole over her head, feeling the rush of air on her nakedness like a lover's breath. She looked out at the world.

The Prince was arched over her, pale and trembling, his muscled alabaster flesh as vulnerable and omnipotent as a Lancelot stripped of armour. Lily assessed the reticence and the lust in his eyes, and blessed them both.

"My God," he said, his regimental swordgrip bracing her breasts, "you're the most beautiful creature I've ever seen."

Lily reached up, seized the engorged sceptre with both hands and guided the royal seed-pod home.

10

1

Lily was cleaning out the stalls of Benjamin and the Guernsey – as well as that of Gert, the little Jersey they'd acquired from Old Bill. Both cows had been bred to an itinerant bull who showed up at their gate one day with his master in tow, but it appeared as if only the Jersey was about to bear the fruits of that brief, awesome fusing. Lily poked at the mess in front of her. At least in January there was little smell, and the frozen manure and straw could be forked rather than shovelled. Aunt Bridie and Old Bill were in the woodlot see-sawing the stiff pine logs into portable lengths – finding the packed snow and tightened earth a convenient, almost hospitable, environment in which to labour. Uncle Chester, walking, unaided now, would be keeping himself "useful" by replenishing the wood in both stove and fireplace, and peeking out the window every once in a while in order to be amazed by the filigreed snow on boughs he was now seeing as if for the first time.

As Lily jerked a forkful of manure onto the sled, she felt a twinge in her lower abdomen. She stood stock-still as the wavelets of pain worked themselves ashore. She leaned on her fork, catching her breath and waiting for worse. Something fibrous and alien cramped in her, seeking expulsion. I'm going to faint, she thought, I'm going to fall face-first into that cow-shit and smother, and then maybe the thing will abandon me.

The sharp air in her lungs brought her steadily upright again. Well, she thought, I can't do this sort of work anymore. I'll have to tell Aunt Bridie. The question is no longer when but how much?

Lily waited until Old Bill had tucked Uncle Chester into his robes and set off in the cutter with him for a leisurely ride through the oak ridge to Little Lake, where it was reported the town's best mingled with the township hopefuls upon the ice-pond. Uncle Chester had even talked of fitting himself out with skates. "So's he can sprain his other wrist an' his neck to boot," Auntie said not unkindly when they had disappeared into the snowy woods.

Not having spent long enough in polite society to become practiced in its subtle arts, Lily could think of no indirect way of conveying her news. "I got somethin' I have to tell you," she said when they had settled at opposite ends of a half-finished quilt.

"I figured so. You ain't stopped fidgetin' once since dinner. A body'd think you'd contracted St. Vitus' Dance or somethin'."

"I'm pregnant," Lily said. "Four months and three days."

Whatever story Bridie Ramsbottom had braced herself for, this one was not it. Over the next hour her responses, largely monologic, bridged the generational silences in that intense woman's room.

"That's not possible! What on earth do you know of such things?"

Then, following the succinct disclosure of certain irrefutable biological events: "My lord, child! Do you know what you've done? You got a babe inside of you, growin' away in there. Do you have any idea what that means? What that can do to you?"

Lily said she assumed she was going to be a mother, in June.

"You feelin' all right?"

"I'm fine."

"Don't you go shovellin' manure now, you promise me?"

"I can't work in the barn no more. I'm sorry."

"I knew I never should've let you go with that woman. Look at what she's done! I told you the city ways'd destroy you, didn't I? But I don't blame you, child, I really don't. I put the blame onto the shoulders of Alice Templeton, I do. An' somethin'll be done about it, I promise you."

The life and mores of the Templetons were recounted at length.

"But want can we do, eh? You an' me? If I go rantin' an' ravin' across town, everybody'll know, an' your life'll be in tatters. I warned you, Lily, I did, why didn't you listen to me, why didn't you listen to your...Auntie?"

As simply as she could, Lily suggested that no one had seduced or deceived her.

"Who *was* the scoundrel, then? You can't tell me a girl of your age an' your innocence wasn't abused by some blackguard bent on corruption. You forget, child, I lived in Toronto an' London, I went out to service with no family to back me up. There's nothin' you can tell me about 'gentlemen' I don't already know twice over. Why do you think I tried so hard to keep you here? An' I went an' trusted that woman who calls herself a Mayor's wife, with her fancy flowers an' her fancy manners an'—"

Lily refused to divulge the name of her seducer.

"Every girl who's ever been in your position – an' I say plenty in Toronto – has said the same thing, at first," Aunt Bridie said with surprising gentleness. "But there's no other way out of the mess, lass. He will have to make amends. We've got the law, such as it is, on our side. You are still a minor after all. If you can stand him, then he must marry you. If not, then other arrangements can be made."

"I can't tell, ever," Lily said. "No one'd believe me anyways."

"Not the *Mayor*?" Aunt Bridie went white.

"Not anybody you know; besides, he's gone off to another country, where he's from. I'll never see him again."

"Not a Yankee?" She went green. "One of them visitors from the Port?"

"He's gone, Auntie," Lily said firmly. Then: "I don't want to see him again."

"Don't talk such drivel! Look at me. Look me straight in the eye. I'm goin' to tell you what it means if we can't get redress from the father of this babe. You are an unmarried young woman, a minor, an' you are pregnant. In another month your belly will swell up an' stick straight out for all the world to see. An' when it's seen, the tongues of the town will start waggin', an' you can't dream in your worst nightmare what they'll say as they pass along the 'gospel truth' from one to the other – they'll whisper that your Uncle is the father or Old Bill or worse, they'll say you've been seen down by the railroad shacks just like Violet hangin' round them navvies an' deservin' everythin' you got from your sinnin'."

Lily had no reply.

"You won't ever be able to go into town without bein' accosted by ruffians believin' you're a scarlet woman an' free game. Your Uncle an' me will have people whisper an' snicker behind our backs when we're in Cameron's or McWhinney's. Now you know I don't give a sweet fig for the opinion of such people, but will *you* ever get used to them churchin' ladies thinkin' an' callin' your child a bastard an' keepin' it out of school an' makin' it an outcast. What I'm sayin' to you, Lily – you are the most precious thing that's happened to me since ever I was born – what I'm tellin' you is as long as we stay right here on this plot of land, our lives are our own, but as soon as we step off, they belong to those people out there." For a moment she looked weary, beyond recovery. "We are women, Lily, an' poor; the world's not ours to make."

"I know," Lily said.

"Then there's no hope of the father bein' found?"

"No, Lily said softly. Then more strongly: "I want to have the baby. Here. At home."

Bridie saw in the girl's face the very strength and determination and fragile naiveté that had coalesced early in her own life and led to rebellion, flight, engagement and exile. For the first time in two years she felt a surge of the old, lost, pure anger uncorrupted by doubt or the angst of repeated failure. Once again her girl's mind was abuzz with plans and stratagems.

"*We'll* keep the babe," she said. "No one, not even Old Bill will know it's yours. We'll move you into the kitchen for the winter, make you some large housedresses, keep Chester in the dark as long as we can. An' after it's born, we'll say the child belongs to my cousin, an' I'll…go off to London an' pretend to come back with it an' –"

Auntie's eyes glinted with intrigue.

"Oh, Lily, we'll manage," she said. "We always have."

Lily fell against Aunt Bridie's chest, pulling her arms about her, wanting to feel in the mere closeness of flesh some mutual future. For a second Bridie permitted the contact – a brief transfer of energies and vulnerabilities – then drew resolutely back.

"We'll have to be strong, little one," she whispered.

Moments later – pretending to stir the fire, her back turned – she released her tears. But these were not the now-familiar sobs of rage and recrimination that shook through her bones in the deep of the night; these were a woman's fresh, unguarded, outwelling tears of sadness and joy-of-being and irretrievable regret. They poured unabashed down the unfamiliar terrain of Bridie's cheek as she turned to marvel again at the slight marrowing swell of the girl's abdomen.

"After that thing with Bertie," she said. "I wanted so bad for Chester an' me to have a babe of our own."

2

Two days later as Lily was preparing a mustard plaster for the cold Uncle Chester had caught while travelling to the ice-pond, the patient whispered behind her: "Love, if you have anythin' you need to tell your Uncle, go right ahead. You can trust me. And if I need to, I can handle your Auntie." The last remark was qualified somewhat by a spasm of coughing. But the import of his commentary was clear. That evening when Aunt Bridie shuffled in wearily from the woodlot, Uncle was sworn to secrecy and taken into the conspiracy. He beamed for days.

The plot went well throughout the winter. The ruse of having Lily work exclusively indoors was quite plausible, though few of the stray accidental visitors who found their gates in the muffling snows of that season bothered to persevere with their inquiries, and Old Bill simply had none of any ilk. Ever since Violet had been taken away, he had become even more taciturn and withdrawn, though his work for Auntie was done with a conscientious concern verging on the sycophantic. Occasionally he would consent to take Sunday dinner with them, but most of the time he ate on the job or took Auntie's offerings back to his hermitage. Two or three times that autumn they heard the discordant strains of the mouth-organ seeking some elusive harmonies, and would know that he had 'fallen off the wagon' again. Mostly though he slept off his excesses and popped up a day later at dawn ready for work as if nothing had happened. One December night after an exhausting day with Aunt Bridie in the woodlot, Old Bill went to his hut, downed a couple of slugs of 'rheumatism juice', and took up his instrument. The disjunctive jangling of tones startled him more than it usually did, and be blew all the more stridently – desperate for some chording, some key he could recognize as his own. But the discordances mocked him, skirled to a mad laughter – their decibels jarring and random. Old Bill's wild shriek brought Lily upright in her sleep. It was followed by two sharp howls of pain, then the long silence of the nether solstice. Aunt Bridie marched across to his hut first thing in the morning, expecting the worst. Old Bill was slumped on a pile of filthy rags some of which had been his clothes. Dried blood coated his mouth, jaw and throat. He saw Bridie and gave a clenched grin. The stumps of his last two teeth flashed at her jaggedly, their blackening nerves adrift in the icy air like sprung lute strings.

"They fell out," he laughed, and winced horribly.

If old Bill, in seeing Lily shuffle flat-footed about the kitchen, had any suspicions, he kept them locked away with all the other secrets, precious and malign, he stored away for a future he'd already given up on. Nor did the occasional traveller caught in a January squall or one of the ice-storms of February, do anything more than smile their gratitude for the warmth of Lily's hospitality. In fact the only visitors to arrive with a predetermined purpose were three gentlemen who said they were from "the railway" and asked to see Aunt Bridie alone. Lily and Uncle Chester went for a slow walk through the arbours of snow, holding each other upright and sending their laughter skyward. When they got back, Aunt Bridie forced a smile to acknowledge their evident happiness, but Lily recognized the subtle signs telling her the news was grim. "They wanted to buy us out," she scoffed. "I told them where to go, and it ain't cool there."

One of the side-effects of the conspiracy was that more quilts – some with an interesting new design that could have been interpreted as either a mushroom or a baby's fist – got made that winter than last, and the woodlot was cleared on the north-east side right back to the Grand Trunk property. Only a windbreak of pines on the north-west side separated them from the village-to-be. Auntie could now cut and saw and haul and also keep an appraiser's eye on the phantom townsite wherein so many of her hopes now lay. In March during a great snowsquall, Bridie was called from her woodlot and Lily from her stove to attend the birth of the Jersey's first calf. Lily took a more than usual interest in the event.

Old Bill was already in the stall, thick with fresh straw, part of which was dusted with snow blown in through several cracks in the planking. Gert, the Jersey, was bawling out great wrenching cries, pelvic and vascular. Her eyes alternately lolled and stabbed. Her legs quivered, registering each spasm. Aunt Bridie hurried to help Old Bill who was trying to jam his hand into the cow's slavering vagina.

"Quit the jumpin', Gert," Old Bill yelled. "I ain't the bull!"

Gert wheezed as if she'd been kicked in the stomach; Old Bill's wrist disappeared. Aunt Bridie went around to Gert's front end, grasped her by the neck and began to murmur into her ear. The next cry shook the planks of the barn. Lily felt her blood curdle; she couldn't swallow. Uncle Chester left.

"Comin' out feet first," Old Bill announced. "I can feel its little hooves." He gave a yank, as if he were trying to jerk his axe out of an oak. Aunt Bridie was thrown against the wall.

"Here she comes!" Old Bill hollered.

Lily saw the spasmic undulations of Gert's belly muscles, heard the fierce dry-heaving of her breath; and then riding as it were on the death-scream of its mother, the calf slid into the world on a toboggan of blood, mucous and membrane that splattered across the snow and the straw. Old Bill looked like he had been shot with ruby-glass. The calf, wobbling in the pool of its afterbirth, peeked up at the snowy universe. Gert dropped to her knees, reached for breath and, unable to ask why, died.

What surprised Lily about the baby taking shape in her body was how disconnected its existence seemed to be with the event that initiated it and with the life of the person housing it and feeding it. Certainly the pleasures of the Prince during their lusty encounter and the gentle, almost effeminate, afterword, did not have *this* end in view. Nor did her own surrender have any purpose but the immediacy of its joy and pain, the need to feel that something mattered. Not only had the creature inside her proclaimed its own existence, it continued to evolve in a manner that was both impudent and independent.

It lay in her womb like a young vegetable marrow with a nozzle attached, hose-like, to the host-vine. Her abdomen, as Auntie predicted, puffed outward and inward as well, pressing against her back. Her belly felt like a rind or a casing that might harden and burst without warning in the night. It cared little that she could walk or sit or lie with ease. Moreover, when she wanted to sleep, it decided it wanted to swim. One of its errant back-strokes would jar her out of a dream. Huffing and panting at the end of a day's work, she could feel it sucking on her flagging energies, pulling the best of her blood into its own. Always she referred to the thing as "it", never him or her. And not simply because she couldn't see it to know or fantasize: even her dreams reminded her that it was a creature, a tadpole seeking out a shape for its eventual humanness, and more powerful than any ordinary infant – boy or girl – because it was still ungoverned potential, raw ribs-and-blood with no future yet to lose. For Lily it had organs and cartilage and nerves – but no face. I will bear you, she thought often, then I will name you, and love you. Forever.

By mid-April the snows had vanished. The crocuses and stove-pipes dotted the lawns and gardens of the town by the River and the Lake. The rains fell, gentle and inevitable. The surveyors arrived to lay out the streets and lots of yet another village destined to germinate and bloom within a single season. Aunt Bridie looked on this event and at the unswaddled belly of her niece, and permitted her heart to leap – once – in expectation.

3

No one at the great western station that April evening took any particular notice of the impeccably attired, distinguished gentleman – complete with an entourage of well-dressed but undistinguished lackies – as he disembarked from the first-class Toronto car and crossed to the livery at the east end of the building. After all, Sarnia was an important town: moguls and politicians and pretenders of all sorts stepped off the 6:40 almost every day of the week. Such anonymity seemed to be to this visitor's liking for the exchange which resulted in the rental of a democrat – *sans* local driver – was done with despatch and discretion. One of the lesser apostles took the reins, while the two secretaries and the Honourable Charles Gunther Murchison settled down into leather and velvet, and studiously ignored the regional scenery. Little notice was taken of them as they turned north-east up the Errol Road and drove into the dusk of early spring. It was almost dark when the driver, following some route previously committed to memory, veered into the lane of the Ramsbottom place.

Only the Honourable Charles Gunther Murchison remained in the kitchen. The others, having been courteously introduced, were banished to the democrat, where they were stared at by Old Bill as if they had just dropped from the moon. Inside, Uncle Chester perched on the edge of his chair and watched in awe as Bridie and the distinguished arrival occupied the middle of the room. In her bedroom Lily was just waking from a restless doze.

"I have come on the most urgent of matters, Mrs. Ramsbottom, straight from the office of the Governor himself. I apologize again for the suddenness of our appearance so late in the day, but when you hear what news I bring, you will understand our need for covert action. Several lives are at stake."

Uncle Chester leaned forward; Bridie blinked but gave no ground. "Whose lives?" she asked evenly.

"Before I am permitted to offer detailed explanations, I must talk with your... niece." He was like a bald eagle at home in this strange eyrie, his bronze pate feathered at the sides with grizzled whiskers, his aquiline beak and assayer's eyes piercing every shadow in the coal-oil gloom, his bearing regal as befitting a man who has twice been a cabinet minister, who stared down a dozen rebel guns in 'thirty-seven and prevailed.

"My niece isn't well," Bridie said. "She's not available to you, sir, nor to Sir Edmund Head himself."

Murchison took no offense. "I'm afraid she must be. The orders I am under, you see, come from Her Majesty."

Uncle Chester fell part-way off his chair and barely recovered in time to abort the trick in his back. Lily opened her eyes.

"Queen Victoria?"

"Yes. Directly from the palace, through His Excellency in Quebec. I have been asked to seek out and speak with your niece on a matter of the utmost delicacy and urgency."

A glimmer of insight reached Bridie's eyes, they faded in disbelief.

"With all respect, sir, my niece is ill and can't be disturbed. If you tell me what you need, of me or her, I'll talk to her in the morning. Surely even our Queen would understand the need not to upset a sick child."

Lily's legs cramped to the bedstead.

"I appreciate your desire to protect your niece, Mrs. Ramsbottom, and I know His Excellency and Her Majesty would applaud your loyalty and solicitude. But it is imperative that I at least *see* your niece. If she is ill, I can return to speak with her tomorrow."

"Please, sir," Uncle Chester said, his voice quavering, "Lily ain't well. An' that's the truth."

"Chester, you keep –"

"It's all right, Auntie," Lily said coming slowly into the shadowy light.

Aunt Bridie was now sitting down in the straightback chair by the stove. Her face was ashen.

"You see," Murchison was explaining in lower but no-less-formal tones, "I had no idea whether the girl had informed you of the possible paternity of the child. Indeed, we did not know for sure that the girl was 'enceinte', though one of our sources, a young man disguised as a lost traveller and sitting now in my carriage, reported the possibility to us two months ago. All this was carried out, you understand, at the request of the Monarch Herself after a belated confession on the part of her son. Then, of course, we had to use the utmost discretion possible to ascertain the moral character of the girl. It proved, as I'm sure you know, ma'am, to be unimpeachably stainless." He was speaking directly to the stunned Aunt Bridie, averting his eagle gaze from the lumpish, squat figure seated to his right.

"It is the Prince's babe," Lily said again.

The Honourable Mr. Murchison shifted tone and stance, as if he were a lawyer changing from defense to prosecution. "Now that these most difficult and delicate matters are clear, I have the awful duty to inform you of the decisions taken, as I have said, at the highest levels of state. I have been commanded to explain to you that these decisions have been reached after full consideration of the best and just interests of all parties concerned. The Prince, you will be pleased to know, is contrite and eager to make amends for his youthful indiscretion." He looked about for some confirmation, but only Uncle Chester was nodding ritually.

"Now that we know the babe will have royal blood in his veins, we are under the strictest obligation, as citizens and subjects of the Empire, to treat that fact with the awe and respect it deserves. Her Majesty expressly wishes the child to be born in circumstances most conducive to its general health, including the utmost care of the mother during the crucial days of her lying-in. The best doctors and midwives are to be consulted; a hospital or surgery must be close at hand in case of emergencies."

"We got no hospital here," Aunt Bridie said.

"Precisely. You take my very point," the solicitor said, wheeling to face the invisible jury. "We have come to take Lily to a place where all of these conditions obtain, where both her well-being and that of the child will be assured. Moreover, we are not insensible of the social difficulties associated with a child born out of wedlock; the Prince himself was particularly concerned about this point. Hence, the immediate and secret removal of the girl to a house we have arranged in London will be of benefit to all concerned."

"And after the babe is born?" Aunt Bridie said coldly into the ensuing silence.

"Mother and child can be returned here, of course. Not right away naturally. Perhaps a husband can be found for her, or a reasonable story concocted to account for the exceptional circumstances. Whatever arrangements are decided *post partum*," he said relishing the Latin, "Her Majesty has commanded Her viceroy here in the dominion to disburse appropriate funds for the maintenance of the child till he comes of age. Furthermore –"

"We don't want any of your money," Aunt Bridie said.

"Now, sweetie –" Uncle Chester said, but was cut dead by a stare.

"Would you kindly get the girl's things together as soon as possible? There's a freight train leaving here in an hour; we've arranged a special caboose to be attached."

Aunt Bridie stood up. "The girl, as you call her, only goes if she wants to. Please tell Her Majesty that we are quite capable of taking care of our own – royal blood or not. An' we don't take charity."

"May I see Lily alone, then?"

Lily nodded to her Aunt.

"If you must."

The privy-councillor and ex-Grenadier was disconcerted by the way the girl stared directly at him while he lectured her, with just the slightest hint of impending disrespect. Moreover, the thumping of the foetus on the drum of her abdomen was scandalously audible.

"We understand your reluctance to leave home, but we ask that you reflect on all the advantages that will accrue to a positive decision to go to London. The lady who has agreed to care for you is a woman of the highest quality and discretion. We also recognize that you are part of a working family and that your loss over the next three months or so will impose serious hardships on your Aunt and Uncle. Thus, though your Aunt sees it as charity, His Excellency will, with or without her consent, deposit a hundred dollars in her account at the Bank of Upper Canada for each month you are away, for as long as it takes to resolve matters in a satisfactory manner."

When Aunt Bridie and Uncle Chester were waved back in, they found Lily standing by the stove, her eyes brimming with tears.

11

1

Mrs. Edgeworth's walled garden in May was as beautiful as the East Gate to Eden, as that lady iterated often over the irritation of teacups and silver spoons. When the ladies of London were gathered there, as they were each Thursday afternoon during the warm season, Lily had to observe the ritual proceedings from her room on the second floor of the red-brick mansion. She was not to be seen in public and particularly *en silhouette*. Those were the principal terms of her confinement. But when it was not Thursday afternoon, Lily was free to roam the gardens at will, protected from prurient view by its fieldstone walls, rampant privet and gothic elms. Hedges of honeysuckle and wild lilac marked out avenues for the eye or the weary step, arrested by arbours of budded rose, beds of thrusting tulips, and the prodigality of peony and rose-of-sharon. Here Lily whiled away the weeks and hours of her twenty-first spring.

Of London itself she had seen little since that night in mid-April when she had been lifted from the caboose of the highball freight and placed gently in a closed carriage to be driven through the dark to the Edgeworth home. The full moon in concert with the spring stars allowed her to catch glimpses in outline of the largest, most imposing buildings she had ever seen. The road beneath them was firm gravel, the horses' shoes ringing reliably upon it; the gas-lamps along Richmond Street glittered like amethyst and cast across their path the shadows of railings, newel-posts, pitched gables, startling spires and other eccentric castellations alien to the imagination. There appeared to be no trees except for occasional decorative saplings of maple or elm on the steep lawns of the palaces along North Street. As they wheeled onto the latter to go east, Lily drew in her breath at the sight of two cathedrals whose grand martellos carved the night-sky up in Protestant and Catholic halves. She could, if she stood here on the stone bench by the iris-bed, see the many towers of the saints stretched out against the sun: rooted, durable, and unquestioning. In this 'forest city' they were petrified trees.

So this is civilization, Lily thought. This is what the Millars and the Partridges dreamed of as they hacked their trees to death – slashed, burned, pulverized and ground the very ash of them back into the resisting earth. This is what the burghers of Sarnia – with their muddy streets and clanging foundries and clapboard shells – yearned towards? Is this the dream Papa dreamt the night he wrestled with his demons and left forever? What dreams could Mama have ever had, looking as she did each day on her wizening flesh and knowing in the interminable night that death was perched like a leper on her shoulder?

"You can't *read*? My gracious Godfrey, what *have* they done to you in that dreadful bush-town?" Mrs. Anthony Edgeworth's questions were usually pointed comments on the deteriorating human condition. "Well, we'll soon rectify *that*! We shan`t have a son of the aristocracy grow up in a family of illiterates now, shall we?" She blushed then, as she did easily and often. "Oh, I am sorry, dear-heart. I am expressly forbidden to mention things like that. Walls have ears, you know." And she dropped her voice a decibel and half-an-octave.

"I had no upbringin'," Lily said helpfully.

"Well now, that isn't *your* fault. We'll just see what we can do in the few weeks at our disposal," she said with determined cheeriness. Then she released a bosomy sigh. "If only the Colonel were alive, he'd take you in hand."

So it was that just as the first lilacs sprang into bloom, drenching the air with the sweet phrases of their perfume, Mrs. Edgeworth donned her best brocade and ushered the freshly attired Lily into the grotto where Lamb's *Tales From Shakespeare* could be suitably worshipped. "She's very quick," Mrs. Edgeworth said consolingly to the vicar after another of his less-than-successful exchanges of catechism with the unlettered and unrepentant girl. "She took an instant fancy to Portia and Rosalind. Isn't that intriguing?" The vicar thought not. "She can tell you right back, quick as a pedlar's wink, the whole story of *The Tempest*, or *The Winter's Tale*." His reverence thought perhaps *Pilgrim's Progress* would be more suitable fodder.

To Dr. Hackney, essaying an escape after the bi-weekly check of the patient, she said, "And yesterday I decided to read her some of the Bard himself. Of course, as you remember, I don't read nearly as well as the Colonel, but do you know that wisp of a girl understood those speeches! I swear she didn't know half the words in 'The Quality of Mercy' but she got the gist of it all right." How she wished she could confide in the vicar and the doctor, but only *she* knew that the father of the child was some important figure-of-state from Toronto and that secrecy was imperative. The doctor, the vicar and Lucille, her servant, were told only that the girl was the daughter of a friend from the country, and that discretion was requested. Lucille was, alas, "dumb as a post but ever so sweet" and fully devoted to her mistress. Lily soon discovered that Lucille was not at all dumb, only French, and that to her own surprise she recalled a great deal of the French she had heard so often so long ago. The two girls, barely a year apart, chatted amiably in both tongues during the drowsy afternoons of early spring with the earth greening around them and the air as clear as claret.

For the first time ever, Lily found she did not enjoy being alone. She loved to listen to the funny stories Lucille had to tell about her crazy relatives down in Essex; the slither and scrape of her *joual* was like the low notes on a slow fiddle. Lily sat entranced by the tales Mrs. Edgeworth read to her and she committed to memory some of the strange, cadenced phrases of Shakespeare's women – all the more powerful because they swam in her head only half-understood, hovering and forever about-to-be. One night she woke up already sitting, and heard a voice say, "The crow doth sing as sweetly as the lark when neither is attended." She lay awake for over an hour trying to feel the meaning under such words.

When not reading to her, Mrs. Edgeworth took full advantage of her captive pupil, and proceeded to give her a singular history of England from the narrow but no-less-illuminating perspective of her own family and, where verisimilitude demanded, that of the late Colonel's. "Oh how my Aunt Fanny laughs when I tell her in every letter that I live in London on the Thames in Middlesex County. She's of the opinion that we all live in log cabins and spend most of our days swatting flies." Then she would sweep the garden and environs with her Canterbury gaze: "Ridiculous, eh? But the Colonel, bless his memory, helped to make it what it is today. My only worry is that my dear nephew, Tippy, the Colonel's sister's boy, who I've raised since he was a tot of ten, will not be the kind of man his father and uncle were." And on she would go about Tippy's modest indiscretions – his poor grades in school, his truancy, his current "escapade" in Toronto, where he was supposed to be learning the law in a respectable firm there, but was more often seen elsewhere in unmentionable places. Lily listened, quite content to nod assent or demurral as the moment dictated, watching the concern and vulnerable kindness play across the face of this stranger who without doubt was coming to love her. Is this the way it is, the way it's going to be? Lily thought. These sudden, powerful, random bondings followed by the wrenching of separation, bleak rides in the night towards dawnings we have not even had time or the wonder to dream of?

Finally, a month after her arrival – with the creature inside her growing increasingly bulbous, lopsided, counterclockwise – Lily got a letter from Aunt Bridie. She spotted her own name in capital letters on the envelope, and could even make out the name of the street and city. But the letter itself was written in Auntie's scrawl, and even Mrs. Edgeworth had a little difficulty in reading it aloud.

> Port Sarnia, C.W.
>
> May 2, 1861
>
> Dear Lily:
>
> Sorry to be so long in writing to you. Word has been got to us that you are doing fine. Things are so confused here that I ought to wait until the news is good before sending it along to you. Uncle Chester is getting stronger by the day. Old Bill is about the same. We all miss you terrible. Just after you left, some bigwigs from the railroad came over here and made an offer to buy our property. I told them no, this land was our living, we would never leave it. Then they said the railroad needed the land for the townsite of Point Edward. They now own all of it but our section. They said they would expropriate it; that's a two-dollar word for taking it and paying us as little as they

can get away with. If they take the farm, I don't know what we'll do. A friend of Uncle Chester's has written from London with a business proposition but nothing is about to happen very soon you can rest assured. So we don't want you to worry, just stay healthy and bring us back the babe. We'll be here waiting. We've always got by and we always will.

Love,

Aunt Bridie

xoxoxo Uncle Chester

But Lily did worry. Aunt Bridie's hopes, pinned so precariously to the railway's expansion, were about to be dashed by the very instrument expected to fulfill them. Whatever happened with the farm, she knew it would not fatten itself at the expense of the Grand Trunk.

So Lily waited, and was pampered. The form within her prospered. No more letters came. June did, and the time for her lying-in.

2

Lily did not lack for either care or advice. Lucille's household duties were lightened so that she could play the role of nursemaid, a part she relished, though her ministrations in the stuffy, darkened room where the victim was forcibly detained, were more collo-quial than therapeutic. Mrs. Edgeworth herself supervised the serving of the meals and spent part of each afternoon and evening reading to or talking at her "dear-heart." Dr. Hackney now arrived once a week to ceremonially take her pulse, depress her tongue and then poke and stroke the protuberance that used to be her belly. Giving it a fare-well pat he turned, on his last visit, to Mrs. Edgeworth and proclaimed: "It will come on time, Elspeth. Of course it's not great accomplishment to predict the exit day when the entry point, so to speak, has been so accurately documented." Being a woman of the world, Elspeth did not blush, much. Then seeing the entreaty in Lily's eyes, he said for all to hear: "A son: one week: the fourteenth most probably."

Unbeknownst to Dr. Hackney, his visits were invariably followed by the arrival, through the back-garden gate and woodshed door, of Elsie Crampton, the regional midwife. Elsie's examination was more probing, inquisitive and jovial than the good physician's. Lucille and Elspeth followed her in, trailed by her assistant, a buxom, over-blown Irish girl named Maureen, who had recently delivered a son to the skeptical world. The midwife's smile was lop-sided (she had teeth only on the left side) but gener-ous, and Lily felt strangely comforted in her presence, even though her confinement in this canopied, curtained, velveteened chamber seemed out of tune with the raw, rooted germination inside her. Mrs. Crampton held her hand, talked to her, and gave her instructions for the ordeal of the birthing day.

"It's gonna be a bit late, I think," she announced to the curious assembly. "About the twenty-second or twenty-third, I'd say. Which means she's gonna be a stubborn little cuss, but a genuine beauty."

The women of the chorus agreed.

"On my birthday?" Lily said, looking at Lucille.

"Could be, dearie, but I wouldn't pray too hard for it, 'cause the longer you stay penned up here the paler and weaker you get. I don't believe in all this lying-in stuff. Why, Maurie here was hoein' spuds the day before little Mikey popped out."

Lily didn't pray but she hoped, all the same. The fifteenth passed with no signs of the contractions she'd been alerted to. Dr. Hackney arrived for his weekly check, feigned puzzlement, let his fingers linger affectionately on Lily's pumpkin bulge, and muttered to Mrs. Edgeworth at the door: "No question: I'll be back before the night's over."

Other than Dr. Hackney, no man had run his hand over her belly except for the Prince himself. Their love-making had been swift and narrow. His Royal Highness had wheezed twice and slumped lengthwise upon her. For Lily there had been pain, cutting and revelatory, her body moving almost on its own, as it did when infused with the music of some dance, though here there was no time to ensure mutual cadence, no culmination except the fierce clutch of skin to skin, a second of total accessibility broken by the boy's sobs as he rolled away and saw the escutcheon of blood on the duvet. Instinctively, forgetting her own discomfort and sense of incompletion, Lily reached up and brushed the tears across his cheeks. He stared at her in awe; never had she seen such a look in the eyes of another human watching her. For a moment she felt not sundered but whole, not colonized but possessing – extravagant even, imperial. Then she lay back, settled in her own kind of amazement, and let her lover's hand replicate in minor keys the brute affection of their coupling. Deep down Lily knew it was not her body – with its elastic, cursive allure – that the future king worshipped with his caresses, murmurings and bunting glances, but something beyond it yet not exclusive of it. As the days grew closer to her own birthdate and the high solstice, Lily began to feel at last come connection between those events on the *Michigan* and this thumping, reciprocal being waiting to be born.

In the early hours of the morning of the twenty-first, the first spasm struck. Lily was startled by its severity, and not a little frightened. She had been well-prepared for the sequence of calamities to follow: Lucille was the middle child of a family of thirteen and reported graphically upon the numerous, horrific births she claimed to have witnessed. Mrs. Crampton had described to her in clinical terms the necessity of these discomforts and added the assurance that "when you see the babe you'll have already forgotten the pain." Cold comfort that was here in the dead of night in a stranger's house in a foreign town with her belly squeezing her stomach into her throat and her bowels into her spine. She gritted her teeth and let the aftershocks knit their way through her flesh; she would not cry out. She tried to wipe away the images of Lucille's encephalitic brother ripping his mother's vagina like a tear in a button hole, or the Jersey's eyes in the snowy coffin of her stall, but the only picture she could replace them with was that of a shadow-green cove in Papa's backwoods – with the spread flesh of the faceless squaw, the propulsion of the tiny head treeward, the corolla of flung blood, the silence into which it dropped petal by scarlet petal.

When the third contraction gripped and held, Lily reached over to pull the bell-cord.

In the blackness of her pain, Lily was aware that she was surrounded by women. Their faces, their detached, consoling hands floated intermittently above her: Mrs. Edgeworth disguising her anguish, Mrs. Crampton too busy to register feeling, Lucille agog with fright and devotion, Maureen impassively efficient, Maryanne (the new chambermaid) pale and chattering. Lily felt like one of those fish Papa used to catch in Brown Creek, floundering on the grassy bank, its muscles jerking without purpose or hope. Just after sunrise her body, now totally outside her own control, gave one last convulsive heave and banished the little beast forever to the far outports of air, space, time and consanguinity. The pain was now bearable; she released her grip on Lucille's hand. She could feel the midwife's fingers stretching, pulling, yielding.

There was a smack like the crack of a rifle, followed by a stuttering wawl that rose to a series of well-defined shrieks and settled into the universal enunciation of the newborn struck by breath, by the fuel of its own blood.

"It's a girl," said Mrs. Crampton between commands.

"How wonderful!" said Mrs. Edgeworth, hiding her disappointment excessively.

"An' it come real quick an' easy, eh Maureen?"

"Like a squaw's in a corn patch," said the Irish girl, swabbing up blood and afterbirth.

Moments later as her pain ebbed, the baby – wiped clean, its umbilical cord neatly knotted – was laid beside Lily on the linen sheet. On the canopy overhead she noted the cherubs and the lambs and the crenellated walls in the distance. Then she gazed across at the child curling in the arch of her shoulder and breast. The eyes peering back were her own.

You've given me great pain, she thought, as its miniature mouth nudged towards the expectant nipple, but you needed the pain to separate yourself from me, to put something between us, to be yourself. Now I can hold you, love you, and give you your name. And she did, saying the syllables in a low murmur over and over as sleep closed in, and she did not feel her daughter being gently extracted from a mother's grip.

3

When Lily woke it was afternoon. Of what day she really didn't know. She was fevered and ached all over. She reached for the baby. It wasn't there. Her breasts throbbed, the milk pulsing inside like the Guernsey when Uncle Chester 'fell asleep' before milking her. In the hazy light allowed by the curtain she could make out across the room the form of Maureen seated in the armchair. Her blouse was open with one puffed breast shining and stiff-nippled and the other hidden behind the head of the suckling child.

The noise of its feeding filled the room. Maureen's eyes were slitted, glazed with contentment; her thick pelvis was rocking back and forth in an unconscious parody of intercourse.

"Now don't you worry, dear-heart," Mrs. Edgeworth soothed a few minutes later, her brow creased with worry. "Everything's going to be fine. Dr. Hackney says you've got a slight infection. I must say he wasn't too happy arriving late and finding Mrs. Crampton on her way out, but he's been a dear anyway. He's left this medicine for you and –" At last she noticed Lily's nod towards the baby and its nurse. "Oh, *that*. Dr. Hackney says with your fever and all, you wouldn't have enough milk, so Maureen, who God be thanked has more than enough for her own and yours, is helping out, *aren't you, dear?*"

Maureen responded by changing breasts and sighing with satisfaction.

"Believe me, love, it's all for the best."

"What day is it?"

"You've been in and out of a doze for three days now. But you *are* looking real good today. Shall I get you something to eat?"

"Could I hold the babe, afterwards?"

Lily *was* feeling better. She ate some soup spooned lovingly in by Lucille. Then her daughter was laid beside her, and when the women left for a moment, she eased a nipple into the nuzzling lips. She felt their pull upon her, amazed by the strength and depth of the need there, the compulsion of bonding it brought. Together they drifted to their separate sleep.

When she woke the next morning, feeling ravenous and fully alert, the room was empty. Moments later the door opened and Mrs. Edgeworth entered in the wake of a strange man who strode to her bedside and sat down on Lucille's chair as if it had been set out there especially for him.

"This is Mr. Clayton Thackeray, M.P.P.," she said to Lily with a tremor in her voice. "He's come all the way from Toronto to see you, *if* you're feeling up to it."

"I'm feelin' all right," Lily said, staring at the intruder from the city. He was formally attired in spats and morning coat and stiff collar; his face was obsessively whiskered with a pair of hooded eyes like two chips of anthracite. No amount of girdling could control the overbite of his belly.

"I'm glad to hear it, child," said the M.P.P. to the opposition benches. "We have important business to discuss, *vital* business."

Mrs. Edgeworth closed the door to mute as best as possible the booming rhetoric of his delivery, then stood leaning against it and watching.

"I would like you to listen carefully to what I have to say. While you may find parts of it distasteful, I want you to remember that my communication to you comes from the highest authority in the land, that the decisions which have been taken have been thoroughly and humanely considered, and that the best interests of all concerned will be served by ready obedience." He paused but no 'hear! hear!' was to be heard, not even a heartening assent from the back-benches.

Lily stared right at him – conceding nothing, offering nothing. She recognized the official timbre of the voice and braced herself. When he turned slightly to Mrs. Edgeworth for support, she was staring at the carpet.

"Well, then," he began again, glaring at the eternal opposition, "I've been asked by the Honourable Charles Gunther Murchison to convey to you the following information. We have it from the *highest authority*," and here he glanced at Mrs. Edgeworth and then back at Lily with an absurd wink, "that the father of your babe, a man of pre-eminence as you know, wishes to have his child raised in the most congenial and appropriate circumstances. With the welfare of the child uppermost in mind, certain investigations, shall we say, were carried out in Port Sarnia. Alas, the results were not favourable. I'm sure I do not need to tell you that the financial and particularly the, ah, *moral* circumstances of the Ramsbottom household leave much to be desired."

Lily looked straight ahead.

"What the gentleman means, dear-heart, is that your Uncle and Aunt don't go to church regularly," said Mrs. Edgeworth.

"What the gentleman means, child, is that the *mother* of the babe's father insists that it be raised in the Church of England, a not unreasonable request, you will agree."

Only Mrs. Edgeworth, faintly, agreed.

"And in this instance the *grandmother's* wishes are paramount, as only you know," he said to Lily with another wink that came down with the clank of a coal-shute. "Hence these decisions have been taken in the best interests of all concerned. The child will go to Toronto with its nurse to be adopted by a prominent family there who know *generally* about the circumstances of its conception and birth and, in spite of such, have, in the most magnanimous and humanitarian of gestures, offered to give this poor creature life and hope."

Lily flinched, and recovered. In the silence the breeze worried the curtains, a robin in the garden gargled its breath and ripped a worm from its burrow.

"It is all for the best, Lily. I believe that," said Mrs. Edgeworth near tears.

"Indeed so," said the M.P.P., as the thunderous clapping of colleagues rang in his ears. "The wet-nurse is delighted to be relieved of the burden of her overnumerous family; she is packed and ready to go, as is the infant itself. Mrs. Edgeworth will have the satisfaction of knowing that she not only saved the reputation of a wayward girl but that the illegitimate offspring of the unfortunate union will also be given a second chance at life. You, my child, will suffer briefly at the loss of an infant not yet dear to you, but may return to your own family purified and renewed. As a bonus for any inconvenience, I am also authorized to tell you that a cash settlement in compensation has already been deposited in your Aunt's account in a Port Sarnia bank."

Clayton Thackeray sat back waiting for some response – tears, rage, thanks. He got nothing. Finally rising, he said to Mrs. Edgeworth, "Not a soul in Port Sarnia has gained a whiff of this. It's been handled with the utmost discretion and concern for the feelings of those involved. The girl will return with not a single blot upon her character."

With that he swept out, startling the pages and footmen. A moment later Mrs. Edgeworth returned. Lily had not moved.

"Oh, Lily. Mr. Thackeray asked me to find out something important for him. It seems the lady in Toronto who's going to adopt the babe wants to know, just for herself, the last name of the babe's mother. I'm to write it down on this card."

Apparently Lily didn't hear.

"It will all work out, dear-heart," Mrs. Edgeworth said, dropping all pretense. "We'll work it out together." She took Lily's hand, its calluses now grown smooth, its flesh pink again. "Can you tell me your name? Not Ramsbottom but the one you had before you were taken in."

"Fairchild," Lily said.

Mrs. Edgeworth wrote it down.

4

It was July 4. If she were home now Lily would be watching the fireworks display across the River as the Yankees celebrated the seizing of their liberty. Many people took the ferry across and stood in the grounds of Fort Gratiot as the skyrockets soared independently starward, the army band struck up the victory march and the guns that had driven the British back where they belonged boomed over the non-partisan blue of the fresh-water sea to the north.

According to all observers Lily was "recuperating nicely." She left her room for daily walks about the garden. She let Lucille chatter on at will. The colour flowed back into her cheeks. The freckles reappeared with it.

Lily knew this hurt was permanent, like so many others before it. Somehow it seems safer, she thought, to stay inside the ache, to let it be continually numbing, and build whatever remained of her life around it. But, as before, the sun rose each day with impudent optimism, the elderly rosebushes stretched and infected the garden with their ungirded profligacy. The wind sweetened her chamber each morning. She ate and grew lithe again. At night she held the talisman in her fist, and waited for a word of its magic to re-enter the world.

In the meantime, she realized she must write to Aunt Bridie. In fact, Mrs. Edgeworth helped her the very next afternoon following the baby's swift departure by writing down Lily's words and mailing off the letter immediately. It said this: "Dear Aunt Bridie: I love you and Uncle very much. I am fine. The babe was born dead. I will be coming home as soon as I get strong enough. Soon. Love, Lily." Despite her careful monitoring Mrs. Edgeworth detected Lily crying only once: the evening after the letter was sent. She was left alone.

Lily was now quite concerned that she had heard nothing back from Aunt Bridie. She understood why her Aunt had chosen not to write before the birth of the child, but fully expected some response by now. Two weeks had passed with no reply. Lily began to feel that something momentous was about to happen, though she was uncertain about whether it would be happy or sad. The talisman was strangely silent, as if it had already spoken on the subject and was surprised that Lily was not able to interpret the obvious.

What neither Lily nor the magic stone knew was that Aunt Bridie had actually sent a reply to Lily's letter by return mail. In her haste and anxiety, however, she had addressed the envelope to "Lily Ramsbottom, North Street, London, C.W.," omitting "in care of Mrs. Anthony Edgeworth", and a summer-time employee of the post office dropped it into the general delivery slot where it remained for several months.

Just as Lily – on this beautiful fourth of July – was about to suggest to Mrs. Edgeworth that she ought to consider returning home in a few days, she had a slight haemorrhage and was put back to bed with stern warnings. However, in the late afternoon she persuaded Lucille to help her into the wicker wheelchair and push her into the garden, where she sat alone by the rose arbour in the westering sun, letting the tears flow and dry on her face. What am I doing here? she thought. I want only to belong to some place, to someone besides myself. I reached out blindly to the young man inside the Prince's suit, and he reached back. It was an act of faith on both sides. What has it come to? What did it bring? She thought of her lover, guessing at the special kind of loneliness he too must be suffering. Her heart went out to him across the distance between them, in the dream-memory which was the only mutual thing left to them. Beside her a hummingbird dipped its beak into the nectar of a tiger-lily.

"My word, look who it is!" Mrs. Edgeworth's voice cracked with some of its former zest. "Lucille, come here quick! It's Tippy coming up the walk!"

There was a scuttle and scurry in the household behind Lily. She turned away, letting the sun caress the nape of her neck. Below the female greetings and oohhing-and-ahhing came the rumble of a man's response. For a while all was quiet within. Lily grew tense. The hairs on her neck rose. Her heart pitched and yawed. She heard the slap of the screen door, the steady step, the coolness of the shadow blotting out the light behind her. She turned in her chair to face the silhouette framed by the setting sun.

"Tom," she said, steadying her voice.

12

1

"I don't remember much about my parents except my mother was beautiful and my father was tall and stern in his uniform. It was him who got sick first, consumption according to my Aunt, then mother went down with it and I was torn away from them. For my own good, of course. I remember my mother's face in the window too weak to smile or cry or comfort my screaming. Weeks later I was taken by the Colonel and Aunt Elspeth to their funeral. All of London was there, she said. Except my parents. They're over there." He pointed vaguely south-west to where the pink spire of St. Paul's glinted bravely through the trees below which the granite, engraved stones proclaimed steadfastness.

Lily lay her head back on the pillow behind her head, half-closing her eyes. Along the ambling lane and its weathered zig-zag fences, hollyhocks flung their petticoats shamelessly into the sun's gaze. The breeze, perfumed by a penultimate rose, eased her lids shut. Some beneath in the shape of a hand fluttered on her own.

"I guess you could say I was rich and spoiled. Aunt Elspeth finally got the child the Colonel was too busy to provide her with, and she made the most of it. She had an ensign's uniform made for me to prance about in when I was barely eleven and very small for my age. But rich, no. My father left me a small sum to be given out as an annuity from my eighteenth to my twenty-sixth year. That ends this fall."

Lily squeezed his arm to get a firmer grip as they started north on Colborne Street, on this her first excursion around the block.

"Take it easy," Tom said. "Nurse's orders."

"Your Auntie bought you the wrong costume," she said lightly.

"I was a real rebel; I must've come close to breaking my Aunt's heart. Especially after the Colonel died in 'fifty. I hated school. I hated Latin. I hated Greek. I wouldn't do my sums or the dusty old histories of the Empire. I played hookey to go fishing or help the boys build huts and forts and kites. I was pretty good with my hands then. I liked those scruffy, bad-mouthed kids…"

Lily stumbled and gave a stifled cry at the sudden pain. Two powerful arms held her until she forced back the tears, found her sea-legs and peered up at him wanly.

"You try to do too much," he said. "You want to get better soon, don't you?"

Lily gave him an ambiguous smile. Letting go his arm, she teetered up the path – confident, bathed in the green praise of the high summer.

"It's funny, don' t you think, that even though I loved to scuffle and carry on mock battles with the ruffians down by river – we even built rafts and men-o-war – my Aunt decided I was too undisciplined to follow in the footsteps of my father and uncle. She decided I was to be a scholar, she had an eye on the law or the new university in Toronto. But, of course, you know enough of Aunt Elspeth to see that she just couldn't ever be too firm or mean enough to corner a character like me. But she kept me in school, one way or another, mostly through bribes or long bouts of weeping and sighing and calling up the ghost of the Colonel."

In the field before the Thames where they were walking for the first time, wild daisies with single-eyed resolve contended with the twitch grass and still-stemmed blue devil.

"But I got even, I guess."

"You joined the militia," Lily said, holding a daisy under her chin as if it were a dandelion.

"Yes," he said after a pause. "Major Bruce's Volunteer Corps."

"Do I have butter on my throat?" Lily said, raising her face dangerously close to the voltigeur's. He took command – though the kiss was brief, almost brotherly.

"We drilled every other Saturday over there in Cricket Square," Tom said. "I was determined to show the world I could make a soldier out of *myself* and not my upbringing."

"I had no upbringin'," Lily said.

Tom released her arm. "Why do you say things like that?" he said with that mixture of hurt and anger she was growing accustomed to.

"Because they're true," Lily said, walking ahead with a steadiness that was now only partly feigned. She leaned back against the fence for support, letting the bough of the overhanging apple tree – its fruit as hard and tiny as buckshot – fall across her shoulder, her white dress and her freckled arms set against the last spray of hollyhocks, the sun incendiary in her hair.

"Are you comin', Sir Tom?" Lily called.

Tom was starting in her direction. At last he came up to her, but when they resumed their stroll, he kept rigidly to her left as if he were marching in rank. Lily, sensing the change, made no move to touch him.

"It's all right," Lily laughed, skipping and tilting her way down the steep river bank below Westminster Bridge. "I won't break!" To prove her point, when she got to the bottom she fell face-forward into the consenting grass, as if she were making angel-figures in the snow. When she bounced back up, though, there was little record of her daring. Breathless, Tom reached her side, his eyes wide with disbelief.

"For God's sake, Lily –" he said with an edge of anger, then softened and finished: "please, please be careful."

"I'm not fragile, you know," Lily laughed, doing a little jig and whirling in the breeze to some inaudible fandango.

"I don't know *anything* about you," Tom said, sitting on the bank and staring sulkily into the water.

"You know I had a baby," Lily said in that tone which left him puzzled and occasionally seething. "And I got no husband. And I'm your Aunt's charity case."

"For God's sake, quit talking like that! It's… it's –"

"True?"

"– disgusting and…reeking of self-pity."

Lily stared at her face in the shivering water. With his blue epaulettes flashing in the light, a kingfisher broke the surface with the bayonet of his beak.

Tom's arms were around her in a most unbrotherly fashion. They gripped her like braces; she let him pull both her softness and her strength against his rigidity. Some of the tension flowed her way. His lips brushed her eyelids, her cheeks, then met her own rising. They simply held each other that way for a long time, as if there were a question to be raised and no one to utter the first syllable of the answer.

Tom let go first. "I'm sorry," he lied.

"I'm not," Lily said. "An' what for?"

"You're in my care," Tom said feebly. "My Aunt, she's trusted me, she's –"

"An' you," Lily said, "have taken advantage of a fallen woman."

"Why *do* you say things like that?" he said.

"Now that we've kissed," Tom was saying as he dropped the sour cherries into Lily's apron, "you must tell me more about yourself. Fair's fair."

"Nothin' to tell, really," Lily said. "I'm a farm girl, born an' raised."

"You were no farm girl that night we danced in Sarnia." He held a cherry aloft and she captured it with her teeth, the tart juice stinging.

"Even farm girls dance," Lily said equivocally, and saw right away that he was hurt.

"We've come too far," Tom said. "You sit right here and I'll fetch the buggy."

"Let's just rest a bit," Lily said, puffing and laughing from their run down the lane.

They sat. In the thicket a veery's note soared and sighed, surrounding solitude.

Tom said, "Don't you…don't you, ever, well, feel sad –"

Lily turned her solemn eyes his way, puzzled.

"About the baby, I mean."

"It died," Lily said.

"That's what I meant," he said, patting her wrist.

"All the time," she said.

It wasn't the answer he expected.

"You'll find it hard to believe but I'm known among my cronies as the strong and silent type," Tom said. They were walking hand in hand in the countryside just north of the city after a pleasant ride in the surrey. The country lane was fringed with young goldenrod and late-blooming, orange-throated lilies.

"I'll be goin' back home soon," Lily said. "I ain't heard from Auntie in a month. I'm worried about her. Things ain't been goin' good for us the last while."

Keep talking, Lily, his eyes said.

"Why do you want to be a soldier?" she said.

After their picnic under a huge elm beside the creek, Tom reached for her but she drew back ever so slightly.

"Well, I guess I started out just wanting to prove something to my Aunt and her friends. I was never too good at it, even then. By the time I was eighteen I was running around with Mad-Cap Dowling and that fast crowd, drinking and…carrying on."

"With fallen women," Lily added.

"Scarlet women is the term used in polite society," Tom said, scanning her face. "I had my own money at last and spent it as fast as it came in. So when my Aunt suggested I go off to Toronto, not to the University but to clerk in a law firm, I said yes. I wanted to travel, to see the country and the big city. I discovered that the Dowlings of this world are not confined to London."

"An' then?"

"Then I decided one morning last fall that with my income about to be ended this year, I had to look at my life, my future. And I did. I joined the Canadian Rifles volunteer brigade the next day. I attended all the drills, read the manuals, bought my own uniform and was made a corporal. Then I heard that the British Army was going to allow Canadians to join regular units to serve here and abroad."

Overhead, cicadas announced mid-afternoon August with a reedy voluntary. In the meadow grasshoppers dozed in the heat.

"What do soldiers do," Lily asked, "besides killing people?"

Tom was taken aback, then sprang forward at the ready. Her directness was something he could find no antidote for. Had she just asked a question or made a cutting appraisal? Nothing in her steady gaze could help him. He gathered his dignity and said overly loud: "The British Army and our militia do not kill people. Our job is to protect the lands and homes and lives of our citizens – ordinary people like your Uncle and Aunt who would be prey to thieves, murderers and foreigners. None of us would be safe without them. None of us would be *here* without them. Surely you've heard of the Rebellion? The Patriot's War?"

"I had no schoolin'," Lily said.

He pretended to ignore this remark. "Even now there's rumblings of a war between the states over there, a big fight over slavery. We've been put on alert at all the border points. The boys are growing real excited about it. There's a good chance I'll get into the regulars by September. That's what I want. To be a defender of my country. That's what putting on the uniform is about." His eyes were glistening, and in spite of herself

Lily was held by the brilliant, earnest, frightened power in them. "The army's about the things that are most important to any man anywhere: honour, duty, loyalty, service and patriotism."

He sought the confirmation of Lily's hand; she allowed him to take it, but said after a bit: "I've heard of them words."

He gave her a grateful, jittery smile.

"Where's Tom?" Lily said to Mrs. Edgeworth at breakfast.

"Tippy's been called away to Toronto," said the good lady, her face reflecting both the panic and bemusement with which she had been observing the month-long convalescence of Lily and her nephew.

Lily finally got up the courage to ask Lucille if she knew anything about Tom's call to Toronto. Lucille didn't, but speculated that he might be home either the next day or not at all – depending on her mood.

Lily could not sleep. Two nightmares recurred and competed to keep her edgy and restless. In one a pulpy-pink fish with her daughter's eyes lay belly-up at the bottom of an ebony stream where fierce currents roared by, carrying with them ribbons and braids and colophons of infant-flesh until its idiom-bone showed through and let the tides polish it to fossil; the eyes alone remained in their jellied pools, like orphaned pollywogs. In the second dream she and Tom were riding on a train, not in a passenger coach but on top of the tender; they were roaring through a night-blizzard with the engine's boiler red-hot and sizzling; the two of them were laughing and tossing their clothes into the white wind, and the train was rising up off the tracks and driving skyward into the throat of the maelstrom that contended, in its own accelerating screams, with those of the locomotive and the lovers posed to collide...

Mrs. Edgeworth changed the sweat-soaked sheets each morning, and thought of calling the doctor. She feared that Lily was having a relapse, and fading fast.

Then Tom returned – in the regalia of his militia unit, and a rapid recovery ensued.

"It's a wonderful city, Lily. Full of parks and brick buildings and a beautiful lake. You must see it sometime. When you're better."

"I am better, Tom. Really."

"You look pale."

"I been indoors too much."

"I never should've left you!"

"I'll be goin' home. Probably next week."

Lily held her hands like a prayer in her lap. The sun, through the scrim of trees in the garden gilded her face. In a voice about to break Tom said, "You're the most beautiful creature I've ever laid eyes on."

Lily felt herself on the edge of a precipice. She shuddered – memory and dream propelling the commotion in her blood. She longed for the unknown yet knew too much. She needed to surrender unconditionally to some mystery, some hazard beyond these torturing certainties.

"I heard them words before," she heard herself say. "Just before he ruined me."

"For Christ's sake, Lily, why *do* you take your bitterness out on me? I'm trying to help you. I'm your *friend*."

"I know."

"I love you," he said to stop the pain.

Lily studied him. In a voice that was an echo of a whisper, she said, "I can't love a man who pities me."

The distant door slammed like a cannon-shot in a barracks.

"Why haven't you written me? Lily asked her Aunt between the alternating night-mares. Mrs. Edgeworth had persuaded her to send a telegram to Port Sarnia, but it was returned with the curt message: "No response". On the third day of Tom's unexplained disappearance – even his Aunt looked anxious – Lily announced that she was better and would leave for home the next day, the fifteenth of August. She had been away for over three months.

Mrs. Edgeworth teetered on the brink of panic; all her breeding was about to dissolve under her. "He'll be back," she said, dropping all pretense. "I know him, dear-heart."

"I got to see my Aunt," Lily said.

"Oh, I know, Lily, I know I can't keep you. I've been too selfish already. But you are such a sweet, such a kind thing –"

"Can you buy a ticket for me?" Lily asked.

"Of course, I can. You can have all the money you need."

"Just the ticket, please. And I'd like to send another telegram if I could, asking them to meet me at the station."

"Of course, of course."

Lily slumped in her chair. Mrs. Edgeworth came over. Without looking Lily reached for her hands, and the two women held each other that way, rocking gently back and forth in the midst of their mutual helplessness. In the kitchen they could hear Lucille's grotesque whimpering.

2

Lily was just about to settle into one of her nightmares when she was awakened by a loud scuffle and bumping below. Mrs. Edgeworth's scream shot up to the gables of the house. "Come back here you – you blackguard!"

Lily sat bolt upright, her thin gown pulled down to the tips of her breasts, as the door popped open and Tom staggered in behind it. He had not removed his boots nor his cloak; his eyes were wild with fatigue and fading rage. She fully expected to see him foam at the mouth.

"Goddammit, I *will* have you! I will!" He flung his cloak across the room, spilling the figurine of a mermaid which cracked lengthwise on the carpet. Lily didn't move. If she were aware that most of her bosom was exposed in the dim light from the hall and in the lamp her demon lover now swung towards her, she made no move to cover herself.

The lamp fell to the floor, and Tom lurched onto the bed beside her. "I will have you, I will, I will," he muttered into the slurred haze in front of him. His hands clasped her bare shoulders and in their rough urgency jerked the nightgown down to her waist. He froze. Her sharp breath and his heaving gasp for air filled the room. He stared at her breasts.

He rocked back, chin sagging to chest.

Mrs. Edgeworth, having found a candle, could be heard huffing up the stairs.

"It's all right, Auntie," Lily called. "Tom got in the wrong room by mistake. He's comin' down."

After breakfast Lily asked to be alone for a while in the garden she had seen through its best season and come to love. She was there after mid-morning when Tom came up to her. He looked wary but was shaved and trim in his uniform.

"Lily," he said, "I can't live without you. I have every reason to believe you have strong feelings for me. Last night was the last time you'll ever see me drunk."

Lily gave him no help, but even in his turmoil he could see that she was alert and listening. "I love you. I don't pity you. How can anyone pity a person who is twice as strong as they are? I may not know what love is, but I can still say I love you and know I'm telling the truth."

"Yes," Lily said.

"Here is a token of what I feel," he said shyly, opening his fist – his sword hand – and letting the sun catch the facets of the ruby stone set in a gold ring. "My mother's," he said. "For you. For us."

Lily made no gesture towards the words or the gift.

"I'm asking you to marry me right away, to go off to Toronto with me. I've got word that the Regulars will take me; that'll mean a salary, a home for us, perhaps by the lake or on the island."

Lily looked as if she were struggling to interpret the speech of an earnest but thick-tongued foreigner. Surprise, wonder, doubt –all contended there as Tom talked on.

"I'm almost certain to be stationed at Fort York, unless some foreign war broke out, but there's little chance of that. Lily, I'm asking you to take a chance on me. I'll love you like no other man will ever love you."

Lily had no doubts about that.

"I do love you, Tom."

"Then you'll marry me?"

Lily looked away, then back. "I can't," she said.

"But *why*?"

She felt the full weight of his hurt and her own.

"I can't marry a soldier."

3

"I've sent the telegram," said a chastened Mrs. Edgeworth. Over and over she apologized for the behaviour of her nephew, last night and again this morning when he smashed the glass on her china cabinet and stomped off to his drunken pals again. "I'm just thankful the dear Colonel was not alive to see it," she said, wishing he were here to help, to share the guilt, to give her life some point once more.

"I'll come to visit you," Lily said, tucking the baggage tickets in the little leather purse Lucille had insisted she take.

"You're not just saying that?"

"Soon as I'm sure everythin's okay at home."

"God bless you, child."

"Thank you for everythin'," Lily said shyly. The locomotive let out a peremptory blast.

"Last night," said Mrs. Edgeworth, "when you called down to me, did you…die you mean —"

"Yes, *Auntie*," Lily said, ending the embrace. She stepped aboard, turning her back on London and all it had brought with it. Over the shriek of the whistle she mouthed, "Goodbye, Auntie, I love you."

In less than ten minutes the train had left the city and plunged straight into the bush. Lily sat by herself on a bench and gazed blankly at the landscape fleeing past her. In two hours she would be in Port Sarnia, a journey that only three years before would have taken her a full day in ideal weather. She thought of her own two-day's trek up the River so long ago.

Here and there, as the coach rocked and swayed, Lily noted the gaps in the trees where a farm had been cleared up to the right-of-way, an occasional cabin in the distance with its chimney-smoke indolent in the afternoon haze, the flash of an apron or chemise signalling life, and hope. Beyond the thick border of woods on either side of the track lay hundreds of partially cleared farms like these. The bush had been broken.

Lily soon found herself very drowsy. The repetition of tree-line and the rocking monotony of the wheels below her made her heavy-lidded. Though she was certain she was not asleep, the images of sleep rose up and fell away. She was in the cabin brushing her mother's hair, pulling the livid sun through it with every stroke, and Mama was smiling at her and saying what a sweet voice she had even though Lily's lips were not moving except to record the cadence of her combing. Then Maman LaRouche appeared, her cheeks buffed by oven-heat, the sweat bubbling through her grin as she bent down to the wee sprite of a girl and wrapped her in the great loaves of her forearms. Behind her at the verge of the North Field, Old Samuels waved at her, and as the girl danced towards him, the smoke from his calumet whitened around him and he dissolved tenderly in the green backdrop of his own words – *take me with you, take me with you, I will tell you their meaning* but the waif trips on a stone and when she looks up the figure is gone and the grave-ground under her is ice-cold and she is about to cry when Papa comes to launch her upon his shoulder and they stride through the umber dawn towards a sun rising in the east, there is the rhythm of skin-drums and a ululating chant as the wood wakens to the ancient tribal roundelay, and the girl is about to dance when out of the river's silver surface slides a black hand and arm and shoulder and – eyeless – the thing is beckoning her down where the currents run as deep as blood in the antechambers of the earth.

The train jogged, bucked, shuddered and squealed to a halt. Lily looked out. They were not in Port Sarnia.

"What are we doin' here?" she heard a male voice ask the conductor farther down the coach. She could hear the confusion of people collecting their belongings and shuffling to the exits.

"Wyoming Station," said a deeper voice. "Gotta stop here now. It's the oil boom south of here. Dozens of people every day, carryin' their life on their backs. Diggin' for oil. Crazy, the whole bunch of them."

When Lily opened her eyes again, they were moving cautiously through the environs of Port Sarnia, now referred to by the natives as just plain Sarnia. She picked up her carpetbag crammed with the gifts she could find no way to refuse, and walked through the stifling air to the end of the coach where she waited quietly until the train stopped. The conductor took her bag as she stepped down, and held her arm.

"Watch your step, ma'am," he said, following her with his practiced eye.

Lily stood in the bracing air of the open platform, unable to look around her. In a few minutes she was almost alone. No one called out her name. No one was waiting for her. She went over to the baggage-man and asked if he could find her a taxi. He took all of her in – slowly – then said , "Yes, ma'am. Just here for a visit, are you?" He whistled towards the livery area.

Lily smiled her gratitude. Moments later Pig-Eye Poland, who had driven cart and cab for two decades, pulled up with his pair of bays. Lily gave him the instructions.

"You from London?" he asked when they were underway.

"Just arrived," Lily said to the man who had waved to her every Saturday as she trotted Benjamin up to the back door of the St. Clair Inn.

Pig-Eye's steady chatter ceased by the time they left Exmouth Street and headed northeast up the Errol Road. He sensed the tension in Lily's laconic replies, and respected her need for silence. At the gate she paid him twenty cents from the silver coins Mrs. Edgeworth had pressed on her "for emergencies, dear-heart". It was late afternoon and the August sun still burned hazily over the western sky. Lily looked at her home.

The fields had been planted, but instead of the neat rows of beans and potatoes Lily saw ragweed and wild mustard and Scotch thistle choking in their own glut. The little barn and south coop struck her with their old familiarity, but not a sound came from them. Only the flap of a stunted corn-leaf in the wind reached across the waste of Aunt Bridie's prized garden. On the pond near the house, Booster the gander swam alone in a single circle. No smoke in the chimney. Well, it was afternoon and very hot. As she approached she saw that the door was shut tight, and the windows pressed against the sashes. She listened. Behind the woodshed a groundhog rubbed its back against the rim of its burrow; a garter snake sawed through the grass; a mouse sneezed.

"*They ain't there!*"

Old Bill had emerged from his hut and was calling to her as he hobbled across the cucumber patch. She waited for him to come up to her before she said, "Are they in town?"

"Then you *ain't* heard," Old Bill said, suddenly looking at the ground and smacking his gums together nervously.

Lily waited.

"Bridie wrote you a letter about it," Old Bill said.

"Where've they gone?"

"Packed up an' went off to the oil fields," Old Bill said. "Down there Petrolia way," he added, seeing her puzzlement.

"Left the farm?"

"Yup. After fifteen years they just up an' left. God-dammedest thing I ever seen," he said, "if you'll pardon my French."

"For good?"

"Yup. Had their bags packed by noon an' just left the house an' the doo-dads and all standin' pat, an' hitched up Benjamin an' headed for the oil. Dammedest thing I ever seen."

Gradually Lily got the whole story from him. She took him inside where she found everything still in place: the breakfast dishes on the table infested with flies; the kettle on the stove, half-full and waiting. The beds were unmade, as if they had discarded their occupants only moments before. Lily started a small fire, made some tea, and tried to keep Old Bill settled long enough to achieve some kind of coherence.

Aunt Bridie and Uncle Chester had gone to the Petrolia area about the time the baby was born. Bridie had put all the details in a letter which, of course, never reached Lily. The Grand Trunk had served the expropriation papers on them in early June. Old Bill's hut and yard were exempted, as were the house, barn, coop, shed, pond and kitchen garden of the Ramsbottom property – about an acre and a half in total. The rest – the fields, woodlot, cleared fallow, planted gardens – were needed, they said, for the sprawling company town already starting to unfold on the ordnance grounds of Point Edward. Naturally since the GTR was a humane, Canadian-directed enterprise, the Ramsbottoms would be permitted to harvest this year's crop or take a small sum in lieu thereof. A reasonable – even generous – offer was made for the seized acreage and pinery. That such money was of little value to a couple who had depended on developed land for their continuing livelihood was an argument considered by the directorate to be seditiously Luddite in nature and intent.

Uncle Chester had mentioned the business proposal of his friend from London, who had written during the winter to say that he had put capital into an oil-drilling company under the command of a fast-talking, knowledgeable New Yorker, and that they were looking for another partner. Aunt Bridie suddenly began quizzing Uncle Chester closely on the matter, and within a day the decision had been made. Old Bill was to sell off the Guernsey and the remaining chickens and take what he could use or sell from the garden, They left him some money, but he had hidden it so well he could no longer find it. As he talked, he dunked chunks of mildewed bread into his tea and slurped them through the sieve of his gums.

"Why?" Lily said.

"Dunno, little one. Never seen the like of it. Woman like that farmin' all her days, then just up an' leaves it all. I saw her walk out to them cabbages that mornin', an' she mumbled somethin' at them, an' then kicked one of 'em square in the head."

"She hated it," Lily said.

"All she said to me was: 'I can't let Lily an' the babe come back to a patch of ground. You take care of them front teeth now Bill,' she says to me."

"The babe died," Lily said. "She knows that."

After a while Old Bill said, "They sent a fella here a while back to tell me everythin' was goin' good down there. They're stayin' in a fancy hotel somewhere – it's wrote down for you – an' you're to go there soon's you get back. They'll send a buggy to Wyomin' to take you an' the babe down. You're to live with them there."

"The babe died."

Old Bill went to the cupboard and pulled out some rumpled papers. "Here's where it's wrote down," he said. "You're to send a telegram the minute you arrive."

Lily looked around at all that was familiar, at nine years of her life spent in this kitchen with its own seasons of disappointment and delight, of love and its absence.

"This here paper's specially for you," Old Bill said, flogging his memory for some gist of significance.

Lily took it. She recognized her name in print and her Aunt's signature, and a bit of the date.

"What does it say?" she asked.

"It's a deed," Old Bill said, showing the purple of his gums as he stuttered over the legal script: "It gives you – Lily Ramsbottom – what's left of the farm when the railroad is done."

Lily stared in awe at the official stamp.

"Your Aunt says to me, Bill, she says, you tell her the patch is hers, so's she'll always have a home to come back to no matter what happens to us down there."

Old Bill munched the last of his soggy tea. The kettle was humming again, but Lily made no move to tend it.

"I can go to the telegraph first thing in the mornin'," Old Bill said at the door.

"Not yet, Bill. I want to wait a bit. To think."

"Okay." He was about to leave when he pretended to remember something. "By-the-by," he said, "when you was down to London way, did ya happen to see anythin' of my Violet?"

4

The hoe in her hands felt good again: astringent, righteous. She worked without rest in the steaming humidity. Blisters formed on her palms; her back ached like a loosened tooth; at night her muscles buckled. Her hair was a frazzled rope. Still, the weeds died and the vegetables – chastened, attenuated – took shape and then heart. She herself ate whatever had been left, scraping off the mould with a jack-knife and splashing pump-water over her bone-weariness at day's end. By the third morning she smelled worse than Old Bill. She couldn't get out of bed. Her back had jammed at right angles to her hips. She shuffled through the shed to the back door where she eased herself down on the bench so that the morning sun would catch and soften the seizure in her back. She pulled up her nightshirt and moaned softly as the heat soaked in. If anyone saw me like this, she thought, they'd think I was a crone tuning up for flight.

She heard Old Bill coming faithfully up the path to the front door, as he had each morning only to see in her face the answer to his question about the telegram. She poked her head around the shed corner to intercept him. The sunlight rolled in a horizontal wave across the frayed garden and struck the approaching figure with indelible illumination.

Lily saw the carpenter's tool-kit first, then the overalls, bib, and navvy's cap.

"Good mornin', ma'am," Tom said. "I'm lookin' for work."

PART TWO

Tom

13

1

Besides the wedding of Thomas Marshall and Lily Ramsbottom, *née* Corcoran *cum* Fairchild, the autumn of 1861 produced several other events of moment in what was known throughout the province as 'the Lambton swamps'. Alexander Mackenzie – who was later to prove that stonemasonry and Haldane Baptism were no obstacles to the highest political office in a country that was still a pipe-dream in George Brown's head – had succeeded in overthrowing the old reformer, "Coon" Cameron, and delivering the counties of the West into the political jaws of the Clear Grits. The gum-beds of Enniskillen ceased harassing wayward oxen and began oozing oil, in commercial quantities plump enough to be noticed in Chicago and New York. Twenty thousand barrels – each one constructed on-the-spot of the finest, most perishable oak – were hauled through bogs and sloughs up to Wyoming Station, in spite of every attempt by the County to provide a road for such traffic. Within a year the town of Oil Springs was confected to match the expectations of the drillers, dreamers, and exploiters of the human condition.

Less ostentatious but no less bumptious was the rise of the village around the railway terminus on the old ordnance grounds. What boundless optimism it was – in the face of Darwin's grim gospel and the resuscitated silliness of Bishop Ussher and the mute unglory of Balaclava – to lay out a town site crammed with streets without the ghost of a house to grace them, and each one meridian-straight, square to the intangible North, and festooned with a denomination derived from the Royal Egg itself: Emma, Maud, Alice, Alexandra, Albert, Alfred and, of course, Victoria – *regina and imperatrix*. By the summer of 1861, besides the makeshift workers' shanties sprawled around the sheds and yards, several clapboard houses and one less doubting brick establishment had aligned themselves with the future forecast by the unpeopled street. Some attempt was made by outsiders to call the new municipality Huron Village, but the Point it had been, was, and is.

2

The nuptial ceremony did not take place until early September. Lily herself didn't know why but she set up a room for Tom in Benjamin's barn, where Chester had so often hibernated, and to the amazement of Old Bill who watched till his eyes glazed and he fell asleep propped up on the sill each night, the lovers parted half-way down the garden path just before dark, each to a cold bed. If anyone had asked Old Bill for an opinion, he would have said, "Looks to me like a marriage made in purgatory."

Tom had proposed on the day of his arrival, and Lily had said "yes". "Tomorrow?" "Soon." The groom-to-be then bedded down in the straw, grateful that the pony had been gracious enough to move his quarters to town a month before. In the weeks before Lily announced that she was ready to set a date, a daily routine was established. In the morning they worked side by side to save what they could of the garden and to prepare for a more productive season of their own next spring. Lily tried not to laugh at Tom's ungainliness in the field, where he would attack in a frenzy – his sickle stabling like a bayonet, decapitating as many allies as enemies – then retreat *sans* dignity with his hands blistered and rebellious. Working at the steady pace she had learned so long ago – with her body low to the earth, her legs apart in an unmaidenly but resilient squat – Lily would pass her sweating lover, only to hear him wheeze and rally his forces behind her for yet another volley-and-retreat. As they rested in the shade periodically, she would kiss the blisters on his palms, but he tensed like a trigger before her soft insistence triumphed and he eased himself into the grass where she could stretch alongside him and let his hands find solace where they would. In the afternoon Tom would take up his tool-kit, fling it like a haversack over his shoulder and, whistling a grenadier's march, tramp through the parapet of pines separating them from the townsite, and head for the rail-yards through the grassy streets. Lily watched him till his sandy hair was no longer distinguishable from the goldenrod in full bloom. Most days he came back at dusk, whistling and telegraphing his coins in his pocket: the Grand Trunk in its benevolence had found some occasional task for his limited skills.

"Almost got enough to pay the preacher," he'd say each time, going through a mock counting-ceremony till she laughed and made a grab for the half-dollars, whereupon he would seize her wrists, pull her to him and give Old Bill a quick seizure by kissing her full on the lips. "What do you charge, mam'selle?" "More 'n you earn in a year, laddie." "Then I'm off to seek my fortune in the big, bad world!" "I'll be waitin', if you ain't too long." Always Lily would turn away first and head for the house. Once, she heard his footsteps right behind her; she stopped. The crickets all leaned one way. He said nothing but she recognized the sharp breathing that signaled suppressed anger. She longed for Aunt Bridie's voice to give her some warning or assurance, but none came. That night she lay awake in a silence of her own composition.

The railway expropriation left them with so little land that they dismantled what was left of the hen-houses to make room for more garden. A make-shift coop was rigged up near the barn, but no chickens were to be installed until after the wedding.

In the meantime, Booster the gander was made a gift of three lubricious females, whom he trod regularly and flamboyantly near the pond below Lily's window.

On the last day of August she heard Tom's step in the field; he wasn't whistling. She came out to meet him, apprehensive. He stopped just where the stunted sunflowers grimaced in the thinning light.

"What's happened?"

"Nothing much. They've finished the new freight-shed."

She brightened.

His smile was genuine but guarded. He was looking directly in her eyes, as if searching for some valuable that might not ever have been lost, for some certainty the knowledge of which could have been as deadly as it was redemptive.

"They're taking on stevedores. Full time."

Lily waited.

"I'm one of them."

After supper they set the date. The harvest moon – ovular, increscent – was almost wholly above the horizon before Old Bill saw the cottage door open and a male figure bound towards the barn in a step that was somewhere between a quick march and a gavotte. He smiled toothlessly, and thought again of Violet, and absence.

3

The ceremony itself took place on a warm Saturday morning in September 'on the porch' of the Anglican Church, the latter expedient being resorted to as the best compromise, considering the lapse faith of the groom and the apostasy of the bride. "It would mean a great deal to Auntie," Tom had said and Lily replied, "Well, one of our Aunts anyway," and smiled in the hope that Bridie herself might savour the ironies. Mrs. Edgeworth was too ill to travel, and so it fell to Alice and Maurice Templeton to serve as witness and as family for the occasion. Mrs. Templeton was deliciously horrified at the thought of a semi-sanctified union under some shady portico in the far reaches of the nave. She insisted that Lily wear the dress she had worn to the Great Western Ball three years before, and though it needed some alterations, Lily was happy with the results – and the appropriateness. *He* won't remember, she thought, but I will. A small reception – just tea, cakes and chilled champagne among the rusting flowers – with the Templeton's daughters and their prospering husbands down from Toronto to supervise the move of their parents. For Mrs. Templeton, and Lily, too, that was the only sad aspect of an otherwise happy series of events. Maurice had at last been persuaded that his business and political fortunes lay ahead of him in the provincial capital, and his wife – eager to be near her first grandchild – was in no position to second his reluctance. The decision had been made. Both Lily and her benefactress well knew that, despite the miracle of railroads, a separation of two hundred miles and a full social stratum in that day meant it would be many years before they were likely to meet again, if ever.

Aunt Bridie and Uncle Chester did not come. Lily had got Tom to write them a letter a few days after his arrival, telling them of the impending marriage, and several days later a long letter arrived from "Oil Springs, Enniskillen Township." Needless to say, Aunt Bridie was relieved to learn that Lily was all right, and delighted with the proposed union. No mention was made of the baby's death." "We are doing fine," she went on. "Please don't worry. When you come to us I'll explain why we did what we did, though I'm not sure I even understand it myself. Anyway, I reckon you won't believe this but Chester and me took all the money from the sale – robbery – of the farm and all the savings in the bank we all helped to earn, and we packed up in one day and moved down here. Your Uncle's friend in London said we should join up with his friend from New York and form a company to search for oil. I didn't know anything about oil but I'm learning fast. Mr. Armbruster is a wonderful man. We're all living for a while here in the Lucky Derrick Hotel. We have a huge piece of land out by Black Creek. Uncle Chester is back making things like barrels and rigs. Mr. Armbruster and I look after the business end. We are doing very well. We may be rich some day. But you know, Lily, your happiness means so much to us. We want you and Tom to come and stay with us as soon as you can."

As it turned out, after several exchanges of correspondence, Aunt Bridie and Uncle Chester, because of their work it seemed, were unable to come to the wedding, but Tom and Lily were to go to Oil Springs for their honeymoon, and then go on to London for a week to visit with Mrs. Edgeworth.

For Lily none of this seemed real. For her the only grip upon reality in the days leading up to the ceremony was the presence of Tom: in the flesh she clove to daily and in the dreams she cherished and prolonged through the solitary nights. I must not believe in such happiness, she thought. I may enjoy it, regret it, kindle it, remember it – but it's not mine to possess outright. But her dreams whispered 'yes'.

4

After the morning vows and the afternoon champagne and the extended goodbyes, Mr. and Mrs. Thomas Marshall were carried off by the engines of the Great Western Railway as far as Wyoming Station, where they disembarked in preparation for the fifteen-mile journey south to the gum-beds of Enniskillen.

"At least we don't have trunks to lug about," Tom said, looking around in bewilderment at the prospectors and their families as they dragged steam-trunks, roped-in suitcases, haversacks, tool-boxes and assorted bundles of blankets and clothing along the plank platform and down the improvised alleys of the shantytown. Babies squalled, draymen cursed, women wept, husbands railed and cuffed. Somehow bag and baggage managed to find its way onto the waiting carts. Driven by the fearsome oaths of the teamsters, the horses lurched and skidded southward on what appeared to be a road through the bush.

"Plank road all the way to Oil Springs," a grizzled veteran of these wars yelled whiskily into Tom's face. "Just built her last month. A joy to ride on!"

Lily squeezed Tom's arm in a reassuring gesture. It struck her forcefully how much of an urban man he was. She wondered if he knew or would be upset to know how much at home she felt here looking beyond this ephemeral paraphernalia and seeing the rows of farms backing sleepily onto the right-of-way, a team of oxen currying the earth with unfathomable patience, the distant chime of an axe in some field-to-be, the curl of woodsmoke from homesteads secure among the trees, a small girl near the tracks gathering wild columbine.

"There's our coach," Lily shouted.

Anyone remotely prejudiced by the romanticism of the stagecoach in the American wild-west would have been shocked by the contraption that went under that guise in Lambton County in 1861. Tom was speechless. What he saw was a sort of haywagon on which had been erected five backless benches set in theatrical rows and over which there perched a wooden roof held up by several stilts that also served to lend the allusion of windows and doors. Some prankster had tacked an orange fringe around the perimeter of the roof, on which were hand-printed these already-fading letters: 'Enniskillen Coach Lines: the Road to Oil'.

"Let's snuggle," Lily said, climbing onto the last bench, arranging her dress, and pulling Tom and their suitcase up. "Nobody'll see us back here."

"We'll get all the mud from the wheels if we sit here," Tom said. "Your dress'll be ruined."

"What chance has it got anyway?"

Finally he laughed and moved in beside her. "You're a funny one," he said, putting the shawl around her.

"I'd like to be," Lily said.

Ten minutes after the coach, its foul-mouthed driver, its four horses and ten passengers left the 'depot' at Wyoming, they were swallowed by the bush so thoroughly and so possessively that the effronteries of the makeshift town were instantly forgotten. Even the farms cut only one concession deep into the glacial alluvium of hardwood stands, festering swamps, treacherous sloughs and gravel-beds, and oozing boils of pent-up petroleum – none of which were sympathetic to road-construction. Three times the Road-to-Oil express had to be reactivated by the passengers themselves – the lurid imprecations of the driver-conductor seeming to lose their miraculous power the further they penetrated these wilds. On the first two occasions, where sloughs had simply gulped down both planks and supporting logs, the three women passengers were implored to remain aboard while the combined animus of the seven gentlemen and the verbal efforts of the owner-operator succeeded in disgorging the wheels long enough for the horses to reach secure ground. Tom was soaked and muddy; Lily wrapped a shawl around his shivering: "You need somethin' to warm you up," she whispered. There was no reply. On the third occasion, when a ruptured plank caused one of the front wheels to snap off and flung the coach and all into the muck beside the road, even the ladies had to descend and pitch in, after brief and less-than-dignified trips into the underbrush. Lily looked as if she had just danced the night away in a hog-wallow. Only the intervention of two burly passengers prevented Tom from dismantling the driver's cursing-apparatus.

"Damn your Aunt anyway!" Tom said, putting the shawl between them and grabbing at a strut to steady himself.

Lily held her laughter firmly in check. Half-an-hour later she was snoozing on his broad shoulder.

"I don't believe it," Tom was saying in her left ear. "Civilization. Of a sort."

"That there's Petroli-ar!" shouted the driver in his best tour-guide voice. "Don't blink now or you'll miss 'er!"

To their left they could see a broad clearing, the steeple of a church, several brave storefronts, and a scattering of shanties, tents and open-air camps. But what caught every eye in the carriage except the driver's was the huge brick refinery with its sixteen stills and its chimney towering above the highest elm or pine. In the distant clearings the passengers saw their first three-poled oil-rig, the jerker-lines pecking away at the earth below like robins after a rain.

"My God," Tom said as they plunged again into the bush, "where *are* we going? Three hours ago we were sipping champagne in a garden."

"Auntie says it's a grand place for a honeymoon."

"If you're a toad," Tom said.

Lily laughed out loud, waking the woman in front of her.

"You must have *some* Aunt," Tom said, struggling to keep a straight face.

It appeared Aunt Bridie may have been right. Towards the end of their third hour of jouncing, with the sun beginning to weaken over the western rim, they saw the unmistakable signs of human habitation. No farms of any kind, but rugged clearings – large and small – had been hacked and slashed out of the wilderness. It looked like a war zone, as pines lay rotting where they had been slaughtered, stumps protruded and tilted every-which-way, while still other trees – giant ash or ironwood – remained afoot, though horribly gashed and left to cure themselves. A tent or a shack were the only visible dwellings, usually squatted right beside a tri-pod log-derrick or a mound of greasy clay or occasionally near a drilling-rig pounding into the rock below. Everywhere the odour of oil hung in the air – like the aura of temptation itself.

The town proper began like most other pioneer communities: razed clearings with cabins or plank shanties arranged more-or-less along roadways that might – with effort, imagination and luck – become streets with names. Gazing upon the mud-spattered beauty of his bride, Tom felt his heart sink even lower, beyond anger. Lily opened her eyes and brushed his cheek with her lips.

"Look!" she said.

The rutted road had mysteriously flattened and smoothed to the gritty bounce of gravel. In the midst of the outlying shantytown, they now beheld – like a palm-sweetened oasis or some miracle akin to the loaves-and-fishes – a self-contained one-street town. The silvery dusk-glow may have lent it more allure than it deserved, but it was a wondrous sight to the travel-weary arrivals.

King Street, so declared by the black-and-white signs on either side and repeated at the two crossroads interrupting its quarter-mile length, was a freshly planked broadway extending as far as the eye could see, surmounted by sidewalks of finer board and trim railings, and overlooked by posts carrying the telegraph wire and bearing what appeared to be lamps of some sort. The building and shops on King Street – many more than two storeys high – faced one another, complacent in their painted splendor, proud of their false fronts and perfectly satisfied in their mutual adoration. The coach rattled mechanically along, passing other, more elegant carriages and making the gleaming glass-and-clapboard facades of shops, taverns and offices a magical blur full of undefined promise.

"Six hotels, five gambling dens and a dozen oil companies!" proclaimed their indefatigable guide. "An' this here's the one we stop at."

Lily looked up, and guessed from what she saw printed above the upper verandah that this was the Lucky Derrick Hotel. It was the second-to-last building on the broadway. Next to it at a little distance lay the livery stable, bustling with activity. Beyond that, bush reasserted its hegemony.

Now that they were stopped Lily could see that the town was awash with people. Ladies with long dresses and parasols strolled along the walkways, gathered at corners, or sat happily on benches surrounded by flowerboxes and pink paint. Men in formal coats buzzed in front of the taverns, tradesmen rushed here and there with purpose, and the twilight air shook with the cries of draymen, the muted roar from the gambling dens and the barbed hilarity of loose-tongued women.

"Well now, here's the honeymooners!" boomed a voice with a twang as clear as a Liberty Bell. "You must be young Tom," it carolled, and Lily saw the puffy flesh of an outflung hand. "Welcome to the oil capital of the world." Tom was pulled heartily onto the boardwalk. "And by golly this has to be the blushing bride. We've been waiting for you, sweetheart. Now don't you look a beauty." Lily felt the pulp of his grip on her fingers and hopped down, as gracefully as she could manage, beside Tom.

"I'm Melville Armbruster," said the man with the florid face. "Just call me Mel." His grin was as brisk as a shoeshine.

Standing under the shadow of the porch roof of the hotel were Uncle Chester and Aunt Bridie. Lily went to them, the four months away feeling like four years. Uncle Chester stepped forward and without a glance at her despoiled dress or the mud caked around her left brow, hugged her with arms that said: 'this is it, we're not letting you get away again.'

Lily turned to Aunt Bridie, who met her extended hands, and they held one another at elbow's length, letting their eyes do the greeting, probing, forgiving. Too soon Lily had to disengage, not fully satisfied with the brief tenderness she glimpsed at last beneath the new layers of toughening brought on by the latest calamities. More-than-that, though, Lily was puzzled by the presence of some eccentric note of hope, barely disguised as most of Bridie's feelings had been out of long habit. Does she really believe in all this? Lily could not help asking herself. Had Auntie let her guard down after so much straightening experience? Had she given up? Surrendered to some final, lethal euphoric?

Aunt Bridie cast a speculative eye across the handsome form of Tom Marshall. She took in Lily as she stood beside him.

"I'm afraid we're a bit of a mess, Mrs. Ramsbottom," Tom said, releasing her hand.

"Aunt Bridie will do," she said firmly.

"Now don't fuss about the mud, folks," said Melville Armbruster. "We got rooms and a bath and as soon as you're changed we're all going to sit down and have us a king-size family dinner."

Lily saw his gold tooth flash – like a fang.

5

During the dinner, between the polite conversation and explanatory narratives, Lily kept one eye on her beloved and the other on Aunt Bridie. Armbruster's boasting about their 'suite of rooms' was not much exaggerated. The company formed by the unlikely trio, New York and Upper Canadian Oil Explorations Ltd., had leased the back quarter of the Lucky Derrick – two floors that included a living room and dining area and huge bathroom downstairs and three bedrooms upstairs with a water-closet at the end of the hall. They had their own entrance. "Twenty dollars a day," the New York half of the company informed them before they could ask. Auntie had smiled ever so slightly at that, with a quick lilt of the brow, and Lily had picked up the message though she could not decipher it. What was even more curious – perhaps distressing – was the way in which she sat so close to Uncle Chester, spooning sugar into his coffee, turning to him for confirmation of a point not in dispute, and once even patting him on the hand affectionately when he described for Lily's benefit the especially efficient method he had devised out at 'the works' for making barrels on the spot. "Your Uncle's workin' on a new kind of jerker-line," she said. "He's the king-pin in this operation," said Armbruster, jiggling the champagne glasses. Uncle Chester blushed, then beamed. Lily felt the stanchions give way under some part of the world she had deemed substantial. I'm being foolish, she thought as she poured cream into Tom's coffee; I want my own happiness to be so perfect I can't rejoice in theirs. But I want the whole world to be happy, she said almost aloud. I do.

"We're not exactly rich *yet*," Armbruster was saying, steak sauce a-drool on his woman's chin, "but as you can see, we ain't precisely starving either. We're scooping up the surface slop quite regular and shipping it out to London and even to Boston, thanks to the railways. Greatest invention since the Lord pulled the rib out of Adam and gave us the fair sex." He included Bridie and Lily in his generous assessment and no doubt the ample serving-girl who brought in from time to time silver tureens and bulging platters of food for their conspicuous consumption.

"To the railways!" Uncle Chester blurted out, glass raised foolishly before he realized his blunder.

"To the Great Western for bringing us together," Tom said quickly into the embarrassed silence. Aunt Bridie gave him a look bordering on approval.

The company president insisted that they all take the world-famous taxi-ride up and down the King Street mall. When they stepped into the handsome buggy awaiting them outside the hotel, it was nightfall and the landscape was transformed yet again.

There may have been starlight generated in the heavens that evening but its sheen was annihilated by the blaze of manufactured incandescence along the entire broadway of Oil Springs. The southern arch, from which the wedding party sallied forth on their grand tour, was set aglow by two fiercely beautiful gaseliers, their dragon-tongues decimating dark at the menacing edge. Along each side of the street the largest kerosene lamps in the known world flickered bravely against the canopy enclosing them. Every window of every shop, every tavern, every den of iniquity flung out its own ersatz luminosity so that the whole city seemed to shimmer and reverberate in the vast blackness around it, like the rings of Saturn. Lily snuggled against Tom and watched in disbelief as the boardwalks, verandahs and alcoves – shadows in the omnipresent light – hummed with the motions of human intercourse. Never had she seen such colour, warped and fantastic in the weird moon-glow – scarves, bonnets, bustles, coifs, bosoms, top-hats, canes, waistcoats. Flesh was flamingo, falsetto, iridescent. At the northern arch under the braggadoccio of 'Oil Capital of the World', they wheeled and started back. Lily closed her eyes and clung to Tom as if he were the last capstan on a dissolving wharf. Around her she heard voices unhook and drift towards disconnection, towards the far harbours of loneliness. Beneath her the wheels seemed now to be turning faster, the horses' canter transgress to a gallop, the night-wind wail past the vacuum of her eyes till she could no longer hear the drumming of hoofbeats or the rolling of iron on wood – only the breathless rush of starlight through sudden wings.

After an interminable day that had been given over to others – the Templetons, Aunt Bridie and Uncle Chester, condescending clergymen, foul-mouthed stage-drivers and would-be tycoons – the bride and groom at last found themselves alone and unencumbered in a room they could make their own. For a moment – drained by the shock of departure, the travails of the journey, the hut and puzzlement of abrupt reunion – Lily wondered if she could recover that special part of her she had conserved for her lover and husband. As Tom slipped in beside her – naked under the linen sheets, the feather mattress offering no resistance to whatever shapes they might wish to compose – all doubts vanished. Even the thought that this whole episode might be a charade, a little girl's doll-house dream with a fairy princess and her toy soldier and a bloodless conjugation. Tom, too, might well have been wondering what he was doing here miles from the nearest parade ground, pledged to a future he had not even the pleasure of imagining, unbuckled and vulnerable beside a stranger (whose past he dare not mention) in a room overwhelmed by Persian carpets, rococo wainscoting, and Venetian wallpaper replete with ambidextrous angels in comprised configurations.

So, like many others before and after them, emprisoned by the past and fearing for the future, Lily and Tom gave themselves up to love. They let their bodies be ambassadors for what they felt, hoped, craved, had no words to say. They foraged in the other's flesh to take the pulse of their own. In the aftermath they clung together, even in sleep, like sole survivors.

6

After breakfast the next morning, during which Melville Armbruster managed to wink and drop his voice an embarrassing number of times, they all drove out to Black Creek to examine the oil-drilling operations of the new company. "There's a bit of walking to do out there; hope the kids've got some energy left!" Wink. Wink.

But it was Uncle Chester who had to stop every hundred yards or so as they hiked from the edge of the bush-trail towards the drilling site. "You go ahead, I'll be okay," he gasped, but Aunt Bridie said with genuine warmth, "Don't be silly, Chester, we're in no hurry. That oil's been there a long time before we come lookin' for it." "Yessiree," Armbruster chimed in on cue, and began explaining to Tom all about the geologic formations and glacial events that had miraculously convened to produce the very petroleum they could smell seeping out of the earth around them. Uncle Chester caught his breath, took his wife's hand and strode forward. Aunt Bridie, Lily noted, turned briefly to Armbruster as if to say "Thanks".

A half-mile or so into the dense bush brought them to a ten-acre clearing, the home of New York and Upper Canadian Oil Explorations. Here Armbruster took full control of matters, guiding Tom firmly away from Lily and leading him from one piece of machinery to another, certain that his exposition was both fascinating and necessary. To Lily's surprise, Aunt Bridie followed them, listening intently to the details, turning from one to the other as the monologue broke down occasionally, and even offering one or two comments herself – which seemed to please Armbruster. If Tom were bored he gave no sign of it, relying upon the engrained courtesies of a proper upbringing, Lily felt a twinge of something close to envy. "Show me your woodworkin' place, Uncle," she said more loudly than necessary.

Having got his second (or third) wind, Uncle Chester smiled freely at her. "Lily," he said, "you're still a wonder to me. I want to tell you, while I got the chance, that I'm very, very happy for you. An' no one in this world deserves happiness more than you."

"What's this?" Lily said, pointing to some metal contraption off to the north.

"That, my girl, is a little invention I'm workin' on. To speed up the barrel makin'. Come on over and I'll tell you more about it than you'll ever wanna know." He offered her his arm.

They crossed the litter of broken trees, gouged roots and scorched pits towards a series of shacks and wooden benches that formed the cooperage section of the operations. To the south, where the others had gone, lay the three jerker-lines perpetually pumping the thick oil from shallow wells that had been dug out several months before. A single steam-engine, shrouded somewhat by the nearby trees, provided power for the pumps and for Uncle Chester's carpentry works. Lily could see several men in the bush, cutting and preparing firewood.

"We got five young men workin' for us," Uncle Chester explained. "Two of them help me with the barrels an' shippin'. Nice lads, they are, from over Moore township way." Lily could see the pleasure, so long absent, now in her Uncle's face, some sense that the world was not only still evolving but that it held some place for him in it. But she knew him too well to be totally taken in. As he hopped about the area showing off, as modestly as he dare, the intricacies of his efforts and his plans for the coming winter, Lily was faintly aware that his eyes more and more reflected the hysterical hope of an orphaned child who's found a home as perfect as it is temporary.

"You gonna stay on that land, with Tom?" he asked in a sudden shift of tone.

"Maybe," Lily said. "It's not *that* far away."

"Oh," Uncle Chester said, "I didn't mean it that way at all. It's just that your young man, well, he –"

"– don't look like a farmer."

"I wouldn't've said it quite like that," he said, smiling as she did.

"He was a lawyer's clerk and a militia man," said Lily with as much pride as regret. "He can be whatever he sets out to be."

Uncle Chester was a bit puzzled by the latter remark but said cheerfully, "I don't doubt that for a minute. Not a minute."

Just then the door to one of the shacks opened and a young man about Lily's age emerged, blinking and then blushing.

"Don't be shy now, Jimmy," Uncle Chester said to him. "This here's just my favourite niece come to see whether we're doin' a decent job."

"I'm Lily Marshall."

"When he gets his tongue untied," said Uncle Chester, "he'll tell you his name's Jimmy Millar, won't you, Jimmy?"

"From Moore Township?" Lily said.

"They got a lumber trail now goes from Black Creek here straight west to the big river," said Uncle Chester into the sudden silence.

Jimmy Millar even remembered the day when Lil and Papa left, though he was only eight years old and hiding behind his mother's apron as they stood at the end of civilization and perhaps envied father-and-daughter as they headed north to cities and roads and talk of railways. Urged on by Lily's soft but insistent questioning, Jimmy Millar related the details – embellished by local legend – of the deaths of Maman LaRouche and the Frenchman.

"Some of the boys're still there," Jimmy went on, on his own. "But the place is a mess. They mostly hire out for booze money. None of 'em got married. Luc sometimes lives with a squaw. Madeleine died."

For a moment Jimmy did not understand Lily's next question. "Oh, *them*," he said, as light flooded in. "That squatters' camp broke up right after you left. The government opened up those back lots and Old Samuels an' his brood just melted into the trees. Nobody's seen or heard of 'em since."

Lily didn't respond.

"What about you," Jimmy said. "How's your Pa doin'?"

"He's dead," Lily said, knowing deep down this was not a lie.

Tom and the others came into view. Uncle Chester lay snoozing in the shade. Armbruster's voice reached her. "And this is just the part that pays the bills, Tom my boy, the real bonanza's in the deep-drilling rig we're moving in next week. Yessir, we're going as far down into that rock as we can 'cause there's an ocean of oil just waiting there to make us all millionaires. If I was you, I'd talk turkey to that Aunt of yours in London. A little capital's all you need."

Tom was nodding his head politely. Aunt Bridie was walking between them. She seemed so much smaller than the men.

"What's the matter?" Tom said, rolling into the feathery shadows of their afternoon bed.

"Nothin'," Lily said, leaning over him and planting a series of frantic little kisses along his great chest and massive shoulders. "Nothin' you can't cure."

And she sighed extravagantly as he gripped her breasts and eased her towards acceptance.

Nothing you *can* cure, she thought sadly, her loving of him trebled by that awful knowledge.

7

Aunt Bridie looked right at her and said, "You want to know *why*. Well, you've got a right to."

They were alone in the 'sitting room', the men having gone off to try their luck at the casino two doors down. "Men need their toys," Auntie had said as she closed the door after them.

"Not really," Lily replied, "if you don't want to tell –" She waited for her Aunt to move away from the window and sit down on the divan beside her. "I'm so happy I guess I just wanna make sure everybody else has a share."

Aunt Bridie appeared to be trying to recall something important, then brightened and said, "Yes. You've always been like that. That's why Chester an' me feel like we do about you."

"Then…"

"Why did we up an' leave you?"

"Not that. I left you, remember."

Aunt Bridie was fiddling with the tassel on the oversize drapes. "We never felt that," she said softly. "We knew why you went. It came near to breakin' Chester's heart when he found out. But it saved him, too, in a way. All through that horrible business with the railroad, he was a great strength to me. Imagine that. 'Lily's comin' back,' he'd say. 'She'll need a home more than ever now.' An' so I got mad, madder than I've been for a long time." She peeked over at Lily and forced a thin smile.

"At the railroad."

"An' the damned government and all the petty do-gooders that made my life hell since I been a girl. So when they come an' took what all of us built up with our sweat an' bones for ten years, I must tell you, Lily dearest, I was about ready to call it quits.

When I saw that Grand Trunk man drive those red stakes into our land, I felt like they were enterin' my heart an' splittin' it in a dozen pieces. If it hadn't been for Chester an' they thought of you sufferin' down there in London, I don't know what I'd've done. I really don't." Her voice, always so strong and clear, shook with the memory of those weeks.

"Auntie," Lily said, reaching out.

Bridie was not to be forestalled. "So when Chester's friend in London suggested we pack our bags an' take all our savings an' make the craziest gamble of our lives, I took about thirty seconds to make up my mind. Chester's still shakin', as you can see."

"But all this," Lily said carefully, "is so new an' different from what you're used to. This place, these…people."

Aunt Bridie smiled. "You mean Mel," she said.

"No, not just –"

"Lily, you're almost as smart as your Auntie. And as dumb, thank the Lord."

"But all this –"

"Phoniness an' sin an' greed? It's just another version of livin'. Remember, before I was a farmer an' fruit vendor, I was a housemaid, an' before that a rebel daughter who gave up her family an' her country with less than a night's thought. When I married your Uncle Chester, I knew less about him than you do about Tom."

The mellowing late-afternoon sun flowed into the room and around them. Bridie was still talking.

"When you see Fate comin' down on you, there's nothin' you can do, Lily, but get out of its way before it crushes you, an' hope there's one more run at the world somewhere else. A body can only fight so long without winnin'. After a while you're not a fighter, you're a fool."

Lily was only half-listening. She was thinking how fragile a thing the human heart was, whatever flesh or will or faith pretended to represent its spirit.

"Pardon?"

"I say you'll come an' live with us again?"

"Here?"

"Not right here, of course. As soon as the big well comes in, your Uncle an' me we'll build a cottage on the outskirts, with trees and a garden. A flower garden."

"We ain't made any real plans yet," Lily said.

"Don't you worry about Mel now," Aunt Bridie said. "There's a good man under all that blarney. I know. I'm Irish, remember?"

"I'm sure there is," Lily said.

"All I'm askin' is for you to talk it over with Tom. There's plenty of work. Lots of opportunity for a man of his upbringin'."

"I'll talk to him," Lily said, catching the strange look in her Aunt's eye and searching for the source of some thought or feeling that fought to stay hidden there.

"Tell him you gotta take chances in this world," Bridie went on in the same tone.

Lily crossed the room and took her Aunt by the arm. Bridie tensed. "*But you left me the deed*," Lily said.

Bridie gave a wry smile full of tenderness and doubt. Then she stared out at the setting sun. Some time later she whispered, "It wasn't for you."

"Oh —" Lily said. Then she put her arms around her Aunt and held her as she might her own daughter. Bridie's body shrank, then the tears came, irregular and fugitive, not so much the release of pent emotion as a gentle questing for some feeling almost beyond remembrance.

"There'll be another one," Lily said. "Soon. I promise."

14

1

Although they lived on the far edge of the new village, shielded from it by the last rows of aboriginal forest, Lily and Tom felt their lives growing in parallel with it.

Very soon after their return from a week with Mrs. Edgeworth, now Aunt Elspeth, Tom took up his job with the Grand Trunk and settled into a daily routine that Lily wished to go on forever. Each morning just as the sun reached the tree-line and their cockerel reannounced his lustiness, Lily detached herself carefully and reluctantly from the cocoon of warmth she helped create with her lover's body, and got a brisk fire going in the stove. The kindling she had chopped the previous afternoon snapped and thirsted after air. She would then pump the kettle full – the autumn dews cool against her bare skin, the hushed morning wordless with expectation – and having placed it over the open flame, would slip into the bedroom again and watch her husband's face in its sleep. How pleasant it must be, she mused (noting his limbs fret and unwind beneath the comforter) to be wakened every morning by the crack of kindling, your home filling with heat to welcome your rising, your wife with her kettle on and bending down to bless your lips. She had to be quick, of course, or the day's natural timing would be set ajar; Tom, pawing his way out of some dream or other, might ring her with his powerful arms – now thickened by the hauling of hundred-pound kegs and sacks – and pull her back into his lustful reverie. Beyond an initial cry of surprise and protest, she made on these occasions no resistance, for Tom's loving would be slow and dream-like, drawing her down into her own fantasia, and she was glad she'd had no one to tell her exactly what love could or shouldn't be. If Tom were somewhat taken aback by her aggressiveness at night, he very soon adjusted to it, and here in these improvised and illicit mornings they found a mutual pace that left them both adrift, dreamful, awash in desire without appetite. It was during one of these sessions late in September on a misty Sunday morning that Lily unexpectedly broke the spell and thrashed her way to a first, shuddering, eye-popping climax.

"Good morning," Tom said when he'd caught his breath and some of his dignity.

Lily shut her eyes and clung to his shoulders, letting the last wavelets of shame and ecstasy fend for themselves. "Nobody told me about this," she breathed against him.

"Me neither," Tom said. "And on a Sunday at that."

She felt the laughter rumble through his chest, and she hugged him, and marvelled at the whimsicality of the world's working.

Except for Sundays, she had learned to discipline herself to the point where Tom would have to dissemble sleep as she started breakfast and then spring like a lynx at her when she bent to watch him wake. She soon learned, also, that a sudden giggle or a quick tickle under the arms deflated his desires or the fancies that fed them, after which they would tussle and cavort like a couple of cubs until one of them toppled onto the cold floor and breakfast-and-work reasserted their sober priorities.

Tom liked a heavy breakfast, so Lily cooked him back-bacon and eggs (provided by their own hens now), then joined him for toast, jam and tea. She didn't mind in the least that he was often grumpy in the morning, as she was accustomed to rising at dawn and found herself unable to contain her humming and good cheer. Besides, she wasn't eager to talk too much over breakfast since one of her recurring fears was that they would soon run out of things to say to one another, and barely a month had passed since the wedding. Once, walking through the oak-and-maple bush east of the house with the leaves crackling underfoot, Tom had turned to her and said: "Lily darling, if you and another just like you inherited the earth, there'd soon be no talking left at all." Aunt Bridie had been more blunt: "Child, you're about as gabby as a rabbit in shock." But she was sure Tom loved her precisely because she was such a good listener. After supper or after a stroll through the woods on Sundays, he loved to tell stories about his wild school-days, his escapades with Mad-Cap Dowling and his 'bunch', or the absurdities of the characters he'd encountered in the practice of law in Toronto. Not that he wouldn't try to prompt Lily herself to open up: "Why don't you ever talk about yourself? You don't have to *tell me all*," he would laugh. "I just want to get to know as much of you as I can. Love is sharing, isn't it?" So, on neatly spaced occasions Lily would take up the burden of story-telling, for that is how she conceived of these exchanges before a blazing fire or sometimes after early-evening love-making, with Tom puffing away at the clay pipe Aunt Elspeth had given him. As she cast back for suitable material she found herself selecting the happy, nostalgic events – her trips to Port Sarnia to peddle her fruits and vegetables, the eccentric Misses Baines-Powell, the boozy warmth of Char Hazelberry and her girls Betsy and Winnie, Mrs. Templeton's kindness, Bachelor Bill's antics. Moreover, she discovered that as she gathered momentum in the wake of Tom's encouragement, she was using voices and phrasings – even cadence and intonation – that belonged more to others than herself: Aunt Bridie, Bachelor Bill, Mrs. Templeton, Maman LaRouche. Finally she realized that she was reliving these simple events through a variety of lenses, so that they came out fresh, droll and unscathed by repetition.

However, for much of the time Tom continued to do a lot of the talking, and Lily found herself somewhat envious at the ease of his delivery and his confidence. Even now she had an intimation of the difficulty she would later have in this community – particularly a community of women where gossip, reminiscence, familial history and chronicles of daily life, and the comforting reciprocity of small-talk were the principal means of social intercourse and of dealing with the world at large. Here at home, though, during the honeymoon of their love, Lily discovered that while their talk for much of the time was being reduced, it was also being transformed into a much richer kind of communication, one at which she herself had always excelled. Over breakfast, for instance, Tom would raise his left eyebrow and Lily would fill his cup with tea. When he left for work they no longer exchanged 'Goodbyes'; Tom would embrace her with one arm (his lunch-box in the other) as if to say "It's all right, I'll be back soon", and she would briefly detain his outstretched hand and give it a single pat, intimating "I know you work hard, but I'll be here when you get back." So subtle had this range of gestures and subvocalizations become – even in a month or so – that one variation from the norm could be devastating. One day Tom seemed particularly grumpy over breakfast, and later when he put his arm around her on the stoop, she sensed the tentativeness, and as he withdrew it for her to bless, he pulled it back too quickly. Her caress ended in mid-air. It was like a slap in the face. But when he returned at dusk, he hugged her till he felt her forgiveness. The periodical evenings, then, when they exchanged narratives or speculated on the months to come were, like their carnal interludes, events of a discrete kind with their own indices of joy.

Being a man of easy words, Tom was also more easily stung by them than she was. "You've got a midget's tongue in your noggin'," Aunt Bridie would say to her, "but it's as tart as a bee-sting." To Uncle Chester she said one night: "She may not talk a lot, but when she opens her mouth it's trouble with two *t*'s. She'll rue that sharp tongue of hers one day, mark my words." Lily on the other hand was more hurt by an unthinking shrug of the shoulder than by any direct complaint Tom might make about his food or her not dressing up enough when Aunt Elspeth was "good enough to give you that trousseau of beautiful things" – *salvaged from the outcasts of the daughters or Shakespeare* she might have replied but bit her tongue, or more tartly still and more to the point: *I thought you preferred me dressed down.* I guess I've spent my life not reacting to words, she thought; I seem to prefer to observe them, absorb them, or find out what lies under them. But then women are better at absorbing things. And better, too, at waiting.

For Lily, much of that first autumn was spent in waiting of one kind or another. Tom would trudge in to the early dawn, and she would stand in the partly redeemed garden and watch him till he disappeared through the trees. There was lots of work for her during the day – cleaning the house, tending the last of their meagre harvest, 'doing down' some of the wizened cucumbers, baking bread, and then – in the afternoon hours – chopping wood, mending, sewing, and planning the robust suppers Tom required. Several times a week she went over to see that Old Bill was all right – taking him baked goods and vegetables, and seeing that his cupboard was stocked with staples. Old Bill was growing worse, it appeared. More and more he seemed distracted and forgetful. Lily often had to remind him that he had promised so-and-so up the line a day's chopping, or even point him in the right direction.

Nonetheless, it was a day of waiting. Tom was everywhere: in the sock she was darning, a sweater she was knitting him for winter, the food she prepared sweating over the stove in the warm Indian Summer, his smell in the sheets as she changed them. The memory of his lovemaking, his stark worship of her flesh and its unpredictable surrendering, rippled through her all morning long or ambushed her at odd moments. Or some imagined, interrupted slight would fester during the interminable hour when she would expect his figure to rise in front of the setting sun and bring with it the kind of healing possible only at the end of day. At least the waiting-out of his absence was over. But there were the other, more minute types of waiting – visible only perhaps to women. Waiting to see what sort of toll the labour-of-the-day had taken upon his body – sore back, bruised arms, crushed finger – and upon his spirit – fatigue, anger, rebellion – and for her the myriad adjustments to be made and tolerated and woven into the harmony of home. And waiting to see what response, if any, he might make to the signals she gave of her own needs – to be touched, to be soothed with stories, to be his accomplice in lust. If Tom were watching her in the same way, she could not detect it, nor, she guessed, would he ever know how much giving – beyond the visible – she was offering him each day. When Tom was late, compelled to work overtime as the ice threatened to close down the shipping lanes for the season, the waiting was unendurable. I have made him my life, she thought, and even though I ought to, I seem to have no regrets.

2

One day late in November, a week before the ice froze over the River and long after Tom had begun his nightly trudges homeward in the oppressive, autumnal dark, Lily sat beside her lamp and waited for her husband. Overtime again, she thought resentfully. For two nights in a row he had come home at eight o'clock too exhausted by a twelve-hour shift to eat his supper or do anything else but fall comatose on the bed. On the first occasion he woke her up and made perfunctory, routine love to her out of some misguided sense of pride or perhaps some ordinary sensitivity to her needs – she knew not which, though the result was a surge of depression she had not had since waving goodbye to her Aunt and Uncle in Oil Springs. The next night when she again felt his weary gesture, she murmured that her period was starting, and he slumped gratefully to sleep.

It was past eight o'clock. The fire was almost out below the congealing stew. Never had Tom worked this late. Even the Grand Trunk admitted the limits of exhaustion. Her only comfort was that one more week of this and Tom would be transferred to the new car-shops beside the round-house. Here he would ply his carpenter's trade, fixing broken boards in box-cars and other rolling stock. Lily had seen the glaze of defeat in his eyes these past few weeks, and she had done what she could. The labouring job, she recalled, had been all along a mixed blessing. Early on, it had put muscle on his fine frame and added a masculine air to his stride and his proud smile as he counted out the dollars on the table every pay day. Sometimes as he dressed in the mornings, Lily would effect a trip to the woodshed so that she could pause and watch him unobserved through the open door. Always he slept naked, and she would gaze – fascinated and ashamed – as he stepped into the chill air: clapping his arms across his chest like some haughty gorilla in a Congolese dawn, then pressing his palms between his legs like a little boy, and finally stretching for his undershirt so that for a second his body froze in a singular tableau of muscle and unreleased sexuality. She thought: he could crush me with one flex of a forearm. His man's instrument, driving towards its own pleasure, could sunder her like a peach, those tiger-teeth on her breasts could mangle without a flick of remorse. Then, his sandy curls just emerging from the undershirt, he would spot her and grin innocently, and be her Tom again.

But that body and that power had their own forms of vulnerability, she soon found out. Many an evening during late October she had repaired the damage of the day – rubbing liniment into his aches, putting plasters on his cuts and scrapes, and when those remedies failed, helping him forget in the yielding opiate of her flesh. But tonight he was not here to choose. It was at least ten o'clock by the moon's position in the southern sky. Perhaps he had been seriously hurt; barrels and cartons were forever toppling and injuring the men. Already two workers had had arms broken, and disappeared – without recompense, of course: an incapacitated man was a threat to the health of the company. My word, Lily thought, what will we do if Tom can't work? What we've always done: *get by*. I'm as strong as any man in my own way. He wonders why I don't wear those London ladies' dresses, but *I* don't. I don't have any flesh to fill them out. I've got no need for corselets, my backside is muscled, my hips are as lean as a boy's, my breasts small and unwomanly. My skin is sun-burned, my hair blotched. I felt a fool in that wedding dress even though it was made for me. I don't know for the life of me why a man as handsome as Tom would feel so passionate about me. But, then, I don't intend to ask him. I only want him to come home safely, now, in one piece.

During this reverie Tom came noisily up the path and flung open the door.

"Hullo, Lily love," he grinned loudly. "Think I might be a wee bit late."

Lily could smell the whiskey before she could rise to face him. She brushed by him to the stove, where she began poking aimlessly at the corpse of the fire.

"Ah, the little woman's saved supper for me. Thank you, darling. Thank you very much," he slurred. He stumbled, caught a wary table, righted himself, and managed to land one buttock on a chair. "If that's Irish stew, love, I can't smell it from here."

"The fire's out," Lily said, blowing on some paper in a pathetic attempt to rouse it.

"We worked some overtime," he said, "then Gimpy and Bruce and me went down to the bunk house to toast our good future at being dray-horses for the Grand Trunk Railway."

The kindling had caught, smokily, and Lily shook the flaccid stew across the stove-lids.

"*Stop that infernal racket, woman!*" Tom yelled. "I don't need anything to eat, can't you see that? Are you deaf and dumb? I'm *drunk*. Glorious and stupid falling-down *drunk!*"

Lily headed for the bedroom.

"Where in hell are you going now?"

"To get the bed-warmer," Lily said in a shriveling voice. "An' the liniment."
"*Come over here!*"
Lily stood her ground.
"For Christ's sake, woman, come over here before I puke in your stewpot!"
Lily edged over towards Tom. He was sitting with his head between his hands, shivering no doubt from the cold and false embrace of the alcohol. Lily stopped about four-feet away, near the stove, but she made no move towards the simmering stew. Tom coughed in a series of ghastly spasms, but when she started to assist, he raised a warning hand. Finally, taking a deep breath, he looked up at his wife, the one soul on this earth he would give his life for, and said through the press of tears: "For God's sake, Lily, why can't you get made or scream or sulk or curse me or hit me with a frying pan. I'm no damn saint, you know. I'm a human being." And to prove it, he sobbed into his hands and could not be consoled.

3

For a while Tom seemed pleased with his winter job. Since all the rolling stock in those days was made of wood and the climate of those times no less inclement than now, the repair business was secure and lucrative. In fact, the 'car-shops', as they were called, were to be a stable source of employment for the inhabitants of the Point for decades to come and eventually the centre-piece in the Great Betrayal of the 'nineties. But in the cold winter of 1861-62 there was no tunnel under the River St. Clair or bridge over it; the great highballs from the American mid-west thundered up from Chicago laden with corn and wheat and roared back with over-priced implements and calico from the factories of the eastern seaboard and now – thanks to the Grand Trunk – from the fledgling foundries of Montreal, Toronto and London. Situated on the narrowest neck of the mighty St. Clair, Point Edward had had its destiny already appointed: it was to be the gateway to a westering continent. However, by mid-December the River was jammed with ice, its own and that crushing down from the vast lakes above it. The same ice that silenced the freight-sheds – with steamers, paddle-wheelers, sloops and yawls alike out for the season – stilled the huge barges and ferries that wheeled up to a hundred box-cars a day back and forth between the two nations. Occasionally, during a January thaw or a freak contortion of the ice-pack, the fierce current would surge in the sunlight and a wild dash would be made across the divide – box-cars, deck hands and ferry-boat tilting, skidding and slewing in the northerly gales. On these occasions all the company hands were pressed into service, including the carpenters and joiners. The box-cars, many of them fully loaded, had to be pinioned to the ferry's deck with ropes and blocks. Often several of them pulled loose in the lurching swells, and the desperate crew would try to jerk the lines back into place, sometimes improvising an ingenious brace but mostly using the brute strength of their backs, while icy spray broke over them and jagged floes flashed by at every turn. That winter they didn't lose a single box-car. Three men were crippled, and dismissed.

Tom insisted that Lily "get out of the house" and come down to watch one of these adventures. Finally, she agreed. As it turned out, the crossing was relatively uneventful except for one stock-car full of chilled cattle (on their way to Flint, Michigan) that tore loose from its moorings and slid part-way into the water before it could be winched back into place. Lily could see the commotion and hear the vivid cries of the terrified beasts, but she lost sight of Tom, and when one of the men flipped into the water, her heart stopped. Seconds later the fellow was hauled back in on a safety rope, striking the deck with the thud of a frozen seal. In a minute he was up, and Lily was sure she could hear laughter; then the man who had engineered the rescue peered towards the wharf, towards Lily, and, she was certain, waved at her.

Tom escorted her up to the little tea-room in the grand concourse of the station. Lily made no mention of the luncheon she had shared with royalty in the adjoining ball-room, and certainly no one present on that occasion would have recognized her as the object of a Prince's attention. Lily was not thinking at all of such things. She was trying to understand the gleam in her husband's eye, the sureness of his stride beside her, the jauntiness in his voice. He paid no heed to the rope-burns on his hands as he sat across from her, with his tea cooling, and recounted every detail of the crossing and the rescue.

"We did it again," he said. "You see why I wanted you to come down and watch. I only wish I could bring you on board. You can't imagine what it feels like out there with the wind howling in your ears and the ice bouncing all around you like big boulders and the ropes stretching and everybody holding their breath waiting for something to break loose and knowing that one slip and you'll either be crushed to death or dumped into the drink and froze like a brick. Did you see me yank ol' Mason out of the pond? He's not thawed out yet!"

Lily said something she instantly regretted.

"How many of them cows died?"

4

By mid-January winter had settled in for a long stay. No ferries challenged the ice. The snow bloomed and foliated in the hardwoods behind the house and plumped the pines along the lane towards the Errol Road. It was a soft, blanched, filigree world that threw into sharp relief those few surviving angularities of landscape.

Lily found Aunt Bridie's quilting frame in the shed and, near it, a bundle of scrap cloth collected from the cast-offs of Sarnia's *petite-bourgeoisie*.

"What's that contraption?" Tom said that Sunday afternoon, glancing up from his labours over the broken chair.

"It's Aunt Bridie's," Lily said. "I'm gonna make quilts."

"Oh."

"An' sell them," she added.

Tom went back to his repairs, but soon he was seated behind Lily as her hands played with the myriad shapes and hues of cloth scattered on the floor, out of which she was improvising patterns later to be meticulously duplicated and sewn into their own interim kind of landscape.

"How do you know what goes where?" Tom asked quietly. Lily shook her head and continued. These were not like any designs he had seen at his Aunt's or the bazaars she sponsored. Lily herself didn't know what prompted her to select one piece and place it a certain way over another. She fiddled and nudged and tested – barely aware that some triangular, kendall swatch might have called to mind the corner of an elm once visible at a window's edge, a maple leaf quartered by shadow, or a slice of fern thirsty for light. Under her fingers' urging, bits of colour and cotton became half-cast suns, ovular moons, any-tree's boughs arched, corniced, magically magenta in the blue, blue shade.

The afternoon was gone. Tom was still there.

That night he slowed his love to the most forgiving of rhythms, and Lily – released into gratitude unencumbered by guilt or diminution of self – sailed at her lover's pleasure into the ecstatic and unconditionally sensate realm shared by fool-saints and madmen.

"You are a marvel," Tom whispered as if in church, his forefinger caressing the sweat from her brow. "You're so much more than I deserve."

"Don't say such a thing," Lily said when she was able to speak. "Ever."

Christmas had been one of those serene familial interludes appreciated in retrospect more for its happy interposition between events of more boisterous moment than for its own special ambience. A few days before the holiday two train-tickets arrived from Aunt Elspeth along with a touching invitation and word that Bridie and Chester were in London on business. Thus, Christmas day – its religious significance noted only, it seemed, by Mrs. Edgeworth and that "fine American gentleman" Melville Armbruster – was spent in feasting, toasting and voluable good cheer. Lily found herself tingling with a queer sort of pride at the sight of Aunt Bridie holding her own in such a household – her new clothes, serviceable yet always carrying one hint of extravagance (a bow at the waist, a tiny yellow hanky at the sleeve, a violet hidden among the folds); her upright bearing; her country speech undercut with wit and calculated humour; the ease with which the topics of the day were discussed and dissected. Mrs. Edgeworth was in awe; Armbruster was enthralled, kissing Bridie's hand with Yankee hyperbole, sliding her chair in at the strategic moment. Lily reminded herself that, after all, her Aunt had once been an urban woman waiting on table and attending *toilette* in the bed-chambers and anterooms of what passed for high society in the provinces. Notwithstanding, Lily was puzzled by the nameless resentment that welled up at such thoughts. Aunt Bridie, in turn, waited for news that Lily could not deliver.

Uncle Chester looked pale but happy and full of enthusiasm for his projects, as their drilling was to continue even through these winter months. Tom seemed in his element also, and after Christmas dinner he went up to his room and came down in uniform to entertain the guests with funny stories about the Battle of Montgomery's Tavern and other escapades of the Province's military past. Lily was seen not to be laughing.

When it became obvious that winter had closed the river traffic for some time to come, Tom was unable to disguise his frustration. Lily had picked up every tic of irritation, careful now not to overcompensate with excess cheeriness or solicitude, though she did kill one of the hens for Sunday dinner and stuff it with Tom's favourite dressing. He seemed pleased, and asked her to show him how the quilt was coming. Lily felt that she herself might have been the cause for Tom's irritableness because she had been having bad dreams for the past while, which left her tired and shaken. One scene in particular was powerful and recurrent enough to obtrude into her daylight existence. Try as she might, she could not erase it. She saw a clearing at night, engulfed by moon-shadow, and yet in the centre of it a sort of tower made of some ghastly, luminous metal reared upward on its own – stark and imperious; and then without warning the entire land-scape quivered epileptically, and the top of the tower burst apart in a cloud of spouting emulsive that might have been smoke or steam or some rabid foaming of the mouth; then all went black, the clearing empty and silent except for two objects that glistened in the grass like discarded wall-eyes.

One day in early February Tom came home late, and slightly drunk. He seemed cheer-ful enough, however, and beyond banging a pot or two for effect and serving supper in its lukewarm state, Lily did nothing out of the ordinary. Tom seemed amused by her performance, and later his love-making was as playful as it was prolonged. For two days thereafter he arrived home on time in spite of the near-blizzard that buried the hen-house and erased the international border.

"The men are organizing a sleigh-ride for the families and girl-friends," he an-nounced. "Next week. Be a good chance for you to meet some people."

Lily feigned interest, watching for signs.

The following evening he was drunk again and decidedly uncheerful. He uttered nothing decipherable, fumbled with his supper, and finally vomited all over the freshly-scrubbed floor. By the time she got it cleaned up and dampened down the two fires and freshened the chamber pots, Tom was snoring, fully-clothed and stinking on the bed. Lily slipped into her old room. The dreams were not happy ones.

At breakfast she said, "I'd like to go on that sleigh-ride."

The weather would be perfect for the 'tallyho', as the locals called it. The blizzard had been followed by five days of clear, below-zero skies; the snows had settled in the bush, been tramped smooth on the village paths, and deceived the eye into accepting the altered horizons. The night before the planned festivities was immensely beautiful. The stars shone with such clarity even prophecy seemed possible; the completed moon sailed alone, serene and sibylline. Seated on a stool near the west window, putting the last stitches into a quilt pattern, and gazing for long moments at the universe expanding beyond her, Lily was hardly aware that the evening had passed her by and her husband was not yet home.

It might have been midnight for all she knew when she saw two figures staggering through the drifts of the garden towards the house. The moon sketched their antic in cutting silhouette. They were singing a bawdy shanty of some sort, and laughing heartily as they pitched and yawed through the yard. The stranger, she guessed, would have to be Gimpy Fitchett: there was an extra stammer in his swagger. As they navigated in the general direction of the door – arms interlinked, voices joined in the hunt for harmony – Tom changed the tune, bellowing moonward in a mock-heroic Irishman's lilt:

> In Dublin's fair city
> Lived a maiden so pretty
> Her name was sweet
> *Lil-lee my love!*

At least they're happy, Lily thought, poking the fire into life and hoping for the best.

"Come on, duckling, come over here and say hello to Gimpy," Tom said as he tipped another dollop of whiskey into the coffee Lily had prepared.

"I said hello to Gimpy," Lily said. "Five times."

"I mean say *hello*, not just say hello," Tom said.

"It's okay, Tommy. Just take it easy, eh." Gimpy, more sober than when he'd first arrived, put a soothing hand on his buddy's shoulder.

"Don't tell me what to do," Tom said. "I get enough of that horse-shit at the shop all day long."

"Maybe some more coffee, missus," Gimpy said with exaggerated politeness.

"Are you gonna come over and say a nice proper hello to ol' Gimp or aren't you?"

"You oughta have some supper," Lily said. She stared at the lukewarm pots on the stove.

"Ain't that sweet now, Gimp ol' boy, the little lady wants me to have some supper. I think maybe she don't like me drinking coffee, eh." He winked with the wrong eye.

You go ahead, Tommy. But if it ain't too much trouble, I'd like a bit of that grub, ma'am. Smells real nice." He grinned, exposing his rotting teeth, and adjusted his stiffened leg, the result of an accident during his glory days as a trainman.

"If you like horseshit," Tom said, and started in with a barrack's version of Molly Malone:

> Oh her blooms were so ample
> The lads love to sample
> The sweetmeats of –

The grub which Gimpy alluded to had abruptly left the stove and was already on its way to an unexpected target. The potato-and-roast-beef hash struck the Irish balladeer flush on the tonsils. Tom blinked in disbelief as the sludge oozed onto his workshirt. Still dazed, he looked up just in time to receive the full venom of the vegetable soup. Before he could recover to mount any response, Lily had her boots and her coat on and was slamming the door with resolute finality. She heard the scuffling behind her, and as she marched towards the north-east woods, she heard their voices rise and then wane.

"Goddammit, you come back here, woman! You hear me? You goddam well come back here!"

"Now Tommy, Tommy. It don't matter none."

"You get your carcass back here or I'll –"

"Let it go, eh. Come on now."

"Lil-eee!"

"I think I better be goin'."

"You stay right here. Don't you move. I'm gonna fix her wagon good. *Lil-eeee!*"

Lily let a deer-trail lead her into the woods, into the silk oblivion of silence and deep snow. Here, thought was obliterated. She gathered the rhythm of her breathing from anonymity, she felt her heart pump with every stride, she let the wind-chill anesthetize the blood under her skin, she walked and walked till she found again some part of her being she could inhabit with impunity.

She found herself sitting in a tiny cove of snow along the frozen creek. Underneath the camouflage she was sure she could hear the water still moving, its voice faint, tinsel, palimsest – like a dolphin's song from a distant sea. She heard the weasel's ermine belly dragging at the burrow's edge, felt his ferret's glare on her heart. Then he was gone, scrambling underground, his ears picking up the same sound that made Lily leap straight up and freeze.

It was the crashing of masculine boots against the snow, punctuated by the snap of brittle twigs. Lily swung round in time to see a black figure staggering through the stark trees, its exaggerated shadow slashing and dissolving into the chiaroscuro of the moon-lit forest.

Quickly Lily picked up the deer-trail to her right and fled as quietly as she dare. Against the hammering of her heart she heard the attacking footfalls fade, and when she stopped – it seemed like miles later and after a dozen curves and backtrackings – the silence of the bush had reasserted itself. Who could it have been? A drunken railroader? Not Tom, that was certain. What did he want? She let the aftershocks shiver their way out of her system, and then took her bearings. To her relief, she concluded that she had ended up less than a quarter-of-a-mile from the house. What time it was she could only guess. She headed south-west towards the remains of the pinery.

A few minutes later she could see the opening in the trees ahead. She was almost home. The figure surprised her completely when it leaped out of the shadows to her left, flung its arms overhead like uncoordinated wings and stumbled forward, its eyes – if it had any in the black blur where its face lay – aimed at Lily. As she stood mesmerized, the creature seemed to half-fly, half-stalk towards her, the way a rabid crow might seize upon some fatally silver trinket. The cry that came from its torture was not a caw. It was a lament, a plea, a wail – and utterly human. The force of it stunned Lily so much that it was several seconds before the words were decipherable. By that time the creature was upon her, and she slipped to one side, grasped one of its wing-cloaks as it sank past her and tipped it into the snow, where it lay crumpled, as if dead.

Gently, Lily drew back the fur flap of the Russian helmet.

"I been lookin' everywhere for Violet. She's run off again. I been lookin' all over and I can't find her no place. You seen my Violet?"

"Violet's safe in London," Lily said, trying to get Old Bill to his feet. "Let's go home now."

"You ain't Violet? I can't go home without my Violet."

Lily ignored his desperate questions. She dragged him to his feet, and once up he seemed a bit more oriented. "I know you," he said. "You're Lily, Bridie's little orphan girl."

Lily forced his arm over her shoulder. He was not much taller than she but he was still muscled and a dead-weight. She gasped as the stench of his breath struck her: something besides his teeth had died in there. One step at a time, through drifts and over felled trunks with the zero-chill icing up sweat and saliva and stiffening muscle against bone, Lily carried Old Bill the four hundred yards to the edge of the expropriated property. It took close to an hour because every few steps Old Bill would sag, then suddenly straighten, like a corpse sitting up in its coffin, and howl into the muffling night his one-word lamentation.

The sudden illumination of moonlight-on-snow in the clearing seemed to jar something in Old Bill's brain, and he said softly to Lily, standing on both feet, "You're Lily. Are we home now?" And they tramped together towards his darkened hut. Lily saw a dim glow in the window of her own house as they passed it, but no sound carried outward. The chimney was smokeless.

In the candlelight, Old Bill's kitchen was dank, cold and stinking of rotted food, mould, urine, sweat. Her teeth chattering and her fingers numb, Lily found some bits of wood and paper, enough to get a smudged fire going in the ancient stove. She removed Old Bill's outer clothing, shielding herself from his asthmatic breathing with one forearm. From a pile in a corner she retrieved a wool sweater and pulled it around him like a shawl. He leaned towards the fresh heat as Lily rubbed his stiff hands in her own. The flesh on his face drooped, sallow and cadaverous.

"Ya' see, Violet ain't here. She run off again."

"When did you last eat anythin'?" Lily said, casting about for any signs of recent cooking. "Didn't you cook up that bacon I brung you Tuesday? You like bacon a lot."

"Violet always cooks the bacon," he said warily, his head slumping onto one shoulder.

Lily managed to get enough of a fire going to warm the pathetic little room and start a kettle boiling. She made some tea and then threw into a pot some of the oatmeal she'd brought over for him. But Old Bill was asleep, breathing in double-time. Lily put an arm around his neck, held his head back, nudged his lips apart with the tin cup, and gently poured hot tea into the sump of his mouth. His eyes opened part-way, and lolled expressionless. When the oatmeal porridge was ready, Lily tried to set the spoon in his hand but it fell away. He was helpless.

Very patiently she filled the wooden stirring-spoon with porridge and brought it to his lips. Old Bill's tongue circled it, then he spit violently, sending the stuff all over Lily. Again she brought a fresh spoonful to his lips, this time holding his jaws open and slipping the food in, then clamping them together until he gulped and swallowed. She felt him shiver, and knew it wasn't from the cold. Time and again she raised the spoon to his lips, struggled to establish a comforting – a pacifying rhythm. When or why she began to hum she didn't know, but she felt Old Bill's neck muscles relax under her grip, and then heard her own voice, deep and instinctive. At first there were no words, no need for them, but they surfaced on their own and bore no meaning beyond the memories of the time and place they evoked.

Hi diddle dum, hi diddle dare-o
Hi diddly idly, hi diddle air-o
Hi diddle diddly, hi diddle um

Old Bill settled into a profound, restorative sleep – snoring like an exhausted horse – his fingers, softened by the heat, curled in his lap like a baby's.

Lily didn't leave. She sat in that befouled and moribund room and thought of Maman LaRouche baking bread in the open-air oven; of Mama's hair unfolding in its last sunlight; of Old Samuel's flow of words as smooth as hickory smoke; of Southener's face as the sea-sands over it erased the sky; of Papa's grief as he stood fixed behind some tree watching his child dissolve.

When Lily came in, Tom was sitting in the glow of a single coal-oil lamp. He had heard her step in the yard and was fully awake to face her. He had plotted both an offense and a defense, but when her eyes came into the light, all premeditation was swept away. He wrapped her in his arms, even as he knew that forgiveness would never be enough.

Lying with her lover before their mutual fire, half-way between midnight and dawn, Lily Marshall told of the things she had dreamed, then remembered, then realized – the words uttered as easy as spider's silk towards a web. But even as the pain mellowed with each successive sentence holding out the possibility of accommodation, she sensed that she was passing the private burden of her own past to the public and unpredictable mercies of her husband. From this moment onward, these events of her history with their attendant joys and griefs would become part of the *materiel* of their relationship, unimmune to interpretation, retraction, emendation. By the time she'd finished talking, the fire was a low smouldering, the light in the room radiant.

Tom rose beside her, the quilt slipping off the bare flesh of his torso, bronzed and promethean in the demi-dark. His voice bore the cut of a scimitar. It hacked at the air.

"God damn me to hell, but if I ever get these hands on any one of the bastards that hurt a single hair on your head, I'll squeeze the living shit right out of them."

When he stopped shaking, Tom took Lily's hand in his sword-grip till it softened inevitable in hers.

The daylight brought them news of Uncle Chester's death.

5

On February 19, 1862 Hugh Nixon Shaw's drilling crew struck oil hundreds of feet below the gumbo surface of Enniskillen Township. It was to be the world's first recorded gusher. It was also the world's first uncapped wildcat. History does not record what the *enfant terrible* of Black Creek expected, but it was certainly not the gas-propelled blowout that shook the early-morning chill and began founting a hot, black syrup onto the snowscape around it. For three weeks the locals came and watched it spume, as the ground for miles around darkened and sagged. Oil was seen oozing in sticky rivulets towards Black Creek, where it slithered a ways in the ice and congealed. At last someone from Pennsylvania arrived who was able to improvise a method of staunching the wound. Meanwhile, thirty thousand gallons of oil were estimated to have been lost. Only temporarily, though, for in the spring an exotic sheen was observed on Black Creek and on the Sydenham River, and by early summer vast surfaces of Lake St. Clair and Erie glistened eerily. The world's first oil slick had been achieved.

The echo of that February blast reverberated far and wide, and the oil boom took on the intensity and surreality of a California gold rush. The town of Oil Springs would boast two thousand greedy souls by the year 1864 – before all boasting became bravado, the wells died of superfluity, and the rich and the broken departed on the same trains; already the steady, stable, Presbyterian good-sense of the burghers of Petrolia (five miles north) was reasserting itself. Ten years after the Oil Springs' boom, the last board of the last saloon was consumed in some anonymous hobo's bonfire among the twitch-grass and scrub hawthorn. Mr. Shaw was asphyxiated in his own well on February 11, 1863.

On the morning of February 20, 1862, Chester Ramsbottom shook the sleep out of his eyes and stepped out of his warm shanty into the winter air. He liked staying out here alone even though Bridie worried about his occasional blackouts and his desultory eating habits. Here he could think and dream and conjure his little plans for the days and weeks ahead – as he had done so many years ago before the fire had destroyed his shop and that part of his life.

The boys had already arrived; he could hear the steam-engine starting up in the drilling area, a cacophony he could never quite get accustomed to. Bridie and the Yankee fellow had gone over to the Shaw site yesterday afternoon and not returned. A loud blast had been heard from that direction and already rumours were flying. He could hear the excited buzz of the drillers under the relentless slamming of the bit into the rock fathoms below.

Chester decided to take it easy. He was a bit short of breath this morning and, besides, he was well ahead of schedule: they would have more barrels than oil by spring. The Millar brothers had been sent home to attend the funeral of their youngest sister, felled suddenly by diphtheria. He thought of Lily.

Near the lean-to which he had rigged up with boughs and furs, Chester built a slow fire, fried some bacon, found he couldn't eat it, and lay down with his head against the supporting tree with a buffalo robe across his knees. Despite the nipping air and the thudding monotony of the drill, he drifted into sleep.

Sometime about noon on that day, New York and Upper Canadian Oil Explorations also struck oil, at a hundred and fifty-two feet, a well only half the size of the Shaw strike, but a bonanza nonetheless. It too came with mere seconds' warning, the crew scattering at the hoarse roar of underground breath released after eons of capture, and falling stunned into the brush as the top blew off with a volcanic crack and thunderous remonstration.

Uncle Chester popped upright as if he had been struck by a dinner-gong – his eyes sprung from their dream, as wide and as vacant as a doll's, and blue as ball-bearings.

The funeral was held quite sensibly in the village of Petrolia where the Wesleyan Methodists has already erected a six-hundred-seat edifice to the glory of their version of the Divine Creator. Uncle Chester's mother had been converted, once, to this church. The good Reverend Kilreath reminded the tiny, shivering band of mourners of that fact, though he could think of few others to include in a necessarily abbreviated eulogy. The wind was cold enough to make a trespasser confess.

Lily stood beside Aunt Bridie and gazed at the casket ("Shipped straight from London by express," Armbruster said in the hushed shout he had concocted for these solemn moments) set over a pit gouged out of the frozen earth. Tom was a step behind her, ready to take her arm. Nearby she could feel the bewildered, estranged presence of the Millar lads, three members of the crew, and the owner-operator of the Lucky Derrick. Who else *was* there? Old Bill had sobbed like a baby when Tom told him the news, but an hour later he said, "When did you say young Chester was comin' back?" Lily had a feeling she was watching her own interment or that of someone who would become close to her far away in a future which seemed at this moment improbable.

Aunt Bridie as usual contained her grief. She did not weep. Lily saw pain in her Aunt's eyes only when she looked at her niece, her lips opening to say something (that might have – just a while ago – offered some solace, explanation, consolation even) but then closing again in reluctant resignation. But as the minister drew the cross of sand over the coffin-lid and murmured the final words 'dust to dust', Aunt Bridie went faint, slumping against Lily's grip. Melville Armbruster stepped forward and steadied her, and Bridie let her head fall gratefully against his shoulder. Lily scarcely noticed. She was staring at the only other gravestones in the newly consecrated grounds: three white tablets in a neat little row, each bearing the same name: "Morton: Elijah, age 6; Sarah, age 3; Joshua, age 1; taken into the bosom of Our Lord in September of the year 1861." Last fall's scarlet fever epidemic.

Behind her, Jimmy Millar sobbed without shame.

After the others had walked down to the carriages, Lily remained for a moment over her Uncle's grave. Here, alone with whatever remained of his spirit, she was able to find thoughts of her own to give some meaning to these windfall happenings. Something Old Samuels said came back to her – about how the soul leaves its earthly housing only to seek some finer refuge out there in those spaces and seasons and harmonies that all along gave it nurture and definition. What spaces, old man? What seasons for Uncle Chester? What sense did his flesh make entering this ground? Earth that was forest only a year before? Oil spouting from its slaughtered heart? Your hands, she thought, were a shopkeeper's hands, a woodcarver's at home with a doll's cradle or a toy gismo. What sort of place has been reserved for you, here?

Suddenly the incongruity of it all struck her so forcefully that Lily wanted to laugh, and she wanted Uncle Chester to join in and share the joke as he used to when Auntie wasn't looking. Finally, she was able to weep, but not before she heard herself say – to Old Samuels or to the benign divinities wherever they were skulking on such a macabre afternoon – "Does all loving end like this?"

"Are you all right?" Tom said, cradling her.

"We missed the tallyho," Lily said.

6

It was the kind of spring that made prolonged grieving seem an unwarranted indulgence. Crocuses and trilliums festooned the walkways in the woods and the more timid recesses beyond them. Winter wheat tossed its maiden-fuzz in the fields along the Errol Road. The earth turned easily under the spade. The air smelled of lilacs and orange blossom and wild crab. Along the creek banks, jack-in-the-pulpit promenaded his stationary lusts. The sun feigned perpetuance.

Lily found she did not have to seek out private moments or places – dust settling on the workbench, the tools untouched, *Last of the Mohicans* under the washstand with its marker still there – in which to remember and work out her grief. The natural rhythms of her day were conducive to the kind of semi-reflection best suited to recalling the aura of loss, shorn of all cutting detail. Moreover, in the evenings with Tom she was able to share some of these feelings, not always by direct discussion – though she noted how Tom contrived to raise Uncle Chester's name as often as he thought appropriate – but mostly by just having him in the room, breathing and caring somewhere beside her. It was a comfort she could not recall ever having had before in her life, and even as she allowed herself to soften into its consolation, she was only too aware of the evanescence of all things cherished-too-much.

On one of their long Sunday walks, Tom steered her gently through the windbreak and across the wide meadow towards the townsite. Though the only sounds were the cries of killdeer over the grass and the clarinet rasp of redwing blackbirds among the reeds of the marsh, Lily could see from the skeletons of half-built houses that dotted the horizon ahead, that on weekdays the air must have clanged with the sounds of progress. The prevailing wind no doubt had carried them away from her to the Lake beyond: she had not known. The transformation of the ordnance grounds was well under way, and it was awesome. Almost four blocks of dwellings were completed or under construction, mostly single-storey frame cottages set in civilized rows along the premeditated streets named for Queen and Empire. Along Michigan Ave., the only anomalous face among the royal suite, several brick buildings announced the arrival of commerce: a post office, Redmond's grocery, the Black Bass Inn and Tavern. Along Prince Street, facing the fields below the River, the first of the Grand Trunk hotels was rising brick by yellow brick.

"Three stories and thirty rooms," Tom said as they strolled by it. "The bigwigs will stay here, not overnight like they do in the Grand Station, but when they're assigned here for a sizable stint – also, I expect the boosters and carpetbaggers we see getting off the trains more and more." He grasped her hand tightly. "Come on over this way, I've got something to show you."

They walked east along Victoria where a block of cottages had been completed late last fall. Already the window boxes sprouted petunias and several families sat on shaded verandahs or under a leafy tree, digesting Sunday dinner and perhaps the sermon gathered in at one of the services in Sarnia. Tom stopped beside a cottage lovingly painted white, with a well-dug garden in back and a brand-new rose arbour in front.

"My boss's house," said Tom. "He rents it from the Company."

"Are all these Company houses?"

"More or less. It owns all the land, but it's selling lots to the business guys, and if and when you can afford it, you can buy your house and property back from them. They don't care as long as they make money."

"Oh."

"Well," Tom said, "do you like it?"

From somewhere inside they heard a baby squall and subside.

From the foot of Michigan Ave., these or any other lovers could look north to the dunes and the Lake beyond them, west to the River and Fort Gratiot on the American side, and south to the vast railway yards and the great wharf. What had, only two years before, been merely fields, swamps and a pinery awaiting the arrival of soldiers, was now an octopus of energy and purpose. The Grand Trunk station-hotel loomed highest against the horizon and around it sprawled the freight-sheds, bunk-houses, round-house, repair-or-car-shops, and seventeen sidings each with its own shunting locomotive. Along the wharf and further on around the bay, the masts, rigging and funnels of dozens of ships could be seen – schooners and sloops and steamers and mail packets and fishing trawlers. The flow of goods and people was phenomenal. No one but the workers, of course, stayed put; all else was in flux. Here, motion was money. Those who must pause – to rest or reflect or indulge illicitly – found their wants, however eccentric, amply provisioned.

As Lily and Tom walked towards the dunes, they noticed, where Prince Street ended in scrub-alder and sandburs, several makeshift shacks – like pencil smudges in the backdrop o a Sunday sketch. "Squatters," said Tom. Lily flinched.

Though no pact was formally signed, the accumulation of cash for an eventual move to the new village became a mutual endeavour for Tom and Lily. Tom worked as much overtime as he could get. Lily sold her quilts at the Baptist bazaar with the aid of Mrs. Salter. She extended the garden as far as their shrunken acre would go, and set up a stand at the end of the lane on Errol Road, now busy with traffic to the northern counties. She arranged for two township farmers to take some of the produce to Saturday market, though the profit was miniscule. They just could not afford to buy or keep a pony. Through the Misses Baines-Powell Lily got orders for quilts to keep her busy throughout the winter, as well as occasional requests for mind-numbing seamstress' work. Their lovemaking suffered somewhat as their enthusiasm became tempered by common fatigue (or worse: one weary, one not); by the counter-romance of sweat and pickling juice; by periodic martyr-philia; and the sheer exhaustion of possibility. Nevertheless Lily felt their love itself was prospering. All around them things were greening, lives were changing, and civilities multiplied. It seemed improbable that they too should not be swept along on such an irresistible tide of progressive evolution.

At night they continued to probe in one another the limits of trust, vulnerability and commitment – dimly aware that the flesh has its own disguises and dissemblings. Time after time Lily let Tom's seed wash over her blood-lit gill where she kept in escrow some tiny variant of herself awaiting rescue. And though Tom sat one August evening at the kitchen table and wrote out a letter to Bridie in Lily's words, then helped her read it back and watched her append her own name, shakily, to the bottom of the page – Lily had no news of the kind that might bring solace to a new widow. For weeks Lily waited in vain for a reply.

One evening early in September Tom did not come home for supper. He had assured her that there was no overtime work to be had for several weeks to come. At first Lily was worried, then annoyed, then scared. There was still a little daylight when she saw Gimpy's unmistakable silhouette crossing the fields towards the windbreak. She met him just as he was coming through the opening in the pines. She had known by the pace and tilt of his stride that something was wrong. His expression confirmed it.

"He's been hurt?" she said, trying to remember if the stove were okay to abandon as is.

Gimpy shook his head, out of breath, his eyes casting about for some place safe to rest.

"How bad?"

"Real bad, ma'am. We can't wake him up."

"Please take me to him," Lily said, tightening her shawl.

"You got a Bible?" Gimpy rasped, trying to be helpful.

Tom was lying on the dock in the open where a barrel of nails had struck him on the head and felled him more than two hours before. Someone had covered him with several dusty sacks. His eyes were seized shut, a dried trickle of blood in his hair and over his left eye. His breathing shallow but regular.

"We tried, tried everythin'," Bags Starkey, the foreman, said to Lily as she bent over her husband. "Cold cloths, ice from the barn, slappin' his face, pinchin' his cheeks, everythin'. He's been lyin' just like that ever since it happened."

"Where's the doctor?" Lily said.

"The one on Front Street, he's drunk an' can't be rolled over. The other one's out in the township somewhere on a call." He turned to the others for confirmation and consolation.

Lily leaned over the death-mask of Tom's face and spoke softly but clearly into his ear. "It's me, Tom. It's Lily. I need to talk to you."

The onlookers were startled, even moreso when Lily put her arms around her husband and pulled him into her embrace, sitting beside him and holding his dead-weight with her own litheness – her knees and thighs inadvertently exposed to the stevedores. Several looked away. Lily continued to talk. Lily continued to murmur sharply into Tom's ear until all of the men had averted their gaze, not knowing what to do or where to direct their pity.

Moments later, Tom's eyelids fluttered. He let out a huge, purging breath that sent chills up the spines of the men. Then a low groan as some particular pain was identified.

"Tom, I need to talk to you. I got somethin' important to tell you." She pulled his limp hand across her belly. "I got your baby in here," she said as shyly as she dare.

A month later, when a scar on his temple and a crackling good yarn were all that remained of Tom's brush with death, Lily was no longer lying.

Tom took the letter to Aunt Bridie – jointly composed – down to the Post Office in Sarnia so it would reach her more quickly. When he came home from work that same evening, he had a different letter in his hand. "It's from Aunt Bridie," he said. "I picked it up at our own Post Office a few minutes ago."

He began to open it. Bridie's familiar script graced the envelope. "What are you shaking for?" Tom said teasingly. "It's your *Aunt's* writing."

London, C.W.

October 20, 1862

Dear Tom and Lily:

Just a short note to let you know that Melville and I were married today at the Middlesex Court House. We leave tonight for New York. We've sold everything at Oil Springs. I'll send details from the City when we get there. Take care, Lily.

Love,

Bridie Armbruster

15

1

By the winter of 1862-63 the world, or that part of it that was interested to know, realized that both the Great Western and the Grand Trunk railways had come to stay in Lambton County. Each, moreover, despite other more commercial intentions or manifest destinies, was foreordained to establish in its feverish wake a settled and hopeful community. Port Sarnia, later Sarnia, had begun corporate life as a deep-water harbour on the Great Lakes system, but the welcome arrival of the Great Western had opened it up to the hinterlands behind it and sealed its fate as county town. Point Edward, on the other hand, was an afterthought of the Grand Trunk, a place where the workers and their burdensome families might live while temporarily serving the noble cause of British mercantilist expansion. Where houses were necessary, so were streets – of a sort – and these must have names. Of more importance certainly were the station-hotel itself, the construction of a chain of subsidiary inns of lesser comfort and repute along Michigan Ave. and Prince Street nearest the rail-yards, and the erection – in the spirit of free enterprise – of several capacious, rambling three-storey clapboard houses to serve as warrens for the dozens of often itinerant and less-than-trustworthy navvies and stevedores. By the spring of 1863 such facilities were well in place, along with several stores, two taverns, a post office and a barber shop. It was a motley, uncoordinated, boyish hamlet – mere appendage to a grinding dynamo – and unlike its ambitious neighbour, puffed with Scots' bravado and cunning, it had no sense at all of itself, of what it might become, of the pain it would eventually suffer merely to be born.

South of the border, meanwhile, a much more murderous rivalry was still being played out with gun and hacksaw, pomp and propaganda. Over there, truths, it appeared, were not self-evident: America's dream-of-Eden-regained had been momentarily stalled by fratricide.

"You must stop working so hard," Tom said.

Lily almost said: Well, it didn't do me no harm last time, but thought it best not to raise that topic at all. "I'll let you know when I'm not up to it. Besides, I ain't protrudin' yet." And she pushed him out into the overnight snowfall – the first of the season – and watched him plant his bootprints all the way up to the windbreak. Inside, she could feel the child clinging to her with both of its tiny hands.

Humming, doing a shy two-step, she cleared up the breakfast dishes, banked both fires, ate an extra slice of bread-and-molasses, and settled in beside her quilting frame. This one's for *you*, she thought aloud, whatever your name shall be. When her eyes grew strained and her leg cramped, she got up, put her coat and boots on, and walked across to Old Bill's.

"You gotta eat, Bill," she shouted in his ear, the steam of her breath filling the hutch. She wrapped his shoulders with one of his stinking shawls and got a bit of a fire going. He had not eaten any of the bread or salt-pork she'd left him.

Old Bill grunted something, but she was unable now to understand any of his words, if indeed any were intended. At times she thought he might be trying to sing or to recite some faded chant from his boyhood. He would open his mouth wide, his lips would freeze in some abbreviated contortion, and the air would sail up from his lung over the exposed chords and vibrate, it seemed, off the back of the tongue or the throat itself – for nothing in the front of his mouth moved. Yet out came an eerie, wavering note as if an errant breeze had blown over a castaway fiddle. Then he would reach out and clutch her wrist, hurting her. It was her turn to hum a tune from her own childhood – sweet, reminiscent, lullaby-low – until his grip softened and a mute rattle gathered in the back of his throat, and he would lie back in his chair by the window. Sometimes, then, he would eat.

Lily had never seen Tom so happy. On most mornings they woke up in the dark, made cautious illicit love, then rose together into the bracing chill of the cabin to light the fires and watch the sun animate the snow that lay its gratuitous beauty everywhere about them. On Sundays they would go for long walks into the village, along the River, up the beach and then across the oak-woods to Little Lake, where they cheered on the skaters, some of whom brandished curved sticks with which they relentlessly pursued a frozen horse-bun.

"I'd like to skate," Lily said and despite Tom's protestations and then his pleas, she did. Gimpy Fitchett borrowed several of the blades-and-straps from his cronies at work and all three of them made their maiden attempt the very next Sunday. Gimpy sort of levered his way along the margin of the circular pond as if he were rowing with one oar, managing to stay upright though deriving little other pleasure from the sport. Whenever he spotted Tom or Lily he would weigh anchor a moment, spin perilously as he waved and laughed, then laugh even louder as he retrieved his balance and continued his sounding of the shoreline. Tom slashed away with both blades, aiming himself at the centre of the ice-pond. He scissored, and fell on his nose. The blood had barely begun to congeal in the cold when his wings tangled and again he crashed spectacularly – this time on his nether side – to the unsuppressed delight of several young toughs out for an airing. Dazed and bruised, Tom slid across to the safety of the nearest snowbank, where he pouted, then looked up for Lily. She was floating twenty yards before him – a swan with its wings an inch from the glazed surface, its feathers lighter than breath cutting perfect curves in the glassy wake it left for all sckeptics.

Twice a week Lily walked into the village to do some shopping at Redmond's store and occasionally at Durham's Dry Goods. The store-keepers nodded pleasantly to her, often called her by name, sometimes chatted about the weather or the progress being made down 'at the yard'. Lily smiled a lot and gradually, as she assured Tom over supper, she was learning how to chat idly and even enjoy it. Twice the Grand Trunk had let the round-house and car-shop gang use one of the small rooms in the station complex for a Saturday night gathering, and Lily and Tom attended both parties. The men drank whiskey by the cup from a barrel while the wives and lady-friends coaxed them away to the dance-squares or bunched in corners gossiping. Tom kept himself free from the whiskey and danced with Lily most of the night at the cost of much barbed teasing from his mates. Lily talked to several of the wives whose husbands she felt she knew thoroughly. They seemed to like her. She was invited to tea. She surprised herself and Tom by going.

"Well, how did you like Maudie Bacon?" Tom asked, finally.

"She's very nice. She was raised on a farm in Moore township near Froomfield. She remembers the Millars. She was friends with the Partridge girls."

"So you did more than chank cakes and cheese?" he said, reaching for the muffins Lily had made on her return from the tea. "Well, this time next year we should be thinking about picking out a place of our own. Maybe in the same block as Maudie's. You'd like that, eh?"

Lily nodded. "First things first, though," she said, glancing down.

Lily went again to Maudie's house, a neat white cottage with a brick chimney and a fancy metal stove to keep it cozy through the winter. Maudie was friendly and incurably chatty; she quizzed Lily on every aspect of her history in Moore township, and to her surprise Lily found herself not only answering but volunteering extra detail, embellishment, even. The ladies – farm girls every one of them who had married young and willingly trailed their husbands to the excitement of the new towns – seemed particularly titillated by her stories about Old Samuels, Sounder and Acorn. Sometimes they tittered in the strangest places. Afterwards she felt vaguely guilty and if Tom asked her how her 'hen session' went, she would snap at him or keep a morose silence as long as she could bear to. He put her moods down to the delicacy of her 'condition' and kept smiling.

Tom smiled because he was genuinely happy. He liked the winter work, in part she supposed because he hated the slave-labour of the summers in the freight-sheds. But also because in the car-shops he could use his hands and his brains. He could work in concert with a select crew assessing problems and improvising solutions as the rolling stock limped or was dragged into their repair depot with all manner of fracture and trauma – after a rough stint on the open rails that now stretched from Portland, Maine to Chicago. And even though Tom would never be a master carpenter, he liked the challenge, the camaraderie and the unpredictability of their daily routine. And of course there were the thrills of emergency ice-jams, of which he was forbidden to speak over supper. And the son growing in her belly towards its own day.

Early in March, after Lily had complained of unusually severe cramps in her stomach, Tom arrived home from work with a brisk little man in tow.

"This is Dr. Dollard from Sarnia," Tom said, unwrapping him from his black beaten-lambswool coat and looking for an appropriate place to install it.

"How do you do, Mrs. Marshall," the doctor intoned absently, waving her to a nearby cot.

"I've had some crampin', doctor. Maybe somethin' I ate."

Dr. Dollard ignored this and all subsequent remarks from Lily and from Tom who was determined to be helpful. Primly he drew Lily's skirt and half-slip away to expose the stretched skin beneath. He tapped, tamped, and plumbed, giving out every once in a while significant but untranslated 'ahs' and 'hmmmms'.

He wheeled around to Tom.

"What is it?" Tom said, afraid to look at Lily.

"Your wife is at least seven months pregnant," he announced. "She is not eating enough to sustain two life-systems, hence the stomach cramps. She is getting too much exercise, hence the general faintness and the wan complexion. I recommend a bottle of *Ayer's Sasarsparilla* for the stomach. That'll be sixty-three cents for the medicine and a dollar for the visit."

Tom blanched.

"Pay me when you can," Dr. Dollard flashed an avuncular smile at Lily. "The young lady's health is the main thing. When she goes into labour, send a message for me, day or night, and I'll come straightway. You know where I am." He put a bottle of patent medicine on the table, shook Tom's hand, rescued his coat and decamped.

"Tom," Lily said, waving off the *Sasarsparilla*, "I want you to promise me one thing."

"Anything," he said.

"I want a midwife for this baby."

By the next day Lily was feeling fine. She got some food into Old Bill and walked him out to his privy and back. When he spotted the medicine bottle in her apron pocket, he grunted avidly. She left it beside him on the arm of his chair and by the time she got the door jammed shut, he had consumed it all. I hope he's not pregnant, she thought, skipping through the snow to get the baby's attention. It responded with a surly kick. No sense of humour, she laughed, and stretched her lungs against the brisk late-winter air.

Tom was waiting. "Your informants are correct," he said. "There *is* a local midwife. I went to see her. She said she knows where we live. In fact, she seemed to know all about us. She'll come when you need her."

"Thanks," Lily said. "But you look worried. Somethin' wrong with her?"

"She's got a terrific reputation around here," Tom said slowly, selecting his words with care, "but she lives down there in that place, you know, down past Prince Street towards the dunes, where the squatters are."

"Oh."

"She lives in a sort of – well – a hovel."

"You don't think she oughta come?"

"I didn't say that," Tom said and his glance told her: *don't remind me, I know, I promised*.

No more was said on that particular subject.

2

On the first day of spring the screw-prop grain-carrier *Lake Erie* nudged its bulk through the scattered ice-floes of the River St. Clair and docked at the Point Edward elevator. A day later Tom was moved from the car-shops to his summer job in the freight-sheds: lugging crates from ship to box-car and box-car to ship. The new regional manager, Warden Hargreaves, who set up temporary personal quarters in the luxury suite of the Queen's Hotel on Prince Street, promised Tom that there was a good chance he could be made part of the permanent repair crew by the following spring. That hope and the more certain promise of a child to carry on his name buoyed his spirits considerably. So much so that only Lily could detect the minute signs of tension and strain that habitually afflicted him at this time of year. Although her own back had begun to throb – especially after a full day over her quilting (she'd sold two to Mrs. Salter, and Tom had put the cash in the Sarnia bank) – she spent the evenings of early April rubbing liniment into Tom's back and arms. Outside, the snow-flushed creek and sudden freshets chattered their way across the wakened landscape.

"We oughta start diggin' the garden," Lily said.

"We don't need a garden this year," Tom said. "And next year somebody else can worry about this place. Don't you go near it, you hear?"

Lily heard. Nonetheless, she did slip out as soon as the sun was up and burning through the green gauze of the trees and bushes and shrubs and looping vines. But the baby had dropped and she felt as wobbly as a pear, so she merely pruned the perennials as best she could and scraped away the detritus from the fall harvest. No spading, she thought, I've got to be very careful. Unless I can rouse Old Bill to some work. She could tell by the sun that it was barely mid-afternoon. She turned and started over to Bill's hut when her eye caught a movement near the windbreak. It was Tom, coming at full tilt across the field which lay between them and the village proper. She met him, breathless, at the tree-line.

"It's Bags Starkey," Tom said. "A crate carrying half a locomotive boiler fell on his legs. Crushed both his feet. He's bleeding real bad. They don't want to move him too far. They need sheets for bandages."

Lily was running across the dead garden towards the house. "For God's sake, Lil!" Tom yelled, but he fell to his knees, panting helplessly, tears spurting from his eyes.

Lily rubbed and rubbed as if the ache might take advantage of the slightest let-up on her part. She lay her breasts – engorged and twingeing not unpleasantly – against the small of Tom's back and listened to his heart thumping.

"He's alive, but that's about all you can say. He wasn't supposed to be in there lifting, but the crate was badly built and it got stuck, and ol' Bags must've thought he was still a spring chicken the way he tore into it and swore away at us till the damn thing came loose, and buried him. We had to get it off with a block and tackle, and not once did the man cry out."

"Don't Tom, please."

"*I gotta talk about it, woman!*"

Still, he didn't turn to look at her, and when her hands reached for the ache between his shoulders, he leaned back into them. "Both feet crushed like tomato pulp, blood was squirting everywhere. Gimpy was sick all over himself. But Bags is a tough bugger. He's alive. And the doctor says he'll likely have both his feet, though the bones won't ever set straight and there's still a chance of gangrene. His cousin came down from London; they're holed up in a dirty little rooming house on George Street. We went to see him today. The company's gonna dock us a day's pay, but we went anyway. *Fuck them!*"

"We could take up a collection or somethin'," Lily said very quietly. "I got lots of preserves left."

Tom didn't answer. Then he said, "He's got no job, Lil. They told him yesterday. He begged them for an office job, he swore he'd be better in a month, he'd be able to get 'round on crutches, he knew the work, he'd been with them for six years, from the very beginning. Warden Hargreaves said he was sorry but he was only carrying out company policy, orders given way over his head and all that shit. You know the line."

Lily nodded. A thrill of fear shot through her.

"I've made up my mind," he said. "I'm going to see Mr. Warden Hargreaves tomorrow. In his office. I'm going to get Bags Starkey's job back."

"Don't go," Lily said.

"I've got to. I don't expect you'd understand, but this is something I just *have* to do. If I don't, I won't be able to live with myself."

"I know that," Lily said. "I know why you have to go. And I know what'll happen. I'm only askin' for the baby's sake, not my own."

"Nothing ever happens in this world," Tom said angrily, every trace of gentleness erased in his gathering rage, "because nobody is willing to stand up and be counted. Nobody wants to fight. *Nobody!*"

Lily wanted to reply, but she held her peace. She might have said this: *there are many ways a body can fight, though I don't know of any ways of winnin' – yet.*

"Well," Tom said to her, his fury undiminished, "I got the satisfaction of telling that cowardly bastard what I thought of him." His hands shook as he poured himself a mug of cold tea. Lily was knitting in the rocker by the south window. She felt Tom's stare on her, keen as an accusation.

"An' he fired you," Lily said without emotion.

"He certainly did not." Tom pounced on her presumption. "I put the fear of the devil himself into that yellow-livered little weasel. He didn't dare fire me. I told him where he could shove the Grand Trunk."

Lily continued, starting a new row after re-counting her stitches.

"He only had the guts to suspend me," Tom announced triumphantly, and Lily heard him scrabbling under the sink for the big jug. "I got a free holiday till October," he laughed. She heard the gurgle of raw whiskey. "Can't do without me in the car-shops. What do you think of that, eh?"

What Lily thought of it mattered little. What it meant was that without a garden and at best a bit of casual work for Tom over the summer, they would have to spend every cent of their savings just to survive. There would be no white-walled cottage in the new village. Lily continued to knit.

"You keep your nose clean all summer, he tells me, and I'll let you back next winter. Sure, what he means is I kiss enough company arse, they'll let me keep on working for them. Who knows, maybe I'll get good at it, eh? *Eh?*"

Gimpy arrived shortly to chaperone his friend through the bleak evening ahead. Lily went to the bedroom and lay down. Even with the comforter wrapped around her, she found herself shivering. She caught no words from the other room, only low mutterings and occasional jabs of sound accompanied by the steady clink of crockery. With her teeth chattering she rose in the darkness, fumbled under the bed till she felt the leather sachet in her grasp, opened it and drew into her hand the familiar talisman. She left it burning there till its allusive warmth spread through her whole body and beckoned sleep her way. When she woke, the magic jasper lay on her bare throat, beating there like a hummingbird's ruby heart.

She stepped into the quick heat of the big room. The kitchen stove throbbed jovially. Tom was standing by the door, fully dressed, his walking boots agleam. In the crook of his arm lay the twelve-gauge double-barrel.

"Where're you goin'?" Lily asked.

"You all right? You had a lot of covers on you."

"Where're you goin' with that?"

He grinned, and she saw with relief the blend of daring and reserve she so loved and trusted. "I'm going hunting," he said. "Rabbits. Got to put food on the table, now don't we?"

With the baby due in a few weeks, Tom tried very hard to adjust to the situation he had put himself in. Lily sensed that his resentment was directed only partly at the Grand Trunk. He was positively heroic in his attempts to keep himself busy and useful. He went hunting up in First Bush almost every morning. He helped Gimpy and Maudie's husband, Garth, trap a few tardy muskrats down along the verges of the swamp. Their skins hung stretched and reeking in the little barn beside the latest slaughtered cotton-tail. He walked over to Sarnia to hang around the boiler works or one of the sawmills in hope of picking up some casual and very menial labour. In these ways he managed to keep out of the house till suppertime and arrive home with a Tom Marshall grin on his face. Sometimes she would stretch out on the cot after supper, and Tom would run a caressing hand over her belly for what seemed like hours on end, neither of them saying a single word, the slow sunset easing darkness into the spaces around them, as if a spell was about to be cast and auguries about to be tested on a sympathetic wind. This baby was even more active than the first, throwing tantrums of fist-and-feet in several directions and at times of its own choosing. Her back ached with the weight. It's all right, she kept telling it – him – you just keep kicking all you want. I want you big and strong and alive.

While they were eating supper one evening early in May, Gimpy arrived with a piece of paper stuck to the fingers of his right hand. "It's a telegram," he said. "Come in on the telegraph 'bout an hour ago. I told Farley I'd bring it on up here. I thought I'd better."

From the last remark, from the anxiety on his face and his reluctance to hand over the fretful paper, Lily was certain that he had seen the news and that it was dreadful.

"It's your Auntie," he said, looking away.

Tom ripped the envelope from Gimpy's hand and tore it open.

Seven months and not a word from Aunt Bridie. For weeks Lily had waited; she had gone to the post office whenever she was in the village, hoping not for an explanation but simply a word, a greeting from afar, a wave from some other life in which she was still, for a while at least, Aunt Bridie. But no news of any kind had come, and the postal watch ended. I don't even know where you are, she thought not without bitterness; I can't comfort you if you need me, I can't give you a better reason for living, I don't know what to do with this stored-up, useless love.

Tom was mumbling over the words to himself. She saw him go pale, and while her heart sank, she knew perfectly well that her Aunt was not dead. All winter long, she recalled, I've heard your voice in the silences of my morning kitchen, in the hollows of my sleep, in the dream below my dreams – not as it used to be, brave and clear and certain, but very very faint, a voice calling out yet too weary or bewildered to compose a full cry for help, too proud ever to slip into whimper. You are alive, Auntie: *what are you trying to tell me?*

"It's Auntie," Tom said. "She's had some kind of attack. She wants me in London, as soon as possible."

Tom's letter from London, which Gimpy helped her decipher, said that he would be away at least a week. But she was not to worry, as Aunt Elspeth had merely had a good faint one morning and fallen down against her bedstead. She had a nasty bruise on her temple, was as forgetful and cheery as ever, and determined to spoil him and Lucille, now her sole companion. She was wildly excited about the expected arrival and bent on living long enough to see it heading a regiment someday. The doctor reported to Tom that she may have had a mild stroke but did not see any cause for alarm. In the last sentence – delivered with a wondrous blush from Gimpy – Tom urged her to cross her legs tight till he could get home.

Lily herself was not concerned about actually bearing the baby. Gimpy came for a while every afternoon and Maudie brought her some goodies one morning and helped a bit with the house. Lily was having some trouble getting to sleep, and when she did, the dreams that assailed her from the deep part of night left her sweating and exhausted in the morning. Something was coming apart. Tom should be here. She needed him close. She felt he had to be close when the time came. Every night since Bags' accident Tom's body had coiled away from her, a trigger of muscle without a target. If anything were to happen to Aunt Elspeth…If something were to happen to the baby…She just remembered she didn't even know the midwife's last name.

The night before she thought Tom might be coming home, worn out and fretful, Lily surprised herself by falling into a dreamless sleep. The evening had been very warm for mid-May, the air was suffused with lilac and wild-apple blossom. She lay down on top of the comforter with only a cotton nightshirt on, gazing at the swell of her flesh until sleep relieved her of all speculation. Some time towards dawn the wind shifted to the east and blew with the usual abandon of a spring storm. When Lily woke, the sun was up but smothered by a skyful of nimbus cloud bullying its way westward. The wind howled out of its secret, zigzagging centre and roared through the pinery and fern-leafed hardwoods with the hoarse clamour of a doomsday horn. She sat bolt upright. Her nightshirt was a sail. Her sweat cooled and receded. She punched her son; he punched back.

Before she was certain she was even awake, Lily found herself outside. The nightshirt flapped about her waist as the storm's breath claimed every part of her nakedness. She felt her nipples sprung like crocus-buds under snow. She felt the obscene, clammy, overweening presence of something so vile even the wind disowned it and the rage of rain that now struck her could not assuage or cleanse.

Soaked, shivering, wild with dread – she seemed to be running without any sense except that of flight itself. Within seconds she found herself standing in front of the battered door of Bachelor Bill's hut. She stood there until her breathing came back to normal, and longer. A deep calm pervaded, body and spirit. It's happened, she thought. She pushed the door aside and went in.

Bill was dead, though she had to walk over and touch him to confirm her fear. He was sitting where he always did: in his chair by the south-east window – the only window – with a clear view of the lane, his neighbour's cottage and the rising sun over the tree-line. His eyes were wide open, full of arrested anticipation, and aimed down the lane that ended at the Errol Road, as if he were at any moment expecting the arrival of someone dear to his heart.

Lily was still sitting by the stove wrapped in a shawl and wondering if she could walk all the way to the village through the gumbo left by the storm, when she heard Tom's call from the road. She went out to greet him, embarrassed by the flush of joy she felt but unable to stop herself from trotting awkwardly towards the bend beyond the gate. What she saw stopped her breath. Tom was striding down the lane waving to her, and behind him, skipping to keep pace, bounced a slight female figure, also waving. Lily waited until they were almost upon her before she allowed herself to believe it was Lucille.

Bachelor Bill, as they were to always remember him, was buried in the public cemetery of Sarnia less than half-a-mile from the property he had occupied so long no one could recall him ever not living there. Tom had sent a telegram to the asylum in London, hoping they could find some way to tell Violet. In the meantime the sheriff's bailiffs arrived to claim the valuables. It appeared that Bachelor Bill had not paid his taxes with the money Tom gave him and that the Grand Trunk bought him out for the sums owed. Warden Hargreaves, it was said, had personally intervened to keep the acquisition quiet and permit the old fellow to live out his days in security and dignity. The day after the funeral Tom received word back from the authorities in London.

"Violet's gone," Tom said. "It says here she ran off three days ago and they haven't found a trace of her anywhere."

3

Tom informed Lily that Aunt Elspeth was well enough to travel to Toronto to make an extended visit to the Colonel's sister-in-law, long a widow and now, it seemed, quite frail and in need of companionship. "I haven't laid an eye on her for ten years, since the funeral, but the dear old soul isn't strong, you see, so I really can't say no." Hence, Lucille was to be despatched, at great personal sacrifice, to oversee the baby's entry into the world, after which she was to come to Toronto and escort Aunt Elspeth back to Lambton to inspect and approve.

Lucille was a joy and a wonder. Freed from the supervisory affection of Mrs. Edgeworth, she became a volatile blend of wood-nymph and street-urchin. She never walked where she could flit, saunter, glide or dart. She assaulted the objects in a room with her flung glances: "Oh, Lily, what a *beautiful* quilt!" "What a sweet little tea-pot!" "Where on *earth* did you get calico with them colours!" She filled the kitchen and big room with a quarter-acre of lilacs stripped from every lane within a mile's radius. They strolled and they tumbled (one of them) through the May woods searching out the red-tongued trilliums hidden amongst the ivory millions carpeting the forest floor. Lucille picked up a dazed garter snake, made as if to fling it at a giggling Lily, then abruptly dropped it down the front of her own dress, after which she engaged in an hysterical jig of exorcism and mock sexuality. When she was excited, which was a good deal of the time, she lapsed into a headlong patter where French and English vied for supremacy, to the detriment of sense but the sheer delight of any listener. In the midst of such paroxysms, Lily would suddenly put two fingers across Lucille's lips and the girl would stop in mid-syllable, her eyes bulging and an enormous giggle burbling in her throat.

"My turn," Lily would say, and begin to talk. They told each other the stories they had rehearsed back in London, but now with more flair, more dazzle of detail, and a lot less crippling veracity.

"My *Maman* had a lot of kids, you know. She swell out like a pumpkin every spring and *woosh*, down she go every September. But Maman always wear a big dress, like a tent, an' so we never got to see what shape the pumpkin take under all that. Always I wonder, eh?"

Lucille and Lily lay at ease in a grassy hollow in the hardwood forest not far from the brook. The sun was morning-mellow. Both girls had their skirts thrown back far enough for it to bless the skin all the way to the thigh. Languidly, with no particular forethought, Lily unbuttoned her skirt and pulled the cloth back to expose a bevelled expanse of skin.

"You gonna warm him up a little?" Lucille said.

"It's *my* turn today," Lily said, widening the breach.

"You gonna toast that bun-in-the-oven!"

Lily closed her eyes, trapping the sun under the lids.

"I never did get to see one of them kids in there," Lucille murmured, her fingers already treading across the rippled drum of flesh. "Hey, I can feel its head. I can!"

Lily shifted slightly to one side.

"Hey, he kicked me! I felt him! The little bugger!" Lucille's fingers softened, they lathered and soothed. "You like that, little fella? You like this? Eh?"

A voice murmured sleepy assent.

Lily eased herself up, her clothes falling back into place. She took Lucille's hand in hers and moved them both up to the girl's cheek. The tiniest pressure tipped her back onto the grass. Lily brushed Lucille's hair from her forehead, then with utmost tenderness stroked the sunlight across her brow, along the edges of her smile, in the furrows of her throat. Then she watched her own shadow fold across the girl's face as she leaned over and kissed her as lightly as a butterfly touching milkweed.

"I ain't never had a man yet," Lucille said.

Since the baby was late – it was already the first week in June – and Lily seemed to spend much of her day with Lucille, Tom took more and more time away from home. He hounded the numerous small factories in Sarnia but got precious little work for the hours he put in to the search. Though he refused to admit it openly to her, Lily knew that somehow the word had been passed along from above and was being routinely obeyed. Even the Great Western, avowed enemy of the Grand Trunk, could find no spot for an experienced hand. When Tom took up the spade and headed into their garden, she knew for certain that he too had given up.

But he was still her Tom, a man of spirit, and she loved him till her heart ached whenever he came into the kitchen smiling and teasing 'his girls': "Gimpy and the fellas think I got a harem up here!" he'd say, leering at Lucille. "Well, ain't ya'?" she'd say right back. Or he'd come across to Lily at the stove, wheel her about for a kiss, give her belly a lustful bunt and say, "You'll have to lean forward, missus, there's somebody standing between us," and Lucille would pretend she'd heard the line for the first time and topple back into Uncle Chester's chair as if she'd been felled by an axe. Later, in the gloom of dusk Lily would watch him hacking at the clods in the garden, harrowing his hands twice as badly as the tough heart, trying as always to overwhelm it, or cow it with a quixotic show of force. Come on, you little urchin, she'd say to her full-time lodger, we can't wait much longer. On the fifteenth of June he walked up the Errol Road and hired on with the first farmer he saw behind a team of plough-horses. Two days later she saw him sneak into Benjamin's stall where he kept a jug of soul-restorer poorly hidden. When he came to bed in the middle of the night, he curled his body behind hers as close as he could fit it, slid his scarred hands around her breasts, then let them drift down to assume some other shape more promising than their own. "I do love you," he whispered.

After breakfast that Sunday – while Lucille was helping Lily with the dishes and mimicking her Maman's defense of the 'lumpy' suitor who owned a whole township next to them and who had heroically offered to readjust his 'sights' in order to secure the services of a 'well-brought-up' farm girl – Tom poked his head into the room and said, "There's horses in the lane." Still wiping their hands on their aprons, they got outside in time to see a matched team of Belgians hauling behind them an over-size and vacant buckboard very like the one used to deliver beer barrels from the new brewery. Only a driver, swatting occasionally at the reins, and his assistant, with both hands grappling the bench beneath them, managed to steer the vehicle anywhere close to a single direction.

"Whoa! Gee! Haw! Whoa!" yelled Gimpy Fitchett with a slap of leather on leather.

"Ya-hooo!" yelled his partner, sparking the horses to greater effort.

"Whoa back! Whoa back!"

Fortunately the veteran team had had enough brisk exercise for a Sunday morning and drew themselves sedately up before the gate of the Marshall place.

"Where in sam hell did you learn to drive horses?" Tom hollered as he dashed across to the visitors.

"I worked for a week in an abattoir," Gimpy said. "Good mornin', ladies. I hope you'll pardon the intrudin', but me gentleman friend here felt the need of a little airin'."

The gentleman was Bags Starkey. Thin, wan, shivering in the gathering heat of the day – he unhooked his hands and flashed a huge smile at Lucille and Lily as they came over to the buckboard.

"Mornin', Mrs. Marshall, Tom. I don't believe I've had the honour of –"

"Lucille Verchères," Tom said.

"Ah, ça va bien, ma'amselle? "

While Lucille blushed and attempted to find a dry hand for him to kiss with a flourish, Lily and Tom tried not to look at his feet, or rather the white blobs of bandage that had been wrapped around them and that, except for the stipple of dried blood, might have been mistaken for giant baby booties.

"This here's Bob Starkey," Gimpy said. "He speaks English, too."

"Just call me Bags, everybody does except my mother," Bags said. "Could we interest anyone in a drive through the countryside? Best of accommodations."

"We got Barney and Sue here for the whole day," Gimpy said, never taking his eyes off Lucille. "We're tryin' to dry 'em out."

"Might even rouse the interest of someone we're all waitin' to meet," Bags said, gripping the bench with his left hand so he could teeter over to wink in the general direction of the yet-to-be-born.

"Why don't we take *you* for a ride," Lily said.

Tom was staring uncomprehendingly at Bags' crushed feet.

Bags fitted very nicely into Uncle Chester's wicker wheelchair, retrieved from the wood-shed, dusted off and padded out with several pillows, at least one for each of the blobs to rest upon. With Gimpy pushing and Tom stationed at the vehicle's left wheel, Bags, his lady companion and her duenna promenaded past the garden, where they admired the fine froth of early radish and the flutter of escaping crow and starling, while the veery in the bush offered his see-saw siren in lieu of a melody. They whirled at the barn and headed back by an even more circuitous route. "Quite splendid! Simply charming!" Bags shouted, "And only the servants live there, you say!"

"*Oui, capitaine-le*" Lucille giggled, skipping to keep up with the postilion's pace.

"*Wee, wee!*" Gimpy yodelled, accelerating to break Tom's grip.

"Wheee!" called the lone rider.

Bags pulled a mouth-organ from his back pocket, wincing a bit as one of his legs hit bottom, and began to play a jig, sprightly and yet ever so delicate, as if the notes had hopped and glided to their independence only after being pummelled through silk. As Bags' eyes dances and pursued them, Lily and Lucille joined hands and performed on the lawn of their dooryard a somewhat gallic and oblong version of the Irish national ditty. Suddenly the music got louder and faster, the notes ripped at the air, the girls' feet began whirling and pointing, bruising the blank spaces around them, maddened by grooves just beyond gravity – till Lucille let go and Lily went sailing backwards to make an ungainly two-point landing in the long grass by the stoop.

Lily popped up, laughing and panting, and brushed Tom's hand aside. She and Lucille fell giggling into one another's arms. Gimpy blushed to his Adam's apple, with his lame leg still pumping to the echo of the beat. Then everyone stopped.

Bags had begun to play again: a soft, melodious air that sang wordlessly of something lost and green and never-again-to-be-possessed. Part-way through – no one really noticed when melody and lyric were as seamless as bunting – a tiny voice joined in and made the morning complete:

> *Un Canadien errant*
> *Banni des foyers*
> *Un Canadien errant*
> *Banni des foyers*
> *Parcourait en pleurant*
> *Des pays étrangers*

Bags Starkey smiled again at the ladies, winked at Tom, and then waved one brave hand from his perch on the buckboard. Gimpy whipped the horses to life, Lucille's kiss still burning on his cheek. The rig clattered down the lane and muffled all farewells. Just before it disappeared into the trees at the big bend, Bags hunched over, as if he'd taken a cramp, and let his head hang helplessly between his knees.

Lily squeezed Lucille's hand. Then she looked for Tom. He was stomping away from them – in the direction of the barn.

"You better fetch Tom," Lily said.

Lucille went white. "*Le bébé?*"

"Uh huh. Tell Tom to get the midwife. It's not gonna be long."

"He's gone, Lil. I don't want to wake you up for supper, you look so peaceful –"

"Where'd he go?"

"Off to the town, I think. Oh, Lily he was –"

"Don't start cryin' on me," Lily said. "Please listen. Stoke up that stove real good. Fill the water tank all the way up. Get out that supply of clean flannels I put in the hamper. Then go into the village. Ask around for Tom. If you can't find him, see if you can find the midwife."

Lily let out a wrenching cry that caused the saucepan to leap right out of Lucille's hands. "What the matter? *Mon Dieu, mon Dieu!*"

"It's just a labour pain," Lily said when she could feel her heart again. Sweat dropped off the end of her nose. "The little bugger wants out."

Lucille didn't laugh.

"But you know all about this," Lily said, "Your Maman had a dozen after you."

Lucille was fumbling with the hardwood faggots, spilling them on the floor in front of the stove. "I don't know nothin' about it at all," she whimpered. "I run off an' hide in the woods – every time."

"I'll tend to the fire," Lily said. "You go for Tom."

"But how do I find this – this *sage-femme?*" she said.

"Just *ask*, you silly girl," Lily snapped. But Lucille was incapable of asking anything. Lily waved her over to the cot, put her arm around her, and then holding her chin gently in place, said to her: "Don't worry, *ma petite*. We've done this all before, haven't we? Just go to Mr. Redmond's place, the grocery on the main street. He'll still be there. Ask him to fetch the midwife for you. Then bring her here. Okay?"

"Okay."

"Her name's Sophie. She lives where the squatters stay down by the dunes. That's all I know."

As Lucille reached the door, Lily let out another cry, and Lucille started back.

"Hurry," Lily gasped out. "Please. *Go!*"

Lucille disappeared into the withered sunset.

The pains were coming about seven or eight minutes apart as far as Lily could judge. They were as raw and frightening as the last time, perhaps moreso because she knew how long they would continue, and how much more frequently they would come to remind her how cowardly and insignificant and dispensable she really was, a mere web of birthing nerve and muscle; and knowing that she too – like the millions of child-bearers before her – would cry out for relief and expiation, would curse the universe that could look on with such unfeeling while the pain wracked from within as if it were ripping your skin apart from nose to navel with a single, whittled fingernail.

Why did you leave me? she heard a voice like hers shout from the underworld of her pain. *I need you, Auntie. I do.*

"Only the glow from the stove-pipes offered any light to the room when the door burst open and a burly moon-fringed figure strode to stage-centre and stalled, as if wondering in which direction the audience lay.

"Jesus-Christ-in-a-butter-box! Where in hell's the light?

Lucille, a trembling silhouette in the wake of this large personage, flitted across to where she had left Lily. "It's *la sage-femme*, she's come with me."

"So I hear," Lily whispered in a voice that caused instant paralysis in the girl.

The midwife was already at the stove menacing it with a series of ferocious manoeuvres. Flames shot up through the opening and smoke retreated up the chimney-flue. Wielding a lighted chip, the midwife broached several lamps and within seconds every object in the room softened into view.

"Well now, ain't that a damn sight better? You must be the victim," she said, ambling over to Lily who was struggling to sit up, a cautionary hand on her abdomen. "I'm Sophie Potts."

"I'm Lily. And I think you come in the nick of time."

"I've heard all about you," Sophie said, and she bent over Lily, easing her gently down with a fleshy hand that looked as if it had just milked fifty Holsteins and triumphed. "My, my, you got a live one in there, my girl." Without turning from Lily she barked softly at Lucille: "Get fresh wood on that fire, Frenchie; I want that water hot enough to boil a baker's bowlin' balls. Then haul the oil-cloth off of that table an' throw it across the bed back there. Then bring all the pillows an' sheets you can find. We gotta make this young'un as comfortable as we can. Right, dearie?"

Lily cried out; her body thrashed as if it were being jerked on a fish-hook attached to her belly-button. Quickly both of Sophie's hands were laid on Lily's convulsing muscles, like a phrenologist's divining truth from a skull's topology. "Wonderful… wonderful…Such power for a pretty little sunfish like you." She kneaded and soothed. Her milkmaid's fingers seemed to communicate directly with the rolling, berserk musculature under them.

"We got about half an hour, I'd say," Sophie said, "so let's get you off of this junior-cadet cot and on to somethin' soft an' motherly."

Lucille started across the room to help. "I told you to stoke that fire, *ma'amselle from la dell*, and I mean it." Then she reached down, wrapped both arms around Lily, and lifted her into the air where Lily floated, at ease. Sophie's arms were like goosedown lined with stanchions. Lily could see the lamplight wash across plump, pink flesh – not in the least fat or lumpish but rather more like a peach or nectarine that's just passed the penultimate point of its ripeness. It exuded vigour and lusty health. Its sweat slid over her own. However, when Sophie breathed extravagantly on her, Lily caught the echoes of garlic, herring-smelt and improvised whiskey.

While Sophie held Lily aloft, Lucille controlled her trembling satisfactorily enough to cover the bed with the oil-cloth and several layers of clean sheets. She fluffed up two feather pillows. Sophie laid Lily down as carefully as she would a bruised baby. "Hang on," she said, clasping Lily's right hand just as the convulsion struck and double-struck. Lily's scream brought Lucille to her toes with an hysterical snap. "It's okay, *la petite*," Sophie said in a different voice. "It's Nature's way. I been through this myself many times. You gotta holler or you'll bust open like a milkweed pod. Now you go on outside an' bring Sophie in her medicine kit." The cramp had eased off, but Lily kept her hand in Sophie's.

Suddenly there was a clatter and a thump outside the house – on the stoop or just off it.

"Shit," Sophie hissed, "I forgot all about the bastard." She rumbled past Lucille spilling her onto the bed, and could be heard intimidating the door, cursing, and then returning with a kind of scraping clutter across the plank floor of the big room. The tea-table Tom had made for Lily's birthday went over without a whimper. Sophie's generous figure ballooned in the bedroom doorway. She had one hand behind her back. She glared at the startled women. Lucille had begun to sob again. Sophie then laughed. And her laughter was gargantuan. It rose like throttled thunder from the paddled drum of her belly up through the great organ-loft of her lungs whence it whistled through the bass-tuba of her voice-box, thrummed over a tongue that could stun an ox and roared in ecstatic release across the countryside of parlours, vestibules and unresisting gardens.

"I found him pissed to the gills in Car-teer's pig-sty," Sophie said, and hauled out her catch for display, letting it dangle a bit from her hammerlock before she dropped it on the rope-rug in a shaggy heap. "Carted the silly-ass as far as the back-garden an' plunked him down in the compost heap where I figured he'd feel more at home. Some sight, eh?" And she released another trumpet-blast that made the baby lurch in its nest. "I reckoned he belonged to you!"

Tom moaned and tried to sit up, in which position he hoped that his eyes might actually open and see something familiar.

"I couldn't find him nowhere," Lucille sobbed to Lily. "I try real hard. When I get to Mrs. Potts, she says she knows where he be an' she goes –"

Lily came right off the sheets, her nightshirt flung as wide as her cry.

"Oh *Maman, Maman*," Lucille sobbed.

Sophie put one paw on Lucille and the other on Tom. "Go put some coffee on," she said to Lucille with such force that the girl stiffened with more resolve than fear, "stick a funnel down his throat an' start pourin'." With that she jerked Tom out of the room and dumped him onto the cot. It collapsed. There was a shriek, like cloth tearing.

"I'm sorry, Lil, real sorry," Tom said with great effort, not realizing no one was near enough to straighten out his slur.

"You stay put," Sophie shouted back to him from the doorway. "We don't need you. You done your damage about nine months ago, though I'm damned if I know how you managed it."

"Would ya' like some coffee, Mr. Marshall," Lucille said from a safe distance.

"Just keep him quiet and outta the way," Sophie said. "The missus and I got work to do."

Lucille got the coffee boiling in a saucepan and somehow managed to administer it to Tom, who was progressively jolted out of his fog by the staccato of cries from the other room. Tom winced, then shuddered as each one nicked him like a sniper's bullet. These cries were not Lily's: they had no voice; they were not even animal; they surfaced from something farther down the chain of being, some phylum where salt-blood and the composition-of-bone contended, or perished.

Sophie came out of the bedroom with the baby in her arms, Lucille at her side. Tom was seated almost upright at the kitchen table. "It's a boy!" Lucille cried.

"How's Lily?"

"Lily's fine," Lucille said, beaming and peeking into the blanket.

"Thank God," Tom said, rising.

"Thank me an' Mother Nature," Sophie said, opening her treasure to display the bawling, rubber-red being, blood-smeared with its knotted umbilical sticking out raffishly.

Tom peered into its bluish eyes, astonished that already they were staring back, that some primitive, fearful thought about the world was even now collecting in its tiny brain. Tom reached out and touched the protruding umbilical, its ruptured stub.

"That ain't his do-hickey," Sophie chuckled, "if you was worryin'."

"How can I ever thank you," Tom said.

Sophie gave him a steady, mocking appraisal. "First, I charge five bucks," she said with a sort of sly cackle as she turned to lead them all back into Lily's room. "An' second, I'd like a nip of that hair-straightener you tore into this evenin'."

Lily, pale as the flower of her name, held the child close to her; her eyes were drooped with fatigue but refused to give up consciousness, wanting to seal the baby's presence with their unceasing adoration.

"He'll be here when you wake up," Lucille whispered tenderly in her ear. "So will we, *certain*."

Sophie took several jars from a knapsack and put them on the dresser. "Now Lucille dear, you soak them cloths in this here linseed oil, then put on plenty of this powder, then put the whole shebang onto your lady's injured parts – three times a day. An' throw out the rags when you're done."

"What's this bottle for?"

"That's nerve tonic. Special recipe. Good for just about everythin' bad."

"How often do Lily have to take it?"

Sophie snorted. "It's not for Lily," she said. "It's for the patient."

Lily smiled just before she fell asleep.

Tom walked Sophie as far as the windbreak. The night-air was bracing. He held onto Sophie's arm. She turned to him. "She's gonna be fine, Mr. Tom Marshall," she said. "Your son came out slick and easy."

Tom gave her a thankful squeeze on the wrist.

Suddenly the moon landed in both her eyes. She flashed Tom a broad-beamed grin. "There's really nothin' to it," she said. "You oughta try it sometime. It's as simple as shittin' a watermelon."

Tom lay beside Lily. In the kitchen Lucille hummed a Norman ditty of some kind. The kettle steamed. Young Robert had both chubby hands on his mother's breast, sucking health and strength into his sturdy body with abandon and no particular thanks. Lily was quite happy to have their firstborn named for Bags Starkey. It seemed right, in so many ways.

"You get to name the girl," Tom said.

I already have, Lily thought.

"And ain't that Pott's woman the fattest, most foul-mouthed creature you ever laid eyes on?"

Lily changed breasts, and smiled. "She *was* nice, wasn't she?"

16

1

Robert Marshall was born into the pastoral world of Canada West on June 19, 1863, just about three weeks before the Union armies under General Meade and the Confederate rebels under General Lee butchered one another among the meadowlands of Gettysburg, Pennsylvania. No odour of the exhalations of the dead made its way this far north on any prevailing wind. Not even the drought which had scorched the crops from Kingston to Windsor could disturb the quietude that had settled over the Marshall homestead this summer. Robert suckled lustily and his green limbs grew apace. The Grand Trunk, inspired by a government loan, took on extra help, including past miscreants, so Tom went back to his part-time labour with a light and willing step. Lucille stayed on, her good cheer interrupted only by occasional periods when she would stop in the midst of an act – scrubbing a pot, feeding the stove – and stare across at mother-and-child, overcome by a sense of wonder, pure and inexplicable.

Lily felt little separation between herself and her baby. He was never more than an elbow's length from her, day or night. She cupped her breasts for his pleasure and satisfaction alone, feeding them like succulent pomegranates into his avid 'O' and gauging the crease of ecstasy across his eyelids as the hunger inside him overwhelmed them both. She could not yet bring herself to call him Robert; he was just 'baby', then 'nubbins' – a miraculous miniature-being she and Tom had formulated out of their own ecstasies and who, for the moment, served only to extend and refine the sensual tips of her body: lips, nipples, grazing fingertips, nuzzling nose. Thus it was that sometime about the middle of July when Tom lifted the sleeping babe from between them, laid it in its bassinet, re-entered the warmth of that vacancy and draped his angular, urgent length along her own – Lily was astonished to find her legs opening, as of old, to accommodate her husband's pulsive lullaby stroke, yet finding it equally strange, as if the connectors among her senses had been scrambled and recomposed. She was not completely surprised, then, when the climax (that shook her sideways and brought her upright with gazelle's eyes) propelled her exaltatious salute for miles over field and fallow. Lucille moaned in her sleep, and hung on.

Only two things eventually made a ripple of discontent over Lily's perfect summer. Lucille was asked by Aunt Elspeth to accompany her back to Toronto, permanently. That good woman had, as promised, made the train trip unescorted and breathless on the Grand Trunk day-express, which she was convinced, with all its shaking and clatter, had designs on her sanity. Nevertheless, she arrived safely at the Point Edward station, where she was greeted by her 'dear Tippy' who had at last settled down and made a man of himself. If she needed further proof of his conversion, it was forthcoming on her arrival at the Marshall homestead, where she was introduced to Robert, the spitting image of the dead Colonel, and pleased to offer her blessing. She was also discreet (or resigned) enough not to ask if the babe had been duly Christened: not knowing was, in this particular case only, the more bearable of the alternatives.

In almost every way Aunt Elspeth seemed her old, vital self. She showered Lily, Lucille and the infant with small, lovingly selected gifts. Her unaffected warmth spread through the household and the neighbourhood. During her week's stay, she left her mark (and money) in every store and establishment along Michigan Ave. She had set up 'rooms' in the Grand Truck station-hotel, insisted on dining lavishly there with Lily and Tom, then Lily and Lucille, and finally Tom alone. She left a trunkful of clothes for Lily – "Use them for rugs or your quilts if you find them too old-fashioned, but I don't need them any more, a woman of my age and advanced reputation," and she laughed in that wonderful way she had of including herself in the joke and sharing it with the listeners as if she were doling out secrets one joy at a time. On the day of her departure she spent a long, quiet minute alone in the bedroom with Robert while Lucille fidgeted by the door and Tom held the horses of the buggy he'd rented for the occasion. Aunt Elspeth had insisted that she sleep at least one night "in the abode of the people I love the dearest." They put her in Lily's old bedroom with Lucille. Everyone, it seemed, had spent most of the night listening to the baby's soft, unanxious breathing. Aunt Elspeth smiled bravely through Lucille's weeping as the goodbyes were said. "Buck up, girl, we'll be back for Christmas, that's a promise. And as soon as the little tyke's old enough, we'll have him on the train to Toronto to see us."

When she hugged Lily goodbye, Lily felt the crushing, desperate clench of the embrace. She felt herself shuddering through her own smile.

Tom's face told most of the story. He told her the rest at noon when he returned from his half-day's work in the sheds.

"Her health's all right. The stroke left her weak but you can see she's capable of exerting herself when she has a will, and a reason."

"What's wrong, then?"

"She's broke. Bankrupt."

"But how?"

"She had to sell the house and everything in it. Last month. The sheriff and bailiffs did it all. That's why she moved to Toronto, I think. She didn't want to be there when it happened. The Colonel left her little but the property. She should have sold half of it and lived off the money, but she had no head for business. She just mortgaged the place twice over till it was time to go. Her sister-in-law's taken her in. My eldest aunt; she's not well herself. Aunt Elspeth sold some jewellery to pay for this trip. I got it all out of her at lunch on Thursday. I've been sworn to secrecy."

"What can we do?"

Tom shook his head. "She always detested my Aunt Sylvia."

One evening in September, Tom and Lily walked farther than usual. They turned north at the River to skirt the squatter's shacks and strolled along the beach below the dunes. It was an Indian summer evening, thin yet still mellow, the heat of day snoozing on the cool night-air drifting in from the placid lake. Small waves nibbled at the stretch of sandy beach curling before them. Herring-gulls hovered, letting their wings sing for them. Sandpipers skittered at their approach. Somewhere past the dunes, the last bluebirds gathered for a valedictory chorale. Lily and Tom continued to walk, afraid to add any word to their walking. 'Nubbins' slept – as always: peaceful, free of colic and dream – in the papoose frame Tom had made and strapped on to his broad back.

Out on the Lake several ships were visible in the middle and far distance, their funnels puffing smoke that barely smudged the vast ocean of sky overhead. Then as they reached the end of the curved beach at Canatara and turned to retrace their path, a large four-masted schooner hove into view around the bend at Sarnia Bay and entered the Lake. Among the last of its breed, the old grain-carrier seemed cocky and defiant as it caught the southerly breeze square on its main-sails, its lacquered masts bent to the limit of their deep, ravelled grain, its rigging dotted with nimble circus-creatures adjusting the jib as they gambolled and tossed aloft their swallow-cries of delight. Slim, wind-sure, graceful as an aging eland, it angled into the open water and nosed its prow towards the unmappable horizon where it was said magnetic north linked up with a polar star.

Just then a spotted dog with floppy ears came skidding down a dune ahead of them, closely pursued by two young boys. Lily watched them tumble in the sand while the dog snapped at their heels and fists. The more they giggled, the louder the dog barked. Lily felt her hand tighten in Tom's. She stopped, involuntarily turning with the pressure of her husband's grip until she was beside him once more. He had paused with his eyes on the schooner, and as it sailed into the hazy, westering sky, he had turned with it, and his gaze never left it till it was a faded dot indistinguishable from the horizon-line.

"I'm expectin'," Lily said.

"What?"

"Gonna have your baby, sailor."

The winter in its own way was as happy as the summer. The baby was weaned, answered happily to 'Robbie', began to crawl over the floor and furniture – terrifying everyone but himself – and started crying for more than his food. He was a robust, healthy creature with his father's sandy hair and clear blue eyes. He rode his father's arms like a bronco, giggling hysterically as he was whirled through the high air and complaining only when he was let down. On hands and knees he trailed Tom into the bedroom or into the forbidden territory of the woodshed and worse. When the snow came, Tom built him a wooden sled, and only Tom was permitted to tuck him in, in a special way, before they all set out for Little Lake or a hike to the village to be shown off. When he was tired, his sweet temper turned decidedly cranky, but Lily didn't mind at all. She let him thrash some in her arms, her breasts reminding him of what he had abandoned for these risky new pleasures, her lullaby as soothing as ever against the edges of his fatigue. "Go to sleep, little Nubbins," she'd say, and look up warily to check on Tom who was always watching. I must not be jealous, she thought, inexplicably frightened. The child is between us, we made him together, he can never be outside either of us, he likes it here: *between, being one and then two.*

Tom went back to the job he liked in the car-shops. They had spent all their savings just to survive Tom's partial lay-off and the disastrous drought that sent food prices soaring. Neither of them mentioned a new house in the village; it would be a while, but still it *would* come. For Lily this third pregnancy did not go as smoothly as the first two. She had morning sickness all fall, was intermittently nauseous and cramped thereafter, and did not seem to gain any strength from the general state of well-being she felt. However, when Gimpy Fitchett announced in January that he was going to marry Clara Grocott, a farm-girl from up the Errol Road who worked in Redmond's grocery, Lily was overjoyed and for a while, at least, stopped feeling sorry for herself, as she told Maudie Bacon. Clara was added to the Wednesday teas at Maudie's, and Lily found that she liked the girl. She even joined – when she could – in the many discussions about the wedding dress and the details of the reception afterwards in one of the parlours of the Grand Trunk station. She promised Clara a quilt for her wedding night and set about completing it with considerable zeal.

Aunt Elspeth, of course, did not come for Christmas but sent a lovely note and an heirloom silver cream-and-sugar set rescued from the bailiffs. Her letter informed them that Lucille had become engaged to a British regular stationed at Fort York, but had promised to 'stay on' as long as she was needed. Once January came, though, all attention was focussed on the Fitchett wedding. Particularly happy was the arrival of Bags Starkey with his cousin from London. He was manoeuvring quite well on his own with the aid of two crutches and a disarming grin. He marvelled at the vigour and wholeness of his namesake. Unfortunately he had to return to London right after the service because there was a chance he might get a job selling tickets for the Great Western there.

The ceremony was held at the Methodist Church in Sarnia, where the Reverend Elmo Noseworthy managed to smudge with his homiletic proclivities an otherwise colourful and spontaneously joyful occasion. After the formalities of a dinner at the Grand Trunk, where the toasts were charged with apple-juice, the older folk said their farewells and the younger ones, including the bride and groom, remained to continue the celebration. Or start a new one. A cask of whiskey was discovered nearby, with a dozen bottles of iced champagne for the ladies. The working men and their wives sang, danced and caroused until they were kicked out at ten in the evening. The happy couple then repaired by cutter to the bride's home, left vacant for them, where they were to spend the night before setting out on the day-express for Toronto and a week's honeymoon.

What they didn't know was that they were not to be alone during their nuptial greeting. A charivari, or shivaree as it was called hereabouts, had been cooked up by several of Gimpy's crew and avidly agreed to by at least a dozen others, including – against all entreaty – Lily herself. As soon as the couple left the station, the participants pulled out two canvas bags containing their costumes and instruments. While two fellows hitched up a team and sleigh, the others donned their cloaks and masks and hopped aboard, singing badly enough to wake even the most unappreciative sleeper. Under a crisp, condoning moon they floated across fields and through the cathedral arches of First Bush on to Errol Road. They sang and hugged whoever came within range. Silver flasks returned the silver moonlight.

They arrived not more than fifteen minutes behind the lovers themselves. "Just time enough to get their nerve up!" some wag remarked to more laughter than he deserved. As they approached the isolated farmhouse of the Grocott's, the revellers shushed each other repeatedly until only the comic jingle of the harness-bells could be heard. A wan light showed through the blind on an upstairs window. The buskers leapt soundlessly into the fresh snow and, as prearranged, formed a loose ring around the building. Lily had on a sort of bat's costume with a black beaked mask, that had holes for the radar of her eyes, and a flexed cape attached to the wingbones of her arms. An outsize tambourine readied itself in her left hand. All I need is a broom, Lily thought, hoping the baby would not complain too loudly about the night's ride. She'd had only one glass of champagne, hours ago, but her heart hammered with excitement and she longed for the signal to be given. Near her she could see Tom in a botchy deerskin coat with a set of rusting antlers strapped to his brow and shoulders. Between his legs he held, with both hands, a bulbous blood-sausage. Further down she spotted Maudie's husband dressed like *Bonhomme* with coal eyes, a carrot nose and a waxed turnip where his legs should have joined. A battered bugle – flotsam from Sebastopol – sat poised for action. Maudie herself, habilled like a milkmaid in dramatic need of her own service – raised the alarm with a single clang of her cowbell. The din – sudden and relenting – would have stunned a deaf-mute: tuneless bell, oak rachets, soured horns of every ilk, tea-kettle drums, and underneath it all a thumping, manic tambourine. The window above shot open, and Gimpy, wrapped diagonally in a towel, blinked unbelievingly into the soft darkness, then staggered back as a chorus of chanting voices joined the accompaniment – each chorister contributing, in no precalculated order, one or more words or syllables to a love poem that might eventually have been translated thus:

> Gim-pee Fit-chett!
> Gim-pee Fit-chett!
> Give your all,
> Limpy, Limpy
> Ain't no ball!

Clar-ra Fit-chett!
Clar-ra Fit-chett!
Give him some
Limpy Gimpy
Ain't any fun!

Clara's ghost appeared beside her husband, and a further cheer went up from the troupe who speeded up their continuous circling movement and began a new chant:

Come down! Come down!
Or we'll wind you up
And blow your house down!

This encouragement was assisted by a tumultuous fanfare from all sections of the band and much lurid waving of props and appendages. Clara's blush turned the snow on the sills pink.

At last the wretched couple, hastily clothed, opened the front door and the troubadours entered en masse. Some untapped champagne was produced, toasts and cheers rained down upon Gimpy and Clara, who responded with the remnants of their dignity and good will. Following traditions as old as the *habitant's* arrival itself, the well-wishers departed meekly, sat motionless in the woods for twenty minutes, and then when the time seemed propitious, sent up a final, deflating barrage of congratulation.

Tom leaned over in bed and put his hand on her stomach. "You all right?"

Her eyes shone past him in the dark. "We're fine," she said sleepily.

2

At Robbie's nativity the father was drunk and the attending physician sober; at Bradley's birth it was the reverse. Which was, when you looked at it from the long view, only appropriate. After all, nothing about the pregnancy had seemed normal, and certainly the birth itself was spectacularly unordinary. Bradley would not kick, as the other two did. Even by the seventh month – the middle of March – Lily had to lie on her side and press her fingers firmly into her abdomen at a point where she figured his forehead ought to be and then repeat her invitation before she got a faint 'tunk' returned to her from within, like a single tap on a toy drum. At least it's alive, she thought, though it doesn't seem anxious to come into the world. "It's probably a girl," Tom would soothe, "as shy as her mother." "It don't feel like a girl." "And remember, you get to name her." If by chance it should turn out to be a boy, Tom had already got Lil's approval to call him Bradley, Aunt Elspeth's family name. *I've already named my little girl* she wanted to say aloud.

Lily suffered from cramps and from nausea, which struck her down at odd and inconvenient moments. She had missed two of the Wednesday teas because of it, even though Clara Fitchett had offered to give her a ride on her way past (she and Gimpy were living with her parents on the Errol Road until their new house in Sarnia was completed, after which Gimpy was planning to take a foreman's job at the Great Western). She was beginning to feel quite isolated, but with Robbie now crawling about like a rambunctious baby-coon she was kept busy and alert and often laughing at his antics. He's a show-off, she concluded, and we're spoiling him rotten with attention. What else would I do? Her heart would skip a beat and stall while she watched him climb Uncle Chester's chair, test the limits of his agility against the vindictiveness of gravity, then having breathlessly escaped, look up and laugh as if he had just played a joke on the universe and won. When he toppled, which wasn't often, he would lie stunned, waiting for the pain and trying out his arms and the air tentatively – like a chrysalid with its limp wings – and then, reassured that the world's kick was not lethal, snap his head across to glare at his mother: sometimes crying (more often not) but always letting her know that this humiliation was, deep-down, *her* doing, *her* failure to govern the forces aligned against him. Only in the most extreme instances – when the terror inside was wild and formless – would he consent to collapse in her arms for consolation. If Tom were watching, he never cried.

Despite these daily joys and minor catastrophes, Lily found herself missing the company of Maudie Bacon, Clara Fitchett, Alice Bowls and the other regular workers' wives who visited one another, chatted on Michigan Ave. between shops, exchanged recipes and gossip, and admired one another's children – to provide some relief from the never-ending labour of days and weeks. Like Lily these women were young and were new to town-life, just as the towns themselves had had to be improvised to circumstance. On their farms they had shared the labour with siblings and cousins and spinster aunts. Here they had increasingly to rely on one another. Little wonder, then, that the churches easily became the focus for social activity, and much more. As the wife of a fellow-worker Lily was accepted into their company cheerfully, but she found that most of the organized social events revolved around the church – its physical facility and the natural calendar it provided for the seasonal flow of Canadian life: Christenings, weddings, confirmation, baptism, concerts, temperance meetings, strawberry socials, bazaars and bees – each with its own sectarian colour and sanction. "Oh, just come along, Lily," Maudie said again and again. "We love you. And I don't believe *half* of what that old fart up there goes on about, nor do most of the girls." "I can't," Lily told them, and she knew that after a while, when the village built its own churches and she kept on saying no, it would begin to matter more and more. "You *do* believe in God?" Clara once asked, shocked at her own question. Lily could find no words to answer her, and was immensely relieved that whatever look she was giving Clara was sufficient. "Well, then, come along, for Christ's sake!"

For the time being, though, she felt only that she missed their company and their curious kind of affection – given so freely, unencumbered by any expectation beyond the pleasure of her presence. But then she would gaze at Robbie asleep in his rocker-bed, feel the weightless burden of the baby at the centre of her, think about Tom's coming through the kitchen door, and wonder how she could ever again feel sorry for herself. At such moments she was able to say: I have changed, my life is becoming what it is to be, I am Lily Marshall.

The day before All Fool's Day Tom came in for supper looking grim. He waited impatiently until young Mary Bacon, who had been helping with the housework and minding Robbie while she napped, left for the village. Then he spoke at length as if he were delivering a rehearsed speech whose import could not be changed no matter how it was presented. "I didn't want to get your hopes up," he said, "but before Christmas I wrote to the lawyers I used to work for in Toronto and asked them, as a favour to me, if they would check into the existence of an oil company controlled by Melville Armbruster in or around New York. I got a letter back the saft."

Lily flinched, one hand absently on her abdomen.

"Maybe I should save this for —"

"Go on," Lily said. "It's just the usual."

"They did find a company, a real estate company, registered in New York City, with Armbruster as president and chief owner. But it was sold – very suddenly and very mysteriously – in the spring of last year. After that, there is no trace of him anywhere in the business world of that area, as far as they can tell. They also wrote to his solicitors, Van Diemen and Cruickshank, and they said that he had gotten out of big business altogether, and if he had a forwarding address, they were not free to give it out."

Lily began clearing away the dishes.

"I'd like to go down there and thrash it out of them!" Tom said.

She's alive, I know it. I hear the underwater voice, pleading.

"Was that all?"

"Uh huh. That was it." And a dunner for twelve dollars.

Lily flinched again, bent double by the pain.

"Oh God, I knew I should've kept this till after," Tom said, hurrying over to her. He got as far as one of the kitchen chairs.

She was smiling through her grimace. "In a few minutes it's gonna be after," she warned him.

"It can't be! You're only seven months —"

"Started earlier this afternoon. An' this ain't false labour," she said, and squeezed a scream shut to emphasize her point. "Feels funny, but it's real."

"Damn, we should've kept Mary here. Never mind. I'll get you set up in the bedroom. If Robbie wakes up, just let him cry. I'll be back in forty minutes flat. With Sophie."

About two hours later, well after the sun had set and the night-chill was settling in over the trees, Lily heard the sound of multiple footsteps along the back-garden path. Nubbins was awake at her side, but restless and irritable. She felt numbed and disoriented by the pain. Blood had oozed and stiffened on her lower lip. The sheets were soaked twice through with her sweat. She was terrified the boy would tumble off the bed, strike his head on the floor, and lie helplessly dying while she lay equally helpless above him. However, he seemed to sense that something was very wrong, clinging to her damp fingers and complaining only fitfully. All this pain, Lily was thinking, and nothing is happening. The contractions seized, rolled downward in fierce, expulsive knots, sighed and hovered menacing until the next nerve trigged them again. But the foetus gave no sign of its willingness to be so crudely dislodged; it seemed to be fighting back, to be pounding the little battering ram of its brow against her stomach, her lungs, her heart, some place more secure and secret than whatever lay at the other end. But the expunging muscle was not to be denied. It was a sledge with breath and will, needing no name to intimidate or be moved, it was autonomous, life-lending, suicidal. It was driving the baby backwards into her heart like a tomahawk of raw flesh. She screamed as loud as she could but no sound reached her ears. She heard a distant thump. Robbie, fallen away, skull punctured...dead. The cramp eased and her mind let the room back in. Robbie was crying.

"Cut that snivellin', Marlene, an' get the little tyke outta here! Hurry up or I'll give you another cuff." It was Sophie's voice. Lily began to weep quietly with relief.

"You go right ahead an' cry, sweetie, Sophie's here an' everything's gonna be all right." She had gotten the lamp lit and was leaning over Lily, a plump, certain hand on her fevered head. Through her tears Lily saw the familiar but somewhat distorted face of the *sage femme*, swollen and lopsided, the colour of a fresh bruise.

"Get that stove goin' out there an' set up my things, girl," she shouted back to the other room. "I brung Marlene with me to help out," she whispered to Lily with all the tenderness of a rasp on wood. Then she snickered gigantically in stinted bursts, as if part of her lungs were popping at will. Her large frame, which, through Lily's blurred vision, seemed pudgier than ever, wobbled backwards towards the stool, landed one buttock unsuspectingly on it, and slid with it at an acute angle – clattering – to the floor. Her eyes bounced once, like a sturgeon's hitting bottom, and stuck open in permanent surprise. There was a slithering sound as her fat, hydrocephalic flesh caught up with the escaping bones, and for a long second she sat beached on the floorboards.

"*Jesus-Murphy-and-a-pig's-fart!*" she hollered through her bull-horn. "Marlene, get your arse in here."

Marlene was already at the door, quailing. She inched towards the embayed whale – wedged between terror and fear – held out a quivering hand, and when it became attached, heaved back with all her fifteen-year-old might. Sophie came upright, wheezing and not overly grateful. Marlene scooted off to her duties. Lily could smell the alcohol breath that Sophie was spraying like weed-killer into the room.

"Don't worry none, Lily dear," Sophie said, trying to blink. "I've had a bit to drink today. Hubby left me for the boats. Kind of a sad affair, eh? Gone for the whole month, he has. Don't you worry none, 'cause I brung Marlene with me, an' she's got the coffee goin' an' I'm the best damn midwife in this county." To prove it she belched and sat back on the stool without calamity.

"Where's Tom?" was all Lily could find the strength to say.

Sophie snorted. "*Ha!* He's gone after that quack, Dollard. That makes *two* aresholes I gotta deal with."

Marlene appeared several times with mugs of coffee which Sophie swallowed at a gulp. Robbie's giggle bubbled above the girl's soothing lilt. The wick on the oil-lamp singed and threw blotched light onto the wall. From the swamp, frogs sang as if they were the first and only spring. Lily remembered these things long afterward, as if, coming between the self-destructing spasms of pain, they were held to be precious beyond all normal possibility.

As last something clicked and turned over in Sophie's brain. She got herself up, roused no doubt by one of Lily's shrieks-dissolving-to-a-wail. Shrieks she was accustomed to, she read their special code as easily as braille, and suddenly she did not like what she was hearing and what her brain had finally cleared enough to register. She put both hands over Lily's flinching abdomen and kept them there while the spasms continued.

"Holy shit," she murmured. "*Marlene!*"

Marlene was ready, with the cloths and steaming kettles. Right behind her came Tom.

"What's happening?" he said. He was gray from exhaustion and worry. He had run into the village and then all the way to Sarnia and then all the way into the township.

"We got trouble," Sophie said without turning to greet him. She waved Marlene to the other side of the bed.

"Sons-a-bitches are all gone somewhere," Tom cried to no one in particular. "Dollard's on a call to Corunna. Benchley's on holiday. Nobody bothered answering at McElroy's on the London Road. *Nobody.*"

"Marlene, you get her to drink some of this if you have to choke it down her. Then keep the sweat outta her eyes, an' this towel between her teeth when she needs it. An' you, ya' dumb untrustin' bastard, get your butt over here an' hold a leg. I can't do this without you."

"You're *drunk!*" Tom shouted. "You're pissed! You think I'm gonna let you kill my wife?"

"Hold her gently just behind the knee," Sophie said. She had to force his hand there and close it.

"Cry later", she said. "Right now, I'm all you got."

"Tom," Lily said. "I can't see you."

"I'm right here, love. Everything's goin' to be fine now," he said, biting into his tears.

"Just pray to Heaven she's a strong one," Sophie said.

Marlene managed to get Lily to drink the potion.

"It's a narcotic," Sophie said towards Tom. "Old Indian recipe," she winked. "Christ, I can't work up here. Come on, we'll lift this mattress onto the floor."

They lifted the mattress and its tender cargo as gently as they could onto the floor, where Sophie then heaved her own beluga bulk between Lily's spread legs and set to work. "A breech birth," she said, "little bugger's tryin' to come out feet first."

Tom kept his eyes averted, occasionally peeking up from his station to read the agony on his wife's face, and worse: that glint of first-terror when the mind begins to doubt the body's daunted vigour. He could not, however, close off any of the sounds that filled the room: Lily's coughing gasps as she fought for each breath and then re-pulsed it as if it were a poison gas; Sophie's grunts and coarse whinnying as she pushed and wheedled, grappled and comforted; the sucking noise between Lily's thighs as Sophie's fingers began to probe, stretch, demand; the drip of blood – one bubble at a time – onto the oil-cloth; Lily's voice: a continuous whimper containing no ghost of a word, fading down down until interrupted by a stiletto cry that confirmed the depth of pain and the resistance of a life somewhere within.

Tom heard a vile curse from Sophie, felt a great shifting of her amphibious flesh, and could not help looking up. He saw a gush of purplish blood splatter over Sophie, followed shortly by a guttural, clenching moan from Lily in a voice he had never heard or imagined. Sophie's hands were buried in his wife's body, in regions that resembled none he had been witness to – grotesque, stretched, blood-pummelled flaps of flesh.

"Come outta there, you little fucker!" Sophie commanded. "Marlene, get that towel between her teeth before she bites her tongue off! Tom Marshall, bring in hot water an' fresh towels. We're gonna need 'em."

When Tom came back in, Lily was arched fully and breathing like an asthmatic near the end. Sophie was hunched over with her flippers stiffened and jerking back. Tom saw the child's legs in Sophie's grasp, blood pouring over them like pus.

"Gotta hurry, gotta hurry," she panted. She gave a wrench that would have stripped a calf of its intestines, Lily coughed and moaned sweetly, and a rump popped into view, followed immediately by a curved back and the rim of a skull.

"My God, it's coming !" Tom said glancing up to check on Lily. Her scarlet saliva had stained the towel between her teeth.

"Holy Jesus," Sophie whispered.

"What's wrong?"

"The fuckin' cord," she wheezed, panic in her swollen face. "It's wrapped around his neck. Help me!"

Tom's hand shook, his teeth chattered, and the sweat poured into his eyes, but somehow he managed to take hold of the eel-slippery, half-born foetus and, forgetting it was alive and humanoid, squeeze its body mercilessly while Sophie reached one finger through the flensed crevice and with a series of deft manoeuvres somehow coordinated with Lily's last spasms, managed to slip the cord over the baby's head as it propelled itself – at last, reluctantly, perversely – into the air above the ocean.

Dangling it upside down as the afterbirth gushed in a fetid pool at her feet, Sophie tapped on its heels and it howled triumphantly, as if it had made this journey, thank you, on its own merit. Bradley Marshall had uttered the first of his million syllables.

"I'm gonna leave Marlene here," Sophie said. "Lily's very weak an' ripped open a bit. Marlene knows how to put on the special plasters I'm gonna leave you. She'll need the narcotic, too, and the tonic later on. I'll come by if you need me. Just send Marlene."

Tom poured himself another mug of coffee. He had no emotions left to exercise, but if he could have, he would have felt puzzled and sad at what he saw across the table from him. This woman, who had just saved the life of his wife and his son, looked utterly wasted, drained of all vitality. She must have put on a hundred pounds since her visit here last year. Everywhere she wasn't bloated, she sagged. It was more, he knew, than mere fatigue from the ordeal of the birthing room. When he had arrived at her house, hours before, she had barely recognized him. She had fallen on her rump and cursed him out of her house. Even now, she bore the same badge of abuse he had recoiled at earlier in the day. The left side of her face was swollen to twice its size, leaving only a puffed slit for the dark, gypsy's eye to manoeuvre through. The flesh there, previously a sort of scorched red, was now souring thickly: a purpling, yellowish, aborted tumour. When she slumped on her elbows, it dripped – like a smashed pepper-squash.

"Who did that to you?" Tom asked.

Sophie glared balefully at him, then smiled as best she could and said, "My hubbie, of course. With his stokin' fist."

The shock must have registered on Tom's face for Sophie said: "You don't think I'd let anybody *else* do this to me, do you?" She straightened up. "Now where in hell do you keep the pain-killer around here?"

"The minute I'm feelin' up to it, I'm gonna walk over there an' thank that woman myself," Lily said.

Tom tossed Robbie into Uncle Chester's chair, then nuzzled into him till the boy screamed in delight.

"I may just bake her the biggest pie I ever baked," Lily said. Then, "*Ow*, I swear this little jigger's tryin' to bite me."

Tom came over. "She lives on squatter's row," he said.

"Does that matter?" Lily said.

3

Lily felt guilty at waiting so long but finally she did find time to bake an apple pie with the first crop of green cookers from Clara Fitchett's orchard. It was almost September. She was in no particular hurry to pass through the meadows still half-a-mile wide between their property and the outskirts of the village: the goldenrod was new, the bobolinks and killdeer sang in the distance, the sun was warm on her bare arms. As she neared the houses on Charles Street, several with partly finished rooves, she tried to think of all the things she had seen and heard about the squatters.

"Bunch of hoo-ers an' pimps," she'd heard Gimpy say to a pal at one of the Saturday dances, and Tom had a difficult time explaining the terms to her afterward. "Railway oughta clean them gypsies right outta there," was one variation of a recommenda-tion offered by numerous storekeepers and rate-payers along the main street. "They squat on Grand Trunk land, an' just 'cause it ain't good for nothin' else don't mean they shouldn't kick their butts clean to London an' back." "Marg's hubby slips over to Car-teer's come Saturday night," Maudie whispered, assuming she would know what a bootlegger was and was for. "Could be worse," Clara countered. "Hazel's ain't far away." Hazel's Heaven it was called – where the pimps and hooers went to commit their anti-social acts. "When we get our own church here next year," Maudie said, "that'll be the end of all that filth. Then maybe honest folk won't have to lock their doors at night or keep an eye out on the boardwalk for the riff-raff that comes floatin' up from that sewer."

Lily herself had seen children – freckled, orange-headed, streaked with dirt – bounding over the tracks from that direction to be shooed and badgered by the neighbouring townsfolk as if they were chickens out of their run – laughing and cursing merrily as they dodged all blows and melted into the scrub-bush. "Them's the McCourt brood," Redmond sighed over his scales, "leastways the redheads is, the others are most likely bastards of dubious origin, if you know what I mean. Old Jess McCourt died under a hopper-wheel up in Camlachie two winters ago – cut him right in two, clean as a fire-log. His old lady scrubs out toilets for the Grand Trunk; they don't care if she squats in that shack, long as she don't mind swabbin' up other people's you-know-what."

Lily turned off Michigan Ave. onto Prince Street. Several sailors lounged on the patio outside the Queen's Hotel; she let their whistle sail amiably by. A number of large boats were in port. Prince Street, named in honour of His Royal Highness, was less than a hundred yards long, ending its brief north-easterly path a few feet before the Grand Trunk main-line which entered the village farther to the east, looped around its northern limit till it came close to the lakeshore, and then swung south along the riverfront to the docks and station. Beyond the track where it almost intersected Prince Street lay a screen of runt hawthorn, soft poplar and red-willow and beyond it a patchy piece of open ground covered with sawgrass and sandburs that rolled northward till overtaken by the dunes and the beach below them. As Lily reached the end of Prince Street, she spotted a walking path through the grass, followed it over the tracks, picked it up on the other side and went through the curtain of bush into what had already become known, inside and outside the community, as Mushroom Alley.

And there *was* a kind of lane or alley, about as broad as a dog-cart's track, that might have been labelled a street if it had not so flagrantly meandered and ox-bowed its way among the residences on either side. The first two dwellings Lily saw, partly hidden away among some poplars, were not luxurious enough even to be called shanties. They were confected out of the jetsam of the Grand Trunk: rusted corrugated iron, chipped packing cases and chewed-up graindoors. Barred rocks skittered in the dirt where grass had been, then fluttered aloft in the wake of the children who came hurtling from behind one of the shacks. Copper-topped and black-haired, mostly naked, of every size and sex – they roared past Lily without a nod, intent on some ritual game more compelling than the arrival of a stranger. McCourts and McLeods, she thought. From the edge of a hog-wallow, Lily felt the cold eyes of a woman, who did not wave when she did but watched her until she had veered out of sight. Suddenly she began to wonder how she would ever discover where Sophie Potts lived. She would have to speak to *some*one.

Next she came across a genuine shanty, a barn-like structure with vertical boards and proper crossbeams and a slanted roof bearing an iron-plate cover, rusted with moss. The siding had been undisturbed by paint, and while not yet rotten, it had decided to rest a little by leaning fifteen degrees to the left. The single window was covered with greased paper. Like the cabins used to be, she thought. Behind this house, and to a lesser extent beside and in front of it, had been dumped all manner of junk, refuse and castaway valuables: broken tables, backless chairs, two iron stoves irrevocably cracked in different places, piles of gunnysack, burlap, wretched bits of clothing, and utensils of every kind, many of them taking root in the inhospitable soil. A thin figure in an outsize flannel shirt stood over one of the racked stoves holding a piece of sandpaper poised above one of its incurable blemishes. Lily waved and took a step off the path. The figure, male and possibly advanced in years, started to raise its right hand, then stopped and turned back to its labour. Lily could see the left sleeve of the man's shirt flapping in the breeze.

She looked away towards the river mouth, whose contrary currents she could hear even from this distance. Where the grassy field sloped away towards the water, she could see the smoke from several campfires and, partially obscured by the uncertain undulations of the ground, the smudged outlines of the hoboes and bums just off the trains. They slept down there in the open or in makeshift lean-to's; some of them, it was widely rumoured, were deserters from the Union Army or spies from the Confederacy. None had ever been apprehended. Lily quickened her pace. Around another bend she encountered what appeared to be a deserted shack on her right and a bit farther on the left a sizable-looking house with a verandah, glazed windows, several rambling sheds somewhat attached to the main structure, a see-through barn behind, along with a coop, pig-pen and two smaller huts, possibly for implements. Some attempt had been made to grow vegetables in the thin, wind-bitter soil. The clapboard had once long ago been painted – a sprightly blue perhaps. Seated on a wicker rocker on the verandah, Lily spied the unmistakeable profile of young Marlene.

Lily waved and started through the burdocks, balancing her pie with its gauze cover. Marlene appeared to be startled, squinted into the sunlight, then bolted off the porch and into the back yard where she disappeared behind one of the outhouses. Lily stopped. The grasshoppers see-sawed around her. No sound came from the house. She glanced farther up the Alley. In the distance among the trees she could discern two other dwellings, the nearest quite large, its canary yellow and mauve exterior glinting seditiously. Well, she'd come this far. Faintly came the echo of children's voices, the ebb and flow of their carefree play somewhere among the pliant dunes. She walked boldly up to the verandah, slipped on a wobbly step, righted herself noisily, and rapped on the screen door, an action which stirred up a harem of flies drowsing there. Half of them plunged into the dark interior through one of the several portholes.

"Anybody home?" Lily called softly. The flies had noticed the pie. As she turned to go, she heard the squeak of a wicker chair, as if someone had just shifted their weight from one buttock to another. "You there, Sophie?"

"*What in hell do you want here?*" It was a male voice, deep and angered.

"I come to see Sophie. Is she here?"

A long pause, a stretching of wicker mesh, then: "An' who might you be?"

"Sophie Potts live here?"

"Who in Sam Shit wants to know."

"Tell her Lily came to see her. I'll come back another time."

A shadow filled the doorway. The flies danced and disappeared. Two black eyes, like chiselled coal, burned flamelessly in the bearded face suddenly peering out at her. White teeth flashed in a friendly grin. "Hey, you don't go runnin' off, Miss Lily Whats-her-name. Don't you know a joke when you hear one?"

Lily paused without turning back.

"Better brush them flies offa that pie," he said. "I like my sweets nice an' clean."

Lily looked back up at him. "Is Sophie home?"

"Why don't you come inside like a proper lady and I'll see if she might be."

"I just wanted to –"

He opened the door with a flourish and she saw him fully in the light. He was a large, well-proportioned man with a handsome, bearded face, arms that bulged with a surplus of muscle, and ape-size hands that were scarred with calluses as thick and layered as a toad's skin. His teeth were wonderfully even and his eyes rolled in their lively sockets to express and disguise. The only thing to mar an otherwise striking impression was a slight crook of the spine, camouflaged somewhat by his loose workshirt, as if he had spent too long arched in one position.

"I said come in. What're ya' scared of, eh! I'm Morty Potts, Stoker to them that hate me. I crush big bugs an' little mates who get on my nerves, but I ain't killed a sweet-lookin' woman yet. Least none that I know of."

"Sophie home?"

"You got a one-track mind, girl." She caught the blast of his whiskey breath. "Soph'll be real mad now if I don't invite you in to wait for her. You comin' in or not?"

"Where is she?"

"She's down at the Lake bathin' the kids, for Christ's sake. There's only me here."

"An' Marlene."

His stare darkened. Flies were pouring into the house as he held the door wide open. Lily caught a whiff of urine and festering diaper. "Marlene's gone off," he said. "Most likely she's fetchin' her momma right now, so why don't you just come on in an' have a drink …of tea."

"I better not wait. Please tell Sophie I'll be back."

"Hey!" he called down to her.

Lily stiffened, then turned slowly.

"You gonna leave that pie?

As Lily made the first bend in the Alley, out of the corner of her eye she saw Marlene emerge from the bushes and tiptoe up to the house. Lily sped up but she wasn't fast enough. The smack of hand to cheek flew past her towards the foul hearth-fires ahead. She heard the girl shriek once like a reflex. She thought of a stoker's hands, ferrying coal from bin to blast with Beelzebub's grip.

"Well," Tom said, grateful for her return. "Did she like the pie?"

"She wasn't home," Lily said.

"Oh. That's too bad." He looked away. "You going back?"

"Soon as I can," she said with no conviction. "How've my boys been?"

17

1

By 1866 the War Between the States had passed through denouement to catastrophe and uneasy resolution, just as its wily protagonist – the Great Emancipator – was gunned down front and centre by a bad actor who hadn't read the original script. The million casualties – dead and maimed and orphaned – did not return for a curtain call. It was said that an epilogue to this melodrama was already in rehearsal under the working title 'Manifest Destiny'. Farther north, the hastily arranged marriage of the two Canadas was heading, after twenty-five years of mutual incompatability, towards certain divorce – unless some close relatives could be persuaded to share the misery in a more encompassing family unit dubbed by its proponents 'confederation'. The papers were full of little else but news of the scheme and of the tub-thumping Fenians below the border uttering the most horrible threats against the peace of not only Canadians but also and especially New Brunswickers, Nova Scotians and Prince Edward Islanders. The hue and cry went up everywhere, no more so than in those towns unfortunate enough to abut an American state bristling with Fenian brothers determined to liberate Ireland by decapitating the silos of every barn between Fort Erie and Sarnia.

In the teeth of such infamy it is little wonder that scant attention was paid to local concerns: like the continuance of the rate wars between the Great Western and Grand Trunk, to the embarrassment of the public purse and two dozen bankrupt municipalities; like the rumblings of discontent faintly heard from the New West where Canadians were already wearing out their welcome among the puzzled half-breeds; like the visiting phrenologist from Boston who proclaimed in the Town Hall of Sarnia that man was a 'developmental creature' and the earth around him eons old, only to be scientifically refuted, to general approbation, the next week by a learned Doctor of Theology from Pittsburgh; like the death of Mrs. Elspeth Edgeworth, widow of the late Colonel Edgeworth of London, who passed away quietly in her sleep at the home of her sister-in-law in Toronto. The good woman was laid to rest beside her husband in their home city.

Lily insisted that they could not afford train-fare for both of them to attend the funeral in London. She even believed it as she said it, and was secretly hurt when Tom showed no inclination to accept her argument. "Of course we can," he snapped, "and we both know very well why you won't go." She was about to say something in her defense when Brad's whimper from the boys' room sent her scurrying off. Pulling the child close to her warmth, feeling the cold shiver as it clutched at her – she heard Tom slam the door and go out.

Later, into the silence she said: "I loved her very much."

Tom leaned over and held a piece of meat on his fork until Robbie drew it, teeth flashing, back into his mouth and smirked up at his father. "Nice little puppy," Tom said and gave him a pat.

"I wish she could've seen Brad."

"Brad go, Brad go," the little one chanted, secure on his mother's lap.

"Gimme another one, Da," Robbie said and spilled his milk.

"I take it you haven't changed your mind."

"She was the kindest person I ever knew," Lily said. She sponged at the milk with the end of her apron.

"Da, gimme another –"

"Shut up, Robbie. *Shut up!*"

It took Lily an hour to quiet Robbie down, and while she hated to see how a cross word or a sideways look from his father could devastate him so, she cherished his flesh curled into hers so close she could hear his heart palpitate like a minnow's gill out of water. Naturally Brad fussed all the while, complaining that his "tummy ache", and finally throwing a tantrum to prove his point. She held one child in each arm until Brad fell asleep and Robbie just let his head slide onto her shoulder, in which haven he could nestle down and prepare for the wonderful dream that always came just before sleep. Very quietly, so as not to disturb her boys, Lily wept for Aunt Elspeth, for the walled garden, for Lucille in the morning room, and for all that had happened there.

Tom slept on the cot. At breakfast he picked Robbie up, spun him around in the clouds and tousled his hair. Robbie responded by punching Tom on the stomach with mock ferocity. "Can I go with you, Da? Can I?" Tom gave him a manly sort of hug. "Soon as I come home tomorrow, I'll take you hunting," he said.

Tom was eerily polite until he was ready to leave for the train. Lily noticed the dark hollows under his eyes. She reached out and straightened his tie. Tom raised her hand with his. He gave her the strangest look and said tonelessly: "You'll have to leave him some day, you know."

When Gimpy aimed his father-in-law's buggy around the bend in the lane, Tom turned and waved at the boys. Robbie flapped his hand like a pennant.

From the moment of his unorthodox entrance into the world Bradley Marshall was a difficult child to cope with. Being premature, he seemed to try and compensate by constant suckling, demanding service at any hour of the clock, overcommitting his capacity and upchucking the lot. Whereupon he would cry with doubled hunger and indignation. When he did manage to feed satisfactorily, he would be wakened by colic, wailing his grief far into the night and the wary dawn. Where Robbie had been cherubic, Brad was wizened and irritable; where Robbie was robust and outgoing, Brad was sickly and withdrawn, as if his arrival had after all been some perverse mistake. When his colic subsided, he picked up a touch of whooping cough from his brother, then the chicken-pox, and most recently the red measles. Lily had two sick children to care for, and a husband with little sleep to sweeten his shortened temper. Robbie suffered his maladies gallantly, lying in his bed (Tom had made them single 'bunks' for 'their room') and letting Lily minister to him, smiling bleakly when she had to leave to attend Brad, hugging her to him when the pain spilled into occasional tears. In many ways, Lily often thought, these were their best moments together: Robbie knew for certain who she was, what she was for, why she couldn't be done without. As a result, Robbie responded easily to treatment and was soon over the afflicting, bruiting his appreciation to the wild woods and fields he loved to roam in – within a mother's shout of the house.

Poor Brad, being a year younger and never quite recovered from one malady before the next one struck, suffered badly and without dignity. He would shriek till his nose ran and slathered his chin, and Tom would give him several sharp shakes, stilling the fit but ushering in a pathetic, unceasing series of whimpers and mewlings that made his tormentor instantly contrite. But when the whimpering continued unconscionably, Tom would plop the child into Lily's arms wherever she was and stomp off without a word. Usually she could hear him take his gun down and head off for First Bush, with Robbie trailing him ineffectually to the edge of the garden, then returning to Lily to cry out his anger or, more likely, making certain that her attempts to soothe Brad were unsuccessful. When both boys were sick together, Tom would bring young Mary Bacon out from the village to help. Mary was always cheerful and efficient, chattering away to Lily, to the boys, to the lilac bushes, to anything that moved or was beautiful. Robbie had someone new to show off his acrobatics to, and was, Lily thought, excessively affectionate to the girl. Brad did not 'take to' Mary, who failed to notice.

After Brad's second birthday, Lily detected a distinct change in his behaviour and in their relationship. He had begun to talk early – at sixteen months – but despite the facility of his speech he used it mainly to establish the urgency of his wants. Lily cradled, hummed and sang to him often during these stressful periods, and he had responded in a curious way: he consumed the lullaby syllables thirstily, drawing them into his discomfort like a tonic, giving nothing back but the grateful easing of his tense little body in the singer's arms. The songs Lily sang to him in those early months – born out of desperation and sometimes even panic – were those she remembered, however obliquely, from her own mother's lips and imperfectly copied in her sudden need. They did as much to soothe the nurse as they did the child. Most of the ditties had no words she understood, but she felt that somewhere, way back, she had known their meaning or something near enough to meaning to be comprehended and prized. She could not describe even to herself the pleasure she derived from watching the fretful child respond to the lilt and dance of her own deep music, not with his eyes (which often twisted in resistance) but with his skin, his unstiffening body, the green thrumming of his miniature bones, the easy rhythm of animal sleep.

But just last month, all that had changed. For one thing Brad was a bit stronger now, even though he would always be a pale, thin towhead and prone to infection – all the way into his adolescence, where he would choose to capitalize on these 'failings' in unexpected ways. For the most part his abrupt shift in behaviour came with his increasing command of speech. He could not only string sentences together that would have dazzled visitors (if they had had any), he could take a word or phrase, as Robbie might a rubber ball, and play with it – tossing, balancing, testing its resilience against foreign objects – for his own endless amusement. One of those objects became Lily, who tossed the phrases right back – daring, taunting, smiling. Slowly, tentatively, they were returned until the rules of a new and wondrous game were realized, a game for two players – full of laughter, quick slides, dizzy trapezes almost-over-air, shivering hugs when they both at last touched ground and waited together for the spinning to slow. While Robbie foraged out-of-doors, toy rifle at the ready to stun the first squirrel, Lily and Brad spent the mornings in perpetual conversation. Sometimes when Mary Bacon came out to help with the housework, she brought her little brother, Mitchell, and while the two older boys rampaged through the wilds out back and Mary hummed over the kitchen stove, Lily sat in Uncle Chester's chair and began to tell Brad all the stories she knew. Brad did not always stay silent and enthralled; at a signal from Lily he would jump straight into the narrative and help her make it up, and when it broke down, as it must, in rambunctious nonsense, they would both laugh till even Mary would start giggling and Brad would freeze, tug at Lily's apron and grow sullen for the rest of the day. At night he would say: "Put some words to the song, Mama, *please*." "But they *are* words," Lily would say, indignantly, then relent and improvise some English ones. "That don't rhyme!" Brad would shout gaily. "Not supposed to!" "Make it rhyme, Mama, *please*." So she would, happy that the child was content with her quarter-rhymes pulled out of the air and away from objects they shared intensively in their small fabular world. Of course, Lily had also sung Robbie to sleep with her lullabies, and did still when he was in need, and she loved also the way Robbie's eyes, like acorns tinted blue, rounded drowsily and welcomed sleep. Rarely did she finish a song or story with Robbie at bedtime; his gratitude was quick and sonorous. During the day he would merely fidget and long to be outdoors despite the rain or driving snow. She loved Robbie passionately with a kind of aching she had never anticipated as she watched him gambol alone in the garden, stride behind Tom when they marched towards the wood, when he lay breathing in his heavy, recuperative sleep each afternoon. When he was sick or rejected, she got to hold him as tightly as she wanted to.

Tom was quick to notice the change in Brad. Lily was aware of his glance saying to her 'Well at last there seems to be a little human being under all that crying and carrying on'. Lily in turn was quick to include Tom in the conversations as they developed. As first she had little success; Brad would simply clam up and sulk if Tom hung about too long on the fringes of their dialogue. "You're too big," Lily said to Tom, trying to make light of it. "Why don't you get down on your hands an' knees an' just peek over the table, like you done with Robbie way back." Tom was puzzled but went along. It worked. Gradually Tom was let into the word-play, where he did quite well, and occasionally Brad would say something he thought amusing and then look only at Tom and smile. Whereupon Tom would fall backwards and laugh and kick like a tipsy mule. This latter manoeuvre usually brought more laughter from Robbie than any of the other spectators.

But Tom just wasn't around enough, Lily concluded. It didn't seem fair. So for the time being, at any rate, Brad was unwilling to transfer his antics solely to Tom, even though Lily increasingly found opportunities to leave them alone together. "C'mon, Robbie," she'd say, "You an' me'll go down to the creek an' see if those trout are still there." Robbie would glance anxiously at Tom – torn between loyalty and desire – and then give in to the latter. The only way she could keep him happy was to let him lead *her* to the secret pool and point out to *her* all its cumulative mysteries. Often they returned to a silent house.

Tom himself seemed a lot happier in general. No longer would he have to switch over to the freight-sheds every April. He was made a permanent (and veteran) member of the car-shop. His specialty became the repair of crippled stock cars; he would tear out the splintered sections and improvise replacement schemes at minimal cost to the Grand Trunk. "I'll never be a cabinet-maker," he'd say, "but at least these hands are good for something." The only sad news was that Gimpy and Clara had settled permanently in Sarnia. Though they still saw them on special occasions, some of the old intimacy was lost. Tom had a number of acquaintances – pals – at work, some of whom he hunted and fished with, but with Bags' departure (no news) and Gimpy's defection, Tom had so far not found friends to replace them. Though he never said it aloud, with Gimpy gone to the Great Western, Tom had a better chance at becoming assistant foreman.

Soon, Lily thought, we'll start talking again about that cottage in the village.

It was late April. Brad was asleep inside; his glands were swollen. Lily was digging in the garden. Robbie was 'helping' with his toy shovel. After a week's lay-off Tom was back at work. Lily's mind was full of plans for the coming season. She hummed a waltz tune, one she remembered dancing to long ago. Suddenly Robbie peeked up and said, "Ma, what's a Fee-neen?"

"Where'd you hear that word?"

"When me an' Da was fishin'."

"Mr. Bacon use that word?"

"Uh, uh. Da did. What is it? Da won't tell me."

"They're bad men, but they live a long way over the River. They can't hurt you none. So don't you go worryin' about them, eh?"

He paused, then brought his shovel to his shoulder and aimed it. "I ain't scared," he laughed and pulled the trigger; the weapon went off with an explosion of spittle. Lily said nothing. After a while the instrument resumed its more humble duties.

When Tom came in from work, Lily was bent over the rabbit stew. She listened in vain for the rattle of his bucket and 'thunk' of his cap on its peg. She turned to look, the hair on the nape of her neck rising.

He was all in green, tunic and breeches, with black unbent boots. A bit of gold piping winked here and there. The rifle in his fist gleamed more brightly.

"I joined up," he said.

2

The Fenian scare had reached its zenith. Enemy troop movements were being reported daily all the way from New Brunswick to the Niagara frontier. For several months the spanking new Canadian militia, side by side with British regulars, had been patrolling the borders of Canada East and Canada West. Point Edward was a critical spot, the nexus of two great transportation facilities. The Grand Trunk round-house and yards harboured at any given moment more than fifty locomotives. The economy of the united provinces could be crippled with a single surprise strike across the St. Clair River. Near the railyards stood an elevator crammed with last fall's wheat reserves. Beyond, the Lambton countryside was dotted with Irish Catholic farms reported to be longing for emancipation and two-hundred-years' vengeance. Three militia groups with local commanders were formed as part of the 27th Battalion: the Sarnia Infantry and Artillery Brigade, and two units from Point Edward known as the Grand Trunk Companies. Eventually they took on the name they had already chosen unofficially for themselves: the St. Clair Borderers.

To assist them in defending the vital installations of the region, the Government sent several companies from elsewhere in the Province, and these were billeted in what remained of the original Ordnance Grounds – a flat, grassy plain between Mushroom Alley and the lakeshore. The spring breezes billowed the white tents and the sun shimmered on bayonet and buckle. Flocks of truant boys crouched breathless in the bushes nearby, then dashed off to the dunes to replicate the dress-parades and menacing battle tactics they had been permitted to witness. Many a hummock and foolish milkweed felt the slash of a sabre and quick, voiceless death.

The Borderers joined the outsiders for combined exercises, but they also rehearsed independently on the Sarnia parade-ground or among the dunes themselves, firing their rifles into the air, hurling imprecations into the wind blowing impudently from Fort Gratiot, showing curious lads who longed to be a year older how to fix a bayonet without severing a finger. One rumour, widely believed, suggested that a Gatling Gun had been smuggled in from the States and cached somewhere near Mushroom Alley. Ordinary folk bolted their doors and kept the curtains drawn.

With a logic known only to the Irish, the assault did not come against the vital, vulnerable Western region but across the Niagara River against loyalist strongholds rooted in that countryside since the expulsions of the seventeen-eighties. Despite the advantages of a familiar terrain and a spy system which informed them of every twitch made by the enemy, the Canadian militia, in their maiden engagement, set a standard for ineptitude that only the fiascos of the Great War would surpass. Heroism there was aplenty, even a victory of sorts. But the soldiers weren't cheering.

Because John A. Macdonald's agents knew that the Fenians under O'Neil's able leadership were about to cross the Niagara in force, a masterful battle-plan could be hatched with time to spare. The regular army units from Toronto under Colonel Peacock were to sail across Lake Ontario and effect a lightning-swift landing and an inland thrust below the Falls. The militia units – eight-hundred strong – were taken overnight on the Great Western to Port Colborne where, as the sun rose, they were to move slowly, by rail, to a point well below the marching line of the Fenians, who were now disembarked and heading straight for the Welland Canal. The militia commander, Colonel Booker, either forgot to set his watch or was simply overeager, because he started his northern drive two hours sooner than scheduled. Hence the pulverizing pincer-movement – Peacock's regulars from the north, Booker's militia from the south – was somewhat miscoordinated, particularly when the militiamen bumped into the Fenians near Ridgeway, to the astonishment of both parties. The Queen's Own Rifles from Toronto charged into the invading hordes and sent them in full retreat – right through a festering swamp known locally as Smuggler's Hole. Both armies were up to their thighs in muck and pond-water. The battered Fenians, backing up, discovered soon that they were all standing on a dry hill staring down on the sloshing, foot-weary Canadians. It occurred to them to start shooting back. They did, and several soldiers toppled into the sludge, blotting it with their blood. Reinspired by this, the main body of the Fenians charged down the hillside, while some of their units fanned right and left in an attempt to outflank the Canadians and trap them in the quagmire they had accidentally arranged for themselves. Colonel Booker succeeded in effecting an orderly retreat, hauling the wounded with him, until one of his officers, hearing perhaps the triphammer of his own heart, cried out "The Cavalry are coming!", whereupon with no further evidence to sustain him the Colonel called for the formation of the famous British 'square'. When duly formed, it was discovered that there was only one horse within a mile and it was pulling a plough. Meanwhile, the Fenians' flanking manoeuvre was able to be completed with ease; the rear units of the Canadian militia broke and scattered; and the Queen's Own continued bravely and stupidly to retreat in order – until their backs were cut to pieces and fifty-three of them had fallen, seven not to rise again.

Only the news that Peacock's army was coming full-force saved the Canadians from being slaughtered. The Fenians pulled back to Fort Erie where an even more inept confrontation took place.

The Fenians, again by misadventure, barged into a platoon of militia who were guarding enemy prisoners aboard a tug called the *Robb*. The Canadian commander here, Colonel Dennison, who it must be said was exonerated later on at his judicial hearing, ordered his fifty guardsmen to attack the six hundred approaching Fenians. Naturally they had some reservations about the order but gallantly followed it, sustaining seven wounded before capturing twenty of the invaders and abandoning the effort. They tried to retreat with some composure to the tugboat, but it had pulled out in a panic and left them on the dock to fend for themselves. They broke and ran for the houses nearby. Their Colonel scuttled into a farm-cabin, donned the garb of a hired hand and slipped away to take up the fight another day. News arrived at Fort Erie that the American government had decided Canada was not worth the risk and was cutting off all the aid it had denied giving to the Fenian Brotherhood. The war was over. Both sides claimed victory. As they usually do.

"They're keeping up an alert till the end of the summer," Tom said. "We drill three times a week. The Company is giving us a day-a-week off to go on sentry duty. With half-pay," he added with great emphasis.

Robbie was fiddling with the bolt on his father's rifle.

"Stop that, Robbie," Lily said.

Robbie looked at Tom, and continued. He was stunned by his mother's stinging slap across his fingers.

"For Christ's sake, woman, you're impossible!" Tom shouted. He cradled Robbie in his trigger hand. "What in hell do you *want* from me anyway? What in hell do you expect me to *do?*"

"You do what I say," Lily said to Robbie, but all the strength had gone out of her voice.

Robbie's lips quivered but he didn't cry.

From the other room Brad whimpered in his sleep. Lily started towards him, then froze.

"Go ahead," Tom said, more in exasperation than anger.

"I hate her! I hate her!" she heard Robbie say as she entered the room where Brad was thrashing in his bed, his jaws swollen shut by the mumps.

"You say that again," Tom said, "and I'll stuff your mouth with soap." Robbie wailed as loud as Ariadne on her island: I know how you feel, Lily thought.

That night in bed Tom reached over, uncoiled her arms, softened her neck with his stroking, lay his head on her breasts, and when she was ready eased her thighs open and entered with only ecstasy he was still certain they could share. He wasn't wrong. His timing was off, but he gasped to a climax, then held on as she hurried to join him. His ribbed strength ebbed into her; she translated it into something of her own, the alien wonder of her high cry never failing to leave her lover transfixed and triumphant. They stayed together. He tried to ease her burden by shifting onto his hands, but she pulled them away and down towards her breasts until his whole weight fell lengthwise along her and she pinioned him with her ankles. Without seeming to have moved, hours onward he climaxed again. She brushed his eyelids with her tongue, implanting there secret words that would blossom only later under light and speak goldenly of love. Her legs dropped away; he drifted onto his side.

A long while after, he said: "They're beautiful children. I love them both. Almost as much as I love their mother."

He expected no reply. Her fingers, as naive as if they had just been released from their cocoon, roamed the reaches and most delicate places of his body.

The sun was just signalling the false-dawn when she said with no particular emotion, as if the thought had just occurred to her: "Why does there have to be a world out there?"

When they awoke well after sunrise, Tom said, "The Company's giving a special dance on Saturday. We should go."

"We must," Lily said.

Early in September two survivors of the Battle of Ridgeway were brought to Point Edward, courtesy of the Grand Trunk, to tell their stories to the local troops and invited guests. Following setbacks in Quebec and New Brunswick, the Fenian threat had subsided, but the Government was eager to keep patriotic fervour on high beam. After all, the Quebec Conference on Confederation was due to open in October and it never hurt to keep one's citizens emotionally primed and not a little frightened of the bogey-man. The Grand Trunk felt much the same as the Government itself did.

When Tom got home from the gathering well after midnight, he roused Lily from bed (but not sleep): "I need a cup of coffee," he announced with understatement, dropping his watch and stumbling after it in the gloom.

When Lily shook up the fire and boiled some water, Tom told her the whole story of the Canadian triumph over the cousins of Antichrist. What had begun at the start of the evening – before the booze was decanted – as mere fiction or harmless soldierly boasting graduated precipitately to fable and then soared blissfully towards fairy tale. Tom had an alcoholic grin on his face that wouldn't be erased till morning. He kept pulling playfully at Lily's nightshirt to make her look at him, at his happiness and at the pleasure he was having being himself in a world that once-in-a-blue-moon went right instead of wrong. She ignored the clumsy promise his fingers made against her breasts as she poured his coffee, and spilled some.

"Hey, watch the equipment!" he laughed. "Ain't got spare parts for *that* piece."

When she could no longer avoid it, she looked him in the eye, and through the whiskey-sheen she saw a far more compacted, more flammable brand of excitement.

Later, as he thumped and wheezed against her body, she was grateful for the dark. When he sighed and salivated his pathetic little drool of semen into her, she gave a correspondent moan which he mistook for joy. He skidded sideways into a slug's sleep. I love him, even now, like this, she thought, fighting her drowsiness. I love him even more. How can that be? Did love need an edge of panic, the wallow of sentiment? She envied his dreamless slumber, his lying there as if the peace that had seized his boy's body had been deserved or sanctioned by some force beyond the muscle pumping plasma into his imagination.

When she fell asleep she dreamed, as she feared she would, about the soldiers of Tom's story – floundering in Smuggler's Hole, their lungs boiling with blood they coughed onto lily pads, their hands spreading out like flippers in prayer as they sank oceanward, the sudden preponderance of their bones heavier than brine, they slipped under and down till the tip of their heads touched the earth's eldest crust, and as the tadpoles and pollywogs and fingerlings adjusted their nether-dance above them, the soldiers' eyes rolled up and cursed the sun with their death-gaze. Moments later a soldier in a different uniform, beardless and panicked, slipped to the edge of the pond, darted his eyes here and there like a spooked fawn, then pulled out his penis and, holding it as if it were a piece of slack rope, urinated into the murk.

18

1

It was spring again. Because it was unlikely they would be able to afford the move into the village for at least another year, Lily decided to spruce up the homestead. She had planted bulbs in the fall and they were now green spires aimed at the sky. Tom had built a trellis beside the kitchen window and helped her transplant a rosebush from Maudie Bacon's garden. Traces of pink were nudging through the bud-tips. Tom had made her a white flowerbox and set it under the front window in the south sun, and soon she would try her geranium cuttings nursed indoors throughout the winter. She and Brad made up a song about flowers. "Tu-lips, two-lips, do-lips" Brad sang, then rubbed his forefinger through his own lips, amazed at the world's happy coincidents. Another year here, Lily thought, and neither of us will want to move. Tom was taking Robbie on his shoulders down to the creek to fish every Sunday afternoon. Brad routinely trailed after her as she spaded and harrowed the garden (though he didn't much like getting dirty), distracting her with his banter and shy teasing.

On a bright windless Sunday in May, Lily was sitting on the stoop cutting the roots out of the last of the winter potatoes when she heard Brad say with a sinking whine, "Some people comin', Ma."

She looked towards the lane. Trouble. She could tell from the way the two figures held themselves sturdy in the black carriage, as if they were brunting a stiff Northerly. She could sniff rectitude at fifty paces. The horses, frothing against a strict rein, wheeled through the gateway and into the yard, where they stopped – much relieved.

"Good morning, missus," hallooed the large parson down the long nave of the lane. He wrapped the reins firmly in place and proceeded to dismount. He waddled around in front of the horses, giving their baleful stare a wide berth, and stretched out a pudgy hand to his companion. She took it automatically, as if lifting a latch-key, and stepped onto the grass with a practiced swirl. Hand-in-glove, they trundled towards Lily.

"I am the Reverend Dougall Hardman," the parson announced, "of the Wesleyan Methodist Church of Port Sarnia. And this is my good wife, Mrs. Hardman."

"Charity," said the good wife without defacing her smile.

"Yes, and you must be the young Mrs. Marshall we've heard so much about," the preacher said, reaching unsuccessfully for her hand and glancing past her towards the house.

Clara, thought Lily.

"Lily, isn't it?"

"Yes, how do you do?"

"And who's this darling little creature?"

Brad ducked behind Lily's skirt.

The Reverend Hardman cleared his throat with pre-sermon vigour. "Ah, we've come on official business."

"I can make some tea, if you can wait a minute. Would you like to come in?"

"Is your husband at home, missus?"

"No, he ain't." She hesitated, then said, "Him an' Robbie are off fishin'."

The parson swallowed his astonishment long enough to say, "We'll come in and wait, if it isn't too much trouble."

"What a pretty little cottage," Mrs. Hardman said.

The Reverend Hardman was obese: his jowls jigged contrapuntally with the jawbone somewhere inside driving the bellows of his windy sentences. His cleric's collar lay buried in his neck-flesh so profoundly that only a thin ring of it showed through, like a band on a turkey. When he sat at his ease in Uncle Chester's chair, his great belly dozed on two bony knees; his plump fingers fed on the macaroons and tea-cakes like loose grubs. Notwithstanding, there was something different here from the usual parson fattened up by too many teas, bake-sales, middle-age, and ecclesiastical doubt. From the slim leg, the curse of the shoulder and the quick feet came the hint of a once-muscular frame, leathered skin, and agility. A circuit-rider, Lily thought, the memory striking deep.

Mrs. Charity Hardman was a bosomy but well-proportioned woman, trussed, corsetted and handsomely turned out in a mauve dress whose flounces, cuffs, and lacy appendages might have been described by some as bounteous. She sipped her tea with white gloves intact; she resisted all temptation to indulge further. From the edge of her chair she kept her wifely eye on a point just below her husband's lower jaw where his chins converged, and nodded ritually on some cue from him which Lily was unable to detect.

Working from the general principle that anything he had to say was of rivetting significance to any bystander, Reverend Hardman proceeded to orate – with pauses to detassel a cup-cake or disfigure the odd macaroon – the long history of his Church in the country, winding his way eventually towards the good news that next autumn the Wesleyan Methodists were going to build a church in Point Edward that would rival the Anglican once now there in size, expense and depth of devotion. And in the true spirit of ecumenical Christianity, the edifice would be open to use by such demi-infidels as Congregationalists and Presbyterians (no Baptists, please) until such times as they could afford their own houses of worship.

"You will agree that this is a signal achievement, indeed an honour for such a small and as yet unincorporated village?"

Mrs. Reverend nodded.

"Of course, I was quick to volunteer my services. As Mrs. Hardman can confirm, I have always been a man to take on a fresh challenge for the sake of Our Lord."

Mrs. Reverend tilted her petalled hat in Lily's direction.

"As minister to a new flock my duties are manifold," he said, crushing a maca-roon on the downbeat. "First, we shall need commitment, real commitment from our doughty band of believers."

"Money," murmured Missus, delicately.

"True, true. We are looking for pledges, for tithing in the old-fashioned sense."

Lily brought out the last of the macaroons made especially for Robbie and Tom.

"Secondly, we'll need the use of all the talents, the combined gifts, as it were, of our supporters." He stared wistfully at his tea, dotted with crumbs.

"Men to assist with the stone-work and the roof," offered his help-mate.

"Precisely. And finally we shall need the love and spiritual wishes of the whole Christian community, we need their prayers for our success as we seek most humbly to establish a fellowship of adherents among the workers of the Grand Trunk and their loving families."

Mrs. Hardman started to nod but was ambushed by a yawn. It went unnoticed.

"As you can tell, missus, I am a blunt, straightforward man. Always have been, always will." For the first time Lily felt his gaze encompass her, even though he had been more or less pointed in her direction throughout the service. "We would like you and your husband to think seriously about how much you can afford to give us in sup-port of God's work. More important even, we are hoping to open a Sabbath school in September. It is our understanding that your eldest – the one now, ah, fishing with his father – will soon be four-years old."

So it *was* Clara, Lily thought.

"Mrs. Hardman has agreed, on top of all her other onerous duties, to take on the little ones, suffering them to come unto her, as it were."

Mrs. Hardman lengthened her smile a notch.

"He ain't been baptized," Lily said.

The parson showed no surprise. "Don't be ashamed, my dear girl," he said, glancing sideways at the vacant plate. "Remember, I've been a circuit rider, I know the country ways and country feelings. Things get put off. Spiritual matters are often suspended by more pressing demands of the moment. We shall make arrangements for both your children to be baptized. Why, we could inaugurate the Church with such a happy ceremony!" He smiled as if he'd just thought of the notion.

"Such a beautiful child," Mrs. Hardman said, looking about for Brad.

Lily stood up. "When Tom gets home, we'll talk over what you just said. It's been nice meetin' you."

Charity Hardman came back for her parasol. Lily met her at the door. The smile on her face had crumbled. Nothing remained but the pain of a frightened eye. She seized Lily by the wrist and whispered fiercely: "Clara's told me all about you, Lily. Won't you think hard about comin' to the new church? It gets awful lonesome out here in the country. Besides, we got to stick together, you know. I mean us women."

"*Mrs.* Hardman!"

"*Coming!*" she shouted back. With a desperate sort of malice she said to Lily, "An' you don't have to swallow all the malarkey you hear from *that* source!"

As the carriage disappeared, Lily heard the crack of the whip over the horses' heads.

2

The Fathers of Confederation set aside July the first as the day when the citizens of the new Dominion of Canada were to celebrate this historic act of collective paternity. That there may have been more cause for excitement in the boardrooms and on the front benches of the nation did not in any way diminish the general enthusiasm of the magic hour. Even before the ink was dry on the British North America Act, the yearning for a united land from sea to sea was already being translated into affirmative action. On June 28, 1867, *The Sarnia Observer* noted that a complaint had been received from the German emigrants heading west for Manitoba via rail, ship and cart-trek; to wit: the cattle cars that had been rigged out for their comfort contained (they said) only one bucket of water to last five-dozen souls from Toronto to the Point Edward wharf; naturally such ingratitude was dealt with curtly and correctly in the Grand Trunk's statement of denial. Thirsty or not, the movement westward had begun, and was inevitable: a new destiny was becoming manifest.

No town celebrated the nativity more avidly than Sarnia. The local press accounts tell the whole story. 'During the morning a large number of loyal yeoman from the neighbouring townships, accompanied in most cases by the members of their families, came into town by all the leading roads, until ultimately there was a larger influx of strangers than was ever before present, except on the occasion of the visit of His Royal Highness the Prince of Wales.' Two infantry companies from Moore and Sarnia marched to the parade-grounds led by the Sarnia Cornet Band, bugles ablaze in the sun. Here they were joined by the Grand Trunk Rifle Companies from Point Edward under Major Riley. 'After going through a variety of evolutions, the Companies were formed into line, and fired the *feu-de-joie* at noon.' A grand procession then took place back through the town's thoroughfares, bedecked with bunting and spruce-boughs and lined with crowds cheering and waving Union Jacks, as if Wellington himself were marching home from Waterloo. Right behind the band came the volunteers – their combat dreams still warm – and then the town clerk with Queen Victoria's Proclamation and, wonder of wonders, 'four young virgins in white, in a carriage and four, as representatives of the four Provinces'. Following on the heels of the Fire Brigades of Port Huron and Sarnia were the Sabbath school children – skipping, hitching, sidling, scooting and tumbling in egregious disarray. 'On the whole, the Procession was the largest and most imposing ever found in the Town with the exception of that which proceeded from the Town to Point Edward on the Prince of Wales' visit.' Particularly impressive were the volunteer companies of the St. Clair Borderers, all in green, rifles erect, bayonets glinting, their synchromeshed strut signalling their martial pride, warning of borders to be defended to the death, and boasting of heroics certain to come.

When the soldiers fired their rifles at noon, Brad screamed and jumped into Lily's arms. Robbie hopped up and down, searching for a face among the uniforms. She had just got Brad settled down – standing with the boys at the corner of Christina and George – when the bugles struck up a battle hymn right in front of them. She could feel Robbie's body – through his hand – keeping time to the quick-step. The green tunics of the Borderers swept into view around the corner. They seemed to be striding into the vacuum left by the imperial alarums of the trumpeters, a capsule of silence designed to exaggerate the thud of every jack-boot, the clink of tunic metal, the rasp of martial cloth against pink flesh. But if you swung your head rapidly past the moving ranks, the silver bayonets might have been mistaken for the quills of a chieftain's headdress.

Brad started to whimper; he buried his face in Lily's skirt and trembled. Softly into his ear she hummed something gentle, but the crowd noise rose around her like an ambuscade as the Proclamation coach was spotted, and deafened them both, so that they almost didn't notice Robbie leap up with a body-length salute and cry out, "Look, there's *Da!*"

3

Tom came in from work. Since his promotion to assistant foreman (Warden Hargreaves had been transferred temporarily to Ottawa for strategic purposes), he was invariably all smiles.

"What's wrong?" Lily said.

"We got a letter, from New York."

Lily stood beside him and watched him read it, seeing the words and hearing the strange voice of Melville Armbruster ricochet inside them, and hearing under them – like the echo of a sea-conch under oceans – a tiny, compressed cry that might have been her own.

Long Island, N.Y.

August 5, 1867.

Dear Lily:

I am writing to tell you that your Aunt Bridie passed away yesterday. She died peacefully in her sleep, and now rests in the arms of her Maker. Let me tell you what has happened since those happy days when we last say you. I hope and pray that you will understand.

When Bridie and I got to New York after the wedding in London, we stayed only long enough to meet my family here on our estate, and then we were off on a honeymoon and business trip that lasted three glorious months. We travelled first-class by train to Baltimore, Washington, St. Louis, Chicago and as far west as St. Cloud, Minnesota. We stayed at the best hotels, several of which we invested in, and I showed your Aunt the heart and soul of democratic America. She said it was the happiest time of her life. Certainly it was that, and more, for me. Let me say also that Bridie never forgot your Uncle Chester or you and Tom. Whenever we'd tour a lumber mill or carriage maker's, she'd say, 'now wouldn't Chester just love a set-up like this' or 'I wish young Tom could see all this, all the opportunities for a man with his talent and education'. Of course she never stopped talking about her Lily, and praying she'd hear news when we got back about a baby-on-the-way.

She never got back, though – at least not the Bridie we all knew and loved. In Buffalo, on our return trip, she caught some kind of influenza and by the time we got home to New York, she was gravely ill in a coma. I was about to send a telegram to you when she suddenly awakened and seemed miraculously to recover. A day later, however, she suffered what the doctors called a stroke. It left her paralyzed all down the left side. But ill as she was, she could still talk in a slurred sort of voice only I could understand, and when I suggested I ought to telegraph you people and send money for train tickets to New York, she said *no*. At first I refused to believe her, but I could see in her eyes and in the tortured twisting of her body every time she spoke that she really meant it. She did not want her Lily to see her like this, though she would never tell me why. I honoured her wish, though I've been wracked by guilt and unease every day and night since.

For almost five years now we have been living on my family's estate, Bridie and me. I've been taking care of her every need, and she has been as brave and wonderful in her dying as she was in her living. I have no regrets, save the fact that caring for her meant cutting us off from you. But her eyes never once said *yes*, not in all these months of pain and even in the last serene moments when we both knew the end was near. She is gone now, and I can tell the whole story. She was a remarkable woman.

She will be buried in the Armbruster mausoleum tomorrow. I sincerely hope you can come to visit the gravesite and I trust that I'll have the opportunity to learn from you more about this great woman I only got to know a little, so late in my life.

All my love,
Melville Armbruster

Something fell out of the envelope. Lily picked it up. It was an American one-hundred-dollar bill.

Tom held Lily in his foreman's arms all that night. At breakfast she said to him, "I think it's time we moved."

"Soon," he said. "That's a promise."

4

By May of 1870 when the troubles began which would be unresolved even a hundred years later, the Confederatory experiment was not yet three years old. Older by far, indeed celebrating its tenth year of existence, was the company town at the nexus of the River and the Lake. From the outset Point Edward was no ordinary or typical small community of Canada West (or Ontario as it was now nominated in official circles and on the fresh maps of the new Dominion already intimating the imminent annexation of Prince Edward Island, Rupert's Land and British Columbia). It was not of village size, some seven hundred souls, and growing weekly. But it would be some years yet before any move were made to incorporate it as a self-governing village. The paterfamiliality of the Grand Trunk lay heavily upon it. Though many of the properties and businesses had been purchased outright from the Company, it still owned five boarding-houses on St. Clair Street and most of the undeveloped land to the east and south-east which rested in fallow, and appreciated. Eighty-per-cent of the men in the village worked for the Grand Trunk, the others ran businesses or supplied services directly dependent upon the railway. Because the Company's facilities were concentrated along the waterfront, the town grew around it in a horse-shoe shape. Here, then, there could be no village green flanked by churches, library and town hall with quaint cottages idling among the grasses and flowers in trim ranks all the way to the outskirts where a tannery or mill or furniture factory might pull their pastoral smoke into the serene evenings of Middletown, Ontario. There was nothing sleepy about Point Edward. Night and day three-dozen locomotives ran their own version of the anvil chorus. Screw-prop freighters churned into the berths along the Grand Trunk wharf and hooted for attention. Twice a day, passenger trains – local and express – roared to a stop before the gothic grandeur of the station-hotel, discharging political hacks, carpetbaggers and commercial bashaws of every breed into the luxury and corruption that only a first-class colonial hotel can guarantee. Occasionally there arrived a cattle-train with Icelandic immigrants heading for the about-to-be-annexed New West, but temporarily herded into one of the engine-barns to wait for a refitted grain-scow to ferry them Huronward. The noise of their appreciation was often enough to keep a Christian awake at his prayers. Surrounding the din and hubbub of the rail-yards were a dozen thriving but obstreperous enterprises linked to prosperity by rail and sail – smithies hammering out plates and spikes, welders scorching metal into submission, even a manufacturer of barrel-staves who preferred to labour at night. So it was that the town proper did not begin for half-a-mile from its commercial heart – on Prince Street in fact, which ran parallel to the River and was unique among small-village boulevards in having buildings only on its east side and each one of them a hotel or something with pretentions in that direction. While the Grand Trunk station-hotel accommodated those worthies staying overnight on business or waiting for water transportation, smaller hostels like The Queen's served the drummers, gamblers, mountebanks, beached sailors and low-brimmed capitalists seeking illicit pleasures of sundry kind. When the beverage rooms closed, one could drink one's way into a whiskey stupor in the sanctity of an upstairs boudoir complete with country courtesan and douche. If more daring (or desperate), one could slip over the tracks into Mushroom Alley where the gormandizing was as licorous as it was revulsive. At night all the decent burghers of the village clamped shut their shutters and their curiosity. On Sundays the harbingers of virtue inveighed thunderously from three pulpits but did not extend their pastorates quite as far as Prince Street itself.

Point Edward by day was also unique among the insular Christian communities of those days. In most Ontario towns everyone on a main street would be instantly identifiable – along with his pedigrees, the direction and purpose of his movements, the said-value of these latter and the likely consequences thereof. A stranger's presence would be noticed as quick as a bur between the toes and be almost as popular. But here, Michigan Ave. and Prince Street – even a back street if it led to the beach – were daily invaded by exotic creatures from every class, the identification of whom could often form an amusing but inconclusive pastime. Tramps, sailors, stockbrokers, escaped felons, failed poets, even Sir John A. Himself might pass by Redmond's store without a second glance being taken. Notwithstanding such an incongruous cosmopolitanism, there existed alongside it – or within it – a typical ingrown, self-generating community of the Ontario variety. Amazingly, the two societies rarely blended, even at the edges, though they were materially responsible for each other's welfare. The 'village' of Point Edward provided the Grand Trunk with a sober supply of respectable workers with families to ballast their commitment and a church to teach them their manners. The Company – despite the noise, moral squalor, and crass commercialism – ensured the permanent citizens a life of modest affluence and certain progress in divine concert with the Dominion itself.

5

Lily Marshall stood at her kitchen window and surveyed the wonders of her small world. The tulips she had planted along the garden path bloomed gaily in primary reds and yellows. Clara and Gimpy – returned to their circle of friends once more – had made a special trip out in their new Burlington buggy just to admire them, Clara's frail teeter and pastel stare reminding them of her recent ordeal, Gimpy joking bravely and poking his leg in jest at the boys. Along the lane the lilacs that Bachelor Bill helped Uncle Chester plant so long ago exploded a dozenfold in mauve and evening indigo, their underground runners popping up everywhere around, stitching earth to air. Along the edge of the spaded vegetable patch, Robbie, dreaming of his seventh birthday and instant manhood, roamed like a scout for King Arthur – nose to the ground, wooden sabre cocked and ready (made for the young paladin by his aging father), and muttering *abracadabra* oaths to keep his courage charged. With no visible mercy he cut down every milkweed corpse who had dared to survive the winter with a fearsome blow, then scampered into the woods in the direction of Big Creek or Camelot. Ever since Gimpy had read him those King Arthur stories during his stay with them (while Lily nursed Clara alone), Robbie had been wild with them. Tom borrowed the book and read him more, indeed read to them all around the winter fire. Robbie could hardly sit still long enough to hear the end of an adventure; he would be itching to act it out, to get outdoors and stretch his legs and his intrepid arms. He never wanted the same story repeated, and would threaten a tantrum whenever Brad, as he usually did, asked for the one about Gawain or young Lancelot again and again. Lily watched Brad's eyes, the flame dancing in them, as he lay on the sheepskin and formed the words in his mouth a second before Tom pronounced them, as if he were tasting them, until all at once they struck his imagination with the impact of tattoos. Lily sat beside Tom on the arm of the big chair, matching the letters to her husband's lips, herself no longer amazed at the magic congruence of letter and sound, the marvelling transformations of the heart it allowed. She could read. Not all by herself yet. But almost, soon. When Robbie went off to school, in the village in September, she would have him bring the gray-covered primer home, and they would learn together. And Brad too. Lily and her boys.

That's what people whispered behind her along Michigan Ave. when she pulled them into town on the toboggan Tom had made them. She wanted them to say it out loud, to sing it to the congregation. "An' how are the tow-heads this morning?" grocer Redmond would say, ruffling their hair under the tuques and slipping them an appeasing sweet. "Like two beans on a platter." But of course they were as different as two humans could be. For Robbie the objects of the variegated world around him were put there by some benign gamesmaster especially for him to explore, expose to delight or plunder with desire. When he rested, they did too. He could watch with dispassion as his father skinned a freshly-killed rabbit, not connecting the clouded eyes in the death-clench of that animal's face with the bright kinship of those that peered out at him from a brush pile or turned their tender curiosity upon him when he disturbed them over lunch at the lettuce patch. Brad, too, as his health improved, loved to be outdoors in the summer. When the family went walking together, Brad would lag or meander, sometimes even stop in mid-stride as something in the air struck him still: a thrush's sigh from the shadows, beads of dew along a leaf trapped by light, a crow raking the silence with his caw, a bullfrog's eyes bobbing in the slime, the flick of a trout in a pool with no bottom. From this window she could, if she were careful, watch him out there – listening, touching, reaching for the roots of awe. At such moments she wished she could bring him – and Robbie as well – to Old Samuels and hear them talk together or not talk in those silences-between-souls she knew were gone now from her own life. Robbie would have bounced into the woods on Sounder's heels, chattering all the while and then going perfectly quiet for hours, like foxes in the deep grass waiting for prey. Brad and Acorn would have been fast friends, nothing could have stopped them.

Naturally Tom found it easier to relate to Robbie, taking him off to fish in the creek, sometimes letting him come along while he hunted, the boy carrying the lumpy burlap with two dead cottontails on his sore back, blood tickling his bare leg. The boy worshipped Tom's presence and filled his absence with reverent re-enactments of their pleasures. Brad, horrified by the barn, the stench of carcasses and the accusing eyes of slain creatures, took to Tom slowly and obliquely. At last Tom seemed to understand this and accept it as what would always be between them. Tom had that disarming smile – quick and unprepared for, flashing news of its warmth, its fear of being hurt, the sense of its own helplessness in the mess of emotion and desire that made up his larger being. Gradually and very reluctantly, Brad caught sight of those parts of Tom she herself had loved outright from the moment of contact across a faraway dance-floor. By the time Tom began reading to him, Brad was not surprised. Months later he eased himself up onto Tom's knee, and Tom kept right on reading.

They are each an extension of one part of Tom, she thought. Does he know that? Is that why he can love them in such different ways? How much of me lies enfolded in them, I don't really know. I can't see such things because I think of my love for them as complete and whole – as an unending ache when I fear for their safety, panic when their bodies shiver on the brink of fever, as joy that swells out of my heart and leaves me without breath when I see them laughing together with Tom with nature with the world around that loves them this moment. What the women who will love them later might see, I can never say. The affections that bind us here and now are a web of wondrous intricacy, of inseparable elements: Tom and me, me and Tom, Tom and each of his boys, me and the boys. We are. I never hoped for more.

Tom was more than happy when he was offered the foreman's job starting in September. He felt vindicated. He wrote to Bags Starkey's cousin in London to offer Bags a job, but word came back that he had 'gone off' without telling anyone where. On the first sunny Sunday in April, Tom had borrowed Gimpy's old buggy and taken the whole family for a drive in the country. On the way back home they detoured into the village, and Tom, going strangely quiet, pulled the horses up at the corner of Albert and Ernest. Tom pointed his whip towards a newly-built frame cottage covered with cedar-shakes, whose aroma sweetened the air for blocks around.

"It comes up for sale," Tom said, "at the end of the summer."

Lily took hold of his other hand. "The school's just down the street a ways," she said to the boys.

"I don't wanna go to no school," Robbie said.

"He's just mad 'cause we took so long," Lily said quickly to Tom. He just laughed and embarrassed the boys by hugging her in public. To the north Lily could hear the waves repeating their chant on Canatara.

What more could I want, Lily thought, watching Brad from her kitchen window as he sat on the oak-stump in the May sunshine staring past his brother's antics into the woods beyond. The move into the village would be the last link in the chain of connection Lily felt all around her these days. They would at last become part of some larger community, one in which, though she herself might never feel fully a citizen, the boys could grow up inside so naturally they would think later on they had invented it. For Tom, it meant committing himself more certainly to a life he had taken up in large measure because of his love for her; company and family and town would be his domain. But there was a part of him – as with her – that would always remain irreconciled to domesticity, to the predictable rhythms of civility, to a God who hurled brimstone one moment and puffed on a pipe the next. I loved that in him too, she thought, I must have – that perverse will to hazard, to ride the flux, to play truth-or-dare with the random deities of the universe.

Old Samuels was right: the gods don't disassemble when the hedgerows and the houses and walled gardens go up. When the white man cleared the forest of the great trees that were left in the wake of the fleeing ice, the demons who lived in them did not perish in their ash, they were released into the volatility of air where they still whirl and collide and howl like schizophrenes. Even now they ride the winds of pestilence over the corrupt earth, mocking and vengeful.

Lily had heard their mocking laughter many times. When Clara's boy was stillborn and she had come down with childbed fever, Lily had wrapped the foetus in a blanket and covered its drowned eyes and begged Clara not to look. She had sat beside her friend for weeks, watching her twist and grimace with dreadful pain and with the dream of the dead child's face. Most of the time they were alone in the dark, where Lily's hand on a brow, a cheek, over the eyelids was Clara's only link with life and its manifest horrors. When the fever broke and Clara was surprised to find herself alive, she gave Lily a look that said: so it was *you* who brought me back to all this? Later on, when Gimpy arrived and Lily had bathed the stink off her and washed her hair and put a bit of rouge on her ghastly face, Clara smiled and was able to offer something that was almost gratitude. Lily was not in the least offended.

During the winter there had been a diphtheria scare. Quarantine signs dotted the village doors. Lily didn't go into town for weeks. The boys complained but were not taken to Little Lake to skate. Word came via Tom that Maudie Bacon's youngest was stricken. "She's got Mary there to help," was all Tom said. A week later Maudie's little girl was dead but not before suffering the bewilderment of pain that no mother's arms could diminish or explain. She was the first human creature to be buried in the cemetery grounds just donated by the Grand Trunk to the three churches. She's near the woods and the shy trilliums, Lily thought, blotting out the nasal sentiments of the Reverend Hardman. Old Samuels would approve. But what would he say about Aunt Bridie encased in knickerbocker granite lintelled with a family name that would have shrivelled a leprechaun's laugh. Or Uncle Chester buttoned up in the chaste Methodist grave of a sometime oil town, the name on the headstone a perpetual puzzlement to the locals ever after. Where were their spirits now?

A few weeks after the funeral Lily caught Robbie in her room with a leather pouch wide open on the floor and one of its objects in his hand. "Uch!" he snorted, "a dead rabbit's foot." Lily scolded him more severely than he thought necessary, and then gently replaced the cross, pendant, stone and Testament. The rabbit's foot she kept in her hand till it warmed. "Did Da shoot that?" Robbie said through his dried tears.

Lily put the token in her apron pocket, and when Tom took the boys off to watch the ice break up on the creek, she put on her coat and scarf and headed into town.

She went around the northern perimeter, avoiding the streets, walked along the tracks a ways till she could see the smoke from the shacks in Mushroom Alley, then veered north through the brush, coming out after a while into the windswept clearing she knew so well. She sat down and caught her breath. Soon the voices began, one by one, to detach themselves from the wind. She heard Acorn say something to Sounder and caught Sounder's shrill laughter. Southener repeated words to her she had almost forgotten. She saw the outlines of his grave, now sunken below ground level with the weight of a dozen years. Where is he? She asked soundlessly, afraid that even a jarring step might be catastrophic. Slowly she felt her head turn to the north-east, and perhaps ten minutes later – how could she tell? – she was able to discern a slight rectangular hump in the sand, well disguised by grass and young aldershoots. She approached the grave, knelt down, said something reverential in a strange tongue, then scooped up a little sand, placed the rabbit's foot in the hollow, and covered it. *Goodbye, Old Samuels.*

Lily stood in the kitchen window remembering when Uncle Chester used to hold her aloft to see over the sill into the green world. It was hard to believe that by this September her life would have completed one of its great seasonal shifts, that the Grand Trunk would at last exercise dominion over Bridie's land, in return for which they would put down fresh roots in the very village her Aunt had dreamed so intensely it had become real. *What would you think of that, old Shaman?*

In the yard, Robbie had talked or bullied Brad into joining his game. Brad had been offered the sword with the broken blade as a bribe, while Arthur brandished Excalibur possessively. On these rare occasions when Brad was moved to enter into his brother's fantasies, he did so, unbeknownst to Robbie, on his own terms. While Robbie pursued the treacherous Mordred or the cowardly two-faced Saxon (Hengest-and-Horsa), while he jousted and sallied and cut-to-ribbons – Brad played his designated parts, but Lily could see, as she did now, that in the kingdom of his own imagination he was reinventing a world for his pleasure alone. She could hear him humming or chanting away to himself as he dodged the wrath of Galahad's forays. For Brad, no re-enactment of the old stories was real without the words tumbling through his head in magic metamorphoses. Suddenly, Galahad's sword slashed spitefully across an exposed calf. Lily heard the smack and saw Brad fall into the grass. Robbie was stunned by the deed as the victim; he stood gazing at his weapon as if about to accuse it of some crime. Then he turned to watch his brother. Brad's lower lip quivered as the red welt on his leg rose up, stinging. He glanced towards the house, straight into the morning sun. Robbie waited, something faintly pleading in his face. Brad began rubbing the wound, silent tears sliding out and down. Robbie suddenly sat down beside him. Instinctively Brad started to edge away but was stopped by Robbie's arm as it came across his shoulder and gripped it. Very slowly Robbie opened the fingers of his brother's left hand and placed in them the diamond-stubbed Excalibur from Camelot.

Lily was watching it all from her window. A wonder, she thought. The random gesture. Love's accidence.

Lily had just begun getting Tom's supper ready when he surprised her – standing in the doorway the way he always did when there was news.

"It's all right," he said, seeing her reaction. "We've been called up, but it's nothing to worry about."

Lily found herself sitting on the arm of the big chair, a kettle steaming in her hand.

"We're going west. There's been some trouble with the half-breeds out there, but nobody expects we'll have to do much shooting."

Lily felt the kettle brush the floor.

"Say something, Lil. Don't just sit there looking at me like that. You know I got to go."

"You're a volunteer."

"You know I got to go."

Yes, I do know, she wanted to say. And I've tried to understand all these years, I really have. And maybe, too, its partly my fault for loving that unknowable night-thing in you, for being afraid of it, for wanting to bring it too close to the sunlight and tame it with familiarity, yet all along secretly cherishing it as I do those kinds of things in myself I keep hidden from you. I *do* know. And I know also that I could reach out at this moment and touch you in a way that would make you want to stay. If I do, I may regret it for the rest of my life. If I don't…

"We're going to sail into the north," Tom was saying, settling her into the chair and sitting beside her on the arm, "all the way to the lakehead, then cross the Rainy River system in canoes like the old voyageurs. Then we march over the Prairie to Fort Garry where we stay for a while to make sure the new province gets off to a proper start. No fighting, no war. Monsieur Riel won't be there to greet us."

"Think of the boys," she said.

"I am," Tom said. "With the money I'll get from this stint we'll be able to buy furniture for the new house, clothes and books for the boys when they go to school. You'll be able to throw away that wretched quilting frame forever. We'll come back here and put a torch to this old place and make sure it stays a part of our past. Lily, you don't understand. I've got to go. Now."

Yes, it may be the last chance.

"I'm gonna come back, you know."

Lily picked up the kettle. "Supper's ruined," she said.

"I promise."

"I ain't goin' down to the boat."

Lily said her goodbyes at the gate. Gimpy had come with his buggy to take Tom and his gear to the troop-ship waiting at the wharf, and to supervise Robbie who was being allowed to cheer the soldiers off with his hankey-sized Union Jack. Lily waited until the horses had almost reached the bend before she began to tremble all over. Tom turned in his seat and waved back to her, his manly figure caught for a second in a burst of lilac-spray. It was an image she would hold unchanging in her heart for a long, long time.

A few weeks after Tom left, Lily missed her second period.

6

Early in May of 1870 the new Dominion under the stewardship of Sir John A. Macdonald undertook its first large-scale mobilization and transfer of troops to a distant war zone. Railroad, lake-steamer, bateaux and forced march were splendidly coordinated so that in a mere ninety-six days Colonel Wolseley's army of twelve-hundred volunteers and regulars arrived at the outskirts of Fort Garry, Manitoba to claim the province for Canada. No resistance was met. Not a soul to shoot at. A member of Wolseley's staff recorded in his diary that day: 'We were enthusiastically greeted by a half-naked Indian, very drunk'.

But the getting-there was itself a triumph of Canadian ingenuity. Troop-trains left Montreal and Toronto, picked up volunteer units along the main-line and deposited them on the wharfs of Collingwood and Point Edward, where troop-ships – refitted freighters – whisked the battalions northeastward along the ancient fur-trading routes of Champlain, Radisson and Groseilliers, Marquette and Joliet, and the mighty La-Salle. At Fort William they disembarked, seasick but singing, and clambered into hastily constructed bateaux which were three-quarters canoe and two-quarters sailboat. In mid-May they disappeared into the bush and did not emerge again until August 23. Occasional scouts, of hardy native stock, returned to Base Fort William to report on morale and on progress made to a tense and bored populace. These messengers also brought out mail destined for the home front.

So it was that Lily received five letters from Tom written over a span of six weeks, the last one dated 'August 7, 1870, near Rat Portage'. Gimpy and Clara (who was pregnant again) came over, and they read through them. Though Lily found she could read much of Tom's elegant script, she preferred to let Gimpy read aloud so that she could close her eyes and picture every event and hear the words Tom chose: to make each a part of him.

Tom was attached to a forward unit, his company the only volunteer group to be so honoured. The first few days were jolly ones because the recruits could stretch out the muscles cramped by several days in steerage. The sun warmed them by day and the crisp stars overhead at night seemed to bless their enterprise. Then the rains came and the forty-two-mile portage up to Lake Shebandowan. Fire and torrential spring storms had destroyed the primitive right-of-way. Tom's crew headed into the bush with axe and whip-saw. 'I felt like one of the pioneers out there, hacking and cursing and blistering in places I didn't know I owned.' It took three weeks to clear a path wide enough for the rearguard to dismantle and carry their boats through, along with two-hundred-pound barrels of salt-pork, cannon, cannonballs, rifles and cases of ammunition. The bulkier craft had to be pushed ahead on rollers which disappeared into the muskeg as fast as Tom's crew could cut them. Now did the muscles rebel in the wet bivouacs of a chilling dark, the mosquitoes take up the flies' leavings and the rain wash entire tents away from their frail moorings. Exhausted but undaunted, the raw troops reached for fresh inspiration and found it on the smooth straits of Lac des Mille Lacs and the resurgence of July's best sun. While the paddling arms had strengthened and spirits brightened again, the jolting pattern of shooting rapids, driving hullward into stiff winds on open lakes, making sharp, brutal portages, and searching hopelessly for a dry bivouac – these soon took their toll. The food worsened. Dysentery and the grippe left dozens of men to languish in the rear, slumped among the supplies, moaning to keep each other company. But Tom miraculously grew stronger, healthier, happier. He was placed in the vanguard of the paddlers, in the slick canoes manned by Iroquois and Métis scouts. He sang with them. He seemed to forget where they were going and why. He did not wonder at the arrival of Métis scouts sent by the 'rebel' Riel to welcome and guide them in. He revelled in the challenge of the white water, the muskeg like quick-sand, the raw cold of the rivers lit by sun but never warmed even in the sweltering heat of early August. Lily could hear him singing, she could see the reddish-blond beard circling the elementary blue of his eyes, she could yearn to be under him anywhere, always, below the altar of the stars.

On August 8 the expedition neared Rat Portage, passing through an uncharted narrows in the Winnipeg River. Lily held her breath as she watched the war-canoe tossed ponderously by the frantic rapid, tilting and dextrously righted by a dozen pad-dles with a touch as silk as a pianist's, battered sideways by a furtive boulder to an edge of balance, only to be slung straight by the current itself as it hurtled westward blindly, without cause. All at once the lead canoe pitched left as if a sail had been punched by a gust; it yawed, skidded rudderless along a flat patch in the eye of something sinister, spun counter-clockwise like the earth itself only flatter, only laughing at gravity as the paddlers swung free of its burden and tumbled with military precision, one by one, into the gorge below. Lily saw her Tom strike the surface, lean on its buoyancy for a long second, wave his arms at some invisible rope in the air and go under, his head only – mouth, eyes, nose – bobbing up again farther down the roiling half-mile narrows full of rocks that had broached many a birch-bark or the drum of a man's belly. He made so sound at all and after a while his eyes quit looking anywhere. When his body was hauled ashore, floating blissfully in a trout-pool miles away, the underwater rocks had battered it beyond recognition. They knew it was him because some of the white skin showed through the bruising. There was no bleeding because his body was frozen; the cold had killed him, they said, before he could be drowned or bludgeoned to death. Just as well.

Still, there on shore it was August with a rotting sun overhead. Nothing to do but bury the soldier with as much dignity as possible, with due notation of his incredible valour, his unshakable patriotism. They gouged a shallow grave out of the muskeg and laid him there in a spruce coffin girdled by a Union Jack. The volunteers shivered in the heat as the Last Post rang emptily over the Barrens – haunted by stunted cedars, wreaths of sphagnum, and brackish moss-water still shaken by the memory of the Great Glacier rumbling backwards overhead.

Two months later, after many of the troops had been quietly returned home by rail through St. Cloud and Chicago, Major Bolton came to the house to tell Lily the story of Tom's heroic death. The details he provided her – in a kind and fatherly manner that genuinely touched her – added little to what she had already seen in her own way.

After he left, Lily sat for some time, by herself, staring out of the kitchen window she had for so long now used to measure the ebb and flow of her small being-on-this-earth. She tried not to imagine a world that would no longer acknowledge the absence of Aunt Bridie or Uncle Chester, of Bachelor Bill and the moon-sad face of his Violet, of Old Samuels and all his kind, and Mama and Maman and Aunt Elspeth, and Papa wherever the woods was hiding him. She tried not to imagine a life without Tom, without the kind of love engendered only in the dream-songs of the young for whom the future is as real as a moment of touch-and-surrender. She tried not to think of such a place nor the gods mad enough to have contrived it. No deity – whatever its hue or cry – could have invented this, she thought. I cannot accept it. What do you think of that, old Shaman? Do you hear me calling out, shouting over and over again – as if my heart were stone-deaf – *I am Lily Marshall, I am Lily Marshall, I am Lily Marshall*. And who is there to care?

Something urgent was poking itself into her ribs.

"Mama," Brad said at her side, still prodding.

"Not now."

"Tell me a story, Mama, the one about Sir Galahad. Please."

And somehow, she did.

PART THREE

Sophie

19

In the middle of October 1870 Maudie Bacon's husband, Garth, returned home from the wars to a hero's welcome. Riel and his Métis hooligans had been routed without a shot being fired; Manitoba was salvaged for the Confederation and the federalist cause materially advanced. The Grand Trunk – already rumoured to be vying with some up-start pomposity calling itself the Canadian Pacific for the rights to extend their brand of evolutionary capitalism all the way to the salmon-basins of British Columbia – hon-oured Corporal Bacon and four other local boys at a banquet held in the concourse of the station on the Point Edward wharf. Major Bolton, representing Colonel Wolseley, toasted the valiant and spoke reverently of Tom Marshall, the fallen comrade no one more than he, his commanding officer, could have wished to have been present here amongst them. His sentiments were echoed all round. The hero's widow – alas – was not there to acknowledge them.

Just as Lily feared, Robbie took Tom's death very hard. For a little while he seemed al-most pleased with the notion that his father had died in uniform while leading his men valiantly through impenetrable bush and over raging torrents and across waste marshes – every thicket treacherous with Indians who could twist their shadows at will into the shapes of monsters and trolls. From her place at the window Lily watched him slash his way into the underbrush, heard his bullying ululations rise and startle and scatter, then waited, heart-in-mouth, for her brave warrior to tramp out of the woodlot, his weapon trailing in the dirt like a sad plough, all the buoyancy vanished from the large eyes that periodically rolled from side to side in a vain attempt to identify the enemy who would not show himself. Carefully she had explained to him that his father's body had stopped being – like the stilled rabbit's or the frozen sparrows on the window-ledge, like Bachelor Bill under the earth a mile away – and that his spirit, his soul – the things they loved most about him, the way he smiled and listened and spoke – had flown back into the air and even now, if you closed your eyes quick, you could see them and hear them and almost touch them. But five minutes later he would scowl over at her and say with innocent ferocity, "When's Da comin' home?" When Lily suggested that he was seven-going-on-eight and that his Da would be proud of him if he would walk into town each morning and go to the big school to learn to read and write and start to become a man – he said shortly, "I want Da to take me." That was that. When Lily propped him up on the chair-arm and began to read the story of Ali Baba to him (she'd memorized it word for word, though strangely enough she actually felt the letters crystallizing on the page, having their full miraculous say), he kicked the book out of her hands and stomped off. Later he allowed himself to be held while he cried, and cried out at the trolls and ogres whose deaths he had marked in black on his avenging scroll. Even then Lily knew these compulsory tears were but a tiny portion of the huge rage shaking him in her arms. That this would become for him the unanswerable anger of his life. When she wept – for herself, for Tom, for the deep absence no accumulation of days or other joys would ever fill – most of her tears were for her son, for the life he had dreamed that would not be, for the consolation she would be forever called upon to give and be rebuked for. Perhaps I am better off, she thought, because I never learned to dream too far ahead; Old Samuels taught us how to dream backwards and be content. Teach me to be lucky, she begged him one terrible November night as she sat in the dark swaddling her son's fury

Brad was different. He seemed to accept her account of body and spirit, though she could tell it had no more reality for him than the rhymes bouncing in his head at night or as he lay among the spent clover of the meadowlands above the village – flat on his back, extinguishing the sun with an Ali Baba command. Avid for company the boys often played side by side, but only rarely now did their discrete fantasies intersect, and when they did, the outcome was usually swift and violent. Brad accepted Robbie's sudden unprovoked fists as part of his lot in the scheme of things, even his due – but when the latter added, if he remember to, "I hate you", Brad would stop crying at once and grow very still. This seemed to please Robbie almost as much as the tears, for he could then carry on his own game without even the background annoyance of his brother's silliness. As a result Brad drew even closer to her. He ventured out less. He begged her to read to him, and as soon as she had got beyond her repertoire of memorized pieces and slowed to a near-halt at the balking print, he would then throw a tantrum, sometimes yelling out with impudent mockery the meaning of a word that would not come off her tongue. Later, in bed, he would nuzzle against her and start to sing "A froggie came a-wooing" till she relented and joined him part-way through and they finished up with a harmonious roar. I'm spoiling him, she thought, but she couldn't think how else she could love him. Once when he called out to her from his sleep, she came across to the boys' room in time to hear him say, "I saw Da, in my dream. He talked to me." Robbie awakened too, said, "Da's dead." She held them both. When she woke up in the morning, they were still there.

"Ah, there goes Lily and her boys," grocer Redmond remarked to a customer during one of Lily's infrequent visits to town. Lily and her boys. That would be it – her life – at least as far as she could see.

There was so little time, it seemed, to think about the pregnancy, now in its eighth month. Fortunately it felt like the first one, lively and healthful. She had no discomfort except for the weight of the girl herself – she knew it would be a girl and addressed it always as 'she'. This one will be mine, my private treasure, she thought, tasting the bitter sweetness of the notion, there's no helping it. I shall try to give her father to her – when she's ready – but by then she'll be bonded to me. You have your Papa's smile, I'll say to her, and we'll hug one another, feeling your absence, Tom, in our separate ways. Stop it, stop this, remember Old Samuels – dream backwards, dream of your lover blessing your flesh with the fire you stirred and vanquished with your own desire, his seed tucked away already bequeathed.

November of 1870 turned out to be a cold and nasty month. Sleet storms roared in off the Lake freezing the last leaves to their branches while gusting after-winds snapped them free again. Every morning Lily had to get a fire going early in order to boil gallons of water to unlock the ice choking the well-line under the sink and the one in the yard as well. Robbie and Brad carted wood in from the shed – several of Garth Bacons pals had come out in September and cut four cords – but already she had used too much kindling trying to get fast, hot fires going, and Robbie was coming closer each morning to cutting off his foot as he wielded his father's hatchet uncertainly. Young Mary Bacon was sent out by Maudie every Saturday, but had to return weekdays to go to school – "A whim she'll get over soon enough," Maudie promised. Mary helped to clean and prepare food ahead, but she was less proficient with an axe than Robbie. One day she walked Robbie in and out of the village several times – once in the dark – to make sure he could find his way to Maudie's house at any hour, should the baby decide to make an impromptu entrance. From Bacon's a buggy would be despatched to pick up Dr. Dollard in Sarnia. "Sophie's out of business," Maudie said through Mary, "too drunk to deliver." Robbie was delighted with his role as scout and forerunner. Lily was sure he rehearsed it secretly during the afternoons when she had to lie down to rest and he was ordered not to leave the yard. Brad 'never told', though he was treated as if he did – daily.

At any rate, Lily could see that life was going to be no easier after the baby came. She would need help. Help would cost money, even if one of Clara's sisters could be persuaded to give up school for a while and come. And money there was little of. They had saved almost a hundred dollars towards the cottage in town, and the Government had promised some compensation whenever they could find time to pass the necessary legislation. She could live for a year or more on that. Perhaps longer if the boys didn't go to school, an option she had never seriously considered. What then? The whole acreage could be turned over and made productive, provided she was strong enough in the spring. But prices were uncertain as the new Confederation sorted out its priorities, the weather was fickle and the competition fierce. As Maudie would say not ungenerously, "You see now, Lil, why so many of us cling to the church; what else've we got to protect us when we're down, when our men desert us?" Late one afternoon when she was out in the garden area looking for Robbie, she saw his tiny figure zigzagging through the withered bull-thistle of the meadow, and her eye caught the pines on either side of the opening she stood in. The windbreak. Uncle Chester's barrier against the encroaching world, Aunt Bridie's signal to the Grand Trunk of defiance and separateness, Lily's beloved evergreens that sang softly in the summer and held the stars aloft in black winter skies. The last of the ancient horizons, old sagamore, she whispered to his presence somewhere beside her. Say yes. Robbie's death-shriek shook her awake. A bull-thistle toppled. Another. He waved to the sentry.

They must go. This winter, white-pine would still be fetching a good price, before the peninsula was opened up for systematic slaughter. Also, she realized, it was time. The smoke from the cottages was less than half-a-mile away. Some of the timber she could take back as sawn boards; she'd get someone, perhaps the timber-cutter, to put up two chicken coops. Chickens she knew. Eggs were a sure living. She'd trade vegetables for grain. Her thoughts raced, full of figures, schemes, possibilities. She barely felt Robbie's petulant tug on her sleeve.

When Mary Bacon came that Saturday – the last in November – Lily was still excited, and some of her enthusiasm had rubbed off on the boys. "I'm gonna help cut the trees down!" Robbie announced, "an' Brad an' me's gonna collect the eggs every mornin', ain't we, Brad?" and he demonstrated his technique for terrorizing any hen who harboured thoughts of saving an egg for her own pleasure. Lily came out with Tom's writing pad, his quill pen and a bottle of thickened ink. "I'd like a message to be put up in the post office," she said, and Mary, wide-eyed, picked up the pen, eager to display her newly-achieved skills. She left, skipping through the wet snow.

"When the hens get too old to give eggs," Brad said, "what'll we do with them?"

"Chop off their heads an' eat 'em!" Robbie said. "Eh, Mama?"

Lily didn't hear. She was clutching her abdomen with both hands.

"The baby kick you?" Brad said, open-mouthed.

"You okay, Mama?" Robbie clasped her arm and steadied her.

"Yes," she hissed, sitting down, dredging up a thin smile.

That was no contraction, she thought.

2

Whatever fears pursued him, Robbie Marshall acted with a courage and sense of purpose that would have made his father whistle with pride. Despite the galling pain that stabbed incoherently – spitefully – at her body, Lily found time to worry about her seven-year-old melting into the snowy dark, lamp in hand, the map of his voyage floating a foot beyond its shivelled glow, her life in his care, his life suddenly lost to hers. As each scream jolted through her clenched teeth, Brad jumped in the invisible ring that pinned him to one spot on the earth. Between jolts she was at last able to ask him to bring her some water and another blanket. A long time later, hours it seemed, he meandered back in, humming to himself. He put the blanket on and began tucking her in, one tiny fold at a time. There was no water. Her throat burned. The pain no longer sliced into her in slender arcs, it scoured at the entire abdominal cavity, as if some drunken ploughman were dragging a harrow-disc cornerwise across it. Then the air around her went numb.

She dreamt of Maman LaRouche in her ice-house, the soothing cool of ice on the skin, a sunny room shorn of flies.

Dr. Dollard arrived with a rush and a clatter that woke Brad out of his dazed sleep. He started to cry as if he would die were he to stop. Mary went straight to him, forgetting that Robbie was still in her arms dreaming he was awake and strong and not really lost. Maudie and the doctor headed for the bedroom. Garth Bacon tethered the horse and sat in the democrat shivering between 'belts' from his flask. He was only thirty but looked fifty – already he'd seen too much of this. Nothing could ever brace him against the kind of screams that came, undeflected by wood or grass or muffling snow or alcohol, straight into this brain. He thought of a pig being gutted alive by a deaf-and-dumb butcher. She'll die, he thought. We'll all die.

Dr. Dollard, puffing and sweating like a lumberjack, swore at Maudie, the fickleness of chloroform, at God's indifference – wishing to Christ the woman would stop rising out of her death-drowse just long enough to disembowel him with an accusing shriek. "I said give me the forceps, you stupid girl. Quick! I might be able to save the child!"

Maudie stood frozen to her feet. She couldn't understand what was holding her upright. She could see nothing but a brace of female thighs wrenched apart; a battering, bloody child's skull driven back and up and in by some bellicose, furred sphincter the doctor's paws plunged into with fury and disgust. Around her the air stank, like an outhouse in Hell. Mary caught hold of her sister-in-law just as she gave up the ghost. Then Mary herself handed Dr. Dollard his forceps and positioned the lamp so he could see. She saw the dried blood on their pincering grip. She wondered how she had been born, then forgiven, then loved.

"Gotcha by the ears, you little bugger," the doctor gasped, pulling back as if he were rowing a coal-barge upstream. Lily made no sound to interrupt the whooshing blast of blood and pus that greased the baby's slide into the air. The force of it knocked the doctor back onto his rump. The foetus dripped onto the bed. Maudie was awake now. All was in motion. The age-old rituals. Garth had come in and was stoking the fire. He listened for the signal, the all-clear. It didn't come.

Lily opened her eyes to see the tears in those of the women. "Thank God, you're alive," Maudie said. "It's a miracle."

"The baby's gone," said Dr. Dollard wearily. "Probably died yesterday."

Lily whispered something in Maudie's ear. "She wants to know if it was a girl," Maudie said.

The doctor appeared puzzled. "As a matter of fact, it was," he said. "But it was all for the best, Mrs. Marshall. Your little girl was hydrocephalic, a Mongolian idiot."

Maudie and Mary both shuddered. The Lord moved in mysterious ways His wonders to perform.

"Come on, ladies," barked the doctor, "we've got work to do."

Three weeks later Lily, always a marvel to the skeptics of the medical profession, was feeling well enough to send Mary back to her studies. Brad had slept with Mary every night since the stillbirth of little Kathleen. When Mary left he crawled in beside his mother. Robbie announced he was ready to trek into the village to give school a try. After the holiday, Lily promised, and he dashed out into the snow to re-enact the legend of his pilgrimage he was longing to find an audience for.

Lily was sound asleep on the kitchen cot when Brad shook her awake. His eyes directed her towards the doorway. She felt the draft over her bare legs, the thinness of her shift under the blanket. The door closed and before it, filling most of the space there, stood a tall dark-skinned young man whose moustache rubbed against his smile. He pulled the tuque off his head and held it in front of him.

"Your boy," he said with a grin that was both sheepish and bold, "he tell me to come in." Robbie popped out from behind one of the powerful legs; he had an axe in his hands.

Lily sat up, still blinking.

The accent was familiar. "I come about the notice in the post office," he said and ruffled Robbie's hair.

3

Ti-Jean Thériault swung his big axe and another of the great pines went crashing to the ground right where it was supposed to. The boys, well out of the way, jumped up and sprinted through the snow towards Ti-Jean, who posed for them, one foot on the fallen tree like a hunter beaming over a bull-moose. He grinned wickedly and flung Robbie through the air, laughing at his squeals of terror and glee. Brad laughed, too, seated as usual about three feet away from Ti-Jean in a place where he could observe him, secure and rapt. Often Ti-Jean would make teasing lunges his way but he always stopped just short, just in time. Robbie grabbed his father's hatchet and under Ti-Jean's tutelage soon became proficient at stripping away the small branches of a felled tree. Brad would follow behind, trailing his fingers along the bark and stubs, humming to himself, keeping an eye on Ti-Jean in hope that he would burst into his strange, loud, off-beat singing – as he often did when the work had eased a little. Once, while they sat on a log sharing jam sandwiches, Lily saw Brad lean over and press his face into Ti-Jean's rough Hudson's Bay shirt; Ti-Jean kept right on talking to Robbie.

> *Voici l'hiver arrivé*
> *Les rivières sont gelées*
> *C'est le temps d'aller aux bois*

> *Dans les chantiers nous hivernerons*
> *Dans les chantiers nous hivernerons*

trolled the timberman, and Brad, dawdling behind Robbie and his chattering hatchet, repeated the music with his high, boyish flute, the backwoodsy accent flawless. Soon he drifted off into the shelter of the hardwoods while Robbie kept hacking dutifully and Ti-Jean lit his clay-pipe and uttered puffs of smoke through his frozen breath. Later on Brad circled back, coming up unnoticed behind the busy labourers – the song still singing in his head, possessed.

Every morning now the boys were up before Lily. Robbie got a smoky fire going in the stove while Brad discomfited the embers into the fireplace. Moments after sunrise they headed out to the windbreak to watch for the jaunty figure of Ti-Jean cutting across the fields from the village. Lily could hear them arguing about who had seen him first. Robbie always won. Ti-Jean was boarding at Green House, a dingy hostel run by the Grand Trunk. He came every morning, Monday to Saturday – whistling, singing, puffing on his pipe, wool shirt open at the throat – and worked until four o'clock, when he waved the boys goodbye across the fields and disappeared. Lily made him and the boys a lunch, and brought hot tea out to the worksite from time to time. Robbie insisted on drinking out of a tin mug.

Lily assumed that Ti-Jean would be returning home to his family in Woodston up in Huron County for the Christmas holiday, so she was surprised when he asked, in the diffident manner he invariably used when talking to her, if he might join them for the occasion. "Yes! Yes!" Robbie said before Brad could get in. Lily, who could deny her boys very little, said yes. Tom had always maintained the traditions of Christmas he had inherited from Aunt Elspeth and insisted that they keep them up 'for Auntie's sake'.

When Ti-Jean asked her to come with them to select a tree, she said no, that she wasn't feeling up to a walk in the woods yet, and he understood perfectly and the three men tramped off, axe and hatchets aloft, into the bush. Lily watched them go for a bit but had to sit down shortly. She felt dizzy; her heart fluttered and slammed. Get up, woman, she said aloud, you've got work to do and a life to lead.

Somewhat later she put on her macintosh and boots and went out to wait for them. She noted that Ti-Jean was more than half-way through his work. He had cleared an opening in the windbreak almost fifty feet wide. She could see straight across to the village. When the job was finished, she realized that she would be able to stand in her kitchen window and view the entire sweep of the town from the rail-yards and docks in the south-west to the dunes and First Bush in the north and north-east. Between these extremes lay the cottages of the labouring folk, already four-streets square with hearth-fires aglow, smoke from their chimneys welcoming and insular, the cries of their children carrying freely over the fields. She thought she could see the tall brick chimney of the new two-room school on Victoria Street. Above the low snow-covered landscape before her, the winter sun burned without solace.

At Ti-Jean's behest Lily brought out the little Testament with Papa's writing on it. "I read in English almost as good as French," he announced after dinner, "that's what my Maman say, an' she's never wrong, eh?" He winked at the boys and grinned shyly in Lily's direction. "Always my job to read the Christmas story." "After mass?" He laughed, went red in the face, then said, "*Ah non, nous sommes Hugenots.*"

He read the St. Luke version of the nativity in a halting cadence that soon established its own authenticity, its own sort of flawed beauty – at least in the mind of one of the listeners. Though Lily had heard it before, she never lost her sense of the story's magic, of its having happened in a longago time when such mysteries were radiant with possibility, as probable as the rings of Saturn or the moons of Jupiter. She glanced over at Brad and was not disappointed.

Some small presents were exchanged. Robbie's eyes lit up at the sight of a bone-handled knife in its own leather case. Brad clutched the wooden carving of a Gryphon as if it were greased and likely to slip away. Lily blushed when she saw the Irish linen handkerchief. She went back into the shed and came out with a quilt under her arm. Ti-Jean stopped smiling. He took it in his hands, and she saw them shake a little. "Maman makes these," he said. "But not like this."

"Not that one," Lily said. "You can keep that one for now, but I'll make you a proper one in the new year, when I'm feelin' better."

Ti-Jean jumped up and went over to his haversack, the one he'd pulled the presents out of. He had a leather case in his hand. He drew out a fiddle, perched on a stool and began to play. And sing.

> *Quand tu retourn' chez son père*
> *Aussi pour revoir ta mère*
> *Le bonhomme est a la porte*
> *La bonn' femme fête la gargotte*
>
> *Dans le chantiers, ah ! n'hivernerons plus!*
> *Dans le chantiers, ah ! n'hivernerons plus!*

They all joined in on the chorus, several times.

With both children asleep on the rug in front of the fire, Ti-Jean held the Testament in his hands for a moment, stared at Lily and said, "Who is Lady Fairchild?"

"Somebody who lived a long time ago," Lily said.

Just after New Year's when Lily arrived one morning with a jug of tea, Robbie looked up with a smug smile on his face and said, "Ti-Jean's in the barn, ain't he, Brad?" Brad's smile confirmed the conspiracy.

"There's an old stove in there," Ti-Jean said when he came up to them.

"And a sleepin' cot," Robbie said.

"We moved it there when Bachelor Bill's place was torn down by the railroad," Lily said.

"A bit of glass on the broken windows an' it could be fixed up real nice," Ti-Jean said.

"Nice an' warm," Robbie said.

"But you'll be through cuttin' in two weeks," Lily said.

"Not if I rent a team an' haul these logs to the mill before the break-up."

"I couldn't afford to pay you."

"We'll help, won't we, Brad?"

"After the mill pays you, that's okay with me."

"It'd be cheaper in the long run," said Lily slowly.

"I could get some boards sawn," he said, nodding to the boys.

"To build the coops," said Robbie.

"For the chickens," said Brad.

"I'm real good with my hands."

Lily smiled. "Accordin' to Maman," she said.

Robbie promised to give school a try as soon as Ti-Jean no longer needed him in the woodlot. It was nearing the end of January. Lily was feeling much stronger. She accompanied Ti-Jean and the boys to Little Lake but did not join them on the ice. Brad cried because he fell and couldn't keep up with Robbie and Ti-Jean, but settled down when Ti-Jean sat and whittled a strange sea-monster out of a piece of frozen driftwood and told him a story about it half in English, half in French. Robbie found some older boys and showed them how good he was on skates. In a week or so the horses were due to arrive and both boys would get to drive them, Robbie first, then Brad. Ti-Jean fixed up Uncle Chester's hideaway so that it was indeed warm and cozy. He loved the rope-rug Lily gave him for the floor and the curtains she adapted for the window over the bunk. He even had a little shelf where he kept some books – in French. "Junior Book Three," he said proudly. "Best in the family."

Lily began to think ahead, to get herself organized for the spring. She hauled out of the shed Uncle Chester's boxes and containers, still bearing the stamp of his patient hand. She set up the quilting frame once again, hoping to get four or five completed by April. With the boys out of her hair, even on Sundays, she could work miracles. However, she discovered she was short of rags and swatches. She knew she should go over to see Clara, who would supply her ten times over, but still she hesitated. Later, when I'm ready, she thought. Then she noticed the trunk where she'd tossed all of Tom's clothes last August. She opened it quietly as one eases open a closet where some ghost has slept forever undisturbed. She lifted them, squeezed them, smelled them, let their hues and textures become vivid again. Then she took her scissors and one by one she cut the shirts, trousers, underclothes, socks and his navvy's cap into neat geometric shapes she would weave into remembrance.

Not every evening did Ti-Jean stay with them after their supper was done, though the boys made his periodic escape difficult. He had some young friends in town ("a *girl* friend," Robbie breathed) or he had a book to finish reading in his refurbished quarters. But sometimes he stayed on for a few moments after the boys were ordered to bed to have a quiet cup of coffee with Lily. As soon as they were alone, he became very shy, and only by gentle questioning could Lily – knitting or sifting patches for her quilts – get him to talk about himself. It wasn't long before she learned to their mutual surprise that although he was born and raised in Woodston, his mother had come there from Sandwich in 1835. As a girl she had known Maman LaRouche, a LaPeche like her and a second cousin. Lily found it fascinating to hear of the Frenchman's exploits in the War of 1812 narrated once again, but this time through a different set of filters. Maman herself came through as lively and as special as she had been in real life. Lily added some of her own favourite 'Maman' stories to the legend, the happier ones, the ones she cherished. Lily and Ti-Jean lapsed so easily into French that Lily was often unaware of it until some exotic phrase momentarily jolted the flow of their evening-soft, embering soliloquies. It was much later – and sandwiched between longer, more reminiscent narratives – that Lily was able to piece together his own story, and then only as a fragmented outline. His father had come to the Huron Tract with John Galt and Tiger Dunlop. He was a lusty primitive who lived for cutting trees and trekking miles into the snow-bound bushlands of the county. Ti-Jean was the oldest of eleven children, his mother wanted him to stay in school, he wanted to stay in school but at thirteen he was side by side with his father in a pinery. His father roughed him up on a whim or in a whiskey rage, he slapped his wife when she dared to intervene, and Ti-Jean, who was almost twenty and no longer *petit*, blackened both of his father's eyes, keeping him out of the bush for a week, and his mother cried over her son and said she was ashamed of him, so he left to seek his fortune out of the bush, on the docks or the railroad or in a factory, he didn't write and he didn't go home for Christmas. He would never go home again.

"It's a beautiful baby girl with the sweetest big blue eyes I've ever seen," Maudie said, then flushed and looked at her tea.

"When was it born?" Lily asked.

"Just before Christmas. A few weeks late."

"Clara was never one for bein' on time," Lily said and saw the puzzlement in Maudie's face. "I'm kiddin'," she added. Maudie appeared to be thrown into worse confusion, but after a strong dose of fresh tea she recovered.

"You need to get into town more," she said.

"Sarnia's a long ways for me."

"You know I mean the Point. Us. Our Wednesday afternoons."

"I know. I don't want you to ever feel I'm ungrateful. You an' Garth saved my life. I'll come. Soon."

"Clara wants desperately to see you, but she's shy about bringin' the baby out here. She'd like you to come to the Christenin' next Sunday."

Lily listened for a while to Robbie barking his hopeless commands at Dick and Diamond, the team of Belgians with a mind of their own. "I just can't, Maudie. Not yet."

"We understand, we honestly do. But will you think about comin' to the wedding in March, then? We're cookin' up a shivaree." Lily smiled on cue. "You know Steve, Garth's younger brother, an' his girl Elaine is just the sweetest thing you'd ever wanna meet."

Lily waited for the codicil.

"'Course, she's Baptist, but still an' all –"

Ti-Jean let out an oak-rattling whoop and the horses, chained logs, master and apprentices could be heard moving through the woods towards the winding road that led all the way to Sarnia.

Maudie dropped her voice into a deeper, minor key, full of inescapable regret. Lily leaned back. "You know, of course, it don't mean nothin' to me, or Garth for that matter, but I wouldn't be much of a friend if I didn't tell you what kind of ugly, disgustin' gossip is goin' around town."

"Folks don't like me cuttin' down the windbreak?"

Maudie skidded a bit but got right back on the rails: "It's about...*him*."

"Who?"

"You know who, the Frenchie."

"Ti-Jean Thériault?"

"Lily, I'm serious. I'm worried about your welfare even if you ain't. You gotta remember your boys're gonna be in school next fall. Think of them, for God's sake."

"They like the Frenchie."

"That ain't the point an' you know it perfectly well. Folks are sayin', out loud mind you, that he's livin' out here, that he used to be seen comin' home from here every afternoon at a respectable hour but after New Year's he's only been back to town three or four times." She cast a furtive glance towards the bedrooms, blushed, and plunged into the mire: "People are wonderin' just where he's hangin' up his socks, if you get my meanin'."

"In the barn," Lily said. She followed Maudie's gaze around to the window and out across the drifts to where the smoke hung sweetly nicely above the chimney-pipe Ti-Jean had rigged up. "Ain't that where Frenchie's usually live?"

"Thank the Lord," sighed Maudie, depleted and relieved. "I'll spread the word." She finished her tea, took Lily by the hand and just squeezed it. For some occasions even Maudie had no words.

"I *will* think about the weddin'," Lily said and brushed her friend's forehead with a kiss. "By the way," she added, handing Maudie a package wrapped in tissue, "I made this little quilt for the baby."

The windbreak was down. The west wind that blew over the village now continued across the open fields and ruffled the shingles on the house where Lily Marshall and her boys lived. All the logs had been taken to the mill on Sarnia Bay. Ti-Jean received his pay. A wagonload of sawn boards and joists arrived in the last week of February and were stored in Benjamin's stall until the first crack in the winter weather. A few days later it thawed a bit, and Ti-Jean and his helpers cleared the ground and drew the outlines of two coops in the softening earth. Indoors, they sketched plans and Ti-Jean explained the intricacies of squaring and gabling. The boys begged to go with Ti-Jean into Sarnia to buy nails and two tack-hammers. But Brad came down with a hacking cough, had to stay home, and despite having made up his mind to sulk all day, he was delighted to discover his mother could sing in French as well as that other weird tongue. He fell asleep and when he woke she was sitting on his bed.

Just as Ti-Jean and Robbie came up the lane, the wind changed direction, slicing down unopposed from the north-west. By the time they had their boots off, the snow had started in earnest.

Robbie was exhausted. Lily managed to get a little soup into Brad before he fell into a deep slumber beside his brother. She drew the comforter lingeringly over them. Ti-Jean was behind her in the doorway, watching. She kissed each of her sons, and when she turned to slip out, Ti-Jean was no longer there.

She found him in front of the fire, propped on one elbow and staring into the flames, enlivened by the storm swirling above them. On the window sills fresh snow flowered. The room drew itself inward. Lily sat down on the sheepskin next to Ti-Jean, then lay back, succumbing to the languorous, sleepy heat of the fire already beginning to wane. Ti-Jean slipped his sweater over his head – his skin rubbed copper in the ebb of light. Behind her, the kitchen lamp sputtered, and she felt the darkness against the calves of her legs, her bare arms, the nape of her neck. Outside, the snow ceased, as if touched by a wizard's wand.

Ti-Jean rose up slowly dreamily – his torso bent like a paladin's shield, burnished and rippled from splendid use, his eyes as bright as Lancelot's might have been above Guinevere's sudden beauty. He leaned over, captured her wrist and drew her up with him so they were standing together, only the fold of their hands fluttering between the reach and yearn of their bodies. His open hand folded around her waist, he eased her breast against his, he launched her clasped hand outward with his, upward like the wing of a revived bird, he was moving his legs against hers, nudging urging coaxing them into sensual motion. They were dancing. Hesitant, anapest, with no music but the song they were singing – separately – in their loneliness. They were dancing, in a circle no rounder than the moon's on All Hallow's Eve. His teeth crushed her lips; she nipped his tongue with her own. A wave of chilling air shot between them.

"I got to go home," he said. "For a little while."

Lily gathered her breath, some strength and said, "Of course, you must. They been waitin' a long time for you."

"I'll come back."

"Don't promise."

Lily helped him pack his few belongings. She was surprised to note that it was only about eight o'clock. The wind had eased off and fresh snow glittered as the moon sailed in and out of the thick clouds. Ti-Jean said that there was a way-freight leaving for the north from the rail-yards in about an hour. He knew the engineer; he could be home by midnight. He was a long time in the boys' bedroom, though he did not wake them up to say goodbye. He held Lily again at the door, and for a second neither of them was willing to admit the impossibility of what they both desired. Then he turned and left. He didn't stop to wave, as he did with Lily's boys.

Lily fell exhausted into Uncle Chester's chair. Only the feeble glow from the spent fire gave any relief to the gathering gloom. Before she lit the lamp beside the quilting frame, she spoke into the darkness: "See what you've done? See what you've brought me to? Why did you leave me, Tom?"

20

When the snow stopped falling early in the evening, it seemed providential to the roisterers at the wedding of young Stevie Bacon and Elaine. The dining room of the Richmond House had scarcely been able to contain such exuberant well-wishing during the lengthy toasts and fractious dancing that followed. Several carollers toppled out-of-doors into the alleys behind, where they butted and boasted uproariously, making repeated use of the goosedown drifts. Nevertheless, there was a hearty cheer when the wind died and the moon intermittently winked their way again. It was nearing ten o'clock and almost time for the bride-and-groom to board the royal carriage and be whisked away to reconsummate their passion in the snug bower prepared for them at the very end of Victoria Street – where First Bush loomed and offered sanctuary to conspirators. Conspiracy had been afoot for days, led by the groom's treacherous sibling, who had selected the brightest and the best only to take up the roles in his shivaree. "Just give 'em fifteen minutes," Garth commanded with a fratricidal leer, "I know my brother!" A special 'theme' had been chosen for the costumes and musical score – wild creatures of the wood and tundra, a great notion somewhere confounded, however, when ten of the fifteen elect arrived wearing the ceremonial outfits of Blackfoot Indian Chiefs – the kind of natives invented to meet the original expectations of the first Europeans. But several pygmy-lie trolls, a diaphanous jinn (female class), and a brownish bear of indistinct origins served to vie the troupe-as-a-whole a more representative cast. Tom-toms abounded as well as horns to simulate the sounds of Arcady gone beserk.

The wedding-sleigh had no sooner turned the corner at Edward Street when the revellers emptied out of a dozen secret places of the Richmond House into the vacant lot next door, where they hooted, admired, tested and tumbled towards assembly. The bear ambled after one of the squaws, licking her chin as if it were a honeycomb until she was, alas, rescued. From The Queen's livery stable across the street a beer-wagon, devoid of barrels, came skidding behind the bit-chomping fury of matched Percherons. The coachman had some difficulty in checking their devotion long enough for the carousing tribesmen to come aboard, but even the bear was pulled, rump-first, into this racing, four-masted schooner of delight. The runners over the snow sang in sibilants only; the wassailers tipped their flasks starward and hugged and rehearsed the ages-old scenes of *carnivale*.

As prearranged, the sled was brought to a halt a block away from the victim's house. Garth Bacon, straightening his eagle's feathers, called for silence, then peered ahead of him, looking at the ground in a puzzling manner that sent an icy shiver rippling back through the crowd. "No tracks." The news was passed along in a sinking whisper. Garth came back from his inspection of the house and peered disconsolately into the faces agleam with war-paint and blazing, expectant eyes. "They sure didn't come here," he said loudly. "There's no sign of horses and no footprints anywhere near the place. We've been hoodwinked." "Where in hell'd they go?" Much fruitless speculation here. Two braves came to blows; no one noticed. Harvey Shawyer spoke up. "No wonder my Bess was actin' queer all day." "Queerer than usual, you mean." "Shut up, Digger." Harvey was the bride's uncle by marriage. "She blushed every time I mentioned Woodston for the last two weeks." "Woodston?" "Bess's sister lives up there. An' her husband's the engineer on the way-freight!" "An' the way-freight was sittin' there, an hour late, waitin' for them!" "Hoodwinked," Garth said, his regalia adroop. "C'mon, Mose, turn 'em around, we still got a bit of the night left."

Most of the revellers clambered back onto the wagon and let it carry them at a forlorn trot back to the Richmond House, where a few would try to revamp their gaiety. The bona fide roisterers, however, remained – half-a-dozen strong: male, thwarted and bearish. They sat down on a snowbank outside the dark house and drank from a common flask. Digger Smythe stood up. His eyes ballooned in the moonlight like Bacchus before a binge. "Fellas, we might've missed some cozy bundlin' in this here house, but I know where there's some fresh snugglin' takin' place right this minute. And it ain't been blessed by no minister and it ain't been properly shivareed!" A chorus of whoops confirmed the righteousness of the suggestion, and the motley band of make-believe savages set out to the south-east across the fields in pursuit of pleasure. They were not a third of the way when the wind began to gust through their merriment. Then the snow came back in broken flurries, periodically blotting out the orange glow on the horizon ahead of them.

The chieftain halted his troop with a raised palm. He bent over and out of his ample quiver a number of cattails fell into anxious hands. A match flared. The flames from the kerosene-soaked torches leapt wildly in the dark. The snow sizzled and retreated. A tom-tom began to search for a stag's heartbeat. On the faces of the war-dancers the slashes of chrome and ochre shimmered like harlequin masks under gaslight. As if they were circling a wagon-train, the roisterers – fired by whiskey and disappointment and ineradicable envy – swarmed about the isolated cottage, beating the drum of their own pent passion, waving their flambeaux like flags from purgatory, and chanting over and over till the syllables separated one from the other and smote the air like incendiaries:

> Shame, shame, double shame
> Shame, shame upon your name

In their zeal several of the harrowers broke ranks and dashed up to the windows of the seraglio, thrusting their torches against the tainted glass and grinning hideously, as if to deliver the devil a blow in kind. In their haste, two of them bumped into one another, stumbled, left their torches where they dropped, and began slugging it out. Around them the litany of mortification continued.

At first Lily was not frightened. When she heard the shouting she got up from her quilting in time to see the torches flare up, then watched them approach raggedly through the snow. She recalled that Stevie Bacon was to have been married earlier in the day, and she guessed that this was the spillover from the customary shivaree. Their bizarre costumery and the derisive, taunting chant merely reinforced her suspicions. She decided to douse the lamp, slide the bar across both doors and wait them out: whiskey-valour, she knew, had a short life. And the boys were in a deep, safe sleep. But when the wild, uncoordinated whooping started and several of the savages made daring, unauthorized charges at the house, Lily decided that it might be better to waken the boys and tell them what was going on. Tom's shotgun hung where it always did, near the main door.

She had just started towards the boys' room when she heard Brad shriek. Fumbling with the lamp, she ran in to find him paralyzed with fright in front of the tiny window over the bed. The afterimage of the demon's visage still glimmered in the glass – a distorted grimace so real it could have been the Bogeyman stepped right out of an innocent's nightmare. Then the torch-flames rose up and incinerated it. Brad leapt across the bed and grabbed Lily around the waist and buried his face in her skirt.

"Mama, Mama, Mama," he screamed. Lily picked him up and carried him into the big room; Robbie trailed them with a lamp.

"It's all right, it's all right," she murmured, cradling him on the cot, "it's only the men from the wedding, come to give us a little scare, like Hallowe'en. They'll go away soon. Shh…shh…"

Suddenly Robbie yelped as if he'd been stepped on. "There's another one!" he cried. Across the kitchen window, Carcajou flashed through a gauntlet of fire and perforated shadow; a rabid Coyote's grin swallowed his eyes, and his mouth became a wolverine's howl, hovering and thinning. Robbie began to sob with fear and shame, reaching for his mother's hand and jerking it away from Brad's shoulder.

"Make them go away, make them go away." Brad's screams connected and became one hysterical plea. Lily jumped when something thudded against the shed wall behind her. They're coming in, she thought. Where are the shells?

> Shame, shame, double shame
> Shame, shame upon your name
> Marshall, Marshall, Marshall, Marshall
>
> Shame, shame –

The chant stopped. Soft but urgent footfalls in the snow. Silence. They were gone. Brad was now blubbering contently in her lap. Robbie had let go.

"Mama!" he shouted. "The shed's on fire!"

Lily whirled around. Smoke was pouring under the door to the shed. She ran across and flung back the bar. When she looked into the back room she saw the woodpile was ablaze, as was the outside wall behind it. Above her she watched the first, hopping blue flames take hold of the cottage roof.

Lily spoke quickly. "Robbie, get your boots an' your coats. We gotta get out right now." She slammed the door shut and raced across to the bedroom, fighting the panic that was clutching at her throat and paralyzing her thoughts. Blankets, she muttered, it's freezing out there and half-a mile to the nearest house. She grabbed whatever was nearby, stuffed mittens and scarves into her pockets and rushed back to the boys, neither of whom had moved an inch. The room was full of smoke and the roof over them seemed to be melting. Struggling with her own fear as best she could, Lily dragged both her boys through the front door and out into the night. She did not even know which direction they ran in, but they kept on running until she found herself winded and kneeling in a huge drift.

"Mama, we're freezin'," Robbie sobbed with his arm around Brad, who was speechless, and coughing.

Lily found two blankets still tangled in her arms. She wrapped the boys up and squeezed them against her. They had no boots. The boys had their thick night-socks on. She was barefoot. She looked back. She could hear the crackling of wood ablaze, but saw nothing but the wild blizzard raging around them. The barn, she thought. We should have gone to the barn. Ti-Jean's stove might still have been warm. Where was it? A charred beam crashed noisily, but she could not tell which direction the sound had come from. The wind-driven snow muffled and warped. We'll freeze out here, she thought, in fifteen minutes.

"Come on," she said to the boys, "let's start walkin'; we gotta get to town."

"I know the way," Robbie said, "even in the dark."

There was no darkness to be seen, not a jot. They walked in what Lily prayed was a straight line. She picked up Brad and carried him swaddled in her arms. All the feeling left her feet. Robbie dissolved in front of her. She cried out his name. The wind blew it back. He rematerialized in her hand. "I saw a light," he said, "I *think* I did. Over that way." Her legs were gone, she couldn't tell if they were moving or not. "Come on, Mama, come *on!*" She allowed herself to be dragged along. Suddenly, all the feeling and power returned to her legs, she was running swift as a deer towards an obliterating white light as big as the sun, it had a halo shimmering around it, she called out some words of welcome. "Get up, Mama, get up! *Please.*"

She was being carried bumpily, head dangling, the snow melting and seeping down into her eyes. But the arm around her was powerful, and the stride under her was sure and unrelenting. Her feet were burning. She heard Robbie's breathing, somewhere behind her. Where was Brad? They were slowing down. Some light pierced the snow-haze, then a wavelet of warm air as gentle as that from a baker's oven. Kitchen smells. Feet on fire.

Lily had been looking at Robbie and Brad for several moments before she realized she was awake. They smiled warily at her. They were alive. She peered around. They were sitting on a mattress of some sort on the floor of a shanty. She recognized the smells, the drafts, the excessive heat. Someone had rubbed her feet and slathered them with grease. She could feel the blisters rising against it. She looked for their saviour. He emerged from behind the stove, his arms loaded with elm. He smiled at her.

At first she thought it was a trick of the candlelight or a result of the dizziness following her blackout, but in a moment she realized that what she was seeing was real. The man – grizzled, in his sixties, hair askew as if in a state of permanent fright – had only one arm, an elongated ape-like appendage that had grown in strength and bulk with the uses it had been put to since losing its coordinate. He had taken off his musty sweater, leaving only a sweat-creased undershirt that exposed the socket where the left arm had once joined his torso – a pouch of flesh as puckered as the grin of a toothless crone. His face was animated by wrinkles and abrupt gesticulating eyes unchecked by brows (that seemed to have been singed off while he leaned too close perhaps to the campfire along the hobo-glens of some distant rail-yard). A thin scar wriggled over one side of his grin.

He was gesturing with his fingers and arm like a mimist drawing a map of his words with his body; Lily felt the tension and frustration in his eyes as she shook her head and tried to find her own voice. Suddenly, with a magician's celerity he was out of the door and gone. Lily leaned over and drew Brad into her embrace. He was silent and still – deep in shock. Robbie crawled next to her and hung on, crying softly to himself. Wherever they were, they were safe, and together. She gritted her teeth against the searing pain in her feet, closed her eyes, and waited.

Minutes, hours later, the door swung open. Lily felt the breeze of a great bustle and flurry against her eyelids but could not persuade them to open. The door rattled shut with resolution. Lily smelled garlic, whiskey, fresh sweat: a huge presence in the room.

"Christ-take-me-ridin'-in-a-teacup, it's Lily Marshall, an' the two bairns I brung into the world!"

Lily opened her eyes and saw the familiar face beaming down at her. "Sophie," she whispered.

"Spartacus here tells me your house burned down an' he found you an' your lads wanderin' up Michigan Ave."

"He saved our lives," Lily said.

"Only Spartacus is dumb enough to be out in a storm like this, eh? But thank the Lord he was. My, my, look at those feet. C'mon, you old fart," she snapped, "help me carry them across to my place."

Spartacus was peering over Sophie's shoulder like a genie waiting to be recognized. Lily saw his eyes clearly in the light. She knew them. He hopped to one side and swept Robbie up onto his gnome's shoulder. Brad clung to his mother.

"We better get a sled," Sophie said. "Don't worry, Lily. We got lots of room at our place. You're safe now. You're in the Alley."

Spartacus went out carrying Robbie. Lily tried to get up.

"Don't worry about him, he looks queer but he's okay. Can't talk a word to strangers. Used to be a pedlar south of here years ago until some mark he was skinnin' ripped his arm right outta the socket an' then beat him over the head with it like a Chinaman's gong. Ain't been right since."

Brad moaned in his dreams. Lily was shaking all over.

"Just a little fright," Sophie soothed as she turned Lily's feet over in her soft, soft palms. "And a twinge of frostbite." Then she reached up and unhooked Brad from his mother's death-grip. The child settled against her bosom – cradled by two sturdy, rocking arms – opened its eyes and then closed them peacefully. "He'll be all right. One of my boys'll be along in a minute with a sled."

"Thank you," Lily murmured drowsily.

"What's that you got there?" Sophie said.

Lily had pulled something out of the large pocket in her skirt. It was clamped in her left hand. She looked down. It was the leather sachet from under her bed, bearing its treasure. As she slipped into unconsciousness, she was sure she could feel the pulsing of the jasper heart.

21

1

Sophie Potts was something else. Everybody in Mushroom Alley said so in one odd way or another, and Lily wasn't about to deny one dram of the praise due her. From the moment she entered Spartacus' hovel and saw Lily's boys shivering with dazed refugee's eyes, she took charge of the situation. "Bein' a midwife, as I used to be, you kinda get used to fear an' confusion," she often said in her defence. "Some women used to think I was an angel an' some tried to spit in my face like it was all *my* fault. Either way I just plunged in an' did my job. You don't expect thanks in this world or you'll wait a long time for the train to come in." The next day Sophie sent her older boys, Stewie and John, out to see what had happened. In the meantime she put salve on Lily's burns, lay her down in her own bed and fed her broth a teaspoonful at a time "My Peg's takin' care of your boys," she said, "they ain't got a scratch on them." The smell of bacon frying and singed toast floated through the house and lingered; Lily heard the skirl of children's laughter and Robbie's voice, low and brave, saying "It's all right, Brad, everythin's gonna be all right." John and Stewie reported back, out of breath and saucer-eyed. Sophie came in and sat down heavily beside Lily on the bed. "Nothin' left of the house. Just charcoal. Even the stove melted. The snow stopped it from spreadin'. Your little barn wasn't touched."

Lily tried to take this in. Robbie suddenly peeked around the curtained doorway, half wrestling with two black-haired male replicas of Sophie Potts, and grinning. "We could set up in the barn for now," she said. "Then..."

"You could stay here, too," Sophie said.

And they did.

As soon as Lily was able to walk, Sophie led her across the cart-path that served as a road towards a barnboard shack squatting forlornly among the scrub alders. For a big woman Sophie moved adroitly in a sort of ambling trot. When they came up to the shack, she eyed it with the zeal of a horse-trader, kicked the door open and seemed delighted that it stayed upright on its rusty hinges. "Solid wood," she said, entering and motioning Lily in after her. "Christ knows where them Icelanders hooked it from." To emphasize her point she slapped both palms down upon a thick table that dominated the large main room. Dust skittered into the thin sunlight offered by two narrow windows with glass. Sophie pointed to a misshapen stone hearth unadorned by andiron or grate. "Only place in the Alley, except the hoorhouse, that's got one of these. I don't think the poor buggars knew what a stove was. Most of 'em live in igloos back home, I'm told." She tested the resistance of a doorless cupboard over the washstand, loosening one shelf but otherwise seeming to approve. "For your best china," she winked. Then she flung back a curtain that once might have been a velveteen skirt, and when the dust cleared she said, "*Voilà*, they left the beds! See, you could put a screen down the middle an' have yourself two bedrooms, one for the boys." Lily's eyes were casting slowly about the room. "Back there?" she asked. "Ah, that's what I really brung you over for," Sophie said, and she pushed open the back door and squeezed herself through. "Them Icelanders, there was two of them, brothers we reckoned, sneaked off the train headin' for Manitoba an' set up house in the shanty that used to sit right here. Then they built this place, real sturdy. Didn't talk to a soul, but I liked them. We could hear them jabberin' away in their crazy lingo – either laughin' to bust a gut or arguin' fit to murder – and as the Alleyfolk usually do, we left them some food an' essentials when they wasn't lookin'. We figured they was plannin' on becomin' fishermen 'cause they went down to the shore every day an' stood watchin' the pickerel netters real close. One day they started buildin' a boat, just back of here, an' then they added on this big shed." She waved at the luxurious, spendthrift space all around them. "An icehouse, we thought. Who knows? One day soon after, some 'official-lookin'' gentleman come up the Alley an' before anybody could figure out a way of warnin' them, the two brothers was hauled away in irons, lookin' awful sad. We never did find out what crime they committed." The shed had no floor but it was spacious, had windows on the east side, and boasted several homemade tables and benches and two enormous cast-iron pots.

"You can set up in here," Sophie said. "It's perfect."

What Lily set up, with a lot of help from Sophie and others, was a laundering room. After the Icelanders had been taken off to the wilds of the Manitoba Interlake, a woman named Mabel Trout had moved in with her two daughters and established herself as a washerwoman. She had five customers from the 'big houses' up on Victoria Street, and sometimes handled the overflow from the Queen's after a ship or two had debouched its crews upon the lower town. "A hard-workin' woman, I'll give her her due," Sophie said. "She deserved better than those sluts of hers – lazy as sows in the sun, they'd sit an' watch her scrubbin' her hands raw an' never lift a finger. Had fancy ideas, they did, till one got the clap workin' part-time up at Hazel's an' the other got herself knocked up an' dumped by her so-called respectable gentleman-friend from Charles Street. Went bonkers, dear old Mabel did – scrubbin' shit off too many nappies, I reckon. Anyways they had to cart her off to London, screamin' all the way. And I'm tellin' you, you gotta be far gone to be taken for crazy in *this* part of town!"

Mabel's place had subsequently been taken up by a number of transients and hopefuls over the course of the winter. "None of 'em lasted much longer than a pig's fart," Sophie said. "People see these empty shacks an' they think all they got to do is move in an' settle down free-of-charge. Ain't that easy. I seen a hundred come an' go. It takes a special breed to live here for very long." She paused, then grinned: "We got rules, you know."

Although it seemed obvious to Lily that Sophie felt some special affection for her, the latter made no effort to explain the intricate code of behaviour that governed the lives of the permanent residents of Mushroom Alley. "You gotta learn them on your own, so you'll know for sure whether you can stay," Sophie told her. Lily learned some of them every day during those first few weeks in which, though no overt decision was made, Lily began to clean up and repair the Icelanders' shack for habitation. Sophie was able to supply Lily and her boys with clothing to keep warm, drawing upon her vast, motley stock of wretched hand-me-downs. "When you got eight kids, nothin' gets wasted." Lily wore a moth-eaten sweater of Marlene's, wondering where Marlene herself was and why Sophie, who gabbed on relentlessly about her children, never mentioned her. Robbie and Brad were well supplied with assorted tuques, mittens and piebald macintoshes. Spring was only weeks away.

There was no furniture, however, and not a single utensil. But the day after Lily began sweeping the filth out of the main room, she found several pots and pans and a kettle, well-weathered but intact, sitting on the table. Next day there was a chipped chamber pot and accessories. Then four shell-shocked wicker chairs. Finally a sofa desperately in need of a good home. When queried, Sophie just shook her head and jammed a spoonful of porridge into Bricky's clenched jaws (Bricky was short for Baby Ricky, Sophie's five-year-old, loudly proclaimed 'love-child'). "Maybe it was the good fairy," said nine-year-old Wee Sue, who still persisted in believing in such things. However, the moment the gifts stopped arriving, Sophie said, "Spartacus brung them over. If you don't like them you can go over to his junkyard an' pick out better ones. He likes to choose things himself for the first time. He won't be hurt if you take them back for tradin'. He likes to trade. Got little use for money."

"I got money," Lily said. "How much do I pay him?"

"He likes coins best," was all Sophie would say.

When Sophie suggested that Lily take over Mabel's defunct business, Lily agreed mainly because she could think of no other course of action to pursue. She could not bring herself to return to her own property, to gaze on the ruins of the house she had spent nineteen of her thirty years living and growing in. Nor could she consider trying to stay, even temporarily, in the barn where Uncle Chester had gone to escape from himself, where Benjamin had waited so loyally all those years, where the jersey had died giving birth, where Ti-Jean had lain awake nights dreaming of her hurt eyes. It would be a long time before she went back there.

Right now they needed a stove to heat water, they needed firewood, they needed mangles and scrub-boards and irons (Mabel's had been looted – "Here, we call it re-usin'," Sophie explained). Lily had some money left in the bank but she was afraid to spend it. As soon as she could, she and Robbie walked down to McHale's General Store and loaded up a sled with groceries. When Sophie was out, she stocked her shelves and pantry. Nothing was said.

"Don't buy a stove," Sophie said. "Stewie says there's a good one in your barn. We'll haveta get it here before all the snow melts."

As far as Lily could see, no plans were made for moving the stove. She continued to fix up the Icelanders' shack. The boys helped, still somewhat dazed by the sudden changes, but like most children unable to cope with being inactive. Without any advance warning the stove arrived on top of a large sled. "You Lily?" said the grizzled driver from his bench. In the keen air his odour preceded him by several rods. "Yes." He put two fingers in between his toothless gums and sent an icy whistle up the Alley. Then he dropped his chin on his chest and appeared to doze off. The boys ogled the horses, easing up to them and venturing a pat or two. A quarter of an hour later several bulky young men – McLeods, McCourts and Shawyers from their genetic trademarks – trudged in from sundry directions and Bachelor Bill's stove was carried into the workroom and its pipes set up and adjusted to fit the hole already in the roof. When Lily come out to thank the driver, he was gone. "Belcher, the honeyman," Sophie said later. "An off sod, that one." "How can I thank him?" "Leave him alone."

By the time spring came and the earth around her heaved with tendril, bulb and root, Lily was ready to leave the rambling comforts of Sophie's house. At first she thought there should be some ceremony to mark the occasion, but it soon became clear that none was called for. Sophie went off with Peg and Stewie in search of morels, and when she came home hours later, Lily and her boys were gone.

Lily got a rousing fire started and baked some extra biscuits in Bachelor Bill's stove, whose whims she knew intimately. She sat on the boys' bed singing softly to them and keeping one ear tuned to the outdoors. When Brad fell asleep at last, she sat at the table looking into the dark towards the River. No one came, that day or the next. Finally she walked over to Sophie's house, knocked, and getting no response, eased the door open and sat down to wait. The kitchen felt queer. The objects in it began to sway. She grabbed the table-top to steady herself. A great emptiness was swelling up inside her, she was a little girl afloat on her own body, a wafer of ice on a steaming, featureless sea – she was marooned unalterably estranged. The tears, copious and scalding, assuaged nothing, purged nothing, not even the rage she aimed at her own heart.

When she looked up again, Sophie was standing off to one side; she had been there for some time, it seemed, from the stillness of her pose and the resolute composure of her face. "Cryin' won't help," she said gently. "But not cryin's worse. I done my share." She went over to the stove, thrashed the grates and put a kettle on for tea. "When you're ready, love, we'll sit down an' talk about the launderin' business. An' anything else you care to tell."

2

Peg used to collect and deliver the laundry from the 'fancy houses' on Victoria Street, taking John or Stewie along to help pull the wagon over the tracks or through the mud of the Alley itself. Crazy Mabel gave them a nickel apiece. But according to Sophie, Peg was now too old for such a menial task, she was seventeen and ready to go out 'into service' if she wanted to. Although Sophie nattered and swore at all her kids indiscriminately and cuffed them whenever they were unwitting enough to loiter within range, she seemed to have almost no impact on the direction of their behaviour or their lives. "My Peg's got the kinda boobies gentleman wanta use for door-knobs," she'd sigh, but when Peg announced she intended to go to work as a maid for a bigwig at the refinery in Sarnia ("a notorious rake" who had "sprinkled the county with his bastards"), Sophie ranted and huffed like a storm-warning, threatened to "set your Pa on you", sighed, and let her go. She even helped her pack her bags, and said to Lily, "Jesus, I envy her." Thus it was that Fred – or Blubber as he was affectionately called – with Robbie dragged along 'for training', became the delivery boy for the Alley's newest washerwoman. Lily didn't ask how Sophie managed to regain the interrupted business, but all five customers returned to the fold. "I know more about them ladies than their priests," was all Sophie had to say on the matter. It was more than enough. Spring arrived in full force. I may not be alive yet, Lily thought, but I'm living. That's something. On April first they celebrated Brad's seventh birthday.

Whenever Stoker came home Sophie was a different person. The changes in her, which Lily came to know intimately in the months ahead, began a week or so before he actually made his appearance. Blubber or Wee Sue would detect more sting in her glancing blows and glare back with lips aquiver. Sophie – who was rarely quiet for more than twenty seconds at any stretch, carrying on a marathon gossipy tale while giving Lily a cooking lesson, boxing the ears of the nearest 'brat', and breaking up a skirmish in the yard outside with a lash of her trumpet tongue – now fell into pockets of silence from which she had to be periodically roused. Her good humour, that often seemed as indigenous to her as the jowls that telegraphed it, began to fail her, and she would sting the handiest victim – child, neighbour, kettle – with a fearsome, Bible-shaking curse. "I lost forty pounds since I brought your Brad into the world," Sophie said one day when Lily came into the kitchen and found her settled and steaming in a tin vat, formerly used to nurture beer and now being filled with an endless supply of hot water by Pet and Wee Sue. Sophie plopped a sponged into Lily's hand and she automatically began to scrub the great dame's back. Sophie released an elephantine sigh and then lay back among the cleansing suds; her voluptuous breasts, liberated from their natural function, floated before her like plump, spiced offering. Sophie was very vain about her skin; at the beach she had John and Stewie erect a portable sunshade over her, and when she bathed in the Lake, she donned a bonnet bigger than most parasols. "Stoker's comin' down from the bush," she said languidly, probably not even aware that her fingers had reached up to emprison her engorged nipples. "Gonna be here five days before the boat leaves. Five whole – goddamn you, girl, that's *hot*, you wanna *scald* my skin, you want your daddy to warm your ass so's you won't be able to sit down from here to next week!" Wee Sue ignored the comment on her work – being already well out of range and on her way for more healing-water. "Stoker's real fussy about my skin," Sophie said. "After all, the man's had nothin' to rub his hands over but the bark of a tamarack for almost three months." At this point several mammoth towels – once white – were brought in by the servant-girls and held theatrically along one side of the tub. Lily offered her hand and Sophie rose out of the petal-scented waters – all pink curves and voluminous coombs and licorice curlicues and mahogany thatch and acres of scrubbed skin inviting touch.

"Get outta here, Stewie! You some kinda *pervert* or somethin'?"

Stoker Potts came home the next day, hopping off the way-freight as it slowed down for the curve behind his house and sprinting across the flats towards what appeared to be a flag-sized chinese-poppy waving to him from his verandah.

Lily was not introduced to any of the Alleyfolk. "They know you're here," Sophie said. "You'll get to meet most of them, if they want to be met, and on their own good time." In the early weeks Lily could not be sure that anyone in the Alley knew anyone else. One day a gangling black man, decked out in tie-and-tails three sizes too small for him, walked by and waved as if he knew her; an hour later he walked back up the Alley and studiously ignored her, even though she was pulling weeds right beside the path. Nobody was actually seen visiting anyone else; but information – fact, rumour, gossip – travelled quickly and certainly. A woman, vaguely familiar, in a purple-flowered dress and unmatched sunbonnet strolled past and smiled broadly at Robbie; "You must be Lily's eldest" she was heard to say, but she kept on walking. "They'll let you know when they're ready," Sophie said. "'Round here we give people whatever privacy they want. But that don't mean we ain't friendly." Sometimes Lily could see Sophie herself in her back yard feeding Duchess, her sow, or urging on Stewie and John in their labours, and she would come right up to the fence and stand there, waiting, till finally she could wait no longer and called out "Good mornin'!" Many seconds later Sophie might glance over and give the intruder the meagrest nod of acknowledgement and then continue on with her own work. Even the children – the dozens of McLeods, McCourts, Shawyers – when they roved over the whole of the Alley in the dusk playing hide-and-go-seek, never hid out in Lily's yard, nor did she ever see the catcher – desperate as he might be – venture across the invisible boundaries of her 'property'. "Don't ask me why," Sophie said, "*why* is a question we don't have to ask in the Alley."

Stoker stayed for a week, as the ship on which he was chief fireman, the *Princess of Wales*, had been delayed in drydock at Collingwood. Lily knew enough to stay put; besides, she was busy setting up the laundry equipment in the Icelanders' shed. John and Stewie soon arrived – exiled or prudent, she knew not which – and proved to be of great assistance. They came every day and helped Lily move the two cords of wood into the shelter (the arrival of wood purchased by Lily from the local supplier was a cause for much amusement along the Alley, as Sophie told her much later, since no one could ever remember an Alleyperson actually *buying* fuel before this; "How do you get it?" "We swipe it," Sophie replied, "but only what we can use"). They made two spacious windows for her in the south wall and did the glazing perfectly. They walked out to the old property and hauled back some lumber out of which they constructed benches and tables. They promised to add a wooden floor before winter – "when we can pick up enough lumber," they said matter-of-factly. Robbie and Brad watched every move they made. "I'm goin' up to the bush with Dad come next fall," John told them. Robbie asked him if he'd found a little hatchet when he went through the house that got burnt. Then he looked at his mother and said, "When's Ti-Jean comin' back?"

The day before he left, Stoker came over to say hello. Lily was in the workroom when John and Stewie came in looking irritated. "Dad wants to meet you," Stewie said. Lily put down the pot she was holding and brushed her apron. "He's out on the road." "Oh." Lily walked through the house and waved him in from the front door. He had no recollection of their earlier meeting. On Lily's side, she was seeing a different man. He was still bearded, a bit more angular than muscular, with rugged handsome features and a bluff, engaging manner of speaking that seemed out of tune with long months spent isolated in the bush or hunched alone in front of a blazing furnace. His eyes danced lasciviously, like coal-dust in the fractured sunlight.

"Glad-ta-meet-ya, Lily," he boomed. "When I come back from my layover in a couple of weeks, we'll have ourselves a drink together, eh? In the meantime, anythin' you need these lads for, you just whistle. They're good boys, they are."

There was no expression of any kind on the boys' faces.

That evening as she lay in the sort of drugged semi-sleep she was getting used to, Lily heard a commotion from the Potts' house across the way: escalating laughter as raucous as it was hollow, followed by male shouts – barbed and threatening – and a series of haranguing shrieks carrying their own brand of venom: taunting and mocking, a calling-of-all-bluff. Then silence. Lily dozed, grateful. The crashing of glass, as loud and as ominous as if Orion had just burst overhead, brought her wide awake. Brad stirred beside her and she put a hand on his fevered head: sometimes he coughed all night. *"I'll kill you, you fat bitch!"* The words sailed clear and free down the whole of the Alley. Then a sort of muffled scuffling, as if heavy furniture were being abused and feet reluctantly dragged. A low pleading voice against the grim music. Nothing more – though Lily waited till the sun trembled over the window-sill and exhaustion claimed her.

Two days later when Lily came in to fix the boys' dinner, Sophie was sitting at the table. This was a custom Lily was just beginning to understand. Though it seemed you never asked anybody his business or initiated a conversation without invitation or invaded his privacy in anyway, it was all right among genuine friends – indeed it may have been a symbol of such – to simply enter their homes or yards and 'sit a spell'. Mind you, it put the host under no particular obligation; apparently you could keep on about your business if you chose without jeopardizing said friendship, and sooner or later the visitor would just leave. Like Old Samuels, she thought, in some ways. But it was also clear that such special intrusions often indicated a desire to talk. Lily sat down and squeezed out a smile. Sophie, the smudges of fatigue below her eyes almost completely faded, grinned and said "I hate to brag but that Stoker's *some* man. If Christ was hung like that, there wouldn't be a female heathen left upon God's earth." She stropped the nearest thigh and then snorted with the force of a crushed walnut.

Later, after tea and a few nibbled-at biscuits, Sophie sighed and said, "Burton didn't come back from the bush with Stoker."

"Who's Burton?"

"Our oldest boy," Sophie said.

3

During those first few traumatic weeks Lily kept a close watch on her sons. In some ways the shock of their loss and removal was easier for Brad than Robbie. Brad developed a bad cold and an asthmatic cough that made him continually fretful and hence in need of constant mothering. He clung to Lily's skirts everywhere she went during the day, and at night he slept beside her. He cherished her attention so much that it seemed to compensate, at least momentarily, for all the privations and physical discomforts. Robbie on the other hand would not stay put, he wandered beyond the margins of her supervision, his eyes fixed on the exotic rituals of the boy-herds and girl-flocks who ya-hooed, frisked and caromed among the bushes and dunes for much of the day ("Don't none of them go to school?" "Some of them, sometimes," Sophie said) and all evening till the moon went down or got swallowed by cloud. When a gang of boys about his own age would roar by on their way to the beach or the grassy flats, Robbie would stand in front of the house and watch them pass, his own feet longing simply to follow their own instinct and to take their own chances with rejection. Occasionally Lily would see one or two of the lads – dirt-streaked, barefoot ragamuffins – glance over at the motionless creature by the wayside (so much a replica of themselves), and then carry on as if impelled by the demands of some game none of them ever remembered learning the rules of. At last a few days before his eighth birthday, Robbie edged out to the road at the first yip of the approaching horde, so that when they swept by – spears poised for some imminent slaughter – he was almost naturally drawn into the irresistible current of their energy. So intent was this tribe upon the annihilation of its enemy that not one soul noted the addition of a whooping, fleet-footed brave whose heart was soaring with joy and relief and the gratitude of those forever-to-be-included. From that moment on, Lily's main concern was the whereabouts of her eldest. "Don't fuss," Sophie soothed, "they always come back sooner or later."

Neither boy was able yet to sleep without violent dreams, that shook them in their beds like scarlet fever or St. Vitus' Dance. Often just before bed, Brad would see behind the lamp-lit window some configuration of shadow – severed, truncate, bloating ogre-flesh – and shriek. And he would continue whimpering, even when Lily turned the lamp down so that only the blunt shadow of the night was visible anywhere. Even Robbie was susceptible to these sudden incursions from 'out there', and so it was not uncommon for Lily to have to sit with an arm around each boy, singing and murmuring them towards sleep, while the window-images continued to travel on through their dreams. Even so, Lily thought as she watched them fret, they're lucky; the gremlins they're scared of are the only ones that will do them no harm.

Of course Robbie, who was unused to sharing his exploits and triumphs, had some difficulty adjusting to the inviolable rules of the Alley games. Three times in one week he came home with a bloody nose and scuffed knuckles. For hours he would sulk, never telling the horrid details of whatever humiliation he had suffered and glaring at his mother as if it were all her fault. But he always went back, grim-lipped. Lily felt proud of him and yet somehow betrayed, left out, found unworthy. She thought of Sophie's Burton, and was ashamed.

When Brad finally recovered from his cough and when Lily herself felt comfortable enough, she and her boys walked up Victoria Street to the Edward Street Common School. Up to this time Lily had not ventured out of the Alley except to go briefly along Prince Street past the Queen's Hotel to the General Store for supplies or to walk along the cinder road to the rail-yards where she bought the firewood to get her business launched. For some reason she could not bring herself to go up Michigan Ave. to the familiar shops – Redmond's, Durham's Dry Goods Emporium – where she knew she would meet a dozen friendly, and perhaps even anxious, faces. Soon, she promised herself. Victoria was the last east-west street running parallel to Michigan Ave. and to the railroad tracks a hundred yards to the north. It boasted the largest private houses in the village. Robbie proudly pointed out the residences of their customers. "That's Mrs. Saltman's, the baker's wife, she give me a penny for myself!" They came to the frame building that served as the public school – three teachers and eight grades. They stood on the boardwalk in the early morning sun and looked. The windows were wide open, a breeze was billowing the blinds. They could hear the scratch of chalk on slates. "There's nobody in there," Brad whispered. "Stewie won't go to school," Robbie said, "Mr. Grindly whips him."

"Shush," Lily said. "Stewie's just tryin' to spook you. Come September, you boys're gonna walk up here every mornin'. You're gonna learn to read and write." And that's the only thing I know for sure, she thought.

On Dominion Day most of the village turned up on the river flats to celebrate the beginning of summer and incidentally the fourth anniversary of the Confederation, now six provinces strong and still counting. The main attraction was a five-match lacrosse game between the Point and the Brantford Mohawks. The local squad was composed of all the healthy young men from the settled part of town, which meant the exclusion of Alleyfolk and most of the transient railroaders who populated the boarding houses on every block. "Gotta be baptized to play lacrosse," Sophie said, "unless you're an Indian."

The Alleyfolk set up some tents and marquees along the fringes of their own property adjacent to the proceedings, and sold refreshments (some of them legal), rented shade, and gave directions to gentleman tourists in search of a less strenuous but more invigorating sort of exercise. When the Point Edward Spikes scored to win the first match, the Alleyfolk cheered. When the Mohawks won the second one, they cheered more loudly. The Indians eventually triumphed, four rounds to one. "We gotta let them win *some*time," Sophie chuckled.

The races that followed later in the afternoon were open to all contestants. Lily sat in the shade of Sophie's tent and watched Robbie head out to the starter's spot with Stewie and several of the McLeod boys. The athletes were sorted according to age and size by Sunday-school teachers with a keen nose for prevarication. Robbie was the smallest of the 'ten-year-old' group. "He's got spunk, that one," Sophie said. Lily waited for the starting pistol and then let out her breath. In the scramble of the start, Robbie was elbowed and knocked to his knees. He got up and pursued the pack, already ten strides ahead of him – a lot to make up in a two-hundred-yard (or so) dash. Robbie was robust and surprisingly quick. He caught up in a hurry. He took an outside position, and with twenty yards to go drew even with the leader, a rather elongated 'ten-year-old' who was obviously winded and fading fast. From the shouts of endearment that emanated from the wagering crowd nearby, he seemed to be the favourite. Robbie flashed ahead, but not before a stinging elbow caught him in the ribs. He kept his balance, teetered briefly into the larger boy, and then pulled away to win by five full strides. The Alleyfolk and the Mohawks let out a patriotic cheer. First prize was a silver dollar. The judges later determined that the winner had fouled the runner-up and asked that the award be returned. The happy recipient had already disappeared – without a trace.

"My word," Lily said, turning from her beaming son and looking anxiously around, "where's Brad?"

"He was right here a minute ago," Peg said without interrupting her survey of the silver dollar's bas-relief.

Lily dashed out from under the awning; no one else took up the alarm. Sophie had consumed a lot of mineral water and was snoring contentedly under cover. The whole area was bursting with children, all in motion. Lily didn't know where to start. Peg, home for a brief visit, called out behind her, "They're over there!"

Lily saw them under a nearby alder: Brad was curled in the shade of the late afternoon, his eyes closed but his face tensed, listening; and Wee Sue, not two years older, was seated beside him with one arm around his shoulder and the other propping a book open on her knees. Her lips were spelling out words that bound them for this moment together.

Lily decided it was time to walk up Michigan Ave. She picked out a sunny July day and in the glare of noon she came up from Prince Street all the way to Redmond's. "Sorry to hear about your place burnin' down," the grocer said. "No insurance, I take it." Lily nodded and gave him her order. "Bring the boys along," he said. "I always got a licorice or two for my favourite tow-heads." Lily promised she would, said goodbye to Mrs. Redmond and started home. Standing in front of Durham's Dry Goods, chatting with three of the women from the Wednesday tea group, was Maudie Bacon. Shaking just a little inside, Lily walked towards them so that she could be face-to-face with Maudie. A few feet away, Lily opened her lips to say 'hello' just as Maudie's eyes cornered her own for a telling second. The word froze in its frame, unspoken. Maudie turned back to her friends with a snap of her head, that conveyed to Lily so much more than the simple, lethal snub intended.

Lily kept on walking down to the docks. At the coal company she ordered enough coke to last her the winter.

22

1

Sophie was right. By the time the boys started school in September, Lily had met in one way or another most of the regular denizens of Mushroom Alley. One bright morning in early June as she was hanging out Mrs. Christie's washing, Lily heard someone calling. The sound seemed to be coming from a clump of trees to the north of her yard: a high-pitched, plaintive call that could have been a command or a cry for help. That's odd, Lily thought, there's nothing between me and Hazel's Heaven up on the dunes. Maybe somebody's caught up in the short-cut running down to the beach. She craned her neck, and the call came again, a man's voice echoing thinly in the empty morning of the Alley. He must be in a tree, Lily thought as she dropped her work and started through to the scrub, watching out for the sudden hawthorns.

"*Ship ahoy!*"

Lily came out into a little clearing which she was surprised to discover. A wretched hovel not much bigger than a pup-tent sat between two hummocks of sand. An open fire was smouldering in front of the entrance. There were no windows. Lily's gaze was then drawn upward to what appeared to be a scaffolding erected on a steep hummock a few rods away but turned out to be the frame of a barn or coop that some previous tenant had begun in earnest and then abandoned.

"Reverse engines! Reverse engines! Three points to the starboard, Mr. Collins. Steady now, steady on."

Perched on the upper rafters, with his feet on a cross-piece and his arms on the top-joist, was a tiny gnome of a man with snow-white hair frothing about his face like the first foam of a breaker, and a captain's hat, and a uniform whose brass buttons glinted authority, glinted pride. One hand was on his brow shielding his eyes from the fierce sea-sun, the other steady as a rock on the bridge-rail. His knees swayed with the pitch of the waves, leaving his upper body resolute, the nerves unshakable.

"Funnel off the port bow! All hands on deck. Prepare for May Day, Mr. Collins. No panic, please. No panic."

Suddenly his horizon burst apart with a dozen howling children, who dashed out of the bushes as if on cue, washed past Lily without a blink, and swarmed all over the scaffolding like tars littering a mainsail. Of indeterminate sex, they scrambled, hurled threats and boasts aloft, enacted duels to the death, sent pirates to their graves upon impossible planks, and steadfastly ignored their captain's call to abandon ship. Neither the old man nor the children fully acknowledged the presence or legitimacy of the other, but they seemed intricately bound up in a similar game, never quite out of the other's reach. Pirate kings lunged and skewered the old man countless times, and he in turn pleaded in vain with the blackguards to let the women and children enter the lifeboats first. It seemed to Lily – watching, ignored – that they had stumbled into each other's dream.

"Batty as a bull with three balls," Sophie wheezed, "but harmless. Nice old guy, really. Billy Whittle's his name, but everybody here just calls him Cap. That's what he was. Used to pilot the *Erie Shore* till she cracked up in a tornado back in 'sixty-five. He got everybody off an' then lashed him an' his wife to the mast. He begged her to get into the last lifeboat but she wouldn't. The storm broke them up. They were both washed ashore up near Port Franks. He was still breathin'. She wasn't."

It was at the Dominion Day festivities that Lily formally met the three women whose celebrated fecundity had produced almost three-dozen offspring, neatly and incontrovertibly identifiable by their hair-colouring, a genetic miracle that might have delighted Mendel – red-headed McCourts (actually a hybrid orange shade unremarked anywhere else), tow-headed Shawyers (with characteristic cowlick) and black-haired/whey-faced McLeods (with pointed snotty noses that made them resemble starlings on the run). Until puberty, which attacked them disgracefully early, the sexes were indistinguishable by manner, instinct or dress. By age twelve, though, nature decided to have its way with them: the girls willowed and billowed shamelessly through the village, sending one kind of shudder through every respectable father and another kind through their curious sons. The boys toughened and grew lusty, and decent mothers everywhere locked up their puzzled daughters. Though Lily did not ever get to know them well – they were clannish, exhausted from day-labour and child-bearing, and not quite ready to admit they were stuck in the Alley for a lifetime – she admired and felt sorry for them. Later on when she herself was more settled, she was able to help them in the small, unobtrusive ways allowed her; she had tea and chatted with Mrs. McLeod on many occasions and once or twice with Mrs. Shawyer and Mrs. McCourt, but never with all three together. In that regard they formed an exclusive club, sharing their common miseries, shrivelled hopes and the need to exchange petty, emancipating spites. To these ends Lily was, in their limited view, a washout. Miseries they had aplenty: each had husbands who were unemployable because they were alcoholic or alcoholic because they were unemployable. Their men were rarely at home, eternally seeking odd jobs 'digging ditches' up north or down in Kent or in the States, coming home long enough to terrorize the kids, quench their abbreviated lusts, and contribute to the steady advance of progress-through-procreation. The older boys would get work, help support the brood for a bit, then take up with some girl and move off. The older girls went into service and helped feed the younger ones until they found a spouse or let their master get them pregnant, after which they returned home to bear the bastard and take up permanent residence among their own kind. These few families proved to be an endless drain on the charity of the three churches whose auxiliaries competed mightily in fruitless attempts at reform and repudiation. "Even typhoid wouldn't wipe them out," an exasperated elder was heard to say one Sunday morning in the vestry. Nonetheless, it was generally conceded that the girls were good workers: there were at least seven of them serving as maids or scullions throughout the village and the town.

Lily's business was almost more than she could handle. She needed a much larger tub for soaking the huge bloodied sheets sent down to her from The Queen's. She mentioned this to Sophie. Several days later she heard Honeyman's wagon stop in the road near her front door, and when she went around to see what was up, Belcher waved to her and pointed at a shiny, coppery object behind him. Spartacus was already trying to wrest it loose, and soon three boys materialized to help carry it into the workroom. It was a brewer's vat, somewhat tarnished and battered but otherwise serviceable. "Where'd he pick this up?" Lily asked Honeyman, who chewed his tobacco and looked at his toeless boots whenever he talked to a 'lady'. "In the brewery junkpile down on Front Street. Surprisin', ain't it, what a sane man will throw out." Nothing in Mushroom Alley surprised Lily. "Old Spartacus here, he's got a keen eye for junk." Lily got her cookie-box and counted out two dollars in change.

"That's too much, Lily," Spartacus said in a clear and slightly accented voice.

Honeyman was so startled he swallowed his cud.

When Lily went to the beach, as she often did that sultry summer of 'seventy-one, she took the short cut that ran from the road past her place through the scrub and curved below the back-yards of the last two houses before the Lake – Hazel's Heaven and Baptiste Cartier's blind-pig. The boys were curious about the faded clapboard house with the mauve trim, the only house of unnatural tint in the Alley. They were equally puzzled by the flounces and underclothing that curtsied in the breeze off the water: pinkish corsets that drooped like parboiled lobsters; pennant-sized pantaloons fluttering in cerise, marigold and Kelly green; and innumerable pairs of silky stockings so sensuously fanned by the slightest kiss of wind. They kept their distance, though, because both boys were afraid of the bootlegger's pig – Aquinas – kept in a pen very near the path. He was a gargantuan Polish China boar, who snorted and bristled at them, pawing the muck with his cleft trotters, ramming his malodorous snout into a trough of slime, and casting the baleful glare of his blood-puffed eyes at the smooth, white morsel of little boys who might venture too near and be eaten in a wink. As far as Lily could learn, John the Baptist (as he was known here) kept Aquinas as his pet, throwing the most dreadful tantrums whenever anyone – denizen or stranger – came too close to the creature or made some drunken slighting remark about its potency or suggested that it might be of singular service to certain females along the lane. Often he could be heard talking to it – in French or perhaps in some private *joual* they shared to keep mankind at bay. John himself was a morose man, utterly taciturn except when conversing with his pet or cursing trespassers. But he made the best and safest hooch in town, and try as they might, neither man nor boy inside or outside the Alley was able to trail him long enough to discover the whereabouts of his still. Once, a gang of toughs had set watch on his place day and night for a week. As far as they could tell he never left his yard, coming out only to feed Aquinas or sit gabbing with him in the middle of a moonless night. Yet, fresh supplies appeared for the weekend crowd of sailors and the overspill from Hazel's.

On the way back from the beach, Lily often walked around the long way, up the little cliff and onto the lane itself, where the boys could gawk at the big windows beside the verandah on the whorehouse, hoping for a peek at the exotic plumage inside. The girls never came out in daylight, and Lily had warned them away from here after dusk. Across from Hazel's and next to Honeyman's place was another gray shack remarkable only for the fact that behind it were five or six sheds, several of them merely lean-to's, and an old army tent that looked as if it had been recently shelled. "Stumpy lives there," Sophie said. "He thinks God was a fish." One day in July just as she and the boys climbed up the slope onto the lane, she spied a strange man coming towards them. He obviously saw no one ahead of him for he swung onto the path that led up to Stumpy's shack. It was his way of walking that alerted Lily and half-prepared her: an ambling, rolling, almost bouncing gait that a deckhand might use in a high sea but only if his legs had been frozen from the shins down. Stumpy, Lily thought. He was dressed in overalls and a wool shirt, his beard and gray hair were as tangled and forlorn as fish-nets on some deserted tidal flat. Lily never would have recognized him from that face so completely altered in seven short years, but the walk was unforgettable. She told the boys to go on home, and then broke all the rules by trailing Stumpy into his house, and when he looked in astonishment at her intrusion, she smiled sadly and said, "Hello, Bags."

"It's Stumpy now," he said with both resignation and pride. He sat out on a bench overlooking the beach below and told Lily his story, but only after she had told him as much of her own as she could bear. He had got a job in London as a clerk in the office of a stagecoach line, but he had been too miserable at being cooped up or just too ornery, because he was soon fired. He took straight to drink and got so bad even his cousin threw him out onto the street. Finally some preacher found him in the gutter, taught him to see God in all His glory, and sent him abroad to bear witness and teach the world how to overcome the accidents of fate. He cared nothing for material goods now, he lived only for God and to serve the outcasts of mankind. So he worked in the fish plant in the warm seasons to get enough money to aid the down-trodden and the lost all the year long. He showed Lily the shelters he'd erected in his yard to accommodate the hoboes and unemployed and outlawed who jumped train at the end of the line and wandered in here dazed, cold, crippled, without hope or the will to hope. Here he fed them, talked a little religion, listened to their woeful tales, and then showed them the stumps that God had blessed him with as proof of his own temptation, apostasy and resurrection.

"We all need God, Lily. I do hope you've found Him. Is there anythin' I can do to help you? If so, you just holler an' Stump'll be there."

Lily touched the back of his hand, felt how benevolent the sun was, recalled the cool clasp of the waves on her legs, the soaring delight of her boys at play. "I'd like a little music," she whispered.

2

About a week before school was to open, Robbie came panting up behind her in the workroom and said, "Come quick, Mama, there's a naked lady gettin' beat up over in the dunes! She's cryin' an' blubberin', we heard her, didn't we, Brad?" Lily looked at Brad who'd come running in just after his brother. "A big black man's beatin' her up," he said. "Beatin' her to death!" Robbie added, and Lily knew she must go.

The two boys dragged her along through the scrub to the edge of the dunes just behind Hazel's place. Robbie was about to point triumphantly to the exact spot of the murder when Brad yelled, "Up there!" and they all turned and looked towards Hazel's just in time to see a flash of leg, buttock and arm – bald as the sun, black and white blurred together as they disappeared hastily beyond the flapping bedsheets.

"She looks quite alive to me," Lily said, pulling her hand free of Robbie's.

"He took all her clothes away," Robbie said, "an' I heard her cryin'."

Lily was about to drag her boys home and find some way to explain what they had probably seen, when she was stopped in her shoes by a rasping female voice.

"Goddam you, Shad, I told you to keep that black pecker in your pants and I meant it. Betsy Riley, I'm ashamed of you, runnin' around starkers where anybody from the town could see you plain as porridge, I'm ashamed to know you, girl. Now get in there, both of you, before I take the rug-beater to your butts." A door slammed amid some less-than-contrite giggling, and the woman with a voice like a claw-hammer emerged at the top of the rise and began jerking pegs out of the sheets as if they were hairs on the head of her victims. Her quick eye spotted the strangers below. Lily saw the sun ricochet from a gold tooth. The woman's arm was waving them a welcome.

"You boys go on ahead to Sophie's, don't forget the carnival's on the saft," she said.

But the boys slipped into the bushes and watched from below as long as they dare. When Lily came up to the woman, they both stood stock still for a second, then spoke almost simultaneously.

"Lily Ramsbottom!"

"Char?"

Char Hazelberry, now known as Hazel, reached out with her scullion's grip and pulled Lily to her bosom. "It *is* you, I can't believe it, you ain't changed a bit, Winnie said she was sure it was you but I didn't believe her, now I got to believe my own eyes, don't I? Come on in an' meet the girls."

Hazel added a dollop of whiskey to her coffee, sighed across her bosom and said, "We was all doin' just fine, thank you, Winnie's sister took the babe – real cute little fella, wasn't he, Win – and our business was goin' great guns. Then I decided to accept the job at the St. Clair Inn when the new owner took over. I was chief cook with my own staff – naturally I carted Winnie an' Betsy along with me, an' for a time we run the best cookery in town. We heard that from the drummers an' regulars, didn't we Bet, all the time. But that owner an' his snooty lady was somethin' else! Remember that wart on his nose?" She glanced at Winnie and Betsy and was rewarded with reminiscent snickers. "Well, to make a long story longer, the old geezer – he must've been *sixty* – corners me in the pantry on St. Patrick's day an' tries to lift my skirt, pretty as you please. Naturally I resisted an' even threatened to tell his Bible-thumpin' wife. That backed him up real quick. But not for long. I discover he's been pesterin' both Win an' Bet, poor dears, an' them not havin' the wherewithal to resist, an' so I goes straight to his office to have it out, an' the very mention of his sin must've set his gong a-clappin', 'cause he reaches over an' flips both my bosoms right outta their harness. Well, I let out a screech that would've shook grandpa outta eternity, and in rushes the wife. Naturally I appeal to her as a woman and a believer, but you'll never in a hundred years guess what happened. She sided with the old goat! She called me a slut and a hoor and a panderer, an' she told me to take my girls an' depart on the instant. An' the last I see of them hypocrites, she's soothin' and' cooin' up to him an' we're out on the street without a pot to pee in. And, can you beat this, she blabs it all over Sarnia that we're bawds an' harlots, an' we have no hope ever again of gettin' work in a respectable place."

"So we come here," Winnie said with the bubbling natural giggle she'd had since she turned fifteen and that now seemed, in the tired and creased flesh of her forties, eccentric – as if she had just adopted such a youthful mannerism for effect. "What's *your* excuse!" she laughed.

It took almost two hours for histories to be exchanged, but in this strange, enclosed space time seemed even of less importance than it did on the lane outside. The parlour where they sat might have graced the seraglio of a second-rate sultan – with its faded Armenian carpets piled and overlapping on the floor; damask curtains with gold tassels to repudiate the prying sun; sofas that were all curve and cushion and invitation; a myriad of tiny lamps with Oriental shades, the afterburn of incense still in the air; a black-skinned, white-shirted Dahomey cross-legged, with hookah, on the albino bearskin spread before the portico which led to purdah and its languorous, mediterranean pleasures.

"This here's Mr. Lincoln – I understand you met briefly out back – Mr. Shadrack Lincoln. We call him Shad."

"And a few other things," said Betsy, unable to take her eyes off Lily, whom she found to be so much the same and yet so much different and wondering if Lily were thinking the same thing about her.

"Shad might look dumb, but he's quite smart, ain't you, Shad?" Shad smiled dreamily, but Lily felt his eyes scan and appraise her. "He don't talk, so folks around here think he's stupid. But back in Philadelphia he used to be a lawyer's clerk, readin' law books an' writin' out lawyer's briefs. He was a regular black gentleman. He's still got some of his master's suits given to him when he was set free."

"What happened to him?" Lily asked, looking his way and letting their glances lock for a second, then peering through the opium daze, the comic's costume, the mute pose of the face, and knowing full well what she might find in the dark history unreleased behind those eyes.

"After the kafuffle at Harper's Ferry back in 'fifty-nine, you know when the niggers took a run at the federal army an' got butchered, there was hell to pay among the slaves everywhere. Some vigilantes come in the night an' drug poor Shad outta his bed an' hauled him kickin' an' screamin' off to the nearest woods." She paused and checked out the victim. He now lay on his back upon the rug, the pipe beside him, breathing deeply.

"I think he's left us," Winnie whispered.

"Well, Lily dear, shame-to-say but them vigilantes went an' cut his tongue out an' they smashed all the fingers on his right hand so's he couldn't write no more an' left him on his master's doorstep, bleedin' an' sobbin' his heart out."

"But they didn't know Shad was left-handed –"

"I'll tell it, if you don't mind," Hazel said sharply, not quite ready to forget the recent transgression on the dunes. "Anyways, Shad recovered an' was able to write but he couldn't talk no more an' from time to time, as he do now, he went a bit crazy in the head. So his master set him free an' sent him up to Canada to work on the farm of a friend. We're glad to have him. He's a dear man, smart as a whip, an' when them sailors get rambunctious in here on a Saturday night, all he has to do is roll them eyes, froth a bit at the mouth and start gargling out his dumb-language an' they head outta here in a hurry. He does all our shoppin' in town, too." She sighed. "Poor Shad; he's got to listen to Win an' Bet chatter all day an' night an' he don't get to say a word!"

When Lily got up to go, Hazel hugged her again and said, "We have tea up here every Monday – our day off – so why don't you come? Sophie usually does. You can meet the other three girls – they're still young an' need their sleep – and of course our housekeeper an' chief pot-scrubber."

"That's Vi," Betsy said.

"She's down at the beach for a swim," Winnie said.

"*Always* down there, it seems to me," Hazel added.

"Talkin' to the waves."

"*They* can understand her," Winnie tittered.

"Hush up," Hazel said to her. "Vi's a sweet thing an' you know it. You'll come an' see us, then, Lily?"

Lily nodded and waved goodbye several times before she came down to the path behind the brothel. Something urged her to turn towards the Lake, so she did.

The beach was deserted. Though it was a sweltering August afternoon, all the children were off to a travelling carnival and freak show down in Bayview Park. The immaculate sand, cleansed in the endless sieve of soft wavelets against the shore, glittered under a Grecian sun. Lily took off her shoes and stood wriggling her toes until they touched the cool damp granules below the surface. For a few moments she stood perfectly still and listened to the waves, scarcely nudged by a westerly breeze as they broke idly on the shale of pebbles and seashell that ringed the water's edge as far as the eye could follow the miles into the northern haze. Farther out the Lake was calm, without current or direction, indifferent to the winds, an abiding and lucid blue beyond the reach of any sun or season. It *was*, and it shone for any eyes to see. Lily closed hers, and it was still there.

When she opened them she saw something move across the plane of the water's dominion, about twenty yards out just where the bottom sailed from under your feet and you were adrift on your own weight. A swimmer – made elegant by buoyancy, the arms lifting in slowed sequence closer to the blood's own beat, with a leg-kick like the silver spray of a mermaid's fin, hair fanned out behind in winged ebony, the body aimed through some vital dimension with the grace of a dolphin's dance. For a second Lily herself felt that wondrous free-fall moment between stroking and surrender. The swimmer touched down reluctantly – and only when the knees scraped bottom and the bones' angles re-emerged – then stood upright among the taffeta froth of the rollers near shore.

It was a plain, female body clearly visible below the homemade bathing costume pressed wetly against the outlines underneath: lumpish curves, knob knees, a slack belly, masculine feet. Thick black hair was matted against the face, browned unevenly by the sun, the large eyes darkly innocent, the right side of the jaw crooked where it had grown accustomed to the hare-lip above it.

"Hello, Lily. They said it was you livin' down there in the Icelanders' shack, but I didn't believe 'em. I ain't allowed to go down that way."

The words, distorted only by the narrow wheeze of the cleft palate, came out as clear and as natural as a gossip's whisper. As Lily walked towards Violet she shed her outer clothing – skirt and blouse – and covered only by her shift she took the swimmer's hand and together they turned back into the waves. When the first breaker foamed against her thighs and flattened the shift to their shape, Lily jumped and giggled and Violet let go of her hand and laughed and then began to run across the Lake lifting one foot out of the water and splashing it emphatically down just as the other one broke the surface. Lily came skitter-splashing behind her, laughter bubbling and evaporating from her throat, and moments later it was too deep to run, the Lake had them and they capitulated with a wild, surrendering dive into the green looking-glass dream of its depths, oh the cold total possession of its grip on the nippled breast, the silenced eardrum, the pinioned arms, on the knees and the thighs and, ah, upon the paradisal vee at the soul of sensation. They rose again to the icy-hot surface, they were amphibian, they swam in unison as whale and dolphin do, they rolled dorsally, they lolled weightless on their backs facing the firmament, they turned in their own time and swam with slow synchronous ease back to the dry island of the beach. Linking hands again they walked up onto the white sand and lay down to contemplate the sky and bask in the body's long thaw.

Why here, why now? Lily thought. What is it we do to deserve or not deserve such fitful collisions of joy? What is the sun seeing now, gazing down at us? Can it care the way we do? Do we make *anything* happen? She reached over and touched Violet's hand. "I love you, Lily," Violet whispered. "I always did."

Yes, we do. We must.

23

1

Robbie and Brad started school in September. Lily felt she ought to accompany them on the first day but Sophie warned her away from such foolishness. Robbie was delighted to be able to walk ahead with the older boys, while Brad took hold of Wee Sue's hand and headed up Victoria Street humming out loud and skipping inside. All summer long Wee Sue had taken Brad under wing – except for the two weeks he was quarantined with chicken-pox – and taught him how to read. They were both excited about the possibility of startling Miss Timmins into a moment's silence, and Wee Sue squeezed his hand possessively and smiled at the envy in the eyes of the other nine-year-old girls who flocked about them from the adjoining side-streets and lanes. "I'm to take care of him," she announced at every opportunity.

If Miss Timmins, the maiden lady who taught Primer and Book One were startled, she did her best to conceal the fact. Nevertheless it was clear that Brad could read the second primer-book with ease by the end of the month while others, like Robbie, were still stumbling through the recitation of the ABC's. When his printing improved in October, Brad was moved into the front seat of the second row, a bona fide member of Book One. Brad loved school. He loved Miss Timmins. He stayed in at recess and helped Miss Timmins clean the blackboards. Wee Sue rejoined her own troop. On the way home from school he had to be saved from the fists and taunts of the other boys by his older brother, who returned him to his mother shaking but unscathed. While Lily could sooth Brad's feelings in her arms, she could not explain away the bewilderment in his eyes, the child's hurt questioning of the unjust order of things, of secret burdens already inherited without understanding or consent. A few feet away she could hear Robbie running cold water from the pump over the cuts on his knuckles, and the other chamber of her heart contracted. She knew better than to go to him now – to say one word of praise or consolation. Later, sometimes.

Though Wee Sue no longer dared to befriend Brad at school, she continued her affection guiltily at home. She smuggled over to his house a bundle of books, mostly readers and texts which the older Potts had 'forgotten' to return to the school following their various unorthodox departures. They had been locked in a trunk in Sophie's room because no books of any kind were to be exposed in Sophie's presence, on pain of death. Lily wanted to ask Sophie why, but could not find the opportunity to do so. "Mama hated school," Wee Sue said. "Her teachers were mean to her." This grievance notwithstanding, Sophie never complained when Principal Grindly took the strap to any of her charges, and she advised Lily to do likewise. "I got a simple rule: for every whack on the calluses they get there, I give 'em two on the backside when they get home. And if that don't do the trick, I threaten to tell Stoker."

Lily sat beside Brad on the battered settee Spartacus had recently picked up for them, and together they read their way through the first two primers. At first Brad was faster than she was, guessing the words quickly and triumphantly, running his finger under the magic letters a second in front of his nimble tongue, never forgetting a word once he had sounded it out, and prompting his mother's halting efforts with wondering delight. After Christmas, though, Wee Sue brought over a large tome called *McGuffey's Fourth Eclectic Reader*, and the stories and poems in there frustrated even Brad's obsessive efforts. Lily herself found it hard to believe – impossible to understand – but she began to get the sense of such pieces as "The Wreck of the Hesperus", Mrs. Moodie's "Burning of the Fallow" and "Little Daffydowndilly" by Mr. Hawthorne, even without knowing all the words, while Brad became dazed, then numbed, then furious as the indecipherable phrases accumulated and mocked him. Brad went back to his own Reader and after a while, when he settled down, they would take turns again, reciting and listening, giving and accepting, till Brad fell asleep on her shoulder and she could open the big book silently and astonish herself once more by reading it – on her own, unaided, the ancient stories and fables coming off the page at her as if the bards themselves were sequestered among the shadows of this room and chanting towards eternity. I am thirty-one years old, she thought, and something magical is just beginning. She shivered but made no attempt to pull the shawl around her.

Robbie's first season at school was not only difficult, it was a foreshadowing of the troublesome years to follow. In some ways he was as bright as Brad; by the end of the first grade he could read, print his letters, and do the simple sums required. But in temperament he was too much like his father – headstrong, impetuous and fiercely proud. In vain Lily searched for the first signs – any portent – of Tom's redeeming qualities: his good humour, his trusting affection, his courage. Only the latter was visible for very long as Robbie continued to defend his brother, risking not only the inevitable bruises and scrapes but much much more – the fellowship of the ruffians and outcasts he needed unconditionally as companions. Somehow he managed to maintain their fickle admiration even while he punched out the bullies among them whenever he had to. They were a strange lot he hung out with, Lily thought. She made no pretense of understanding the contradictory laws of their code, and she had no doubt about the claims it made upon Robbie's loyalties. Unfortunately in defending his brother for reasons which to him grew more obscure and untenable each time an enemy was silenced,

Robbie's feelings for Brad began to swing from blinding love to intermittent revulsion. When there was affection it was no longer of the open, trusting kind. Strangely Robbie did not seem in the least jealous of Brad's brilliant progress in reading and writing, almost as if he didn't consider achievements of that kind worthy of any response whatsoever. They existed in a world he had no desire to enter.

"He's just like all my boys," Sophie consoled. "Not one of them ever liked school. An' why should they? They went there long enough to learn to read an' write their names an' count up to a hundred – just enough so's the bigwigs an' bosses won't be able to cheat them outta their drawers. What else do you need to know to dig ditches or sling flour sacks on the docks, eh? My John's gone off to the sheds this year, an' Stewie'll go next. For the girls it's even sillier. How is book-learnin' gonna help you be a parlour maid or save you from gettin' knocked up by your mistress's hubbie or son or stableboy?" She spoke this latter sentence with some bitterness.

"Peg?" Lily said.

"You guessed it, an' the silly bitch didn't have enough brains to go for the top, where there's some money at least. A stable hand she tells me, who says he's gonna make an honest woman outta her as soon as he can find another job. She can't come back here, Stoker don't approve of them kind of shenanigans. He's got his pride."

One day in the spring Robbie came home from school in the miidle of the morning. She stood up from her steaming wash and saw him standing forlornly in the open doorway of the laundry shed, his chin on his chest, his hands – always active, alert, poised to clench or welcome – drooped at his side. She heard him swallowing his tears.

"He sent me home. I ain't goin' back." It was not a boast nor a threat nor a defence; it was spoken as an inevitable, regrettable truth. The pathos of it struck Lily so forcefully that she had to busy herself with taking off his sweater and getting him some tea and a cake before she could bring herself to get the whole story. Apparently he had used blasphemous language in the presence of several girls and within earshot of Miss Timmins. Mr. Grindly subsequently interrogated the blasphemer in his office and declared him, in official tones, to be a "little heathen devoid of any sense of the Christian religion." He had been sent home to learn the Lord's Prayer, after which he was to recite it ten times for Miss Timmins as punishment – a gesture of mercy since the alternative was the strap, and even Mr. Grindly did not recommend such extreme retribution for those in the first form, even if it was almost June.

"Robbie, you must go back," Lily said, and in words she hoped he would understand she told him about her own brief career in school and the drastic effects it had had upon her life ever since. He nodded – dumbly, faithfully, letting his trust open up once again to her. While he watched her every move, Lily went to her bed and from under it drew the leather pouch. She took out Papa's Testament and found printed in the front section 'The Lord's Prayer'. She read it through, puzzled. "I'll teach it to you," she said.

She was at a loss to explain the words to her son. They defeated her. She sensed some power under them, in their oracular cadence, but it was the potency of a charm, felt yet untranslatable. She exhorted Robbie just to commit the phrases to memory like learning a nonsense rhyme or a skipping song. It didn't work. He tried, not because he wanted to return to the schoolroom but because he still had faith in the woman who was always at home when he came back, who had not gone away and died on him, and because the underworld of masculine loyalties and camaraderie associated with school had put its brand on him. He tried but he could not do it. He couldn't memorized the meaningless words and he couldn't yet read them himself.

The next morning Lily persuaded Wee Sue to walk Brad to school. She was very abrupt with him, and he left in a sulk. Then she sat once more with Robbie and together they failed again the test before them. Lily took his hand in hers. Very quietly she said, "Robbie, you gotta go back to school. Your life depends on it. Do you follow me?"

Bewildered by his mother's tears, he said, "If you want me to. I ain't afraid."

Lily walked beside him half-way up Victoria Street. He let her hold his hand until they were within sight of the school; then he broke away and strode ahead, his stiffening posture warning her off. She watched him hesitate before the large door marked in stone 'BOYS', and then enter. She followed after until she stood in the schoolyard a few feet away from the building but on the side without windows – unobserved, listening. Long moments later the crack of pebbled leather on stretched skin resounded down the hallway, through the senior and junior rooms, out the wide-open windows and over the spring gardens of the neighbouring houses. The cruelty of the sound stunned a robin in full flight. Lily let her heart disintegrate.

2

Lily worked hard to make her business a success. "I get exhausted just watchin'," Sophie would say, settled in her director's chair by the south window of the shed. Lily had added two more customers farther up Victoria Street, and the new owner of The Queen's, Kevin Malloney, doubled the number of items she had been assigned under the former management. However, he did insist that she herself pick up and deliver them as he didn't trust his property to wayward boys. Lily knew quite well why he preferred her to come in person. "He just looks," Lily said in her own defence, but Sophie shot back, "No man only looks." In the summertime the work was hard because the stove had always to be on, heat wave or no, the steaming water boiled your hands as well as the clothes and reddened your cheeks permanently, the iron skidded into palm and fingertip, the bulk of wet sheets hung out to dry bent the back into spasms and left the shoulders burning with aftershock. Sophie recommended brandy, then reluctantly some Indian herb tea she happened to have around. Sometimes the latter did help Lily to sleep, but the surest cure was a trek to the beach with her boys, with Sophie and her trailing ménage, or sometimes alone with only Violet to talk to and swim with. After the boys were in school, she got Hazel's permission to walk with Violet to the Sarnia Cemetery where they lay white chrysanthemums on Bachelor Bill's grave. On the way home they swung back through the woods and came out into the clearing where they had first met. No trace of the shanty remained, but Violet stood and stared at the rusting gate and at the mutilated tree-line behind it. Lily's house was charred rubble. She was tempted to go through it, searching for *what* she had no idea, but resisted. Instead, like Violet, she stood watching the ruins and waiting in vain for some definable feeling to take shape out of the general numbness. They held hands as they hiked across the fields towards their village.

In the winter months Lily found that the front half of her got steamed and scorched while the back half froze. No amount of heat could warm the laundry room itself. The constant fog from the hot water rose and stiffened into rivulets of ice along the north wall, and over the course of the winter they became stalactites perfectly suited to the dark, cavernous atmosphere of the place. Lily developed chillblains, rashes and a continuous cold. So it was with as much relief as pleasure that she began to accompany Sophie up to Hazel's on most Monday afternoons for a long, gossipy, hearth-cozy tea. Often Lily was too weary to say much or even be a good listener. At Hazel's no one seemed to notice.

On his own or occasionally with Brad, Robbie continued to pick up and deliver the laundry, collecting the money and presenting it to his mother. He now chopped all of the wood. Some of his cronies began to tease him about being a 'washerwoman's suck', and so he often returned in a black pout. But whatever standing he might have lost during the week, he made up for on Saturday when he used the nickel Lily gave him to buy it back. He needs a friend, Lily thought, not companions.

In June Robbie was promoted to Book One and Brad all the way to Senior Book Two. With her winter cough completely gone, Lily put up fresh gingham curtains and wondered who she might offend by trying a little paint on the outside of her house. Already bored by the forced vacation, Brad looked up from his reading one July day and said, as if he had thought the question out carefully, "Mama, are we really Alleyfolk?"

24

1

In the early hours of Wednesday, August 23, 1872 the gunboat *Prince Alfred* slipped unnoticed from its berth in Goderich Harbour and steamed southward through the soft summer darkness. Just as the sun rose over east Lambton, the ship and its precious cargo eased into the first down-currents of the St. Clair River and docked at the Point Edward wharf. The sun lifted fully into the sky, sizzling and solitary. Nothing stirred on the *Prince Alfred* until about nine o'clock when stewards in white suits were seen fluttering from cabin to galley and back. As the morning advanced, the movements aboard seemed to take on a greater urgency: dark marine uniforms were noticed trailing or leading the stewards, and always at double match. Several doors were slammed in undisguised anger. The stevedores on the dayshift stopped to watch. Something momentous was at hand.

This latter suspicion was confirmed around eleven o'clock when a private coach-and-four were spotted coming down Michigan Ave. with as much haste as was compatible with the decorum of its occupants and the occasion. The vehicle wheeled onto the wharf, clattered woodenly to a standstill before the gangplank (just lowered), and debouched two distinguished gentlemen already sweating in their morning-coats and stiff collars. They brushed past the paid help with the unmistakable briskness of the provincial politician. They were observed entering the captain's quarters on the rear-deck. Fifteen minutes later they re-emerged, blinking straight into the sun and sweating more profoundly than before. A crowd of thirty people had gathered on the wharf as rumour continued to sweep through the village. The local hosts were now seen to be moving along the deck in a decidedly deferential manner, Uriah-Heaping their way towards the gangplank in the van of the very-important-person, who upon espying an audience tipped his hat and uttered an automatic smile. Several persons below cheered mightily as Sir John A. Macdonald, the Prime Minister of the five-year-old Dominion and the first Father of Confederation, stepped shakily towards their approbation.

August twenty-first had been designated as nomination day for Lambton County in the federal elections of 1872. Candidates for both parties, the Conservatives and the Reformers, would take the stand, make their pitch and be judged by the members of their own group. The hustings had been erected only the day before in the middle of Market Square in Sarnia, and in the gathering heat of mid-day, sawdust and pine-tar perfumed the air. The rumour that Sir John A. himself would attend to speak on behalf of Mr. Vidal and directly confront, in his own riding, the man he feared and disliked the most had been actively disseminated by the local Conservatives even though they themselves had learned of its legitimacy only moments before the *Prince Alfred* had departed Goderich. After all, Sir John A. was not well, the weather was semi-tropical, the County was a bastion of Brownite Reformism anyway, and not much could be gained by contending with Alex Mackenzie, Sarnia stonemason and Leader of the Opposition, on his home ground. But then, the story went, Sir John A. had never been a conventional politician, so even Mr. Vidal and his Tory colleagues did their best to swallow their astonishment when the great man himself stepped out of the coach onto the soil of Market Square for the first time and glared at the raw hustings in the way an exhausted tragedian might glower at the bare, unlit stage before him.

Sir John A. was not well. Although recovered from the kidney stone that had almost killed him two years before, he had been drinking and travelling and speaking and drinking for nearly six weeks as the election dragged on – according to the sequence he himself had arranged – for that whole wretchedly hot summer. At fifty-nine, he was already old, a grizzled veteran with a long record of victories and defeats behind him. But, he said to himself in the nightly coma he had substituted for sleep, he had one last mission: to get the railway built to the Pacific and thus consolidate the nation's grip on the continent and its vast resources. Re-election was necessary if the country were to survive. No means to that glorious end was to be excluded. Sir Hugh Allen's support – bribe money it would later be called by the impious – was not to be eschewed whatever its colour. But the revelation that the Montreal financier's consortium for constructing the C.P.R. was two-thirds American; the presence of one of those Yankees in the Premier's own office at three in the morning to bully and condescend; and the telegram from Sir Hugh which had reached him *en train* between London and Goderich on Tuesday morning, threatening to expose the whole sordid mess – all these were the burdens upon his conscience that made sleep impossible. Now here was his eldest enemy seated across from him – composed, plebian in his open shirt, unsweating as befits a man accustomed to the sun, his probity as rigid and unyielding as the stonemason's trowel he flashed like a patriot's badge wherever he went. When the several hundred participants and onlookers had gathered by one o'clock, Sir John was already in need of a drink. Mr. Vidal passed him a crystal goblet brimming with ice-water.

Mr. Gemmil of *The Sarnia Observer* has recorded the details of the political square-dance which ensued. Sir John with obsequious humility and a clear sense of occasion deferred to his rival, begging that he of local prominence should speak first and foremost, etc. Beginning to feel the heat a bit himself, the stonemason conceded and the proceedings got underway. Alex Mackenzie was duly nominated by a regional worthy, Peter Graham Esq. of Warwick, who pointed out, not for the first time, the unique virtues of the candidate: he was a genuine, not a self-dubbed member of the working class who required no well-stocked purse to win elections nor did he need, as Mr. Vidal apparently did, the support of outsiders like the Knight of Kingston and his posse of political hacks. Mr. Vidal himself was then nominated in yet another lengthy, uninformative speech. More interest was shown when Sir. John A. himself was nominated (a ploy to allow him to speak later) along with half-a-dozen other nominal candidates with a thirst for rudimentary oratory. Thus it was almost three o'clock when Alex Mackenzie himself rose to accept the nomination of his enthusiasts still able to cheer in spite of the heat, the absence of shade and the petrifying boredom of the speeches to date.

The stonecutter stood up to thunderous applause. His angular features forewarned the weak-at-heart that here was a man of little compromise when truth and honesty were at risk. His eyes were as sharp as a jeweller's chisel. First of all, he said that he was flattered to have the Premier of the Dominion, who had so often supped with the gods, among them. He, as a common mortal, might indeed feel abashed in his presence. His tone now darkened, cumulonimbic and foreboding. He attacked Sir John's pretense of a coalition government, ridiculed the Tories' attempts to pass themselves off as 'progressive', and excoriated the Government's ruinously generous terms for British Columbia's entry into Confederation especially in light of the fact that Ontarians had had to give their own land gratis to the railroads and feed them besides a million dollars a year from the public trencher forever after. It was quarter to four when he sat down to prolonged cheers. In the eaves of the Town Hall behind them even the pigeons had wilted, dreaming of cool breezes and evening dews.

No one left the square. A number of marketeers and strays who had entered the drama stayed to see the outcome. All eyes were on the Prime Minister, who, if his supporters had not known better, might have been thought dozing through some of the lesser encomiums. However, the fireworks that erupted at this point brought everyone out of his stupor as the arch-tory Mr. Vidal popped up to read a damning letter which clearly discredited Alex Mackenzie on a local drainage issue. The crowd, ninety per cent of them Reformers, roared their disapproval and just as fisticuffs were about to be deployed in settlement of the question, Mr. Vidal — realizing that he was not destined to be the butt of the afternoon's entertainment — finished reading the last half of the letter, which — coincidentally — happened to exonerate his opponent. *The Observer* reported that 'a scene of uproar and confusion ensued that beggars description'.

It was only the figure of Sir John rising and assuming the podium that instantly calmed both the outraged and the outrageous. At four o'clock the heat had reached its zenith; in the far south-west, convection clouds were building. Sweat, unthinned by alcohol, thickened on the statesman's upper lip, dribbled down his pale, beardless face and hung in parchment nodules from his chin like cast-off syllables from old speeches. He tucked his left hand in his waistband to keep it from quivering and with his right he sawed the air erratically as a conductor will when he has lost his place and must read the score from memory. In front of him, where his eyes refused to focus, he heard in his mind a cacophony of rejoinders, putdowns, exordia, crippling witticisms, perorations, bombast, retorts, sentences in the old clean high style: a phrase (a word even) with some touch of the truth still unuttered in it. The shallow applause from a thousand previous masterful efforts hissed on the whiskey-drum of his skull. He needed a drink. The sun's heat congealed in his gut, malarial and maggoty. He would open his mouth and he would vomit all over Mr. Vidal's handshake. From the left side of the platform Mr. Mackenzie skewered him with his presbyterian eye. He blinked, and began – one more time.

The Observer comments on the speech thus: 'We regret that our limited space will not permit our giving a detailed report of Sir John's speech in this issue. We will merely say that for a gentleman of his fame, it was one of the most miserable attempts at public speaking we ever heard; while it was at the same time so full of misrepresentations and misstatements…that it has led to the conclusion that he was either so much *indisposed* as not to know what he was saying, or that he purposely occupied his position in the hustings in order that he might wickedly and maliciously traduce and slander a man infinitely his superior. Such reckless, unfounded and abominable charges…coming from the lips of the Crown in the Dominion of Canada is sufficient to cast a stigma on the whole population, in the eyes of every civilized people'.

When the token candidates had withdrawn, the preordained nominees were confirmed and the meeting disbanded. Partisans kicked their dogs and horses awake and set out to slake their thirst. Some stayed to watch the demi-royal party disappear into the Town Hall for a formal dinner and self-congratulatory toasts. There was some spirited wagering as to whether His Highness would make it past the soup course, but he was definitely seen boarding a carriage under his own impetus about nine o'clock that evening, just after the equatorial fury of the summer storm had subsided. By the time he reached the safety of his gunboat at the Point Edward wharf, the master builder could look up, if he so wished, and remark upon the orderly revolution of the starts along their appointed orbits.

2

It was one of those flash-floods that cuts through the brooding heat, cleanses and re-vivifies the air for a precious hour or two, and leaves the browning grass superficially refreshed. Along the lanes and alleys of the Point it also left vast pools of murky water, child-size puddles, dizzying rivulets and thick patches of gumbo. The Alleykids filled the twilight with the dissonant song of their happiness. As darkness descended, more steeply now as September nighed, their voices dwindled and thinned. By ten-thirty the Alley was silent except for the occasional hushed exchange of sailors approaching Hazel's Heaven in twos and threes. The moon rose unobserved.

Around midnight a pair of sailors, having satisfied their thirst at John the Baptist's and their lust at Hazel's ersatz Eden, sloshed noisily down towards Michigan Ave. One of them apparently slid into a slough, cursing and coughing up slime while his buddy sniggered in sympathy. Pressing a damp cloth against Brad's fevered brow, Lily heard them clearly somewhere below her front path, but Brad just moaned a little and turned over. In a while his breathing became steady. Lily slipped back to her own bed. She was very tired, having washed and ironed the hotel's weekly quota of sheets in the intense heat of the day. Even the flies had capitulated. She peered out the side window and in the moonlight she could see the puddles and sudden bogs glistening all the way along the lane. The two sailors had recovered and disappeared. Lily lay her head on the sash and sucked in the damp-cool air.

When she looked up much later, she was surprised to see a solitary figure making its way towards her. At first she thought it might be wounded because it was staggering and then stopping up short, as if calculating the extent of some pain, only to step out again and teeter its way forward another few feet. The man, for so it was from the cut of his gentleman's coat, grunted out a curse every time a wayward foot deposited him in a puddle, but to no evident effect as the splashing and cursing continued at an accelerated pace. He'll never make it to John the Baptist's, Lily mused as she turned away. It was not an uncommon sight, but she was a little puzzled by the clothes and by something unique in the gestures, something melancholy and alone. Just as she was about to blow the night-candle out, she heard a loud splash, then nothing.

Wrapping a shawl over her shift, Lily went out into the yard and looked down the lane. Grass and mud oozed between her toes. She whispered sharply, "You all right out there?" Nothing. Drunk and passed out, was her first thought. Well, he won't freeze out here tonight. But something urged her to continue, and a few yards farther down where the curve widened the path, she saw the man, as she had surmised, face-down and unmoving. But he was not on the ground, he was in the middle of a small slough with his hands stretched out in front of him, his feet splayed, and his face completely buried in the six-inch slime. He's drowned, she thought, racing over and grabbing him by the shoulders and flinging him on his back. His eyes were sealed shut with mud, the nostrils plugged, the mouth gagged. On her knees in the water, she wetted her fingers and scooped the muck out of his mouth, at the same time splashing him all over the face with handfuls of water. Then she struck him on the back with her balled fist as if he were a newborn resisting breath. A wheezing rattle started up from somewhere deep inside, and the man coughed once wrenchingly, as if scraping the catarrh from his lungs. His eyes popped open and welcomed the pain of the grit against them. For several minutes he gagged and spat, swinging between disgust and fury, it seemed. Then he began to weep softly just before he slid into unconsciousness in the arms of his saviour.

One minute longer, Lily thought as she carried the frail victim up the path to her house, and he would have been a dead man. Maybe he wanted to be.

When Lily woke it was still dark. A fresh breeze fluffed the curtains beside her head. She uncrooked her neck and peered across the room. The fire she had set in the hearth glowed weakly; the clothes-horse she had brought in from the shed still held the suit-coat, trousers, socks and linen underthings she had removed from the soaked, shivering, comatose body of the stranger. He sat exactly where she had propped him up on the settee with pillows and a quilt, but his eyes were wide open. They were staring at the last nugget of firelight, which in its turn kindled some flickering vitality in them. Lily saw at once that these eyes were intelligent, guarded, caring, and as alert and quick as a hare's in the open field. He had been awake for some time – watching her perhaps – because he seemed quite settled in the coziness of the room with his chin resting comfortably on his chest, his breathing regular and his face pallid yet void of any real tension. He appeared to be a man who was accustomed to waking up in strange places with colossally harmless hangovers and no memory of what indiscretions led him thence.

"Don't be alarmed, madam. I've just been watching you sleep."

She picked out his Scotch burr somewhat undercut by the vowels of the countryside. Though softened to suit the room and the occasion, the voice was deep and resonant.

"You'll pardon my dishabillement, I trust, particularly because you appear to have taken a major role in effecting it." His eye twinkled and she sensed the effort behind his words. "I hope the sight of unaccommodated man has not discouraged you forever from respecting the species?" He pulled the quilt across the upper reaches of his hairy chest, and his lip curled towards a smile.

"You one of them politician fellas?"

The smile completed its trajectory. He was scrutinizing her through the semi-darkness. "Could we have some light?"

"Of course." Lily got up and lit the small lamp beside her. She glanced over at the curtained-off section where the boys slept. Then she realized she was dressed only in her shift, so she went into her own cubicle and returned wearing the floral kimono Sophie had given her ("Don't worry, it's Marlene's, she don't need it no more"). She stirred the fire and put the kettle on for tea. For a moment she felt embarrassed to be standing here with a man clothed only in a quilt and his most intimate apparel displayed on a rack before them like the severed parts of his body set out in the sun to be cured. Then she recalled – with a slight, rueful smile – that she had dragged him through the mud of her own yard up the steps and into this room – only hours before – and with no other course open to her had stripped away every shred of clothing from his tremoring body and laid his unconscious form on the settee. Then she had proceeded to rub him dry with a thick towel from The Queen's, apply a vigorous sheen of liniment, and mummify him with blankets. When she had made him comfortable and was certain his breathing was normal, she took his clothes into the shed and by the light of a candle, scrubbed the mud and vomit off them. She lit a fire, despite the warmth of the night, and set them on the horse to dry. What a pathetic withered creature had been revealed to her beneath the gentleman's disguise – hardly an ounce of flesh to float the brittling bones into old-age, every rib registering its own protest, the shrivelled penis and hairless seed-sack as smooth as a boy's after a chilling swim in the great wide waters of the Lake. Lily could make no connection between that flesh and this voice, these darting eyes.

She handed him his tea and sat down in the chair near him. "You been up to that meetin' in Sarnia?"

"I confess that I have."

"Government man?"

"I must plead guilty to that also."

"How'd you get way down here?"

He chuckled grimly and sipped his tea with a greedy, unsteady hand. In the lamp-light his complexion had the pallor of a gutted mullet. "That's a long story, only part of which I can recall. I'm staying on the big boat docked up by the station; one of my friends from the town was in the process of leading me to a local watering-hole with the refreshing name of John the Baptist's when his legs went numb and he retired to the wayside. Being the intrepid type, I continued apace." He held out his cup for more tea and when he had trapped her glance, he said, "You are definitely not John the Baptist."

"You give me a terrible fright, I thought you was dead for a minute."

"No doubt I was," he said, letting fatigue take hold of his face for a few moments. He dozed off, and Lily just caught the teacup before it tumbled to a certain death.

The clothes were dry now. The false dawn told her it must be close to four o'clock. The boys still slept soundly, undisturbed by the deep snoring from the stranger on the settee. When the snoring stalled suddenly, she turned around and looked into his wideawake, bemused smile. There seemed to be no border land between his sleeping and waking states. Probably he doesn't even dream, Lily thought. She held the quilt up as a screen behind which, labouring for breath, he donned his gentleman's vestments once more.

"We lead a difficult life," he was saying. "Politicians are a greatly misunderstood breed, especially in this wretched, ill-informed country. You take this county, for example. It's one of the richest places in the Dominion, on the whole continent. I see farms from the train and the shoreline, wealthy beyond description, and owned by men who were, like my own parents, slaves and vassals in their home country, without a pot to spit in. Naturally, they attribute their success to their own hard work, clearing and ploughing and harvesting – and we know all about that because most of us are the sons of farmers. They don't seem to understand that it was the government and their politicians who negotiated the Reciprocity Treaty which kept the wheat flowing to the United States throughout the Civil War, and yet when that treaty is abrogated by the intransigence of the Yankees they are quick to blame *us* for their troubles, including, if you please, the foul weather and the bugs. We have done everything imaginable for the people of this county, and what is our reward? Vilification and perpetual calumny! A hotbed of unrepentant Reformers whose *laissez-faire* mumbo jumbo would ruin every farmer in Lambton. But can they see that? Why aren't they grateful? What have we to do to please them?" He looked at Lily.

"Maybe they just want to have a little say in what's bein' done for them," she said.

He opened his mouth to say something profound or orotund but nothing came out. She went over to the clothes-horse where his morning-coat still hung and began brush-ing the residual dried-mud off it, one speck at a time.

"The railroads are an even more egregious example of ingratitude," he continued while she worked. "What was this town before the Grand Trunk? How did the farmers move their wheat to the markets of the whole continent or the lumbermen their timber to the mills of America? Would there be an oil boom without rail-cars to deliver crude to the refineries? Would there be a factory of any kind in Sarnia? They whine and they complain about the expense, about the loss of a few acres of land in a county that has millions to squander, about a few tarnished hands in the till when there's enough in the general larder to make all of us rich. But everyone wants it *now*, wants it *cheap* and wants it without *pain*. They have no vision. But I tell you there will be no country from sea to sea without the Canadian Pacific to bind it into one. Again, they cry *foul*! They cavil and belittle, laughing at a band of steel stretching across prairies occupied only by a scattering of aborigines, but I see those grasslands full of people and wheat and British towns and villages. The same detractors wept their crocodile tears when we sent an army to establish dominion in Rupert's Land. They fussed and channered over a ragtaggle band of half-breeds as if the world could be stopped long enough to grieve over lost causes. But even out there – with their own province now and their own government, they grumble and claim they are misunderstood." He sighed, intermittent between exhaustion and the ignition of fresh fervour. He turned for sympathy, anywhere.

Lily shook the suitcoat and held it up to the lamplight. "Did anybody ask them Indians what they wanted?" she said.

He looked irreparably aggrieved but soon recovered sufficiently to say "I take it you don't approve of railroads, either?"

Lily nodded.

"You have a personal grudge?"

Lily thought for a moment, then said, "No." Something in her face and in the manner of her denial arrested his attention. He peered around at the room, at the shabby furniture, the cracks in the siding and the patchwork roof as if he were seeing it for the first time. "Why do you live here?" he said softly.

"My husband died. Then our house burned down. We came here, me an' my two boys."

"I have a daughter," he said. "She's not well."

"Sorry to hear that."

"Your husband had no insurance? No pension?"

"No. He died up north." She hesitated as if contemplating some revelation which might alter the course of the strange feeling that now lay between them as vivid as it was precarious. Then she said, "But we get along here just fine. I got my own work, an' my boys are goin' to school. We're all right."

"Yes, I can see you are," he said. "And things will be better for all of us, soon. You have to believe that the sacrifices you've made – that all our forebears made – are for the best, that life *will* get better. You are still young, you are a vigorous and attractive and kind woman. You will marry again."

He put out his arm and she slid the coat over it. Suddenly he winced and clutched at his eyelid. "Damn, got something stuck in here," he said.

Lily bent over him with a damp cloth and gently rolled the upper lid back till the mote was revealed. "Just a piece of grit," she said, swabbing it away.

She felt the chuckle rumble all the way through him. "It's not *clear* grit, I hope?"

"You make sure you keep your boys in school," he said, letting her do up the buttons and straighten the lapels. "Right now ignorance is our only enemy. We're going to need an educated populace if we're to preserve this democracy from the corruption of Yankee republicanism and from the excesses of our own greed. I want to see the schools of this county bulging with happy, learning faces. Maybe then, long after I'm dead and buried, they'll be able to understand what we've built here out of a wilderness and against all the odds. I try not to let the whining and the ingratitude get me down too much, I do try to remember that few of our citizens have had time to learn much history or comprehend the difference between tyranny and constitutional freedom. When they get particularly vehement I just skewer them with my Scot's glare and I say: 'You registered your opinion with your vote – a privilege shared by few in this irksome world – so kindly shut up till the next election'. Of course, over half the people in this county don't even bother to vote and when they do, they haven't a clue what the issues are. No, you tell your boys to stay in school as long as they can. We'll need them. No democracy can long survive if its citizens don't inform themselves of the issues and go out and vote. Is that not an absolute truth?"

Lily handed him the leather case she had retrieved from the puddle beside him, carefully tucking the official-looking papers and letters back in. "Can't say," she said. "I don't get no vote. I'm a woman."

They were on the wooden stoop. The sun was up, simmering and blood-shot over First Bush, and whorls of mist skittered above the vanishing pools along the grassy lanes of Mushroom Alley.

"Thank you, Lily Marshall. I shall never forget what you've done. I shall not forget *you*, either." He leaned back to take her in just one more time. "You must believe in Fate," he said, "in your own personal destiny. It's the only way."

She watched him till the mist clothed him in its own kind of obscurity.

25

1

The five-year reign of the reform Government from 1873 to 1878 was not a happy one. In the winter of 1873 the Pacific Railway Scandal had broken over its authors' heads so resoundingly that it has been capitalized ever since. The succeeding Liberals under Alex Mackenzie of Sarnia tried hard, and proclaimed their virtues even harder, but there seemed to be no quick cure for the economic ills of the fledgling nation: it had caught the world's disease, or rather the fallout from its ceaseless wars, famine, pestilence, and all the human skulduggery that kept the maggots jigging in a carcass which could rot but not perish. Free trade or reciprocity, responsible government in a chastened monarchy or the licensed chaos of republicanism, *laissez-faire* or the Temperance Act – the shibboleths that men lived by and shaped their existence to were falling all over the earth like the pillars of Sodom or the columns of Gaza. The Great Depression – that was to last the whole decade – settled everywhere at once with the stealth of the ash from Aetna. The railroad to the Pacific inched ahead, then rusted in the prairie rain. Tricked out of their inheritance in Red River, the Métis slipped through the shadows and reappeared a thousand miles from the nearest spike. No one noticed. Wheat, unsaleable, fermented in the field; factory workers were laid off; the employees of the Grand Trunk had their pay cut in half. In the township, Clara Fitchett's brother hanged himself in the family barn.

In the Point the depression was felt everywhere except in Mushroom Alley. The railway slump affected every respectable household and incidentally stalled the attempts of its most prominent citizens – storekeepers, foremen, civil servants and clergymen – to wrest the village from the benign paternity of the Grand Trunk. Though almost all the homes and shops were now owned outright, no one in such uncertain times wanted to ruffle the king's feathers. By mutual unspoken consent, all talk of incorporation ceased. Still there was some excited, under-the-counter buzzing when a distinguished gentleman recently retired from the railway wars arrived in town without prior notice one day in the summer of 1876 and within weeks had established an independent industry not fifty yards from the round-house. It turned out to be a factory of sorts, bigger than a hay barn and clanking with impressive machinery. Ten local men were immediately employed; Hap Withers was made foreman. By September the facts were irrefutable: the entrepreneur himself had purchased the Blakely home on Victoria Street and was settling in to oversee his handiwork. Every morning at nine, Stanley R. 'Cap' Dowling promenaded down Michigan Ave., offering his profile equally to the shop windows on either side of the thoroughfare before disappearing down the cinder path to his foundry. Independent industry, he was heard to say at the haberdashers, that's what we need at this moment in our history, and the words were repeated with annotation and gloss all over town. Just how independent the industry was, was a matter of personal interpretation, however. The welders and smithies inside Dowling Enterprises manufactured plates, spikes and various latches used in coupling devices on box-cars. Most of these, it was rumoured, were transhipped fifty yards or so to the Grand Trunk Railway. Nevertheless, people kept an eye on Cap Dowling, entrepreneur.

Except the Alleyfolk. They were too busy to notice anything for long. Depression or no, the necessity of the services they rendered remained unchanged. There was no diminution in the number of clients demanding to be inspired at Hazel's Heaven. Someone had to scrub off or bleach out the weekly blood and semen splashed on the bedsheets of McHale's and The Queen's. Respectable householders defecated at the customary rate and so the talents of Honeyman Belcher were in steady demand. Not a single McLeod, McCourt or Shawyer lost her job as maid, though the salaries were attenuated and the after-hours requests somewhat more importunate. Spartacus had to pick more judiciously through the corporate garbage for gems, but with his magpie instinct and his carrion's pride, he kept the boulevard as impeccable as ever. The only businesses to increase their trade were those of John the Baptist (whose inexhaustible still frothed away like Parnassus in its secret bower) and Stumpy's elymosenary institute now overflowing with the destitute and the dazed who dropped off the way-freight every morning and evening. Sophie Potts bred her sow every season and sold the suckling to Duckface Malloney, and she tended her chickens with the same smothering carelessness she offered her children. "We always do okay for ourselves," she would tell anyone within earshot. "After all, mushrooms come rosier in manure, don't they?"

2

For Lily these would be remembered as good years, growing years. McHale's Hotel and two large boarding houses on St. Clair Street were added to her business. She asked Spartacus if he would act as her delivery man and even though it meant a drop in his status, he smiled and shook his head yes. Then one Monday, when the afternoon session at Hazel's had been prorogued, she asked that good woman if Violet could come down several days a week and work for her. Hazel was almost too quick to agree, Violet was ecstatic, and the arrangements completed within the hour. "You're putting the money you earn in a safe place?" Lily asked her a few weeks later. Violet nodded her head vigorously. Hazel's taking every cent, Lily thought. When she saw the panic in

Violet's face, she patted her on the arm and said, "You can give some to Hazel, for your room an' board." "Anythin' you say, Lily."

Violet was a wonderful, joyous companion to Lily's own labours, which continued every day of the week except Monday afternoons. The good part of it was that they could take an hour or two off whenever the weather or mood tempted them. While they worked side by side they hummed – to themselves or mysteriously in sudden, improvised concert – and sometimes they swapped stories, though Violet's speech always tightened and splayed as the momentum of an anecdote increased. Whenever they were together, they felt the overpowering presence of the shared space between them – lending its shadow to the body needing it most. When the clothes could be hung out in the breeze, they sang the French song Lily had learned from Ti-Jean and taught with ease to the 'idiot' daughter of Bachelor Bill. They sang it lustily like an extravagant surrogate for joy, and loud enough to shiver the testicles of Baptiste Cartier's bachelor boar.

With the profits she made from her work Lily began to make the house more comfortable for her boys. What Spartacus couldn't salvage for her, he managed to purchase second-hand and deliver to her door. He loved a cup of tea but always drank it from a mug with one foot on the front stoop. Lily got proper beds and ticks for all of them, a plush chesterfield and chair, two large reading lamps, a set of dinner plants and cups that almost matched, a small cooking stove for the main room, and a handsome walnut bookcase with glass doors only one of which was cracked. Hap Withers supplied two of his many sons to rebuild her floor, partition the sleeping quarters, seal the windows and eaves to discourage mosquitoes and drafts, and put a slatted platform over the bare dirt of the laundry room. Lily tried knitting again but she was too exhausted, and so she had to spend precious dollars on clothing for her sprouting, handsome schoolboys. After Violet came to help out, Lily tried putting in a garden, but nothing would grow in the sand on her property except burs and sawgrass. She gave up even though a few shrunken vegetables would have meant more money for important things. Like books for Brad.

Brad was a wizard at school. He did everything with an ease and a confidence that was absolute, even arithmetic. But reading and writing were the things he loved most. Lily marvelled and worried. Miss Timmins kept him only two years before she passed him along to the senior teacher, Miss Constance Stockton, newly arrived in relief of the footsore Mr. Grindly. Miss Stockton had a First-Class Certificate from the Normal School and she came to them from one of the better academies in Toronto for reasons still being speculated upon. The village folk were honoured merely by her presence among them. Brad thrived under her aggressive tutelage. Though such preferment usually spelled disaster among one's peers as it had that first year, Brad's start was so high and so bright that he became an object of wonder among them, a person wholly apart from them and hence immune from the cruel sanctions of their fraternity. In his second-last year – Junior Book Four – he wrote a play for the Christmas concert and the lesser breed of the senior school allowed themselves to be flattered and bullied by his direction of it. Lily sat in the back row with Sophie and watched in awe. "You better put the kibosh on this schoolin' business right now," Sophie said afterwards. "It starts to go to their heads an' then all hell breaks loose. There's nothin' you can do once they get too much of it in their blood. Like Marlene."

Sophie demonstrated her views by taking Wee Sue out of school in the middle of grade eight – a few months before her Entrance Exams – and shipping her off to keep house for a retired shed foreman on Alfred Street. "At least he's too old to get her in the family way," she laughed. "He might be able to get it half-way up on a good day but he sure as hell can't catch her." Wee Sue continued to read books despite her mother's embargo on them in the Potts' house, smuggling them in from her employer's surprisingly interesting collection and lending them in turn to Lily and Brad. When in 1875 a proper street railway was opened to connect Sarnia and Point Edward with an hourly service, Lily could take Brad and Wee Sue with her to the new public library on Wellington Street. Brad loved fiction and poetry, devouring the romances of Scott and much of Palgrave's Golden Treasury. For a while Lily tried to read along with him, to feel vicariously some of the pleasure she could see in his eyes and the way his whole frail body bent towards the book he was reading – sucked willingly into the vast rebellious landscapes that dazzled the white side of the page. But she was just too tired; her eyes silted with fatigue; the print crumbled into meaningless alphabets; and she would shake the book with rage, then resignation. Often she would come awake, still sitting with a book in her hand, the chimney-glass scorched, and discover Brad in the other chair with his eyes alert and tirelessly skimming page after page. Sometimes she would sit beside him and put her arm around his shoulder and he would snuggle against it, continuing to absorb the magic print before him but letting her take a full part in his own joy, imperceptibly acknowledging the primacy of her claim, her uncertificated love. When she prompted, he would recount the seven wonders of Midlothian or leave her breathless by reciting those poems about Lucy and the last green field. At other times he would stiffen the moment her hand touched his shoulder and she would be shut out, even if he relented later, as he often did, and included her in his re-enactment of the story. When typhoid fever struck the village in 'seventy-six and swept away two of the Sawyer children, Lily kept her boys at home; she wouldn't even let them out in the yard.

Brad didn't mind much, but Robbie did. Robbie could never be cooped up for long. Maybe that was why he had so much trouble in school. He longed to be outdoors, and the stuffy, fly-ridden weather of Miss Timmins' room was more than he could bear. He never got out of the junior division, though he stuck it out – uncomplainingly – for almost six years. What he loved most was fishing and hunting with the older boys of the Alley and Fred Potts in particular – now known simply as Blub. Robbie skinned the rabbits they shot (with Blub's twelve-gauge) over at Potts before he brought them home for Lily to cook. He was saving the furs for a jacket he hoped his mother would make him. Sometimes he and Blub would 'borrow' a boat from the fishery and head out into the Lake for the day. Fresh perch could be sold in town for cash; Robbie was saving his money for a gun. When Lily expressed her concern about his truancy and his passion for hunting, Sophie gave a ruminative chuckle and said, "He's just tryin' to wear a man's socks – a little bit too soon maybe but then Blub's almost three years older, ain't he? Why don't you just give in an' let the kid quit school? Let him get a job an' make his way in the world. We don't *own* them, you know." I know, Lily thought, thinking of Sophie's own brood scattered and dissident all over the province.

"With John and Stewie off workin' for the Great Western in Sarnia an' Peg married to that no-good-nick *chauffeur*, I only got but three left home myself. But if we don't let go of 'em, they let go of us."

Lily gave in. After driving the truant officer off her place with a broom and then sitting for an hour in the privy before she stopped shaking, Lily said yes, and in the spring of 1877, two months before his fourteen birthday, Robbie left school for good. Mr. Redmond, true to his word, gave Robbie a part-time job on the delivery wagon. When Lily suggested that he might rent the wagon to deliver laundry as well, he stared at her with a resentment that dumbfounded and then cut deeply. She saw the word of assent on his lips but recovered in time to say, "Never mind, really, it was a silly idea." Relief flooded his face but did not wash away the other, darker emotion. At least he has a friend, she thought, watching him dash off towards the Potts' house, trying not to resent in her own fragile way the hundreds of sleepless nights and restless afternoons she had already spent worrying – wondering when and if he would come home, and what new bruise he would have to camouflage in the coming days: any healing words of expiation or remorse stitched like scars in his throat. They spoke little now beyond the brief courtesies of the day. Moreover, Robbie and his brother seemed merely to coexist, chillingly polite in her presence. I am losing them, she thought one day in her desperation. The more I love them and want them to be themselves, the worse it gets. How can that be? If not love, then what?

When Brad came down with pneumonia in the terrible winder of 1877-78, she sat at his bedside night after night cooling him with iced cloths, steadying with her own strength the terror that flickered in his eyes as he began for the first time perhaps to question his own immortality, to doubt the voices prophesying glory to the credulous. Often when she fell into a doze in her chair, she would rouse to his soft moans and find Robbie across from her cupping his brother's flaxen head in a hunter's hand and spooning fresh soup onto those limp poet's lips. Lily closed her eyes and pretended to sleep. After a while she heard the low murmur of their little-boy voices. If not love, she thought, then nothing. That's all I know.

3

Like most relationships in the alley the one that developed between Lily Marshall and Sophie Potts over the depression years was marked by both intimacy and independence. Whenever Lily felt down or in need of company, she would slip over to Sophie's place where, summer or winter, the iron stove crackled and the kettle whistled. Without knocking she would slide into the rambling kitchen where 'her chair' would be waiting. Likewise, Lily would often look up from her scrubbing, bathed in steam, and gradually make out the ample silhouette of her neighbour fixed to the old rocker by the south window. If Sophie were busy – cajoling Duchess' farrow towards plump-ness, doing her own never-quite-finished laundry with a bare-bottomed Bricky hop-ping behind her, or hacking at her garden lathered in sweat and cursing the ill-fortune that made her soil the most arable in the Alley – then Lily would simply make herself a cup of tea, talk to Wee Sue or play cat's cradle for Bricky. Sometimes she would just sit and let the myriad little dramas of the Potts' household absorb her interest and draw her gratefully away from herself for that one hour she needed to recuperate or to become aware once again that there existed other lives, other acts of caring and slight and needing-more-love-than-there-was-anywhere. If Sophie were about to go out on an errand, she would nod at Lily – usually – and then simply disappear down the lane. No offense was meant or taken. In the summer Lily might hear the cries of Sophie's youngest ones, and pulling Brad out of his chair, drop her scrub-board and head up the path towards the beach with towels and swimsuits in hand until they caught up with the Potts' clan, already augmented by several McLeods and Shawyers. Lily would fall in beside Sophie, who pitched and yawed in the sand, and together they would lead the children down to the water, certain that they had established a bond for the long, laz-ing afternoon. It was only on holidays and other rare occasions that formal plans were made to picnic or go skating on the flats or sledding over the dunes. In the Alley it was better to let things happen. Somehow word was passed along as needed, movements were detected by some inner radar, random sound was read with the clarity of print. Here, a pact was signed without recourse to clause or declaration, and rarely broken, and yet the independence of each participant was re-established as soon as the hour or afternoon or safari was complete. It was as if, not having any legal claim to their prop-erty, they chose to guard themselves – their time, feelings, rights, dreams – with double the zeal of any mere ratepayer.

For example, Lily knew that two days before Stoker came home for his three-day layover in the summer or week's rest-and-recreation in winter, she could not engage Sophie in anything but the most superficial conversation. Even then Sophie might lash out at her or cuff little Bricky without cause as her anticipation took full possession of her – with its eccentric blend of fear and longing. And when Stoker did waltz up the lane, braying out some bawdy sailor's song loud enough to alert the entire Alley of his arrival and his territorial imperative, Lily knew enough to stay away and mind her own business no matter what concatenation of squeals, groans and leathery collisions breached the night air. In the Alley no one interfered. Lily did not speak five words to Morton Potts in five years. She saw him only from a distance – bare-chested in the sun, sleeping off a hangover on his verandah, tilting after his little ones in some mock fable he was the ogre in, roaring out loud as they squealed with laughter and scampered away at will. As far as Lily could see, Stoker was either shaken by uncontrollable hilarity or he was comatose. What she knew of him she heard from Sophie who spoke of nothing else for three days after his departure – until she had exorcised whatever demons had driven them both through these furloughs of ecstasy and retribution. Always she would downplay the bruises on her arms and neck – even though no one ever remarked upon them. "The tokens of love, Lil," she would sigh. "When you marry a lumberjack and a stoker, you gotta expect some rough lovin'." Then she would roll her eyes theatrically to mask any feelings she might let free, and say without fail: "As my old granny always said, you can't make a primrose out of a preacher's arse." Then she would manufacture a belly-laugh that Boadicea might have borrowed to stymie Caesar's waves.

Monday afternoons were reserved for tea at Hazel's, but of course there were no invitations and an absent guest was under no obligation to explain or justify. Most of the regulars arrived, feigned surprise at the sight of the pewter tea-service and sweet-cakes, and stayed to chat. Sophie was almost always present – except when Stoker was at home – as was Lily, yet they never walked up the lane together by design, and often returned according to their own schedule. When they did share the walk home, they might well continue a discussion begun earlier or simply stroll silently along, happy in one another's company. Hazel had two favourite topics – local gossip and politics whenever it could be reconstrued as local gossip. With the constant comings-and-doings of many powerful but undertitillated gentlemen through her portals and bedsteads, the latter bit of legerdemain was not too difficult. Shadrack Lincoln, the mute, was often seen reading the radical newspapers – abandoned by the clientele in their haste to pursue less intellectual delights – but he could not contribute to the debates except by grunting approval or disgust or occasionally, when his frustration built to a point where no other release was possible, by scribbling upon the schoolboy's slate Lily had brought for him one day (Stewie had 'forgot' to return it when he quit school). Sophie often dominated the political discussion though no one knew where she acquired her extensive knowledge of provincial and federal affairs. Her source of local 'intelligence' was well-known: every week or so and never on the same day twice in a row, she waddled past the General Store in McHale's where most of the Alleyfolk shopped, and headed straight up the street to the main concourse of stores and services, the hub of respectable gossip and social interchange. Dressed in her orange smock or her squirrel-fur with the heads attached and chattering – according to season – Sophie paddled her way blithely upstream, deliberately fixing victims in her wicked sights and greeting them with boisterous familiarity. The ladies of the town had no choice but to respond: she was too large and garrulous, and besides she knew more about them and had seen more of their flesh-and-blood than they themselves had. It was in these brief shell-shocked exchanges that vital information was spilled into public view, or in the longer conversations that Sophie-the-Wise carried on with the storekeepers, who genuinely liked her and much appreciated the stir she made among the village hens and their imperturbable pecking-order. It took days for the dust to settle. Once, after Sophie had lampooned the Prime Minister for two-and-a-half acts ("He's got a voice like a crow with the palsy!"), Shadrack motioned Lily over to his corner and pointed at the words on his slate: 'I give her the papers every week'.

"No wonder this country's in a depression. Every one of you thought with old Alex up there in Ottawa we'd all be shittin' shamrocks. Now don't get me wrong – Alex's a good man, got a heart as big as a squash – but he's got the brains of a stonecutter and he's as straight-laced as they make 'em. Wouldn't say poop if his tongue got tangled in it." She paused for effect or breath, then said "Every muscle in that man's body is stiff as a steel poker – 'ceptin' the one that oughta be!" Her cackle shook Hazel's hens out of their four-o'clock drowse.

When Lily got to know Sophie well enough, she asked her why she had given up being a midwife. Sophie gave various answers depending on her mood – "Too many of them damn quacks from the university tellin' me what I didn't need to know," or "All the women out there want the doctors anyway, why should I fight it," or "I gave it up in 'sixty-five just a little after your Brad was born – I could see the writin' on the wall, I was just a woman with not a shred of schoolin' to my name," or "Women feel safer with a man rummagin' around down there, they're used to it!" – but finally one morning after Stoker had left, she sat bathing the cut on her cheek by the stove and confessed to Lily that Stoker had ordered her to give it up because he said it interrupted their brief times together and "he accused me of neglectin' my own kids for the sake of other people's. He said I was a piss-poor mother. What could I say, I was already pregnant with precious little Bricky, our love child. What could I say, Lil?"

So it was that the women of the village had to rely upon the distant charity of the Sarnia doctors several miles and sometimes desperate hours away. Mildred McLeod, the youngest of the McLeod servant-girls, got herself pregnant ("By immaculate conception, it appears," Sophie whinnied), and one night near her time, Lily was awakened by a savage scream that sounded as if some cat was being flayed alive under her window. She hurried through the dark down to the source of the agony and met Sarie McLeod with her gray hair fanned around her face like a shriek and not one word in her wild eyes.

"Calm down, Sarie," Lily said, trembling all over. "Has the doctor been sent for?"

"Hours ago, hours ago," Sarie mumbled at last and could find nothing better to say for some time. Lily was thinking: these screams will wake the whole lane, Sophie will hear them and come down. But she didn't. Lily went in to the stricken girl and before she realized what she was doing, she was giving orders to young Kathleen and Frieda and soothing Mildred who was suffering more from terror than pain. Lily whispered into her ear the things she remembered being told herself by the *sage-femme* who had brought her comfort in her own labour. She found her palm resting on the girl's spasming belly like a benediction of some sort, and though she had little idea of what she was supposed to feel there or actually do, she soon had Mildred relaxing between contractions, turning her fawn's gaze up at the visiting angel, and inhaling deeply when she was told. Behind her, preparations for the event itself seemed to have fallen into place as they would have if Sarie, exhausted by one-too-many of these melodramas, had not panicked and sent the household into chaos. Moments later Dr. Dollard arrived, himself exhausted from twenty hours on the road, and together he and Lily gave nature a brief assist and the child nosed its way into the world. It had not occurred to Lily, or anyone else, to go up to Sophie's – Sophie *had* heard, and once that fact was known, nothing else could be done. That was the way it was in Mushroom Alley.

Word spread beyond the Alley, however, and during the middle years of the Liberal regime Lily was called out into the village proper to 'assist' Dr. Dollard in the safe delivery of six or seven babies. Along her own lane she guided another McLeod, a McCourt and a brace of Shawyers into the waiting air, occasionally before the arrival of the harried doctor. Lily described each trauma in detail to Sophie, and Sophie felt not the least embarrassment in commenting and dealing out advice. Or in reminiscing about her own glory days: "So there I am washin' the blood an' muck off the baby's bottom, an' Missus Christie perks up and says to me, 'do it look like it's Da?' and I says 'I can't tell, dearie, I ain't seen your hubbie with his pants all the way down yet!'" When the baker's daughter, Fanny Saltman, gave birth to a foetus so deformed that Dr. Dollard didn't even try to smack breath into its misery, and when Fanny died later that day with her eyes open and the sunlight streaming over the bed, Lily told Dr. Dollard that she couldn't help out any more. And she didn't, though she lived in dread that some female scream would jolt her awake some night and she would have no choice. It never did. "You got the brains for it an' the heart," Sophie had predicted, "but not the stomach." The closest Lily ever came to discovering what might have happened the night Sophie did not come down to McLeod's, was when she suggested that Sophie return to the service as it was obviously needed, even if she could only do it in the winter months when Stoker was away for six weeks at a stretch.

"Once I quit somethin', I quit it," she said with virtuous finality.

"Like you did with readin'?" Lily said.

4

"The kids wanna go to the circus," Sophie announced.

Robbie and even Brad had talked of little else since the posters went up on the fenceposts of the village: Darling Brothers Circus and Travelling Sideshow, they boasted in black capitals, the place and date hand-stamped below the engraved horse with the mane like a mermaid's hair: Bayview Park, Friday and Saturday. Most of the village was waiting in formation for the circus train when it pulled into the Grand Truck station and then backed down a siding which took it past the grain elevator almost to the edge of the park that lay between the town and the village.

Though it was less than a mile's hike, the Potts and the Marshalls climbed aboard the new Sarnia Street Railway that Saturday and rode in style 'on the rails', even if the smart leather-seated carriage was drawn along by a single dray who clumped over the fickle ties. Sophie had her two youngest in tow, Wee Sue and Bricky, and Brad sat with them imagining he was really older than Sue. Blub and Robbie had run on ahead of them, with their own well-rubbed coins jingling in their pockets.

"We'll be lucky if we get a 'hello' outta them two today," Sophie said, fluffing up the tired ruffles on her pink party dress and sniffing at the toilet water she had spilled on the flanks of a partially exposed bosom. "Fred's been in a devil of a mood lately, ever since they laid him off at the sheds. I keep tellin' him his brothers'll get him into the Great Western, but he won't listen to me or anybody else. He oughta be more like your Robbie – content with his lot."

By the time the trolley stopped at the park and the bright minarets of the circus tents floated into view across the green green grass, Sophie had forgotten all about Blub and any other sorrows she may have been harbouring. Brad decided he wanted to see the show under the Big Top with the clowns, animals and acrobats. So did Wee Sue, but since the first performance was not due to start for an hour, it was decided that the mothers should escort Bricky through the kiddies' section – complete with roundabout, a pony-ride, and a corral full of exotic but harmless creatures deemed to be 'cute'. Brad and Wee Sue headed in the direction of the side-show tents with their striped cupolas and brass balls and grisly promise.

"I hope we're doin' the right thing – lettin' them two go off together on their own."

"Brad'll behave," Lily said.

"Ain't Brad I'm worried about, " Sophie laughed, and jammed another taffy apple into Bricky's face. He was looking somewhat peaked after a mere four rides on the roundabout. "You want a meat-pie to settle your tummy?" Sophie said.

Lily loved the colours and sounds and odours around her. They stopped to admire the visible music of a steam-organ and then a leather-skinned man who played an Irish ditty on slender bottles bubbling with melodic dyes and then a juggler who defied geometry with his dizzying blue triangles. Barkers and grifters called out to them to come win their fortunes, try their luck, take a chance, carry off the main prize – in a lingo as old as bazaars or gypsies or the wind-swept Caucasus. Hawkers from the shadow of awnings spread their walnut eyes over every patch of pink female flesh that passed them by.

Sophie sat Bricky down in the shade of a tree, jammed two fingers down his throat and ducked as he brought up the excess of her affection. Wee Sue and Brad came up, flushed and giggling. Sophie gave them a searching look, then said to Wee Sue, "Why don't you an' Brad stay here with Bricky for ten minutes. We'll meet you at the entrance to the Big Top."

Before Lily could say anything, Sophie was trundling ahead of her towards the games-of-chance. She stopped to catch her breath, her great breasts flexing like independent bellows unsupported beneath the frumpery of her costume, garish as a hollyhock. "Did you get a gander at him on the first round?" she puffed and without waiting for a response, aimed her slow-motion trot in the direction of a sign which said: *Guess Your Weight Within Five Pounds or You Win*. Standing below this standard near an impressive set of scales was a dark muscular man with a Moroccan's moustache and Neanderthal eyes. They lit up with larceny and other lusts as soon as they spotted the two women approaching. Lily felt herself skewered and turning slowly on a spit.

"Ready to give away one of them kewpie dolls?" Sophie blared with the brass section of her voice.

"Haven't lost one today," said the grifter, his voice swarthy, salted, montenegron. "But you look like you could fool a man, even a man of great experience such as myself."

"How much is it gonna cost me?"

"Depends on what you're willin' to give, but a nickle'll do. For a start."

"I never start nothin' I can't finish."

Lily slipped back into the small crowd that had formed around the scene and its possibilities. Behind them she could hear the 'thunk' of a hammer and the clank of a rusty bell. Sophie turned just enough to acknowledge the claims of the spectators without actually looking at them, and then made a surprisingly nimble pirouette somewhere inside the gaze of the guess-your-weight man. The onlookers gasped as if they had just seen an elephant do a cartwheel, then applauded both the feat and its elegance.

"That's all of me," she beamed, "or almost all."

"Could there be more?" said the carny, winking to the front rows.

"You gonna frisk me for hidden objects?"

"An' where would you hide them, eh?" the carny said, brandishing a white card and ostentatiously writing down his educated guess. "Three hundred and ten pounds," he announced, "of the prettiest pink flesh this side of Chicago."

Sophie snorted and stepped onto the scales. "With or without my bonnet?" She flipped off her enormous hat and shook out her curling, chestnut hair. The contrast between it and her Irish skin, uncaressed by any sun, was dazzling. Several cheers went up. The carny slipped the weights along the scale as dextrously as if he were milking a cow, but the outcome had never been in doubt. He was more than twenty pounds out.

"Your lucky day, madam!" he cried to the 'marks' gawping at the prize-table, and he waved the biggest, rosiest kewpie past their avid stare and placed it gently on the upslope of Sophie's bosom.

"My lucky day," Sophie said. She wheeled to her supporters. "And I didn't even haveta put that brick between my tits!"

A grown man in the crowd blushed, but the carny laughed and said, "Honey, you couldn't get a toe-nail down there!"

Then he did an astonishing thing. He glanced curiously at Sophie for a long second, then pushed his way through the throng over to the sledge-hammer game, yanked the ten-pound mallet out of a customer's hand and cried out, "Another kewpie for the great lady!" He raised the hammer as easily as a match to light his pipe and brought it crashing down on the button; the clapper shot up the stiff pole as if it were greased, and slammed into the bell so vehemently the ringing shook the lions awake in their cages a hundred feet away.

Of all the magical fairy-tale acts in the centre ring Lily was thrilled most with Mademoiselle Mimi and her Flying Arabians. A fanfare of trumpets and a drumroll heralded their entrance through the beribboned portcullis at the east end: six snow-white geldings surmounted by six beautiful female riders clad entirely in florescent red satin that shimmered under the arc-lights leading them into the ring. The crowd, still stirring from the acrobat's mile-high sleight-of-hand, was drawn reluctantly towards this fresh commotion of colour and brass and galloping drum. Into the ring they pranced, steed and maiden, jogging in happy tandem to the music which – the moment the beasts formed the unbreakable circle of head and tail and head again – quickened to a brassy canter. The scarlet riders took the cue, jettisoned the reins and all hope of control, as the pace of the geldings accelerated – their manes and tails blown back in immaculate fans – Mademoiselle Mimi stood upon her alabaster saddle and uncurled her scarlet arms like a tanager's wings on a morning breeze. One by one her nestlings did the same, and while the crowd applauded with appropriate awe, the Arabians began to gallop with a rhythmic frenzy that pulled the music with it – trumpeting and martial. Mademoiselle Mimi, with no expression on any kind on her face, did not return to the safety of her saddle; she lifted one foot in the air whirling past her and using it as a rudder or fantail she titled outward from the centre of the vortex, and by the time her chorus had repeated this folly, the chargers were circling so rapidly they began to blur at the edges, till Lily could see only hoof and flank and flared nostrils and wild desert-eyes and music-driven muscle and a halo of centrifugal hair; and above them in a separate corona of motion, attached to the lower one only by six fragile stems, whirled the scarlet forms skating some incredible edge of gravity and cadence. Just before the band stopped and the tableau ended, Lily was certain that Mimi's toe floated free of its pinion, her body, already blurred and insubstantial – a mere penumbra of blood brushed into air.

So it was that Lily did not notice little Bricky had fallen asleep in her lap.

Lily carried him into the sunlight where he awoke, pale and peevish.

"Funny, we ain't seen Blub or Robbie all day," Brad said, blinking at Wee Sue.

"They went to the freak shows, I bet," said Wee Sue, reluctant to let go of Brad's hand.

"You take Bricky along with you on the trolley," Lily said right through Brad's frown. "I need to walk some. Sophie'll likely be home by now anyway."

"I never knew Ma to get sick to her stomach before," Wee Sue said. But she picked up her brother and gave Brad a look that brought him trailing along after her, muttering. She's two years older than him, Lily thought.

With the music of the Flying Arabians still echoing inside her, Lily set out across Bayview Park. Something more than music had made her anxious, she was sure. Something to do with Brad or with Robbie who'd been depressed lately, or with Sophie herself. If I walk it off, perhaps nothing will happen, she told herself. The unlandscaped section of the park was very pleasant. She avoided the stone bridge, took off her shoes and waded across the drain thick with aging lily-pads and young jack-in-the-pulpit. On the other side she veered off the path into the swail that wound its way through the scattered maples and brought you out behind St. Clair Street.

Lily was upon them before she could stop herself. They were sprawled in the tender grass at the bottom of the swail. The carnyman lay on top of her with neither his hands nor feet touching the ground, his knees braced on the promontories of her thighs, his torso nestling in the crevasse of her breasts, the gnarled brown root of his back twisting and flinging the buttocks forward in frantic spasms. He seemed to be floating entirely on flesh, a-bob on the blood-tinted acreage of her skin like some scorched Casanova riding the cornucopia of Aphrodite's thighs, the coral shell of her bedchamber, and the resurrecting wave under it. Against the sea-heave of his paramour's breath, the carnyman exhaled a sequence of abrupt barking sounds, like a dog being kicked repeated in the ribs. Sophie opened her eyes and through the glazed lattice of her lust she looked up at Lily, then twirled the kewpie doll on one finger, like a trophy.

"Don't stare at me like that," Sophie said in the kitchen an hour or so later. "I ain't pissed in the Holy Grail, you know."

"It's not that, really," Lily said. "It's just, I thought all them things you said about Stoke, you know, whenever he –"

"I meant 'em, every word. Stoker's damn good to me, we been good together for as long as I can remember. But how often is he here, eh? How many times does he leave me high an' dry an' hangin' out there like a wash in the wind? You think the bugger keeps it in his pants all those weeks in the bush, or up in Fort William overflowin' with squaws an' hooers?" She was slowed by a new look of amazement in Lily's face.

"Then the carnyman…"

"Of course he wasn't the first, don't you listen to what a body tells you? But I ain't no hooer like them floozies up at Hazel's or them harlots of Sarie McLeod's. You ain't thinkin' that sort of thing?"

Lily touched her friend's arm. "I ain't thinkin' anythin', Soph, you know that. If you want to tell me, fine. It don't matter, really."

"I can't help myself," Sophie said. "I try real hard, but then some night a young sailor boy comes totterin' down from Hazel's lookin' sad an' lonesome, and I call over to him and ask him if he'd like a good cup of tea, an' sometimes he comes in, an' usually he's been disgusted by what he's seen up the hill or he got to the porch an' turned back while his buddies made fun of him, and I just settle him down an' we talk in the dark, real quiet like, an' once in a while I just take him into my bed, and it's as warm an' toasty an' nice as you could dream of."

"Does Stoker know?"

Sophie went white. "Stoker must never know. I'm no hooer. What's done in the Alley is never told."

"An' the park?"

"The only time, I swear it." She shivered. "Never again, not like that."

They sat in silence for a while, listening to Wee Sue's laughter and Bricky's squealing from the other room.

"Are you tellin' me you ain't been with a man since Tom?" Sophie said casually as if they had been in the middle of a conversation.

Lily nodded.

"Then you mean that devil's shivaree an' your house burnin' down was all for nothing?"

"Ti-Jean wasn't there, he left to see his mother."

"He was one handsome fella, eh?"

"Uh huh." For the first time Lily was able to smile, feeling once again the undefiled kinship between them.

"You need to take a lover," Sophie said very quietly.

Lily was just putting Brad's supper on his plate and beginning to wonder where Robbie had got to, when Sophie pulled open the front door and stood on the stoop trying to catch her breath.

"What's wrong?"

"They've run away with the circus," she gasped. "Stumpy saw them gettin' on the train at the park."

"Who, Sophie, *who*!"

"Freddie, an' your Robbie. They're gone."

Lily grabbed Brad and pulled him past Sophie. "Run up to the station an' see if the circus train's left yet. Hurry." Brad was already off, his whippet legs flashing in the sunset over the river flats. Lily followed only yards behind him even though her heart, after the first convulsion, refused to make another move. Sophie rumbled after them, sobbing and thrashing her hands. The circus train with its purple and yellow-striped coaches and box-cars could be seen against the orange glow of the horizon ahead, moving slowly and inexorably around the curve that would take it north out of the country, out of all reach, beyond the range of forgiveness and regret. The derision of its chattering bogie-wheels stunned the two women as they came to a foolish halt among the milkweed and the wild mustard and the evening swallows overhead.

"Stoker'll kill me," Sophie said.

Suddenly Brad shouted and the women turned to stare across the space just cleared by the deserting train. A male figure, only a shadow against the perishing sun, was trotting towards them and holding something aloft in its right hand like an offering. No one moved an inch until Robbie came right up to them, the fishing rod over his shoulder and a string of perch thrust out for admiration and approval.

"Can we have them for supper, Ma?" he said amiably.

Sophie sat in the swelter of her kitchen wrapped in a shawl and sipping from a glass of brown liquor. "Go on, have some, it won't kill you. John the Baptist makes his pig try it first. Go on."

Lily let a drop of the hooch slither its way over her tongue.

"He'll kill me, you know. He never got over Burton stayin' up in Bruce County, an' he keeps askin' why Stewie an' John don't come home to see him no more, an' I tell him they're busy gettin' their lives started on the Great Western, an' he yells 'yeah, two fuckin' miles away!' and I can't think of a thing to say back except that Peg brought her little one over here last month an' he was so happy with that baby I thought he'd cry, but then he an' Peg got to arguin' about religion an' how her husband insisted on havin' Peg dunked in Perch Creek an' gettin' the baby baptized too an' then Peg just up an' leaves, and I want to say, 'See, it ain't all my fault, you can't blame me for Peg nor for Marlene, no sir, it ain't my fault Marlene won't ever come home or even see her own brothers an' sisters or tell anyone where she's livin'.'"

"I'll stay with you," Lily said. "I ain't afraid of Stoker."

"No. You mustn't do that, you mustn't ever think of doin' anythin' like that." She drained her glass, keeping her lips sealed to trap the afterwaves of the whiskey. "You promise me that."

"Why don't you leave him?"

Sophie flinched at the question and the long look she gave Lily ran the gamut through incomprehension to resentment, hurt, self-loathing and resignation. "You don't understand, Lil. I deserve it."

26

1

One Monday in June of 1877 Lily was a bit later than usual in arriving at Hazel's as she and Sophie had been up most of the night sitting with Bricky who was down with the mumps and having a bad time of it. Sophie said she was too tired and too hot to come so Lily walked on by herself. As she went past Stumpy's and waved to Cap Whittle on his bridge, she felt a deep unease inside, and quickened her pace. Violet had not been well, Winnie was thought to have got herself pregnant again and was very depressed – there was something waiting for her in the yellow and purple house at the top of the rise, of that she was certain. She leaned on the newel-post, her head woozy, her breath staccato. I'm just tired, she thought, and went in.

Everyone was listening so intently to the newcomer that Lily was able to slip unnoticed into her usual chair in the corner by the south-east window, and note with relief that both Violet and Winnie were hanging on each word being spoken by the tall, silver-haired man. He was like no other Negro she had ever seen – with his gold-rimmed spectacles, his trim business suit, white shirt and cravat, his patent leather shoes and the pearl-knobbed cane he leaned on from time to time for rhetorical effect. His voice was baritone, beautifully cadenced, and urban to the last vowel. He was a sixty-year-old American gentleman – whose skin had been accidentally charcoaled. Lily caught the very end of what had obviously been a detailed story of hairbreadth escape and considerable pathos. You could hear the whisper of Hazel's taffeta all the way across the room. A single gold tear rolled down the right cheek of Shadrack Lincoln who was seated, or kneeling, at the feet of the stranger and peering up with adoration and awe.
  Winnie leaned over and spoke into Lily's ear: "He's Mr. Abraham Jackson, from *Philadelphia*." And, Lily learned later, come to the County in search of the long-lost cousin of a friend in Pennsylvania who turned out to be their own Shadrack Lincoln. The story, just completed, had been one of a series Mr. Jackson had been urged to tell about his days on the Underground Railroad.

"Those were exciting days and they were dreadful days. But of course even now we have much work to do. Many of the committees we formed then are still in operation, but instead of helping people to escape to freedom, we're involved in a variety of Negro causes, including this one – searching for missing relatives and trying to put back together families who were so cruelly broken up by the heinous institution of slavery. We're also helping many of the people who fled here to Canada without wives, children or parents to resettle back in their home counties if they wish to." He glanced at Shadrack.

"Tell us more about the Railroad, Mr. Jackson," Hazel said, as if she were coaxing a reluctant diva towards an encore. "Did you ever get up as far as Canada?" She looked about for support and got it. Betsy filled his cup with alacrity for they all knew he had to catch the late-afternoon express for London.

"I worked out of Philadelphia. I worked for Stephen Smith, a wealthy lumberman of my own race who financed much of the local operation, which was centred around Mr. William Still, whom you've heard about. I was supposed to be an agent for the lumber company, but my travels in Pennsylvania were really designed to keep supplies and money flowing to key points along the line. We were the principal relay station on the main route from the Carolinas over what we called the Great Black Way of the Appalachians and thence on to Ohio. And no, I never did get to Canada myself, but naturally I heard detailed accounts of the bravery and dedication of Canadians, and a number of them came to work for us on the American side. In fact, it was through the Partridge family in Moore Township that we were able to get a line on the whereabouts of Shadrack here. Many of the old railroaders continue to help us out in any way they can. I talked with Harry Partridge before I came up to Sarnia, and we reminisced about the old days. In particular we talked about the Canadians who'd served the cause so well back in the 'fifties when the Fugitive Slave Law made it a very dangerous business. You may already have heard of the exploits of Bill Shepherd, Harold Flint, Michael Corcoran –"

"Quick, get the smellin' salts, Vi," Hazel cried, holding Lily in her arms.

Here in the Alley, no questions were asked; Hazel had given them her own sitting room where the curtains, carpet and plush chairs combined to soften voices and accentuate intimacy. Abraham Jackson sat no more than a yard from Lily and delivered his soliloquy in a hushed, umber, elegiac tone, as if the theme itself might overwhelm the solitary listener or crush the fragility of the words themselves.

"I knew your father long before I met him; he was an early organizer of the Railroad at the Michigan-Canadian border-crossing, one of the most dangerous spots on the line because after the Fugitive Slave Law the bounty-hunters concentrated on these crossing-points, and they didn't care who they killed to get their quarry. I heard of your father's courage from the great Harriet Tubman herself. So when he came over to our side of the border in 1851, he had many influential friends to help him. I met him that fall in William Still's living room in Philadelphia. We never asked him much about why he had to leave Canada, but I could see that he was suffering a great deal as a consequence. Later on he confided to me that he had, in a vengeful rage, accidentally killed a man who had committed some crime against his family. He feared there was a warrant out for his arrest. Only a few years ago did I learn that there never had been any such warrant. Nevertheless, the Lord saw fit to bring him to us, and we were grateful. Your father became the most important person in the human chain of ties, rails, siding and way-stations that made up the Underground Road to Freedom during those grim years before the War. His job was to pick up refugees along the edges of the Carolinas and direct them or lead them himself over the Appalachian Way, with bounty-hunters and bears and renegade outlaw bands all looking for the same helpless prey. Twice he was shot, frost-bitten many times, cut his way out of a southern jail before a lynch mob could take its revenge – he was a legend among the Negros and Abolitionists everywhere. He was a man possessed, a man with a mission." He paused as if to let that much sink in, but Lily's querying, avid eyes urged him on.

"I met him often at Still's house during our many strategy sessions, and it was there that I saw him for the last time in March of 'fifty-eight, almost twenty years ago. I remember ever detail of that evening because all the important people on the Railroad were there to meet and listen to another legendary figure of the day – John Brown, Old Brown of Ottawatomie. He was there with his son, John Jr., looking for money and for recruits. That night he got both. I tried to talk your father out of it, but like so many others, he too had glimpsed the apocalyptic blaze in Old Brown's eye, and I guess he felt the same frustrations that Brown did after a decade of danger, miniscule hopes, senseless death and no sign of victory anywhere they looked, only the trickle of lives they had redeemed with such expense of body and spirit, while the principal evil festered and gloated on every side. They were ready to chance Armageddon, to drive the money-changers from the temple with a single, sacrificial blow; they were willing to use their bodies like sword-blades and ultimately as fodder for gibbets and the poles of crucifixion. We never saw him again."

He paused, swallowed thickly and continued. "He died at Harper's Ferry in the blood and horror of that wonderful *débâcle*. His name is not recorded among the official twenty-two, but his bravery there is well-known among the people he died trying to liberate. He was guarding the Potomac Bridge with Oliver Brown and others when the militia arrived and drove them off. Apparently your father refused to retreat and was shot on the bridge. Before the local troops, slavering for blood and souvenirs, could reach him, he jumped or fell into the river below, where the current swept him gently towards the sea. The Virginia guardsmen stood on the bridge and used his body for target practice till it drifted out of their range of interest. However, when the Federal Marines went looking for it later that evening, it was gone, spirited off by a group of free Negroes who carried it upstream to Chambersburg where they buried it secretly in their churchyard. It's still there under a plain white stone marked simply: 'Mr. Corcoran'. Every year hundreds and hundreds of people – black and white – slip quietly into the shade of that little cemetery to pay their respects."

Lily was about to speak but sensed there was more.

"Your father came back to Canada once. I learned this from Harriet Tubman, who told me about it only a few weeks before my trip up here. He had been present at the famous Constitutional Convention John Brown held in Chatham in April of 1858. Still afraid of being apprehended by the Canadian authorities, he dyed his hair black, shaved his beard and sneaked into the province for the two key days of the Convention. However, he told Brown he had to take part of a day to ride north to visit his sister and daughter in Port Sarnia. She recalled this because she said she had rarely seen him so agitated. When he got back late on the Friday, she took special pains to talk with him about the trip, and he told her – in a calm, sad voice – that he had found his sister's farm easily enough, had walked up the lane till he heard voices in the garden beside the cottage, and then stopped. The two women, he said, were in the garden, working and humming and seemingly content despite the Black Frost that had ravaged both our countries that spring. He told Harriet that he watched them for a long time, hoping that they might glance up and see him and force him to come out of his cover, but they didn't, and he found he couldn't speak, and then he left."

"After a while Lily said, "Did he ever talk about us?"

"Ah yes, Mrs. Marshall, all the time. He told me once that as soon as his mission was ended, he planned to go back and bring his daughter to live with him in the States. That thought was on his mind constantly."

From the sadness of his smile Lily knew he was lying.

2

When Lily came around the bend towards her house, her thoughts were so roiled that she almost bumped into the woman standing patiently by the front stoop. A white glove shot out.

"I'm Miss Stockton," announced a voice crisp but distant. "Bradley's teacher."

"How do you do," Lily said in a tone she herself didn't recognize.

"May I come in?"

Lily stood by the door, puzzled.

"I'd like to discuss your son's future with you," Miss Stockton said, avoiding the railing as she lurched up beside her host.

Inside, Lily became aware of the lunch dishes piled in a basin where the flies were noisily congregating. The dank odour of wet sheets and soda drifted and adhered.

"I'll get a fire goin' for some tea."

"Thank you, no. I've got an appointment in a few minutes uptown."

"Please sit down, then."

Miss Stockton's reserve came close to failing her as she searched about for a safe place to deposit her petal-pink, delicately flounced dress. She decided the middle cushion of the chesterfield was the least lethal of the available sites and perched on its edge like a fledgling on a wire. Lily sat opposite her on the easy chair and waited.

"You may not be aware of it, Mrs. Marshall, but your son is the brightest pupil I have seen in five years of teaching, here and in Toronto. Inspector Whitecastle was here last week and fully corroborated my own intuitions."

"He's a real good reader," Lily said to be helpful.

Miss Stockton flashed an ambiguous smile and continued. "What I'm saying in practical terms is that your son will undoubtedly score highly on all of the papers of his Entrance Examination next week. He will be eligible to go to the high school in Sarnia, and it is my considered opinion that he will be a first-class candidate for the University of Toronto, in whatever field he chooses."

Lily appeared to be absorbing this revelation.

"You *have* thought about sending Bradley to high school?"

"He's been askin' me about it, yes."

"Good, good. With the extra coaching I've been giving him in the evenings this month – I do hope you don't mind his being away from home too much –" and here she chanced a more searching appraisal of the second-hand ambience of the room: the blotched window-glass, the marauding flies, the absence of a study or desk, the pathetic little titled bookcase in one corner. "But I fully expect him to get straight A's." Lily gave no sign of being overwhelmed by this news. "The main reason I've come is to discuss a very delicate matter, and since I've always been a straightforward person, I'll get directly to the point. While there are no tuition fees for the high school, Bradley will have to buy his own books, mathematical instruments and supplies. He will have to take the trolley to Sarnia every day. He –"

"He'll need some money," Lily said.

"Precisely, Mrs. Marshall, how quickly you see my point. He'll also need, how shall I word it, a more fashionable kind of clothing – not to show off, mind you, or get a swelled head, I certainly couldn't approve of that – but just so he won't stand out for the wrong reasons or be picked on by city pupils who can, you know, sometimes be quite cruel in these matters."

"I been puttin' money aside all along," Lily said.

"Splendid. And since we're obviously seeing eye-to-eye on these critical matters, may I make one final suggestion. If you can see your way clear – perhaps not the first year since Bradley's just thirteen – but by the second year or so, you might consider letting him board at one of the many fine homes near the school."

Lily's eyes narrowed slightly.

"That way he won't have to spend an hour a day on the trolley, and more important, he'd be able to use the school library after hours or the public library down the street, and –" she aimed her pity towards the cubicle where the boys slept, "– of course he could have a quiet room of his own in which to study. My purpose today, Mrs. Marshall, has been to relay Inspector Whitecastle's enthusiasm for, and my own endorsement of, Bradley's genius to you in order to make these decisions more comfortable for you to consider."

Lily showed her visitor out.

Miss Stockton suddenly turned on the stoop and said in her own cabbagetown cadence: "You're gonna let him go, aren't you?"

Lily nodded, and touched her reassuringly on the arm.

Back inside the warm room, Lily felt woozy and sat down at the kitchen table. Must be the heat, she thought. Robbie clumped in from the back shed. "No supper?" he said.

"You seen Brad?"

"Yeah, he's up at Redmond's fussin' over that Potts' girl. They were stuffin' their faces with chocolate the last I saw of 'em."

"Miss Stockton, his teacher, was just here. I thought he'd be home to find out what was goin' on."

Robbie went over to the tinder-box. "He knows, all right," he said bitterly. "But he won't come home till dark."

"Why not?"

"He's ashamed to."

27

1

Dominion Day that year marked the first decade of the new nation and in Sarnia the opening of Lake Chipican and the surrounding Canatara Park. The new recreation facility – yet another outward sign of man's steady ascendance to perfection – festooned with picnic benches, a bandstand and a mammoth open-air dance pavilion big enough for a whole village to jig upon. The grand *debut* of the facility would be celebrated with the usual political speech-making, boosterism and fireworks, but by far the greatest attraction was to be the regatta on Lake Chipican itself, starring no-less-a-celebrity than Ned Hanlon, the legendary world-class punter. Sophie decided that Lily ought to go because she had been down-in-the-dumps lately and needed a little music and dancing to cheer her up. When Lily protested mildly that Lake Chipican was just their own Little Lake with a fancy name attached to it to make it sound vaguely Indian, Sophie appealed directly to the boys seated nearby, and the day was carried.

As it turned out, almost everyone from both the town of Sarnia and the unincorporated village of Point Edward came out to watch the races and the mighty Ned Hanlon – whose combination of strength and agility, power and grace, bravura and humility appealed in their different ways to the ages and sexes that rimmed the pond seven-deep that Saturday afternoon.

Sophie and Lily spent the day together. The young people went off by themselves in twos and threes, returning only for supper or an extra nickel. Wee Sue and Brad took Bricky swimming. The sun shone benevolently down upon the festivities, glistening on the muscular arms of the rowers and deepening the contrast of their white-duck trousers and red-striped shirts. They pulled in furious unison, skimming the surface of the pond with the seeming ease of Argonauts, their rhythmic, guttural grunting muffled by the adulating crowd and the evergreen-and-oak of Canatara Park. Sophie was apparelled in a peach-yellow sundress and a billowing bonnet that gave her the appearance of a ruffled bobolink. She clasped Lily by the hand and pulled her here and there in order to improve their view of the racers and get a close-up gander at Ned Hanlon himself. Sophie's ken, however, soon narrowed to the hefty coxswain of one of the row-ing eights, the largest of the shells in the competition, requiring men of fortitude and amplitude to propel her manfully forward, stroke and counter-stroke. Lily preferred the scullers, the solitary racers whisking daft as dragonflies, commuting water to air.

During the picnic supper the Sarnia Bugles entertained from the bandshell and the husky athletes mingled with their worshippers. Several of them had volunteered to supervise the children's races. Robbie won a prize and was presented with a ribbon by Ned Hanlon himself. With the sun behind them making them mere silhouettes, Lily watched her son and this illustrious Torontonian during the brief ceremony in which she knew much more was being exchanged than a mere ribbon. He's just like Tom, she was thinking; he can't live long on small rations of hope. The smile he flashed her way was like a reprieve. When Lily looked around for Sophie, she was gone. Bricky had been laid under an oak to sleep off his indigestion, the young folk had disappeared again, and in the distance the orchestra was just striking its first chord in the new pavilion.

By the time Lily got over there, the hardwood dance-floor was already covered by couples enlinked in a Strauss Waltz, animated by the strings and muted horns of the Detroit City Orchestra just arrived by lake-steamer. The underside of the pagoda-like roof over the raised platform was hung with coloured lanterns and pastel ribbons even though the sun would provide all the illumination required for two hours yet. No one noticed the anomaly. The air of early evening was cool, the music exotic and seductive. Sophie was dancing with the 'eights' man, who was smartly attired in yachting white. Lily could see that he too was surprised – and not a little flushed and exhilarated – by the nimble ponderance of her step, the grand sway of her circling: a panda's waltz on its home ground. Lily was so absorbed in observing this scene that she hardly felt the pressure on her arm guiding her gently into the slipstream of music and dance. Did I say 'yes'? she thought, settling into the stranger's embrace. I must have.

He was one of the scullers, who had come second only to Ned Hanlon himself. In his oar's grip he held Lily as lightly as he would a falling rose-petal. His sandy hair fluttered in the breeze of their own making. In the whirling fandango his fingers on her back praised and applauded. In the slow waltz she put her brown against his bare chin, and they navigated the shoals and eddies of the music with such mutual acuity Lily could feel no part of his motion but the point where brown and chin swivelled on a single bead of sweat. During the jigs she lifted her skirt above her knees and closed her eyes until she could hear, somewhere behind the fiddle's slither, the bounce of a breath-driven harmonica. When it stopped, she leaned against the railing to steady herself; her *premier danseur* – Shamus O'Huguin from Burlington – was catechizing her with insatiable sea-green eyes.

As dusk descended and the mosquitoes began rising from the swamps and pools around, the music slowed to a last waltz, and young and old and many between clung together in pairs and danced as if they believed such bonding – such congruence of purpose and desire and hope – were as permanent a part of the human condition as war and depression and the facing of fidelity. "We're all goin' over to the Grand Trunk for a party," he whispered. "You'll come?"

Around her, jostling couples pushed towards the steps, a bass-viol accidentally groaned, illicit laughter percolated from the shadows, Sophie Potts was waving goodbye with her baby finger and ambling into the brush with her amiable paramour. Lily turned back to the young oarsman and she could tell from the smile on his face that she was about to say yes.

"You comin', Ma?"

It was Robbie, at the bottom of the steps, alone.

"Yes," she said, and released her lover's hand.

2

Next day the Sunday hush lay more heavily than usual upon the village. The church bells importuned as lungfully as ever, but empty places were duly noted in a number of pews, and even in the choir-stall itself. Lily listened to their familiar, reassuring ring as she ironed a clean shirt for Brad, who was to go down to Sarnia tomorrow for his interview with Mr. Axelrod, the principal-designate of the recently constructed, independent high school. Brad lay on the chesterfield pretending to be absorbed by some verse-saga called *Don Juan*, a gift from Miss Stockton – daintily inscribed – in honour of his extraordinary performance on the Entrance Examination. Lily had taken some of the cash she had been putting away in a crockery jar under her bed and purchased her son his first store-bought oxfords, suit, vest and tie. Robbie was off by himself hunting cottontail in Second Bush.

It was a hot and humid July day without the relief of a breeze. Lily was thinking that she should go discreetly over to Sophie's to see if the kids wanted to have a picnic and spend the day on the beach. If Wee Sue came along, then Brad would also. She was mulling these thoughts over sleepily – her dreams had been deep and disruptive for weeks now – when she was startled by a commotion in the back shed. A laundry pail clattered, pursued by a mutilated curse. Sophie.

Lily arrived in time to help her upright. Sophie glared at the offending pail, then flashed a teeth-stretching grin at Lily, catching her frontally with a boozy gust of breath. Her eyes hovered, radium red. The thick humus of her hair shrieked outward. The look she gave Lily (just before the mask of her face closed over it) skidded on the edge that separated ecstasy from desperation.

"C'mon, Lil, we're gonna have us some fun, some *real* fun," she said in a voice amazingly unslurred, riding its own energy.

Lily took her friend by the arm: "Let me get you home to bed, Soph. You ain't had much sleep, I bet."

"If you're suggestin' I been drink' an' screwin' all night, then you're absolutely right," she laughed, pulling away and grabbing Lily's hand in turn. "C'mon, you an' me's gonna haul old Duchess's ass up the hill an' give that bachelor pig up there the thrill of his life!" She rocked back on her heels, sat down on the cushions of her rump, and let out a dry, rattling cackle like a pullet with a kernel in her craw.

Lily allowed herself to be dragged across the lane to the Potts' yard, where it became clear that Sophie had already put her plan into action. Beside the pig-pen sat the rickety trundle-wagon Stoker used for hauling logs or vegetables up to the house. Duchess had been lured out of her shady retreat with a bucket of milk-slops strategically set near the gate to the sty.

"C'mon, Lil, I need a little help gettin' her up on the wagon. Mind you, if she knew where she was goin' she'd hop up there like a toad into poop, but she won't listen to a word I say to her." She flung open the barrier and called out in saccharine, seductive tones: "Soo-ee, soo-ee, soo-ee!"

Duchess pricked up her floppy ears, blinked pinkly, but decided not to abandon the slop-bucket in spite of its barrenness. She was a fine Chesterwhite sow with rosy-hued skin, a soft, lecherous snout, and fold upon fold of self-satisfied fat. More than a dozen litters had suckled from her contented teats, and whenever she was in heat, like now, she lazed in the mud and dreamed of nipples ripening and Farmer Holly's Yorkshire boar rearing up behind her, his cleft trotters flailing against her roused flanks, while she prinked her golden bristles and joyfully sucked out his seed. But Farmer Holly's boar was much overdue.

"Son-of-a-bitch up an' died on us," Sophie explained, circling the wary sow. "The old man, not the stud," she chuckled. "Now you put that there ramp up to the wagon while I push this barrel of grease-shit from the rear," she shouted.

"Soph, you're crazy. You can't get Duchess up on that contraption, an' you can't let her in with John the Baptist's boar. He'll kill you."

"He ain't home," Sophie said triumphantly. "Gone perch fishin' with Hap Withers' boys, out on the *lake* for the *whole* day!"

"He ain't gonna like it, you know how he feels about Aquinas."

Sophie glared over at Lily. "Hey, you an Alleywoman or not?"

Lily grabbed the two planks and tried to make a ramp out of them. Sophie managed to get downwind of Duchess and plop a hand on each of the sow's haunches. She grunted and heaved the animal forward, and was making some headway when she decided to expedite its progress by twisting its tail about three hundred degrees counterclockwise. Duchess squealed like a bruised bagpipe at the outrage and lurched sideways. Sophie lost her handhold, overcompensated and flopped flat on her back in the slime. Lily leaned forward and put a gentle arm-lock on Duchess while Sophie yawed fitfully in the mire, gained a knee, and then let her jaw slacken like a hippo's yawn.

"You *blubber bucket! You bulb-bellied slop-cunt of a pig's hooer! You fat-tit, slant-eyed son-of-a-boar's bitch!*" She hollered through her megaphone at the stunned sow – its eyes red as raspberries – and continued improvising her medley of curses, whose foul effluence rose into the air above the Alley and like an irresistible spoor drew to it all manner of curious creature. Indeed, by the time Lily had seduced Duchess to one of the trundle-wagon's uprights and pulled Sophie to her feet, they were surrounded by McLeods, McCourts and Shawyers of every size and sex. All were eager to help.

Sophie, canary-yellow from the front and mud-umber from the back, re-established what she took to be her dignity by hurling commands into the chaos, and somehow, amid much laughter and several temporary setbacks, managed to assist the terrified sow up the plank and into the wagon. Lily hopped aboard and tried to sooth Duchess

with some nonsense patter she thought might approximate a porcine lullaby, a manoeuvre which, while having little evident effect on the beast, did succeed in reducing
Lily and Sophie to a state of paralyzing mirth. Sophie leaned the mighty ballast of her
body against the rear of the rig while a dozen ululating children pushed from the side
and pursued some invisible Pied Piper up the dusty trail towards the bootlegger's shack.
Other pleasure-seekers, large and small, joined the procession en route. Cap Whittle
was seen scrambling down a yard-arm. Spartacus and Stumpy fell in behind, and Honeyman Belcher left his pony to graze where it stood.

As the tumbrel lumbered past Hazel's Heaven, the hoots and cries of the cavalcade
awoke the drowsy concubines within, and by the time it reached the stamping ground
of John the Baptists's soul-mate, the afternoon was aflutter with petticoat and tinkling
laughter. As the circus crowd gathered and jostled for the best view, Sophie halted the
carriage with a toss of her head and waddled aggressively towards the abode of the victim. All commentary ceased. Wavelets could be heard stroking Canatara beach.

Aquinas had come out of his sanctuary to accost the intruders. In some ways his
pen was the sturdiest and most impressive structure on the Alley. A commodious corral – of stout split-logs and deeply-augured posts braided with chicken-wire – allowed
him freedom to exercise his bulk, loll in the soothing mud, or intimidate children and
idling strangers by stamping his trotters on the gravel pad and grunting like a tusked
peccary in the wild. Behind him stood a hutch-like affair lovingly constructed by his
friend and helpmate. It was water-tight, being shingled with cedar-shake, and the south
side of it could be opened completely to the air merely by raising the two wall-size shutters on their hinges and laying them flat across the roof. This transformation occurred
on warm sunny days when Aquinas preferred to lie in his manger, shaded and content,
and peer out at the fevered world beyond – his feed trough less than a head-loll away,
and if he were pressingly hungry, as he often was, he might even nudge open the lid of
the large grain-box where the goodies were stored.

When he espied the crowd ringing his demesne on three sides, he stopped in his
tracks and tilted forward the horn-shaped ears he often brandished like the sabres of
his jungle cousins. Aquinas was a purebred Polish China boar, black as silt except for
the tufts of white on his feet, tail and snub-snout that made him look, no matter how
fiercely he agitated his bristles, slightly comical. But his grunting in itself could be
awesome, and when the foolish or unwary ventured so close as to touch the walls of
his monastery, he swung his bullocks in a frenzy and stabbed the air with his progeni-
tive wand. Unfortunately, the only sins of the flesh he had ever committed were those
of gluttony and gormandizing. His celibacy was the talk of the Alley, and beyond.
Baptiste Cartier, if he himself knew why, would not say. He treated the boar like a favoured pet, feeding him grain and Jersey milk and windfall apples and a lap or two of
homemade stout when he was extra good. After dark Baptiste could be heard gabbling
in *joual* to Aquinas, who listened with exaggerated politeness and allowed his itching
brow to be stroked and stroked. Sometimes it would be three in the morning before
John the Baptist rejoined his customers in the shack at the very end of Mushroom Alley.

At this moment, though, with the afternoon sun blinding him, Aquinas was alone, surrounded by silent, gawking faces and under siege from a large female who had just – incredibly – entered the gate beside the open hutch as if she were waltzing into church. Trying hard to ignore the presence of those arrayed behind her, he pawed the turf with his right trotter and stiffened his jowls like a rooster's wattles. He belched volcanically and aimed a vicious snort in Sophie's direction. As he looked about, ready to mount a charge of some sort, his beady eye caught sight of Duchess, who was being escorted down the wagon-ramp right behind the invading force. His nostrils flared, appraised the available odours, and tightened. Sophie hauled Duchess by the ears fully into the pen and Lily slammed the gate shut in back of them. This acted as a signal for the silent chorus to erupt in a series of whoops, hollers, lewd anatomical suggestions and general merriment.

Aquinas froze, and waited in the middle of the sty as the dust from his terrible stomping settled in pools around him. He didn't seem to know which of the approaching hags he ought to be most chary of. Something in the aura about Duchess – with her pink plumpness, her undulant softness, her wobbling, fetid underparts – prevented him from outright retreat, from unqualified terror. He watched in rapt trepidation as Duchess, veteran breeder that she was, waddled into the muddy wallow a few feet away, tipped forward on her knuckles and presented herself for servicing.

A rasping cheer went up from the well-wishers. Sophie picked up its inspiration. "All right you black-balled son-of-a-bitch" she yelled at Aquinas, "Let's see what kinda stud you really are!" She turned to the crowd for support, rocking with belly-laughter, and brushing off the mud dried on her backside with lewd aplomb. Aquinas, tempted and shivering, stumbled forward two steps, all caution momentarily overpowered by the incense of passion just beyond his nose. At the last possible second, however, with Duchess braced for capture and rude entry, he lunged diagonally, splashed through the muck and headed for his manger. But the lady's duenna was even swifter; Sophie cantered after the spooked hog, cutting him off at the corner of the opening to his hutch, where they collided with a blubbery thud. A collective 'ooh' was emitted by the throng. Both combatants went down but Sophie was up first, spitting sludge and umbrage. She flopped on top of Aquinas, who made no pretense of resistance. He had given up all emotion but fear, and as she threw a choke-chain of flesh around his neck and jerked him vertical, he closed his eyes, squealed like a piglet without a nipple, and then howled as piteously as a barrow staring at his clipped testicles.

"Grab him by the handle!" someone offered.

"He ain't got one!"

Sophie was dragging him stiff-legged across the wallow towards the puzzled sow, and might actually have succeeded in carrying out such a forced congress if Duchess herself had not decided she required more privacy than this to satisfy her procreative longing. She stood up, unstuck her front trotters from the mud and stumped past the purblind Aquinas towards the shelter.

"The other way! The other way!"

Sophie uttered an oath that sprung something inside the boar's head and he went limp, all six hundred pounds of him. Undaunted, Sophie gripped him by the knuckles and inched him back towards the sow now settled in the shade of the manger. The crowd whooped. Suddenly Lily was at Sophie's side. Together they tugged Aquina's deadweight slithering through the slough, tumbling into it themselves, popping up again with only their eyes and teeth to signal the manic delight of their laughter and fury, and finally – riding a crest of hysterical cheering and good-will – they pitched the wretched male creature into the straw beside Duchess. Lily fell back against the stool John the Baptist used when conversing with his bachelor friend, and let the tears wash over the mud on her cheeks. But Sophie – fuelled by some darker, unspoken purpose – belly-flopped between the dazed beasts and made a lunge for Aquinas's crotch. There was no need. In panic or dread or desire – who would ever know? – the Polish China boar rose up and then down, and with a savage thrust did his pedigree proud.

Before the crowd could confer its ultimate accolade on Sophie's daring, however, two more unexpected things happened. First, Cap Whittle, athwart an alder branch, cried out, "*Man ahoy*," and John the Baptist was spotted tearing across the flats towards the *mêlée*. Second, the combined plentitude of sow, boar and human attendants caused the ground to give way under them. Not all at once but steadily, like quicksand, and accelerating with each floundering second. Straw, dirt, pigshit, rotting timbers, splintered floorboards – all caved inward and down and swept a cargo of flesh into the vortex. Moments later, through a maze of squeals, whimpers, gasps and settling dust – first Lily, then Duchess, then Aquinas, then Sophie clambered up and rolled onto firm ground. And just in time.

As the throng parted and drew back to allow for the entrance of the aggrieved party whose French oaths and howl of desolation preceded him by two hundred yards, they gasped as one when the earth under them rumbled and exploded, and a geyser of smoke-and-steam shot up no more than a handspan behind Sophie's rump. The shock of it bowled her over against Lily, and, arms enlinked, they followed the goose-white plume as it hissed skyward from its underground eruption. Moments later Cap Whittle caught the first whiff of raw whiskey.

A few weeks later Sophie stopped Lily on the lane and said, "Hey, I got news. Duchess is up the stump." She grinned her most wicked grin: "Must've been the holy water!"

28

Stoker had left for the boat. Lily watched twelve-year-old Bricky trail after him across the ragweed fields towards the docks. She waited a full day, then slipped across to Sophie's.

Lily found her in the back shed sprawled on a pile of sheets and scraps of clothing, half of which was dirty and half in one or more stages of being washed. She was absent-mindedly sipping homemade beer from one of the brown pint bottles once used for some medicinal end. She made no sign to acknowledge or sanction Lily's presence. Lily came gently up beside her and eased down onto a stack of overalls. Sophie was staring at one of the cracks in the siding where the morning sun pounced. Lily reached over, detached the bottle from Sophie's hands, and took a large gulp. The beer was warm and fizzy.

"Needs to settle a bit," Sophie said. "Stoke made a batch special for me. He made me promise I'd wait till it settled for a week."

"How long's he gone for?"

"The usual."

"Where's Bricky?"

"Who gives a shit. Quiet around here, ain't it?"

"It's not bad, for not bein' settled."

"Since when did you start likin' *any* kind of beer?"

Lily swallowed an ostentatious mouthful.

"Christ's sake, gimme that before you waste it all!"

Lily rolled away, holding the bottle aloof and foaming.

"Shit, woman, you're drippin' it all over my laundry!" Sophie heaved the flotsam of her flesh forward in an effort to sit up, almost made it, but teetered backwards, wobbling towards gravity.

"Come on, Lil, I ain't kiddin'. That's the last goddam bottle. Stoke's puttin' me on a diet." As Lily danced close to her, Sophie lashed out with her right hand and cuffed a pair of men's underwear.

"You skinny bitch! You bag o' bones! You fly-titted little Jezebel! *Gimme that booze!*"she snorted. "That's a present from my husband. That's sacred stuff. *Put it down!*"

Lily set the bottle down, and while Sophie floundered through heavy seas towards it – her shark's eye on its last trickle – Lily scurried about reorganizing the laundry and restarting the fire in the kitchen stove to heat more water. Later, when she came back into the shed, she brought two brown bottles of beer with her, pulled the corks out with her teeth and squatting beside Sophie once again, handed her one of Stoker's precious gifts.

Sophie sighed: "What on earth would I do without you, eh?"

It turned out that Sophie was in one of her periodic states of false inebriation, where the alcohol merely puts a glaze on the lethargy or despondency or glee already present in its own right. For no sooner had Lily finished up the wash and begun to gather it together to hang outside when the comatose Sophie revived on the instant, climbed onto both feet, and flashed a mischievous grin.

"Come on," she whispered. "It's time I showed you something'."

They took a bit of the medicine with them.

The windowless old relic of a shed had always been locked. Its rusty tin roof sagged preposterously, its vertical barn boards split apart like a sprung barrel. The sun riddled its secret interior unopposed, yet not once did Lily or anyone else in the Alley remember seeing anyone put a key to the seized padlock or in any way disturb the sanctum behind it. At least not for years. Several of the oldtimers did recall that back in the 'sixties Sophie was seen entering the premises with a lantern and several twelve-quart baskets.

Lily followed Sophie up the shaggy path towards the shed. Sophie was navigating with some difficulty, using her arms for balance.

"I reckon you're old enough to see certain sights," she said confidentially as they reached the padlocked door and set the empty bottles down. "Damn lock's gone an' seized up," she said. She grabbed the hasp and jerked it backwards. Screws popped everywhere. Sophie let the whole door fall out of her grasp. "Son-of-a-bitch," she muttered and disappeared into the darkness ahead.

Lily followed. The odours of the dank interior wafted over her and rolled on out into the August sunshine: must, mildew, the mouldy cob-webbing of neglect, the tuberous pungency of root rot and festering, imploded bulbs. But something else as well: an emanation only; an afterscent of something not quite sweet nor tart – herbal perhaps; something that had been lovingly dessicated till only its quintessence remained to impress the believer. Lily was trying to adjust her eyes to the gloom when Sophie pulled up a hinged shutter and the sun shot in from the south with the force and clarity of a lightning flash. The room, unillumined for a dozen years, leapt immediately into view, garish and eerie.

What caught Lily's eye first were the brown leaf-like rags draped over several clotheslines that crisscrossed just above her. Some looked as large as tobacco fronds, others as tiny as mint or thyme. Still others, she now saw, were whole plants – roots, stems, leaves, stunted flowers – dangling from clothes pegs like the shrivelled corpses of aborted, unnamed creatures of mythology. Sophie reached up and flicked her finger against a spade-shaped leaf so thin the sun lit up its bloodless veins. There was a gasp of dust as fine as powdered gold.

"Ground that stuff up in my cough medicine," she laughed. "Over here," she said.

Lily saw the workbench and thought of the chemist's lab in Sarnia – with apothecary jars, mortar-and-pestle, burettes, filter screen, gas-burner and bottles of every contortion and hue imaginable, some still winking. Sophie slapped her hand down on the top of the bench and two shallow dishes coughed their bluish powder effortlessly into the air.

"Didn't know your dear Soph was a witch, did ya?"

In a butter box at the end of the bench Lily noticed three neat rows of dried roots stacked four or five deep and looking quite forlorn. They're like the wizened penises of capons, she thought, as a giggle tickled the back of her throat.

"Not funny, Lil. Not funny at all. That's what all the decent folk thought, and even some of the loonies 'round here. Why d'you think I had to build this here shanty an' put a burglar's lock on the door, eh?"

"What did you do in here?"

"Mixed up potions," she said. She held a fruit jar up to the slanting light where its contents glowed like honey. "Pure linseed oil," she said. "Made it myself. Used it on some of the poultices. Now *this*," she said, displaying a jar in which some purplish precipitate quivered ominously, "is a gen-u-ine witch's brew. Kill a Tomcat in heat at twenty rods."

"These are Indian medicines," Lily said, suddenly serious.

Sophie ignored the remark and went rummaging among some boxwood cases in a shadowy corner still unopened by the sun. She caught her sleeve on an offending nail. "Jumpin' be-Jesus," she hissed, "that's the last of my party dresses." She peered blearily at the slight tear, grabbed the sleeve with her other hand and extended the fracture all the way to the armpit. "That'll teach ya' to trip on a nail," she said. "Now where in Christ's Calvary are those little buggers?" There was a clatter of shaken glass and some further profane encouragement.

"Them medicines you gave me for Robbie an' Brad, you made them yourself?"

"I know they're back here somewhere. Jesus-be-jumpin'!"

Lily heard the other sleeve go. "Where did you learn all this?"

"Here they are, right where I left them."

"Why did you go an' give it up?"

Sophie had a crate of wobbly medicine bottles flush against the folds of her bosom and was struggling to find her way into the light with her treasure. "Goddam quacks, that's why. Just too many of 'em, dearie. I got sick an' tired of fightin'. Besides, people get money an' they want real doctors, don't they? I quit before I wasn't wanted any more. Just like that."

The crate of bottles clattered down onto the bench. For a moment Sophie pretended they weren't there and turned to face Lily for the first time since they had come into the arcanum. "You'd never guess by lookin' at this baby-pink complexion of mine that I got Indian blood pumpin' in these veins."

Lily showed her surprise.

"Told ya' so. Though I reckon Stoke suspected right from the start, if you know what I mean. My Mama's mama was full-blood Ojibwa, from Kettle Point. She was the daughter of a medicine man from Manitoulin. She passed the lore along to me."

"Where'd you grow all these things?"

Sophie guffawed and the manic gleam was suddenly back in her eye, as if all the alcohol from Stoker's store had been holding its potency in check till now, as he himself sometimes tried to do – wondering if, unleashed, it would stretch and burst inside them both in a paroxysm of pleasure and fiery demise. "Not on this singed arsehole of land, that's for sure. And even if I did manage to coax anything' up out there, some brat would piss all over it for a penny." Her chuckle, rumbling up through her, toppled her against the bench where her elbow struck the crate. "No, my cousin used to bring me the supplies down from the Reserve every couple of months. But I made up the potions and poultices right here, right on this bench, early in the mornin' when the sun would shoot right through that window, when nobody was around to unsettle me except the babe kickin' at me from indoors." She patted her belly reminiscently. "They were good medicines, Lil, an' don't you ever forget that."

"What are those, then?" Lily said.

"Hey! That's what I wanted to show you. To show you how good I really was. You wouldn't believe it, Lil, but Stoker, he was proud as punch of me in them days. People couldn't pay much, of course, but they'd bring the kids little presents an' do favours for Stoker around here when he was off on the boats. An' when he'd come home, he'd give out an Indian whoop an' say, 'C'mere little squaw-lady, give big chief some of that wampum.' An' he didn't mean a cup of rose-hip tea!" She stared at the dusty bottles as if waiting for them to speak for themselves.

"But these're drugstore medicines," Lily said after a bit, picking up one of the bottles. "Real old ones."

"Yup. Every one of 'em. I got each of these from a person I helped in my rounds. Whenever my medicine worked for them, they always said, 'Here, Sophie dear, take this quack stuff an' throw it in the River.' But I always brung it straight back here an' put in my trophy case. That's what Stoke used to call it."

Lily started to read one of the labels, a syllable at a time: "*Doc-tor Maur-ice's Cel-e-brated Worm Can-dy.*"

Sophie chortled and hiccoughed at the same time; her eyes bulged and narrowed raffishly. "That ain't as funny as *Sir Astley Cooper's Worm Tea!*" she said, dumping the bottles onto the bench and then lifting them one at a time to the naked light. "Or how about *Ayer's Sasarsparilla*: 'cures scrofula, ulcers, pimples, salt rheum, scald head, syphilis, dropsy, neuralgia, tic dolour-eux, debility, dyspepsia, eruptions, erysipals an' St. Anthony's Fire." She snorted: "Want your fire put out, luv?"

"They left out St. Vitus' Dance," Lily tittered.

"How about *this* one. *Holloway's Pills For Sickly Females!* 'Can be taken with safety in all periodical and feminine disorganizations. Its effect is all but miraculous'," she read with a barker's zest. "Now what in Sam Shit is a 'feminine disorganization'? A busted hen party?"

Lily started to giggle in earnest, the flume from three of stoker's brown ones taking belated effect perhaps.

"Here's a dandy!" Sophie said. "*Bryan's Pulmonic Wafers*: 'a blessing to all classes and constitutions'. You an' me now, we got the constitution of a lady ox but no more class than a squirrel-nut."

She had got herself fully launched. She belched, took a lungful of air and carried on. "*Judson's Mountain Herb Pills*: 'they purify the blood, remove obstructions of all kinds, cleanse the skin of all pimples and blotches, and bring the rich odour of health to the pale cheek'. Ain't that enough to make you puke pennies? The only rich odour we got here in Mushroom Alley is the *per*fumery of pigshit!"

Lily, her giggle askew, handed her another one. Sophie's eyes glinted. "*Dr. Chessman's Female Regulating Pills*: 'the oldest regulator for females'." The backwash of her guffaw pitched her forward and she tottered helplessly against Lily's shoulder and they staggered in loose tandem through the door and outside, where they collapsed into the bent grass – debilitated by laughter and the sudden zaniness of the ordered universe.

"And all this time," Sophie said, trying in vain to keep the punch-line primly swallowed, "all this time, I thought the oldest female regulator in the world was that little pulmonic wafer between Stoker's legs."

"You mean the one that cures all classes an' constitutions," Lily said, and they rolled onto their backs, side by side, letting the excitement of the alcohol, the sun-drenched sky, the woozy delight of their own improvisation flow through them and across the maddening divide that kept their beings temporarily separate. The grass and the heat and the afternoon enfolded them.

Lily drifted in and out of sleep. Hours later the shadow of the shed fell upon her exposed face like a bat's wing.

She sat up. Sophie was sitting up beside her. Lily reached out to touch her sleeveless arm. Sophie looked down at her.

"Every night I pray to God he'll sail away on one of them goddam boats an' never come back. Sometimes I even wish the bugger'd fall overboard an' drown, or trip an' go headfirst into the fuckin' furnace."

Desperately she tried to read the response in Lily's face. "I'm wicked, ain't I, Lil?"

29

1

In September of 1878, after flinging their slogans and exordia fruitlessly into the machinery of the universe, the Liberals lay down and let the Tories take up the torch with their cries of 'National Policy' and 'Reciprocity of Tariffs' that must have sent a shudder rippling through the outer galaxies. Hopes were raised much faster than the fallen economy: The North-West Mounted Police cantered onto the plains to save them from whiskey and Indians. The Métis retreated even farther up the North Saskatchewan to obscure enclaves with immemorable names like Duck Lake and Batoche. With Sir John A. – resuscitated and breathing fire – at the throttle, the Canadian Pacific Railway took lethal aim at the Rockies, and the shockwaves of its revived thunder rolled into the Ontario boardrooms of the Great Western and the Grand Trunk. Talk of amalgamation was in the air that autumn. Retrenchment and consolidation were dusted off and re-presented as bywords of conventional wisdom. At any rate – whatever the reason – the Grand Trunk did decide that it was no longer expedient to supervise the daily comings and doings of its foster-child, Point Edward. Incorporation was hastily added to its list of bywords. After all, the company had more reserve land than it would ever need for future development, had already sold off the choice commercial lots it could not use, and even had a fine locally-situated candidate in mind to act as reeve and avuncular guide. Accordingly, the necessary legal trivia were arranged in the summer of 1878, elections for the first council announced for early October, and a proclamation date set for the transfer of power: January 1, 1879.

2

It was probably Hazel who first raised the question, but it soon became general up and down the Alley: what would be the fate of squatters and outcasts in a village controlled by its own elders and *grandees*? This question took on more biting import when it was learned that the Railway was ceding – gratis and as a gesture of its good-will – all

347

such marginal territories to the corporation for 'future recreational or industrial development'. The town council would own the Alley – outright. When the elections in October returned two clergymen, a shop foreman and a druggist as councillors, and acclaimed Stanley R. 'Cap' Dowling as reeve-elect – no doubt was left about the precariousness of the Alley community. So when they gathered at Hazel's on the Saturday following the municipal election – more than two dozen of them, including even old Angus Shawyer sobered up for the day – they were not unaware of the irony of the situation: a town meeting of people who had settled here so they wouldn't ever have to worry about politics and who had never been called upon to publicly confess that they were a community of *any* kind, even renegades.

Stump Starkey, Bible clamped akimbo, ascended the dais and accepted the burden of explaining the legal details as far as they were known, and when each of these had been thoroughly depreciated by argument and imprecation, he went on to recite the actual words of the Reverend Clough, councillor-elect, who had declared from the sanctity of his altar that the new village would be 'purged of that empustulated rot by spring'. A number of suggestions were made for remediation, all of them indictable, and then the mood of anger changed to frustration and finally to sullen resignation. At the point where the meeting was about to break up, Sophie Potts was helped up onto the makeshift platform (Shadrack Lincoln's steamer-trunk). The silence turned from sulky to expectant. Braced on either arm by Stumpy and Spartacus, she began to speak.

Sophie was now a truly gargantuan figure. The hummocks and drumlins and foothills of her flesh were housed in a cerise-and-violet-striped awning which Spartacus had filched from a Sarnia squire and Lily had fashioned into some sort of presentable container. Her cheeks, unbusked by sun, were nonetheless puffed with scarlet striations merely from the effort of breathing. The spoor of her sweat knocked dogs to their knees. Her chickory-dark hair sprouted up anywhere in thicket and thew. When she spoke, her voice, though unmistakably female, reminded her listeners of hickory smoke, licorice and deep-ground peppercorn.

"First of all, I'm sick an' tired of this whinin' an' gabble-gruntin'. Won't do us no more good than a tinker's fart, an' it's not worthy of any one of you. I know you all. I met you one at a time. I liked an' I hated you as I saw fit an' you deserved. We all came here for our own special purpose, an' we don't have to tell one another why, now or ever. We like it here for our own peculiar reasons, an' most of us wanna keep it that way. Most of us won't do too good out there in the other world: we know too damn much about livin' to last long out there. The question for us is not 'do we want to stay?' but 'how can we swing it?' Well, I'm gonna tell you how, right now."

Stumpy and Spartacus got a firm double-grip and eased Sophie forward till she caught her breath – huffing in the most frightening manner. She continued.

"You're all tryin' to dream up ways of defendin' your rights or gettin' back at the respectable folk or cuttin' your losses before you hightail it outta here like a jarful of spooked jackrabbits. Well you don't need to. This town ain't gonna toss us out on our noses no matter how much hot air the Reverend One-Ball Clough bellows out his belfry. This town needs us, an' they know it. All we got to do is remind them a little bit."

No one present had ever heard Sophie Potts talk like this before. Her gossipy tales and deadly retorts, her mustard tongue and nettling glance, her Olympian profanity – these were legend on the lane, but not this. The Alleyfolk listened, not quite believing what they heard.

"Think about it. Them people out there may look on us as a cartful of cripples, ninnies, hooers and downright heathen, but they get a lot of pleasure out of thinkin' such things an' feelin' a tad better about themselves for thinkin' them. And all the time they know they can't really do without us. If Honeyman left, who would clean the shithouses an' septic tanks? If they lost Spartacus, who would keep their boulevards clean an' give 'em a pile of cheap furniture from Sarnia to choose from? Who'd keep the tramps safe an' warm outta harm's way if Stumpy up an' left? And if Hazel were shut down, where would all them rutting sailors end up, eh? In the chaste beds of their precious little daughters! They may curse old Baptiste every mornin' before prayers, but half the town buys its hooch from that fine, unlicensed establishment. And if they dump the Shawyers an' McLeods an' McCourts onto the streets, what maids will there be to change the sheets on their beds or wipe the snot off their kids' faces? An' think of the mountain of dirty laundry chokin' the closets an' hallways of the town's best houses if our dear Lily was given her walkin' papers?"

Sophie had struck the chord she had intended, and now she merely played the instrument – with intervals for deep breathing. "Now, here's the plan," she said when the cheering had almost ceased.

She had worked it out carefully in her own mind, trying it out first on Lily, and together they shaped it for presentation. The Alleyfolk, each in the course of his self-appointed duties, would take a petition out among the populace. The gist of the petition, written out in legal fashion for them by Shadrack Lincoln, was this: for a fee to be negotiated the squatters on the lane known as Mushroom Alley would have their properties surveyed, after which they would be given outright title. The lane itself would be formally attached to Prince Street at the south side of the tracks. With the addition by Shadrack of several 'whereas' and 'we the undersigned', the finished product looked impressive. Five copies were made. The strategy, as evolved by Sophie and Lily, was first to talk, in the natural course of business or social interchange, individually with a storekeeping, a lady-of-the-house, a day-labourer resting at Baptiste's or exercising at Hazel's, a satisfied customer, a charitable heart – and when that individual seemed convinced by the justice or necessity of the cause, then and only then would the petition be proffered for a confirming signature. Moreover, only the petition for that designated interest-group would be shown; that is, there were separate duplicate petitions for housewives, shopkeepers, Grand Trunk employees and other workers, tradesmen, and various self-appointed burghers of high standing. Discreetness, subterfuge, a touch of flim-flam – traits revered and practiced in the Alley – were thus to be used to telling effect.

The stratagem worked. On the five documents they amassed three hundred and fifty signatures, more than half of the adult population of the village – though strictly speaking not all by any means were eligible voters. But the moral impetus of the suit was considerable; after all, few of the resident landowners could deny having a father or grandfather who had begun life in British North America as a squatter. Nor was the instinct to poach completely extinguished by the advance of civility.

A delegation was appointed to take the petition to Reeve-elect Dowling. Stumpy was chosen to present the suit and do all the talking, his chief qualification for the task being his gender. Dowling lived in a two-storey brick house on Victoria Street in a style appropriate to a factory-owner, retired railway executive and budding politician. A maid, Carrie McCourt, answered the door and curtseyed before she recognized her neighbours and lapsed into an incurable titter. Before she recovered, they were inside, past the vestibule and fully into the drawing room – Stumpy, Sophie, Maggie Shawyer, Hazel and, well in the background, Lily Marshall. Dowling, his tie askew and his shirt in a rumpus, was caught off-guard and never regained his balance. He read through the papers at a muttering clip – glancing up from time to time at the odd components of the delegation, none of whom he recognized with any certainty. He said nothing for fully five minutes. Then he looked up at Stumpy. "Well, I am the Reeve of all the people here; I'll present this to the council in January. Carrie will show you out."

Sophie brushed Stumpy back with a gentle flipper and rolled her bulk till it was planted solidly in front of the reeve-elect, now trapped between his fireplace and divan. "Take it to them right now. We got to know your feelings on this right away. We don't propose to hang around an' wait for your mercy or neglect. We mean what we say here. All the services we provide are gonna vanish quicker than you can count your money. The people who signed there are tellin' you they want them services an' that they agree we got the same squatters' rights as was given to their parents an' to the lowliest of Negro slaves brung over the border from the States. We want an answer in a week, one way or another."

Dowling gave them all his best smile but there was no mirth in it. He promised a response within a week.

3

I'm thirty-eight years old, Lily thought. It's time I put down some roots of my own. I'll take some of Brad's schooling money and turn the place into a cottage. I'll paint it blue. It'll be a place he'll want to come back to, the kind of place everybody needs once in a while – a sanctuary. For me, it will be home.

It was hard for Lily to believe that Brad was now in grade ten at the Sarnia High School, having completed grade nine with honours in every subject. He was studying literature and grammar and mathematics, even French. But when she attempted a brief conversation in the tongue she had known from childhood, Brad grimaced, then announced that she wasn't speaking any version of French that *he* knew of. She started to explain her position but for some reason stopped part-way through and mumbled, "Well, I guess your teachers would know best." They had more luck in their discussions of history and geography, certainly in the flush of mutual excitement during those first few months when Lily packed him a lunch and walked with him to the trolley and waited by the window in the gathering dusk till she spied his slim figure among the crowd of returning workers and put their kettle on. Lily listened to his tales of the English kings – the wicked and the sublime – and of the odysseys of the mad, foolish, wonderful seafarers who sailed straight off any horizon. Cautiously she would interrupt him, trying anxiously to keep the countries and oceans in their place, not a little baffled by the flat maps in Brad's textbook and by his abrupt expositions. He himself worshipped England, her sanguinary pageant and her heroic verse, and was quickly irked by Lily's persistent questions about Ireland and where this or that minor country might be, as if it really mattered to anyone. When Lily reminded him that his grandfather and grandmother came from there, he simply looked puzzled, then hurt; finally he would sputter, "This is history, Ma, not family." Then that soft and engaging side of his nature, the side that needed to be loved utterly, re-emerged and he would curl up beside her on the chesterfield and read aloud to her from *The Idylls of the King*.

By the winter term, however, these happier sessions were fewer and further apart. He seemed more and more to prefer studying alone, drawing the curtain around his bed or when Robbie clumped through, wrapping himself in a shawl and disappearing into the drafty shed. Several times in January he came home late for supper without explanation, and picked at his food. Finally he confessed that he was going out with school chums to have a coffee at a restaurant where they read the newspapers and talked, and occasionally bought some supper. He said how sorry he was for worrying her and that it would not happen again, he was sure, because the fellows had all treated him so many times he just couldn't throw himself on their hospitality any more. Next morning Lily gave him a silver dollar: "You ain't a beggar," she said. "You need money to treat your friends. Just tell me when you plan to stay late down there." Brad made a solemn promise, and most of the time remembered to honour it.

In June Lily received a letter from Mr. Axelrod, the principal, and read it with wonder and trepidation. In a formal style and script, it informed her that her son was at the head of the class and reported to be one of the most brilliant students his teachers had ever seen. She was exhorted not to reveal such appraisal to her son for fear of unpredictable consequences in regard to the orderly development of his moral character. Nevertheless, it was important for his mother to realize the depth of his talent that still lay untapped by enlightened instruction, and to make preparations for her son's potentially long and certainly fruitful academic career. In short, it was never too soon to start saving money, as even with the scholarships Brad was sure to obtain, a university education in a capital city was expensive. That much Lily already knew, and her intuition about her son's precocity was now fully confirmed. She went immediately to the jar under her bed, next to Sounder's pouch, and counted out sixty-nine dollars – two year's savings. She would have to find more, but there were three years still to worry about that. Robbie was paying her a little board money whenever he got work at the sheds. Violet often refused to take the salary Lily gave her, but Lily merely put it aside in a separate cache – it wasn't her money. We'll make out, she said to Tom, like we always do.

In March she had wondered if that sentiment were true when Brad, studying in the shed to punish his boorish brother, caught a chest cold which rapidly turned into pneumonia. "It ain't my fault, Ma," Robbie pleaded and Lily absolved him with a touch and together they once again nursed Brad through his fever and delirium, but in so doing Robbie expended some small part of affection and faith that was afterwards irrecoverable. Robbie pitched in and helped Violet with the laundering – swearing the household to secrecy – while Lily sat by Brad's bed reading aloud to him (in a cadence almost as good as Miss Kingman's) his current favourite, 'The Lady of Shallot'. When at last he was strong enough to speak, the first words he said were: "I love you, Ma. I'll never leave you. Never." He began to shake, not from the fever but its devastating aftermath. Tears slipped unannounced down his livid cheeks, and though Lily brushed them aside with a soft cloth, they continued to fall. He *knows* already, she thought. One way or another, I will lose him.

As soon as she had finished counting out the precious savings, Lily went fishing for Brad's Easter report card; she didn't know why but she wanted just to look at it and admire the scarlet A's printed there and shimmering like heraldic gules – to hold them up to the light for Tom to see. It wasn't in the apple-box beside the bookcase so Lily pulled out the drawer under Brad's bed where he often kept his papers and notes from school. It was there, but she didn't pick it up. A notebook, half-open caught her eye and held it. She leafed through it, scanning the crabbed printing that was unmistakably her son's. Each page contained a poem, scribbled over and copied out and altered and finally printed in immalleable block capitals. They were Brad's own poems. From the fading of the ink, she concluded that some of them had been written many, many months ago. She could not read them. She closed up the secret book and carefully put it back in its rightful place. She sat down at the kitchen table, shaken, unable to think a single mitigating thought. "Hey, Ma, I'm cleanin' two cottontails out here, you want 'em for supper?" Robbie called, and then came in from the shed to see if she was all right. "I'll get the fire goin'," he said.

With the depression showing no sign of being able to discriminate between *bleu* and *rouge*, Robbie had been able to find only occasional work at the freight-sheds, lugging barrels and crates much as Tom had done in the full heat of the summer. Redmond continued to give him three half-days delivering grocers in the township, plodding along at the mercy of Rocket whose swayback and irregular trot amused children and roused the derisive instincts of the young toughs-about-town. Robbie never complained, and although he was naturally taciturn, he often sank into a black silence that Lily noticed immediately and gave a wide berth to. When Brad blundered into one of them, a brief flare-up ensued with Brad snapping out something elegant and barbed and Robbie stammering an unoriginal curse before stomping off to the woods.

The woods he loved still – to walk in, hunt in, do whatever private ruminating he needed to do when the world flummoxed him as it so often did. He was like a gentle bull with its horns growing inward. One day on his return from hunting in Second Bush, he said to Lily, "I stopped over at the old place." "You did?" "I looked in the barn. Nothin's been touched. There's a bed in there an' Ti-Jeans rocker. I almost forgot about that old place, you know." "It's still ours," Lily said, looking for some defense. A week or so later Robbie did not come home all night; Lily didn't notice until she called out to the pup-tent where he often slept in the spring and discovered it was empty. He arrived shortly after breakfast and said, with a hint of badgering pride, "I slept over at the old place. It's real cozy. You get a fresh breeze out there, all night." During the month of June he seemed to spend more and more of his spare time 'out there'. When she casually questioned him about this, he grew silent, then morose. She stopped asking. But one day when she and Violet were out for their Sunday walk, they found themselves by chance coming out of First Bush by a new path and crossing Michigan Ave. towards the town-line not a stone's throw from Bridie's place. Sensing where they were destined, Violet drew Lily into a direct route and they came upon their ruined homesteads through the rotting stumps of the windbreak. What they saw surprised and then astonished them. A fully developed vegetable garden had arisen like a materialized dream-image exactly where the old one had always been – leaf and vine and tuber and wrinkled blossom. Robbie came out of the barn, blinking. "It's real good ground," he said.

Nothing was said about it but when Lily felt up to it she slipped over to 'Rob's place' (as it was now called) in the early June evenings of 1878 and stepped into stride beside her son, hoe in hand, as of old. She offered no advice and none was asked for. He can't make a living out of this patch, fertile as it is, but he loves it: it allows him to give something of himself completely without the fear of hurting or being hurt, she thought. When the August blights spoiled half of his crop, he was undaunted. He gathered his harvest, sold it at the Sarnia Market every Saturday during the season (she was told), and gave his mother ten dollars of his earnings. She put it in the schooling fund. And when Brad whined and pleaded and threatened over the question of his boarding in Sarnia during his grade-ten year, Lily was able to hold fast and say no. The trust fund had taken on an aura of something sacred between them. Someday Brad would understand it all. For the time being, though, he retaliated by staying away more and more to squander his money and time with school friends she was never to meet.

Just before the elections and the fuss over property title, Robbie received a letter with an exotic stamp on it. He had never before received a letter of any kind. Somewhat guiltily he slunk away to his tent and read it. Lily heard him jerk his shotgun off the shed wall and tramp towards the bush. The letter was floating in the breeze near the tent, abandoned. Lily rescued it, then read it as she knew she was meant to. It was from Fred Potts – Blub – and contained a thrilling account of his adventures with the circus, including lurid descriptions of the southern American towns and backwaters they visited each year, and a narrative of his own rise from stableboy to midway helper to full-scale barker for the girly-show. Fred hinted darkly that the circus would be coming next spring at least as far as London, and that a world of unimaginable, footloose wonder awaited the ruthless and the brave.

When Lily and Rob had finally finished piling the last of the pumpkins onto the barrow, they sat on the bench outside the barn and sipped tea made over the open fieldstone fireplace Rob had built nearby. Lil was thinking of past pleasures and sadnesses so she was startled when Rob said to her in his blunt, unprefaced manner, "I'll never leave you, Ma."

4

It was close to Halloween with a frail bloom of Indian summer on the village-to-be when news reached the Alleyfolk that the council-elect had voted – unofficially of course – three to two in favour of accepting their suit. Nor was their unreserved joy dampened one whit by the various provisos attached to the original request: that the lots be resurveyed as far as possible to conform with the accepted geometric principles, that the winding lane in consequence be 'straightened' into two tolerable curves, that the latter be attached to Prince Street at the tracks and adopt *that* nomination for all time-to-come, and finally that a settlement stipend of fifty dollars per property – regardless of size or length of tenure – be paid within three years to cover back taxes, the cost of the survey and the necessary legal fees, and to convince the legitimate citizens once and for all that the Alleyfolk intended to be ratepaying members of this community. The celebration, fueled by John the Baptist's new still, went on for days.

Lily took no part in it. She was not ready yet to celebrate. She had more than the necessary fifty dollars, and could certainly raise that much again in three years if need be. In the back of her mind she had thought all along that she would sell Bridie's legacy and with it invest at last in something of her own making and choosing: thus the appropriateness of taking possession of this property seemed foreordained. She owed ten or twelve dollars in back taxes on the old place, which the township, noting the rekindled interest in the land, had decided to press for, but even in the currently depressed market, almost two acres of cultivated land with a barn would sell for forty dollars or more. But Bridie's place was now Rob's place. No thought of selling it could enter her mind. It's his, she thought; he's made it his. I'll pay the taxes and sign the deed over to him. What else have I to give my firstborn son? Even so, enough cash remained to buy back her birthright, as she now thought of it. Of course she would have no reserve money of any kind. Brad needed a new suit; the two she'd bought him last year had shrunk around his sprouting frame – he was going to be tall and slim and handsome. But more importantly, the warning in the principal's letter and the burden of her own responsibility weighted heavily upon her. More immediately she was worried about Brad's increasing truancy, and though his grades remained high, he was drifting away from her control and into habits that could be ruinous. She knew she must let him board in Sarnia under the supervision of a respectable family whose influence, though not her own, would be essential to his progress. Painful as it might be, she would have to make the move after Christmas. For that, she needed cash, all she could possibly earn slaving six days a week.

When Sophie heard, she was shocked, then enraged, then consoling – offering to give Lily every dollar she could "squeeze out of Mr. Flintskin, esquire, when he comes home." The only concrete form of assistance she contributed, though, was to tell Lily's story to Hap Withers, Dowling's factory foreman and father of ten. Hap came right up to Lily's place the next day and made the offer in that quiet, direct way of his that had endeared him to both sides of the village tracks. His own house lay on Prince Street, a hundred feet from the Alley. He proposed to pay Lily's fifty-dollar fee to the council himself, take temporary ownership of the property only, and rent it back to Lily for a dollar a year and taxes. "I'll have a contract drawn up," he said, "to say that you have a right to buy me out for fifty dollars anytime over the next five years – and of course I won't be able to sell the land. If you don't want or need the place by then, I'll buy your house and give it to one of my sons."

Well, Lily mused, watching Hap whistling down the lane, I've got half a root down, and five years to grow the rest of it. There's lots in this world who've got less than that. By Halloween Rob had a deed and Lily became a tenant.

30

1

Stoker arrived home unexpectedly at the end of the first week of November. His ship had run aground near Goderich and limped into dry dock there. With only three weeks left in the season, it was possible the crew would not be asked to make another trip. Stoker usually headed north to the Bruce lumber camp on the first of December. So it was three weeks at home – with Sophie. Lily did not go over, of course, but she kept a wary eye on the Potts' place and at night slept lightly, listening for the telltale sounds.

After a snowy Halloween, Indian summer had returned more perfect and fragile than ever – a thin, sweet stratosphere distilled of all impurities. Lily and Violet went for long strolls across the river flats and the blanched, silent marshes. They gathered bulrushes and feathered cattails and milkweed pods whose silk parachutes sailed happily anywhere the wind swivelled them. Coming home from Hazel's late one afternoon, Lily saw Stoker and Sophie with Bricky between them (Wee Sue had gone 'into service' in September), ambling towards the flats at the back of their property with a slow ease that bespoke comfort, familiarity and trust. Against the setting sun they were a single etched silhouette. Lily hurried on, repassing a pang of envy or regret. Next morning she woke with a start at the slap of a screen door, and stumbled to the window in time to see Stoker and Bricky walking north-east towards First bush, their claret hunting caps winking in the early sun. Later in the morning, after her first wash was complete, she saw Sophie flopped in her rocking chair on the verandah, fanning herself languorously. She had somehow squeezed into her orange print dress, the effort leaving her strapped for breath. She waved at Lily. Lily waved back, then rejoined Violet in the steaming laundry room. At dusk she heard singing and looked out to see Stoker and Bricky cavorting around a huge bonfire onto which they were tossing, on the off-beat, armfuls of stubble, husks and other refuse of the spent harvest. Sophie was watching them as the hens eddied about her feet and the sow sighed a few yards away among her suckling.

The next day Bricky went off with Rob to sleep overnight in "the little barn" and join in a squirrel-shoot organized by the McCourt boys. Stoker had given him a new

358 | GUTTERIDGE / *Lily's Story*

.410 gauge with instructions that he was to use it only under Rob's supervision. To Lily's surprise, Rob walked over to Potts' and spent several hours with Stoker ("shooting the breeze, he's a great guy, Ma, he's got a million stories") before leading Bricky off on his first all-male expedition. Even though Brad was staying over with one of his Sarnia chums and the house was strangely empty, Lily fell into the first deep sleep she'd had in some time.

She was wakened, not ungently, by the twang of a banjo, a quarter-note chord – tart and sensual. Then Sophie's laughter in the rich full calliope of its range from skirring giggle to braying chortle – rude, skeptical, and embracing: a chocolate taunt. Then: low musical murmurings that might have been leftover choruses from a dozen love-songs. A long quiet. Then the crash of flung glass followed by a descanting, tittering hysteria (that could have been meant as hilarity) rescued at the brink by the banjo's bawdy accompaniment. This lewd invitation reached Lily's ears intact and aflame, until Sophie crushed it with a stuttering guffaw. Words now: projectile and buckler; Sophie's taunting mockery above the lumbering accusation beneath it. Lily was half-way across her yard and flinging a kimono over her shift when she heard the clatter of struck furniture and Sophie's gloating whoop. Then she heard Stoker grunt reflexively and the smack of flesh on flesh. Lily flung open the door and barged straight into the Potts' kitchen.

Two lamps had been smashed and lay smouldering in corners. Only one small oil-flame illumined the faces which froze before Lily's intrusion. Sophie was sitting on the table where she'd landed after being struck by Stoker, a frying pan distended from her right hand, the left side of her face still bearing the livid imprint of his fingers, her eyes braced for the coming shock of pain but still able to bring a glance of incomprehension and dismay upon Lily's presence. Stoker had raised his fist again in such a way as to strike a backhand blow on Sophie's other cheek, but at the sound of the door opening he had stopped it long enough to stare down anyone foolhardy enough to enter this territory. He turned the alcoholic jet of his gaze upon the interloper: "*Who the fuck are you?*"

Lily edged slowly into the pool of light. "You know who I am, Stoker Potts," she said as softly as if they were at tea together.

"Go home, Lil, go home," Sophie said in a ghastly whisper just before the pain hit and she crumpled noisily to the floor, tipping over the table.

"No good layin' there like a whimperin' pig," Stoker said, turning away from Lily and advancing towards Sophie, "get your fat ass off the floor an' take your lumps." An egg-size bump wobbled at the base of his skull.

Sophie put up a hand, not to protect herself but to sooth the stinging welts on the left side of her face. She began shuffling backwards like a paraplegic tortoise, whimpering and all the while attempting to find a way to get herself upright. Lily stepped between Stoker and Sophie. She looked directly into Stoker's eyes, less than a foot away from him.

They were infernos, not merely of the rage and outrage and brute animosity she expected to see but also of self-loathing and frantic, contending appetites. "Get outta my way, you interferin' bitch, or I'll bash your face in, too."

Behind her Sophie was scrabbling to her feet. "Do what he says. It's none of your business."

"Hear the woman, eh? She wants you to butt outta our business." Despite the slurring of his voice, Lily could see plainly that he wasn't stupid drunk, that he probably *never* was, since he appeared to use alcohol as some sort of fiery fuel which he rapidly consumed.

"Get outta here, Lily Marshall," Sophie cried from the narrow hallway behind them, her words sandwiched between choking sobs. "What right've you got pokin' your nose in here?"

Stoker was trying to peer around Lily to see where Sophie was going, but Lily wouldn't release him from her gaze.

"You hear me, Lily? Get the fuck otta here!"

"Don't you try runnin' off, woman!" Stoker shouted, his spittle sizzling on Lily's cheek. But he didn't move an inch. He was trapped between the sideboard and the overturned table, with Lily ahead and a coward's retreat in back of him. His quarry's sobs were fading down the hallway towards safety.

"You gonna move, bitch, or do I beat the shit outta you, then outta her, an' then come back here an' give you somethin' you been needin' for years!"

"Go ahead," Lily said quietly, "beat up a woman half your size an' brag about it all over the Alley."

Stoker went back on his heels.

"You don't think I'd keep my mouth shut like that poor creature back there?" Lily said.

For a second nothing moved, or spoke. Then a door rattled, squeaked open, slammed shut, and a latch dropped into a slot.

"Well, you bitch, she's safe now."

"I ain't leavin' here till you promise not to touch her," Lily said.

Stoker turned upon Lily the full blaze of the bottled fury in his eyes. They burned like bitterroot. They scalded the tears that assaulted them.

"Have a drink with me," Stoker said, tilted forward in the chair with his head in his hands. "Please."

Lily drew up a stool beside him and steadied his grip as he poured out two glasses of whiskey from a jug. Lily sipped at hers while Stoker downed his in two gulps.

"I need to talk."

"People've told me I'm a good listener," Lily said.

Stoker dredged up a smile for her but it did little for his face which, drained of its prevailing animus, was a hollow, devastated mask. The voice he chose came from a person deep inside and intricately hidden, unaided by external expression. Lily stared into the moon-shadows around the stove and simply listened.

"Nobody on this Alley would believe it, but I love that woman. I never meant to hurt her, not once. We been together a long, long time, ever since we was practically kids ourselves, and I only hit her a few times. I love her; I never, never meant to hurt her." He took Lily's silence as reassurance of some kind, and continued.

"We got married real young, an' God we was happy. We lived in Sarnia for a long while an' we took some boat trips together an' when Burton an' Marlene was born, I was the happiest soul alive. Sophie was beautiful then; I know you find that hard to believe, but she was, and I worshipped the ground she walked on. I swear it."

He paused while they both contemplated such an improbability, and Lily poured herself a half a glass of whiskey. "Everybody on this lane thinks I'm a wife-beatin' bastard, and I guess I am, but they don't know what I been through. It was her idea to move here when I first went stokin' on the boats, an' she promised on her grand-mother's grave we'd move into a nice house for the kids' sake just as soon as we got the money. And I made plenty of money, slavin' in the boiler rooms of a dozen stinkin' tubs an' cuttin' timber in the township before we cut all the trees down. But she would spend it, every penny of it; I'd leave her with the money an' by the time I got back she'd squandered it, spoilin' the kids or givin' it away to her poor relations up in Huron an' havin' buggerall to show for it. It drove me *mad*, so I started hidin' some of it an' savin' up to move out of this, this *pig-sty!*"

He assumed Lily was assessing the room they were in, its smell of unwashed dishes and vegetable rot. "At first I tried to keep it lookin' respectable, 'cause I could see the older kids was gettin' ashamed of it; I built the verandah an' the back sheds an' shingled the roof an' put a coat of gray paint on the outside. Then she took up midwifin' an' things got worse; she was never home night or day, the house turned into a garbage dump, I was desperate to move so I told her about the money I'd hidden away; an' it was then I knew she would never move from this place, she actually *liked* it here. I bought the seven kids we had then some new boots an' clothes and I went off for the winter to the bush up north." He located the whiskey glass and drank. "*I ran away from it all.*"

Lily listened for any sound from the back room.

"I know I'm to blame, that's what drives me crazy sometimes. I should've come home an' grabbed her an' carted her off to a nice home in Sarnia an' laid down the law an' took care of my kids. But you don't know how Sophie can be. She'd see me thinkin' that way an' she'd start to sweet-talk me an' get 'round me like she's done since she was sixteen. Even now, as fat an' ugly as she seems to other people, she's got a way with me. Till I get mad," he added softly.

"Sophie has a way with folks," Lily said.

Stoker finally looked up. He continued to speak calmly but his words were blurred by the aftertaste of rage. "She drove my children away. All but Bricky. She spoiled them an' beat them an' doted on them an' left them to fend for themselves. She was a slob and a heathen. But they loved her, every last one of them, an' yet every time I come home, she's driven another one away."

"An' Marlene?"

Stoker stared at Lily as if realizing for certain what he had assumed all along: that Lily might be made to understand. "Every hypocrite on this lane knows I slapped Mar-lene an' that she left an' ain't never spoken to either of us since. But none of 'em knows why. Only me. An' Soph." He hesitated, then went on with vehemence that was more menacing by being whispered than shouted. "That *hooer* in there did it right in front of her own children! Can you imagine that? Hardly a curtain between her an' Marlene lyin' there in the next room, listenin' to such disgust an' filth." His hands shook helplessly on his knees and he started to rock back and forth in the chair.

"Lily, as God is my witness – and I've never stopped believin' since I was a kid – I've never been with another woman since I married Sophie MacGregor thirty years ago. No one. All those weeks an' months on the boats and in the bush, an' not one woman, though the squaws an' hooers was lyin' all around us – quarter a throw. Not one goddamn time. Then I got to find out from my own daughter that her mother's no better than those pitiful hooers on the streets of Port Arthur. Only worse. An' worse than that, I go an' slap my daughter around – the child I loved the most in the world – 'cause I know she's lyin'; and every time I come home that summer I slap her again, for nothin' at all, 'cause I'm ragin' inside. An' so she leaves, an' then I find out she's been tellin' the truth. That girl ain't spoken to us in ten years, we don't even know where she lives 'cause Burton won't tell." After a while he added, as if it were somehow essential, "We was so happy once, but nothin' turned out the way we planned it."

Lily leaned over and touched the back of Stoker's hand. "Most of the time it don't."

A sharp groan from the other room broke the deep silence that had fallen between them. "I got to go to her," Lily said.

"It's all right."

As she hurried towards Sophie, Lily heard the front door open and then the sound of Stoker's heavy body slumping into the wooden rocker out there.

The left side of Sophie's face was blue and so swollen she couldn't see out of that eye and her speech was as slurred as a harelip's. For a while, seated on the edge of Bricky's bed, Sophie pretended not to notice Lily's presence beside her, letting the moonlight bathe her bruised flesh and breathing asthmatically through a slit in her mouth. She paid for every breath with measured pain. To this, eventually, she added the sting of words. Against the ear, they were gentle and evocative. Lily was not prepared for what she was about to hear from the woman she felt she knew so well.

"When I was Sophie MacGregor I was the cat's meow, an' gloried in it. We lived in a brick house in Goderich overlookin' the river. My Dad was a lowland Scots who dabbled in land an' was sometimes rich an' sometimes broke. He had a laugh that would crack granite. Mother was half Irish an' half Chippewa, though she did everythin' possible to hide that honour. I spent every summer on the Kettle Point Reserve with my Grandma, a daughter of Chief Wawanosh, soakin' up the wild ways my mother hoped a lot of schoolin' would soon cure. Funny though, I liked school, too. I read every book in the common school an' every tome in my dad's library. So when I was twelve, it was decided I ought to be shipped off to a proper school where there'd be enough books an' smart teachers to keep me from gettin' too uppity. My dad's maiden sister, Aunt Harriet, lived in London, so that's where I landed, on Princess Street a few blocks from a private grammar an' continuation school for would-be ladies. Soon I became their star pupil, every teacher's pet, and I played it to the hilt. When I complained of being lonely, my mother sent me a new dress or money to have one made. I still managed to get a couple more wild summers in before Grandma died, but by then I'd decided to like both city-life and education. I sailed into my third year with straight A's an' dotin' teachers an' frantically jealous schoolmates. My head was bulgin' with math an' literature, but so were certain curious parts of my body. I was sixteen but whenever I started to take public notice of my best parts, I got frowns an' horrified stares from my elders. So I plunged into my studies. I had it in mind to sit the normal-school exams an' become a teacher. I fancied a country school of my own where I'd be a queen-bee and empress an' lady-saint all rolled into one. In March of 1847, when I was just a year from gratuatin' an' was headin' for another semester of honours, I met Morton Potts. He'd come up from Windsor to cut timber for the proposed railroad; I'd seen the wagons one mornin' pickin' up the men at the end of Princess Street. Mort was boardin' with a great aunt a few blocks away. He spotted me right off. On wet days when their work was cancelled, he'd follow me home from school, and of course I pretended I was too good to pay any attention to the likes of him. Aunt Harriet saw him talkin' to me at the corner an' threatened him with the constable. He laughed in her face, and I probably loved him from that second onwards."

Lily wanted to say something, touch some part of her friend's sorrow, but she dare not. The voice continued.

"Oh, he was a handsome, clever, devil-take-the-hindmost man. When he kissed me behind the bushes or against a snowbank, the promises I made to my Aunt turned to water. He loved every part of me, it seemed, especially those parts I was so shy about an' so curious to know the meaning of. He made me laugh an' he made me talk a blue streak an' he made me feel good all over. I felt like Lochinvar's bride. Of course I didn't really know as much about love an' life as I thought I did, so when Mort cooked up a scheme to get us alone for a whole weekend, I said yes right off. I told my Aunt I was goin' home for a few days to visit a sick friend, and I *did* plan to do that but not for the five days I told Aunt Harriet about. When the stagecoach reached Lucan, I got off an' practically fell into Mort's arms. He put me in a cutter an' we whisked off into the nearby woods to a cabin that belonged to a chum of his. We stayed there two whole days before I got back on the stage for Goderich. It snowed all the time we was there. Mort kept a glorious blaze goin' in the stone fireplace and it was warm as toast all the time. Which was a good thing because we didn't spend much time in our clothes. I can close my eyes this very minute an' see an' hear an' feel every speck of them days – as if it was snowin' outside right now and I was as round an' innocent an' clear-skinned as I was at sixteen years of age, when my lover's eyes popped like mulberries every time I turned over a new way or let his hand find a new surprise. We loved an' talked an' made eternal promises an' loved some more, we gloried in our bodies an' we cared for nothin' that didn't agree with the feelings we could only make when we were together. We pledged our faith."

Lily wanted to tell Sophie something of her own, but again, held back. After this, she knew, there would be time, lots of time.

"Of course, my mother and Aunt soon compared recipes an' found us out. My God, what a row there was! I was locked up an' chaperoned an' tuttutted over day an' night. If I hadn't been the star pupil I'd've been thrown outta school as 'damaged goods' sure to corrupt on touch. For a while I may have believed, just a little bit, that they were right – I really was seduced an' drugged an' led astray by an accomplice of the arch-fiend himself. But not for long an' not very much." Lily heard the wince of a chuckle, some stinted breathing, then: "Stoker never gave up for a minute, he knew what kinda passion he'd stirred up in that snowy cabin. They'd got a judge's warrant to keep him away from me; they'd have charged him with rape if they thought they could've survived the scandal, but we managed to meet within a few weeks when I ran off from an Arbour Day outing an' we made wild love in the clover that was scarcely green enough to smudge our bare bottoms, but it was so good an' Stoker was big enough an' strong enough to beat the world off if he had to. I was hooked – on sex and all the wonderful sideways feelings it sent bubblin' through me. Lily, I loved that thing between his legs so much and I wanted it so bad, I'd have kissed a parson's arse for it. I would."

Lily felt the jiggling of Sophie's mirth up through her tears, the hurting purge of her unique laughter.

"I gave it all up – my books, my family, the life I dreamt ahead-of-myself. I cut them off like a turnip-top and I never looked back." When she had retrieved enough breath, she said, "So that oughta tell you why I'm the way I am."

2

By the time Lily dragged herself out of bed and back into the laundry shed, Violet was starting the second round of washing. The first was flapping smugly in the last breeze of Indian summer. Lily had slept well once she had reached her bed shortly before dawn. Though she was still groggy and somewhat enervated by the trauma of the night, she found it easy to smile for the faithful Violet and pick up the rhythms of the workday with a fresh buoyancy. By noon she was humming and tattling away to Violet about the crazy time Maman LaRouche set about baking a gingerbread man for her and little Guy and convincing them that she had put one of the Millar boys inside the dough for being *un bébé fou* until Guy started crying and Maman laughed and cuddled him, soothing him with *Ah, Ti-Guy, mon pauvre bébé*, and then accidentally saying *mon bébé fou* which sent him into such hysterics he let Lil eat the entire cookie with Billie Millar baked alive inside. They laughed about this through their brief lunch at the outdoor table. They were suddenly stopped by a loud, clear voice that could only have been Stoker Potts': "Don't you ever throw Marlene up to me again, you hear!" Nothing audible had preceded it and nothing followed, though the women sat deathly still for a long minute. Lily got up and peered around the corner of the house: she could detect no sound or movement over there. After a bit, Stoker waltzed out of the woodshed, a bundle of trash under his arm and, whistling a sea-shanty of sorts, headed for the refuse fire out by the flats.

Lily and Violet worked extra hard that afternoon to take advantage of the good drying weather. Lily was just pegging the last of the sheets from The Queen's onto the line when she heard the thud of running footsteps, a heavy body crashing through the dead-stalk and wizened burdock leaves. She whirled in time to meet Stoker Potts as he plunged blindly into the yard – dishevelled, his face smeared with soot as if he had just crawled out of his engine-room, his look deranged and feral. But the voice was a little boy's – pleading and frightened beyond guilt or reason.

"I didn't mean to, Lily, I didn't mean to, oh Christ-in-Heaven I didn't mean to, it was an accident," he said in a singsong cadence wholly out of tune with his flailing arms that were begging someone *anyone* to come and help.

"Where is she?"

"Hurry, please."

"*Where is she?*"

"Out back, oh Christ, we gotta hurry."

"*What've you done?*"

"Nothin', she just fell, I didn't mean for anythin' to happen," he babbled after Lily who was already racing across the lane towards the river flats, her heart in her throat, flapping and nauseous. "*I love her!*" he shouted at Violet as she ran past him. "*I love her!*" he screamed wildly up and down the Alley, till his legs gave out and he sank to his knees, choking on his own sobs.

"Get back, Vi!" Lily yelled as she neared the trash-fire and spotted something grotesque twisting in the dead grass. "Go get a doctor, *anybody!*" But Vi stood frozen in her own fear a few feet away.

Sophie's huge body lay in the weeds which were still smouldering from the impact of her blazing flesh. Charred swatches of orange cloth had welded to the jellied muscle of her back and buttocks. Lily could see where the pink skin had shrivelled, then puffed, then dissolved, leaving the raw red flesh to thicken in the air. The body seemed to be shaking from within as if the bones had just felt the shock, and Lily heard what sounded like a prolonged sigh on a single note, as if that one sound would have to make do in expressing whatever grief or rage or goodbye were needed. Lily shuddered at its intensity, this pelvic hiss that might in other circumstances have been taken for a woman's cry of elucidation at the apex of love. Then with a gasp of greasy smoke and a stench of singed flesh, the body rolled part-way over and slid bonelessly into the cradle of the grass. Lily looked for one horrified second at the dead face. Stoker's bruises were still visible on the skin of both cheeks now swollen into two ghastly sacs about to burst. Between them the mouth was rigidly ajar, lips stretched back over the lunging teeth, the tongue bloated and immobile – the last grimace of lockjaw, the death-grin she had seen so often on the faces of muskrat or beaver caught alive in one of Papa's traps. Sophie's eyes, buried in the flesh that had never been able to contain them, said nothing, not even for Lily.

31

1

It was the largest funeral the village had ever seen. Not that it was meant to be, for none of the local ministers would consent to give Sophie Potts, infidel and blasphemer, a Christian burial in the non-denominational cemetery, and most gentlemen of public esteem (and ambition) publicly announced their support for the clergy's stand. However, the son of the Methodist minister who had baptized Sophie and ferried her through Sabbath School in Goderich agreed to come down and hold a service in the Potts' home and to superintend the interment. The good weather prevailed, despite the odds, and luckily so, for the several hundred mourners who drifted in one by one from the township, hamlets, backwaters and (thinly disguised) from the respectable avenues of the village were pleased to stand in the sunshine and hear the sacred homilies tolled once again for one amongst them so rudely taken away. Reeve-elect Dowling was there, and even walked solemnly behind the horse-drawn hearse all the way to the gravesite where the closed coffin was lowered with earnest gentility into the wide earth. It was noted that there was an unduly large number of women in attendance. Some puzzled notice was also taken of the native people who, although not appearing at the service, did show up at the cemetery where they stood quietly among the fallen leaves, and watched. As Lily was being led away between Hazel and Winnie, she looked back long enough to see the Chippewa men, gray-haired and austere, slip out of the shadows and across the grass to form a ring about the grave. She was sure their lips were moving, as in song.

All of the Potts' children were present except for Fred, whose whereabouts were unknown, and Marlene. What rearrangement of loyalties and patterns of retribution were to take place among them over the coming months Lily knew little about and could not bring herself to care. At the inquest a few weeks later, Sophie's death was ruled accidental. Stoker was the only witness called since he was the only one who had seen the unfortunate fall. If I *had* been called, Lily said to herself, what difference would it have made if I'd told what I thought I knew? None at all. Stoker went off to the bush as usual, but did not return in the spring.

Back at Hazel's the evening after the funeral, the Alleyfolk decided to hold a proper wake. Baptiste Cartier brought in a supply of newly-minted hooch, Stewie and John carted up a batch of Sophie's own homemade beer, and Angus Shawyer was kept sober long enough to play his fiddle. They might as well have hauled in a dirge-drum and pounded it sepulchrally, for no one danced, no one sang for fear they would weep: the mourners collected in fragile clusters about the haunted rooms where Sophie had presided so often, and whispered into the gathering gloom stories that had once evoked irrepressible laughter.

"God damn it to hell," Hazel blurted out to staunch her pain, "what a shame, what a rotten shame. All her life she lives on this Alley, she slaps half the kids in this town on the bottom before they're a second old, she works an' slaves to make a home for her family, an' just a month before that home is about to become her own for keeps, she up an' dies. Not only that but she's the one with the gumption an' the brains to give us all a chance at owning what's ours. Now where's the justice in all of that, I wanna know?"

"The Lord moves in mysterious ways," offered Stumpy.

"Fuck the Lord!" Hazel snapped.

Hazel's lament set off a wave of grumbling and apostasy and boozy self-pity.

"A year from now an' she'll be a nobody, forgot like all of us are the second we're outta mind," sighed Winnie, snuffling and making a great fuss over the silent, tearless Violet.

"Damn shame."

"But true."

"It don't have to be."

The parlour went quiet, as if the corpse had slipped in and just been noticed. It was Lily Marshall who had spoken, and the mourners were not listening so much as watching.

"I said it don't have to be true. About Sophie. There's one way to make sure the town remembers an' to make sure nobody on this Alley ever forgets what she done for us."

"What're you talking about, Lily?" Stumpy said because no one else seemed ready to ask.

"You all know the council is gonna change the name of Prince Street to Prince Edward Boulevard in January when we get to be a village. Then they're gonna hook it up with the Alley. I say we oughta suggest to the Reeve that the whole street be called Potts' Lane."

The rightness of the suggestion struck home. Murmurs of assent rose from all quarters, and one or two defiantly whispered a call-to-arms.

"You think the Reeve'll go for this?" Stumpy said. "After the pressure we used on him to get the land title? I'm afraid we've used up all our tokens."

Reluctant, grumbling assent to this.

"We oughta try," Lily said. "We're only askin' for what's fair."

Stumpy was appointed sole legate for the task of broaching the question to the Reeve-elect. He returned to inform a grim afternoon session of the rump parliament that their request had not merely been denied but ridiculed. Dowling's words, as reported, were: "What in the name of Satan makes you think this town would name its most sacred street after a whoring, whiskey-peddling tub of blubber?" Or metaphors to that effect.

Honeyman offered to stuff the Reeve-elect down a suitable sinkhole and Spartacus brandished a set of pliers capable of transforming him into a capon, but when such displays of resolution and solidarity ended, Lily asked if she might speak. Violet came and stood beside her and squeezed her arm tightly.

"We'll get him to change his mind," Lily said into the awed quiet, and no one doubted her word. They waited for her proposal.

"Once the Reeve's made up his mind, he'll get the council to do what he wants. Now, I want Shadrack to write down the main points of a story I know an' then Stumpy'll go to the Reeve an' tell it to him. When he hears it, he'll change his mind."

Hazel and Stumpy had urged Lily to do the talking when they went to Dowling's house but she adamantly refused. "I can't talk fancy," she said, and held her ground. The notes outlining the story were tucked into Stumpy's coat pocket. The story was one that Tom had told to Lily during the first winter of their marriage as the hearth-fire blazed and her lover did all things possible to make her laugh and see the world through his eyes. Like all of Tom's anecdotes, she recalled this one word for word, detail for detail. The north-east wind blew a dusty snow in their faces as they trooped up Victoria Street that Tuesday morning: Stumpy ahead with his sailor's amble, followed by Hazel in her best hat, Maggie Shawyer, Honeyman Belcher and Lily. Dowling must have spied them before his maid did because he was on his verandah just as they wheeled through the gap in the hedge, a white silk scarf tossed about his exposed throat.

"I've heard the last petition from you gang of rascals that I intend to hear," he shouted against the wind. "Take your causes henceforth to the council and its official meetings. Be off before I call a constable!" This latter remark was flung into the ear of Honeyman Belcher as his two-hundred-pound bulk brushed Dowling aside and barged through the front door. The others followed, and by the time they had removed their galoshes and coats in the vestibule, the shivering Reeve had decided to join them.

"Five minutes," he snapped with his back to them, warming his hands by the fire and absorbing most of its welcome. "Then it's the constable."

"This won't take five minutes," Stumpy said. "We come to ask you to change your mind about namin' Potts' Lane."

"Don't call it that!" he roared. "It'll never have a name like that as long as I'm reeve of this town. You're wasting your breath. Go home to your seedy little hovels. At least you *own* them, thanks to me."

Stumpy didn't reply. He pulled two sheets of paper out of his pocket, and when Dowling's curiosity was piqued, he said to him, "I brought along a story to help you change your mind."

A flicker of fear or animal wariness passed across Dowling's face but was quickly erased by a belligerent ruffling of feathers. "What in hell are you talking about?"

His hands shaking, Stumpy started to recite the story as best he could from memory and the blurred notes. The gist of it was this: nineteen years ago this month the Great Western Railway held a gala ball in the armouries at London and at that ball the well-known and beautiful wife of the railroad's vice-president was seen to dance more than once with a handsome, young, dark-haired gentleman, also an officer of that company. The lady returned to the watch of her husband as the dancing ended, but several hours later she was observed, poorly disguised in a coachman's cape, entering a nearby hotel and without a by-your-leave slipping up to the second floor and sailing into a gentleman's room without a knock. At six in the morning she was spotted by a drayman skipping down the alley behind the hotel.

From the first mention of the month and year Dowling dropped his bully's stance and started to listen. By the time Stumpy had finished, Dowling's face was an impassive mask, closed to all secrets. He looked past Stumpy and speared each of the others with a questing glance, but found nothing he needed to know. Vaguely he recognized several of the faces or figures but could attach no certain name to them, make no connection between the narrative and this crew of outcasts.

"A droll story, I'm sure," he said at last. "And a nasty one as well. Good enough to smear the reputations of a dozen honest men."

Stumpy's jaw dropped, and he heard the sag of confidence behind him. Desperately he wanted to turn to Lily. He was both shocked and relieved to hear Hazel's voice, clear and cold.

"London House, October 31, 1859, room 218, the lady's name reminds one of a flower, her husband was –"

Dowling stared incredulously at Hazel when he cut her off. "That's enough."

"What you did back then ain't none of our concern," Hazel said, "and won't ever be anybody else's. We only come to ask you for what we think's fair."

The Reeve-elect smiled at her as if she were Dame Justice herself and he a lifelong servant of the helpless blind. "Just so," he said.

On January 1, 1879 Point Edward was officially incorporated as a village, and without fanfare or the world's notice quietly gave birth to itself.

2

The first act of the duly inaugurated village council was to pass a resolution declaring the third Saturday of that month "Point Edward Day", a motion that was declared unanimous (until the principal form of celebration turned out to be a dance, at which juncture there was a Methodist retraction). The second motion, as Lily had predicted, was passed with much grumbling dissent but no audible *nays*: the extended street facing the River along its whole meandering length was officially denominated "Potts' Lane". Even the Prince might have approved, Lily thought.

The dance was held in the newly-constructed Oddfellows' Hall, an imperial edifice of brick and mortar and mitred glass which stood at the edge of the sprawling marsh below and beyond – as solid and respectable as a redoubt or a medieval keep. Inside, though, it had been transformed into a miniature, temporary Camelot. Against the starred January dark that stiffened the myriad mercurial panes, crystal light splashed from chandeliers or blazed defiance from ceremonial rushes clamped to the north wall. That afternoon a soft snow had fallen briefly, blessedly, and then the skies had been brushed clear of configuring cloud by some moon-impelled wind just in time for evening's ascension. Anyone gazing down from that perspective would have seen a village unmarked by tread or traffic of any kind, as if its streets and alleys and byways had just been reinvented for the occasion. By seven o'clock, though, there was not a path or passage of any sort which did not bear the imprint of some one of its citizens – and not one of these pointed anywhere but towards the momentary heart of the village itself, and its communal, celebratory beat.

The band was makeshift – two fiddles, a squeeze-box, a battered army bugle and matching drum, a lone asthmatic harmonica, undermined by assorted, improvised percussives – but it was of local genesis and propelled by an imperturbable optimism. Unfettered by sheet-music or conductor's baton, it poured out the latest waltz from old Vienna, the jazziest lancers from the Buckingham Guard, the airiest jib from Londonderry. At first the Alleyfolk – awed by the garish ostentation of cutaway coat and puffed silk, and ever chary of releasing even the smallest atom of their secret selves to public scrutiny – huddled in clumps under the fiery rushes along the windowless wall. Not one of them, despite the heat and press and sweat, inched towards the crystal bowl beneath the main arch where Reeve Dowling's personal tangerine punch winked and rippled its welcome (though Baptiste Cartier was observed passing an unobtrusive jug of white vinegar from hand to hand among the most reticent of the Alleymen). Then, without warning, during one of the intermittent reels, the druggist's son crooked an errant arm into the waiting loop of Miss Shawyer's elbow and swept her out of her flock and out of the Alley and into the ages-old anonymity of the reel itself. If it was a signal, it worked. If not, it worked anyway. As the fiddles sizzled and sang their ancient solipsisms, one by two and two by three the choruses in the wings of the great hall emptied into its epicentre of sets and squares, where – enthused by a music bereft of word and sign and the tautology of time – they convened, divorced, colloquied, parted forever, resumed at once, met and kissed goodbye, remembered and forgot their names: Shawyer with Redmond, McCourt with Durham, burgher with ragpicker – and only the character of the sexes (and of course the jig-tune itself) remained constant and preserved and happily at odds.

Lily stood alone at the open door. Behind her: the music and the fragmentary revels. She peered west towards the Evening Star, just risen; towards the River, iced tight, its winter's-long scream cached and pulsing blackfathoms beneath all hearing; towards the ragamuffin boys skating out some ritual game on the frozen pond a few rods below her. She listened to the crisp snub of their blades against any resistance, the boasts and yelps and elbowing affection of their careless buffoonery; and she knew that Rob and Brad somehow were among them, or of them, Brad, most likely, crouched in a moon's halo and watching, weighing, reading the shadows and the shapes under them; and Rob, inevitably, buffering headfirst into whatever shoulder offered its challenge, and whooping, with the others, the last and the loudest of their boyhood salvoes.

What would become of them, fatherless as they were? And now growing more out of their own stock than out of hers. And out of this place, too. That was something, there was something here that could not be got round. And we've made it better, Sophie, she whispered into the pure dark ahead of her. We made it more real, anyways. *You* did. But how can we believe in it now that you've left us? It seems like just as soon as I get to know something, it goes and dies on me.

Strange, but just before she had decided – for Sophie's sake – that she ought to come here, Lily had surprised herself by digging out Sounder's pouch where it had lain, dust-covered, for the longest time. Had she given up entirely on the aboriginal promise of magic in this world? Trembling, she'd drawn open the leather sachet and one by one fingered the contents: Mama's crucifix with its forlorn sheen under the muted winterlight; Papa's Testament still unread and the Lady Fairchild of its inscription having long ago relinquished her titles; the cameo pendant with the ivory profile someone said might have been a grandmother undiminished by seas or eons; and Southener's jasper amulet – magic's own heart-chamber once – where no echo now embered anywhere. For a second she had wanted to weep, girlishly, not at her irreconcilable loss but at the absence of feeling itself. Just then Rob had called from the lane, "C'mon Ma, everybody's leavin'!" She put the pouch aside, and flung her scarf resolutely about her throat. The Alleyfolk cheered as the nightchill struck the warmth of her greeting.

Lily laughed, then glanced around to make sure none of the buskers had seen her smiling through the tears congealed on her cheeks. She was remembering something Sophie had said only a few months ago. Hazel had asked her if she was interested in having her picture taken by one of those daguerreotype men who came around to the Heaven every once in a while. "Christ, no," Sophie snapped. "I don't need no picture of myself to be remembered by. Who'd ever forget *this* shape once they laid their unsuspectin' eyeballs on it? Stoke calls me the pink poppy with the purple dropsy, an' he ain't far afield on that one!"

The skaters had started a bonfire near the rink. Its avid orange flame tongued the black penumbras above it. It twisted and grew fabulous as she watched, unleafing its fragile intensities in scrolls ever widening, brightening, taunting the very edges of expiry. Lily shuddered, blood-deep in her being. I am still here, she thought. I don't know why and I never have. I am carried along by urges I can feel but not describe, not even to myself. Perhaps they were the same urgencies sweeping these dancers into the music and the moment. Perhaps not. Hers might be her own, after all.

Yet how indifferent the world's imperatives must be to have passed by so many with barely a sideways glance, their primal promptings seemingly devoid of pity or humanity or even acknowledgement. How little comfort they had been to Solomon in his sea-coffin, to Maman and Mama in their frozen loneliness, to Aunt Bridie or

Uncle Chester or Papa in their grave-grounds as alien as the moonscape above her now. How much time, even, had she herself been given to mourn her lover, wild and brave and cold as the snows that held his faithfulness forever from the true earth? Who had decided then that she should go on? And how often had she yearned to hear the voices of the good, dear gods – the ones Old Samuels had promised her if she could only find the shaman's ground they worshipped from in the midst of their fear and helplessness. They would surely have something to say to her, here, now, not an arrow's toss from the hallowed mounds where he and Southener lay in perpetual something-or-other.

I am here. And Sophie is already become another of those I can weep for only because they are absent. Not so. Not true. The dead drive us forward, onward, headlong towards the dark heart of what haunts them. They ache in their knowing.

Without realizing it Lily had drifted back into the quick heat of the ballroom. She felt the blush of it across the nape of her neck, and instinctively removed her coat. Something whisked it away to her right. Her scarf unwound itself and slithered off. She registered only mild puzzlement. The music rose up to meet her sudden attention. It filled her ears like harp's-wind through a seashell, its echoes celestially infinitesimal.

"It's a waltz. Would you like to dance?"

"Yes. I think so."

A muscled hand, her own gently crushed within it.

"A tad off-key, but our own, eh?"

Eager, masculine voice. Accustomed to command?

She must have told him her name, for it graced his lips as often as he dare allow between the suave stint-and-glide of the waltz they were now so evidently engaged in. Then she did hear her own voice, witty and demure and only-just-withholding. Then the music took them both into the sweet morphia of its all-encompassment, and she felt her body detach itself from something ugly and abiding, and swing free, at last, of its own longing.

Who cared that such music was a prisoning bliss? And not once did she deign to glance down at her partner to confirm what she already knew: that it was Tom on that miraculous night of the Great Western Ball, that it was Ti-Jean tender in the breathless music of their cabin, that it was her husky sculler with arms like oars under the pavilion's perfect light. She was, after all, here. She was alive. She was Lily. She was dancing.

BOOK TWO

Shaman's Ground

PART ONE

Granny

32

1

Granny Coote was dreaming she was awake again. The sun's velvet buzz on her eyelids was almost real, the memory of its insistence sweet and bitter over the decades – but she wouldn't be fooled again. No fool like an old one, she thought, especially one who has learned so little for the effort spent. More and more she was having trouble keeping her dreams and her reveries apart. Yesterday afternoon, for instance, she had sat down at the kitchen table with the fresh tomatoes left for her by the well-meaning Mrs. Buchan, and was about to slice the ripest one with a shaky right hand when the room went dark. She was positive she had not closed her eyes, had not fallen asleep, but the sun had gone down without notice, it seemed, and the tomato lay neatly carved on the breadboard in those little wedges she had been fashioning for more than seventy years. The knife was still in her hand. Arthur and Eddie had been visiting again: Arthur at the piano, Eddie tapping his toes and letting the juice from the tomatoes squirt down his chin, while his blue eyes – replica of his father's – never left his Granny: teasing, tempting, full of the wondering beneficence of the happy child. "Eat your supper, then sing," she had told him, as always. "He's singing for his supper!" Arthur called from his dais, and broke into a verse from 'A Wandering Minstrel' just to annoy her. "Let the boy finish his supper, you old coot!", but both the boy and the baritone broke into unchastened laughter. "He's just teasing, Granny," Eddie said. And she wanted to reach across the table and hug him with her bony arms. Arthur was wailing out his parody of Katashaw's song, his grin as sun-lit as the meadows of Titi-pu.

But of course there was no music here; there had been none since Eddie went away so many years ago. And Arthur, bless him, slept near his wife in the village cemetery beyond First Bush. So she had continued her meal as if she had not lost three hours somewhere, glad to sit in the dark where it didn't matter if she were asleep or not. Still, it worried her, this lapsing, this forgetting in the middle of an action – cutting flowers, mending the old chesterfield Arthur loved so much, where they had made their last, startling love, and where Arthur had closed his eyes so she wouldn't see his treachery as his hand stiffened forever in hers. And she would wake suddenly to find herself away off in the sunflowers or squatting foolishly beside the hedge that kept the street at bay. So this is what it is to be senile, she thought; I already know what it is to be old, I've had lots of practice chewing on my gums and getting out of bed piecemeal with every joint cracking like a rusted block-and-tackle. But this. This is trouble. They'll finally have an excuse to put me out of this place, and lord knows they've been looking for one ever since Arthur died and that thing happened with Eddie and the Ladies Auxiliary suggested a 'good home' in the city she had spent her life fighting. But then the tragedy of 'eighteen had struck like the foul afterbreath of the Great War itself, and she had given them something else to think about.

I'm not senile, she thought, refusing to open her eyes, to acknowledge the supremacy of the dream and the incursions of the night-world. I may be a bit 'barmy' as the Alleyfolk used to say, but then I have cause, we all have cause. When that thing happened to her throat after the news came, she had been unable to tell them it was all right, that she understood exactly why and how it had happened, had had to be. She saw her neighbours turn away, their fright a reflection of her own, the same stunned stare she had already seen in the eyes of the bereft – the widows, mothers, betrothed – most of whom had lost a loved one and a god also. They, too, were speechless in their dumbfounding.

The rattle of pebbles across the glass of the front window confirmed it: she was asleep and about to awake. Her eyes opened to the richness of mid-morning August, 1921. She was, she noted ruefully, fully clothed; her flower-print housedress was soaked with sweat and wrinkled beyond redemption. They'd love to come in and catch me like this, she thought, easing her brittle body off the cot – still slim but no longer muscled, her breasts about as lively as a couple of fallen cupcakes ("The trouble with old age," Sophie used to say, "is your arse gets too tight an' your cunny too loose"). Granny got seated upright, steadied herself on the edge of the cot for a moment, then let the sun pour across her bare feet from the vivifying east. As the circulation pushed fretfully through her warming bones, she felt the rheumatic ache subside to its daytime level. She flexed her legs and stood up. The blood rushed back to her head and she grabbed the dressing table just in time.

Stupid old woman, she muttered to herself. Mrs. Buchan'd love to come in here the saft and find me sprawled on the rug with a broken hip and lolling like a mute. It would be Sunset Glades for sure. The village'd be rid of the last of its eyesores, and the council would get its house back and the urchins'd have to go all the way to Potts' Lane for their amusement.

She felt fine now, just a touch woozy, most likely because she had merely fantasized having supper as the wincing of her stomach reminded her. She glanced about the single room that had been her home for five years, ever since she had shut up the last of the two little bedrooms Arthur had added to the far side of the place – Coote's shack as it was known in the village. However, it was a large enough room with the kitchen area facing the south sun and the parlour with its spacious east window and two 'port-holes' in the north wall over Arthur's piano with his music sheets still opened upon it. The rug was bleached erratically by the sun and stained where the roof had leaked before the Reeve had come over to fix it for her.

Yes, her supper – vegetables from her garden (and Mrs. Buchan's) and some lumpish bread she'd made one cool morning in the oven of the stove she'd picked up from the Lane, and Eddie had squealed with delight when old Badger Coombs had let him take the reins for a while, and pouted all afternoon till she baked him his red-currant tarts. Her blood was flowing again, her muscles loosened in the warmth of the room, the rheumatism in temporary retreat. Granny felt strong enough to face the day – whichever one it was – as surprised as ever at the resilience of her body's flesh and nerve, the unwilled potency that gathered its wits each night and surged forth to greet each anonymous morning. In spring, summer and fall there was the garden to occupy her body's self-renewing restlessness, the passage of people before her parlour window, the cries of children from the fields and swamps below her yard, the bleat and harrumphing of lake-steamers half-a-mile away on the St. Clair, the clatter of the city-line streetcar on Michigan Ave., and the periodic fart of Gassy Peter's flivver jostling with the gravelled lanes of the village. She needed all of them: she had not left her property – except for the epidemic – since that black day in September.

It was the winter that frightened her most: the stark stretches of space between house and trees; the icy desert of ragged swamp all the way down to the St. Clair and the distant snow-shrouded freight-sheds; the river's tongue stiffened blue, vacant of vessel or human save for the odd dot of a fisherman expunged by the slightest drift of wind. Birds fled or vowed silence. The children emerged occasionally, as from cocoons, to test the air or the ice, and on Sunday afternoons their cheers and angel-gliding over the improvised rinks of the marsh saved her from whatever form of darkness that was threatening the domestic and habitable variety she had known and coped with for over eighty years. Though her ancient bones invariably found some fresh and independent source for hope, she was not sure she could survive another winter. Why don't you just pack it in, she often said to her complaining flesh. After all I've given you a good run; there's nothing you haven't tried or survived; no muscle, no gland has gone unflexed or untitillated; no appetite untempted or unappeased. I'm as sick and tired of your whining as you are of mine. I'm ready. I've been ready for a long time. What sort of bribe will you consider? Think about it, because I'm about to embarrass us both.

She remembered the clatter of stones that had just roused her. She went to the only door, on the south side near the sink, and pushed on the sagging screen. On the plank stoop sat a glass bowl covered by a dish-cloth. Granny reached down and lifted it up. Inside the kitchen again, she removed the cover and saw half-a-dozen sweetcakes and a small loaf of raisin-bread, the signature of the handiwork of Leila Savage across the street. She went to the front window and peered about for any sign of the Savage twins or the McCourt bullies who often led them by the nose. The roadway was deserted: the men were all off to work in the City, the wives toiling in the back kitchens or leftover victory gardens, the liberated children at the beach or roaming the dunes and bushland with the eyes of aborigines. Over on the main street, she knew, the post office and mar-

ket provided a hub of activity for the women to shop, gossip and exchange complaints
– for those who could still talk.

There you go again, old woman, she thought, feeling sorry for yourself. It does you
no good and you know it. Believe me, nobody's listening.

The McCourt cousins – five of them from three strands of the same freckled stock
– spent much of their time, it seemed, mimicking their elders by plotting ambushes
against the offspring of the village's half-dozen Catholic families, picking fights at random or on principle to keep their prejudices tuned, and generally misleading the susceptible youth of the Point. When things were particularly quiet or unpromising on
a summer's night, they would skulk into Granny's garden from the marsh and, under
cover of the shrubs and a beclouded moon, would begin their low, repeated, increasingly cantatory verses:

> Granny Coote *is* a witch
> Granny Coote *is* a bitch
> Granny Coote hitched a
> Ride on a broomstick…

(pause, then chorically:)

and the broom bit back!

This latter retort was unfailingly followed by disintegrating laughter before the
charm was again wound up in the moon-filtered dark. What they were hoping for,
naturally, was that the witch herself should materialize, shaking with righteous anger
to the point where she would start to rail at them and they would hear – as they had
only once before – the unalloyed, chilling, magic-babble of wizardry itself. Then could
they scatter in gleeful terror to the four winds awaiting them. Once last summer, from
her gladioli beds in the front yard, she had heard two little girls a block away skipping
rope and chanting as if the words had no meaning beyond the dance of innocence they
accompanied:

> Granny Coote has no teeth
> Granny Coote eats roast beef
> with her
>
> > *gum gums!*

> Granny Coote has no toes
> Granny Coote counts by twos
> on her
>
> > *bum bum!*

She heard the rope accelerate at the end, and pictured the wild fandango of the elfin feet. She too had danced to that irreverent beat, once, when the lily of her name had hung like a bell in her child's heart.

Lately the McCourts and occasional camp-followers like the Savage twins had become bolder. They would appear behind the house at dusk – taunting, daring the village with the sounds of their illicit boy-bravery. Still, the victim did not appear. But one evening last week after a particularly callous variation of their rhyme, the side-door swung open and into the twilight floated a caped figure, its legless silhouette seemingly welded to a large whisker-broom, its arms extended more like wings set to try the wind over the hushed garden. The shadows seemed to hide all trace of human visage except for the yellow pricks of eyes and the toothless hollow of a mouth – beef-blooded in hue and emitting a shrill thread of sound like a scream being squeezed to death. The Savage twins were trampled by the precipitate retreat of the Ulster vigilantes.

Back inside the house Granny Coote shook with laughter and after-shock, amazed that she had once again taken up the cudgel, so to speak, having hauled the cape, mask and whistle out of Arthur's ancient theatrical trunk in order to lie in wait for the pranksters as she had so many times in her eighty-odd years of being on the wrong side of respectability and suffering the consequences, or abetting them. "You chose to be an outsider," Cap had said to her accusingly, and she had shot back: "None of us chooses anything except the form of our reprisals." How she could talk then. As the thumping of the routed platoon through the bushes near the march reached her ears, Granny removed the mask and smiled to herself: this one is for you, Arthur, who showed me the gentle half of men's dominion, who gave me a name and a house to carry me through these final years more to be endured than understood. But then, when had she understood anything even in the midst of love, of commitment to those whose youth or vulnerability bound her to a future she never really believed in. Anyway, sweet Arthur, I shall wear your name, surrogate though it may be, till they chisel it on the granite beside yours.

2

After nibbling at one of Leila Savage's cakes – a touch too much vanilla in the over-beaten batter – Granny Coote went into her garden as she had done for seventy-odd summers without fail. It was, as she herself termed it, a little-old-lady's vanity patch. Showy English-style perennials on the perimeter, a neat elevated vegetable section in the middle, divided off by Grand Trunk ties Arthur had brought here when the railway left and the town went bust. Arthur's wife's hands had been bred to coddle a bassoon not a hoe-handle, so it was with some relish that Granny had undertaken the familiar task of resurrecting a moribund garden. Arthur had been pleased, amazed even as cityfolk often are before the vigour and dexterity of country labours. Of course, it was vanity now, pure and simple. She could not eat a quarter of what bulged and fletched here in the summer heat, nor could she give much away to the thrifty, war-wary householders with well-stocked victory gardens of their own. Once a week or so, young Wilf

Underhill would stop by to collect several packets of peppers or carrots to take down to the destitute beyond Potts' Lane. He had not forgotten her 'service' during the terrible fall of 'eighteen, and shy though he was, he often sat and had a cup of tea with her, content to let the silence ferry its own meaning back and forth between them, occasionally telling her a bit about his life in the Old Country because he could see from the shifting light in her eyes that she enjoyed his company. And now that their baby boy had arrived, there was more joy to share. At times like that she was not unhappy about what had happened to her throat because she would not have to tell him what anguish the world might yet bring to those who dared poach on its prerogatives.

Still, the flowers and shrubs were beautiful; they gave pleasure to the eye and to the village heart shaken by doubt. With every root that delved thumbs-down into this patch of ground and with every corona of colour that took majestic possession of this air, Granny felt she was establishing her right to belong. The council wanted this land back as vacant as the lot they had conceded in their haste to Arthur and his bride. They would not get it. It was never theirs, she thought. It is only mine in trust.

She was hoeing the cauliflower, the instrument perfectly tuned to her intricate gymnastic – learned and repeated and refined and remembered deeply. No thought was required. She could close her eyes after 'sighting' down a row and carry on blindly without missing a plantain or chokeweed. These motions evoked neither pleasure nor pain, satisfaction nor ennui. They were as effortless as breathing, and as necessary.

Granny stopped to enjoy the shade of the only tree left on her lot by the Grand Trunk choppers seventy years ago. It soared defiantly above the marsh below it and the neighbouring houses with their pathetic, prearranged maples. Don't boast, Granny whispered to it, you're here because you're lucky not invincible. She waved to Ethel Carpenter working in her tomatoes, recalling their former intimacies, their shared tragedies and the desperate confusion on that good woman's face when Granny's mouth contorted helplessly and the air was chilled by its alien vowel. Now she just waved, exchanging remembrances.

Granny heard the child's step in the hedge before she saw Flora, Ethel's six-year-old, emerge – tiptoed, head tilted to dart away – into the dazzling light. Elfin, blond, the blue eyes star-fed, she edged into the yard, then stopped. One eye was on the old, old woman rigid under the hickory tree, the other on the harlequinade of iceland poppies at her feet.

Granny felt a rush of emotion, a surge of recognition, but she made not the slightest move. Slowly without stepping towards the child, she indicated in pantomime that Flora should go ahead and pick the flowers her fancy had claimed. The meaning was instantly comprehended. The girl's quick fingers one-by-one gathered in a fragile bouquet. She took one step towards the old woman, hesitated, saw what she hoped for, and came right up to her with a sidling skip-and-shuffle. The shade encompassed them. A breeze tufted the girl's hair, the poppies a-flutter, swept the aged hand upward to accept the gift offered.

Bless you, she said with her eyes, and the girl smiled a shy acknowledgement.

"Can I bring you some cheese, Granny? My uncle brung some in from the farm."

Granny Coote felt the words of response shape themselves in her lower throat, the consonants coil and stretch across the rampant vowels, the inchoate syllables contenting towards articulation rise noisily up the hollow nave to the threshing, trapped tongue gonging madly in its belfry. The consonants froze in their chambers while the vowels twisted and howled in anguished release. The shock of them against the open air stunned even her own ears. She reeled backwards and fell. The child's cry was soundless but complete. Her fleeing form was swallowed by the hedge. In Granny's fist the poppies shed a garish blood.

Bless you anyway, child, she was thinking. Bless you for being. I held you in my arms days after your birth, I held the wasted body of your dying brother in these hands and tried to invent some comfort for his mother. These hands that have pulled many a ruby-skinned pollywog kicking and squalling into this world, such as it is. And to what end? In hopes that one or two of my own would live to soften my dying? Well, where are they? Only a neighbour's child to bring me in her innocence a bouquet of flowers, a nosegay for the old girl – may she soon pop off and leave us in peace.

Granny opened her eyes. The sun had burned her arm right through its leathery tan. When she rolled sideways to see how far the sun had moved, she was jolted by a pain in her right leg. A scab was already congealing on her elbow. How long have I been here? Panic stabbed at her more sharply than her bruised thigh. She touched the dried tears on her cheek. My lord, have I been bawling and jabbering out here all afternoon? They'll be coming to get me, just like they tried that time with old Malloney. She started to get up but the grass swayed and she hung on, closing her eyes to let her breath catch up with her heart.

When she opened them – feeling once again the regular, sturdy beat of her pulse – it was almost dark. She was very cold, but the ache in her leg was gone and she was able to totter to her feet. No broken bones anyway, she thought, you stupid old woman, letting yourself forget that thing in your throat, scaring little Flora half to death, then falling down and snivelling your way through the afternoon, almost breaking a hip and an arm in the process. "Get your arse in harness and giddyup!" Sophie always said when things looked bleakest.

Monitoring each step, Granny walked through the hazy twilight towards Arthur's house. At the corner of the front hedge she spotted Flora, her nimbus of golden hair still ablaze in the fading light. A pale face like a moon's satellite peered out of the shadowed honeysuckle, aiming its amber invitation unequivocally in her direction. She stopped breathing. The figure was fully into view now; it was not Flora. The hair was too native, too radiant; the dress simple and unadorned; the posture questioning, braced against something only half-comprehended.

It was *her*. There was no doubt. She had seen the face, the stance, the elemental flame of the hair too many times not to know it. She had dreamt this very scene, this tableau of Madonna and lost child, many times over.

Suddenly the child's eyes materialized in the otherwise blank face: *save me, save me* they cried for the village, the county, the country to hear. Granny heard her own feet hitting the earth, her heart ricocheting in its prison, her breath catch against her gums. She was running towards the little lost girl, the figure that had beckoned to her just so in a dream they had shared for decades. The name of the child fought at the torque of her tongue, gained her lips, the night-air, the ears of the mother uttering it aloud to make it real.

Granny hit the crushed stone with both knees – snapping her body forward onto her splayed palms and whiplashing forehead, and silencing for the moment the tremor of her hyena-howl which those who heard it afterwards declared to be as much the laughter of the mad as the grief of the inconsolable.

"It's a miracle there's nothin' broken."

I'm all right, I'm all right: she was trying to make the words with her lips, fighting the treachery of tears and trying to get up.

"Don't worry, Cora," the voice soothed. "It's me, Bob Denfield. I'll take care of you."

Yes, Cora thought, the Reeve is a man of his word. Like Arthur.

But my name is Lily, she remembered thinking absurdly – just before the blackness struck again. At least it was, once.

33

It was a January without thaws, that first month of 1922 in the village between the Lake and the River. The snows were Russian-deep and full of forgetting. In their beauteous violence, their Arctic grip and their long quiescence, the memories of Ypes, Passchendaele and the Somme were permitted a momentary absence. The streetcar from the City squealed on its icy rails, the smoke from the war-inspired foundry billowed and froze, the lonesome switching-engine shunted a desultory box-car or two beside the freight-sheds, the pickerel beneath the ice dreamt of fingerlings and white sun. In the meantime, notwithstanding the vagaries of season, commerce or *réalpolitik*, the public business of a municipality must proceed.

The council meetings were held twice a month on Thursdays in the small room that housed the library. Below it lay the four jail cells normally unoccupied till the weekend. Next door sat the newly purchased scarlet fire-engine, close to its crew. If ever there should have been a fire on a Thursday evening during an odd week of any month, the council chamber would have been instantly cleared – to a man. When special meetings of wider public interest were held, as they often had been during the Great War and its dreadful aftermath, the tiny library was given over in favour of the more spacious Oddfellows' Hall next to the old Coote shack. In the opinion of the Reeve, looking at the agenda for this January evening of 1922, the time was fast approaching when such a 'town-meeting', as their Yankee neighbours termed it, would have to be called. Tonight, for the time being, the library-cum-jail would suffice.

As usual, Reeve Denfield was there early, with his recording secretary, the younger of the Misses Robertson, staunchly beside him. She had just finished writing the agenda items on the portable slate blackboard behind the square table (composed of several reading tables conjoined for the occasion). They read:

1. Reclamation of the Coote property
2. Report of the Cenotaph Finance Committee
3. Setting up a Cenotaph Search Committee
   a. Site

b. Designer, builder.

As the younger Miss Robertson finished up with a schoolteacher's flourish, she flashed a hopeful smile at Reeve Denfield. It went unacknowledged, however; the Reeve was deep in a brown study.

"No one is more sensitive than I," Councillor Stokes was proclaiming from his pulpit, "as a minister of the Church of England and servant among you now for these eighteen years, to the plight of this wretched woman. It would take a heart of stone not to bleed with pity at the thought of her living out her last days in utter squalor and loneliness. Our Lord said 'blessed are the poor in spirit for theirs is the Kingdom of Heaven', but shall we stand idly by while Mrs. Coote suffers in her long wait for that Light to shine at last upon her? I appeal to your conscience as Christians," and he gestured dramatically to the far pews.

What did he know about her long wait? thought the Reeve. About the poor in spirit? He, too, wanted her out of sight and out of mind, tucked away safely in a cubicle in an old people's home, condemned to slience. Unconsciously he fingered the smooth, pink scald that was the left side of his face. Behind him he felt the whisper of snow against the window like the breath of a child.

Councillor Garnet Fielding – "Choppy" to his cohorts – was on the counter-atttack, barking orders against the odds to his shell-shocked gunnery. "I mean no disrespect to the cloth when I say we've got no right to treat the widows and homeguard who stood by us so well during the darkest days of the War in such a manner. I was born in this village more than forty years ago, and I was raised to respect, to revere, my elders. This woman who you youngsters and Johnny-come-latelys call Granny Coote has been a citizen of the Point for most of her life. I recall my parents talking about her heroic actions in the 'seventies, and everyone in this room knows what she did for us during the terrible autumn of 'eighteen." Choppy was surprising everyone, even himself, for he was a laconic man despite his high school education and his sergeant's stripes, his clerk's job in the City and the Distinguished Service Medal riveted over his heart. Moreover, his speech was somewhat impeded by the prosthesis which formed the major part of his jaw. "Took my breath an' half my chin away," he always said in recounting the explosion that had kept him out of action for several months.

"Some citizen!" huffed Councillor Harold Hitchcock – 'Half-Hitch' to his wife and other detractors. "Thirty years an Alleywoman before old man Coote went senile an' rescued her." He waved his gloved, wooden hand like a pointer and accepted Miss Robertson's nod.

"Would you like the floor, Hitch?" the Reeve said icily.

"Everyone in this room's been through the hell of war," Half-Hitch informed the multitude, brandishing as he did so a legal-looking document proudly tweezered between his mechanical thumb and forefinger. "Except one," he added, looking purposefully away from young Horrie MacIntosh who somehow – lacking credentials, battle-experience, and years – had got himself elected to council at the troublesome age of twenty-four. "We can't be accused of callousness, we've suffered to much, we've lost too much," he cried through his oscillating glove. "But the facts're clear; so is our duty. Accordin' to this record in my hand, the village council granted Arthur Coote back in 1888 a lease on the village lot number 82 at one dollar a year for as long as he remain organist of the Methodist Church and thereafter if he retire in good standing unto his death." He had spent hours memorizing the heady lingo of the document and found the words in actual presentation happily satisfying, even appropriate. "My point here is this: we've let this woman stay illegally on municipal land for ten years. We've shown mercy and pity for the wretched soul. But enough is enough. Her contributions to the community are well known. But everyone here knows what an eyesore that shack's turned into. All of us know the stories of how Granny Coote has scared the sam hell out of children an' babies with her crazy babble. An' last fall you all know she was ridin' on a broom in her back yard. How much more can we take?"

"Hitch is right," said Lorne 'Sandy' Redmond, the elderly grocer, rousing himself at last in his chair, the thunder of the Boer guns receding, the sting of their smoke sharpened by the jabber of Dutch tongues. "Olive's asked me to remind the council that the City car goes right by that shanty every hour. She says she can't hardly go to a WCTU meetin' down there without some gossip or other comin' up about Granny Coote. How can those of use who're older," and here he fixed the victims of his jab, "forget she was a shantywoman, a crony of bootleggers and" – he glanced at the younger Miss Robertson "– scarlet women, an' she was a boozer and a heathen to boot." He stopped lest the effect be overwhelming. Murmurs of assent suffused the room.

"I am prepared," said the Reverend Stokes, "to suggest that a public collection be taken up for the perpetual support of this ancient citizen who, though she has fallen on sad times, seems worthy of our forgiveness and charity."

And we could cast a bronze medal for her, the Reeve mused, to hang in her miserable vestibule at Sunset Glades.

More enthusiastic yeah-saying followed. Young MacIntosh had not yet spoken. It was three for and one against, so far. Sunny Denfield's views were well known. If Horrie were to follow his own feelings, the best that could be achieved was a tie. Grant Griffiths, the sixth Councillor, was down at the 'hospital' in London being treated for recurring shell shock, and wouldn't be back till God-knew-when. Still, he held back.

"An' what's your opinion, Horrie?" said the Reeve.

Reeve Denfield was on his feet. "The legal aspect of the matter's clear," he said very quietly, a pulsing glow in the garish pink of his war wound. "The lease to Arthur Coote, accordin' to our lawyer in the City, was to last until his death, and if his wife was still livin', she was to be allowed to buy the property at market value. When Arthur died, nobody gave a damn about another vacant lot. Nothin' was done. Till now."

He paused and stared out at the falling snow as if counting the individual flakes in the general mass curling over the sill. Then into the shuffle of embarrassment, he said as if he were confiding to an intimate in a small room: "So we haven't any case, one way or the other. But I'd like to say to you, my friends and fellow soldiers, that I see a strong link between this discussion and items two an' three on the agenda. The buildin' of the cenotaph, the monument to our dead in the War, is the most important thing we've ever done as a village. In 1914 we had fifteen hundred souls livin' here, just over three hundred families. Two hundred an' fifty boys an' men went off to France in 1915 – almost one per family. Almost a hundred of them were casualties, almost half of 'em maimed or dead. I've got the two lists here. Most of you could read the names off by heart. We fought for different reasons, I guess, but all of us were proud to be from the Point. In the past we survived the greed an' the treachery of the railway; we fought off the City politicians an' big-wigs who've been tryin' to get this town for forty years. When I came here from the biggest city in 1901, I was eighteen years old. I saw the vacant lots where the houses had been pulled up by the roots an' carted off. It was a ghost town. We built it all back up board by board. An' the War tried to do us in again, killin' an' maimin' the best of our men. We owe them a monument."

The councillors sat stunned, as shocked as they might have been when the words of a dull sermon suddenly jelled into meaning.

"So what are we doin'? We're sitting around this table jawin' away about takin' a harmless old lady – our most senior citizen who's fought as hard as any of us to keep the political chisellers and city-types out of here – we're actually thinkin' of pullin' her out of the house she's lived in for twenty years an' dumpin' her in a poorhouse run by the riff-raff of Sarnia. We're behavin' here just like the people we've despised an' battled against all our lives. Don't you see the connection?"

If they didn't, none of the municipal legislators was prepared to admit it in this most public of forums. Young MacIntosh wished he had followed his heart. Occasionally it paid off.

The remainder of the meeting now progressed smoothly. With luck, the third period of the hockey match would not be out of reach. When the younger Miss Robertson opened the door to let the starch out of the steam-heat, the councillors could hear the drum of wood on wood and the choric encouragement of the village crowd, could visualize with ease the violent ballet, and hear the music of silence under it.

First, the members fell over one another suggesting ways in which the unfortunate Mrs. Coote could be aided in her final days. It was agreed unanimously that someone should approach her to explain her legal position *vis à vis* the property and assure her that no precipitate action would be taken. Reeve Denfield volunteered, but the Reverend Stokes respectfully pointed out that as a longtime friend and semi-regular visitor to the shack – house – the Reeve might be perceived by the befuddled old soul to be a biased report, when what was emphatically needed was someone official of sufficient probity and evident neutrality who would be seen by Mrs. Coote to represent the will of the council and the village. While the Reeve failed to see the logic of this sophistry, he reluctantly agreed. When the council promptly nominated the good Anglican pastor for the task, however, he revealed his profound humility by refusing the proffered honour and suggesting that in his place go the Reverend Buchan whose Methodism and common touch were ideally suited to the delicacy of the venture. Moreover, he himself would speak personally to that man-of-God on the morrow. The amended motion was passed.

Sandy Redmond then reported that the finance committee for the cenotaph now had sufficient monies – in pledges and cash – to allow the project to move forward to the next stage. He further outlined a series of benefit hockey games, raffles, spring bazaars and government promises which would enable the village to erect a glorious monument. His greengrocer's eye glowed as he spoke, and a round of self-inflatory applause ensued that might have shamed the hockey crowd down on the river flats.

The Reeve resumed the floor. He pointed out that new committees could now be struck to search for a designer-builder and to select a suitable site. The former committee was to be composed of the Reeve, the Reverend Stokes and Sandy Redmond. The latter, less onerous, one of Choppy Fielding, Harold Hitchcock and young MacIntosh.

On a wave of optimism and good cheer they swept out into the snowy night and managed to see the hometown Flyers wallop the hapless Wanderers of Landsend 9-2. The auguries were in place, and they were smiling.

34

1

It had snowed again in the night – in her dream and in the world out there. It must be almost February, Granny thought, lifting the kettle from the stove and staring across the unblemished tundra that fell away to the frozen River and the ice-edge of the Lake as far as the eye could travel to the north-west. She had no calendar except the one over the sink with the bleached buffoon's visage of King George grinning possessively down at his faceless subjects – the one she had left unchanged since that terrible September day. But more than eighty years of superintending the passage of the seasons had left her with a clock more subtle than almanacs or Swiss watches. She had heard the special shout of school children passing by and knew the Christmas holiday had begun. The church bells rang from the trinity of God's Houses in the village, and so she counted the Sundays as they held fast in spite of sleet, thaw and squall. The silence of Christmas Day was as awe-inspiring and as puzzling as it had always been. No one came; the snow lay uncreased over her yard and dormant gardens. Next day, though, Sunny Denfield and his boy, Boots, came around with a dish of turkey and dressing and fruitcake. She nodded her gratitude at the door, and they seemed thankful that she didn't motion them inside. Obviously forewarned, Boots tried hard to smile and not stare at her too long but managed only the latter. Nonetheless, the boy had the inerasable kindness of his father's eyes. He will be another one who will suffer, she thought, watching them leave their eccentric prints in Saturday's drift.

From time to time parcels of food – clothing even – would appear mysteriously on her porch, the tiny trails in the snow betraying the identity of the secret heralds. Bless the children, she thought; they're afraid but they don't hate easily. To some of them Granny Coote's a witch from the Lane, but at least they think of me as somebody, as a creature with her own peculiar power, magic, and brand of terror. What am I to the others? Something that *was*, and got left over.

The snow was comforting. Without it she knew she wouldn't survive another winter intact. Not die, of course. That was out of the question given this body of sinew, gristle, bones of oak. Once the arthritis unstiffened in the morning and the blood honeyed the desiccated veins one more time, her body – with its muscle-memory, its own receding legends, and its mindless optimism – went about its daily exercises and evacuations. Pain she was accustomed to; it was relegated to some lower order of response, and forgotten. You don't die of pain, she thought, or we'd all be soon dead. Nor loneliness.

The snow, re-establishing its beauty every fortnight or so like a goose ruffling its plumage after a roll in the dust, created spaces between the trees, houses and hedges. Into these blank meadows she was able to pour her thoughts – half-memory and half-feeling – filling them until they rebelled and she had to pass her eye along to the next one. Thus she could spend a morning or afternoon, starting with the Carpenter's yard and moving at the pace of her own musing across the windowed landscape section by section till it ended at the high point where the dunes began – cutting off from her vision the vast shore of the Lake. Memories she would never run out of. They returned as whole sequences of events – tragedies, comedies, farce, melodrama – or as a single moment of action radiating endless wavelets of feeling, some of it fresh and uncorrupted, some of it coloured by intruding events that enriched or mitigated, some of it redeemed or crushed by the perspective of eighty years of remembering and pretending to remember. But I can still think , she reminded herself emphatically; my tongue may be as thick as a gelding's fetlock, but these memories don't come sliding by on their sentimental honey without comment or appraisal. I still know a foolish sentiment when I feel one even if the damn tear-ducts don't. I remember so I can stay alive, so I can be myself, whoever that is. But then you don't really want to stay alive, do you, old woman with the sagging breasts and brindled hair? Be honest. You close your eyes every night and hope they won't open again, that something will stop the nightmare machine. Yes. Yes. But I won't go before my body does. I am not my body, though enough people have thought so over the years.

The nights – these winter nights – were eternal and terrifying. Dream was not memory, though it brewed its maelstrom from the remnants thereof. Nor was dream prophecy, though its phantasmic imagery sometimes stunned the future, sometimes held out the illusion of augury. There had been magic in the world, that much she knew, and she herself had had those very dreams which touch upon its tenderest mystery, whose tremors brought the body – awakening – to the brink of belief. No more. In these present nightmares the same tale was told and retold, a masquerade of her own life parading as the truth, calling out to her for acceptance and validation, begging her to accept its mutant reconstruction of reality, whispering to its apostles the soft promise of annihilation. In the daylight she could dream or doze or resurrect; she could defend herself against such depredations. In February the nights were longest. And if the night-dreams ever began to eclipse those of the day, it would be all over. Then I'll be as batty as people think I am, she thought. They'll cart me off to London in a cattle car, and I won't even care. You can't have a nightmare, if you're *in one.*

Even if she should ever talk again and people around here didn't think she was loony, it wouldn't make too much difference. Who would she talk to? There was nobody left from her generation. Not one. Old Duckface Malloney's still alive, she recalled, innkeeping at the Sunset Glades, though he'd had four strokes, none kind enough to do him in. Half the people she had known left after the tunnel fiasco of 1890; the Boer War got a few more. Several had died from the pressures of the Great War – losing sons and grandsons and staring at the gray months stretching forever ahead, and just giving up. As she should have.

All the original Alleyfolk older than she were long dead. She had watched them enter the earth one by one, mostly in sorrow, occasionally in envy. The Potts' Lane crew began to move away and drift off – as she had done – because no one arrived to renew their own naïve faith in that perverse community; even the kids found jobs, respectability and excuses not to visit. After the War and the epidemic had wiped out the last of the Laners along with just about everybody else over seventy-five, the European refugees had begun to discover the shacks and improvised abodes. And Granny knew why. I wish I could go there, she thought. I want to hear their stories. I've heard them since I was six. I would know what comfort, if any, to give them. You don't need a war to make you an outcast, though I've seen four of them if they care to swap miseries.

Not only was there no one of her generation left here, very few of the second and third generation knew her or anything about her. She had lived in and around this very spot for seven decades; she knew every family who'd ever put down roots here. She knew their relatives, connections, feudal histories, pretensions and genial follies. They did not know her. "You've made yourself an outsider," Cap used to say with that arching smirk, "because you enjoy watching and judging, and because you are afraid deep-down to take part in the rituals that sustain their daily lives for fear they will swallow you up. You've judged these values before you've had the courage to try them. I tried them and then, with a little help from Dame Misfortune, gave them up. I may be a bum, but I know who I was, and what I am."

Not true, not so, she found herself arguing with him again – between the hedge and shriven hickory tree. You don't know what I've lived through before I was even an adolescent, what horrors were inlaid already for these old-woman's nightmares you couldn't have survived for one night without a quart of brandy. What-is-more-to-the-point, you were not a woman. To be woman – here, then – is to be consumed by ritual. If I forget, my nightmares remind me.

Many of the basic stock of the village – Brightons, Barbers, McCourts, Carpenters, Savages – had been here since the beginning, but the children of these pioneers would know her only through the stories told of her by their church-going, upright parents. And she had heard them all in their variously embroidered forms; that was the price – one of many – she had paid for living on the fringe. So be it. She had never complained then and wasn't about to start now. Certainly Sophie's yarns and epic jokes about the citizens-in-good-standing gave back more than they'd received. "That old mister Redmond, if you stuck a turnip up his arse, he'd ask you the price-per-pound!" Or, after an Easter Sunday promenade: "By the Judas, did ya see the riggin' on the Reverend Missus? Four corsets wrapped in a mainsail. One fart an' she'd've blown us all to Kingdom Come!" To the children she was just Granny Coote, or worse. To their elders she was queer-old-Arthur's second folly. To others still older she was Cora Burgher, the cleaning woman. Before that there was no one to remember that she had once been Lily. Or care.

2

The Reeve cared. After Limpy Jenkinson (shrapnel at St. Eloi) and his retarded son Wally (Walleye to the kids) delivered a cord of wood in November and again in February, Sunny Denfield would come over after work at the Foundry and split enough kindling to last her through. When it got real cold he would lug a scuttle of soft coal over for the Quebec heater. Granny would smile her thanks, but shake her head when he left: after all, like so many others her age she had been raised in drafty cabins and shacks. She knew how to keep warm, if she wanted to.

Last week following Limpy's delivery, the Reeve arrived promptly and began splitting wood in the tiny shed off the kitchen area. Granny lay on the chesterfield where she often slept since Arthur died and listened to the two-step cadence of the axe on wood – one of the earliest, abiding sounds of her long life. There was comfort in it, and reassurance. She must have dozed a bit, half-dreaming of someone of whom Sunny Denfield reminded her – the questing eyes, the softness unclothed by false masculinity.

"That should carry you through to the spring, Cora," he said, a vee of sweat on his shirt-front. "Goin' to be an early one, they say."

He always called her Cora because she had been that when he had arrived in Sarnia to take advantage of the boom created by the tunnel under the River. Something, lord knows what, prompted him to take up residence in the Point where Prudie KcKay espied him and persuaded him to make the move permanent. "Good mornin', Mrs. Burgher," he would say to her – dropping imperceptibly into the local accent – as he met her each day outside the Queen's Hotel in his brief bachelor period: he heading for the streetcar stop at the end of Potts' Lane and she trudging up the steps towards another day of housecleaning. Even then his reputed good breeding ("black sheep of a fine Toronto family, they say") shone through: a tip of the workman's cap and the impeccable "Missus". Her first thought had been: I've seen those eyes.

Instead of saying good night and returning to his family, the Reeve went over to the stove and put the kettle on.

"Don't budge, Cora. I know where everything is. I'm goin' to make us a cup of tea, an' then I've got somethin' very important to tell you."

Granny was fully awake now.

"It's good news," he said immediately.

I'll believe it when I taste it, she thought.

When he had poured the tea, Reeve Denfield sat beside her on the chesterfield and began talking. For some reason he was the only person besides Wilf Underhill who did not stiffen before her apparent silence – perhaps because he realized that she was not at all silent, that her nods, looks, minute shades of gesture and quick touches of the hand represented a fierce desire to communicate. Somehow she always felt he was talking *with her*. Over the years since he had been visiting her, he had come to know by patient trial and error not only every nuance of her response to his questions or proposals but also what subjects she liked him to talk about, what village tales she wished to be told and retold. He was her lifeline to that part of the world out there – small as it was – which she had marked out for her own. It wasn't a matter of keeping up with the gossip – she'd lost the passion for that when Sophie had died so horribly – but as the Reeve himself soon discovered and approved, a question of maintaining the continuity of one's being, of keeping operational the connective tissue and the nerve-beds of a lifelong existence in one place over time. Lucien's bride, Cora the cleaning-woman, Eddie's granny, Mrs. Arthur Coote, Granny Coote – these lives and the others she had temporarily inhabited were kept coherent and drew their meaning only if the person she now was, was also moving in time – touching, colliding, being broken and revived, fully sentient. If not, then the web of these memories sustaining her would be loosened from all anchorage, and set adrift to be engulfed by the alien Night-Dream itself.

"Don't look so sceptical," the Reeve smiled knowingly. "It *is* good news of a sort."

I told you so.

"You've heard that up-and-comin' types like Harold Hitchcock are keen to get this property back. Yes, I know he's a phoney, but he's also cunning. He's playin' to certain prejudices an' sentiments in town, as you know so well. I was hopin', and I still am, that the spirit of cooperation brought on by the War and the epidemic would carry on. I think it can, Cora, really, I do." Her stare had almost stopped him.

"We're goin' to need that spirit, as I've told you before. This town's in rough shape. No one knows better than you what the village went through during the railroad years an' the tunnel scandal and the wholesale depopulation." Did he know what had happened? The details? Were they written down somewhere? She hadn't considered that possibility.

"When I came here, there were fifty vacant lots and a dozen houses rottin' where they sat. The Anglican Church was boarded up. Even the Lane was half-empty."

I left it, too. A deserter, like the rest.

"You stuck it out as long as you could. Don't deny it now."

She did, emphatically.

"Anyway, you know how hard we struggled to get the stone works and the Foundry in here. Then the War and all those men, our neighbours, gone, *like that*. An' the fever attackin' the young an' the helpless." He paused, seeing the pain in her face, but she urged him on.

I need to cry she said to him, I need to feel.

"Well, times are boomin' again. But just stand at the car-stop any mornin' at seven an' watch three-quarters of our men leavin' town to work at the Refinery or the railroad shops. How long can that go on before they start feelin' like City people? An' how long before Sarnia decides to make another move to take over and fulfil the dream they've had for forty years? The War come close to breakin' us. Unless we get back our sense of bein' a community, we'll go under."

Granny nodded her agreement.

"That's why the monument means so much to us. It's goin' to be bigger an' nobler an' more lastin' than the one in the City. To get the job done, I need to keep the council together. This business of your property has to be settled. Oh, don't be alarmed. You know where I stand. I told them last week that our lawyer said you have the right to buy the lot before any other kind of move can be made."

Granny's eyes filled with tears. Oh damn, she thought, there you go, acting like a half-senile old woman, snivelling at every turn of emotion in the conversation. But as usual the tears just fell.

"I've had the property assessed, without the council's knowledge. What I have to know is, do you have any money? Did Arthur provide for you?"

She nodded, yes.

"Three hundred dollars?" he said with great hesitation.

She was comforted by the concern in his voice. Her smile was all he needed.

"In the bank?"

No. In a much safer place.

"Don't tell me," he laughed, much relieved. "I'll make all the arrangements. The council meets again next week. I'll have the deed, if we can find one, in your hands by then. That is, if you *want* to stay here."

There was little doubt about that. Suddenly Granny got up and went over to the steamer-trunk next to the locked door of Arthur's room. She pulled out a small slate, the one Eddie used before she got him into school. A piece of used chalk lay on the ledge at the bottom. The Reeve was watching her with intense curiosity.

She came back and sat beside him again. She lay the slate on her knees and took the chalk up in her left hand. The Reeve saw the concentration in the furrows of her brow. He saw the tendons mount on her wrist, the skin draped and useless. Then the hand flexed and began to write in shaking, tentative curls across the slate. When she finished she smiled grimly at him and gave him the board. He could just make out the message there: "Tell the council I wish to die in this house."

3

She was thinking back to New Years. Outside, the snow was falling as gentle as confetti on a bride's veil, as it had on that night. She had perched herself on the arm of the Morris chair – Arthur's own – to survey the couples entering the Oddfellows' Hall next door, two by two into the ark. The electric lights inside stretched every quadrangle of glass to the limit (she still preferred the hominess of coal-oil or the dazzle of gas), and soon the orchestra struck up the welcoming number, the horns dominating the strings in the modern style. She closed her eyes and pictured them dancing – a whole village in cadenced, concentric motion in the arms of the music, palpable and reassuring. Through the transmuting snow she detected variations of fox trot and waltz, and somewhat later, as a gift to the elders, the polka and a solitary, fiddle-driven reel. No jig, no fling, no hornpipe. Certainly no galop or lancers. Then something strange, something novel: horns and drums only, the beat fevered, truant, edging towards chaos, held fast by some primitive fulcrum between beat and cadence, sound and melody. She could not imagine what sort of dance they would be doing to such rhythms, such raw choristry, but she sensed it would go well before a fire in the dark under starlight. The snow sizzled and she was asleep.

4

Could it be that after all these years of searching and effort she would have a home of her own? I'll believe it when I've got the deed in my hands – in triplicate with the king's spit on it, Sophie would have added. Not that she hadn't lived in places where she had felt at home. That was a different matter. A home is something no one can take away from you. Ever. That's the reason her forebears and thousands after them had come here: to find a place, build a house, and be at home. This shack, as the villagers called it, with is leaking roof, tarpaper skin, sloping porch and rambunctious gardens was Arthur's gift to her. Thirty-six years ago – installed in the honeymoon suite of the St. Clair Inn – she would not have dreamt such a finale as this. "Life is mainly what happens to you," she had said to Cap, sure that he would agree to such an unexpected admission. "Nonsense," he had replied, rather quickly. "I built my own chamber in Hell. And so did you."

At first she thought the man clearing a path through the yard with his golashes was Sunny Denfield come to tell her about the meeting. Then she remembered dimly that it was far too soon for that. The fire was out and she sat wrapped in shawls by the front window. Too tentative a step for the Reeve. She leaned forward for a better look. The young Reverend Buchan, fresh out of preacher's college. Granny sighed indulgently. How many times had such a scene as-was-about-to-follow been enacted over the years? She knew every line, every cue, even the sub-texts. Has this one come on his own or been put up to it by his betters? From the tiny rap on the door she knew the answer. His baptism, she thought, feeling the whole range of ironies.

"Good afternoon, Mrs. Coote," he said, his voice barely penetrating the puffs of vapour it generated.

Granny dipped her head as she always did in greeting. Reverend Buchan followed her gaze to his feet where he checked to see if he had put his galoshes on the wrong side, again. Granny pulled the inside door further open.

"I'm sorry to disturb you on such a beautiful winter's day," he said, still standing on the porch, "but I'm here on an official mission."

God's or your own, said her silent voice. She stepped purposefully back into the kitchen area.

"May I come in?"

She nodded. Not vigourously enough apparently. She grasped his startled arm and hauled him into the rapidly freezing room.

"Ah, yes. Yes, I'm terribly sorry. I forgot. Unforgivable of me. Will you forgive my stupidity?"

Only if it will help, which I doubt. She indicated Arthur's chair, but either his aim or his eyesight was off because he landed at one end of the chesterfield. Granny placed his galoshes on a mat by the door. She held the tea-kettle up, and he shook his head up and down. She took that for assent and stirred the firebox. Realizing there was no heat in the room, she shook the grates. The gasping of the flame brought the Reverend to his feet, and when she came over with the tea-service, the one Lucien had given her as a wedding gift, he was still erect, as if wondering how he had got into such a posture.

"May I take my coat off?" he said foolishly.

If you prefer to freeze, yes.

He did remove it – with a little last-second boost from Granny – recognized his folly in an icy instant, and sat down with the coat draped around him like a shroud.

She looked at him not unkindly, waiting as she must.

He seemed genuinely overwhelmed by her silence or by the possibility that some exotic and profane speech might at any moment break out of it and anathematize them both.

"I've been asked by the council, by the Reverend Stokes to be precise, representing the council, that is, they wished me as the minister of the church where your late dear husband played the organ, they thought I would be best suited to come and explain the position of the council to you. Do you understand?" He was now shouting as one does when talking at the deaf.

Granny handed him his cup of tea, steaming heartily in the chill air. The heat from the kitchen stove went straight through the old roof.

Reverend Buchan had just found the phrases he had committed to a perilous memory when he spilled his tea on his trousers, and emitted an entirely unrehearsed sequence of expletives.

"Oh, can you ever forgive me," he blustered, wincing and whisking at his soiled pantleg and managing only to overturn the rest of his tea onto the carpet, necessitating a further string of apologies.

Granny did her best to comfort him, but every time her hand touched him, he flinched, and when she fixed him with her eye and appeared about to say something out loud, he panicked and fell sideways onto the floor, the tea-stain stiffening below his crotch.

Granny went over to the table and returned with her slate. Once he had determined that she was not about to hit him with it, he sat back trembling and profoundly curious. Granny wrote on the slate with a stuttering left hand, then let him read the words: "The Reeve has given me the news. You are forgiven."

He stared up at her as if she might be the Virgin Mary reincarnate. Then he burst into tears.

Granny, her own heart relenting, mothered him back into his clothes, got his galoshes on in orthodox fashion, and watched him cut a fresh path through the snow towards his ministry.

"If there's a special spot in Heaven for preachers," Sophie said many times, drunk and sober, "I'll take the other place, and a bed-warmer to boot."

Amen.

35

1

It was snowing again, like ack-ack in a dream, like slow-motion shrapnel. And thick enough to asphyxiate the streetlamps in front of the library, whose eerie rectangle interrupted the blank landscape like a redoubt along the smoky Somme. No wind ruffled this February evening. The snow fell with the absolute illusion of innocence upon the sills, upon the eaves, upon the nervous domesticity of a post-war winter village.

"An' so to wrap it all up," the Reeve was saying to the assembled councillors, "she's an old, old lady who's lived here for three generations; she's got legal entitlement to the property if she's willin' to pay fair market-value; an' she definitely wants to live out her days in peace in that rag-taggle shanty, whatever we think of it. I already asked our lawyers to find out a proper price. Any questions on item one?"

The worshipping hand of the junior Miss Robertson came to a breathless halt at the end of the Reeve's remarks, certain there could be no further question to record. She took advantage of the pause in her note-taking to tilt her calf's-eye upward in hopeless adoration. Hence she did not, as the Reeve himself did, notice that although there were no questions on the issue, the room was electric with anticipation, with secret understandings on the brink of disclosure. Neither the heat undulating from the floor-register (inconsiderately located beneath the table) nor the imperturbable silence of the snowfall against the night could distract the council from the matters of state before it. So palpable was the undercurrent that Half-Hitch inadvertently crushed a tailor-made in the trigger of his artificial thumb. Stubby Fielding's rubber jaw sagged grotesquely. Sandy Redmond felt the Boer's bayonet strike his thigh like a fish-knife. An improbably icy wind burred along Sunny Denfield's cheek. Young MacIntosh's flat feet ached with humiliation and regret. Canon Stokes struggled valiantly with the insurgency of his wife's roast-beef supper.

"Then I'll ask Sandy to speak to item two."

The village grocer, whose own father had come to the Point with the railroad in 1862 and stayed to found a dynasty of shopkeepers (Sandy's son, Red, now returned a hero from the War, was already a fixture in the business), rose and presented the report of the subcommittee for selecting a designer and builder for the proposed war memorial. As luck would have it – or Providence in the case of the Presbyterian Redmonds – they had been able to locate a man who could both design and build a monument to meet any specifications they wished. It turned out that he had done just that for three villages in Grey, two in Huron and one each in Middlesex and Kent Counties. His specialty, veri-fied by references, was erecting impressive monuments – but simple and noble in design – in small towns at reasonable rates. If the stories told were true, it seems he had a grudge against big cities and 'government' types, and had devoted the last three years exclusively to building cenotaphs in underfunded villages that would outshine those overpriced ca-lamities indulged in by the senior municipalities. The man's name was Sam Stradler. He hailed from a hamlet near London. He had been a stonemason and tombstone carver before serving overseas. Once a site was chosen and the ice broke up, he would begin work – about mid-March or early April – and finish in six to eight weeks.

Approval was audible and unanimous. Miss Robertson recorded the verdict with a proud flourish. Sandy Redmond sat down. A feeling that something significant and abiding had been done suffused the meeting place. The snow emptied itself into the darkness outside.

Half-Hitch clicked his hickory thumb-and-forefinger and rose to speak to item three. Stubby Fielding and young MacIntosh, who had fidgeted and looked embar-rassed during the earlier presentation by the Reeve, resumed their fidgeting. Stubby preferred the direct statement of an artillery barrage to all this oblique conniving, but he had been convinced by the devious Hitchcock of the necessity for secrecy. There were times , he allowed, when battle-plans had to be kept under wraps if the strategy itself was not to be jeopardized and the humane goals themselves forever compromised. Stubby had grunted assent and shut up. Horrie MacIntosh, on the other hand, was in no position to argue any side of the matter: he was the recruit, the cadet untested by battle and not yet sanctified by its scarring.

"Our committee's reached a unanimous decision," Hitchcock said rigidly from memory. "We explored every angle of the…the issue-at-hand, and we found only one spot – site – that meets all the requirements." He fished the requirements out of the recall-box: "(1) central location, (2) flat land of at least one-quarter acre in size, (3) property owned by the village or available at nominal cost, and (4) ah –" He flipped the stuck card in his head. "Presence of shade trees."

"Get on with it, Hitch!" barked the Boer veteran. "This ain't church! No offense, Mort."

The Reverend Mort, unaware that high drama was ravelling its sinuous subplots around him, took neither offense nor heed.

Half-Hitch had now irreparably lost his place. He plunged ahead recklessly. "We all agreed, all three of us, there was only one spot to fit the needs we set out here last meetin'. The spot we chose is in the dead-centre of town. It's on a main street where the city-trolley passes every hour. It's got a marvellous big shade tree, an' shrubs an' hedges to boot. You can see across the marsh to the docks an' up to the dunes by the Lake from the back-end. An' best of all, it's almost owned by the village."

The Reeve leaned forward in his chair. He now understood the edgy quiet during his earlier speech. His anger, alas, was tempered by the force of the logic in Hitchcock's report. The only other vacant lot in the middle of town was the one right beside them; but it was the last of the railroad properties: a memorial on its ground would be the ultimate betrayal. Foolishly he had assumed they would choose the original site of the old Anglican Church where the cubscouts pitched their tents. He'd underestimated the opposition.

"I move," Half-Hitch was saying through his smug smile, "we agree on the Coote property as a site for the monument, an' begin legal proceedin's to take back title."

The motion passed.

2

Granny liked the snow the way it was tonight. Once, with Eddie on her knee and nothing but dark days ahead and only two small presents under the tree, she had watched the Christmas Eve snowfall through the child's eye, and called it the snow of remembrance. Back then she had thought 'someday I'll be sitting in another place with times as bad as these and I'll remember the wonderful gentleness of this falling without motive or design'. And here I am.

In the Carpenter's yard she could see the outline of the spruce windbreak, shawled and scarved by the snow – white on green, shape lending shape, all voices hushed inward. This could be any of the snowfalls upon any of the spruces she had lived beside or under in the many seasons of her childhood, girlhood, womanhood, dotage, death-watch. "Who wants to live to be old?" Cap said to her many times, his flesh wan and shivering after a bad bout. "What would you do with a useless body and all that time on your hands? Sit and remember when your elements used to work and your brain could count to three? How many good times can you re-live anyway before they're worn out and you come to despise them and despise yourself for staying alive?"

She had no answer, then; neither of them had been old enough to speak from experience. Well, I'll tell you now, she thought. It's not the way you imagined. Yes, I live on my memories – what else is there? – but they are not summoned up like individual pearl buttons, like heirlooms, to be turned over in the hand and admired till the eyes water. It doesn't work that way, Cap. Not for me. Some moments do come back almost whole, like Eddie and me watching the Christmas snow of 1897 with different versions of hope in our hearts. Like the snowy night of 1886 that was like this one except for the wind that blew through it like an invisible beam when Lucien and I rode out to find heaven on a one-horse sled. Or any of a dozen more – from parts of my life you never surmised – full of sweetness and pain of course, but more often marked by the exquisite surge of innocence against experience, by the raw edge of questions which remain more beautiful and durable than the answers we invent merely to stay alive. You would be astonished, Cap, to hear me talk – think – like this, use words in such a way. Then again perhaps you wouldn't. In any case, you must take the blame for some of it. You maintained, didn't you, that the world wouldn't be a safe or sane place to live in if ever women were taught to read and write. But then you didn't know Eddie, or his father. They taught me that poetry can be gossip made glorious by language. That would shock you. But Sophie knew so, she lived it and died for it. You saw in her only what your prejudices allowed.

And you've got no prejudices of course, you silly old coot, she said sharply to herself. Then laughed. You see, old darling, that is how the memory works, that is how I fill these hours before I am overtaken by exhaustion and the dread of the Night-Dream, the one I fear must have shaken you each day of those last years. Forgive me if I failed to acknowledge your anguish. Anyway, you see how the mind refuses to accept the denial of a present or future. I think of Eddie, of snow, of you, of Lucien Burgher, of Sophie's battered face, of sweet Arthur – separately or together. They have voices, you know, like you; they can be talked to. They can speak with one another in the special existence I lend them, here on a February evening in 1922 with a snow falling that thinks it's special too but is really the same one whose breathlessness drew a little girl's wonder to her cabin window miles from this spot more than seventy years ago. You gave it all up too soon, old pessimist. I am alone. I am ready for death's surprises, if he has any. But I am not lonely. I am still, after all these years, waiting for something to happen.

Like the stove going out, you day-dreaming old fart, she thought, shivering and shuffling over to the Quebec heater. It stared at her, one-eyed and glum. Against the protest of her rheumatism she shook the grates as vigorously as she could manage, but several intractable clinkers had lodged between the flanges. She'd have to get Sunny to clean out the firebox when he came over to tell her about the meeting. He had left her a fine white notepad on which to write out requests and things she needed. She was grateful, though it was very difficult at first to scrawl anything legible there. It wasn't just the arthritis, she knew. Whatever had afflicted her throat had spread to her writing hand. But it was easier now to list the few supplies she needed for either Sunny or Wilf Underhill to take to Redmond's or Turnbull's. It made her feel better about possessing Arthur's house, at last. They won't think I'm completely batty. Just old. Maybe I'll be allowed to die with a little dignity, she mused, trying to recall anyone she loved who had.

Now the good burghers and pewsters of the town would be able to pity her with a clear conscience. However, if they'd been able to observe her wrestling with the paper and kindling in a plugged stove with smoke polluting the chill of her front room, they'd have cried gleefully: "Poor old soul, used to be strong as an ox, you know, scrubbed floors in The Queen's for years, but then age and arthritis gets the best of us all, don't it. And of course she never did take care of herself, you know, livin' in that drafty shack in the Lane all those years, an' never settin' foot in a church or a decent body's house." I prefer the children, she thought. They only think I'm a witch, an outcast – with status.

She felt pain firing through both her knees. She was on the floor among the spilled cinders and ash. The kindling had burned itself out, the smoke had escaped with the brief heat through the cracks in the walls. Had she blacked out? A tumour? Tiny strokes? She winced at the bruising in her knees and the scalding of tears. Get up. Get up. The room spun on the axis of a single candleflame in the front window. Lie down. Let it be.

The temporary blaze was taking the chill off quite nicely, and the hot tea warmed wherever it went. Granny pulled the kimono more snugly around her throat and continued her vigil at the snowy window overseeing the street. Arthur was such a sweet man, so different from the others. He loved to walk, as she did, with no aim or purpose other than the pleasures of being in motion in the woods or along the beaches or among the cattails or under the parliament of stars that had supervised conception and birth and all the rest. Often they would pull Eddie on his sled through snows like this over to the dunes, where he would fling himself into semi-flight down their slick slopes to the borderless prairie of the beach below. When they got home, after a brisk fire and some mulled wine – with Eddie snug in his cocoon – she would make slow mutinous love to Arthur. Always he was too shy, too untrusting of the tender impulses that throve in him, to initiate lovemaking. She would think of him, though she never told him so, as an instrument – say a curling rosewood mandolin – that she would rub and thrum till its music wakened and overwhelmed. "We shouldn't, love, we're too old, too ridiculous," he'd murmur unconvincingly, and she'd say, "Keep your eyes closed, sweet; it's beautiful, it's beautiful in here."

So rare in a man was that refined reticence, that rare combination of resignation and engagement, gentility and passion, music and masculinity that she – Cora Burgher – would have scoffed at the very notion; certainly Cap would have laughed out loud, and Sophie no doubt would have smiled indulgently and offered some devastating quip: "I know he's sweet and kind and does the dishes, dearie, but has he got a dick or a doily down there?"

In a letter she wrote but never sent to Eddie, she said about Arthur: 'He was the kind of man every woman should marry. As lovers only should we take the adventurers, the wanderers, the plunderers; and when we've taken our pleasure on them, we'll turn them loose again to waste themselves upon the world'.

I've had my share of the other kind, she thought. And their children. They're dead and gone, all of them: willing victims of whatever demons drive the male flesh to annihilation. And the innocents along with them. Eddie. Eddie, I can't even say your name out loud. The gods that could have helped us are still in hiding. When Arthur left he took some of the earth's music with him, but you were my last cause for hope. What am I doing here now? The gods won't answer from their skulking-places. Even death has passed me by. Cap was right: waiting is not living.

You're waiting for something to happen. Yes, of course. That's it. I almost forgot.

She heard a commotion in her front yard and turned in time to see the blurred outline of Sunny Denfield, the puffing portliness of Mortimer Stokes and the loping strut of Harry Hitchcock. From the gait and bearing of these harbingers she recognized, from long and repeated experience, the peculiar footfall of officialdom. And the news it bore, she knew, was never good.

3

And Granny again dreaming Lily, dreaming the longago as if it were real or had actually happened or could happen again only differently so everything would be changed in the wake-up world, she was eight and she was alone under the moon and the shadows around her blurred into smoke when she touched them and the night-air was jarred and riven by a music that had no sound to it, no melody in it, only cadence and verberation and blood-thrumming titillation, she was wild with it and as her body's bird-bones sang and sailed in their weightless jubilance, she was aware that the smoke-wreaths and shadow-substances about her were other souls twisting in the same silence, driven by the same yearnings towards the bliss of oblivion, and they shared a simultaneous cry of release and not-a-single-regret as the dark struck back, as the shadow reclaimed its dominion in the fallible flesh of all dancers young and old, native and alien and she awoke to find herself sleeping the sleep of the exhausted upon the shoulder of the Southener, the last of the Shawnees from the legendary battles of the war-with-the-States, his eyes half-lidded and undreaming and his arm around her more fatherly than she had ever known and in the clearing among the Pottawatomie wigwams around them they watched with their separate intensities and under the moon's clairvoyance the midnight ceremony repeating itself before them as for the first-and-only time the virgin among the priests of her family and the ghosts of her ancestors and the wraiths of the children she would bequeath to the future, the shivering Pottawatomie girl-child with woman-needs bone-deep and thriving in her to be blossom and spur, and when all the chanting was done and all the fleshly transformations had taken place within their spheres, she was able to smile into the moon-varnished dark with the face of her new name, no longer White Blossom was she but Seed-of-the-Snow-Apple and all that was promised therein if summer should ever come or the darkness imbedded above the moon ever lifted itself from the dreamer's eye...

36

1

On such a night as this – with the stars frozen in place, the quarter-moon windless with wonder, the inheld breath of all snow – did Lucien the locomotive man, thirty-six years ago to the month, baptize his bride "Mrs. Cora Burgher". To the astonishment of the other burghers and burgesses of the village, no doubt. On the other hand, nothing fazed them concerning the behaviour of any former inmate of Mushroom Alley. In fact, being one of its superannuated denizens, Granny thought, granted one a comforting sense of immunity, a licence to commit extravagant social irreverencies. Not that being made an honest woman by Lucien Burgher was all that irreverent. Lucien: with the great grappling hands; with a laugh titanic enough to be recognized over the competition of steam-whistle, grinding iron and the wail of wind through the open windows of the cab. With a heart as hot and propulsive as the firebox he fed lovingly each night with lozenges of beach and elm. You were the only one willing to take me away, take me out of myself, take me sailing on the white wave that sweeps us clear of our body's weight. We made our secret pact and we kept it without compromise. Less than three months. But I remember still, for both of us. And, Lucien my love, the gods of either hue were watching – in trepidation and cowardly delight. Yes, all that really *did* happen.

Even when you left, I thought to keep your name. I braved the taunting and snobbery to make them say it long enough to forget I'd ever had another. With you gone, I had to grow into it alone. You'd have been proud of me, but pride, as we both knew, was never a substitute for the wonderful meshing of our brief nights together. You would have roared with laughter, or cried, to overhear – as I did many times at The Queen's scrubbing out a room at eight in the morning – the wheezing and whimpering next door, the off-key giggle, the under-rehearsed moans and yelps, the slap of dead flesh, sadness like an aftersmell in the room hours later no scouring could efface. Only the memory of our love and your courage not-to-be kept me going in that black year after your leaving.

I kept your name; it grew around me in the Lane and in the village. The graft took. When Eddie came, he needed something to call me. Granny. I resisted, gently. The child needed a surname. I gave him yours, and mine. When sweet Arthur carried us off together, I surrendered it with reluctance. You know that. We talked it over at the time, remember? I told you what a sacrifice Arthur Coote was making, offering his widower's hand to a woman thrice fallen, risking all for love as one of his theatrical publicists might have put it. Don't laugh. Driving down to the Sarnia Court House in a borrowed butcher's cart to be "hitched" by a judge was one of the most courageous acts I've seen any man ever perform. Of course, I told him to pretend he was on stage and he did, and I gave him rave reviews for a week. You would have come to like the Arthur I was privileged to see. Don't forget, he was an actor, an entertainer. He played The Royal in Victoria and the Lyceum in San Francisco. Being organist and choir director at the Methodist Church was his greatest role, though you wouldn't like me saying that, would you, Arthur?

She was thinking now – in this stasis of starlight and snow, with the gentle foraging of Sunny Denfield back in the woodshed – of that night a few weeks after the ceremony when Arthur sat over there at his piano and began to play, in slow time, the opening bars of "I am a model of a modern major-general" and young Eddie, barely ten and wide-eyed with wonder and fright, picked up Arthur's baton, tucked it under his chin like a swagger stick and started marching up and down to the music. As Arthur, his own shyness finally easing, began to speed up towards the song's regular triphammer gallop, little Eddie's legs hopped in rapid synchronization, his arm jerking up and down in perfect parody, his eyes dancing in accelerating cadence till at last they left the safety of his granny's and garnered their own delight. She herself had grabbed a saucepan and began beating it with a spoon, unable to catch the presto-con-brio of the ditty as it soared to an apex of divine stillness. When the cups on the shelf ceased to rattle from the final chord, Eddie scooted past her waiting arms and flung himself at Arthur, who recovered in time to hug the child so tightly he could feel the diminuendo of music still humming in the tiny bones.

2

The front room was as warm and cozy as it had ever been. Sunny Denfield had removed the clinkers and cinders, and then built a fast, hot maplewood fire to take off the chill. As it died down, he put a chunk of Wilf Underhill's coke on the ash, where it simmered contentedly. Sunny stayed for his tea even though he knew Prudie would get that hurt, puzzled look in her eye again, certain that there was some sinister explanation for his unconscionably long visits with such a strange soul who sat without speech winter after winter cheating death. Charity had its limits. God would not credit such excess.

"I didn't tell you, did I," he was saying, "that I got another letter from my cousin Ruth-Anne in Toronto. Yes, it's true. Seems like the hoity-toity side of the family has decided to acknowledge its black sheep." He was fully aware of her own acknowledge-ment, reflected in her face which he always observed, as he spoke, at a three-quarter angle, reading the slightest quiver of her lip or brow, assessing each shift of labyrinthine light in eyes that had not, he sense, changed their essence since they dawned upon the world.

"You remember, of course, the callow bachelor who set up shop in The Queen's back in the fall of 'nineteen-one. I was only eighteen, would you believe? I didn't tell my parents where I was till after I got settled in the job at the sheds and was pretty certain Prudie McKay would say yes. What few people know even today is that I ran away from private school. My family was, an' still is, high mucky-muck."

Granny acknowledged the accuracy of the term.

"My grandfather was a minister in the old Union government of Baldwin-Lafontaine. My father was a fancy city solicitor in Toronto. He died during the War. Lucky for me, I stopped to see him on my way overseas in 'fifteen. He knew he was dying, I think, because he made a great show of forgivin' me. I was sure I'd die before him, an' maybe he thought so too."

Granny pushed another of Mrs. Savage's cookies in his direction.

"Anyway, it seems my Aunt Grace, my mother's sister, who died just a year or so ago, got interested in her family tree. She'd married Bramwell Beattie, a sort of junior tycoon, a guy I hated all my life. But Aunt Grace was a pet, the sweetest, kindest soul there was. Since my own mother died havin' me, Aunt Grace was the closest thing to a mother I ever had. I wrote to her all along. I'm sure she understood my rebellion. At any rate, she kept my secret. I wrote to her a lot during the War."

Granny's eyes narrowed slightly.

"Well, anyway, accordin' to my cousin Ruth-Anne MacEnroe – that's her married name – who was Aunt Grace's only child, we've got some distant relatives on my Aunt's side of the family who lived in Lambton County at one time. Trouble is, they seem to have moved away an' nobody can now locate them. Since her mother died, Ruth-Anne's been like a fanatic about tracing her roots. You'd think with cabinet ministers an' lawyers an' tycoons on your family tree, you'd be satisfied an' leave well enough alone."

Granny underlined the irony in the remark and Sunny smiled broadly. Reluctantly draining the cold tea from his cup, he rose to go.

"That stove should behave till spring," he said, pulling on his mackinaw. Granny watched every move he made. He reached sort of nonchalantly into his tool kit and pulled out a notepad, the brown wrapper still on it. He placed it over on the kitchen table, then looked across the room at her.

"The mass meetin's tomorrow night," he said quietly. "Right next door. I want you to write out on this paper whatever you want to say to the people of the Point. I'll read it aloud to them. You have some rights in all of this, you know."

Her eyes said neither yes nor no.

At the door, with his scarf tucked in, he said, "I think you should be there. I'll come for you around eight."

An icy draft from the open door struck her a sideways blow before the heat of the cleansed stove replenished itself.

37

By seven-forty-five the Oddfellows' Hall was almost full. More than half the town's six hundred adults were gathered to hear confirmation of the facts which were already public knowledge and spice for the rumour mill. The infirm, of whom there were more than the usual number, sat on wooden benches arranged especially for the occasion. Everyone else stood in clusters, buzzing, or leaned elbows on sills and wainscoting, happy to observe and judge. On the dais at the north end, the councillors peered down at their constituents, secure behind the trestle-table now littered with official-looking papers that were being shuffled more than necessary. The Reeve's chair remained unoccupied.

Just before eight o'clock the door opened and Reeve Denfield entered. Granny Coote was beside him. A stunned hush gripped the assembled: no rumour of this sort had tested the village breeze. What they saw, through their surprise, was a tiny old woman, barely five-feet tall with mottled gray hair pulled back into an uncustomary bun and tamed with a frayed blue ribbon. The Irish-white skin was blotched with liver-spots and yellowed from too much indoor light, but the eyes incandesced in their shrinking flesh, like two jets set in a shaman's mask. Although she allowed herself to be guided by the Reeve's arm, it was plain she wasn't feeble. Indeed, after the flaring of the eyes, it was her bearing that arrested the viewers' attention: she walked with an autonomous, erect grace that reminded the hunters in the hall of the way a white-tail lopes through a maze of brushwood, never once condescending to take a sideways glance; the women thought wistfully of queens at ease in crowded drawing rooms.

To the further surprise of the gathering and to the councillors themselves, Sunny Denfield escorted 'mad Granny' to a place beside him at the table. There they nonchalantly removed their coats and sat: downstage centre. Needless-to-say, the subsequent proceedings were scrutinized with more than usual interest.

First of all the Reeve announced that for reasons which would become clear later on he was turning the chair over to the Reverend Stokes, and then he and Granny Coote moved down to a less ostentatious position at the west end of the table. The old woman did not flinch under the obsessive watch of the assembly. She didn't even take the Reeve's arm, though the impression she left was one of determined fragility. Throughout the speeches that followed, she sat straight up in the wooden chair and looked out at the townspeople she had lived amongst for decades. Her eyes shone with a sanity that shamed them.

There's not a face I don't recognize, she was thinking. That would surprise most of them. I can't put a name to every one, but I know the family stamp: big noses, weak chins, sallow eye, the unmistakable hybrid smile. She could rhyme off their lineage – public and suppressed. She knew whom their second cousins married in Goderich or Petrolia. She remembered the high hopes their parents once had for them. And all these years these good citizens figured it was they themselves who were watching the sideshow of Mushroom Alley and the Lane. Who did they think we talked about? Whose rebels and strays kept our blind-pigs fed and our whorehouses wholesome? We took in rumours like transfusions. We invented the last laugh.

The chairman-pro-tem had begun. He called on Sandy Redmond, who repeated aloud the stale news about the selection of Sam Stadler to design and build the monument. The gathering added its applause to the speaker's own.

"However," Redmond continued when the last clap had exhausted its echo, "I must tell you that the buildin' fund will still need to be added to, as the cost of the landscapin' hasn't been figured in. So we're askin' you to dig as deep as you can. I think it's fair to say your council's stretched a dollar as far as it can go."

Like your wife stretches them behind the counter, Granny mused. You've got a grin and a handshake and a gift for the gab, but it's Olive who keeps the business afloat. Any woman who's been president of the WCTU knows how to dot the 'i' and cross the 't's' in temptation. But does she know you used to slip down to the Lane just like your Dad for a quick snort? I liked your Dad. He had doe's eyes.

"Harry Hitchcock will now give us his report on the selection of the site," said Chairman Stokes. "But before he does, I want to take this opportunity –"

And every opportunity you get.

"– to say a special word about those who have sacrificed, in silence and humility, their time and energy, and in one particular case more than that, for a cause which we are all agreed is a noble one, even a divinely inspired one."

Oh no, he's about to make a platitude out of a beatitude.

"Our Lord said, 'Blessed are the meek, for they shall inherit the earth'," and he bent to acknowledge the frail being at the end of the table, blessing her with his roast-beef smile.

And blessed are the obese for they shall batten on the pastures of heaven. Sunny Denfield touched her hand but she stared straight ahead.

Half-Hitch was on his feet and sailing through his set-piece, which he managed to complete without dropping a stitch. Into the sea of puzzled faces he then said in his own voice, "Of course, you now see the special sacrifice the good pastor was referrin' to. We need to have back the lot where Mrs. Coote now lives. Her house'll have to come down to make way for the monument. We're all dreadful sorry about that. But I'm sure we all know that progress has its price. And there'll be compensation for Mrs. Coote beside the reward of the Almighty Himself. We're gonna decide on it at our meetin' next week. We won't bore you with the complicated details now, but I was asked by council to tell you that Mrs. Coote's generosity will not be overlooked or ever forgotten. After all, a war memorial's all about sacrifice an' rememberin'," and he executed a little semaphore motion with his wooden souvenir.

That's some remembrance you're waving. You don't know that I know how you lost that hand, and it wasn't in the trenches. I got a full description from Eddie of you toppling off that barstool in some bordello at Givenchy during an air-raid and getting your arm crushed between two barrels of beer.

The stingy applause for Half-Hitch was cut even shorter by the Reeve's rising and holding up his hand. Half-Hitch sulked for a moment, but like the others surrendered to curiosity and waited for the chief councillor to speak.

"I stepped out of the chair," he said to them quietly, "because I was the only member of council not to vote in favour of the Coote property as a site for the monument. I didn't want to influence the decision before you all had a chance to hear the explanations. Even though the vote of council is legal and all, I'm sure nobody wants to do anythin' that would go against the conscience of the village. So I feel duty-bound to present to you Mrs. Coote's side of the story."

He waved before them what looked like a handwritten letter. All eyes followed it.

"As most of you know, Mrs. Coote can't speak for herself because she's got an affliction of the throat that stops her from talkin'. But I want to tell you Cora Coote is as bright an' sharp of mind as she ever was, and I have here her feelings on this matter, which she wrote down for me last night. I'd like to read these words if the chairman and council will let me."

There was consternation among council but the assembly made the decision for them. "Agreed," seconded chairman Stokes.

The Reeve then read: "Dear members of council: I wish you to know that I wholeheartedly agree with your selection of a site for the monument. You have chosen wisely and with good reason. I wish you to know also that I will do nothing to stand in the way of your plans. My house and land are yours. They are sacred to me for reasons no one but myself could understand, but then so is the village. I was here when the railroads arrived; I saw the townsite grow block by block, house by home. I cheered when it was proclaimed a village. In a small way I helped to name one of its streets. In all those years this house I now live in was the only one I could really call mine. My hope was to die in it. What I ask of the council is not compensation in dollars, which are of no value to me, but compensation in kind. I want to live out my days here in the village. I do not wish to be cast into a home for the wretched. The property is yours, in any event. I ask only that you think of me as you would any true citizen of the Point. Yours respectfully, Mrs. Cora Coote."

The reform party in council were devastated. No ploy, no plea or manoeuvre of any kind could have been as effective as these words. The old dame's a long ways from being bonkers, Half-Hitch thought. She was giving up her property but throwing her eighty-year-old-frail-pathetic-hard-done-by body upon the mercy of a boastfully Christian community. Even Reverend Stokes was able to discern the sheer cunning behind the move. What could be done? There was no public property to trade for hers, outside of unimproved fringe lots near the dunes, the dump or the swamp. Any solution that appeared in the least to be mean-spirited would crush the communal joy in whose spirit the monument was to be erected.

In the midst of these hushed mutterings, few people noticed young MacIntosh rise and ask for the floor. The Reeve, resuming command, rapped his gavel on the table.

"There is a solution to the problem," said the junior member of council, his voice quavering ever so slightly. "A solution that's fair an' workable."

"Go ahead, Horrie," said the Reeve.

"Well, I been thinkin' about fair compensation for Mrs. Coote all week, and I did some askin' around an' some fishin' in the County Court records. You all know the old lane that used to run between the Savage house and the Waggoner's place right across from Coote's? Hasn't been used as a lane I find for more than thirty years. The Savages now grow potatoes on it, an' Murray lets his grass grow over his half. Well, it seems the actual allowance there is thirty feet, twice the size of the lane. What I'm sayin' is, there's more than enough property to build a small cottage on. My suggestion is this: that we get together as a community, pool our skills, an' with the help of donations and any money Mrs. Coote can spare, build her a cottage to live in an' give her a deed to the property. When that's done, we can knock down the Coote house an' start to build the monument."

As one, the village turned to Granny Coote. She fought back the tears, with limited success. She looked towards Sunny Denfield and – imperceptibly – nodded.

38

1

March of 1922 was one of those late-winter months which people are forever remembering as part of a past that was not only better but more certainly connected with God's Grace and His grand scheduling of events for the world's good – before the rude intercession of wars, pestilence, and apostasy shook the embedded railings of the Divine Throne itself. Even God was growing nostalgic.

But here before the villager's immediate eye was proof of a larger beneficence, a firm hand on the throttle of natural progress. The snow continued to fall but only at night, silent and windless. Each morning it surprised and delighted anew, fostering the hope that it had not fallen from an empty sieve of the universe but rather had grown wondrously from the essence of limb, eave and chimney pot. By day the thermometer held steady at thirty degrees under a velvet sun, coaxing icicles out of warmed gables and generally rounding, curving, mellowing. Rinks glistened by noon but froze tight again overnight. Snowballs packed as neat as baseballs yet struck like puffs of childish laughter. The meanest shanty, suffering the neglect brought on by war and the failure of hope, was transformed by the architecture of ice and snow into a glittering edifice, bemused by the temporary perfection of its impromptu scrolls, prisms, mossy filigrees. Some folk even conceded that the old Coote shack was 'almost presentable', though the latter sentiment may have been prompted equally by the thought that, come spring, it would no longer grace the village landscape in any of its transformations. During this brief, cherished interregnum of the seasons, passers-by could not help but notice the small, still, alert face of Granny Coote in her front window. She seemed, to all her newly-hatched well-wishers, to be staring intently across the street where, despite the weather, several burly young men were to be seen, at noon-hour or after work, clearing the snow and chopping out a rectangular trench that would, when winter had yielded to necessity, hold the concrete footing of a new house. Around them were conspicuously piled a number of sections of 'material' – two-by-fours, joists, cedar siding – purchased out of the public purse and the charity of the citizenry, and carefully covered with several tarpaulins, all of them turned outward to expose the donor's identity: McKeough Fishery, Point Edward, Canada.

Though her attention was from time to time drawn towards the intermittent construction activity – she noted with appreciation (and the pure pleasure of memory) the presence of Charlie Brighton, old Mike's boy, out of work, his 'nerves' still bad from the War; of Wilf Underhill, taking precious time from his new son; of Stu Macdonald and young MacIntosh; and of Sunny Denfield who always came over afterward – Granny Coote was more likely to be thinking back to other days of renewal and starting over, to the gentle remembrance of those few, joyous months with Lucien Burgher, and those years afterward – unexpected, unearned – when she bore his name proudly through some of the darkest times of her long, long life. *Cora. Cora Burgher. Cora Coote. Cora the Cleaning Woman.* She was all of them, none of them. And before that, through a haze of memories deliberately but imperfectly obliterated, she remembered being Lily – of Mushroom Alley, of Potts' Lane…

2

The years between 1879 and 1885 saw the new nation gradually regain the confidence it had lost during the great depression when for a few shameful moments some citizens had suffered a lapse of faith in the ineluctability of their own progress. Aided by crop failures and a cattle epidemic in England and sanguinary adventures in Egypt and the Sudan, the local economy turned pink with health. If good works were a certain sign of election, then who could doubt the divine rightness of Sir John A's national hope, fulfilled at last in 1885: a three-thousand-mile band of iron to weld the faintheart provinces and empty territories together in a singular purpose. And add to this a thousand breath-taking bridges and trestles, mathematically graded inclines, brooding watchtowers, suspended steel arcs and ballooning grain elevators stretched between Montreal and Vancouver. The Canadian Pacific Railway swept all before it, the juggernaut of the transcendentalist dream. By happy coincidence in 1882 the Grand Trunk finally succeeded in swallowing whole its ancient rival, the Great Western, and within a year rumours of a magical underwater tunnel began to circulate, an engineering miracle that would not only confirm God's allegiance to His chosen creatures but also link the Canadian transcontinental grid with the rich, spidering network of iron and affluence south of the border.

In 1884 when the world adopted Sir Sandford Fleming's scheme for Standard Time – made necessary throughout the civilized world if rational and efficient train schedules were to be realized – who then could doubt that the railways, and the foundries forging their steel nervous-system, carried with them the aspirations of mankind and the sanction of the Almighty? True, a number of malcontents and Luddites (who curiously enough preferred to set local time by the local sun) did write strident letters to newspapers complaining of "railroad tyranny" and accusing our noble men of science of "tampering with God's time". But pusillanimous voices such as these were forever silenced by the last spike driven home at Craigalachie.

3

For Lily the first two years following the incorporation of Point Edward as a village were deceptively peaceful. She mourned the death of Sophie quietly and deeply, as she did all those she had lost, but around her the seasons and the lives within them changed and throve. The surveys along Potts' Lane were duly carried out. The new half of the street was a little less rambling than before but certainly not as straight as the town's other ones were (having been drawn on a map with a ruler in some official's study). Except for Lily and her secret arrangement with Hap Withers, no one on the Lane was unable to scrape together the fifty dollars to make their quietus with the council and the railway. The surveyors 'squared up' the wandering lot-lines, driving red stakes in the ground to prove their point. The resulting deeds were then registered, fixed for all time. But if the village worthies expected fences and hedges to spring up along these fresh definitions of ownership, they were disappointed. Nor was there a rush on paint and plaster at Lockwood's Hardware by the citizenry of Potts' Lane. However, over a period of many months some signs of proprietorship did become visible to the discerning eye – a shingled roof (one side only), a single sparkling pane of glass, a thrust of perennials along a barren wall permitted to bloom if they were persistent enough, a stone fireplace that didn't quite get finished but was used and admired nonetheless.

Mushroom Alley evolved slowly in the Lane in other ways, no more dramatic but much more important to Lily and her own life there. People moved away and were replaced – one or two at a time, so at first little difference was felt: a brief break, a hiatus, some memories, a forgetting – and you could reassure yourself that the Lane was still the alley with a better truer name and that the requisite essentials for one's own continuance were still in place. Then one morning you wake up and realize that everything has changed, that it has been changed for some time, and people around you are looking at you as if you're the only thing that hasn't. And you ask, how did it happen?

That Stoker Potts didn't come back from the Bruce was no surprise to anybody on the Lane. The house stood empty all that winter, the screen door slamming in the wind till Rob finally went over for Lily and nailed it shut. Next to Hazel's it was the biggest and best-built house among them. Rumours flew that some entrepreneurial stranger was about to buy it with a view to gobbling up the neighbouring properties to make room enough for a hotel larger than The Queen's – now that the depression was giving way to prosperity and financial adventure. It was soon confirmed that the fifty dollars had been duly paid and a deed transferred. There was considerable relief when Peg Potts (now Granger) and her husband moved in, bringing their own child, and her young brother, Bricky, with them. But Peg, though she still had Sophie's devilish eyes and hair-trigger laugh, had got religion and was quite reserved, 'standoffish' according to Betsy and Winnie. Her husband was a sober man who worked in Sarnia and tried to build a fireplace to please his wife. "Still," Hazel philosophized, "they're really not *the other kind*." Bricky spent a lot of time with Rob, and when Rob was away, with Lily.

Cap Whittle, one windy autumn day in 1880, leaned too far out on his topsail yardarm and tumbled into the billows below, cracking three ribs and jarring another dime loose in his overworked imagination. His lot was sold to the eldest McCourt boy and his girlfriend, who proceeded to live in splendid sin in the neat clapboard cottage they erected and painted pale blue – once. Despite the impudence of the paint, they were deemed to be genuine Alleyfolk (the girl being a cousin of the Shawyers from Bosanquet Township). Lily had known Pippy McCourt for years, and she waved to him every day as he passed on his way to the freight-sheds. He always gave her a big smile. I wonder why, Lily thought, then chided herself for such foolish introspection.

In the bitter winter of 1881-82 Honeyman Belcher caught pneumonia and died alone in his shack. The frozen body was discovered three days later by his friend Stumpy. Honeyman's business was taken over by a man from Sarnia. Hazel organized a campaign to raise money so that one of the Shawyer girls and her husband could afford to buy the lot and make the place habitable. It was something Sophie might have done – they all thought but did not say. Another property have been preserved from contamination, it seemed, but no one was willing yet to admit that each change somehow put the whole enterprise – if indeed there was one – in jeopardy. No one dared to even think that with Sophie's death something vital and irreplaceable had gone out of their collective life, that in some mysterious way Sophie Potts had *been* the Alley and that the Lane in which they had immortalized her name was already something else.

Such sacrilege may have entered the minds of one or two of the believers when in May of 1881, without warning or explanation, John the Baptist capped his still, chivvied Aquinas the boar onto a wagon with his furniture, and moved to another shack in the south end near the recently constructed racetrack and fairgrounds. "Got some French woman hot for his product," Hazel opined freely, but nobody laughed. A few nights later a gang of hooligans put the torch to his shanty when they found the still without sustenance. "I don't believe in signs!" Hazel snapped at Betsy to shut her up.

As it turned out, Stumpy and Lily were the last of the hard-core Laners to survive there. In the fall of 1882 Spartacus, complaining of "too damn much noise an' interferin' in a body's business" moved in with John the Baptist. Both lived and carried on their work into the 'nineties and were missed when they passed on. They never returned to the Lane. Poor Stumpy, whose supply of derelicts was not diminished by Sir John's 'economic miracle', continued his good deeds until December of 1884 when one of his boarders stabbed him to death, mistaking him in the dark for an avenging Beelzebub whom he had seen leaping from the evening express just moments before. The assassin was shipped off to the asylum in London.

Several weeks after Baptiste Cartier's place burned down, Violet arrived at Lily's in tears.

"What's wrong?" Lily said.

"Betsy an' Shad are gettin' married."

"What *else*?"

"We're all gonna move."

To a rambling brick house in Forest, twenty miles to the north-east. "We're goin' legitimate again, Lil," Hazel explained, "in a town where we can start over. Shad an' my girls – Winnie an' Betsy an' dear, dear Vi – we're gonna fix it up an' start a boardin' house. I mean it, Lil, a genuine boardin' house. I'm goin' back to cookin' again. This here's been fun but we're all too old for it. Winnie almost died with her last abortion an' Betsy's insistin' on keepin' the one she's got in her now – at forty-six years of age – 'cause she's sure it belongs to Shad. So I headed off for Forest on the train one day last week and I just up an' bought this old place."

"Who'll get *this* house?" Lily asked.

"Hap Withers has already bought it – for his eldest."

"When're you leavin', then?"

"Next week, after the holiday. Ain't it excitin'? You can hop on the Day Express an' come up an' visit us any time. Any time you please."

"Yes," Lily said, "it's not even an hour, I'm told."

Hazel, almost white-haired now, let her eyes mist over. "I remember when you was a red-haired beauty with the shyest smile in the County an' your little pony Benjamin pullin' you up Front Street every Saturday mornin', an' Betsy an' Winnie were the worst teases ever."

"I remember, Char."

"Christ in Heaven, Lily," she cried, "what's to become of us?"

Violet came in to the laundry shed to say goodbye. When Lily had gathered enough courage to ask her why she wanted to go with Hazel and to assure her that she could stay here and live and work and be happy as long as she lived, Violet looked at the floor and said, "I got to go with Hazel. She's been good to me." Like the mother you never had, Lily was thinking when Violet stunned her with: "She needs me, Lil."

The two women embraced, and it was Lily who let go first.

"I got somethin' for you," Lily said.

Violet glanced at the carpetbag in which Lily had packed some of the clothes and trinkets Violet had left here over the years and into which she had secretly tucked the one hundred and fifty dollars of unclaimed income that Bachelor Bill's 'retarded' daughter had earned as her helper and her friend.

"Not that," Lily said. "Something my mother gave me I'd like you to have, to re-member me by."

"Hazel says you'll come up to see us on the train."

"Of course I will." Lily drew the gold crucifix and chain from her apron pocket and as Violet leaned forward, Lily placed it around her throat where it settled as soft as a butterfly's dream on clover.

"Remember me," Lily whispered.

Lily always intended to visit Hazel and Violet, and did receive one letter months later indicating that all was well: Betsy's baby was robust and black, Winnie's health had improved, Hazel was practically running the village, and oh yes, Violet had found her-self a gentleman friend and specially asked after Lily. With Brad's help Lily composed a stilted letter wishing them all well and promising once again to climb on the train and visit. She couldn't, of course, tell them what sort of chaos her own life was sliding into.

4

Granny: in the belly of the Night-Dream again from which mercifully there was no remembrance, only the aftertaste of ash and self-loathing: Birdsky's child called Rabbit was dancing around her again on his jackrabbit legs, his chestnut face burnished by the uninnocence of the summer's sun and his slim boy's arms undulant as willow and waving, wending them both backwards towards the bush towards the forbidden dark at the reaches of the East Field and beyond the last spot of sunlight reserved for Mama's grave, its honey-heat pouring longingly on her neck, her shoulders bare, on her gooseflesh calves and casting a nine-year-old Lily-shadow upon the ghost of her mother's cold breathing but Rabbit's happy-dance was hopping in the bell-chambers of her little-girl's heart and he was leading her away from the hearth where death dwelt unabashed in the daylight where Papa committed his treacheries upon the copper woman who cried out like a night-jar, her baby Rabbit dancing his two-foot/four-foot Indian jig into the crooked dank into the sweated crotch of ancient branch and Cambrian bole and somewhere out of the black interior the sound of music drifting out of brass and violin and tympany striving towards the geometry of a waltz or galop or durable lancers and Rabbit's hand grew suddenly firmer and in the glow of hoarded moonlight she could see he had sprung taller and light-of-hair and his smile was Tom's smile, a first-lover's smile and "Come on, come on" it crooned waltzing into the intricate distance till it drew her at last into his dancer's grip and she saw that his eyes were pebble-blue, iced amethysts agleam like the stiffened orbs of the long-drowned staring starward as the seasons' rivers wash mockingly over them...

39

1

Bradley, as he was now called, continued to do well in school. Studying was as effortless as breathing to him and no amount of dereliction seemed to interfere with the steady flow of A's on his report cards. In January of 1879 Lily agreed to let him stay at Mrs. Tideman's boarding house a block from the high school in Sarnia. Lily talked for an hour with that good lady and concluded that she was a sober-minded, conscientious Christian who specialized in haltering the headstrong youth of the town. "He'll keep his nose to the grindstone here, and it's lights out at nine-thirty!" She did her best. So did Lily, but Bradley was rapidly turning into an impetuous, brooding young man – taller than his father by a head at age sixteen, with an oddly effeminate handsomeness that both attracted and repelled the young women in whose company he was increasingly seen. He deliberately cultivated the tubercular look of a romantic poet, letting his blond curls droop wantonly over a pale brow and wan cheek. He was supposed to spend his weekends at home, and did so until he entered grade eleven and took up with the likes of Paul Chambers, the solicitor's son.

Even when Bradley was at home, Lily often found herself at her wits' end. Whenever she would cut short his swaggering arrogance with a stare or a retort he was unable to handle, he would sulk for hours, often ending up in a fit of remorse and weeping until Lily wrapped her arms around him and let him feel how deep and complete and unqualified her forgiveness was. For days on end he would be a model son, provoking a smoky fire at dawn and serving her tea and toast in bed, or sitting with her and patiently explaining who the Tudors were or how the United Empire Loyalists came to be and why they were hailed as the founding pillars of Canadian society. He even helped her with her writing which, he insisted, was coming along famously. But even when Bradley was in one of his rare good moods, Rob would not stay at the house nor in his backyard tent; he headed for solitude on his own place – where she herself had lived so long ago with Bridie and Uncle Chester, when she had been – it seemed forever – Lily Ramsbottom. When Bradley left for Sarnia, Rob would arrive home for supper and be so ill-tempered for days that Lily found herself taking out her anger and frustration on the innocent one. With the depression ending at last, Rob was working three days a week at the sheds all year round. Whatever resentment he felt towards Bradley was always swallowed for Lily's sake; she knew this and tried her best to be fair to him. But Rob was not a talker; Lily could feel the currents reverberating deep in his body as she sat in the same room with him, but they were rarely expressed in words – only obliquely in looks. I wish I knew what he wanted for his life, Lily often thought, then I would give it to him tenfold. But I don't.

"He's living out there in that shack with some tramp," Bradley pouted. "Why don't you do something about him?"

"With Sue Potts, you mean," Lily said and Bradley went white, then silent.

But in the fall of Bradley's entry into grade eleven, Wee Sue eloped with the baker's son.

Paul Chambers was bright and ambitious and rich. Mrs. Tideman, throwing up her hands, declared him "a bad influence" capable of leading "the Virgin Mary astray". But vexed and puzzled as she was by the whole affair, Lily was inclined to believe that he was a kindred spirit that Bradley, for reasons she could not yet define, had sought out and bonded himself to. His head is full of words he hasn't found things to pin them to, was one way she thought of the restless, tethered creature he kept inside him; if he stays here he'll suffocate, he'll tear his own brains out. So she watched and hoped, and kept putting money into the crockery jar under the bed. There's love inside him, too, she consoled herself when the rheumatism started up; words are a way of feeling, I know, and Bradley's only got to get them aimed away from himself and towards something bigger and more wonderful, *out there.*

In Paul Chambers he found a purpose for poetry and politics – Canada First, the frenzied ultra-nationalist club of writers and apprentice thinkers that was sweeping the salons and tearooms of the confederation. Chambers had founded a local chapter of the society, used his father's money to rent a club room at the St. Clair Inn every Tuesday and Thursday evening, and gathered about him a group of like-minded believers. It was reported that they smoked cigars and drank French wine. Most of the adherents were between seventeen and twenty-two years of age, youthful, idealistic, bent on literary careers and affecting (without achieving) the Byronic form of ascetic Hedonism. Only Bradley was successful in getting a poem accepted for publication in the society's national organ, *Rose-Belford's Canadian Monthly.* For a time the legendary Goldwyn Smith was their idol and mentor.

On the rare weekends when Bradley did come home during his senior year, Lily was made an honorary inductee and subjected to lengthy expositions of the Canada First manifesto. Bradley's eyes would flash with righteousness and confidence of youth, and there was in them a purity of purpose that frightened Lily, but also amazed and gratified. Mostly, though, she was inundated. It seemed that people like her were representative of the provincialism, the parochialism, the homespun timidity that was keeping Canada from taking her place among the senior cultures of the world; that was holding back the natural development of a larger national spirit, a more capacious transcontinental loyalty and a more transcendent view of citizenhood; that was, moreover, sabotaging the very free and unlocalized and politically independent forms of literature and philosophy which were necessary to the growth of civility itself. When Lily protested that she failed to see how she personally was at fault in these matters, he merely grew more vehement and repeated his arguments with an increasing number of polysyllabic words. And when she had the temerity to ask him how much of the Maritimes and Prairies and Rockies he had seen, or questioned the sincerity of 'St. John' Macdonald, he threw a tantrum, then retreated into his morose/remorse routine. She soon realized that she was not meant to comment or defend or reprove but merely to listen as the lava of his words hardened in the clear air around them, to become – as she had once done so long ago when he had been afraid to sing to the dark – the trustee of his secret self. And so she came to accept in silence his wheedling and badgering and elocutionary harangues until tears shattered and regrouped behind her eyes and Bradley slumped exhausted on the table, staring at her with the look of a pneumoniac. Once, Rob was in the shed chopping wood during one of these gruelling sessions, and came in just as Bradley finished. Bradley glowered and went out, slamming the door. Lily released her tears more in annoyance than hurt. She felt Rob watching her, axe in hand. She looked up at him for some gesture of help, comfort, understanding – anything. He flung the axe-blade into the floor and stomped out the back way.

When Bradley graduated *magna cum laude* in June of 1881, Lily was fussed over by Hazel, Betsy and Winnie until they could declare her 'a regular town lady'. Hazel contributed a fancy hat and Betsy a parasol – both of which Lily politely refused. But she did allow them to stitch and tuck the dress they'd created out of partial cloth until she was respectable enough to pass muster. She did not want her son to be embarrassed on the most important occasion of his life. In fact Bradley seemed surprised and not altogether pleased by the bearing of his mother during the ceremony and the apparent ease with which she made polite conversation with her betters at the reception. "I bet she could joke with the old Queen and get away with it," Paul Chambers burbled. "Where *have* you been hiding your mother, you rascal?" Bradley was not amused, though he too was unable to take his eyes off his mother. When Counsellor Chambers himself asked her to dance, Bradley blushed from half a dozen contending emotions. Rob did not come.

The following week, just after the news of Hazel's decision to leave reached her, Lily was buoyed by word from Mr. Axelrod that Bradley's application to University College in Toronto had been accepted and that a modest scholarship of twenty-five dollars was proffered with the promise of much, much more down the line. That night as an early summer storm raged around them, Lily and Bradley sat down to map out the details of his future. Bradley held the principal's letter in his hand as if it were an executioner's telegram. All the blush and bravado had drained from his face. In his trapped blue eyes Lily watched a boy's fear of the crooked dark, sly moonlight, bat-shadows under eaves, the giant's fee-fi-fo-fum. She braced herself but he would not say it.

"You must go," she said.

"I will, I will," he said, "but I can't. Not yet."

"When?"

"As soon as I have enough money. I was expecting a much bigger scholarship. Twenty-five dollars is an insult."

"How much do you need?"

"Paul says at least four hundred dollars over the four years."

"But I got two hundred an' fifty already – in the crockery jar. An' the principal says you can expect more scholarship money by second year."

"What in hell does he know? He's never been east of London."

"Okay, then, tell me when."

"I need a year off. I've talked it over with Paul and his father. He has agreed to take me on as a clerk for a year; I'll earn enough money to put myself right through, and we won't have to be beholden to anyone."

"Is Paul going?"

Bradley paused before he answered, scanning his mother's face with anger and amazement. "No," he said almost inaudibly. "Paul's going to tour Europe for a year, and then register at University College after that."

When Violet left, Lily tried to carry on alone with her business. But the summer was exceptionally hot and she soon became exhausted. Rob found her one day in a faint, seated beside the mangle as if she were taking a snooze. She couldn't remember where she was or how she'd got there, and when Rob clasped her arm to raise her up, she screamed with pain. She spent three weeks in bed exorcising the fever. Rob was at her side much of the time. Bradley came on weekends.

"You don't need to do this, you know," Rob said in exasperation as she tottered back to the shed and surveyed the accumulated laundry Rob himself had not been able to clear away. "There's only yourself to take care of."

"I'll get a couple of the McLeod girls to help me. They need the money."

And she did.

2

Frieda and Mitsy proved to be good workers and kind, grateful neighbours. But nothing could replace the loss of Violet and the others, and Cap Whittle's fall and Honeyman's death made Lily feel very much older and very, very tired. Rob was lugging freight full-time and talking about adding some animals to 'his place' in the spring, and Bradley was working diligently in the law office and starting to talk again with enthusiasm about university, particularly, Lily noted, after the arrival of a letter from Paul with a postmark from Rome or Paris. So Lily wrapped herself in sweaters and plunged each morning into the frost and singe of the laundry shed in winter. Frieda and Mitsy sang off-key in shy, tin-whistle voices, but sing they must, and laugh – as everyone around Lily eventually did.

Paul Chambers arrived home on the first of May for a month's visit before touring New York, Baltimore, Chicago and the far west by train. Bradley informed Lily that he and Paul were going to Toronto for a few days to inspect the campus and make preliminary arrangements for their entrance in the autumn. "We're going to stay at the Royal York, and see the sights," he said, his guilt at the twenty dollars or so he would have to spend drowned in his excitement. When he left, with an extra five dollars from Lily to buy some new clothes, she sat by herself and drank a slow cup of tea. It's going to happen at last, she allowed herself to think, very quietly and scarcely in words.

When he returned five days later with his tweed jacket torn and a bruised carnation in his lapel, Lily heard little talk of the university. The subject was Wilde, Mr. Oscar Wilde, whom they had heard lecture twice at the Botanical Gardens and spied up close in the flesh during one of his 'progresses' up York Street.

Bradley's eyes blazed with something hard and radium and irreducible. They held Lily in their spell while their author paced back and forth across the kitchen like a frantic Socrates, gesticulating and querulous, his pale, thin body whipped and fanned by a zealot's fire.

"We've been wrong, Paul and me, all along. Not completely wrong because we've been trying to expand our sense of the world, to cut all the ties that bind us here, and to reach for something larger and more wondrous and unknowable – like the spirit of a nation, something beautiful and sacred because it is *bigger* than the miserable little lives that combine to make it up, the wretched lives that have no poetry in them unless they're stretched and broken and consumed by the *idea* of nationhood. Not blind, stupid patriotism but the noble conception of a collective consciousness, an invisible oversoul that moves and directs a country's destiny, just as Emerson has said. And you know how passionately Paul and I have held to this notion, and how we've begun to put our own poetry and our schoolboy philosophy at its service, but then, then to have heard Oscar Wilde speak to us as he did from that dais, and tell us in words I shall never forget – I shall take them to my grave – that we were only partly right, that Beauty, and the arts that create Her, are valuable *for their own sake*, that there's a magic universal truth that inspires beauty and goes beyond the spirit of nation-states, German philosophies and pious moralities. Don't you see, Ma, we were headed in the right direction, we were trying to learn more and more about the world out there, about the unseen powers that regulate its fate, about ideals that would allow us to transcend our petty day-to-day lives, about the forces of poetry and art and history – but we just didn't go far enough. There are universal truths we can't begin to grasp until we've disentangled ourselves from politics and moralizing, until we are ready to devote our lives to the pure contemplation of what is beautiful."

Lily picked up the carnation that had fallen on the table and brushed it partly back to life. "This was Mr. Wilde's?" she said.

Bradley nodded, then sat down, still shaking, and let Lily pin it carefully back onto his lapel. "I'll stitch your jacket up before you leave."

Bradley caught her hand in flight. "You *do* see, Ma, why I've got to go to Toronto. There's so much I have to know. There's so much out there to see. There's so much buzzing around inside my head I think someday it will just explode and that'll be the end of me. I got to keep going, Ma. I got to find out what I am."

Rob was actually the one who found the note on the table and the smashed crockery jar beside the bed. Lily had been over at Peg's helping her nurse the babe through the whooping cough. Frieda, terrified by the look that Rob had given her, came dashing across the Lane to fetch her. Lily and Rob read the note:

> Dear Ma and Rob:
>
> I love you both more than my life. I'm sorry I have never been able to show it or prove it to you. But I must make the break now and for awhile it must be complete. I've got to have a look at the world out there. When I do, I'll be back.
>
> In the meantime, please don't try to find me. Take good care of her, Rob.
>
> Bradley

3

Lily waited only a few weeks before she walked down to Hap Withers' cottage and told him he could have her house as well as the property. He moved the last of his numerous brood into the place and, being a widower and now alone, asked Lily if she would like the use of his two front rooms in return for a few housekeeping duties. Since they were already furnished, Lily brought nothing with her but a laundry bag full of clothes, a bookcase, a few trinkets and keepsakes the boys had given her as gifts over the years, and Sounder's pouch with Papa's Testament, the talisman, and the cameo pendant with her grandmother's face on it. She put the pouch under her bed and left it there.

Rob was very good to her. He stopped by often for tea or supper with her and Hap Withers. He took her down to Sarnia on the trolley for supper at a fancy English tea-room on Christina Street. He urged her to come over and help out with his garden. He was full of plans for expanding the operation. He had fixed up the little barn so that it was comfortable in a rustic way, shingled and shuttered, with white-pine floorboards and a split-log table he built himself. Nearby he had constructed a pigeon-cote full of homers and tumblers, each with a name and pedigree. Below it, his pet angoras lived in luxurious innocence. He'd adopted a stray dog, who slept with him at night and guarded the premises by day. He seemed content most of the time, but still she knew there was a restlessness in him, inarticulate but deep. Only when he got a letter from his only friend, Fred Potts (who had run away with the circus and was now in charge of all the animals and had just married one of the bareback riders in Texas) – did he let his regret and helplessness show. She left him alone, with his pigeons and his dog.

Lily went to Duckface Malloney at The Queen's, who readily agreed to let her do the hotel's wash in the new sheds he'd just added at the back. Her other customers she let go, though she decided that since she was now alone she ought to get out and around more, and so she was often seen during the next couple of years working in the households of Mrs. Durham, Mrs. Saltman, Mrs. Blakely and others – washing, ironing and most of all minding the children. Three mornings a week, then, she toiled at The Queen's where there was company if you wanted it and solitude if you needed it.

She went out to Rob's place two or three times a week during the growing seasons, working away in the garden with Rob at her side whenever he could be. She heard at The Queen's that he was seeing a young lady at Camlachie up the lakeshore a bit, and so on many a summer evening it would be almost dark when he got home, and he'd pitch in beside her, chopping away like a fiend at the offending weeds. Still, despite their joint efforts, the garden seemed always in a state of imminent disorder. One day when she came over in the afternoon while Rob was at the freight-sheds, she was surprised to see a bedraggled young woman and her three children pulling up beets and tearing off tomatoes, trampling as much as they were retrieving. "Rob told us to come an' help ourselves, mum. Sorry if we give you a scare." When Lily casually mentioned the event a few days later, Rob grunted and said, "Yeah, I said they could take what they wanted. Her husband died last winter up in Camlachie." He got up. "I gotta go out for a while. Don't go fussin' too much over the cabbage patch, eh." Lily didn't. She sat on the bench beside the cooing pigeons and let some of the realities of her life sweep over her, one of which was the fact – now irrefutable – that Rob had kept this miserable patch going for her sake alone. He had come to despise the sight of it.

Since Lily never went up to the Post Office for her mail, the postmaster decided it was his duty to deliver the letter to her door. She thanked him and then stared at the florid, feminine calligraphy on the envelope. She could barely recognize her own name. She unwrapped the vellum paper and read:

Toronto, October 10, 1884

Dear Mrs. Marshall:

You do not know me. My name is Sarah Crawford. I am a good friend of Bradley, your son. I met him last year here in Toronto, and we shared the same boarding house. Before he went to Montreal, we belonged to the same literary circle. He was the most promising poet among us. A few months ago he wrote me from England, where he was staying with Paul Chambers, who was there for the summer break. He told me he was on the verge of something great and important in his life, and that he would write again soon. He never did. But I did get a letter from Paul Chambers. He too had decided to give up school and make his way in England. He never mentioned Bradley until the letter that came yesterday morning. Oh Mrs. Marshall, I cannot write this without weeping. Paul told me that Bradley took his own life a short while ago. He left a note begging Paul to tell no one, and just walked into the Thames. Paul arrived in time to see him go under and disappear forever. Paul does not know that

I found your name and address in Bradley's room after he left for Montreal. I felt it my sad duty to write you immediately. I loved your son, Mrs. Marshall. I tried to save him. I hope that some day we shall meet.

Yours respectfully,

Sarah Crawford

I tried too, Lily thought. And I loved him.

4

The second Riel Rebellion was in every way different from the first. Where it had taken a ragtaggle, improvised militia almost three months to traverse the northern wilderness by paddle and portage, the modern Canadian army boarded trains all along the old Intercolonial line and embarked on a three-day excursion to the Saskatchewan River courtesy of the Canadian Pacific Railway Company. Militia or regulars, this was, moreover, a pan-Canadian force of crack troops under seasoned leadership. At the other end, the rebellious natives and half-castes were also better organized and armed than their forebears had been along the Red and Assiniboine. But muskets and religious fanaticism were no match for rifles, the drill of discipline and the spanking new Gatling gun on loan from the U.S. Army, who were anxious to test the latest 'improved feed' model in legitimate combat. It performed splendidly, spitting out a record twelve hundred bullets per minute and scaring crows for miles around. The major battle at Batoche was won in less than a day. The hillsides where the Métis had dug themselves into the earth were littered with their dead, the log cabins behind them where their women and children crouched were razed by the efficiency of six-pounders, and the mad secessionists were silenced for all time. It was a clear victory for mechanized order in the service of benevolent civility. The integrity of the fledgling nation had been breeched, and that breech was not healed with blood. Only seven citizen-soldiers died in the cause. And if this first great national military action was not on the same scale as the American Civil War – with its million dead and million maimed – it was nonetheless a landmark victory for the universal cause of nation-making. It was also, in miniature, a curtain raiser for the horrors-to-come less than thirty years later.

Naturally there would have to be a little political fence-mending in the squalid aftermath of the shooting, but nothing Sir John could not accomplish over time. Certainly few loyal citizens wished to see the publication of those letters sent home by militiamen who, upon seeing the pathetic condition in which their adversaries had been forced to live, decided they had more in common with the Métis than with Mr. Macdonald. Such naive emotional lapses are to be expected under duress, and a generous victor can afford to be forgiving. Louis Riel was hanged.

Rob surprised her in the pantry of The Queen's where she was fetching a jar of marmalade for the cook.

"Hap Withers said you'd be here," he said.
Lily saw the blue of his uniform, nothing else.
"I got to go, Ma."
"Yes", she said.
"I'm not Brad. I'll be back. I swear."
She had heard those very words before.

The night before the battle of Batoche Lily dreamt she was the angel of innocence, floating over the battleground with the folds of her shift swept upward into wings as warm as a swan's throat. In the grassy shadows below here, scythed here and there by a quartering moon, lay the corpses of the seven who died. One by one she settled over them and the winnowing of her angel-arms awoke in them some instinct sharper than death, and each in his turn rolled over, as in sleep, yawned and opened his eyes abruptly, like a doll's. The seventh figure did not respond to the angel's wing-breath no matter how fervently it was offered. Sadly, very sadly the kindly seraphim eased the body over into the moonlight. The face was dead. It was Robbie's.

5

And Granny, once again or still, in the sea-warm, abdominal home of the Night-Dream where all that was precious had to be remembered and re-remembered with all its pristine pain intact and bright as foetal blood against the pitch of almost-morning, had to be re-membered fresh and bruising or be forever claimed by the place of forgetting that lay at the bottom of all sleep whose oblivion was absolute: she was in the Lambton swamp once more, still-called Lil and only eleven and very much alone, the River-of-Light pouring past her mere yards away like some maddened tributary of the Styx through its underground grot-toes and moon-starved dark, she was chilled to the marrow, the chill of abandonment that runs as deep as childhood itself, the prodigal heart orphaned under the indifferent stars, and drifting towards the sleep where death's welcome seemed a kind of comfort, and waking, surprised a second time, in the presence of the stranger from the lost south, the Shawnee or Southener as he was known, but when she reached to touch the warmth his kindness had brought, the robes over his ancient flesh weakened and thinned in the pre-dawn radiance around them, and when she tried to speak to him in one of the ancient tongues she knew his gentle face cringed and clenched, the lips crying no, no before they began to fade and the face with them, the copper flesh first so only the wrinkled outlines were preserved and the old, old eyes grew correspondingly larger till they filled the smoky space around them with their sad brilliance and promise of a thousand sagas curled in the shadows behind them and it must have been the eyes that spoke to her because there was no longer a mouth to utter its oracles, crooked or straight, but the air was filled with its voice and suddenly a hand, no bigger than a father's lovingly in his daughter's, floating in the immeasurable distance between them and on its upturned proffering palm there glowed the jasper talisman – scarlet as a hum-mingbird's throat in the sun's full thrust, as rooted as radium, and the voice shimmered in its carnal incandescence and she remembered the words in their alien consonance – intact – because all that was precious has to be remembered bruising and fresh: "This will bring you luck all your days, it will help you find a home here and in the hereafter; I received this magic stone on a sacred ground, long known as such by generation upon generation of tribes who have dwelt in these woods and waters and passed on, as we all do; the days of its guardianship are almost over, there is little magic left in the forests and the streams, older now than our legends; the locomotives of the white man's soul are on their way, so when you have no more use for the stone's power, I ask that you return it to the sacred grove whence it came; you will know when you are standing on it because it resides beneath the protecting branches of a giant hickory on a knoll just where the forest begins, and when you look west and north you will be able to see, at the commencement of summer, the joining of the Lake and the River set perfectly on a line to the North Star, whom we call the eye of Wendigo" and the words of the Southener echoed and re-echoed in her long dream until daylight came to quench them...

40

1

It was bitterly cold when Lily left the hotel after her shift. Normally the fresh December wind, sweeping across the open water of the Lake and slashing randomly at the village, would have blown her quickly north-eastward towards the shacks along the Lane. Instead she walked west towards the River. There was no hurry in her walking, no evident purpose. The River was frozen tight, its rage arrested. Locomotives languished on sidings, their armour-plate complaining in the cold. One or two lamps glowed feebly in the dockside hotel to her left. Nor was her walking quite aimless, even though she soon left the road that wound its way to the freight-sheds, and seemed to drift into the frozen verges of the marsh. It was as if she were walking towards some end that lay about to reveal itself yards or rods ahead of her, or that lay curled inside her near the heart ready to declaim its desires only when this ritual walking was somehow complete.

Certainly she felt no windburn on her face, her exposed throat, her ungloved hands. Her eyes blurred in the keen chill of the night-air, but she had no difficulty seeing what she had to see. Her heart pumped hotly in her chest, like a featherless bird beating its bony wings against invisible ramparts of ice. But she felt no emotion flow from its exertion. It was connected only to her legs and to its own mechanical instincts. The heart that had once stored her feelings and stoked them out of memory on command was now dead. Numbed, then drained, then irreconcilably dead. Considering what had happened to her over these last months, these last years, the death of feeling was no surprise. Only so much could be borne, lived through, and accommodated to the adjusting heart. To bear more, as she had been asked to after such pain and loss, was not to expand the borders of her humanity but to deny that any of its elements was essential, unshakeable, or rooted in necessities like love and steadfastness. How many times during her travail had she promised herself: I will not live just because my flesh yearns to continue and this flap of muscle in my chest convulses in its own selfishness. I am more than flesh and gulping blood. When I hurt I can feel the pain everywhere,

I can hear it running backwards all the way to my youth, my childhood, the moment of birth.

What was surprising was that she had carried on at all, that right from the beginning she knew her daily trek to The Queen's to repeat the labours of a thousand previous days was not merely the automatic motions of a body not knowing how to do anything different nor the trust of a numbed will in the therapy of familiar routine. 'Busy hands and the seasons will mend the fractured heart' was the village cliché. Well, she had lived enough to know the worth of such homilies. Nonetheless, the very next day after the dreadful news about Robbie had been confirmed, she arrived for work on time. It was on the same day also that she began this nightly ritual of wandering the village paths and byways – in search of something, lost or promised.

Tonight there was more urgency. She felt it somewhere between her frost-bitten cheeks and the haemorrhaging of her heart. She did not notice the snow begin to fall just as the wind died. She failed to hear the shale-ice crumble underfoot. The dark dissolved before her. The air was lit by snow, by moving and motionless bits of the universe, by the arctic friction at the heart of the snow's design. Uninvited, individual flakes touched her cheeks without regret, and made their own tears. Somewhere something incorruptible was melting, gaining radiance.

For a moment the snow lifted and the night sprang back. She was lost – in the marshlands that lay on the peninsula between the River and the Lake. She was not frightened. She felt nothing but this vague edge of urgency. Ahead of her, set out against the shadowy blur of houses and gardens on the rise where the village began, she saw the outline of some fantastic, multi-limbed figure stretched upward through the veil of snow, the etch of its gesture somewhere between yearning and defiance. Over its brief horizon, it presided: heroic and doomed. The snow closed in again. Her walking recommenced. She was moving towards the figure no longer visible. She touched it shadow falling through a white daze. She heard its breath against her own as she neared. She felt suddenly encompassed, kindled, amnesiac, at home. Her back rested against its rooted bole. At last she saw the snow as it was: dancing its intricate, hopscotch, hornpipe fling for her eyes only. *This is it. The reason.* She sat down. She let her eyes close themselves. She let the last magic take her.

"You give us quite a scare," Malloney said. He looked very uncomfortable, not certain whether to sit on the captain's chair that could barely contain his bulk or to stand awkwardly above her with no place to plant his hands. They were alone, in his room at the right-front of the hotel. She cleaned it twice a week.

"It's lucky for us all," he said, glancing hopefully around, "we was havin' our Oddfellows' meetin' down there tonight."

She coughed, and he sprang cumbrously forward with a cup of hot tea in his grip. She saw that it was half-consumed.

"You'll need some more of this," he said, then suddenly looked away.

She was crying.

She thought: poor Duckface. That is what everyone called Kevin P. Malloney, some to his face, others out of earshot. The epithet was descriptive of his large, fleshly face that was pushed inward vertically along the centre-line, resembling a ruffled duck's tail, as if his mother, in shock or despair, had struck her infant with an angle-iron. As a result, his beady eyes had been squeezed even closer together and his mouth, longing to be spacious, pursed and dilated simultaneously. Hence it was very difficult for him to convey emotion, the range of overt expression being limited, as it were, from the outset. Most people were content merely to assume and accept that he was, as his face forewarned the world, a saturnine, obtuse, uncaring sloth of a man. It was widely reported that his Irish eyes only danced to the jig of a cash-register.

She saw that her hands were shaking as she sipped absently at the tea.

"Almost froze to death, you did," Malloney said, automatically drawing one of the shawls more firmly about her shoulders with a shy hand. "I saw this bunch of clothin' through the snow, scrunched under that big tree back of the Hall and I says to old Redmond, I think somebody's fallen over, sick or somethin'. Just your imagination, he says. But I goes over anyways. Thank the Lord."

She felt nothing but the fierce scald – on her tongue, on her cheeks – and a mocking pulse somewhere below her throat. Malloney tried to catch the cup before it toppled off the bed but he missed, burnt his finger, and stifled a curse. All the mutant angles of his face grimaced inward to corral the giant's breath behind it. "Owww," he squeaked, and, pitched sideways by the congested pressure, he crushed the china cup.

She giggled. My word, she thought, I'm alive.

"Nobody's got more right than you to think about endin' it all. There comes a time when everybody, churchgoer or not, thinks about it. Few people in this town or any other have gone through what you have: your husband, your kids, not to speak of poor ol' Sophie goin' up in –". Malloney was clearing away the supper plate he'd secretly brought into her. It appeared to her that he was intent on preserving his reputation for toughness. Certainly he was aware that *she* had no reputation worth saving. She had never heard him string so many sentences together before, but it didn't surprise her in the least. She'd lived long enough to know that even the most taciturn being had inside him whole pages and chapters of the unspoken – lamentations, indictments, confessions, recantations, fervent manifestoes, poems of the beleaguered heart. She had heard them all, in herself and in others.

"What you need most is to get out of here, away from this place. You been here too long. You've had too much grief here. There's ghosts on every street. You been in most of the houses in this dump, so you can't shut out what you know they're sayin', even now. Every one of them cheered when Riel was strung up, you could hear them on the docks. Don't matter to them what the Rebellion did to you an' Rob."

Later, when it was dark in the room, he returned. He lit the small lamp by the bed. His face was scavenged by shadow and lurid light, but the eyes shone out at her, their message clear and unmistakable. Don't do this to me, she shouted, but his was the only voice in the room.

"You've got no hold here any more," he said. "No kin, no land. What you had is all gone. Wiped clean. No reason to stay. You've got to start fresh. You ain't fifty years old yet. You're as healthy as a yearling."

Stop, please.

"I got a friend in Sarnia, works on the railroad there. They need a janitor, a woman. I can arrange for you to have the job, right away. About two blocks from the station there's a boarding house run by the Widow Jarvis, a former lady-friend of mine. She'll take you in. You'll be a long, long ways from this place," he said, "from this, this *shit*."

"Could I have more tea," she said.

2

The Widow Jarvis was an excessively discreet woman and kind-hearted to a fault if obsessive interest in her acquaintances' welfare (present and past) were the criterion of measurement. "Don't you worry now, luv," she soothed and patted in her English mum's accent. "Ducky tells me you been hard done by of late, downright abused, he says, an' I should take good care of you an' not be askin' too many questions about what's happened to you, leastways not for a while, till you settles in an' starts to feel at home with your bones again. Well now, luv, he don't haveta tell the Missus Jarvis a thing like that, now do he? One look at you and I knowed it all, straightway. Cup-a-tea, luv?"

"Thank you, yes. You're very kind."

Malloney had been right about the job. She was taken on immediately. Her duties were simple, repetitive and comfortably numbing. She felt no twinge of irony or resentment at being, after all these years, an employee of the Grand Trunk Western. She was employed. She worked. She walked two blocks to a boarding house made up with ferns, doilies, lace curtains, carpets and comforters to resemble a home. She ate, tolerated the chit-chat of the resident ladies, slept without dreaming, walked to work again. The only change in routine occurred when she switched on alternate weeks from day shift to afternoons – when she worked from four till midnight. The tasks were much the same. She assisted the male janitors in scrubbing and dusting the waiting room of the huge, refurbished station – six passenger trains a day between Chicago and Toronto and dozens of local and highball freights. By herself, she kept the ladies' toilets clean. On the afternoon shift, at seven o'clock, she walked down the platform and across the yard to the new bunkhouse complex where she worked alone for an hour or so, washing dishes and tidying up. Twice a week (she worked six days with Sundays off) she stayed longer, moving to the attached laundry room where she 'did' the dirty sheets and pillow-cases which had accumulated from the men's bunks. In the damp steam-chill of that room, arms up to elbow in boiling water, hands like flails against the washboard, punching into resistant shape these cotton sheets, wet-heaving as drowned flesh – she felt, at last, bone-and-body take full possession of her being. Why did I fight it so long, was all she thought.

The long, empty Sundays were difficult; so were the mornings and early afternoons before the late shift. Usually she filled the hours with walking, often following the old spur-line (no longer used since amalgamation) southward to where it stopped in a field before the River. The late-December wind blew forlornly over it. In the distance, an ice-fisherman's tent shivered.

"That Mrs. Marshall's a quiet one, ain't she?" Miss Spence whispered.

"Had her troubles, poor dear," Mrs. Jarvis countered.

"Still waters run deep," reflected Miss Campbell, who had a high school diploma and was soon to be married.

The Widow and her boarders tried very hard to include the new arrival in their conversation, whether she was present or not. When pressed, she told them about her work, though its fascination waned somewhat after the initial description. They asked about the fashions and manners of the V.I.P.'s from exotic Toronto or scandalous Chicago. She was not helpful.

Miss Spence was an angular schoolteacher (third-class 'local' certificate) of indeterminate age with a voice like a chalk-squeak always delivered at full vent, as if she were trying to start each sentence somewhere in the middle. Perhaps she felt this lent authority to her many strong opinions.

"He got what he deserved, no more, no less. Where on earth would we be if we let rebels and murderers run around scot free? Grandpa Spence fought the Frenchies way back in 'thirty-seven, as you all know."

They knew.

"An' what'd they do then? Let 'em all come back as smiling an' rosy as ever they was. Bad seed oughta be scalded at birth, my granny always said, and if they'd done that for Mister *Loo-ee Ree-al* we'd all be a darn sight better off."

Miss Campbell nodded vigorously, her husband-to-be having just returned from the North-West mercifully intact. Mrs. Jarvis was only half-listening; her eyes were riveted on the one who had not spoken.

The bunkhouse was relatively new and comfortable, having been built only two years previously, following the merger of the Grand Trunk and the Great Western. Being a woman, Lily was not allowed into the bunk rooms, which formed a separate section of the complex. Being a woman, she was expected to be at ease in the kitchen and laundry room, set on the side of the building opposite the bunks. Between these exclusively male and female demesnes lay the sprawling comfort of the 'parlour', replete with tables and chairs (for eating, poker-play, solitaire) and several chesterfield suites of chewed leather (for snoozing, contending, yarn-spinning). Its hallmark was tobacco smoke and the afterbite of spittoons. As a woman, she was allowed in to clear the tables of dishes, to empty ashtrays, flush out cuspidors, and when no one was present, scrub out a week's soil and smudge.

The bunkhouse was frequented by engineers, brakemen and conductors whose homes, when they had any, were not in Sarnia. Since most of the passenger and freight trains plied between Sarnia and Toronto (a few still followed the old Grand Trunk route to Stratford and Berlin), these men were likely to be from the capital city, using the new facility to 'lay over' until they were due to make a return run, usually the next day. Railroaders from Sarnia likewise 'lay over' in Toronto. Many of them, bachelors or *de facto* bachelors, lived in boarding houses near the station here (or in Port Edward), where they waited to be called. She had on occasion been asked to sweep out the Yard Office, where she had seen the huge call-boards listing the names of the running crews and yard gangs. When a train was 'made up' and ready to go, elfin messengers would scatter from here across the south end of the city to 'call' the men to their labour. Sometimes, of course, they had only to dash to the bunkhouse or, as one of the regulars dubbed it, 'Palaver Palace'. Some of the grizzled veterans among the engineers and conductors had routine schedules. Most of the running crew, however, seemed to lead semi-nomadic lives with sudden wake-ups, cold breakfasts, chilling dashes to overheated cabooses or blazing furnace rooms where even the iron stanchions froze as the arctic night whistled by.

"I just ignore 'em, I barge right in there; after all's said, I got my work to do," Big Meg had explained to her at the beginning. "Most of them's gentlemen, really, long as you ignore their cussin', which they can't help, and don't want to help when it comes right down to it." She chortled, and her forearms shook. "If you don't barge right in there, you'll never get the chores done. Besides," she winked lasciviously," they tell a juicy story or two."

But she did not take Big Meg's advice. She quickly figured out – for both shifts – when the peak periods of use occurred and when the parlour would be empty or be occupied by a solitary derelict snoozing away a hangover or sulking with a cigar in a far corner. During the latter times she whisked in and out – tiny, unnoted, anonymous. In the kitchen, with its own stove and gingham curtains and lamplight on the copper pans, with snow sizzling against the glass – she felt able to breathe again, surprised as she had so often been before at the unencouraged robustness of her small body, the gleeful pleasure it took in routine acts. However, because the parlour was separated from the kitchen only by a heavy velvet curtain (the original door having been kicked in by a drunken fireman under the misapprehension that his young wife lay thrashing behind it with her secret lover) she could hardly help but hear, from time to time, the muffled grit of railroader talk, with its blend of scuttlebutt and tall-tale. She could rattle the dishes in their warm suds or hum too loud for comfort, but not forever. Whenever there were three or more men in there, they were constantly gabbing – between hands at poker, slumped on smoky leather, or floating on a whiskey-edge.

One voice in particular insisted on separating itself from the others, not merely because it was loud (they were all loud) or colloquial (earthiness of speech was endemic): there was something in it that was at once hearty, spare, generous, withholding. When this one spun a yarn, the room would be restless at first as some of the uninitiates or the odd interloper would spar with the teller, according to custom and at certain sanctioned intervals; then gradually these exchanges gave way to rapt attention, as the voice took control and the story itself grew larger and grander (though many had told it before) and the laughter at the end not quite as predictable. She heard him laugh too

– at the story, at the teller, at the trapped parishioners. His guffaw would have embarrassed a bull moose.

"You remember the Guffer? Stuffy McGuffin we called him when he first come brakin' on the late-great Western. 'Course the son-of-a-bitch was near fifty even then. Married the leanest of the superintendent's three daughters. Hell of a way to break into railroadin.'" A pause for laughter, then: "She turned out to be a bit too tart for him to ever call her sweetheart, but he always claimed if he caught her downwind on a Saturday night, she give him more bumps an' thrills than a gravel train to Cayuga. Mind you now, these trips didn't happen too often, least not as often as Guffer would've liked, so the poor bugger got to draggin' his caboose into every 'waterin' trough' between Trenton and Ing-arse-hole. Now drinkin' was harmless as long as he was brakin', and even when he fell into stokin', it wasn't too bad – though you all remember the story, denied by everybody but the Guffer himself, about him pissin' his pants in the cab of 1546 on the old Barrie run in the middle of February an' the air cold enough to crack walnuts an' other precious jewels, and' old Fartsy Farmer cursin' beside him an' tryin' to see through the snow comin' as thick as the Governor-General's undies, 'Jesus McJesus, you stupid son-of-a-bitch, do somethin' about that stink or I'll pitch you onto the first siding I can see.' 'Course, it's the ice formin' round his balls that's interestin' Guffer the most, so, driven by the thought of no more gravel runs to Cayuga, he yanks open the firebox door, drops his pants, turns round, and *sits down.*"

"Horseshit!"

Gales of horse laughter.

"I'm only repeatin' what I know to be the gospel truth. The Guffer soft-boiled his eggs so beautifully that night near Barrie, he went straight home and at the tender age of fifty-nine started to assemble his own way-freight. It's true, the son-of-a-bitch had five kids before he retired."

Skeptical, gelding laughter.

"I thought you was gonna tell us a new one, you prevaricatin' bastard!" Hoots, steam-whistles, derisive applause.

"Where was I? Ah, yes. I got the Guffer up to –"

"Up to his arse in bullshit!"

"– Up to his last fateful year of the Festerin' Western, when, in order to save a dyin' enterprise, they promoted the old fart to engineer. Christ, he was like a kid with a hayrake. An' they give him one of the new 2160's, runnin' highballs between here and Toronto. Well, one day in the middle of July he gets all tanked up on his stopover in London, he's so pissed his eyes are settin' fire to the table-cloth, an' he churns up old '62 an' starts to let her loose around Mandaumin, an' by this time he's got her up to eighty miles an hour an' climbin', an' his fireman's hanging onto the tender for dear life and a high wailin' sound can be heard from the caboose a hundred yards behind, but the Guffer he's laughin' an' singin' away like one of them Eye-talian bassoes with a pinched prick, an' suddenly they're only five minutes outside Sarnia Yard, an' wouldn't you know, on the main-line track of this here station was sittin' the doodle-bug from Stratford waitin' to take on passengers. The platform was jammed with people. At first they was all intent on gettin' their tickets an' baggage in order, an' then they heard this god-forsaken screech-a-comin' at them from the east an' their hearts froze – it was the Guffer's song ridin' along in front of old '62, now doin' ninety-five miles-an-hour an' scatterin' car-men, oilers, yard crew an' jiggers in all directions. Mercifully the Guffer brought her untouched an' unscathed – there wasn't a mark on him – clean through to the station. Some say he was pullin' on the throttle 'cause he thought it was the brake, but we'll never know. What we do know is that the engineer, fireman an' conductor on the doodle-bug jumped left an' right an' that the Guffer stopped singin' about two seconds before the collision."

Another pause: to take breath, relight a pipe?

"As luck would have it –"

Raucous response, conspiring and brotherly, checked only by the anticipation of something further.

"As luck would have it, the doodle-bug was not bashed to one side or the other – which would have resulted in the grisly deaths of numerous bystanders or the sudden slaughter of a corral-full of steers – she was knocked straight an' clean ahead, she popped up into the air an' did a series of back-flips down the main-line as tidy as a tumbler across a mat. About a hundred yards from the end-of-line near the old dock by the River, it hopped sideways an' settled into an alfalfa field. Which was a good thing, too, 'cause Guffer an' number 62 was followin' it real close, rippin' up track all the way but stickin' to its line like a trouper. Then, boom she hits the block an' flicks it aside like a flea on your collar, an' *in she went*."

A gulf of speechlessness. Finally, on cue, a miniature "In the river?"

"Christ no, into the river *bank*, an' deflectin' downward so she starts to plough forward, an' the stoker an' crew jump just before she disappears completely into the ground, tossin' back whole gopher-towns of dirt risin' up like a huge sandstorm that covers all of Sarnia, an' some of the passengers on the platform think its Armageddon – with the passin' of the Juggernaut an' the great seals busted wide open for all time, an' the last we ever saw of old '62 was the thrashin' of the caboose before she was sucked underground."

"And the Guffer?"

Wheezing of freshly stoked pipe. The timing was all.

"Oh, *him*. Why, he come up face-first on the other side of the River, smilin' and fartin' and assumin' he was in paradise. Yessir, he done the Great Western a genuine favour; he gouged a *tunnel* straight under the St. Clair from the Dominion of Canada to the U.S. of A. Now all we gotta do is figure out how to get the son-of-a-bitchin' *train* out of the hole!"

Uproarious approbation. A spell had been wound up, achieved, held, and released. She heard the conversation break up into its customary blurred elements. The dishes, rattling and all, had got themselves washed and dried. From the shuffling behind her she knew the men were about to leave, some to work, some to town or to their bunks. She edged over to the curtained doorway, drew the velvet slightly apart, and watched. They were every shape, size and age. They lumbered, sauntered, hurried – only their faces exposed above mackinaws and denim as they turned from the cozy brotherhood of their room to the blizzard outside.

She could not fit the voice to a body.

Most of the times they played cards – poker – and the yarn-spinning was given over to sporadic jokes and what sounded like ritual teasing. Even then, though less often, that grained, seasoned voice prevailed; and no amount of compulsory bluff-and-blarney could completely disguise the grit of authenticity at the core of it.

"Hear the one about the brewer who couldn't swim?"

"Are you in or out?"

"In."

"What'd he do, Luce?"

"Fell into a vat of his own beer. Raise you two."

"See ya'. Did he drown or what?"

"Not right away." Brief interlude of clinking coins. "He had to crawl out twice an' take a piss."

Belly laugh as big as moose country.

"Jesus Murphy, but who laughs louder at his own shit?"

"C'mon Luce, stop laughin' an tell us what ya' got."

"Three aces. Sorry."

"You son-of-a-bitch!"

All the coins see-sawed in one direction.

When they were all gone, clumping into the snowy dark, she waited fifteen minutes and then entered the parlour to clean up. She emptied the ashtrays into a can and was brushing the crumbs off the table when she noticed that one of the overstuffed chairs at the back was occupied. A coal-oil lamp, singed and smoking, threw a shadowed light across the face which was turned towards the door, though it did not appear to be looking at it. A smouldering briar pipe sat discarded on the low table beside the chair. Near it, as if flung aside in the same gesture, lay a puffed, expired hand. At the sound of falling glass, the face belonging to the hand swung numbly towards her, tried to focus on the source of irritation, failed, and swung back.

In that instant she knew who it was. She had an impression of size – of bulk and crag and underpracticed muscle – and a rumpled dignity of dress and demeanour. But it was only the face that registered: the grooved laugh-lines sagged and fleshed around the mouth – generous and quick but fallen now into the very shape it did everything to forestall- and around the eyes also that were capacious and coal-black and used to dancing for reasons the heart behind them kept to itself. At this moment, though, they slackened in their oversize sockets like exhausted gavottes. They saw nothing.

She fought to regain her breath, turning to go.

"Don't, please. You're not disturbin' me."

It was him. She left.

The tenor of the talk in the parlour of the Widow Jarvis had shifted several quarters as December of 1885 drew to a close.

"Herbert positively insists I go straight to Walker's an' order up the fanciest dress in the store."

"It's only New Years once a year," said the Widow generously.

"And it is the biggest ball in town, sponsored by the railroad an' all."

"How'd you come by that invitation again?" Miss Spence prompted.

"All the veterans was given one, as is only right considerin' Herbert risked his life for all of us."

"Usually only the bigwigs an' some railroad people's invited," said Miss Spence in awe.

"I don't suppose anybody knows this but my dear Harold was a fightin' man, a grenadier he was, an' left me a widow almost twenty-two years ago, battlin' them nigger-people over there somewhere near Egypt."

They did know.

"Niggers, Indians, Frenchies, what's the difference?" asked Miss Spence, her eyes pinned to the last row of Senior Book Four. "Can't stop 'em from fightin', they love it. It's born in them."

"Poor Harold."

She was doing the laundry, well away from the boisterous revels in the parlour. It was snowing again and the heat from the kitchen stove could not cut the damp cold that hung everywhere, stiffening the sheets and forcing her to fetch fresh pails of boiling water. Twice she scalded her left wrist. The sudden steam rushed hotly over her face with its illusory warmth, and soaked her hair – that coiled wherever it was struck. She thrashed the scrub-board to beat the blood to the surface of her skin and back again to the chill in her leg-bones. The sheets froze solid against the clothes-horse like opaque window-glass. The rollers nipped her right forefinger, but she didn't feel the pain. Till later.

Long after she heard them clatter out of doors, she slipped back into the kitchen, pulled a stool in front of the stove and sat their motionless, without thought, without the compunction to commit a single redemptive act. Her tresses thawed, tattered, dripped. The fire swallowed its lone sound.

"Excuse me, ma'am."

She turned around.

"Pardon me for interruptin', but I assumed you was finished your work."

She felt her hand in her hair.

"My name's Burgher. Lucien Burgher. The fellas call me Luce." His smile carried his mouth, his eyes and some further part of him with it.

She felt beads of sweat in the tiny hollow of her throat. She was wiping her hands on a towel.

"Of course my mother wouldn't approve. She prefers Lucien. I tell them that, but they don't pay no attention to me. No respect."

"I thought you had –" she began.

"I waited for you," he laughed, flashing his grin full upon her, then dropping his glance for a moment.

She watched his hands. They seemed shy but strong; at this moment they looked as if they could commandeer the world. One of them reached into the pocket of his engineer's tunic.

"Would you like to dance?" he said.

She backed up a step, the heat surging behind her.

"What I mean is, could I have the pleasure of escorting you to the New Year's dance?"

She let his eyes, at last, have hers.

"I can't tell you exactly how I come by it, but this here's an official invitation to the Grand Trunk Ball tomorrow night. Naturally, thought I've tried on occasion, I don't dance too good by myself."

She reached out with her left hand, exposing the scalded wrist, now blistering painfully. Confused, he pushed the white card into it.

"What's your name," he said gently.

She hesitated for a long moment, the invitation poised between them. At length she replied: "Cora."

It was at the very moment of his asking that she had discovered what it was she had been trying to quit forever. A picture had sprung fully-formed into her mind: she was lying in Southener's arms and the Pottawatomie tom-toms were sounding through the smoke as the girl named White Blossom was transformed, by the dance of her elders and the dance inside her, into her new being: Seed-of-the-Snow-Apple. The seed-core. *Cora*. Beginning again.

"Cora," he repeated. "Beautiful name. An old and sacred name. And?"

"Does a last name matter?"

"Not to me," he grinned. "You'll go then?"

She nodded.

PART TWO

Cora

41

By mid-April there was barely a trace of snow to be found anywhere in the village. The sun thawed, stirred, reminisced with the earth. And in the memorable warmth of the afternoons, workmen of every shape and ilk came to help with the making of Granny Coote's cottage: a mason, a joiner, a sawyer, several carpenters, a lather and plasterer, two roofers, assorted painters and paperers, a clandestine electrician, a legitimate plumber, and countless helpers, apprentices, and sidewalk foremen. And each one, novice or seasoned hand, was watched over by the still figure outlined in the front window of the miserable shack across the street – a pale, disinterested ghost looking for new ground to haunt. Not once did she wave, nod, or in any other wise break her silent superintendence.

The workmen might have been relieved to learn that the supervising wraith behind the glass did not spend all of her watching time minutely observing their amateur, though enthusiastic, performance. True, she never left her post, but on most days, shortly after noon, she would cast an eye up or down the street to catch the eccentric stride of one or more of the young men en route to the site, and begin to trace its advance until some moment of sudden recognition occurred, as it inevitably did. Ah, that's young Mike, Maggie Hare's lad, she would think; Bunny, they used to call him and he'd come running home bawling and quivering with hurt, too tiny to fight back, to cast off the name that would dog him all his days, but I would always put down my mop and making sure Maggie was out of earshot, I would let him fling his eight-year-old arms around me and butt me in the stomach as hard as he wanted till he'd slow down real gradual and just hug me, and I'd reach into my apron, as if I'd thought of something special, and pull out a peppermint – like a prize for a clever strong boy who would never again let the bullies call him Bunny. He doesn't remember that anymore. It was a long time ago, of course, and she and Maggie did have a falling out shortly after, and she had been, after all, a lifelong Alleywoman. By the time Granny looked up from such thoughts, the studding for a bedroom wall or a new doorway would have mysteriously come into being across the street. For Sunny's sake, she did try to watch, but it was very, very hard.

There's Slowboat Saunders, Eliza's youngest. She was too old to have any more and she paid for it. Slowboat could drive a nail through his thumb and then wonder why he couldn't pick his nose. Poor dear soul.

I've wiped that nose many a time after Alf got his leg crushed in a coal-tender's bogies and Eliza went back to school teaching. He waves at me and grins, but I'm sure he can't connect what he sees here behind glass with those days before Arthur, before Eddie, before the catastrophes of age. Even the Army wouldn't take Slowboat – flat feet, they said. To her surprise, the last of the roof-boards – magically – had already been put in place. She could no longer see inside. I didn't even hear the hammering, she thought.

Moments later she saw Sunny Denfield climb down from the roof, stand for a while with his arm on Slowboat's shoulder, then detach himself and walk across the street towards her gate.

"I guess you remember the day when my father came lookin' for me. He got the police out by tellin' them I was under eighteen an' pullin' some strings in the government. Naturally they expected that, bein' a young lad accustomed to money and pleasure, I would run off to the fleshpots of Montreal or Detroit. It never occurred to them that I might be runnin' *away* from those very things. To be honest, I didn't know what I was doin' except findin' some room to breathe an' think an' sort out my life. I suppose if I'd had a mother, I'd have stayed away just long enough to give them all a good scare, but I didn't. To this day I haven't a clue as to who tipped off my father that I might be livin' in some little dump of a railroad town called Point Edward. Probably one of the big shots stayin' at The Queen's where I had that room near the back annex, you remember. Unfortunately I'm the spittin' image of my father. Anyway, as you'll recall, it was only a month after I'd settled in at the sheds – in September of 'ought-one – when he comes scoutin' after his lost son." He dunked one of Mrs. Carpenter's cookies in his tea. "The whole village knew somethin' was afoot," he laughed.

Granny had written on her slate. She held it up: 'We all heard him'.

"So did everyone in Port Huron and Sarnia. Imagine, comin' to fetch a runaway back home in a horseless carriage, firin' off sparks an' fartin' bedlam in every direction, deafenin' dogs an' spookin' horses an' givin' old Mrs. Farrow a case of the hiccups she claimed took her ten years to get over."

The sun was now shining through the west window over the sink. She felt its warmth around her ankles. Soon in her garden it would be tempting bulb and tuber.

"He left it sittin' in front of The Queen's, surrounded by townsfolk, an' walked by himself across the fields towards our work gang; we were cuttin' ragweed or somethin', between boats, with our shirts stripped off showin' our muscles an' tan to the whole world. He didn't know I saw him, but he stood near a little hawthorn, watchin' us work an' horse around as we always did, an' by that time I was feelin' like one of the gang, with all my blisters toughened up and all the kinks out of my arms an' legs, an' real *earned* money in my pocket. He never said a word, and I never let on I saw him. He just turned an' walked away. We heard the poppin' and jumpin' of the automobile all the way across the marsh, and I remember one of the fellas sayin': 'Christ, it's like ridin' a Gatling Gun!"

Arthur – bless him for trying – built that little cupboard beside the sink, she was thinking. He let Eddie cut out the scrolls and curlicues with his coping saw. He was so patient, Arthur, with his hands on the piano, with anything in them. We were always going to fix up the outside, but there was never enough money and the property was not really ours and beside the inside was always cozy and full of music, and the nimbleness of Arthur's fingers never did transfer from piano hammers to a carpenter's, though he could never figure out why, staring up at her helplessly for absolution.

"You would have liked my Aunt Grace, Cora," Sunny was saying. "I never could understand how she came to marry such a stuffed shirt as my Uncle Bramwell. You couldn't picture two more opposite types. She cared nothing for money or fancy things: she loved people. Especially children, an' she regretted, I know, bein' able to have but one child. She almost died havin' Ruth-Anne, I was told. I'm hopin' you'll get a chance to meet Ruth-Anne soon. I've been tryin' to help her with her pursuit of her family tree. She insists her mother had relatives livin' in this county, and is threatenin' to come down here an' prove it to herself. I hope she does. You'll like her. She's got her mother's spunk."

Granny smiled as best she could. She wrote a word on her slate: 'When?'

"Two weeks," he said, barely above a whisper. "The plaster an' paint won't take long. It's gonna look real nice, Cora. Just the way you an' me sketched it out. We'd like you to move in by the first of May. The monument man's comin' from London about then. We're plannin' a little ceremony for you – I know you don't approve but it's really to make the council feel good about it all, if you wouldn't mind – but that won't be till later because the lawyers are still sortin' out the legal stuff. But I promise you, you'll have a *bona fide* deed in your hand by June. You'll own that piece of land an' that cottage outright. Nobody'll ever be able to take it away from you. It's the least we owe you, the least you deserve."

She was listening and not listening. She got up and walked slowly to the west window. She looked out over her dozing gardens. Sunny Denfield was at her side. He looked out with her. "I'm sorry," he said, his voice breaking. Her hand on his wrist said, *I know.*

A stranger, walking by, might have caught them in their window – glazed by a westering glow – and mistaken them for mother and son.

42

1

The Grand Trunk Ball was the social event of the winter season. For twenty years – years marked by unparalleled human progress (one or two depressions and the odd insurrection notwithstanding) – the affair had been held in the largest, most resplendent ballroom of western Ontario, the G.T.R. Station-Hotel on the docks of Point Edward. Burned to the ground by revisionist forces of Nature in 1871, it had been immediately resurrected, more capacious and vainglorious than ever. The three dozen Venetian chandeliers, reflected like minor galaxies in the ebony firmament of the walnut floors, were a testament to the depth and longing of the mercantilist fancy that confected them. And though the queenly edifice herself was imperceptibly aging – indeed about to be sacrificed to such commercial inevitabilities as mergers and corporate restructuring – she had fitted herself out for this annual ceremonial with no diminution of splendour and no intimation that the cracks at the edges of her smile might one day be irremediable. And whether by coincidence or design, the last evening of 1885 – a year which had seen the young nation riven by dissent, racial antagonism and rebellion – turned out to be clear, crisp and star-spangled.

Gliding along in their special open sleighs (provided by the Railroad), the celebrants could lean back against their nuzzling furs and behold the earth commanded utterly by the night-sky, so dark and eons-deep that the stars appeared as tiny semaphores chilled forever in bas-relief. Around the carollers, the snow had flattened and blanched an unresisting landscape. The black, unseamed horizon folded down and over the verges of their little world so that it seemed as if they were all afloat on a bone-white saucer, riding an insubstantial ice-floe on the night's immensity. And when their Clydes or Percherons – Pegasus every one – puffed majestically towards the confluence of river and lake, the grand-old dowager loomed ahead like a bejewelled atoll, garish and preposterous against the asperity of those panarctic constellations. Unperturbed, an ambidextrous footman, mustered in gold and vermillion, hopped down before the evergreen welcome-arch and raised a dainty mitt to the first descending lady. The festivities were underway.

The orchestra had been imported all the way from London. It remembered the fading courtly dances – gavotte, lancers, galop – and paid them due respect. Under the steadfast blaze of the chandeliers, the sets and squares whirled to their ancient, magic geometry. Speed, intricacy, the levitation of brass and fiddle – all conspired to project the illusion of momentary anonymity. Nonetheless, it was a modern age, and the sophisticates from Middlesex could bedazzle the countryfolk with waltz, polka, schatische, and once, jovially, they unleashed an exotic fandango. Here – hand-to-hand, face-to-face – even the most jaded romantic could borrow the energy of the sweeping violins, the just-harnessed tympanies, the peremptory surge of coronet and horn, and sail – accompanied or no – into the sweet amnesia of the music.

The performance was non-stop. Sets broke apart but quickly reconfigured; couples clung or recomposed: the dance contained them and carried on. Though the critical complement was never threatened, individual participants would occasionally slip away to the north section, where uniformed waiters filled crystal goblets with champagne that had been chilled in snow. At the south end stood the powder rooms and several improvised salons where a gentleman could find relief and a reassuring cigar. But always the music drew them back, out of themselves and the petty gravitation of their lives.

At precisely five minutes to midnight the orchestra ceased on a pre-arranged downbeat, the indefatigable conductor stepped aside, and the dias was occupied, somewhat unevenly, by three distinguished guests: the Honourable Halpenny Pebbles, deputy premier of the province, on loan for the occasion; Mr. Margison Dilworth, first vice-president of the Grand Trunk Western (who invited himself); and Mr. Stanley R. 'Cap' Dowling, reeve of the village since its incorporation back in 1878, who was present by divine right. This trio of luminaries, further distinguished by a pair of arc-lights, proceeded to lead the assembly, now formed into a huge circle of interlocked hands, in a singing of Auld Lang Syne. After which: much toasting and, as soon as the choir directors could be urged off-stage, more dancing.

Lucien and Cora danced. Lucien and Cora were dancing. Lucien and Cora sipped champagne and anticipated dancing. During the entire eventful evening, they exchanged no conversation other than the requisite formalities of greeting, thanksgiving and good manners. On the sleigh-ride from town (they met at the Sarnia depot), they clasped furred appendages, warmed a common shoulder, and let the stars look at them with their loveliness. Whatever pretence each had chosen for this extraordinary courting, it was accorded the unquestioned blessing of the other. No single note jarred the harmony of their shared narrative. They danced, sometimes alone and sometimes together, each happy to confer upon the other the prize of simple presence, however fragile or fleeting. In the dance, with all motion foreordained, they were released to their own fictions.

Lucien laughed and glided and marshalled his companion with large, commodious gestures, driven it seemed by some inward, transparent, uncalculating reservoir of loco-motion. Cora smiled on her own, choreographed her partner's laughter, and curtsied to the universe in three-quarter time. She danced as if the world cared, or mattered. She believed, for now, in the eyes that beheld her as if she had just been born.

A caress of finely powered snow greeted them as they stepped outside. Still, there were no clouds and the stars glittered over head. It was blissfully cold.

"I didn't tell you," Lucien said as he helped her onto the back of the sleigh, "but I been livin' here in Sarnia for almost a month."

"You left Toronto?"

He hopped aboard. "Uh huh. I hang around the bunkhouse, of course, for obvious reasons."

She smiled and let him wrap his heavy arm about her. She snuggled in, not thinking of any moment before here, content with this.

"I been livin' down by the River. On Front Street." He squeezed against her, testing. "At the St. Clair." He waited for some part of her body to reply. Then, softly so as not to disturb the sleepy revellers on either side of them, he said: "I got a suite. Two rooms."

2

"I started watchin' you the second I spotted you in the waiting room. I found out from Big Meg when you was due to work in the bunkhouse." He poured her a tumbler of champagne from a bottle that had been cooling on the window-ledge, catching her eye so she could nod to tell him when to stop. She did.

"There wasn't much to see," she said. She took the glass, tipped it in his direction, and sat on the edge of the settee in the 'sitting area'. He stood – tie askew, shirt adrift – leaning on a balky commode.

"That depends on how experienced an eye is lookin'," he said. "An' this pair's seen plenty. I'm no yearling, you know." He patted his paunch reverentially. "You tried to fool me, I suspect, with those aprons an' bandanas an' steam-bath hair-do's. You might've tricked a few of the greenhorns 'round the Yard, but not a veteran like me. I know beauty when I see it."

"And I know blarney when I hear it," she said, glancing past him to the other room, the wink of a brass bed just visible.

"But you love it just the same?" His face, flushed from cold and drink, lit up in a broad grin. Only the creases there and the bituminous glow behind the dancing eyes belied the boyishness of the attempt. Somehow, unlike most men of his vintage and temperament, he did not look ridiculous when he allowed his high spirits to overwhelm his fatigued, resisting flesh. Always, there remained a residue of dignity.

"I used to," she replied. "Quite a long time ago."

His face teetered on the verge of collapse, then brightened: "You weren't thinkin' of long ago tonight."

"I don't think either of us was," she said, holding out her glass as he refilled it.

"Happy New Year," he said.

"So you left home," she said.

"Uh huh. Just packed up an' packed it in. Nothin' to it," he said, "once you make up your mind."

"I guess you could say I left home, too," she said, startling him. "Though I didn't come as far."

"Point Edward?"

"You knew."

"The miles make no difference," he said, sitting down beside her, but not close. "The truth is, I saw something in you I can't explain. Me, with the big mouth and a smart story for every occasion. When I asked you to the dance, I'd never done anything like that before in my life. I didn't even know what I wanted or wanted to do – to talk, to have some laughs, to feel a woman dancin' near me again, to turn a caterpillar into a butterfly –"

"No need to talk," she said, unlocking the tumbler from his grip one finger at a time. "It mostly spoils things."

"I know."

"Promise me just one thing," she said, blowing out the lamp and letting the snow-brushed starlight in. "No talk of what's gone before. None."

He followed her – amazed – to the inner chamber.

Neither of them made a move to light a bedside lamp. They undressed, apart in the shadows, and slipped under the nearest half of the comforter. Their bodies met, without ceremony, and gave way to their individual hungers.

Cora and Lucien were past middle-age. They felt no urgency to have their flesh explored nor to be reminded – by an accidental touch or a gesture of forgiveness – of scar, stretch-mark, crease, sag, weathered muscle. Cora needed to know if the dead thing in her belly could be revived long enough to die with her consent. Lucien needed to know that he could waken, with the vestige of his lust, some flesh more drugged than his own.

He was hard in seconds, and she guided him in. Aware of his own craggy weight, his angular need against her seeming-frailty – he hunched, catapulted elbows-first, found some ballast, lanced, withheld, thrashed, and crushed two pillows. She winced joyfully at the pain, then tried to right his lopsided fervour and find some balance or rhythm one of them could use, some pressure-point that would trigger *something* they could ride out together. Nothing worked. Unwilling to call up those memories that might have established some sort of order, however bogus it might have been, and not yet knowing enough of each other to improvise the event – they staggered to separate states of incompletion. Nor was there the impetus of youth to rally them to a further attempt. They had contended in good faith, and discovered nothing but their age and the extent of their weariness.

But the Druid moon, almost full, had risen in the east and was just now tilting over the west edge of the room's window, flooding it with light borrowed and preserved from defunct suns. Side by side they lay just as they had failed to disentangle. No word was exchanged – of apology, consolation, promise, regret. Into a silence fed only by moonlight and across the long hour before dawn, they reached accommodation, and more. A hand that bruised and commanded, settled like a wing upon a thigh. A girl's grip surprised and softened. A whisper lingered in the ear like a long, shy kiss. Someone's lips plucked a tear prematurely from a cheek.

Much later, it might have been in a common dream or in a fantasy shared with the moonless dark, they made love that was both violent and tender, that was as synchronized as the music it was made of, that threatened to touch the ache abiding so deep inside them it had been perfectly protected by the stratum and acre of orthodox pain.

When they woke, it was January.

43

1

Throughout the winter of 1886 Lucien and Cora lived together in the St. Clair Inn on Front Street. Their love, if that term be at all appropriate to their curious co-existential relationship, was founded upon a strict set of covenants, unspoken but mutually – compulsively – observed. They did not speak of their own past, even when – secure in the embrace of a lover or vulnerable in the sinking aftermath of passion – they were sorely tempted. They asked no question that might carry them, however innocently, beyond the moment of their meeting. They took their dark time alone, suffering through it as best they could. When they came back together, though, to make love or talk about the long January afternoons, there was no camouflaging of that private pain, that burden from their deep night-dreaming. They did not use their passion nor any of its incidental pleasures to ease or soothe or sedate. Their lovemaking – frequent, intermittent, often unpremeditated – was a way of transmitting not the detail of sufferings minutely lived and defined but rather their gravity, the bone-density of them, the sudden echo in them of all the ruptured joy that once had been. Such surprise was enough. They accepted the blunt physicality of their comingling almost if it were a phenomenon outside their instigation or control. Each was content to let the other translate the results in his own way.

Their cohabitation quite naturally caused a stir and a buzzing abroad. However, since they were both strangers in a sense, the radius of the gossip was limited to the fringes of the beverage rooms, the quiet corners of the foyer, and the lively but closed network of fancy that followed the main-line of the amalgamated Grand Trunk Western. Percy O'Boyle – Suds to his customers – who clerked behind the registry desk by day and slung beer by night, blushed a deeper red than his hair whenever Cora came down to breakfast sometime before noon and smiled her ingenuous 'good morning' not a foot from his chin. "Mornin', ma'am – missus uh – ma'am," he would blurt out, stuttering without fail, then blush more carnally as his eyes rose up on their own to trail her figure through the doorway to the dining room. Except for Mulligan, the owner and principal waiter, she found herself anonymous among the carpetbaggers, drummers and occasional couples who drifted in and out – off the boats, ferries or trains, and always en route to somewhere else. Sarnia, like the place she had left, was a stopover town, all bustle and hubbub. But seated unobtrusively at her regular table near the west window, she could sip tea shyly (she never got used to being waited on, ever startled by Mulligan's shadow at her elbow, embarrassed by his incessant, waterless hand-wringing) and look over the traffic along Front Street towards the ferry dock and beyond to the thin artery of the River suspended now between frozen shores, rigid and deep. She would keep her eyes fixed upon that blue pulse, its tiny ventricle breath as whispered and hesitant as her own.

"Would Madam like some more toast?" Mulligan would say with his blend of sarcasm and hope.

"Madam don't wish no toast at the moment," she invariably replied, watching his puzzlement, and certain that he never quite managed to penetrate the ironies proffered.

The arrangements were simple. And for two people who had led entangled and encumbered lives, they were made with speed and no touch of regret. Yes, Cora would be pleased to quit her job. No, she didn't mind taking up residence in a second-class hostel. Nor did she object in the least to a lover who would be away more than at home. Lucien was a senior engineer with a regular highball run from Sarnia to Toronto. Leaving Sarnia at noon on Monday, Wednesday and Friday; return from Toronto by three on Tuesday, Thursday and Saturday. Which meant overnight in a cold Toronto bunkhouse three nights a week and four warm ones in a specially heated bower in the St. Clair Inn. After which: a leisurely breakfast-for-two long after mid-morning, an abrupt departure, farewells recalled and nursed till again the sudden arrival, the brisk, physical greeting of flesh in its loneliness. Only Saturday and Sunday were exceptional. When Lucien arrived early in the afternoon, tired from the six-hour trip and the layover in London, they would not make love. Instead, she would draw him a bath in the room at the end of the hall and languidly cleanse his rumpled, gray flesh. The sensual flapping of water and the murmurs of their give-and-take would drive Suds O'Boyle's blush down to the tips of his torso, so that he had to rattle the papers on his desk or bang the bell with his elbow for relief. Refreshed, the couple would stroll down to the Christina Tea Room for supper, and then it was time to prepare for the dance at the Armouries. Though the dances were different – guest orchestras coming from as far off as Windsor – they were both aware that each was a vital reenactment of the first one: they did not speak, they merely danced and lived to dance. They rode the three blocks home in a hired cutter. They drank a tumbler of champagne from a bottle cooling in the snow on the sill. She took his hand and led him into the sanctum, where they made love, now alas coordinated though no less lacking than its original in tough, sweaty, buckling urgence. Afterwards it seemed, to Cora at least, as if they were contributing to this fiction of reenactment more as an assurance to themselves that they *had* a shared past of some sort rather than as a refusal to accept the inroads of time itself on their relationship.

Certainly the enforced absences were crucial to their feelings for each other and the tilting equilibrium they had established. On Sundays, for example – their only full day together – they rented a cutter and drove south or east of the town, down the back sideroads of the township plump with farms and settled prosperity, laughing or singing some improvised ditty as the bells on the Clydes jingled an icicle tune of their own and their big breath left a fading print on the air. Then after a dinner at three, they would relax on the chesterfield (she'd had it exchanged for the spartan settee) with a mug of coffee, and talk. Lucien entertained her with slightly baulderized versions of his folk-tales, stringing a story out till it seemed to float on its own voluableness over the sleepy gloaming of their Sunday communion. Embellished for her ears alone, polished or impromptu, they made her laugh and re-see the world made over by this man who inexplicably loved her, or wished to cast whatever love he had left upon some image of her she was not about to question or deny.

"Now let me tell you about one of the funniest characters ever to throttle an engine or puke up in the back seat of a caboose: old Pokey Burdette. One time when I was workin' in the Yard Office, long before I went on the road, Pokey comes into the place about four in the mornin' an' there's half-a-dozen fellas there smokin' an' warmin' their thumbs by the heater, an' they see right away by the whites of his eyes that he's as mad as a plucked gander. He's just come in from Montreal on a passenger – six hours late! 'Stuck in a snowbank as big as a buffalo's arse,' he cries, 'somewheres between Cornwall an' Trenton. An' you know who went an' put it there?' Nobody could guess, so Pokey swats his cap down on the nearest desk an' yells, 'George McPherson, the president of this here railway, that's who!' Then when everybody's real quiet, he says, 'Well, the son-of-a-bitch goes off on his New Years' toot, eh, gets himself gassed up, goes outside to take a piss in the wind, jerks the wrong lever and accidently lets a fart fly, which starts a fuckin' avalanche rollin' down the main-line all the way from here to Port aux Basques!'"

Cora herself had little to offer to this exchange beyond her enthusiastic response to Lucien's efforts. Under his encouragement, however, she was persuaded more and more to tell him about the odd ducks she'd seen in the dining room or about her running series of *contre temps* with Mulligan:

"Top of the mornin' to you, Mrs…Burgher. A menu?"

"The usual, I'm afraid."

"Oh, I do hope you haven't gone an' lost your wedding ring," – staring hard at her left hand exposed upon a soiled napkin.

"Not at all. As a matter of fact, my *husband* keeps it…"

Pause: the silence delicate.

"…*in his nose.*"

To which Lucien would applaud with a bray of guffaws loud enough to make the clerk's bell jump with alarm in the lobby below them.

But of course there was mainly the long Sunday to fill and a few scattered hours over meals and after naps during the week. There would not have been enough stories to plug the silences that a day-to-day, hour-to-hour relationship would have demanded. Nor could they have sustained the bruising-healing quality of their love-making out-side of regulated absence and joyous reacquaintance. When they were separated, and alone, though, the hours were hard won. Cora walked, made polite conversation with young Suds and several of the benchwarmers in the lobby, and waited for the black moments to engulf her. When they did, she tried to muffle her sobbing with the comforter – Lucien's smell lingering there – but sometimes she forgot or did not care, and woke up in a daze in the sitting room with a broken glass at her side and the window wide open to let the wind howl through – whetted by ice, neutered, pneumoniac.

She supposed that he too suffered such relapses, though she saw only the wreckage in his fatigued flesh as he slumped into sleep after a difficult shift. He works it out, though, she thought, he rides that locomotive through the dark, I can hear its singing whistle in the words of his stories. But I am alone, without work, without recourse. I am mad, with little islands of sanity bubbling up and mocking me several times a week. Then Lucien would come back – needing her to need him. I am sane, she concluded. When I go mad, I won't know it. That's a comfort.

"You need a story," Lucien said, "even though it ain't Sunday yet. A Pokey Burdette story by the look of ya'."

She stirred his coffee.

"Well, Pokey comes into the Yard Office one time an' he's all hunched over an' humble-lookin', an' he's got his cap by the brim an' turned over like an organ-grinder without a monkey, an' this time he waits till everyone's lookin' his way an' he says, 'I'm passin' the hat, boys, and I expect you to be generouser than a church warden 'cause we got a charity case right here in our own little family, an' who might that be, you ask?' Then he says, 'Would you be shocked if I told you it was none other than vice-president Margison Dilworth. Yes, it's true, I swear on my grand-daddy's underwear, so dig deep fellas', and all the time he's anglin' around with his cap outstretched lookin' for donations an' brushin' a tear from his eye. 'Poor bugger's broke,' he says, 'down on his luck so far his kids need shoes, eh, his girls're ashamed to go to school, they are, 'cause of the holes in their last pair of patents, an' the eldest lad's got his feet wrapped up in little red bandanas with G.T.R. stamped on the toe.' By now everybody's laughin' an' whoopin' an' trying' to ad-lib but he keeps it up and at last he jumps up on the counter an' hollers, 'Bleedin' Christ but I ain't collected a red cent, not a copper for a man who'd give you guys the skin off his – nose, if he hadn't of worn it out kissin' arse'. He's got them right where he wants them now, eh, keepin' a perfectly straight face till the guffaws die down, then he says, real quiet, 'Now what am I gonna tell Mrs. Marge when I go over there this mornin' an' she begs me to give her some comfort afore hubby comes back from the office?'"

Cora laughed in all the right places, reassured once more by the unaffected ease of her response and the certain knowledge that Pokey Burdette had never had any existence beyond the confines of this room.

2

Early in February Lucien arrived from Toronto bearing under his arm a cardboard carton tied up with string. "For you," he announced, grinning and wary. She sensed something forced in his voice.

"Nice wrapping," she said.

"Did it myself."

"A shame."

"Go on, silly woman, open it."

She did. Inside were a dozen or so very large books, several of them uncut, their calf bindings unsmudged.

She stared.

"From my mother's old place. She liked to read."

"They're beautiful."

"Dickens, Trollope, some fella named Hardy. A Yankee called Fenimore Cooper; *Uncle Tom's Cabin*. She liked them all."

"They must've cost an awful lot."

"They're for you – to read on the days when I'm on the road."

She was holding the largest book in her hands, as if guessing its weight.

"You *do* like to read?"

"Yes. I do. Really." She seemed strangely touched, and he knew enough to say nothing more, though words of all sorts ached for release. She saw the desperate reconnaissance of his eyes, but could not help.

The books remained on the little mahogany table where they had been opened, and the weekday routine continued as before. The next morning Lucien left for the Yard earlier than usual. She felt the extra tension in his shoulders as he held her.

"When you hold my arm like that," she said once, "I get the feeling you're squeezin' a throttle."

"My hands never leave it," he said, trying to grin.

"You can't set still for long."

"Had St. Vitus dance when I was a kid."

"I'm serious."

"It's not so much that I like bein' on the road," he said at last. "After all, I don't get anywhere. It's just that I can't stand bein' cooped up. Makes me feel like a badger in a hutch."

So he was off again, to ride down whatever demons had chosen him long ago. As usual, though she still felt badly sometimes, she was relieved. The rooms were hers. They were sanctuary. And now there were the books. She went right to them.

At first she treated them like sacred texts, circling them, easing them open, glancing quarterwise at the black type as if it were a set of shimmering runes about to divulge something clandestine. Gradually her anxieties diminished, and though she was not ready to tackle an entire book, she would flip open one of them to a random page, and sit for a long time reading and re-reading a single paragraph. An hour might go by before she looked up long enough to realize that the sun had moved above the sash.

"I see you been readin' a bit," Lucien remarked as soon as he got in. She caught the strained casualness of his tone right away.

"A little bit. They're beautiful books. Your mother must've been a beautiful person."

The book froze in his hand.

"I'm sorry," she said. "I really am. I didn't mean –"

"These were her favourites," he whispered.

"I'll read them, Luce," she said. "All of them."

First, she had to read one of them. It had been a little while since she had read anything, and while the trick of it came back quickly to her, the associations it brought with it were not pleasant. After an hour or so of trying to decipher the opening of *Bleak House* (she was drawn to the title), she found herself dizzy and faint. She went to lie down on the bed. She did not remember reaching it, though she was evidently asleep for the black dream was now upon her, its pestilential winds sweeping her along, as always, while she lay begging that other half of her self – the one that would not speak – to succumb, to give it all up, to let the greater will have its way. When she opened her eyes she realized with dread that she was lying on the carpet in the hallway outside Mr. Stewart's room. The hall table was tipped beside her, its little genie-lamp shattered.

"Are you all right, Missus – un – ma'am?"

Waves of nausea rolled up into her throat. She blinked at the young clerk. His hand was very gently upon her arm, about to lift. Suddenly he jerked back as if stung. He crab-walked away from her down the hall, stumbling, reaching wildly behind him for the railing. Stamped on the *tabula rasa* of his boy's face, she saw the insignia of her misery.

"I'll g-get some help," he called hoarsely and disappeared.

Where? she thought, and was sick on the wool roses.

"Tell me, Mr. O'Boyle," she said to him in the lobby the next week, "what does the word 'chancery' mean?"

"Don't know, ma'am," he said warily. "Somethin' to do with courts and b-bigwigs, I think."

"Did you go to school?"

He looked for help. "Yes, m-ma'am. We all did, I got my l-leavin' certificate. Did real good, my m-mum says. She don't approve of m-me slingin' beer."

"Do you have one of them books that explains all the words?"

"A dictionary, you mean? No, I don't. But Mr. M-Mulligan's got one in the office b-back there. Belonged to his wife, b-before she run off." Then as if he felt the latter remark demanded exposition, he said, "That was all she l-left him."

It was heavy sledding, decoding *Bleak House* with the aid of Noah Webster's Dictionary and her own mother wit. It wasn't merely that the words were long and the sentences interminable, but so much of the world being described therein was itself so foreign. The strange speech; the courts and alleys and traffic of an imperial metropolis; the exotic manners and customs – all had to be learned part by part in a vain effort to get some sense of the whole society, some feel for the meaning she was certain lay locked between the words and their referents. Sometimes, as she used to do, she read quickly, letting her instincts and intuitions catch at the flutter of truth sweeping past her. Gradually, assuredly, she felt the grip of the story, the particulars fading the moment their impression was made. She felt the loneliness and the spirit of the mother-less heroine, her heart went out to the poor and the abused, but most of all she was drawn to Jo – she read the chapters about the abandoned street-urchin many times over, struck by the pathos of a soul so orphaned by the world he had less than half a name to call his own.

"You're gonna wear that one out," Lucien said.

"I *will* get to the others," she replied, and seeing that look in his face, she brightened and said, "but let's get the cutter and go into the country. I feel like a little travellin' today."

The air was clear and cold. The sun shone on them. Across the fields the wind blew soft snow upon the week's bruising. The runners sang in the horses' wake.

"You ain't travelled much, have you," Lucien said, turning for home.

A bit later, Cora opened her eyes, her lashes laced with frost. "This is far enough for me."

"Someday soon, I'll take you for a real ride," he said. "We'll get on the C.P.R. an' cruise all the way over the prairies and up the backside of the Rocky Mountains an' slide down to the ocean out there past Vancouver an' hop the first whale we see an' sail the blue sea to China."

This was a voice she hadn't heard before. Still looking ahead she reached across and touched his hand, tight on the reins. "An' have a decent cup of tea," she said.

When they pulled up in front of McPeck's livery, Lucien gave her a furry bear-hug in full view of the astonished grooms.

"You were right," he whispered. "She *was* beautiful."

And she did get to the other books. For five weeks on alternate days, she read and ab-sorbed and puzzled and thought more than she ever had in her whole life. She began to get some sense of that 'old country' she had known till now only through what she had heard and been told: that old old land where her own parents and the parents of almost everyone she knew had begun their lives, and who gave, through their stories and speech, a temporary credence to exotic landscapes – gardens, hedgerows, wobbly lanes, ancient abbeys among the meadow-growth – and peculiar notions of town and village and dialect as indigenous as the local loam or limestone. In some ways, think-ing as she must about the mighty River and the Freshwater Sea of the Hurons and the vast prairie the scarlet soldiers had crossed, the old world was as exotic as ancient China or some far Hindustan. Somehow, she thought, alone in her brown study, I am one of them, yet not a part of them. Then, like most of her thoughts, it wouldn't stay still long enough for her to grasp it fully, and she would be left frustrated and aching with a great emptiness.

When she began browsing through the other books, she noticed a peculiar thing: the fly-leaf page had been cut out of each, probably with a razor, so neat was the inci-sion. She became aware of this only because in the copy of *Uncle Tom's Cabin* the page had been crudely removed, as if in anger, leaving jagged edges despite a subsequent attempt to disguise the initial violence. Which was the moment she realized that every book was supposed to have such a page, and began examining the others. She said nothing to Lucien. He seemed more and more tense, and absorbed, though at times he could be garrulously happy in the usual manner. She would catch him staring at her at odd angles, the mask of his face dissolved, leaving only his eyes to carry the burden of whatever he could not feel or say. So she found herself beginning to fill some of the more frequent silences by recounting for him the stories, as she heard them, from the great tomes he had brought her.

"We'll make a story-teller out of you yet," he said.

She put on a brave front. When he was away, she thought: this cannot last. We've tried, but it can't be done. Whatever has happened to him, he's needed me in the same way I've needed him – to get through enough days with some feeling, some pretence of caring, some ritual repeated enough to seem necessary: just until we can decide whether there's anything left worth salvaging. But I don't want this to stop. Neither does he, I think. Why, then, should we not keep it going? Who is to tell us it can't be done? Just because it isn't or isn't supposed to. It was we ourselves who decided to make the night we met the first day of our lives. So be it. But it can't last. Love, whatever it's been, has never been enough.

Absently, she leafed through *The Last of the Mohicans*, a novel she had started but left, for some reason, till now. A page fell out. It was blank. A fly-leaf ripped. From *Uncle Tom's Cabin*. She turned it over. She saw the handwriting there, but it was several minutes before she could disentangle it enough to be sure of the sense: 'To my beloved Mary, to while away the lonesome nights, from your devoted wanderer, Luce; Christmas 1875'.

When he arrived home that afternoon – early in March of 1886 – Lucien was all smiles. She'd heard him humming to the banisters. "Get your bonnet on, Susie-Q," he said. "We got business at the Court House."

They did. They were married by a drowsy judge in cold chambers with a scrub-woman and a janitor gaping on. They hurried home to a warm bed and made love as if it were New Years.

"You went an' made an honest woman outta me," she said, watching him smoke.

"Too late for that."

"Too late long ago. An' more than once."

"That wasn't the main reason, though," he said.

"Oh?"

He grinned. "Somebody had to do somethin' about young Sudsy's stutter."

44

1

All across the reunited Confederation it had been a heartless, unrelenting winter. Snow clogged the Laurentian trench, inundated the fields and fallow of the south-west, blew without purpose across the vacant prairielands, and settled like a mocking bride's-veil over the little graves at Batoche and Duck Lake. In March, a week after the wedding of Cora and Lucien Burgher, came the great thaw. The world around them sagged, glistened, and hummed with the promise of heat. Then unexpectedly and just when the severest skeptic was about to admit the possibility of spring, the unforgettable blizzard of 1886 struck home: in the middle of the night, howling from the north-west.

For three citizens of the Province, though, such a dramatic shift in the weather seemed like an act of divine intervention, a pope's blessing on the deed about to be accomplished. Their meeting, if somewhat unorthodox, was nonetheless predestined: sometime just before or just after the trio's singing of Auld Lang Syne at the Grand Trunk Ball, the initial commitment had been made. The Honourable Halpenny Pebbles, Mr. Margison Dilworth, Q.C., and Stanley R. Dowling, reeve of the village, whispered the same word together and decided that after due time for consultation and soul-searching, they should meet again – in utmost secrecy – to put their particular seals upon these first covenants. The word they whispered was 'tunnel'.

It was a word heard before in these parts. Both the Great Western and the Grand Trunk has boasted of blasting a channel below the St. Clair River to link the destinies, common ideals and profit margins of the two great nations so unhappily divided by the inconvenience of a natural border. It was all bluff. No one in Sarnia or the Point took it seriously; before the merger of 1882, that is. With a combined strength and an unabated capacity to plunder the public purse at will, the Grand Trunk Western's boasting about a tunnel was henceforth received with joy in the village and muted applause in the town. Naturally any such tunnel would be built across the narrowest strip between the Republic and the Dominion: where the GTR reached the very edge of Canada: Point Edward. Which meant that some of the advantages gained by

Sarnia at the original merger – main passenger terminus on the principal line between Sarnia-London-Brantford-Toronto, expanded switching yards and car-shops – might well be stunted or, heaven forfend, wiped out by the inevitable surge of power westward towards the heartland of America – via a *Point Edward* tunnel. Strangely, though, little talk of any kind regarding such an engineering miracle had been heard for more than a year. To those in the know, of course – board-room bullies, intimates of the disbanded Compact, the Scottish moneylenders – such silence signalled clearly that the most feverish plans were afoot. However, only the most trusted insiders – the directors of the Railway, the premier's own privy council – and one outsider, knew that the issue was no longer financial or even technological. If the fittest were to survive, then the survivors of this Dominion would be the fittest: the dynamite and the air compressors were ready. What was holding up the orderly advancement of the nation was something more pivotal than money or technique: politics. Though merely a village, the Point had become a symbol to many another small Ontario community that had invested in railway promises only to be left holding worthless debentures and their assigned mortgages. Indeed the government-of-the-day was vulnerable in the villages and hamlets. If Point Edward were seen to have been 'done dirty' by the Railway or what-is-worse by a government in collusion with a railway, then the upcoming election itself might be lost, with the resultant chaos and inestimable human calamity. Word had just come from Montreal by coded message: Hobson, the world-renowned Canadian engineer, had completed his feasibility study. His news was unequivocal and without prejudice: the geology of the terrain at Point Edward absolutely precluded a tunnel ever being built there; the ideal spot lay five miles to the south, near Sarnia.

Enter Reeve Dowling, politician and former railway executive. The trick, he announced, was simply to get the population of the village to actually want the tunnel to be built at Sarnia. Vague promises were to be made, *quid pro quo* – the town gets the dirty, noisy, hazardous tube but the village keeps its lucrative car-shops, round-house, freight-sheds, and will certainly have its port facilities expanded at public expense and the almost certain possibility that a large steamship company – beholden to the present government – would set up house at dockside. *Et cetera.* And who better to present such a package of delights to wary constituents than the Reeve himself. For his part in the melodrama, the Reeve would be offered – without contest – a safe provincial seat to the north, from which redoubt he might well eventually storm the gates of Queen's Park itself. The key to success, all agreed, lay in the Reeve's gradual and delicate revelation of details so that neither collusion nor predetermination be apparent. It was this intricate series of 'one-acters' that had to be negotiated among the three interested parties. The timing was all.

The blizzard of March 15 was both a blessing, then, and a sign. No one except a sleepy yardmaster noticed, through the haze of snow, the arrival, around suppertime, of a 'special way-freight' consisting of locomotive, tender, three empty box-cars and a caboose. The sole occupant of the caboose was deputy-premier Peebles. The conductor had sat shivering in the engine-cab with the driver and fireman all the way from Toronto. Mysteriously, this 'ghost train' was turned around, then backed onto a far siding. Its crew, following prearranged orders, left the locomotive primed and running, and headed for the comforts of the bunkhouse. They had been commanded to return at precisely seven o'clock and, without a by-your-leave, head back to Toronto.

A few minutes after they had left the train seemingly deserted, the doodle-bug from Stratford arrived and debouched a handful of well-chilled passengers (the heating apparatus, clogged with snow and striations of ice, gave up in Ailsa Craig). One of these, distinguished in black, did not enter the faint warmth of the waiting-room, with its windows steamed tight, but instead turned and, pausing to confirm his anonymity, slipped through the snow towards the mystery locomotive, panting inexplicably on its lonely siding. The male figure – at ease anywhere, even in a blizzard as if he might at any second command it to cease at his convenience – glanced up at the deserted engine-cab, nodded with satisfaction, then walked casually down past the three box-cars to the caboose, whose single lamp flickered bravely outward. Vice-President Margison Dilworth hopped nimbly aboard, shutting the caboose door deliberately behind him, disdainful of the privy councillor's teeth-chattering 'hello', and apparently unmindful that his boot-prints were already half-obliterated by the still-falling snow.

A second pair of prints, suffering a like fate, were fast approaching along the tracks from the north where they curved and ran down Front Street towards the outskirts of Point Edward.

2

By six o'clock the snow was deep enough to impede all walking. So Lucien and Cora decided to celebrate the first week's anniversary of their marriage in the dining room of the St. Clair. After a light supper they began toasting one another (and several recruits from nearby tables) with champagne and a heartiness only partially forced. There was in Lucien's eye a manic twinkle that had taken spark sometime before his arrival home early in the afternoon, and that was not in the least assuaged by their fiery coupling nor its amber aftermath, that prospered with each tumbler of elixir he lavished upon it with the abandon of a dispossessed leprechaun.

"Tonight," he said, "I'm gonna take you on that ride I been promisin'."

"In this?" she said lightly, scanning his eyes for some sign of what the fire in them was shielding with its glee-glint.

"Snow never stopped a train," he said.

When they stepped outside, Cora could just discern the outlines of a horse-and-cutter. Lucien silenced the muttering of the driver with a silver dollar, swept his beloved onto the snowy seat, and proclaimed: "To the station, my good fellow. And hurry. We've got a train to catch!"

Cora snuggled against him. His heart was drumming through layers of wool. The sound of the horse's hooves never reached them. It was hard to believe that somewhere behind the muffling veil around them there was a night full of darkness punctured by stars. No lights blinked at their passing along Front to Cromwell. The driver closed his eyes, sagged forward, and gave up the reins. Only the instinct of beasts brought them at last before the looming shadow of the former Great Western depot.

The waiting-room was deserted, its gas lamps blazing foolishly. Brushing the snow from his coat, Lucien said, "You wait here. Scrubby Parsons said we could hop on his way-freight down to the Point. About seven o'clock. I'll see if he's in the bunkhouse."

Cora spotted Big Meg in the doorway of the Ladies, and pulled her scarf further up across her face. She felt a twinge of shame. Meg didn't see her. "It'll be just an hour's run to the Point an' back," Lucien had explained, "but you'll get the feel of it. There's nothin' on this earth like it."

His hand touched her shoulder. "Can't find him anywheres. One of the boys thinks the run might've been cancelled." She saw in his face the deep disappointment, the souring of the champagne's sheen, and beneath it the germ of something black and combustible. "I'll just check the back sidings. They may be out there waitin' for us."

"I'll come with you," Cora said.

"Okay, but wait on the platform," he said quickly. "You can't tell a tie from a T-bar out there."

She followed him outside and stood in the passenger area beside the main-line as Lucien headed across the half-acre of tracks normally visible to the south-east. Within seconds he was gone. The snow beat against her face like the frayed wings of winter-sparrows. She shivered but was not cold.

Lucien reappeared, flushed. "I found it," he puffed. "Six tracks over behind the car-man's shed. She's primed an' ready to go."

Cora hesitated, her head tilted to one side. She seemed to be listening for some sound in the mute threshing about her – a warning perhaps, an all-clear, a starter's gun – like a robin waiting for the ground to heave with the worm's appetite.

"Come on," he said, no longer able to mask the desperation behind his excitement.

Above them the clock hanging over the platform, if it had been unobscured, would have read 'five minutes to seven'.

Hand in hand they crossed the tracks they could not see.

The locomotive stood rigid in its berth, huffing and fitfully sighing to itself. The snow sizzled on its hot metal and, dripping downward, froze instantly into stalactites – which lent an illusion of immobility, of rootedness, of fossilized behemoth. The great gulping steam-chambers, hissing inside it, said otherwise. Lucien pulled her into the cab with a gentleman's grace and slid the flap closed behind them. They were alone.

"Where's Scrubby? An' the crew?"

His broad shoulders were turned towards the dials and levers in front of him. "Slee-pin' it off in the caboose, I reckon. We'll do them a big favour, takin' it down there on our own."

Any response she may have been contemplating was cut short by the shriek of the steam-whistle – two short blasts, repeated. "She's steamed up an' ready to go," he shout-ed back. "All set?" He hopped over to a leather bench on the right, slid open the win-dow, leaned out and with his left hand grasped a lever and slowly eased it towards him.

Everything metallic around them shivered, creaked, strained against gravity. The creature lurched, skidded, lurched again. A tremor of motion hummed through their bones and shook its way back through the coal-tender, box-cars and caboose. Safe in this cab, surrounded by steel, Cora could sense the power of the released steam as it crashed into the cylinders like stunted thunder, and poured its dissipating energies into the pleasures of motion and speed. Lucien pointed to the stoker's seat under the left-hand window. She looked out in time to see several blotched shadows below her. They appeared to be waving. She waved back.

"I got her up to thirty," he called across, peering at a smoky gauge an inch beneath his nose. "She was well-primed."

The only light was cast by two fixed lamps above the benches that shivered and threatened to jump ship with every jerk and skid of the locomotive over the drifted, erratic roadbed. The slitted firebox, near Cora's side, glowed with radiant, welcoming heat, but cast over wall and ceiling scraps of fretting shadow that reminded her of moths caught in a coal-oil lamp.

"Feels like we're curvin' to the left," she said. "Shouldn't we have veered right by now?"

He slipped open his window a little ways, pushing his face into a white flail. "Yup, we would've," he said, "if we was goin' towards Point Edward."

Cora looked out her side. She was certain she could see a ragged horizon line bouncing just beyond the storm's fury. "I see the bush," she said. "We're headin' for London!"

"We were, old sweetheart, until this very second!" As he spoke the cab jumped sideways, spilling Cora onto the stippled steel floor and pinning Lucien to his perch. The screech of iron rebelling against iron pierced the ear, stunning them both. Then as each of three box-cars and the caboose met the crossover switch behind them, they were struck again. The whole train tilted wildly to the right, yearning to roll over into the battened ditches beside it.

Lucien's powerful throttle-hand was under her. He helped her back to her bench, mouthing endearments and apologies, then starting to laugh uncontrollably. Without the least notion why, she joined him. Whatever direction the beast had chosen, it seemed perfectly content to travel on its own. Lucien's lips closed her eyes. After a time, he drew back. They could hear again: the steady, imperturbable cadence of Pegasus en route to anywhere.

"I don't know why we got turned east," he said. "We hit the main-line just past the bunkhouse. I figured we'd spend the night in London, but somebody left 'number-three switch north' where it was an' now we're aimed up the spur-line that don't end till Woodston. Up in Huron County."

"Are they expectin' us?"

"Ain't got much of a choice!" He was laughing and trying to holler over from his side where he was scrutinizing the steam-gauges. "There's nothin' between us an' them an' we sure ain't gonna park out here tonight. In fact, we got a straight run in there. Oughta make it in about forty-five minutes."

"I know someone in Woodston," Cora said. "I'm sure she'd let us stay overnight."

Lucien didn't hear her. He had his window wide open. The blizzard poured into the cab and spent itself in miniature frenzies. "Hang on, sweetheart! Woodston, here we come, and if you don't like it, we'll shove somethin' hot up your ante room!" He pushed his head outside and wailed: "*Ya-hoooo!*"

The whistle skirled in unison with the engineer's taunt. Cora was astonished to find the cord in her own grasp.

"She's losin' pressure! You'll have to take over while I stoke her." He motioned Cora over to him. Carefully he took her hand and placed it on the throttle beside his. Then he eased away. "Hold her steady an' keep an eye on the pressure gauge," he said, starting to strip off his coat.

Cora felt the lever seize her hand. It throbbed in her grip and she felt simultaneously through it the monumental trembling of the whole apparatus – furnace, boiler, cylinders, pistons, driver-wheels, the cold ignition of metal on metal, its hair-trigger touch.

As Lucien flipped open the firebox door, a jet of flame shot across the cab, scalding the walls. He was bare to the waist. His torso gleamed with sweat and the wash of infra-red. She saw the crevasses between muscle and muscle, tendon and bone, as he leaned back towards the opened shute, scooped up a huge shovelful of coals as nimbly as if they were beans on a spoon, swivelled around, and in unbroken arc of motion and strength hurled them into the furnace. At first his pace was slow and methodically beautiful; soon it accelerated, gaining momentum and urgency. The firebox roared, then howled, then frothed into a white, wordless delirium. The stoker's motions became blurred, no one part distinguishable from another. Suddenly the motion ceased and the stoker leaped sideways, kicked the door shut, and punched a knob just below the pressure gauge. A cloud of steam burst from each of the creature's nostrils. They heard its death-scream and the hail of melted snow and ice crystals flung against the windows.

"Can't have her blowin' on us, can we?" His cheeks were as scarlet as a berry harrowed in Hades, his grin was as wide as Beelzebub's. "*Open her up! Let's make her fly!*"

Cora pulled back on the throttle. All the needles on all the gauges flinched.

"Use these," Lucien shouted.

She slipped on the goggles, slid open her window and peered out, not letting go of the throttle, the microscopic value that somehow enflamed the steaming heartstrokes of this leviathan-on-a-toot. She had to see what her lover saw, what he felt, what he could forget to remember. She peered ahead.

The storm had tapered off to intermittent squalls. At this moment, between sieges, she was able to see the glint of the piston-levers, the patina of exertion along the bevelled boiler plates, the thrust of the stack with its charred smoke blanched and flattened by the wind, the head-lamp pinpointing a thousand discrete, induplicate snowflakes for the quarter-second it took them to self-destruct and be replaced. She could see no sign of the track. Somewhere below and beyond must be a meridian, however thin or obscure, guiding them magnetically across a landscape blown featureless by the blizzard and past the reach of star or sextant.

Lucien was at her side. His warmth enveloped her. She lay her cheek beside his along the ledge. She was aware of her eyes closing with his. She held him holding her. They took their breath together. Wherever they were pointed became their destination. In them the snow dazzled, deepened, blossomed with crystal flowers untouched by grief. Without moving, with not a whisper of expended passion, hurtling at seventy-miles-an-hour through a blinding snowstorm in an iron box alternately freezing and searing, dumb-founded by cacophony and inviolate silence – Lucien and Cora made patient, handwritten, memorial love.

Lucien was talking. She had screamed a tacit, unending *no*, he had frozen his lips with her kiss, she had yanked the throttle-lever as far back as it could go until the struts and bolts of the beast rattled like coffin-bones in an earthquake. But no ground can hold a voice whose words must be spoken.

"Her name was Mary. I met her through her sister, who was married to a friend of mine, a fireman like me on the Great Western. I was no longer young but rich, as I thought, an' footloose. I let her charm me, an' she did. But she said she knew from her sister's experience how much hell was in store for the wife of an engineer. I hadn't had a chance to ask, but she'd already said no. Of course, I kept seein' her, an' she was always unattached, so I begun to wonder; an' besides, I was getting a bit tired of stokin' an' cattin' around in Detroit an' them places. So I told her if she'd marry me I'd settle down an' become a respectable family man. When she doubted me, I quit the Great Western an' joined the Grand Trunk, breakin' all my old ties. For two years, though, I stayed on the road, but when Mary became pregnant, I gave in. I hired on as a clerk in the Yard Office. So that's what I became at age thirty-five. I hated it as much as I loved my wife. It was like workin' in a rabbit's den, you couldn't breathe, you sucked in the stink of everybody's body, you had no place to run or feel free in when you needed to. But I did it, for five years I loved an' hated. We had two beautiful children, a girl first, then a boy. But my salary wasn't a third of what I made stokin' on the road. We rented a house in the east and down near the rivermouth by the lake. It was a shanty-town, really, though we painted the place, an' put a fence round it an' planted ourselves a garden. But it was swampy down there and in the winter the snow piled up, thawed an' froze, an' the dampness went right through the wood, you couldn't keep enough paint or pine-tar on it to stop it from rottin' under you. In the daytime the bugs devoured the vegetables in the heat, an' the mosquitoes come out at night to torment us. I begged Mary to let me go back on the road. She said she would get a job as soon as the kids were older – she had a high school certificate. So I went off one mornin' an' hopped on a freight an' never went back to that stinkin' clerk's den. I took only short day-runs. I lied every day to my wife an' kids. I hadn't been at this long, though, when my punishment was revealed to me in all its horror. My little girl complained of a headache after supper one day. It got worse by bedtime. By the middle of the night she was screaming in agony an' bewilderment. When the fever hit the next day, we knew it was typhoid. We'd seen it in summers past. An' shuddered, an' prayed. Her little body was burnin' an' tremblin' at the same time. The diarrhea weakened her terribly. Like a thief, I stole away, I took the money I'd secretly earned an' went for a doctor. Not many would come down to our slum for any sort of money. But I found one who would; he told us it was typhoid fever, that only one of us should stay in the house as nurse, that we should boil our water, an' so on. He gave us some laudanum for the pain an' suggested we pray. He wasn't gone an hour when my boy, barely a year old, was struck down with it. Mary and I did what we could. We knew full well only the strongest survived. We needed more medicine. Mary hadn't slept in three nights but she said I must go back to work to get some money for the kids, an' to keep my job which I could lose at any moment for being absent. So I did. I took a way-freight to Jackson's Point. When I got back that night I was stopped about a block before my house by Mrs. Putnam, our neighbour. 'Don't go there,' she said. 'Come to my place. It's best.' But I tore away from her. I ran down that muddy street like a madman. I saw the crowd gathered 'round the spot where my house had been. There was nothin' left but cinders an' charred bits of wood an' bone – who could tell? 'Just as the sun was settin',' Mrs. Putnam said, 'she come out the front door carryin' a lantern an' wavin' it frantically all about. *They're dead!* she hollered. *They're gone!* An' before we could stop her, she ran back inside, an' seconds later smoke poured out the cracks in the sidin' an' then flames shot into the air, an' we never heard a single sound come from inside the house. Not one.' She died alone, my Mary, without leavin' me a word. Everythin' was gone, burned to ashes. Later I found out she'd loaned her sister the books I'd bought her over the years. They're all that's left. That was eight years ago. I been on the move ever since."

Lucien's hand was on the throttle once more. Cora clung to him, to the terror in him, the exhilaration, the risk. Every needle on every dial had peaked, then snapped, the glass restraining them had shattered. The firebox door throbbed like a fevered eye. The welding scars on the engine's joints stiffened, brittle as ice. One more revolution and the whole contraption would fly apart in a welter of primal steam and lava. We'll die together, was Cora's thought as she heard the shriek of rending boiler-plate, the shudder of disconnecting wheels. She waited out the silence that preceded the impact, holding her breath and Lucien's hand.

But there was no crash, no clatter of wheels on pigiron, no surge of piston in its chamber. No sound but the rushing of the wind behind the snow. They had left the track, the invisible meridian, the groove of all gravity. They were flying weightless and triumphant through the spaces between the snow that rose with them, lifting and blessing, till it turned itself into a constellation of planets, and they soared through its black immaculacy towards the Polar Star whose belly was the Milky Way, whose jasper eye would draw them safely beyond Newton or Darwin or any other calculus of the frozen heart.

Most of the population of the hamlet of Woodston heard the ghost train of 'eighty-six as its shadow hummed past the Grand Trunk passenger station. They heard the muted screech of its futile braking. They flinched as one at the abrupt, epimethean thud of cast-iron on drifted snow. In fact, despite the blizzard and dire storm warnings the good people of Woodston had come out in force to christen their brand-new depot, just completed mere days ago and ready to receive its first passengers on the morrow. The unscheduled arrival of the ceremonial train was more than a shock. Woodston's reeve was in the midst of a passionate toast to the eternal glory of railways in general and the Grand Trunk in particular. The wine-goblets glistened beneath the gas-lamps. The room burbled with the good cheer that comes from unearned contentment and free booze. So concentrated was the assembly's attention on the latter exigency that no one noticed, shortly after the meal began about six-thirty, the rumble and roar of a nearby avalanche. Not more than fifty yards from the station where the spur-line itself came to an end, there stood on one side of the tracks a mountain of stored coal, ready to be used as soon as the connecting spur to the northern trunk-line was completed in the spring. Opposite it was another mountain, this one of crushed stone to be likewise deployed in the expansion project. Over the preceding two days local squalls off the Lake had dumped acres of fresh snow onto these man-made peaks. Somewhere between the roast beef and the baked apple, a huge ledge of packed snow gave way and rolled unimpeded into the valley below. This fracture awakened the trolls in the mountain opposite and it too sent an avalanche bevelling down upon the first. The result was that the end-of-line was now defined by a trapezoid of snow thirty-feet high, twenty-feet across and a hundred-yards in length.

Into this welcome – decelerating at sixty-miles-per-hour – the purloined locomotive irrupted.

What the reeve and the anxious press in the doorway behind him saw as they peered speechless into the haze was this: the rear end of a caboose otherwise burrowed utterly in what appeared to be an improvised dune of snow –where the tracks used to be. The caboose door had been knocked silly by the plundering impact, and was giggling on one hinge. Nothing else moved. Nothing else was visible. The snow, between flurries, fluttered and hung. Further along, a thread of steam or frost began to uncoil from the mountain ridge. Something under there was breathing. Then like a blue whale blowing in some fairy-tale sea, a spume of spittle and geysering breath stunned the onlookers. In terror they heard the hiss of overheated, subterranean flesh.

Which noise seemed also to rouse whatever life lay cowering within the caboose, for on the same instant the reeve detected several shadows emerging from the ruptured doorway. Through a scrim of snow he could distinguish them only in silhouette, but it was clear that they were three men and that they occupied various stations of suffering. The forward shadow was taller, or more erect, striding so as to disguise a twisted knee and wrestling manfully with the impossible task of repositioning his crushed bowler. A yard behind him a second shadow essayed to keep pace with abrupt, paralytic steps. Further back: a hunched, crabbed figure was advancing with painful slowness, as if its thighs were glued together. On the platform, no one moved or spoke. The figures came silently towards them, close enough at last so that they were seen, despite the snow, to have human faces – but dazed, tentative, and slackened by incredulity as if they had just stepped onto the dark side of Pluto's moon.

"Mr. Dilworth!" gasped the reeve.

"Where in hell's *this*!"

"Woodston, sir. But what are you doin' here this time of day?"

"Never mind that," boomed the voice that made boardrooms tremble and second vice-presidents quake in their sweat. He swivelled and pointed at the crippled creature behind them. "Get the deputy-premier to a toilet." The reeve leaped forward. "He's shit his pants." And leaped back.

"Then, round up your strongest men and dig that son-of-a-bitch out of there!" He aimed a gloved finger at the far end of the avalanche where the smoke-stack of a locomotive was materializing fantastically out of snow, steam and the night-air. "I want that renegade's balls broiled for breakfast!"

3

While there are many ways in which a conspiracy may be accidentally disclosed, no more public or more indecent exposure could be imagined than that which occurred when the railway executive, the privy councillor and the ambitious reeve staggered into the Woodston station under the scrutiny of two hundred well-dressed guests of every political stripe – dazed, enraged, malodorous, trembling with the aftershock of an hour's journey into terror. Nor was it convenient to keep from popular view the speculation the presence of a runaway train embedded spectacularly in an impromptu ski-slope. Indeed, the celebratory dinner had attracted several gentlemen of the press and one keen photographer, who between them managed to immortalize the train of events on bold-face and daguerreotype. Nonetheless, both governments and railroads are wont to survive such momentary embarrassments, as they did in this instance. The tunnel was eventually built where God had ordained it, and the ruling clique clung to power for still one more term, though the railway lost a faithful servant and the federal Senate was fleshed out with yet another retiring member of cabinet. The most evident victim of these unfortunate and unpredicted violations of the natural order, however, was Stanley R. Dowling. Two weeks after the catastrophe, with eighteen months left in his term, he resigned as reeve of Point Edward, a position he had held by acclamation since the birth of the village itself. In total disgrace, he faded from the printed page of local history.

Cora remembered the soft surreality of the crash, the sensation of falling into a cushion of cloud, then being pitched forward. That was all. When she woke up, she was in the infirmary of the Woodston doctor. It was noon. The sun shone in a blue sky. Where was Lucien? she asked. The railroad police had already taken him away to London, to jail. It was assumed, since she was a woman, that she had been abducted and was therefore as much a victim as the wretched trio who had bounced about in the lampless caboose. Much solicitude was thus shown her. She said as little as possible, mostly because she could do nothing but think of Lucien. She wanted to go immediately to London, but two days later, when her head stopped spinning, she was taken to the train (the inaugural one having arrived a bit late) and accompanied by an official back to Sarnia. She was left, alone at last, in Lucien's rooms.

The next train for London left at five-thirty. She started to pack, her hands shaking uncontrollably. One image above all others floated in front of her: a badger in a wire cage swallowing its own fury.

When the knock came at the door, she jumped straight up. It was young O'Boyle, his face ashen. He had a telegram in his hand.

"I'm sorry, Mrs. Burgher," he said.

"He's dead," she said, as if telling him the news he already knew.

"Yes, ma'am. Word come along the railroad 'vine' about noon. It's all over town."

"How?"

"Hung himself, ma'am. In his cell."

Ten minutes later Mr. Mulligan opened the door a notch, paused, then came in. Cora was seated on the chesterfield, holding a book bigger than a Bible. When she finally looked up, at his third cough, he said: "I want you outta this place by noon tomorrow, bag an' baggage."

There was little commiseration in his Irish grin.

45

The arrangements were now complete. In the morning they would come and move her things across the street into the cottage they had built for her. Sunny had asked her to come and have a gander at it before the trauma of moving day, but she had refused. I'll see it when I get there, she thought. At my age I may not wake up in the morning, and then I won't get there anyway, so what's the point of seeing something first and getting all stirred up for nothing? I fussed about the future many times, in the nine lives I've had before this one, and where did it get me? All the way to Grief Street, that's where. For Sunny's sake she had feigned some interest in choosing wallpaper from the assorted bundles he lugged over, though none of the ghostly roses, dumpling flags or haplessly cheerful urchins he unrolled for her held any appeal. In the end she selected the plainest and least offensive. What did it matter? She was not really interested in a house which she herself had been tempted to help confect. Houses ought to grow, she had always thought. They should express the lives lived there. They should be surprised, dreamed, mercurial, beautiful to the beholder. I guess that's why I loved the Lane, and why I never could explain it, certainly not to Cap and not even to Arthur, who tried very hard and whose own handiwork was, despite his good-natured disclaimers, done in the same spirit. 'Only the temptations of the church saved you from bein' a Laner,' she used to tease him. 'And only *you* saved *me* from the church,' he'd laugh back.

I'll ask them to move your trunk last, Arthur, she promised. I'll walk beside it. That way we'll keep the ghosties inside. You realize they aren't going to be too happy with the sudden transfer. Being theatrical ghosts, though, they ought to be used to being on the move. They told me you were almost fifty before you settled in one pew. She wished now that she could have seen Arthur in his prime, treading the boards of the great stages of the West, warbling away like his own favourite – the bluebird – with not a touch of winter in his song, with no thought of wings wearied with migration or the unalterable swing of the seasons.

It was May now and unseasonably warm. Her crocuses had bloomed in their usual profusion. The tulips along the house bulged in the trapped sunlight. The vegetable beds lay spaded and expectant. "We'll leave the border flowers an' shrubs, for a while," Sunny had assured her. "But the garden'll be turned into grass. Eventually, the whole area will be landscaped in some manner suited to a cenotaph. It'll be a kind of special ground. There's a bit of land behind your new place. We may have to clear some trees, though, to get enough sun in there."

Granny felt the need to get out for a while, out of Arthur's house, out of the gardens they had planted together, out of the vegetable patch she would never tend again. As far as she could recall, she had not been off her own property since the terrible autumn of 1918. It was high time. I'm going out there and have a look at this town, all of it, one more time before I settle in somewhere to die. If these wobbly old legs will carry me. And if I happen to topple into the River, well, I'll save the council the price of a ceremony.

She felt surprisingly sturdy. She walked north along her own street towards Michigan Ave. She recognized every house she passed, found perfectly familiar every gable, stoop, gate, half-finished dormer, or coppery window with one blank eye unpatched since the War. Each house sent its voices wafting out to her – shredded, grown faint with the years but still unappeased, still desperate for attention, the need for a story to be told in full, an ending to be got right at long last, and a hidden side to be revealed and understood. Too late, too late, she whispered as she hurried slowly past, too late for all that, now.

She passed the houses of the respectable, some fallen since to disrepute, and heard no apologies for the treatment received there by Cora the cleaning woman, or before that, 'that washerwoman Lily from the Lane'; houses where she had been good enough to wash clothes, scrub floors, cook a meal, wipe up the children's snot and shit but not to share a meal, carry a confidence, love them without premeditation. 'But did you ever try to *talk* to them? See life from their point of view?' Cap had asked her many times. 'You kept yourself aloof. You expected the world to come to you. You were a loner by choice. It was your chosen philosophy.' Perhaps there was more to Cap's accusations than she had ever acknowledged during their long hours of reciprocal interrogation. But what did it matter now? They were all dead. Several of them she had walked with to the very edge, helping them across when the props of their respectability cracked asunder, when death dared them to enter his chamber unattended, and they couldn't. 'But you'll be glad to know,' she said to Cap now, 'I felt no satisfaction.'

Some, of course, like Eliza Sanders, had been furtively kind, slipping her an extra dollar when a husband wasn't looking, giving hand-me-downs she was too proud to take home to her boys but others along the Lane were happy to receive.

She passed Redmond's Grocery, the Post Office, the new hotel, the Pool Room – feeling heads turn in shop windows – and crossed the street to the Lane where The Queen's had stood for fifty years. It was a rooming house now, she had heard, but the spirits that poured out of its bowers, anterooms, closets, pantries and wine-cellars stopped her in her tracks, overwhelmed her with their babble. She felt dizzy. Don't faint, you stupid old fool, she thought, not right here on the main street with the sun shining.

She didn't, thought she couldn't be certain because when she opened her eyes she was not in front of The Queen's or any other building, nor was she on any of the village sidewalks. She was in some sort of field. In the summer it would be covered with sawgrass and sandburs, but at the moment it was soft and fern-like, and her legs were carrying her, not willy-nilly through it, but along a wide path that was, for a short time in this young half of spring, plainly visible. This had been a road once, a winding, sauntering one. On either side of her, she noticed clumps of concrete or the shell of what had been a porch or chicken-run, some of its wire rusted as thin as fish-nets in the drying sun. to her left a window, all of its glass intact, stood rooted to the ground where it had slumped and stuck while all else around it had inexplicably rotted away. She almost tripped over the frail skeleton of a child's sled. An icy breeze from the Lake reminded her of more than she was prepared to remember.

The Alley. The Lane. She looked unbelieving to the north-east. She saw the backyards, sheds, coops and rambling pitches of the houses built along the 'official' Lane, straightened by statute. I helped to do this, she thought, long ago, in another name. Now the air was filled with human sounds, voices skewed and thinned by the breeze. Her body was propelling itself towards them. She saw the crazed outline of chicken-wire, caught the thick stink of swine too long in their styes, heard the domestic sing-song of women's conversation as they laboured. Her eyes strained ahead to see them, to know who these inheritors were, whether they knew what ground, what tradition, what spritely demons they had foolishly promised to possess. No one was in sight. She stumbled. The voices arrived, loud and clear: a foreign tongue. She listened, ignoring the burn in her knees: it was no language she knew, or had ever heard. Suddenly the syllables stabbed at her eyes, raced unconnected through her head like bat's echoes in a belfry, spinning her around, deafening, she couldn't hear the last beats of her heart nor the bounce of her kneecaps on the stiff earth.

When the sounds stopped ringing in her head, miraculously she was still walking. It was getting dark or misty, or both. She was in a sort of hollow, for though she could hear the lake-breeze high in the distant trees, she felt no wind at all on her face. The ground beneath her walking was resilient, kindly, sown with the tender grass found only on the graves of children. She was lost, her legs had gone numb, but she was not in the least afraid. She felt serenely at ease. At any moment of her choosing, she could lie down on one of those sandy mounds, close her eyes and sleep the longest, deepest, sunniest sleep of her life. The air around her trembled with invitation. There were voices in it but they spoke directly to the weariness of her bones; they carried the news of consolation. It's time to lie down, she thought.

A shadow flicked, off to her right. A bird, returned from its journey? A mourning dove? Something bright and shifting caught the last of the daylight and transformed it. It's alive, she thought. Am I?

Then a sound, the last quarter of a whimper. She forced her legs towards it, gritting with the pain. Don't worry, she cried, I'm coming.

The voice reassembled. The sun froze in the entanglement of a child's hair: glinting and going out as it twisted in the grip of something perilous. It was a cry. A child's cry. A little girl's cry. The sun went blood-red. It jerked the blond tresses of the little, lost girl upward into a scarlet, lungless scream.

"Mom-mee! Mom-mee! Mom-mee!"

The child's face caught fire. The features blurred and congealed. The hair flared like a halo and cindered. The lips alone remained to surround their one word, emptying it again and again into the empty air.

Granny felt her heart burst. Her knees hit the sidewalk, then her elbows, then her chin. She was looking up. The sun grinned down at her. She read the faded letters of the Queen's Hotel on a yellow brick wall. This is not Heaven, she thought, just before the pain blinded her.

46

1

Granny Coote lay in her new house and listened to the warm wind stirring against the unexpected gables. She heard every errant sound that the house contrived to interrupt her sleep: the complaint of green lumber along the eaves, the slap of an ill-fitted shutter, the rattle of windows not yet settled into their glaze, the fluting of air across the chimney-pot, the exotic tick of the pendulum clock in this strange space. I must not be ungrateful, she told herself a dozen times a day. There was a time when this is what I wanted most, foolish as that notion might seem now. We all want a moorage of some kind; though the space it takes to launch us out of this world is not nearly so large nor so anchored as we would suppose. The day after Wilf Underhill, Sam Brighton, Limpy Jenkinson and the others had moved her furniture and belongings – the baggage of many decades – across the street to this house, she had begun to undo their patient work. They had put the table and chairs in the kitchen at the back with the queer gas-stove and ice-box; the chesterfield and piano went into the front room, Arthur's bed and her cot into the bedroom at the back left, and then they carefully set up her Quebec heater near the tiny vestibule and next to the bay window overlooking the street. Arthur's theatre trunk went into the bedroom. Out back was a neat woodshed with a privy off it so she would never have to brave the elements again. She regarded the electric lamps – donated by the Methodist Auxiliary – with a mixture of suspicion and wonder. But none of this could be. As soon as they were gone, she dragged the cot into the front room, marvelling at her frailty as she struggled to move it a few inches at a time. She set it up across from the heater. She managed to get the table and one chair out of the kitchen and into a spot near the cot. Perhaps when she had a chance to get a garden in, she would eat in the strange, closed kitchen and look out the window at the dense greenery. For now she felt she needed only this solitary room, surrounded by these few necessities and comforted by them. From here she could gaze westward, at a moment's notice, through the bay-window where the empty rectangle stared blankly back at her from across the street, where the familiar side-hedges yet flourished, where the stems of tulips combed the rim of the sky at the edge of the marsh, where the arching hickory allowed its thick-gnarled limbs once again to fringe the breeze with its maidenhair green. "They'll take the front hedges out but not the side ones, and of course they'll leave the flowers as is for this year," Sunny assured her. "The builder an' his helpers'll be comin' in next week. You got a front-row seat."

She tried to get Arthur's trunk into its proper place – she wished she'd just had the courage to tell them she wanted everything in this room, but she didn't want to hurt their feelings. Besides, she thought, they think I'm queer enough as it is. By sitting on it and pushing off with her feet she managed to get the trunk as far as the doorway, where it wedged itself in quite permanently. Sunny arrived just as she was trying to lever it up with a stick of kindling.

"I'll do that for you," he said. And did. After a cup of tea and a scone (Anglican Auxiliary), he said: "And if you want to go walkin' again, you just let me or Purdie know. No need to go off by yourself."

And fall on your face, she added, in front of The Queen's and suffer the double mortification of a bloody nose and having been rescued by Half-Hitch Hitchcock, who promptly assured the whole town that he had told her so but what can you do with doddering old ladies who don't know enough to die when they have the chance.

"The deed should be ready in two or three weeks," Sunny said. "But you know lawyers, don't you, Cora?"

She did indeed.

2

Cora Burgher surprised the village in a number of ways when she returned a few days after Lucien's death. Her coming back to live there was itself a surprise, considering what happened to her, what painful memories must have lain all about her. Second, she did not return to the Lane though the meagre room she rented again in old Hap Withers' cottage was as close as you could get to the Lane without actually being a citizen of that nether-town. Third, she not only brought her new name with her but flaunted it all over the place, despite the fact that it had had only a few months itself to settle in. She seemed obsessed with having herself addressed as Mrs. Burgher or, worse, Mrs. Cora Burgher. When she *wasn't* – even by the gang at The Queen's who had known her best – she appeared not to hear or became merely distracted. But then she *had* suffered more than a body could be expected to bear – without the sustenance and solace of religion, poor thing. What surprised no one who bothered to notice was that she returned to her job at the Queen's Hotel and to that itinerant society still regarded by the villages with disdain and raw envy. For a few months, then, Mrs. Cora Burgher was discussed litigiously, then taken for granted, then forgotten.

Cora herself was so numbed by Lucien's death that she recalled little of those early weeks back in the Point. She did now know why she was here, why she was even living at all, except that any decision not-to-be required more effort than merely going through some deadening ritual dredged up from the past and substituted for existence. Happy Withers found her wandering in front of The Queen's and simply took her in again, as if she were an orphan dropped on his doorstep a second time. What else could he do? When she became coherent, he fetched her things from the St. Clair Inn and then took her down to Malloney. Within hours she was back at work.

When Malloney or Gertie Flounder called her Lily or Mrs. Marshall, she flinched and said automatically in a low, thin voice: "I'm Cora Burgher, Mrs. Cora Burgher," and kept repeating it till Malloney, bewildered as he always was face-to-face with any feeling he couldn't count, would say "Yes, *Mrs. Burgher*," startling the bench-warmers in the lobby. It took Gertie quite a while to say "It's all right, Cora, we know." Thus it was soon 'Mrs. Cora Burgher' almost everywhere. When some of the numbness turned to mere pain, to the slow singe of grief she recognized and welcomed, she carried that name in her heart like a gift, a legacy of their brief love. For a while it would be her reason for being.

Gertie, of course, had been promoted in her absence, so Cora was content to clean the lobby, beverage room, Malloney's suite and the kitchen area out back. This meant more scrubbing on hands-and-knees, emptying spittoons, scraping up grease and crushed cigars, and scrubbing out the foul toilets near the bar. Gertie was the upstairs maid, making the beds and tidying up the half-dozen suites on the second and third floor. When there was extra scrubbing to be done – clogged fireplaces, debauched carpets and duvets – Cora was called upstairs to assist. She didn't seem to mind. She arrived shortly after seven, had a bit of breakfast with the cook, and worked until six or seven in the evening, when she would take a cold supper and trudge the single block back to Hap's cottage.

At first Cora preferred to work alone in the back corners of the place, but gradually she came to like those moments when she could slip into the lobby – a large front room really with a double door and scenic window overlooking the flats leading to the River and the Lake – and quietly dust or empty the brass ashtrays while the commerce of a busy railway village passed before her. The three suites on the third floor were still advertised as elegant and often played host to smartly attired executives, officious politicians or blustering entrepreneurs – all of whom were in themselves worth the observing and who provided fodder for days of follow-up analysis and commentary by those seated on the sidelines. For the lobby, with its hospitable stove, drew to its domain an unchanging cast of locals: a half-dozen or so elderly denizens who spent half the day in the barbershop up the street and the other on these benches (and the two stools given to those with seniority). They called themselves the Smokehouse Gang, comprised of whey-faced pensioners, discarded elderly uncles and a pair of defrocked patriarchs – all from the respectable part of town and all with much to say about the decline and fall of the human race. Some of them Cora knew from earlier days – when they were unwrinkled and God-fearing – Pudge Grogan, Tubby Trout, Ballroom Baker. Others she knew only by their trade names: Wart, Dicer, Shotgun. Through some pact worked out years ago, it seemed, they were never to arrive before two o'clock nor stay later than five-thirty. And though they would always be certain to arrive one at a time to establish their independent worth, the benches were full by three-fifteen and deserted by five-forty. Soon Cora was organizing her chores so that the lobby required her presence in the late afternoon. Malloney seemed relieved, though he never said anything to Cora about that night in his room and made no overture that might be misconstrued as friendship.

More than a year passed. If the great world around her were moving, Cora didn't notice.

"Tunnel don't matter a fig's tit," opined the Wart. "Railroad ain't gonna move the shops an' sheds outta here till the day before doomsday."

"How d'ya figure it?" Shotgun said, watching for an opening.

"They still own half of this here town, that's why. A crow don't shit in its own nest."

"Just in everybody else's," Shotgun said and sat back to bask in the stringy laughter of his easily amused colleagues.

"Never get her built anyways," said Pudge Grogan, who used to build things.

"Why's that?"

"Gravity, that's why. Never heard of Newt's first law of gravitations?"

Before the next riposte could be delivered, all eyes turned in silent appraisal upon two figures just coming through the double-doors. Both were dressed in expensive business suits but the young one – a bright-looking chap with a scrubbed face and soft eyes – was supporting almost the full weight of the older man, who stumbled on the doorjamb, uttered a ghastly cough and fell to his knees. Duckface Malloney stood at his ledger behind the desk-counter, grimaced, but did not look up. None of the onlookers made a move or sound. The young man reached down and as gently as he could raised the older one to his feet. "He had one too many at the meeting," the fellow said. A dozen heads nodded *we know*. "I'll need some help getting him up to his room."

"Elmer, get out here!" Malloney shouted without looking up, and moments later a skinny lad appeared from the barroom and helped gather the drunk into a manageable lump to be carried upstairs.

Cora came in just in time to hear them clumping onto the second-floor landing. Someone up there let out an elongated retching noise, Elmer cursed, and the clumping resumed. Cora went for her mop and pail.

Over the course of the winter, it became evident that there was one spot she was never asked to clean – the spacious bed-sitter on the northwest corner of the third floor, the one with the view of both river and lake. When she asked Gertie about it, all she got was a blush and a forefinger laid against the lip. Gertie herself, as far as Cora could tell, seemed to go in there intermittently. Finally she confided: "He don't go out much, an' till he does, I got orders to stay outta there." No more was said on the subject.

One day early in July Gertie was off sick and Cora was told to do the third-floor rooms. "Stay away from 3A though," Duckface said and Cora detected more fatherly admonition than command in his voice. When she searched his face for more, he swung abruptly away. It was stifling up there, even in the morning with the hall windows wide open and a hot breeze wafting the curtains. When she had finished the other two suites, Cora came down the hall to do the water-closet. As she passed the mysterious bed-sitter, she thought she heard a groan, as if someone were in extreme pain.

She eased over to the heavy door and put her ear against it. Nothing. She was about to leave when it came again, a breathy groan as if someone were being punched, followed a half-second later by the tight whine of a second voice, descant and linked to the pain of the other. Again: in a staggered cadence and vocal accompaniment which she had heard inadvertently many times before from these rooms around her – unmistakably sexual. As she headed back towards the stairway, wondering only vaguely who the lovers might be, she was pursued by the coupled climactic cry, and there was something alien in it, chilled and yearning, not even close to pleasure. She shivered and descended.

Gertie returned the next day and Cora forgot about everything except surviving in the swelter of that summer. She took to walking down to the River in the cool of the mornings and evenings, catching the wind off the water before the parched fields heated it up for distribution over the village. Malloney suggested that she and Gertie lie down in one of the empty rooms during the blaze of the afternoons and finish up their chores after supper. So it was that Cora happened to be scrubbing out the pantry one evening about seven o'clock when she heard a commotion in the lobby. She put her pail down, got up and walked along the hall in the direction of the noise, which now became more clearly defined: men's voices raised in anger and the thump of bony flesh on wood. She hurried into the front room.

First of all she was surprised to see four or five of the Smokehouse gang seated in place; then she remembered that they too had taken to coming in after the heat – with Malloney's grudging permission. The Wart, Shotgun, Dicer and several others were all staring towards the stairs near Malloney's desk. Their eyes were popping as if they'd all just inherited the same goiter. Cora stepped further into the lobby until she could see the stairway itself. She went no further.

Malloney, his duckface squeezed horribly inward in rage, had a huge hand on the collar of a man whom he was, it appeared, dragging down the stairs and across the carpet towards the door. The man was resisting by flailing his arms and digging his black leather oxfords into the rug. His bulk, which was considerable, was entirely in Malloney's fierce grip.

"Get on your feet you fat-assed bum an' haul yourself outta here," Malloney shouted into his ear.

The victim's gray hair was askew, covering a good portion of his face, but Cora could see the flush of humiliation and amazement there. His arms flopped uselessly, girlishly, about him, as if he felt he ought somehow to be striking out though all the time knowing it was hopeless.

"You're lucky I don't call the constables to come down here an' kick the livin' shit outta you!" Duckface opened his fist and the man dropped to the floor. The crack of his elbows shot through the room like a whiskey-glass on a bar-top. The Smokehousers flinched en masse, their mouths agape, salivating.

Cora watched the man. He rubbed at the smudges on his worsted trousers, got himself seated upright, then peered out to see where he was, where the next attack might come from.

"Get on your feet, you drunken deadbeat. You got thirty seconds to haul your ass outta here." For the first time Malloney seemed aware that he was not alone. He whirled towards the benches, his beady eyes defiant and daring. He got no challenge. The old men rocked back onto their seats, appalled and thrilled. Their collective rheumy-eye swept the room with the instincts of a gunsight. Malloney did not see Cora.

The man was now up to a crouching position. The sweaty hair had fallen away from his eyes. He had the look of a pig the second after the sledge hits – when no regret will do. She could see him desperately trying to garner some fury, some outrage, some word of reprisal. Nothing could penetrate his amazement.

With no warning, Malloney kicked out his foot and caught him in the lower back. Stupidly, he seemed to teeter towards uprightness, pause at the suddenness of his ascent, and then he canted forward onto his face. For the first time he let out a cry, high-pitched, a little boy's stunned by undeserved pain. When he rolled over onto one side, blood spurted from his smashed nose.

Malloney, who had his foot raised for another blow, froze. The man whimpered, caught sight of the onlookers and said in a whisper, "Please help me."

Dicer rose from his stool. "What's he done?" he said to Malloney.

"Ain't paid me a fuckin' cent of rent for three weeks. Nor his bar bill of eighteen dollars. So out he goes. You got trouble with that?" He put a threatening edge to the last comment but it was unnecessary. In truth, he had gone as far as he intended to go. Farther.

"You fellas want to help me assist this gentleman to the exit," he said in what he assumed was a jocular, familial tone.

The man had finally managed to get to his feet. He pinched his nostrils to staunch the blood. He was shaking all over. "I can pay, I can pay," he said from under his hand, staggered and fell again. The blood sailed in a wet sheet down his white shirt, his skewed tie, his ripped morning-coat. He may have been crying.

"Leave him alone," Cora said, coming towards Malloney.

Malloney wheeled around, surprised. His eyes narrowed to shut out any indecision. "Stay outta this, Mrs. Burgher," he said. "Ain't your business."

"He needs a doctor," Cora said.

"He can get a doctor after he's well an' gone from here. The deadbeat owes me three-weeks' rent and a bar bill an' he ain't got a farthing to stuff up his nose." He turned to his supporters. "I'm out thirty-nine dollars an' he's got a bloody nose!"

Malloney, his outrage restoked, moved menacingly towards the man, who started slithering backwards, sobbing, daubing at his split flesh, and uttering a slurred jumble of words. Malloney reached him a yard from the door. He raised his fist; the elderly chorus behind him gasped and hung onto their breath; then Malloney gave a quick, clandestine glance towards Cora, winked, and opened the double-door.

"Go tell your troubles to your pals up at the station. See if *they'll* let you get into them for thirty-nine dollars."

"You tell him," Dicer said, delighted to have recovered his voice.

"We don't take to deadbeats an' traitors in this town."

"You had your chance here, fella, an' you blew it."

"There's not a spit of pity left for the likes of you."

"An' when you hit the town-line just keep on goin'."

Quite gently Malloney lifted the target of his abuse to his feet and pointed him towards the sun they could all see sinking below the west bank of the River. Behind it, darkness beckoned.

"Let him be," Cora said.

"Stay outta this, woman, if you want to keep on workin' here."

In the air Cora could taste the stale, desiccated breath of these old, old men and their ancient, jovial hatreds.

"Let him stay."

"What are you sayin'?" Malloney's eyes widened in disbelief.

"I'll give you the money," Cora said.

No one offered to help her get the man back up the two flights of stairs he had just been dragged down. She didn't ask. The cook, Mrs. Suitor, kept Cora's money for her in a little safe in the pantry. Malloney went there to get the cash he was owed but only after he had ordered the pillars of the community out of his hotel, glared at the victim, and muttered brave homilies to Cora about the fate of women being stupid enough to squander their money on hopeless cases. But even in the midst of this petulant tirade, while the deadbeat finally got the bleeding stopped, it was clear to Cora that Malloney would forever-after regard her in a new light – observing her with sidelong scrutiny, a lifetimes' prejudices set off-balance, his natural wariness deepened and yet undercut by doubt, by something akin to wonder.

When Cora got the man to his room – number 3A – she washed the blood off his face, got his shirt and shoes off, and tipped him onto his bed. His eyes were glazed with fatigue. He had said nothing to her; she wasn't certain he knew what had happened. As the blood was wiped away and his hair pushed back into place, his features – the nose puffed – came clearly into Cora's view, and she stepped back at the shock of recognition. He spoke drowsily but in his normal deep voice. She remembered it. "Thank you for helping. You were…glorious."

"I'm Cora Burgher," she said, not ready yet to believe her eyes.

"Glad to meet you, Cora." He spoke now in a threadbare, weary whisper. "My name's Stan Dowling. People used to call me Cap."

47

1

"I told that pinch-faced marmot down there I was no deadbeat. People like that, with no education and less breeding, assume that because a man gives up his worldly goods and vain ambitions in favour of a quiet and contemplative life he must be impoverished, a fool, and a cheat. I told that creature a dozen times my great aunt would not survive this heat-wave, that if he showed the slightest scintilla of patience he would get his money back threefold. If I were a vindictive man, or if I still cared for such normal pleasures as spit and vengeance, I'd have my lawyers on him. But then I've had my fill of lawyers, haven't I?"

Cora, who was dusting off the crystal decanters and watching the boys on the flats playing some ritual tag-game against the ritual sunset, nodded in general approval. Cap was in his plush chair beside the narrow north window, looking across the room at her as she worked.

"There's just enough in dear Auntie's legacy to keep me comfortably here for as long as I wish to stay, and not near enough to tempt me back into those ways I renounced with such flourish and finality." He waved his solicitor's letter at her as if it were a flag. "And of course I shall write my first cheque in your name, with a few extra dollars for you and your loved ones."

Cora finished dusting the sill, sweeping the shrivelled flies into her dustpan. "No hurry," she said. "I don't need the money."

"But your family –?"

"Got no use for it," Cora said at the door.

"Just a minute!"

She waited.

"Ah, Mrs. Burgher, would you tell Malloney not to send Gertie up here any more."

Cora loved the view from here. You were so high you could see both banks of the River where they stretched into the Lake. At eye-level the herring-gulls reconnoitred or bullied the breeze over the soft shoreline. Way below her a fisherman swung his net rhythmically through the current to some slow music inside him.

"I was the son of a struggling merchant in London. My father sold hardware, but he wanted a lot more than that for me. He got religion just so I could attend the right church and go off to study law in Toronto. There, I learned a lot about gambling, the fast track, and how the money is made to ensure that such luxuries are maintained throughout one's life. In short, I met and was liked by the right people. I started collecting that useless pile of haberdashery you try to straighten out every afternoon."

He flicked a finger at the wardrobe with its doors jammed irreversibly open – suit-coats, vests, silk shirts, trousers stuffed in and threatening to abscond. Cora would reorganize these habillements at least once a week, but when he'd had a brandy or two, he'd go fishing for some poignant moment of his past, and though always successful – she'd find him the next afternoon slumped in a flawlessly matched outfit for dinner, dancing or a royal audience, with a bib of vomit down his vest – he left the haberdashery itself in chaos. Sometimes he even managed to get into one of his three-dozen pairs of shoes.

"Why don't you give some of these things away," Cora said, "to people who could use them?"

"They are reminders of what I have repudiated. I don't believe you could understand."

"You don't keep them just in case?"

He began to cough as he often did this late in the day after a dozen cigars. He always seemed to go limp and let the coughing shake him this way and that, then peek over at Cora as if to say "there's no help for this, you know." But a cup of hot tea with lemon and honey was rarely refused.

"I cut quite a figure in Toronto and in London society when I returned there in 1852. It was a small pond and I was, to put it as modestly as I can, a glittering gander in their midst. With a little help from my friends in government, I bought and sold some property that made me at the age of twenty-five independent of my father's influence, so to speak. In short, I enjoyed myself. I explored each of the seven deadly sins with a Franciscan zeal. You may not guess but I was as slim and trim as a birch in those days. The ladies were, as they say, drawn to my company."

Little of that glamorous figure had survived the rigours of middle age: he was now a gray, greasy-haired, obese man with pink, deflated flesh, side-whiskers long ago left to their own vices (Cora shaved him twice a week but was not allowed to trim or cut there), a gourmand's paunch, skinny legs that complained constantly of the burden they had to bear, and milky, shapeless fingers that had spent too much time coddling brandy-snifters, fondling Cuban cigars, and coaxing dollar bills into or out of wallets. Only his eyes gave any sign that a life had been lived here before and remained to tell the sad story. When he wasn't drinking, when he had slept a full night, when Cora found him as she occasionally did in his chair by the north window with a book open on his lap and his face turned outward to the sky above the Lake – then his eyes seemed alone in this jettisoned flesh, grotesquely out of place but to Cora beautiful, shining with intensity of a life lived and only partly regretted.

Most afternoons when she came up after finishing her duties, she found him snoring in his chair, half-dressed or half-undressed, cigar-ash littering his paunch, a snifter overturned and bleeding on the table, and a thick, calf-covered tome open on his knees at about the same place as it was the day before. His snores scattered the sparrows on the sills of the wide west window. Carefully she would wash his face and torso, wrestle him into a clean shirt, and as he muttered his way grumpily towards consciousness, she tidied up the room, humming to herself and giving the decanter an extra clink.

"Stop that racket!" he'd holler, stung by his own voice. After waking he would often ignore her presence for upwards of an hour. He would sit in a sort of stupor as if he were trying to recall and identify the various parts of his quisling anatomy. Sometimes he pretended to read the book before him as if he'd accidentally dozed off and was now resuming his onerous intellectual responsibilities. Or he'd reach over for his toppled brandy glass and appear surprised – amazed even – that it had disappeared without his permission. Cora would continue her work regardless, tidying the pillaged wardrobe, taking fouled garments down to the water-closet where she washed them out in the tub, and finally just curling upon the bay-window ledge to watch the autumn afternoon linger in the fields and resting dunes.

"I'd like some tea now," a small voice would say from a farther part of the room.

Cora then went down and brought up their supper. Cap had the lamps lit. Their evening began.

"The real power and the real money lay in the railroads. And the glamour. Contrary to what most people assumed, I was never that fond of money. In fact I could have made a hell of a lot more in real estate, safe in the arms of the Family Compact, so to speak. It was the sheer excitement of being in a position of power or being close to its centre. It has a glamour unknown to those who've never reached for it." His eyes glinted in the winter light of the late afternoon.

"You got to meet the Prince of Wales and all that."

"Exactly. That's exactly my point. I not only got to shake his hand among the self-professed dignitaries of London, but as an investor and young executive for the Great Western – bless its memory – and then the Grand Trunk, I got to chat with him over dinner in the presence of Lady Marigold and Mr. Dunbar Cruickshank at the inaugural luncheon of that very palazzo you spend so much of your time admiring from this distance."

"It burned down," Cora said.

"Pardon me, but you're right, and the barons of steel from Threadneedle Street built it back up in a wink. *That's* power. And believe me, glamour and romance flow directly from it. You couldn't imagine, I'm sure, how it feels to ride out into that lake on a fragile craft bearing you and the future king of an empire, of a vassalage half the size of the earth, to share a brandy and cigar with him, to wink with him at the lecherous virgins prowling the foredeck. And of course to treasure the flow of that sort of feeling – that brief kinship with monarch or potentate or railroad magnate or dark lady of the drawingroom or boudoir – as it keeps on surging through you for days or weeks, months even, spicing every emotion and sensation you subsequently feel, casting a halo over the most mundane liaison, spiking your lusts in whatever shape of luxury they care to take. Imagine, the prince-in-waiting was mine for an afternoon and for years to come. I saw it in the eyes of others as they envied me, and curried their pathetic little favours. For a time, Cora, I was afire, ablaze, one of the elect."

"I hear you give all that up," Cora said from her window-seat.

"I shocked everyone, especially those who thought they knew me," Cap said, shivering in his velvet robe. Cora had the west window raised so she could put the remnants of the supper Cap hadn't eaten out on the ledge for the sparrows.

"With Lady Marigold, you mean?"

He looked startled. "Close the damn window, woman, I'll shake my teeth loose!" The room was as stuffy and warm as it always was. Cap had been off the booze for two days, having ordered Cora to hide the supply and then yelling at her and cursing her perfidy when she refused to change the rules of his game. Finally he just shivered and sulked.

"Everybody around her knew all about you an' Lady Marigold."

"Oh, that. Sure. That was another part of the glamour – we felt like equals, we could admire or hate one another as we chose. There wasn't much else going on there. Not as much as *hoi poloi* imagined, anyway, though we enjoyed their envy and rancour exceedingly."

She brought a blanket over and laid it across his shoulders. He smiled wanly at her. "It's time," he said.

"You said you didn't really need it."

"I say a lot of things."

She poured him a snifter of his medicine. He sipped it slowly, breathing the restorative fumes. The late-winter darkness seeped into the room. "Don't," he said when she started to light the lamp.

She left him earlier than usual, walked home under the March moon and slept alone, as she always did.

"Quit fussing with those damn clothes and come here."

She continued her work: every jacket had its sleeves pulled inside out, like skinned muskrats.

"What I was referring to the other day when I said people were shocked was my sudden switch from the Great Western to the Grand Trunk. But my motive was simple. I could smell a rotting carp at twenty paces. I decided to put my money on a winner –"

"Money you didn't care about."

"– so to speak. Again, you see how wrong you can get things from your restricted vantage-point. The Grand Trunk was bigger, grander, more ambitious than the Great Western. It had plans to build from sea to sea. It had a lion's heart and lion's pride."

"An' teeth."

"Naturally. But it's what I wanted. And I did well, as you know. I suppose if I'd known I would have jumped again to the C.P.R., but you see by the mid-seventies I was over forty years of age and much of the romance was beginning to pall. It was clear we were going to crush the Great Western, but the C.P.R. had usurped our place in the royal sun, so to speak, and there seemed little left for a man of my temperament. When I sucked caviar through champagne all I tasted was ashes." He drew in a lungful of his Havana and held it in defiantly.

"Must've been terrible," Cora said, tossing clean sheets onto his huge canopied bed and stepping gingerly around those that had been soiled by an uncharacteristic inconvenience the night before.

"But I had a dream of my own, one nobody knew about but me. My parents, who'd long ago disowned me, were now dead, and I felt the weight of some indefinable obligation descending upon me. It filled me with unnameable regret and remorse."

"We call it a bad conscience."

He persevered. "I quit my directorship, I gathered my life's savings and I came to Point Edward, a place I hadn't seen for years but whose beauty had impressed itself upon me in a way I could never forget. I decided to give back to the world some of the things I'd robbed it of. You'll recall much of the rest yourself: my little factory down on the flats – still operated of course, by others – my meteoric rise to the reeveship in return for my influence in persuading the Grand Trunk to let this village *be*."

Cora nodded but had no comment.

Cap began coughing. When his defiance had subsided, he said, "What a waste."

"I can see the smoke comin' from your factory," Cora said. When she came over to help him into bed and fluff up his goose-down pillows, he propped her chin on his soft fingers and said: "Why do you do this?"

Grasping his fingers, she said, "For the money."

As she let herself quietly out, she heard his coughing start up, loose and wayward, as if he were about to embarrass himself by crying.

"I should have stayed there in the factory. Hap Withers was a great manager. I'm glad he's got it now. But you see in this experience how the vanities of life have to be renounced completely, they have to be expunged from the tablet of memory, cauterized from the flesh they've preyed upon. After the glamorous life of civilized debauchery I'd led heretofore, you'd think the temptations of reeveship and regional politics would have seemed petty or beneath my considerable talents."

"Maybe you had more in mind?"

He examined her shrewdly, his teacup at half-mast. "I'm glad you decided you were good enough to share my table," he said with heavy irony, pleased at the power he still held over words. Throughout the winter Cora had served his supper on the silver tray and then retreated to the bay-window where she ate her own meal in a silence which he ignored with particular satisfaction. A week ago – through Gertie, it seemed – orders had been given to have a single meal for two prepared and sent up at precisely six o'clock, winter or summer, sunshine or gloom. Cora now sat opposite him on the stool he used to launch himself back into bed.

Cora poured herself a second cup of tea.

"I'm sure I did at that," he said. "I guess all along I knew that this was not the United States whatever name we chose to call ourselves by. In my heart I knew the corridors of power and the chambers of decision lay in Toronto and in Ottawa, in the legislatures and in the sanctum of the privy council. I was getting old, Cora; I know you can understand that. I had only one more chance for the genuine thing, a run at the crown itself. Better men than me have been o'er-thrown by such ambitions."

"Then you took a train-ride," Cora said, watching his face for signs and portents.

He sat back. His side-whiskers quivered like a tom-cat's in front of the master's cheese. His thin lips tightened, causing the jowl to ripple and rebel. But his eyes danced with the kind of joy a ballerina might feel pirouetting on a sprained ankle. "What a way of putting it," he said, snarling out a laugh. "I took a train-ride I didn't buy a ticket for. And derailed. What a spectacular fall that was! Wolsey would have been envious."

"Who's Wolsey?"

"A fat man who couldn't swim."

"Tell me, I'd really like to know."

Elmer knocked at the door and she took the tray over to him. She felt Cap's eyes on her. She didn't turn around right away. It was still light. The summer wind floated in, bringing with it the swallow's song, Queen Anne's Lace and other intimations.

Next day when Cora came into the room she discovered it was as tidy as a monk's study. Cap was seated in his chair with a smoking jacket neatly vee-ed over his paunch and a gray tome open on his knees. He was turned so that he could observe the motions of the sky to the north; a pleasant breeze lifted the brushed hair back from his strong brow; a bowl of mints rested at his side. He pretended not to hear her. It was only when she let out a cry of surprise that he could bear to turn and face her.

"It's for you. Go ahead. Sit."

Cora put her mop down and stared at the chair which Cap had ordered Elmer to bring up and place opposite his on the other side of a walnut gate-leg table he'd also ordered from the collection he recalled seeing in one of the 'luxury' suites on the second floor. The table had been covered with a lace cloth and graced with a silver tea-setting. The new chair was high-backed, cushioned and beautiful. The mahogany legs shone.

"Please, sit."

She did,

"It's time we had a proper tea and conversation."

After their meal, Cap poured himself a brandy and lit up a cigar. He kept his eyes on Cora, as if he thought she might bolt at any minute like a flushed pheasant.

"Now that you've heard my life story," he said, "it's time for you to tell me something about yourself." When he saw that she was indeed going to say something, he averted his gaze, slouched back into his comfort, and listened.

Cora soon found herself responding to his request. She realized that she had not talked for a very long time. Not merely aloud, to others – for that was only a minor form of talking – but not even to herself in those sinuous dream-monologues she could detach herself from, if she wished, and listen to her own thoughts as clear and necessary as her heartbeat. She didn't tell him very much, of course. Much he would be unable to understand; some would be too strong for a man in his condition; some would not be told – ever.

She had come, by a circuitous route, to Lucien. She hesitated. She felt the strange security of this chamber she had seen only in the late afternoon and early evenings of four full seasons. We are exchanging our voices only, she thought, we do not know or even want to know each other outside the safety of this collaboration. For now, that is enough, it is a lot; it is a kind of miracle. When Lucien's name left her lips, she felt at once like a traitor and glanced across to see how much she'd given away, how much was irretrievable.

Cap was sound asleep.

2

The sparrow lay unresponding in her cupped hands. She waited for the heart's flutter, the spasm of blood in the misted eye.

"Leave go, Cora," Cap said from the hutch of his bed. "You can't save them all, you know."

Several of the dead bird's cousins flapped against the pane, then settled into the snow on the sill, where they pecked away contentedly at the crusts left there by the same providence that caused one's blood occasionally to congeal.

"Bring me the Schopenhauer," he called. "The one with the gray cover."

"I can read," Cora said.

"Pardon me, but I forget little things like that."

Cora brought him the book.

"You don't expect me to read in *this* light?"

"Sometimes, Cora, I think you deliberately try to misunderstand me. Is it your way of getting back at me, pretending to be stupid just because you never had the benefit of an education?"

"I'm a woman, remember?"

"That is an unforgettable verity. But my point, to get back to it, was that I consciously, by choice, by an act of the invisible personal will repudiated my life of vanity and power-seeking. Only I know what went on inside my head during those weeks after the calamity up in Woodston. Just because the world around us assumes that a combination of x and y conspired to undo us, to turn us along a certain path, does not mean that we followed that course for those reasons. What people think is never the sufficient cause. If you'd been listening carefully to what I told you about Schopenhauer's statement on the issue, you'd understand that perfectly."

"And if you'd given it all up one minute before the train left the Sarnia station, then more people would be ready to believe you."

"But quantity is irrelevant here. Only what I do and know is significant. Look at it this way: just because the society I sought to exploit decides to strip me of opportunity and honour – dump me down the shit-hole, so to speak – does not mean that I, at the

same moment, cannot have a sudden insight into the very hollowness of that society
– both its rewards *and* its so-called punishments. The fact is, I did. Long before they
defrocked me and cast me out like a leper, I had decided to renounce both the pleasures
and the pains of that community of hypocrites. That was my way of coping with their
petty retributions and with the horror of my own past. I decided to retire from social
intercourse of all kinds, to follow Schopenhauer's path of ascetic withdrawal to the life
of contemplation, shorn of vanity and pretension. I would devote the rest of my allotted days to studying the great thinkers of our age. Over there you see the expanding
fruits of the labour." He waved a loose sleeve towards the glassed-in bookcase already
filled with volumes which arrived weekly from a bookseller's on King Street in Toronto.
Elmer carried them in reverently, as if they were Bibles fresh from Caxton's press. Cora
had to dust them daily in spite of the glass parapet.

"Seems to me," Cora said, "most of them saints you talk about had themselves a fair
old time before they saw the light."

"Woman, there are times when I'm sure you're a hopeless case!"

Cora jumped up and Cap jerked back against his pillow, spilling his tonic. "Look,
I'm sorry –" he said.

"It's alive," Cora cried. She drew the fluttering creature out of her apron pocket,
lifted it to the window and let it beat its way into the blackness of a winter-sky. Her
thigh still tingled where the bird had made the decision to live.

"I don't need no raise," Cora said.

"That's not the point. You're the best worker that sleazy leprechaun's ever had slaving for him. I told him to give you more money or I'd hire a gang of thugs from the
Alley to break his knees and then his Irish mouth. He seemed impressed by my logic."

"I thought you was supposed to have 'renounced' the things of this world?"

"I have." He gave her one of his philosopher's looks – bristling with protective am-
biguities. "By the way, did you get me those cigars?"

Every evening about ten o'clock, Cora walked to her room in Hap Withers' cottage.
She missed the outdoors, the pleasant walks along Canatara beach, a sleigh-ride to
Little Lake to watch the skaters in the winter, flower-hunting expeditions into First and
Second Bush. The odd time, in the month of June when the sun stayed until almost
ten o'clock, Cap would fall into a brandy doze and she would slip out – sometimes as
early as eight o'clock – and walk briskly in any direction, drinking in whatever Nature
offered the senses and the gluttonous memory it fed without conscience or care. Most
of the time, however, she arrived home by ten, fell into a dreamless sleep, and rose early
enough to help Mrs. Suitor with the breakfast and chat amiably with Elmer or one of
the new girls Malloney had not yet frightened out of a job. At four o'clock sharp she
went up to the third floor – her duties for Malloney completed – and entered Cap's
retreat. How he survived his night or what he did during the morning to recuperate
and justify his existence she could only guess at from the detritus he left about, or read
in the scavenged slag of his face.

"The salient point in all of this, then, is not *when* you discover the truth but the fact that you *have* accepted it into your life to the extent that all your subsequent actions are consonant with it. That is pure Schopenhauer. I read that only after I had come to similar conclusions myself. My disgrace, if you will, was merely one of the means which prompted me to see what was there to be observed all along: that as long as one persists in pursuing one's own desires, which means working against the world's will, one will never be in the position of making a choice. It's strange, I know, but the more you try to be yourself by desiring the things of the world and lusting for dominion over them, the more you play right into the hands of a universe that cares nothing for such vanities or will-o-the-wisps. The only choice we can make is to renounce all vanities, all desires except the pursuit of truth through contemplation. One can choose to do that."

"When you tempt fate, it gets you."

"Well, that's oversimplifying a grand notion, but yes, that's part of it. Sooner or later one of the world's accidents will drop its careless hammer on your hopes – which you thought you could direct and manage to some personal conclusion. Certainly you would concede that an impromptu train-ride at the hands of a drunken suicide was one of the world's more bizarre examples of happenstance?"

"Maybe the German fella was in love," Cora said.

For a second Cap caught the edge in her voice, waited, but when she added nothing more, he said, "Love has nothing to do with it. Love is one of those desires we must purge ourselves of. I speak, as Schopenhauer does, of Eros, not Caritas or Agape. These latter await those who can approach the best in themselves, and thereby come close to the spirit of the World's Will itself, which is suffused with sympathy and the kind of knowledge that cannot help but issue in the complete affection of Agape. When we know fully, then we sympathize, then we love with utter acceptance. That's the hope that Schopenhauer offers us."

"He had no vanity?"

"None."

"Why did he choose to lecture at the same hour as the great Hegel at the University of Berlin?"

"You've been reading these books," he said, astonished and not a little befuddled.

"Only when you're asleep. I don't take them out of the room."

"How long?"

"Just a little while. You seem to be snoozin' more these days."

"It's the damn soft coal," he said.

"But I can only read some parts. Usually the part about their lives. The rest is too hard."

His gaze narrowed. "What else do you know about Schopenhauer?"

"He saw the world as a dark place, full or horrors, from a lonely room. Maybe he needed to get out more."

Cap's face relaxed visibly. He flashed an indulgent smile and surveyed his pupil as from a great height. "You think his magnum opus, *The World as Will and Idea*, was coloured by an unhappy, friendless existence?"

"Some of it, yes."

"That's why women aren't encouraged to study philosophy," he said, fumbling for his silver lighter. "The man *chose* to be alone. To think. As I have."

Cora took the lighter from under his napkin and handed it to him. She waited until he had his cigar lit and was sucking greedily on its adrenalin. Then she said: "He kept a dog with him. All his life."

That second spring Cap had a bad time with his cough. Cora would wrap him in blankets and get Elmer to help her carry him to the bathroom, where she would fill the air with steam from the water, and sit with him till be could breathe again. She begged to be able to stay with him through the night but he insisted she leave: "You're a respectable widow," he would say, winking a smile as best he could. "I'll survive. Or I won't," he added with Schopenhauerian resignation, but Cora knew the look in a doubter's eye – she'd seen it more often than she'd wanted to, seated at many a sick bed with the smell of camphor in the air like a gruesome incense. But she went. Malloney followed her footsteps down the block from his bedroom vigil. Cap survived. He went back to the cigars.

"Can't give them up," he said. "They fuel the gray-matter up here. And I don't mean my hair. But I'm giving up the brandy. You were right. It is a desire, a vestige of my former vainglories. More symbolic than real, but significant all the same. It goes."

The day after these resolutions, Cora arrived to find a pad of lined paper set on the table in front of her chair. There were notes made in a neat, printed hand.

"They're for you. I'm summarizing the main points of Schopenhauer so you can read and study them and ask me questions."

She stared at the notes, wary and elated. "Can I ask *him* questions, too?"

He smiled shakily, and she could see he had both hands tucked into his trousers. His flesh was the colour of grass along the flats in November. "Only if he'll let me answer for him."

When Cora came in she knew immediately that something was wrong. The room was frigid, the charred coke lifeless in the grate (Elmer got it started early morning, she banked it at night). Her eye caught the snow beating its fletched fists against the narrow north window. His chair was empty.

"Cap?"

The bedding had been tossed aside as if in anger, the white sheets glowed eerily in the winter dusk fast descending. Sparrow-wings flapped against glass, begging entry. Cap's moan answered from somewhere behind the bedstead. Cora strode to the end of the bed and peered around it into the shadows that hovered between it and the west wall. Cap had fallen out of bed, the covers had gone one way, their tormentor the other. Automatically she lit the beside lamp and then knelt down to him.

"Go away. Let me die in peace."

He was sitting precisely where he had landed, propped obliquely on one bruised elbow, his brittle spindle-legs flopped uselessly to either side of the fattened toadstool of his belly. The hand that was free pawed compulsively at the fringes of the mattress the way a gutted woodchuck might claw in hope at his burrow wall. The only visible wound was the fractured brandy decanter, forlorn against the wainscotting.

"You people got nothing better to do than sit and stare at me? I'm no traitor. I'm just a man, just like you. So leave me be."

His eyes peered out of their devastated flesh but did not see her, even as she bent and kissed them and her arm slipped under his numbed shoulder to begin easing him up. "It's only me," she said.

"Let me die in peace."

His face came up into the lamplight. The flesh was sallow yet as puffed as if he'd been beaten with a cuckold's fists. His beard and hair were matted with vomit from some previous misadventure, and his speech, his pleading whine, was squeezed through his stunned lips without once jarring them.

Later, scrubbed and remorseful, he said to Cora: "Whatever I said to you, I didn't mean it. I've been told I'm a mean drunk."

"And a sweetheart when you're not."

"Be kind. I fell three bloody feet off the bed."

"An' the wagon."

Cora paused, drew the razor back and seemed to be contemplating her unfinished handiwork. Either that or the opium of the lilacs drifting in from the four quarters of the town had induced a reverie of its own. "You didn't tell me that German fella said there was more than one way to give up thinkin' about the world."

"*Schopen – hauer.*"

"Don't put me off."

She finished the left cheek, wiped the blade and sat back. He reached over and touched her wrist. "A day like this and I'm almost tempted to venture into the chaos out there just to see the trees again."

"Almost."

"Schopenhauer, as you well know and are pretending not to, suggests that although the ascetic life of contemplation is the only permanent way to avoid the wrath of the universal Will, one can indeed obtain temporary relief and insight into the more benign, spiritual side of the life-force by studying and appreciating works of art."

She sat back again. His hand lay where it had fallen.

"Have I got it right?" he said.

"But why can't it last? He don't seem to say much about that."

"I didn't write that part out, I guess."

After a moment she said, "Why?"

He feigned annoyance. "Because it's deductible from the system as a whole. Too much exposure to, or an obsession with, art constitutes yet another form of desire and egocentrism and becomes, therefore, self-defeating. Now would you fetch me my cigars?"

"I don't know what you mean."

He lit his cigar without removing his eye from her. She could see the effort it took for him to concentrate, to keep his fingers steady, to let some of the pleasures so rigidly curtailed simmer again in a glance that once held salons and boardrooms in thrall, that skewered the witless and charmed the unwary, that had never quite become reconciled to its own delight.

"I think you'd give Socrates a hard time."

"Who's Socrates?"

"See what I mean?" he said theatrically, peeking back over his shoulder. Then he sighed deeply, coughed through his teeth without jolting loose his cheroot, and said: "I'll use an example, an *exemplum*, to illustrate. So listen carefully. In England there has developed over the past few years a school of esthetics which promulgates the notion of Art For Art's Sake. To a degree Schopenhauer would have approved. They believe in the creation and contemplation of beauty for its own sake – no other. You see how that view of art precludes the world out there with its phoney social and moral values. Beauty is to be loved for her beauty and that beauty-as-loved gives the beholder a momentary insight into the One Will whose expressive breath activates the heart of the universe."

"The way I like lilacs or you like them cigars?"

He made a brief effort at filtering out the ironies, sighed, and continued. "In a homelier sense, yes, though art – in painting or music – is created by an act of the individual will, and is not merely nature."

"Oh."

"But you're getting me sidetracked. The point I'm making is that *that* school itself, in practice, has become perverted to the sorts of desire that we must renounce – the kinds of the things I have given up to live as I do in this hermitage."

Elmer arrived with hot water and Cora made the tea.

"I'm speaking of young Oscar Wilde of whom you might have heard."

"So I have." The memories stirred by the mention of that name lapped and stung.

"Came here in 'eighty-two. I met him in Toronto, showed him the sights. He was marvellous. He gave a speech in the botanical gardens about making your house itself a work of art. Impressive. He told me he planned to actually *live* the esthetic credo, to be a breathing, walking *objet d'art*. You'll recall I was in Toronto at that time to help with the merger of the railways. My genius had not been forgotten. What few people know is that I was asked by the Grand Trunk in 'eighty-five to go to England and help sell the idea of the Tunnel to the British owners. They thought a little charm might help. What they were worried about, of course, was that Joseph Hobson, the only engineer bold enough to attempt the feat was, alas, a native Canadian."

"You saw Wilde again?"

"Yes. I went to Paris and Rome and when I returned to London I discovered that he was still notorious and that he had indeed tried to live out the purely esthetic life. I was invited to his house on Tite Street, the most infamous household in the Empire. I saw for myself the results of a philosophy based solely on the exigencies of beauty."

His eyes drooped and glazed, as they often did when he talked too lengthily. Sometimes he would just drift into sleep, waking minutes or hours later, not remembering what had driven him to repose and occasionally getting irritated when Cora tried to renew the lapsed discussion. It seemed that as long as he was talking, uninterrupted, his thought was coherent and edged, but if he tired or was distracted, the coherence faltered and could not be recovered – the very thought itself might well be lost for days or weeks, sometimes resurfacing in unexpected intervals as whole and vital as before, and yet as unconnected as ever to any of the other sequences that emerged in their own time and circumstance. It was a mind, Cora thought, in brilliant disarray.

"This life – of Wilde's – it didn't work," Cora said, gently.

He thrust his lidded gaze at her. "Desire," he rasped. "All desire."

She waited. His breathing slowed. He was asleep.

"It looks like another one of them days, almost beautiful enough to tempt you into walkin'," Cora said at the bay-window. "There's no shade of purple quite like the milkweed flower. I used to walk out on those marshes every fall as long as I can remember. With my kids, too. I like to see the pods shrivel an' dry out an' then surprise everybody when they crack asunder and all that white silk billows an' floats in to the air, not carin' very much that winter's almost on it, just happy to be born an' to fly in the little sun that's left."

Cap watched her from his chair, saying nothing, afraid to cough or breathe too hastily. He watched her slim form, and the strength it never telegraphed while it was at rest: the chin set in expectation; hands folded peacefully in her lap, forgotten; the eyes – as clear and blue as the moment they popped from the shell – moving in a meditative sweep over the landscape of their attention, not afraid to let the possibility of some truant beauty penetrate and flense the ancient, sealed wounds underneath. In the autumnal silence, her still-life composed itself for contemplation.

"Of course, not all the arts are equal. Mr. Wilde was perhaps too overzealous concerning the visual. Schopenhauer suggests that music is the highest of the art forms, closest to the sublime, less tainted by the coarseness of individual life. In short, more universal, more in tune with the circulation of the spheres, so to speak."

"You like music?"

For a while he appeared to ignore the question; then: "When I was in Europe I heard the most sublime music, the kind that must have moved Schopenhauer to advance such a claim for it. You have to hear it played by orchestras so grand and multitudinous and cohesive and stirring that no one in this province could even imagine. Sometimes I lie in that ugly bed and try to recall it. I can't. No one can. The old German fella was right."

Cora was helping him into bed. He had talked for almost two hours, in bursts interrupted only by brief forays into the brandy supply or more lengthy appraisals of his audience – Cora didn't know which manoeuvre discomfited her more. He was pallid, palsied in his attempts to get his nightshirt over his mountainous stomach, and yet as she guided him onto the sheets she could feel a strange resolve in him.

"I wish you could have heard it," he said, not rolling under the comforter but turning with great difficulty and balancing, egg-like, on the precipice of the bed. "I wish we could leave this place sometime and go there and hear it. Where else could we come as close to the transcendent?"

He patted a spot beside him and Cora, wary, joined him. She felt light-headed. It was past ten o'clock.

"What kind of music do you people around here have, eh? The bugle band?" He draped his hand over hers. She sensed the fear in it.

"I dance." Cora said.

"Don't go, please."

"You seem awful tired."

She allowed her hand to curl up inside his. Sweated and blood-warm.

"I watched you all afternoon. In that window."

Gently – afraid, unafraid – she tugged against the pull of his hand, the room, the momentum of the seasons behind them.

"You don't even know how beautiful you are. That is the wonder of it. That's what takes my breath away, my shrivelled old-man's breath away. Still…" With his free hand – the other clasped to hers – he reached over and staring steadily at the vee of her throat, he tried to unbutton her blouse. She let him fumble there just long enough to let him know she didn't mind, then raised her hands so she now held both of his in front of her.

"Cap," she said, "I love you in a way I've loved nobody else. That's the truth."

She saw his eyes moisten, his lip quiver, his fingers tense to overpower or take flight.

"But there's no need. Please understand. You don't have to –"

He peeled her hands back, startled at his own strength, and with a prisoning tenderness he took her breasts beneath the thin cotton. She wore no corset; they came willingly into the shape he imagined for them. Then with a sort of forced, grotesque humour, he closed his eyes and whispered. "I must. You've been walking home every night for more than two years now, with every lecherous eye on the street pursuing you. Not once have you stayed till morning. People will begin to think you're a respectable woman."

His grip slackened; she felt the shuddering right through him, and knew it was not desire.

Softly she planted a kiss on his brow, easing herself out of his limp embrace. "It's all right, Cap. My dearest. I know. I've known all this time."

"Know what?" he said, but it was not really a question, for already he was scanning her face for the ill-disguised signs of disgust and repudiation. There were none.

"You always liked the young men," she said.

3

The Night-Dream had pursued her here, as she knew it must, for its abode was in the bone's blood and in the mind that imagined it daily into being, it cared not for Arthur's house or a widow's comforts, she lay in its icy grip and felt its absolute breath against the last tenderness and heard it whisper sinuously of treacheries and mocked promises and she was Lily once again, squeezed tiny and tight into the last of the longago scenes but the branched dark was still vivid after seventy-one years, the ether of mosses and sweating fern and marooned violets awash in the nostrils and shut eyes, and Papa's voice, clear and unquenchable, mouthed its sweet prevarication: "To my dearest princess, the Lady Fairchild, from your Papa who loves you forever" and forever was less than a night, less than the time it took her to dream of a father with arms like brass buttresses and breath as warm as wool and a stare as strong as Sampson's and truer than Troilus under the Trojan wall, and she woke to find Papa gone and the gift of the Testament with its perjured inscription forlorn in her hand, her heart frozen and not caring one whit that the whole greenwood around her was weeping for all its lost children and crying out against the perfidy of a world cursed with the fickle seasons and tides of propagation.

48

"If we look at man with his industry and trade, his inventions and technology, we must admit that all this striving serves only to sustain and bring about a certain amount of additional comfort to ephemeral individuals in their brief span of existence, and through them to contribute to the maintenance of the species."

"Well done! You see, when you *read* you *can* put the 'd' on the 'ands' and the 'g' on the participles. Now why on earth do you pretend that they don't exist in free speech?"

"Tell me what 'ephemeral' means again?"

"Like us. We don't last very long. Plump in the spring, bust by fall."

"I'm sick an' tired of the German fella."

"Me too, but you can't deny the cogency of his arguments."

"Tell me about some of them other fellas you studied before I come here."

"Have it your way, then." He stared out at the Lake, wistfully noting a four-master as it bellied before the south wind, its glory as ephemeral as the June breeze it collaborated with. He proceeded to give her capsule accounts of Hegel, Feuerback, Marx and others, delighting for a while in his own clarity of recall. But the drowsiness of the late afternoon overwhelmed, and when he woke he was ravenous.

"Let me brush your hair, you look like a dandelion."

"I feel like one."

"I want you to write down the main ideas from one of them fellas. They sound interestin'."

"I bet I know which one." He wrote something on his pad.

"That Danish fella."

"I knew it!" He shoved the pad triumphantly towards her. "Soren Kierkegaard." Gleefully he recited his earlier encapsulation: "Existence was for Kierkegaard a category relating to the free individual. To exist means to realize oneself through free choice between alternatives, through self-commitment. To exit, therefore, means to —"

"I didn't say I believed him," she said, cutting him off. "I just said it sounded interestin'."

"The man was a fool."

"But you'll write out his thoughts? Without cheatin'?"

He was wounded. "Of course. A fool never hurt anybody for long."

"I'll get supper now."

When she had the door open, he called over: "Free choice is just an illusion unless it's used to renounce the world that tempts us with it."

Cora came back. "I made my own choices." She looked him straight in the eye. He saw that the game had ended, with no warning.

"So you see now that all those flirtations I was notorious for, even my flamboyant escapades with Lady Marigold, served a very special purpose. When one is known everywhere as a roué, it is much easier to indulge one's illicit proclivities, so to speak. You'd be surprised how many lonesome young men the army produces and how much comfort an older, wiser, more licentious gentleman can provide in times of stress."

Cora was curled in the bay-window seat – reading, half-listening, mildly annoyed at his attempts to shock, to keep the attention flowing his way.

"I knew that pervert of a Calvinist Dane would get to you," he said. He started to cough, *in extremis.*

"Your medicine's three inches from your ring finger," she said without looking up.

The coughing wound down to a pathetic nickering sound: "Cora, come over and talk to me."

She did. "This Danish fella is sayin' that we have to know who we are by makin' up our own minds about what we do, an' being strong enough to take the consequences. The key to it, as you've written out for me, is makin' choices."

"I choose, therefore I am."

"I like that."

Cap shook his head ruefully. "Cora, you've told me more about your life and your travails than any one man ought to know, and I'll be damned if I can see where you had much choice. Like most women you've been devastated by wars you never started, diseases you can't cure, and children who die on you or run off to lead their own lives without a pennyworth of gratitude. The world cares only for the species, and women bear the brunt of that reality."

Cora mulled that over for a while. "May be," she said. "But I chose somethin'. Every time."

"And what would that be?"

"I chose to love."

When Cora came in, Cap was sitting in his chair, but the chair was next to the bay-window where he could see the cardinals in the bushes along the Lane, bright as blood against the fresh snow. She pulled her chair over to his, took up her knitting and sat down – as if this were the spot he had chosen over all others for them to contemplate the rejection of the world. They never again sat by the north window. No explanation was offered.

"That bird, bless his heart, thinks he has chosen to stay the winter while all others have succumbed to the herd-instinct and flown south."

"I'm glad they stay."

"In a sense, we *all* choose to love," he said, his eyes still on the birds foraging hopelessly among the sterile drifts."I loved a young man in my regiment so desperately I would have given my life in exchange for his. Luckily that passion thinned before I was put to the test. By loving so, and choosing to do so, we simply fall prey to a larger desire that does not liberate us or refine our feeling of who we are or who we might become – as the Dane implies – but rather one that pulls us into desire itself and its compulsive yearning after something that threatens to overwhelm us or leave us feeling foolish and often so bitter we're not capable of dealing with the world on any terms. What is left of our precious self then? Our power to choose is progressively reduced as each new passion rages through us, and the indifference of the universe drops its accidents upon us. History has no time for lovers."

Cora was silent for a bit, but he knew from the way she chewed at her lower lip that there was more to come. He sucked on his cigar and waited.

"I admit there's not a lot we have any choice about," she said.

He was poised to make his customary interjection-with-homily but stopped short.

"I mean women," she said to forestall him. *Not that again*, he would be thinking, but she pressed on. "Some people might say I lived my life for others, an' that I took my existence from them. I loved my children but they're gone. I loved my husbands an' they're gone. I don't know now, and I never will, if they knew who I was. But I can tell you this: I was myself long before I knew them. I think this Danish fella was wrong in a way, though I like what he says a lot more than Mr. Arthur Schopenhauer."

The pedagogue's gaze narrowed. "Wrong, in what way?"

"You can be yourself even when you can't choose."

Cap was not prepared for his pupil's sudden apostasy. He blinked, then coughed.

"I loved my children: Rob an' Brad and even the little dead one I never saw the livin' eyes of, an' most of all the little girl they took away from me because they thought I wasn't good enough to –" She saw the flinching in Cap's look and stopped. Then: "They took everything I offered them. So did my lovers. But I tried not to give myself away, I really did."

"I know," Cap said.

Weeks later with the frost-fronds thick upon the glass, the glacial wind howling around the corners, the lamps lit throughout the afternoon – Cap seemed to pick up the thread of an earlier conversation. Cora was surprised because he'd had a bad night, soiling his sheets and writhing helplessly in the grasp of the pain he didn't acknowledge the existence of. She had been reading aloud to him from *Leaves of Grass* (which he informed her was real poetry), fully expecting him to be carried into sleep on the perambulating, narcotic rhythms. When she finished his favourite – 'When Lilacs Last in the Dooryard Bloomed' – she stopped, then looked over at the weary, gray pachyderm's flesh hunched in the chair by the bay-window. He began: lucid and didactic, as if the lecture-hall were jammed with sophists.

"You did make one kind of choice in your life," he said. "From what you've told me and what I've been able to infer from your life's story, you chose to be an outsider. Ironically, it was a choice you admitted only when it seemed convenient – like many of us. When life treated you a bit roughly – and I concede you've had a touch more ill-fortune than some – you blamed your sorrows on the very society you deliberately set out to repudiate. Being hypocrites and sadists they picked on the weak – like yourself – and drove you into exile, where they could increase your suffering tenfold. In other instances, though, it is clear that you never at any time accepted the values of that society – neither its comforts nor its sanctions. You not only made yourself an outcast before they decided to, you secretly gloried in your own superiority, your own capacity to survive nicely without them, thank you. You wanted it both ways. The German fella would say that you were corrupted by two of the world's illusory desires: pride, through which you pathetically hoped to establish an identity of your own; and what-is-worse the projection of your own failings upon the innocent and the guilty around you. The more you tried to be yourself, the less you really were. I know. I've been through it all – twice."

Cora drew his shawl against the icy draft from the window, and held his hand until she felt the relief of sleep take him.

"I can hear the machines hammerin' all the way from here," Cora said. "Funny, isn't it, to think they're a mile under the River."

"They'd burrow into Lucifer's outhouse if they thought there was anything but shit in it," was his only comment.

"They say it'll be finished by the fall. Three men've died so far. One of them was crushed so bad his wife couldn't recognize him."

"A particular talent of the illustrious company I helped to build."

"You want to talk, or read?"

"Talk."

"I figured out what's wrong with all them philosophers you been readin' all these years."

"You have? And in such a short time."

"None of 'em was women."

"Good Lord."

"I'm serious, Cap. I been tryin' for days to find the words to explain it to you. But they just keep revolvin' round in my brain all night and I can't get them to stay put. You know what I mean?"

Cap was very drawn of late. Much of the puffiness in his face had disappeared, leaving flaps of vellum skin with umber grooves between, his cheekbones protruding like a pair of interrogative andirons. His eyes seemed much larger, as if he were hydrocephalic and these couriers had been thrust into the chill to bear the bad tidings. At times they were as clear of thought or malice or desire or hope as a calf's eyes blinking into the flow of its birth-stall. Many times Cora had to lean over and wipe tears from the rungs of his cheeks, though she knew he was not weeping. He'd give her a wink and a shrug to reassure her it was just old age, irreversible decrepitation.

"I'm all ears," he said.

"Well, the way I see it, all these philosophers, as you call them, are tryin' to answer questions about how and why things happen, how they work, an' who might be responsible – us or some greater power, like the God they all seem to miss very much."

"More or less."

"To my surprise, I must admit to you, I found these were questions everybody sooner or later starts to fret about – not just spoiled brats with too much learnin' out of books. Many people I knew used to ask why such-an'-such had to happen, why a nice God would destroy a child's life, why their farm failed when they did everythin' humanly possible to make it work, why old so-an-so was always lucky an' they weren't. These philosophers of yours seem to be obsessed by things to do with actin', the whys an' the wherefores of it."

"Questions about the world of action, you mean, of freedom and necessity?"

She gave him a scrutinizing stare. "More or less."

"Do go on. Your main point?"

"Well, bein' men they seem to look about them an' conclude that all the actions in the world are carried out by men."

If she expected him to be taken aback she was disappointed. "True, but then all the significant actions in the world's affairs are."

"That's what I thought, too. At first. Men make the wars, they start factories an' farms an' make up countries to suit their fancy. They even give their names to the next generation. But there's somethin' wrong, I said to myself. Women. Women's *actions*, as you put it. First I thought: after-all's-said-an'-done, they worked as hard, they had babies, they raised the boys up till their fathers took them away an' they turned their girls into women to serve men. Wasn't that enough? Then I saw what those thinkers saw: that women didn't make the *big things* of the world happen, so they didn't seem important to their questions about how the world works. Accordin' to them, you have to look at the actions that count an' get things done."

"Yes, you do see that these men are not making value judgements about the worth of women; they are ignoring them strictly in terms of the philosophic questions they have chosen to raise. Some day those questions or new ones may involve women in a central way."

"But –" Cora said, letting the word hang weightily.

"The most telling word in the lexicon," Cap murmured.

"But then I got to thinkin', an' here's where the words started to jump about on me. So I'll just tell you where I'm at now an' see if it makes any sense. In my view women *do* act, an' not just doin' woman's things either. They act by not actin'."

Cap came out of his doze like a swimmer who's suddenly decided not to drown.

"I know that sounds crazy, an' maybe it is. But I think it's true. You see the tangle all this thinkin' in words gets you into?"

"Tell me. I'm listening."

"Let me give you an example."

He smiled inwardly, deeply. "Do, please."

"Suppose there's a war. The men an' the boys go off, an' whether they win or not could change the world a lot. It could affect the lives of millions. It can change the future. Like this Buonaparte you're always goin' on about. The women do the usual things: they kiss their boys goodbye; they give support and comfort; they nurse; they pick up the pieces that are left; they cheer or they weep. Mostly they suffer."

"True, and very sad."

"But what if to suffer was in a way – I know this sounds silly – but what if sufferin' was another way of actin', a special woman's way of actin'?"

Cap realized he was expected to say something. She was watching his face strain towards concentration. "Interesting," he said, feeling a flush of shame. In the silence between them, Cora reached over and wiped her handkerchief across his cheek. He tried to wink.

"But how can not-actin' be the same as actin'? That's where it all starts goin' round like a bobbin in my skull. But think of it this way: what if these women refused to suffer? If sufferin' means, and I think it does, that we take in pain, sort of soak it up –"

"Absorb it."

"Yes, absorb it, then if it ain't absorbed, where does it go? You see what I'm headin' for? The actions of men always cause pain, they upset the world, an' most of that pain is simply swallowed by women. If they refused to swallow it, where would it go? What would happen to the world if all that pain were left loose in it? Would the men be able to act at all?" Cap clutched at the gleam from her eye, trying to hold on. "If the women on one side suffered an' those on the other didn't, would the outcome of the war not be changed? Is it just because sufferin's mostly invisible that these philosophers don't see it as actin' and as important to the world?"

Bravely he fought against the waters that closed over him, beating his arms against the green insistence like an eagle's against the four-cornered wind. He needed air – for words, for praise, for wonder.

"Don't you see, Cap. I just ain't got the words yet."

His eyes locked onto hers just before he slipped away.

"I told you to leave that section alone," Cap said in the villain's stage-whisper he had adopted to save wear-and-tear on his throat. "There's nothing there to look at."

Cora pulled the books from the glass case into the beam of the sun from the west window. She read the titles aloud not for his benefit but her own: Whitman, *Democratic Vistas*; Darwin, *On the Origin of the Species by Means of Natural Selection*; Bucke, *Man's Moral Nature*; Carlyle, *Sartor Resartus*; Huxley, *Evidence as to Man's Place in Nature*.

"Stop that magpie muttering, will you. I didn't sleep a wink all night."

"Maybe that's because you sleep most of the day."

He grimaced and clutched his stomach. She saw pain startle the soft points still left in his eyes, before he wedged them shut to keep this penultimate anguish in its own private darkness. She waited until he could open them again before she went over to wipe the sweat from his face and draw the shawl around his shoulders. She would kiss him sweetly along the nape of the neck, massage the tension out of his muscles, hum secretively in his ear, but she would never come around and look at him until he raised his hand to signal that he was ready. He did not want her to see him in his pain as he was: an old, fat man afraid of death.

"You read all those books?" she said, fixing the tea.

He glared malevolently.

"You never talk about them."

"Don't you go hiding my cigars again."

"Let me come in the mornings," she said.

"No need to read about fools, even when they might be right."

"But you told me –"

"Don't listen to what people tell you. Now give me that tea before it turns to ice, and swing me around so I can see what's left of June out there."

All that summer the dreams and meditations of the villagers were accompanied by the steady throbbing of the steam-powered hydraulic rams against the wrought-iron shields they drove inch by battering inch into the millennial rock under the St. Clair River. Children awoke whimpering, afraid of thunder that rumbled past the ear to inner bone. Tornado warnings were ignored in deference to more impressive manifestations of omnipotence. It was rumoured that mothers' milk was drying up. Old men in their cribs at night fretted like babies. In September the noise stopped. On the eighteenth, three days before the sun began rolling backwards towards the equator, the first Grand Trunk express roared unimpeded under the ancient waterway that had stymied bison, glaciers, and herds of brontosauri lured to the faithless sun.

"It's done," Cora said.

"It's never done," Cap said.

Elmer helped her get him down the back stairs and through the kitchen, but he insisted on going the rest of the way with Cora's help only. "I'd like to go for a walk," was all he said when she had come in early that afternoon.

When the warm sun struck him, he blinked like a hibernating bear, and she nudged him forward half-a-step, then let him stop to savour its blessing on his face and hands.

"Don't need this," he growled, and she unwound the scarf. "It's almost July, isn't it?"

Behind the hotel and paralleling the backyards of the boarding houses along the street was a winding pathway used mainly by draymen and delivery boys and lovers out for a semi-public promenade. Aging board-fences lined it on either side, adorned by hollyhocks deceptively frail in the light breeze that now and then lifted their petticoats. Orange blossoms and honeysuckle bloomed wildly over rusted gates and abandoned sheds. Roses, planted with some care or purpose years before, rebelled lustily, overwhelming trellis, rotted arbour, sapling maples. At the far end near Victoria Street, they could see the ice-wagon and the ragamuffins from the Lane trailing it like gulls in a trawler's wake. Their cries rose in delight, tangled in the green branches overhead and then faded as the horse wheeled away up the main road.

Cora held Cap firmly by his right arm, but not as a nurse would: she lay her head near his shoulder, and from time to time she moved her free hand over and patted him possessively.

"People will think we're lovers," Cora whispered.

"They already do."

She hugged him sharply, saying *we already are*. She felt laughter ripple somewhere inside him.

They made slow, halting progress. He glanced from side to side, taking everything in; she watched his nostrils flare as the odours and aromas quickened them; in the tart air his eyes watered but he waved off her handkerchief. Just before the lane ended they turned together, as if they were both reading the same map, and started back. Cap stopped. He inhaled deeply, resolutely. He reached over and seized her hand. She felt the reserves of its strength. He moved forward, pulling her with him. He wanted her to feel the rhythm of his stride – a wonderful, easy, lover's ambling, as if this kind of afternoon, this larcenous beauty, this accidental pastoral bower were designed for those pure and dedicated enough to deserve it.

Elmer met them at the gate and together they carried him back up to his room.

Cap was in a rare lively mood. Some of the old, teasing humanity of the would-be rogue shone through and gave every word and every gesture an extra fillip.

"You're always going on and on about suffering. When I suffer, you call it self-pity; when you suffer, it's martyrdom on the road to beatification."

"I feel sorry for myself every day," Cora said, "but I don't go makin' a religion out of it."

"A philosophy, you mean."

She caught the flint in his eye. "Whatever that German fella called it."

He mouthed the bait but didn't bite. "I meant what I said. I'm asking you to tell me about how you women suffer that makes it any different from men."

"Do I get twenty years in a sea-side cottage to come up with an answer?"

"As you've never stopped telling me, men traipse off to the great capitals to play at politics and death. They deliberately find ways to make wars just so they can play the roles of soldier and field-marshall, so they can take the little-boy dreams their mommies tried to stifle and make the rest of the world believe them, or else. According to your version of reality, they never get over playing *truth-or-dare*. Well, I agree. Nevertheless, they *do* make the world happen. Napoleon ravaged Europe and left it a better place. And in the meantime other boys-become-men are writing great poems and composing great symphonies, and building bigger bridges and faster locomotives."

"Are you through?"

"I have a feeling I am."

"An' they suffer, of course, all through this?"

"That was my main point, yes."

"They get killed an' maimed? They die young? They suffer for their beliefs an' their talent?"

"Exactly."

"So they're the true martyrs?"

"Martyrs to time and history…and circumstance," he said in a different tone, seemingly astonished that the mental apparatus was still operational. For several days now he had been mysteriously free of all pain.

"You don't have to tell me about that," Cora said. "I already lived a good deal of it. I seen it close up."

"There you go," he said, "proving my point again. As a woman you suffered, certainly, and you feel sorry for yourself like all women because you weren't part of any of it, or if you were likely an Austrian virgin casually raped by a French soldier, or your lover was killed at Austerlitz —"

Cora had turned away and was staring out the window at the heat-haze.

"I *am* sorry," he said.

"What for?" she said softly, looking directly at him again and speaking through her tears. "I've never been afraid of my sufferin' an' grief. It's nothin' to be proud of nor ashamed of either. It's there, like my eyes an' my heart."

Cap was devastated. His hands shook. He tried to get up to a full sitting position. Cora was beside him, she had his right hand in hers. Her fingers rose and brushed back what remained of his boy's cowlick. The tremors ebbed into sweat.

"It's all right…it really is."

After a while he was able to rest his head back on the chair cushion. She kept his hand firmly in hers. Finally he spoke. "I really do want to know," he said. "If you could find the words for me."

"Well, I ain't had a sabbatical on the Baltic to think it over," she said, fluffing up the pillows under his head the next afternoon, "but I'm gonna try an' put some real knowledge into that decayin' brain of yours."

He essayed a smile. "Where'd you hide the medicine?"

"You get a dollop when I'm finished talkin'. I been up all night rehearsin' what I got to say, so don't put me off the rails. Just open your ear-flaps an' listen for once."

Through his exhaustion and through the layers of resistance he had learned to build into the face he presented to the world, Cora spotted the wick of curiosity fired, at great expense, just for her. Her throat thickened.

He whispered, "I think *you* need the drink."

She drew a deep breath like a girl about to recite at a Christmas concert, and began. "A great deal of what you say is true because it's already what's happened in the world and is still happenin'. I myself've seen enough to believe it. I'm not so sure it will always be that way. I hope not. *You* say history is made by men who are dreamers an' soldiers an' builders. Women are put here to make sure they do the things well they were meant by their maker to do. That means, I suppose, bein' their mothers an' lovers an' companions an' nursemaids. When wars happen or great changes come like they have in this country since I was a girl, the victims who suffer are everywhere – not just women but children and old people an' the young men who die for these causes. You claim that soldiers an' dreamers suffer somethin' even worse: the collapse of their dreams, the ruination of what they tried to build, an' so on. I agree. But what you can never understand is the special suffern' of the women, and I'm not talkin' just about the loss of a husband or a son in battle, or the pain of bein' uprooted an' havin' to follow your husband wherever, or the anguish of a nurse when she tends the broken body of a lover or a brother. All these kinds of sufferin' can be understood by anybody with a heart to feel them. No, what I'm talkin' about – what it took me all last night to figure out in words – is not the sufferin' that comes at the time of the loss or the inflictin' of the pain or the ache that follows ever afterwards, but the sufferin' that happens *before* all that: the private, invisible sort of sufferin'. Think for a minute about the young wife whose husband marches off in uniform with his head full of glories to be won. Her sufferin' starts the moment she knows he might leave. She'll have fears an' nightmares an' pre-monition, but of course she mustn't let her husband or her neighbours *see* any of this. She holds it all in till the hour of his leavin' when she's allowed to burst into woman's tears for a while an' be comforted by her own kind. But then every single day or hour he's gone, she's sufferin'. And there's no thoughts of glory to keep *her* mind off the hor-rible possibilities of life without him, without means to support her family, without a father for her children. There's no daily action for her that does not remind her of these horrors. She looks at her children an' thinks of him. She looks in her neighbour's face an' sees the same terror she herself is tryin' to hide. At night her bed is empty. There's no lover, no camp-follower to lie between her legs an' help her fall into a safe sleep. Her dreams make love to her but they're the soldiers of Buonaparte mockin' her tears. An' when she hears of his death, it's almost a relief because at least, she says, somethin' vis-ible has happened, I can go out into the town among my neighbours an' grieve an' be consoled, an' play some role in this terrible thing you call history an' progress, an' you claim so loudly to have renounced."

Cap was still awake.

"An' there's more. You say this God, that neither of us believes much in, made women to help an' support men in their hopes an' dreams. Maybe so. But what you forget or don't know is that we have dreams too. You tell me about Christopher Wren buildin' the monuments in the great city of London, but I ask you whether there would ever be villages with cozy homes an' hearths, with meadows for the children to play in, with neighbourhood squares an' markets for gossipin' an' friendliness, an' cottages sur-rounded by flowers an' green growin' things – what I'm getting at here is this: though men may dream up the grand design an' the monuments an' bridges, it's the women of this world who dreamt the home an' the village an' all the little objects of beauty that men learn about as boys at their mother's knees while papa's off huntin' or fightin', an' later when they're grown up try to make into…grandiose – is that the right word? – objects you call works of art. But I ask you, who sings to the babe? Who tells him his stories? I tell you, Cap, there's more to this than I can work out in my head. But I think what I'm sayin' is that at least part of the dreamin' you say is man's contribution

to history is really a woman's. Without women, there'd be no history or only part of
it. Can you follow that? Think for a minute what men would make out of the world
without their mothers an' wives – an' I don't mean just their job as nurse an' helpmate
an' so on. I mean what if they were only raised by their fathers an' fed *only* their father's
dreams an' hopes – what would the world be like? What 'better' world would their wars
bring us? Would the wars ever end? An' one last point. If what I'm thinkin' might be
true, if some of the dream that's made the world as it is now is a woman's dream – if
that's true, then why can't women share in workin' it out? If mankind's dream is really
a village turned into a city full of love an' beauty an' harmony an' justice, then *we've*
got a lot to offer it."

She was finished. Her own words had taken her breath away. She sat amazed, as a
painter might when the landscape he's been labouring at suddenly quickens with sym-
metry. Cap's eyes were closed. For a second she felt like Schopenhauer's dog. Then they
opened and took her in, and she knew he had understood something he had already
prepared himself to believe.

"I'd like that drink now," he said.

Most days now Cap did not get out of bed until Cora arrived. Elmer came in early in
the morning to help him to the water-closet and to prop him up in his chair or help
him back to bed. Cora never entered before the designated hour, though she often
sneaked up to his door during her chores and listened to the wheezing cough that had
replaced his breathing – asleep or awake.

"You're like an old trout gulping air," she teased.

"A sturgeon, amusing the caviar."

He never dressed now. When Cora closed and locked the wardrobe for good, he
applauded like a seal behind her. Instead, he wore a silk dressing-gown trimmed with
ermine that Cora had been ordered to retrieve from a musty trunk. "To remind me of
my past sins," he explained.

One day in late September she arrived to find him sitting by the window. A book
lay open in his lap, several more were scattered nearby.

"I do love that goldenrod along the River," he said. "It seems so pleased with itself."

Cora pulled her chair close, and fussed at his robe.

"I read all of these books," he said, "long before I came to that German fella. I guess
what I found in them – though it was better than the mess I'd made of the world – was
not to my liking. Nonetheless, there's both truth and illusion in them – in their pure
forms."

Cora squeezed his hand and looked out across the prospect they had marked out as
their own: marsh, river, lake, dune.

"Terrifying. Positively terrifying. Mr. Darwin got most of it right. There's more
order and more chaos out there than we've yet dreamed of. What he didn't know – or
didn't care to say – was that man has already freed himself from those laws, he has
loosed the bonds of evolution, he has exorcized the ghost of god; he's inventing his own
future. I've seen some of it already, but it's just begun. We've got the steam-engine, the

gatling gun, the screw-prop battleship, we've got the power *up here* to unravel the laws that've governed our behavior and held it in check for thousands of years. It's wonderful and terrifying. A part of me wants to live longer just to see the outcome. But I'm afraid, Cora. I'm terribly afraid. I look into the blackness where my heart used to be and I say: what will become of us when we have invented everything? How much of our being human depends wholly upon our need to be a part of the mystery itself?"

Cora entered the room as quietly as she dare. The morning brightness of Indian summer suffused the air, coming from no discernible direction, like altar-light in a sunny cathedral. Cap was seated in his philosopher's chair, the familiar German tome, covers closed, on his knee. His gaze was aimed outward, his white beard radiantly professional. His right forearm was raised above the chair, its forefinger tenderly pointing out an error or an omission. Cora moved soundlessly to his side. She looked at him for a long, commemorative second, then reached over and closed both of his eyes.

49

A cold uncalled-for wind with the bite of December in it swept down from the Lake and over the dunes and through the shanties along the Lane and around the cozy homes of the townsite and past the little windbreak of firs at the north edge of the village cemetery, rippling the late-summer grass at Cora's feet. She shivered. The sing-song intonations of the Reverend Baddeley sailed past her, warped by the wind beyond reason or faith. She kept her eyes on a tiny corner of the coffin – red cedar, all she could afford – and the ridge of soil near it. According to the worthies, she should have been grateful that the good parson, placing Christian compassion above Anglican ortho-doxy, had offered to render the burial service to such an apostate – conspicuously un-repentant to the end, cohabiting in squalid sin with a woman who changed her name more often than her address. She didn't care, though it occurred to her, despite the rector's graveside drone, that Cap might well be savouring the ironies of the situation. This ground won't hold you long, she thought. You need an audience.

> Man that is born of woman hath but a
> short time to live, and is full of misery.
> He cometh up and is cut down like a
> flower; he fleeth as it were a shadow and
> never continueth in one stay...

A brief service had been held in the lobby of The Queen's. Duckface Malloney was there, Elmer, Gertie and Mrs. Baddeley, who sang a sad hymn in a high sunny so-prano. Only Elmer accompanied the undertaker, the parson and Cora as they clopped up Michigan Ave., barely noticed, though several workmen mechanically doffed their caps. No church bells offered their petition to the autumn air. The crunch of box-cars coupling echoed past them into First Bush and beyond.

> ...we therefore commit his body to the
> ground,

earth to earth, ashes to ashes, dust to
dust…

Cora glanced around her, once, to see if anyone else had come in behind them. With solemn gaze the undertaker, Josiah Smiley from Sarnia, kindly remained beside the minister as he intoned the familiar words of intercession and false comfort. Elmer stood nearby, watching Cora. She half-expected the two cousins from Toronto to show up, sooner or later, to claim what was left of Cap's fortune. When Cora had suggested that he make a will, Cap scoffed at the notion: "I've never been able to will anything while alive, how could I manage it when I'm dead? Besides, what would the old German think?" But no one had followed them in.

When she had asked Malloney if they could use the lobby for the service, he said yes immediately though without any enthusiasm, without any apparent feeling of any kind. Cap was never discussed between them. That Malloney must have been under some pressure from the community to purge it of this pariah whose treacheries were even this instant being felt throughout the village, Cora had little doubt. How or why he resisted it, she did not know, though she suspected that he, like her, had chosen to come to accept a life on the periphery. Were you right after all? she wanted to shout out loud to Cap.

The minister's orthodox lamentation was suddenly challenged by a stifled sob, then several unstifled ones more or less in unison. All eyes sidled right even as the Reverend picked up the dropped stitch. Two elderly, arthritic ladies – adorned in mourning clothes – had apparently slipped into the quietude unremarked and had been observing the ceremony from a short distance. Overwrought by the holy litany and the sadness of the situation, they had given vent to their sorrow. The cousins from Toronto, Cora thought, and fought against a strange feeling of resentment. Their cries and lyric whimperings seemed heartfelt. She tried to block them out. At least they're weeping: you deserved that, at least. I'm glad they're here. Really, I am.

Reverend Baddeley carried on doggedly, doubling both volume and tempo.

…in sure and certain hope of the Resurrection to eternal life through our Lord
Jesus Christ who shall change our cor-
ruptible body…

The cross he had nervously essayed with the sand through his fingers looked more like a crooked question-mark waiting for someone to 'dot' it. Brushing past Cora, he strode effusively over to the strangers and waited for them to receive his outstretched hands. She heard the ritual exchange, the timbre of inconsolability in the voices of the women.

"We're only second cousins," she heard one say, "but we grew up with him, we went to school together and you never forget that sort of experience, being so young and attached."

"Never, indeed," said the good parson, his relief both obvious and immense. He was back on home-ground. "And you haven't seen him in some time, I assume?"

"Years and years," said a thinner, more aggrieved voice. "But once you knew Emery, you never forgot him. He was a sweet, sweet man."

"Emery?"

"We always called him by his middle name. He wanted us to call him Stan when he got older, but we never would. We always were a bit of a tease with him." She interrupted her encomium with several more sobs that left even Mr. Smiley discomfited. He began mumbling endearments to his horse.

"May the blessings of Our Lord ease your sorrow in the days to come," said the Reverend Baddeley, searching for an exit-line.

"We come all the way down from Owen Sound and then up from London on the train. It was late. The taxi brought us right here from the station."

The taximan's mare, obscured by the cedar-hedge near the road, whinnied in the direction of the undertaker's gelding.

"Emery was from Owen Sound, you know," said the stronger cousin. "The whole family, what's left of us."

Her sister added a sniffle for emphasis.

"But I understood Mr. Dowling was born and raised in London."

A silence deeper than death itself seized the cemetery and its grieving occupants. The gelding's tail whiskered an imaginary fly. Cora turned to look. Mr. Smiley, as shocked as if one of his cadavers had sat up and saluted him, came over to the ladies, who were looking pathetically about them for some explanation.

"Your cab-driver's gone an' made a terrible mistake," he said, hat in hand.

"But we told him, didn't we sis, we was late, we'd missed the church service but would he please take us as fast as he could to the interment of Stanfield E. Dowler."

"And he brought us here."

"Saints preserve us," said the minister.

They were all gone: even Elmer, reluctantly, his great sad moon's face turning away at last down Michigan Ave.; the cousins, poor souls, to grieve all over again at another site; the minister and undertaker to the call of their respective professions. Later, under the cloak of darkness, the sexton would come with his boy to lower the coffin and seal it off, with dirt and grass-seed, from the morning sun. For the moment she and Cap were alone once again. The chill wind sent some of the fallen leaves chattering across the grass, the limbs of a maple stretched and complained, but Cora was no longer cold. She thought of the cousins jouncing and breathless in the taxi-cab, afraid they would be too late to expend their grief so loyally husbanded all the way down from Owen Sound and all the way up to Sarnia on the Grand Trunk, which was, alas-as-usual, late again. And Reverend Baddeley trying to retract his hasty, misdirected condolences, saving them up for a more appropriate occasion. She felt a bubble of laughter disrupt the numbness around her heart, then the tears intercepting it.

As soon as she got back, Cora went to the pantry to continue the cleaning she had started the day before. Malloney came to the door and called her out into the hall.

"You don't have to work today, Mrs. Burgher. Why don't you go home, or just find a place to rest around here. You been through a lot."

"I'd like to work," she said, "if it's all right."

He seemed very uncomfortable, the wrinkles in his face tensed against some certain ambush. Suddenly they relaxed, and his eyes doubled their size, gripping everything in their ken. "Cora," he said quietly, "you been hearin' the same rumours I've been, about the Grand Trunk packin' up an' desertin' this place after thirty years. Well, even the rumours, which I don't for one second believe, are keepin' people away. Business is real slow right now. You can work if you like, but I suggest you take a few weeks off. Go somewhere. See somebody. Get the hell outta this place."

"I got no other place to go," she said evenly.

His face twisted in preparation for some kind of speech or gambit, his eyes shrivelled in their casing, but nothing came out. His drayman's hands swung loosely at his side, and finally he slouched towards the lobby.

"Mr. Malloney."

He looked back over his shoulder, then came fully around. "Kevin," he said.

"You may be hearin' from some cousins Cap had in Toronto, once they read about his funeral in the papers."

He came close to her, alert.

"His aunt left him some money, not a lot, but all the same I expect they'll be comin' down to find out."

Malloney looked straight at her, hesitated, then said: "Dowling's got no money to leave to nobody."

"I thought —"

"His aunt's money run out. He's bust."

Cora could barely get the next words out. "How long?"

"A year ago."

She felt his eyes shiver on her back all the way down the hall. They were as soft as a doe's.

The wind blew harder and colder that night, the last one of September, 1892 – the date some stranger's hand had chiseled on Cap Dowling's tombstone. Doors were locked and shutters tightened. There was talk of a tornado, of gales on the Lake wild enough to send tremors through the sailors' wives alone in their beds, through the captain's helpmate measuring the minutes along her widow's-walk. On nights like this the Point was all maritime. Later on, foghorns would wail against the driving sleet, proclaiming loneliness and fear in the cold tongue below the gut. Cora made a pot of tea and sat by herself in the gloom. Hap was at the factory helping his sons batten the hatches. Above the clatter of rain on the windows, she heard the Grand Trunk express roaring around the bend by the River and steaming towards the station. She thought of the hoboes in their encampment beyond the Lane, rain dancing on the tin of their lean-to's and dripping into the hot, flameless fires below. She thought of the outcasts, the exiles, the forsaken, the unforgivable. She pulled the comforter off her bed and sat down in Hap's rocker. Let it rain, she thought. Let it not rain. I am here.

The rap on the door jolted her upright and awake in one motion. Hap never knocked. The rapping came again, magnified by the dark, twisted by the wind-blown rain. Loud but not regular enough to be official. As she started for the door, candle in hand, it came again, rattling the hinges in its urgency. One of Hap's boys, was her only thought as she lifted the latch and let the door swing inward.

A man stood there blinking at the flame and the wash of interior heat over him. He was a hobo, no doubt just off the express. The rain had smeared soot into grotesque shapes over his face. He wore a battered fedora and a wool overcoat three sizes too large and soaked right through. He was holding a rumpled package in his hands as if it were fragile and some kind of offering. He stared at her as if he ought to know her and were waiting for her to confirm his assumption. For a second she was blinded by the whites of his eyes refracting the bent candle-flame.

As she started instinctively back, he stepped forward, and pulling up the canvas flap shielding the gift in his arms, Bradley said in a consumptive whisper, "It's me, Mama. I've come home."

She fell back as if struck.

"And this is Eddie," he said, lifting the baby's face into view.

PART THREE

Eddie

50

1

Granny Coote sat by the window looking over at the altered landscape to the west, wondering vaguely when Mr. Stadler would arrive to begin the transformation, and finally drifting into a doze. "After wars, pestilence," Cap had told her many times. You were right, for once, she thought. She let the events of that extraordinary month in 1918 pass before her for Cap's skeptical appraisal.

Sometime in the middle of the night of October 1, Oliver Fletcher sneezed. Just a cold but worrisome nonetheless because Ollie had been gassed at Ypres and returned home with half-a-lung. Young boys stopped him on the street and asked to hear him breathe. By mid-day he was running a fever. Five-year-old Barbie Savage, who'd survived scarlet fever and whooping cough, stopped playing with her china-head doll and asked to be put down for her nap an hour early. Chuck Simmers, delivering bread, felt a stab of pain in his lower back: lumbago. He headed for the Richmond House and some afternoon solace.

There was considerable unease along Charles Street at the sight of dear young Dr. Simon, black bag in hand, hurrying up to the Fletcher house and entering without a knock or by-your-leave. By suppertime everyone knew that Ollie had died: poison gas. A hero.

Still, no one was seen going in or out of the stricken house. It was morning before the undertaker arrived from Sarnia. Mrs. Carpenter, a lifelong friend, was observed about noon on her way to Mrs. Fletcher's with a soup tureen, still steaming. Barbie Savage refused to get up from her nap. A fever took hold of her in the early hours. Dr. Simon rushed in. Neither of the Savage twins was seen on the streets that evening. Chuck Simmers had to be carried home from the hotel in his wagon. He swore he'd only had two drafts. By morning his wife had covered him with three blankets and he was calling for more. By the time Dr. Simon arrived, his lips were beginning to turn blue, a deep lassitude had taken possession, and he mistook the doctor for his horse. Mrs. Simmers locked the children in their rooms.

Some sort of collective distemper seemed to have struck the village. Sailors just off the boats were ordered to stay on the docks. Two who slipped undetected into the Mens at the Richmond House found themselves in a scuffle, then a punch-up in the alley, and finally were dragged to the wharf and dumped. Any stranger on the street was eyed with suspicion, rudely dealt with by junior clerks, welcomed out of town. Among friends, customers and neighbours tempers were short: a lifelong word misunderstood, taken wrongly, newly resented. "The war's been goin' on too long," grocer Redmond said to his wife before bed, "people are gettin' squirrely." "Too many false stories about an armistice," Maxie Wise opined to his wife already in bed, "You can't keep raisin' people's hopes like that."

Next day while the hearse carrying Ollie Fletcher's body to the cemetery passed by a weeping crowd of mourners along Michigan Ave., news arrived of the deaths of little Barbie and Chuck Simmers. Turned blue an' died, both of 'em, the rumour rippled west to east following the black cassion of the fallen soldier. *Flu.*

Granny heard the church bells tolling their dark news. She saw the hearses from Sarnia passing her house en route to one of the three churches on the main street. She saw the toy coffin being carried from the Savage's house. She saw the white wreath on the door. She tried to make room in her heart for the grief of a child's death. It was hard.

For days no one seemed to pass by her window, at least not while she was looking. The recess bell from the school stopped ringing in mid-morning. Twice more that week she was roused by a carillon of death – all three belfries lamenting in unison. Dr. Simon went into the Savage house again. He was wearing a surgical mask. That Sunday no bells proclaimed heaven to the faithful. Two figures in white – masked – hurried past and into Mrs. Carpenter's next door. A mother's cry scattered the eerie Sunday silence. For two years now Granny had not ventured beyond the front gate or the back hedge. Her tongue had paralyzed itself. She had nothing to say. She had nothing to give.

On Monday morning she went out to look at the village.

The sun was bright, the air dry and warm. She was alone on St. Clair Street. Not a soul stirred on verandah or waved from hedge or fence. Not a single door or window stood open to the breeze, to the rare sweetness of autumn. As she passed familiar doorways, she felt curtains part and fall behind her. Leila Savage, eyes red-rimmed above her gauze mask, kept her glassy stare aimed straight ahead as she went by. She was carrying a crockery pot wrapped in a towel. On Michigan Ave. several figures, head down, walked briskly towards some overweening imperative, as if any contact with the streets themselves were irrelevant, hazardous even. Several women came out of the back entrance of the Anglican Church – not saying a word – reached the sidewalk and parted company silently, pretending their momentary meeting was accidental. The town gossips, she thought, amazed. She turned into the churchyard. Alien ground. A chill, all over. She was walking on the moon, the back side.

In the vestibule she heard the minister's wife say that they had more food than they could use, wasn't it wonderful how generous people were in a crisis, and so on, but they needed volunteers to take it into the worst houses, some of which, like the McLeod clan farther down the Lane, had not been checked at all – perhaps they were all dead. She felt the astonishment of the Anglican ladies upon her as she reached out for a tureen of soup. Mrs. Stokes handed her a mask. She shook her head no. It had begun. Without a word.

On this part of the Lane noise was usually continuous and varied: babies crying in several keys of displeasure, the shouts of unincarcerated children, the bawl of a calf or pig or battered wife. At this moment not even the chickens flicked an eyelid. Here silence had become something positive, not an absence but an embodiment of something foul oozing out of the cracks in the house, under the doors, through a fist-size hole in a window-pane, and settling over the styes and coops and hutches where animals squeezed in the darkest corners and watched, without hope.

She walked briskly. There was need. She stepped over the debris in the yard of Jessie McLeod's shack, wishing she could call out some warning, some comforting salutation. She banged the tureen, still steaming, against the door. No sound from within. She turned the knob and leaned inward. Then she glanced down and saw the jamb that had been wedged against the world. She waited. She heard breathing on the other side of the door, shallow but quick. A child's. " She fought the urge to speak, knowing what chaos that would bring. Instead she began to hum, searching for a tune and keeping her voice soft and lullaby-low. Something ticked – tentatively, weakly – at the shim. It popped loose. Seconds later, still humming, she felt the door drawn backwards into whatever fear had seized the interior and its inhabitants. She saw a black-haired McLeod child. No mistake. A girl about five-years-old.

Granny smiled or at least she thought she did because the child did too. Granny edged into the gloomy 'front room' of the shack.

"Mommy won't wake up," the child said. "We're hungry but Pa says he'll whip us if we go out." She began to weep, not in the sobbing, physical manner of children but in the quiet, foreknowing way of stricken adults.

Granny put her hand on the little girl's shoulder: the touch was electric. She strode to a table, put the food down, and went through some curtains into a bedroom. Jessie – barely thirty, one of Eddie's playmates – lay propped up on two filthy pillows, her eyes closed, feigning sleep, feigning peace – for the children's sake. Beside the bed was a home-made cradle. Granny reached down to grasp the baby's hand. It was as stiff as a doll's. Closing the curtains, she went into the next room. Three mattresses, salvaged from the dump, had been laid out on the floor. Sam McLeod – Jessie's second cousin, sweetheart, then husband – lay naked on one of them, shivering and moving his lips in soundless, misshapen moans. His three boys were huddled under covers nearby, alive but unable to acknowledge her presence, their eyes glazed, all their weeklong aching passed into painless languor. She felt for fever, there was none. One of the boys, the youngest, let his eyes loll over to try to take her in. Through his puffed lips she heard him whisper: "Are you an angel?"

Granny set about her work, little 'Claire' at her heels. Pillows were improvised so the boys could be propped up, washed and fed a drop or two of soup. Sam was made warm and as comfortable as possible. He couldn't take any food. Claire ate ravenously, and turned chatty. Granny sent her in to cheer up her brothers while she washed and wrapped the bodies in the other room. Then she went next door to Katie McLeod's. Katie's face appeared in the window. "We're all right," she mouthed. "Go away, please." Granny gestured and pointed towards her sister-in-law's place, trying to convey with her eyes the dread news. The curtain was whipped shut. Moments later a male voice said: "Get out of here, old woman, an' leave us alone!"

She walked all the way back to young Dr. Simon's house on Alfred Street. She sat on the stoop and waited for him to return. Out of the surgery window his nurse glanced from time to time, not unkindly. Young Dr. Simon, the first physician ever to have his residence in the village, pale and solemn, followed her to the Lane. When he had finished inside, he said to her, "We need you very much, Mrs. Coote. You come to my office in the mornings if you can, and I'll tell you where to go and how to help." He touched her hand, the way Eddie used to when he needed her approval.

People entered the shops singly – no more than one or two or three at any one time in the baker's or grocer's or post office. No one deemed a haircut necessary. The clerks stayed behind their barricades, pointing and giving directions. When Granny entered Redmond's, unmasked and brisk, the few customers trapped there dissolved into shadow behind the pickle barrel or a stack of canned goods, giving out tiny warning coughs every few seconds. Any movement quicker than the cautious, underwater strokes of the fear-struck was enough to send panic rippling through a store or along the fringes of a street. When people did talk, as those in charge had to, they spoke in slow-motion, in tune with their hushed gestures. Still, rumours managed to slide freely along an edge of communal fear, snuffling at doorways, abbreviating gossip, waylaying the weak and faint-of-heart.

It's the Gerries, that's what! It's them new-fangled electrical lights, interferin' with Nature. It's the foreigners, we never should've let them in. It comes in on the trains, like all our trouble – goddamn the railways! It floats in on the wind: close your windows, close your mouths, close your hearts.

On Sundays the bells held their peace. During the week the whole village waited in dread for their sombre pealing. In Sarnia they had run out of coffins before the ides of the month.

Mrs. Stokes had everything ready for her at the Church each morning, afternoon and evening: food, aspirin, quinine, clean bedding. Dr. Simon was too busy now: he left instructions and disappeared. He looked sixty-years-old, and haunted. One by one the volunteers themselves went down. More were needed; few could be found. Neighbours lived in fear not only of the pestilence – now spread to every street and lane – but of the cry from the door or a child with a name on the verandah begging help, the dreadful decision to be made in an instant and unretractable. Mrs. Carpenter walked down to her sister's with a bundle of food, and stood for ten minutes on the front porch before entering the diseased rooms within. The next day her whole body went numb. She lay helpless while six-year-old David and the three-year-old peered at her with puzzled faces. Eventually David started to cry; Flora wandered into the shed and began to play with her doll. It was still light when Granny came by – her day spent in ceaseless walking, washing the living and the dead, holding the children stiffly in her arms, and bearing the useless medicines of the day – unable to utter a single word of comfort or goodbye. Flora's face was pressed against the front window. Granny turned and went in.

Ethel Carpenter was moving into the fever stage. Granny knew each of the stages well. Delirium had set in. Ethel clawed at her, her features distorted, her words jumbled but perfect couriers of rage. When Granny put a cool cloth to her forehead and tried to get some of the quinine down her throat, Ethel grabbed her arms, glared like a maenad, and spat in her face. She swallowed the medicine with a shocked gulp. Granny put the children in their room, soothing them with her abrupt gestures as best she could, and then walked over the marsh to the railway yard, where she got a block of ice and lugged it back in a heavy bag. She ran the tub full of cold water, chipped some ice in, and went to get Ethel. Her ranting had subsided but she was shaking all over, sweat pouring over the gooseflesh, her eyes goitered and stabbing at their tormentors.

By morning the fever had eased off. Granny woke from her doze to the sound of the children playing in the kitchen. She stirred some aspirin into coloured water; Ethel was able to guide it to her own lips. By afternoon the bloated lips were less black and the blotched skin had regained some colour. She felt Ethel searching her face for some sign; she hoped it was there. By suppertime when Granny returned from the Brownings on the far side of town, Ethel was able to take some soup. She was asking for the children. Granny shook her head. She went out to find some supper for them. David looked pale. She took him quickly into his room and then set up Flora's cot in the parlour. Flora was cranky. She wanted her mother. She was angry at the old woman who refused to talk. She wanted her brother to pull her in the wagon.

Granny went for the doctor. He was out. The nurse, glassy-eyed herself, said he was near collapse, please don't bother him. Granny was back at the Carpenter's gate when she heard the bell over the Presbyterian Church begin its sombre tolling, joined shortly by its sister muses. Flora was sitting on her mother's bed. Ether was in a deep sleep. Granny lifted the child away and after much difficulty succeeded in getting her off to sleep as well. Then she went in to the boy. The fever and aches were upon him. When she tried to get the medicine down, he vomited all over her. She had just got clean sheets on the bed and the shivering lad loosely covered, when the nosebleed struck. Granny shuddered. It took over an hour to get it stopped. Blood sprayed over her and the bedding and the boy himself as if someone had cracked a fire hydrant. David sobbed, then went silent with terror, then slumped back into an incredulous semi-coma, his eyes wide open, taking in every tick and rustle of movement in the room and in his rebellious body. He'll die of the fear, she thought. Like the others. Desperately she moved about as if she knew exactly what she was doing and every move were calculated to bring about instant recovery. She held his hand, stroked his brow, set some kind of hope in her face, and tried to forestall the exhaustion and the bone-deep ache threatening to overwhelm her.

When she woke it was dawn. She felt feverish. Flora was tugging at her sleeve. The boy seemed to be resting. She went across to Ethel. She was sleeping peacefully. She's dreaming of her husband, and the promised armistice, and reunion. Granny went back to check on David; his fever had ebbed, but she could not get the boy to open his eyes. Whenever she touched him, he cried out in a shrivelled, hollow voice, moaned, and went still.

Granny went again for the doctor. He was exhausted and resting for the first time in days. At the Church Mrs. Stokes begged her to take some soup to the McLeod's, then some quinine and camphor to three other families – with all members stricken – along Albert Street. She stayed on there to cook some meals, stepping over dazed or delirious victims who had selected any convenient spot to lie down and rest and refuse to move. They ogled her like a ghost or wraith whose presence was deemed not a little malign. Their arms floated towards a soup-bowl, then drowned in its weight. Eyeballs bulged, tightened, braced for the siege. Eyes pleaded, called out for explanation, justice, expiation. The children clung to their skirts, and put their fingers against her lips' refusal.

When she got back to Carpenter's it was almost dark. David's lips were swollen shut, his skin was scorched, and his eyes were squeezed tight against all the terrors the night would bring, but one. He opened them once, saw the dark angel bending down, then closed them for good. When the sun nudged her awake in the morning, Granny looked upon the dead boy, then his mother – awful in the doorway. Ethel Carpenter stared not at her son but at Granny; her look said: what right have you to save me and not him? Who are you anyway? When Flora came skipping up behind her and grabbed her mother's skirts in play, Ethel whirled and slapped her across the face. Granny started towards the stunned child, and Ethel glared again at her as if to say: *there, you see, you don't have it all to yourself.* The child's scream was piercing enough to startle the dead.

On the third Saturday in October the pestilence reached right into the heart of the village. Within an hour everyone who could listen heard the news that young Dr. Simon had succumbed to the disease he had helped so many to survive. The funeral was held on a Sunday, an unprecedented event. The cortege included most of those who could still walk, had already recovered, or were brave enough to venture out at any cost. The Methodist bell tolled for an hour. The other two bells had been struck dumb by the plague itself.

Granny did not attend the graveside ceremony. She was busy nursing Rose Underhill through the critical period of her delirium.

As she watched young Rose sweat out her fever, she felt the desperate need for speech. She had begun to realize that it was the fear – the unmasked, tongueless, viral fear of death, that tic under the heart's shadow – that was most hazardous, especially at the point just after the delirium panicked and fled, and the victim gazed into a mirror or a loved one's anguish and saw reflected there the bloated flesh, the charred skin, the frog's-stare that they had become – then was the danger most severe. Then came the lapse into the lethargy and ache of the final stage, out of which only the strongest climbed. Afterwards Sunny told her it was because she was unable to speak that so many people claimed she had saved their lives – people who did not even know who she was or whence she had come.

More recently he had told her that many victims still swore she had appeared to them out of nowhere like an apparition. Her silence served only to convince them even more of her incorporeal origins. Whereas they normally looked up into faces full of grief or shock or morbid foreshadowing, they were able in her case to fix on a face that was impassive and yet remotely beneficient with not a hint of fear for itself or the stricken one. With her as miraculous visitant, they had no call for a brave front nor would their cowardice, their pleas for mercy or a warm death, their last-second repentances – none of these be necessary or expedient. Indeed, she would respond to nothing but the courage they needed for the effort at hand – to survive or bear it out to whatever end this spirit from the earth's pantheon had foreordained but would not give away by nod or wink. Sunny had convinced himself that all this was true, that it really happened that way.

Sitting in Rose's bedroom, not knowing then that Wilf would outlast his wounds and return here to give her a son, Granny simply wished she could once again speak to her friend with a woman's compassion: once she had begun, the words would surely fall into place. Instead, she held Rose's hand like the others, and winced at the fever's tremor. I'm as helpless as she is, was her thought. After all these years, I still know nothing.

Granny had watched four people die – close up, and each different. Young David had opened his brave eyes, stretched out a hand to the comforting one offered him, and, released from his pain, walked towards the warm sunshine he sensed in the valley just over the hill. Mrs. Thibeault, who hadn't missed a Sunday school class in thirty years, sang hymns in her delirium, refused to believe her nurse wasn't a seraphic envoy, and shut her ears to her husband's cries of rage and despair in the adjoining room. Moments before the light dimmed in her eyes, though, she'd looked straight at Granny and said, "Cora, I'm sorry for what I done to you; can you forgive me?" A few minutes later she whispered, "Will you come with me? I'm scared of goin' alone."

Gladys Monk, a preacher's daughter, stared at her with the same unspoken questions any thoroughgoing pagan might have raised: Why me with three children and a one-legged unemployable husband? Why Dr. Simon, a saint? Why not you, withered and without speech, feeding on misery, without faith? Granny wiped her brow tenderly and trusted that Gladys' god was strong enough and forgiving enough to absorb the curses these wretched hypocrites intended for the heathen and the lost. When Gladys died, Granny closed her eyes as quickly as she could. "She looks so peaceful," Herb said, hobbling over to her.

In the last shack on the Lane, just before the dunes, Granny found the Wollochuk brothers, come here from one of the innumerable pogroms of Europe to work at the new foundry. They spoke little English. Both were down with the flu. The youngest was in the last stage, but some colour had returned to his cheeks and there was a glint of expectation, of astonishment, in the general glaze of his eyes. His brother, a year or so older, strapping and exuberant only a week ago, lay on the dirt floor, burning with fever. Alien syllables spurted from his lips in a frenzy, wild and sing-song and manic – like a holy-roller speaking in tongues with the devil half-a-note behind him. At the height of this babble, everything stopped. He lay ominously still, the death-rattle beginning to leak up his throat. Granny stood horrified, unable to believe such a powerful man would not make it out of the second stage. Afterward the recovered brother said to her, "Yevi die with the Black Death." His own recovery was deemed a miracle. It had to be.

"The plagues that followed a war," Cap said, "were not unlike the year-long sieges of an enemy castle in the late Middle Ages. The shells or missiles or fireballs or arrows fell at random in no fixed sequence. People died under them regardless of the precautions they took, the prayers they incanted, or their own self-evident worthiness. In such cases over a prolonged period of time, the random marauding of Master Death often cause the victims to blame themselves and prompt the survivors to look for new configurations of the heavens or new canons of blessedness to explain their own good fortune. A plague is a devilishly unsettling affair."

Rose Underhill got well. Flora searched in the garden for her brother. The bells tolled twelve times in all during that month. Five of the souls were Anglican.

Granny returned to the sanctuary of Arthur's shack. But not before she overheard, on her final trip to the Church kitchen, this one-sided 'conversation' between the Reverend Stokes and several senior churchwomen.

"She may be a bit queer – who isn't at her age – but I tell you, ladies, she's a candidate for sainthood, if you'll pardon the expression. You saw the way she worked throughout this dreadful month. A hundred times she risked her own life, going right into the dens of disease where no one else but dear Dr. Simon would venture. It was as if she knew that god Himself had chosen her for this mission of mercy and would offer her all the protection she needed. Rarely have I seen such an example of God's love and the spirit of Christianity 'bodied forth' in the actions of a single parishioner. My own feeling is that the dear soul, even though she's not attended service these many years, decided that during the few months remaining before her own imminent entry into paradise, she would bear witness in a way that would atone for a lifetime of neglect or perhaps even rejection. We must find a way of honouring such valour, such selflessness, such preeminent charity."

Safe in her own kitchen, Granny curled her hands around a cup of tea and said softly into the glow behind the stove: "I'm sorry, Arthur. I'm still here. You'll have to wait a little while yet."

With more than three-hundred-and-fifty thousand German troops incapacitated by the Spanish influenza that had already killed more than twenty million people worldwide, a halt was called to the mutual slaughter in Europe. On November 11, shortly after noon, Granny heard the bells ringing out the news.

2

Across the street a battered, lime-encrusted pick-up farted and coughed to a standstill in front of the vacant lot. A middle-aged fellow, swarthy and lithe, jumped from the open cab and, hands on hips, surveyed the site for the monument. Out of the passenger's seat hopped a very old man, who scuttled over to the younger man's side. They were both smiling.

The stonemasons, come at last.

51

1

The hardest thing Cora had ever done in her fifty-some years on this earth was to start walking up the Lane a few doors in order to tell Peg Granger that she couldn't keep the baby, she'd have to give him up. Peg had been looking after him while Cora nursed Bradley; she had not set eyes on the thin, quaking thing since. Ten years ago any decision not to accept the responsibility of rearing an orphaned creature – especially one with her own blood in its veins – would have been unthinkable. Those ten intervening years, then, had brought her to *this* pass: where, for two nights following Bradley's interment in the Point Edward cemetery (not many yards from Cap's resting place), she had lain awake rehearsing the speech she would deliver to Peg explaining why the child ought to be placed in the Sarnia orphanage. That Peg herself might offer to raise it with her own large brood – two of them almost grown – had not figured into her stream of excuses and pleas. I am old, she had thought, not necessarily in years but in experience, in the expenditure of human feeling. After all there was only so much pity or remorse or hurt, only so many tiny jolts of joy or vacant acres of grieving loss that any one set of flesh-and-bones could be expected to endure. Something had to be kept in reserve: for oneself, for the last days. It took energy to die, as Bradley had just shown her, and reserves of feeling. With Cap, she had known this from the moment she had interceded to prolong his life. There was to be no redemption for either of them, but at their age and in their circumstance something more vital and prized: a rich living-through of select hours, one by one by one. That she was there in his room to shepherd him towards death and towards some version of dying he could accept as appropriate, was never in question. But it had been only towards the end that she had come to the realization that Cap himself began to understand how much it was she who needed him. And when he died, she did not feel the stabbing sense of loss and dismemberment that followed the other deaths small and large, expected and sudden. She missed him, she would have to reorient her remaining days to exclude their daily collaborations, but Cap's voice persisted inside her – not as a lapsing memory or object of endearment (as the others were, still) but as part of her own speech and the thoughts it shaped – a live, thrashing verb whose argument would not be quelled, nor patronized by the simple affection with which the dead are decorated. You will never be anybody's memory, she said. Not like Brad, she thought sadly, resurrected, for what? To die again? To let me play out once again the mockeries of nurse and angel?

But a child, six-months old, who deserved to grow and breathe the wide air and become something in a world partly of his own making – that was asking more than she was capable of giving. That the dark gods were heartless she had known since she was eight or nine, and ever since had gathered evidence for the case against them. That they were capable of such a cruel jest as this, that their laughter was a joker's guffaw –she was now certain. In her own view, she was a tired, worn-out, benumbed creature, disenfranchised of the earth's aboriginal blessings. She desired now only the small comfort of a quiet, brief old-age, a little time to dream backwards, to reacquaint herself with the shy deities of woodland and brook. Then, out of the jester's joke-book – or the world's will as Cap might say – *presto*: the return of the prodigal son, dead twice already, and the babe, the boy – Eddie. How can I play the mother again? she thought in a panic. My fingers are arthritic, the skin droops from my cheeks, I've lost a tooth, my breasts are withered pods, I am a parody of motherhood, I haven't smiled with any semblance of innocence in ten years, the little tad will shriek when he sees me, as he did the first night in his fever. And what if I should dredge up, somewhere, some facsimile of mother's love, some fissure of untapped affection from which to nurture that miniature being – what then? I might die when he's four or eight or twelve, when he's still becoming and mercifully dependent – where will be he then? Who would care for him enough to embrace his orphaned heart? I am alone. I have no one. I rent two rooms in an old man's house. I have nothing to give but the derelict self. And what if some perverse miracle should occur and we both survive? When he's twenty and a man, I will be over seventy years – a creaking, babbling buffoon of a woman with cataracts and a weak bladder and the temper of a nanny-goat. It can't be done, she concluded. It would defy reason and nature. It was just the sort of misguided world-desire that Cap's all-seeing Will found to be as pathetic as it was common.

So when she had left her place that bright morning in October, she had irrevocably decided to have Peg carry the babe straight to the orphanage. She wouldn't even ask to see it. But in the few minutes it took her to reach the tracks and cross them, she changed her mind. She decided to take Eddie back with her. Reasons were never enough. Don't you dare laugh, Cap Dowling, she said, swinging her arms vigorously to work out the kinks.

"He's an angel," Peg Granger said. "Good as gold; you won't ever be sorry for keepin' him."

Cora had steeled herself against the worst: nights of fretful crying, daytime tantrums, the numb suffering under the fever of measles, chicken-pox, mumps, whooping cough or worse. She had seen it all, survived and not survived, and if she must do it again, she'd take the bit as far forward in her teeth as she could and smile through the grimace. Eddie soon let her down. He was a joy, a child with happiness and good humour born in him. He slept right through most nights, and the few occasions when the colic struck he needed only to feel her arms around him and the rhythm of the rocker to be soothed again. And just before he'd drift back to sleep, without fail he would grasp her by one of her thumbs and squeeze it. When he did get the measles, at two, he whimpered with the pain in his sunless room till she thought she'd go mad with her own, but the moment the fever subsided he cast the pale, blue gratitude of his eyes upon her and begged for a story. Even then he never took advantage of an illness, as most children quite naturally do. Whenever he complained, Cora was certain he was hurting somewhere. Whenever he had a choice, he chose joy.

Where did such feeling originate? she often wondered. I loved all my own children as much, doted on them more than I do Eddie because I was then young and vigorous and foolhardy. During the first winter she left him on his own more than she should have – when the arthritis or the black-mood would come upon her and leave her frozen to the bed for hours on end while the fire took its chill from the room. Once in February when he was starting to crawl everywhere and she lay in a daze dreaming of snow and fiery locomotion, she was brought back from the brink of something wondrous and lethal by a tug on her left thumb. She opened her eyes. Eddie was pulling himself upright so that his face was parallel with hers. He grinned in delight at his triumph and her sharing of it. He pushed his nose against her stiff cheek and made his 'choo-choo' sound, and laughed. She let him pretend he was drawing her upright by the thumbs out of her delirium.

Hap Withers, now over seventy, went up to the Lane to live with his son and family. He told Cora she could have all four rooms of the cottage if she wanted, for a dollar a year. All he needed to know was that the couch in his old room would be available on those few occasions when he felt like "coming home for a spell". He never did, and that room became Eddie's when he was ready for it.

When the decline of the village began in earnest, Cora found herself working only two days a week at The Queen's. She bundled Eddie up, tucked him in a wicker basket and hauled him on a sled down there with her, where the staff did their best to disrupt his even disposition. With her savings over the years she really didn't need to work full-time, but she found it helped to get out and around and see familiar faces and places, even though many of them jarred old griefs from their manageable grooves. By spring, Eddie was beginning to toddle and say his first words, and she could see that he deserved better than to be cooped up day and night with an old crone. On sunny days while she coaxed her vegetable patch into reviving, she tied Eddie onto a long rope so he could roam a bit and get the feel of what walking would be like when it was unfettered. Still, he had little company except the maids at The Queen's. She watched his eyes perk up at the animal calls of the urchin boys back in the dunes.

So she went out and arranged to do some housecleaning for Elizabeth Sanders, the schoolteacher and, incidentally, helped mind her slightly retarded son, Sammy (Slow-boat to the kids). She was recommended in turn to Maggie Hare, the wife of the manager of the freight-sheds. From time to time she worked also for Agnes Farrow and Mrs. Thibeault, scrubbing or ironing or helping with a meal on special family occasions. "She's quick and quiet," Mrs. Thibeault said all over town, "and what's more, she keeps her mouth shut afterwards. For some queer reason, the kids go for her."

Eddie was brought along – on a sled in winter, a wagon in summer – and spent much of his second year of life sitting on a pile of laundry, playing second or third fiddle to the children of the household, watching Cora as she watched him, and in general enjoying the constant shift of scene and character. His cheerfulness was so infectious that it often obstructed the premeditated whining of the little brats unofficially abandoned to her care. If Sammy lunged after a certain toy of his, Eddie would look hurt for a fraction of a second, weigh the effects of a pathetic glance at Cora, then pick up a less-prized object and before long begin to play happily with it. Sammy, who was a year older than Eddie but spoke with a slurred stutter, soon started to call her 'Gran-nee', despite repeated warnings from his mother. When Eddie's words began to arrive – fresh and tumbling over each other – the one he chose for her was Granny. And Granny she became, even at The Queen's among the staff and old-timers in the lobby, several of whom remembered most of the names she had accepted as her own in the long years past.

Granny in turn decided to give Lucien's name to young Eddie. Eddie Burgher. Why not? she thought. I have been Mrs. Cora Burgher now for eight years. It is the name I will take to my grave. All she ever told Eddie about his real parents was that his mother died having him in Toronto (which was almost the truth) and that his father had been an engineer on the Grand Trunk, whose locomotives still roared by their back window several times a day. "When you're grown up, I'll tell you all I know about them," she promised him after he'd been teased about it in the schoolyard. And, trusting her with a naive faith which afterwards led her to weep alone in her room, Eddie never once raised the subject again.

Still, many days were spent at the little cottage Hap Withers so generously provided for them. Sometimes Hap could be persuaded to leave his own clan and join them for a Saturday supper. Eddie, normally very shy around males, took to him immediately. Hap whittled him a tiny flute out of willow and showed him how to tease a skidding, dizzy music out of it. The neighbourhood near the tracks was populated not only by Hap's numerous grandchildren but by second and third generations of Shawyers, McCourts and McLeods. Gangs of ruffian boys combed the shadows at dusk with their signal cries, and bruited danger in the long afternoons of summer. One day when Eddie was three, they came for him, and she could no longer hold him back.

"We're just gonna play hide-and-go-seek," he begged her. "I won't go near the water."

From her place in the garden she scanned the flats and the blotches of bush, detecting the tell-tale signs of his running, the glee of his cries on the wind, the teasing crouch behind a shrub or sandbank, the soar of his little-boy voice *"Home free!"* against the derision and mockery everywhere about him. When he came home, he had a scrape and a bruise on his cheek. "I fell down chasing Jimmy Shawyer," he lied. Though he never really became part of the residential gangs, he would gladly join them for games or swimming at the beach, seemingly content to take what the moment offered and always always making up his own mind about what he wished to do or how far he would be absorbed into their tribal rites. Oddly enough they could not cope with his cheerful outlook or his irrepressible goodwill. One day when one of the bullies challenged him by jerking his prize apple out of his hand and chomping into it, Eddie grabbed him so quickly by the wrists that the bully's back was against a tree-trunk with his dignity collapsing before he could bleat out a protest. With the entire retinue watching (and Granny from behind her raspberry canes), Eddie glared at his tormentor, threatened him with a devastating knee, then slowly let a smile overtake his whole countenance, his laugh gently coaxing a guarded one out of the bully till they were both laughing and Eddie relaxed his grip and turned around to let the others know that it had all been in good fun, even the gesture of contempt that had initiated the coward's game. He's going to be all right, Granny thought. Whenever he can, he'll choose happiness.

One of the accidental side-effects of Eddie's playing with the neighbourhood children was his request, the summer before he entered grade one at Edward Street School, to be allowed to accompany Meg and Burt Granger to the Methodist Sunday School. He studied the indecision on her face with growing puzzlement, and the stalling tactic of "we'll see" died on her tongue. "Course you can," she said. She covered her guilt next day by showing excessive interest in his grooming, and when the Granger kids – all five of them – arrived to escort him up Michigan Ave., she said loudly enough for all to hear, "Put on your Sunday smile, Eddie". She was genuinely surprised when he reported that he had enjoyed the experience, that they did a lot of singing and hand-clapping, and a funny old fellow came in near the end and played hymns on the piano and sang till his eyes almost popped out. He went back every Sunday after that. Mrs. Sanders gave him lessons to bring home and learn. Granny sat with him and taught him the verses, one by one. Do I laugh or cry? was her thought at the close of each Sabbath. Not once did Eddie ask her why she herself never went to church.

By that Christmas, though, Eddie was in school and reading well enough to commit the innocent homilies to memory on his own. He's going to be a reader, too, she thought. Like his father. Then what?

2

The effects upon Point Edward of the new tunnel under the St. Clair River were not immediate. Indeed, people in the Point at first joined in the general bubbling of self-congratulation over having one of the century's great engineering achievements. 'Let the Yankees top that one' was a common sentiment. The first cheer was echoed when the passenger service from London – despite the skeptics and doomsayers – was maintained right through to the Point Edward wharf. And even though the ferries, which had begun service before the first log-hut was built on the site, were silenced forever, the car-shops and round-house and the freight-sheds to service the steamships were left intact and thriving – in the last boom years before the depression of the early 'nineties.

But when some strangers arrived one morning in 1893 and began chipping away at the brick and stone of the grand station as if it were some sort of pagan temple whose gods had abandoned it to the conquerors, people began to talk – on corners, in the barbershop, over tea, in smoky taverns. Then when the wrecking crew came shortly thereafter and proceeded to demolish the round-house without a care to what they smashed or burnt brazenly in the fields for all to see – the talk turned to whispers, half-hearted jokes, jittery silences between sidelong glances. No one was consulted. Everyone and no one knew what blow would next be struck or from what quarter. Half the town either worked in or supplied the wants of the car-shops, where every damaged coach or hopper in western Ontario was hauled for rehabilitation. It was discovered that a small local car-shop had been constructed in Sarnia near the new round-house which was near the new tunnel. A few men were transferred there. No one panicked yet. Obstinately the transferees stayed put, taking the trolley to work every morning. They were lauded from three pulpits.

In the spring of 1894, Harmon Hayman, the milkman, and his wife, Billie, returned home from a weekend visit with relatives in Wyoming. Harmon was unhitching the horse by the barn at the very edge of Alexandra Avenue when he heard Billie shout from the raspberry patch, a sharp 'yip' as if she'd been stabbed with tynes. When he reached her side and was relieved to discover no blood or bruises, he looked across in the direction of his wife's trembling forefinger and the sight that had stopped her speech for the first minute since they'd left Wyoming after dinner. Jeb Stuart's house was gone, as was his chicken coop and tool-shed. Posts, fencing, everything that was portable was gone. The vegetable patch was stripped clean. On Friday when the Haymans had waved goodbye, everything had been in its customary place, though as Billie remarked later and often, the Missus had been a 'mite teary-eyed'. The Haymans stood silently together and simply stared at an absence, a failure of permanency they could not accept. The Stuart house may have been the first of the Point Edward homes to be dismantled and removed overnight to the more favourable climes of Sarnia, but it was not the last. Between 1893 and 1901 the village population dwindled from well over two thousand to just seven hundred and eighty. Two of the churches closed for a year because they could not muster enough souls to pray for the town's survival. Folks kept a wary watch on their neighbours, searching for early signs of faithlessness, as they would invigilate sadly the homes of the quarantined that carried in them pestilence enough to undo them all.

Entire streets disappeared, ragweed and wild carrot rioted on the wounds, and boys flew kites over the grassy graves in the autumn. It was a common sight during these years to see a gaggle of wagons, tumbrils and overpacked drays moving up St. Clair Street towards Sarnia, invariably through the mist of a spring morning with the bricks and mortar and salvageable boards of their lives stacked beside chesterfields and weeping children, with forlorn dogs – foolish in their faith – trailing in the dust behind. 'Gotta go where the work is' was the universal plea of exculpation. It was a sad truth no villager would care to deny.

The thriving hotel trade, the verve of boarding-house life, the cosmopolitan flux of sailor, bagman, bigwig, drummer, carny and capitalist – all followed the romance of the rails elsewhere. As one of The Queen's philosophers put it: "We rolled to riches an' glory on the wheels of progress, an' now they just up an' run over us."

Eddie loved to sing, and though he remained shy whenever strangers were about, he announced that he was going to take part in the Methodist Christmas concert. He had agreed to be one of the three kings. "I get to give the gold," he said, "and I get to sing 'We Three Kings of Orient Are'." Granny showed commendable enthusiasm – it would be good for him to get on stage, get over just a little of his shyness, or more accurately, his natural reticence to put himself forward. "What are Kings of Orient?" he asked. "I don't think it matters," she said. "You're gonna come?" he said, and there was no answer but "Yes."

Thus it happened that Granny found herself in the basement hall of the Methodist Church on the twenty-third of December, 1899 to watch Eddie, a few weeks short of his eighth birthday, take his place on a makeshift stage, draped in ersatz gold lamé, with a cardboard crown on his temple and Mrs. Sanders' jewel-box in his hands and the nervous smile of Herod's Innocents on his beautiful, upturned face. Granny nodded politely to several of the older women she recognized, brushing aside their stares and resisting any of the droll rejoinders that echoed easily in her head. Mercifully, Eddie's number – shared with two other regal personages whose soprano was suspiciously high – came early in the programme. Eddie's voice was pure tone, like the A-note struck on the unvarnished oak of a xylophone. It sweetened all the air it sailed through. Granny was irked that several boorish women in front of her began mumbling before the last piano chord of the piece had faded.

For the remainder of the pageant Eddie stood at the back of the stage and poured his kingly gaze upon the manger and a host of other late arrivals. Only once did he allow his eye to catch hold of his Granny's, satisfy itself of something important, and return stalwartly to his duties. Long before the pageant ended with a multi-sided rendition of 'Joy to the World', Granny had ceased observing the drama before her. The music itself began to make an impression upon her, in particular the robust yet nimble choreography of the piano accompaniment. Naturally she was drawn again and again to the instrument itself, and to the fingers that hopped and sprang and babied and ambushed the high-strung keys, till the ancient carols and roundelays shook the cornerstones and belfry-beams of the Lord's edifice. Finally she dared to peek up at the eyes fathering such divine mayhem, and discovered them in search of her own.

One of the odd jobs Granny had taken on in order to supplement her diminished savings was sweeping out the Oddfellows' Hall each Thursday morning after the regular meeting the evening before. Beside the Hall sat the 'Coote shack' as it was known around town. It had not always been so, because when Arthur Coote arrived here in 1888 with his bride, Helen, to take up his duties as organist and choir director for the Methodist Church, a grateful congregation had talked the village council into leasing them a town-lot beside the Oddfellows' Hall, upon which they built with their own hands a pleasant cottage quite suited to a childless couple. Granny herself recalled the whitewashed siding, blue shutters and scrolled flower-boxes straining with geraniums. But when Helen Coote died suddenly around 1894, the place 'went to pot' by degrees. No more paint ever touched its outer walls, the shutters dangled, rotted, retreated into the weeds and stuck up through the winter snows like mangled thumbs. The geraniums had thinned, grown emaciate, sucked at the summer air, and suffocated just before the bottom fell out of the boxes and ragamuffin boys ripped the sides off them to make weapons with. But Arthur remained inside with his piano and his memorabilia. He continued to rouse congregations with unrehearsed Bach or Schubert, patiently assembled the wayward voices of his choir, and even found time to give piano lessons to a number of village prodigies. "I think your grandson may have musical talent," he said to Granny at tea after the concert. "I'd be happy to have him come over. Free of charge, of course." She didn't mention anything to Eddie.

On New Year's eve, the last day of the nineteenth century, an appropriately grand and progressive ball was held at the Oddfellows' Hall. Four blocks away, seated in a wooden rocker reading the 'Tale of the Sleeping Beauty' to a drowsing Eddie, Granny could hear the brass and drums and wild shenanigans, and long into the night and the first dawn of the new age, her sleep was disturbed by the whoops and fireworks and the casual discharge of rusty carbines.

When she arrived in the morning to clean up, she was not dismayed by the mess left by the celebrants. Eddie was safe in the hands of one of the Granger girls, so the whole day lay before her. She surveyed the debris and wreckage around her, mentally plotting a path through it towards a semblance of order. Humming to herself, she started in to work.

She didn't know exactly when but at some point the hum in her head began to match the tune on the piano coming faintly from afar. For a second she thought she might be imagining its coexistence, but when she stopped and arched an ear towards the high windows on the south side, the lilt of the Londonderry Air was unmistakable. It was coming from Arthur Coote's shack. At the tea after the concert she remembered him saying, "They tell me I'm a very good teacher; I wouldn't know about that, but I do get along well with children. You should come over some time and let me play for you". He had glanced down to include Eddie in his invitation, but before he could blush and continue, he was spirited away by an anxious-looking Mrs. Sanders.

When Granny stopped to eat her bread and cheese at noon, she heard the piano start up again. The song was a strenuous marching-version of 'John Brown's Body'. She mouthed the words, and tapped her toe on the dance-floor.

Come over some time and let me play for you.

Now was as good a time as any.

52

Every Thursday afternoon at three o'clock Cora Burgher, the cleaning woman, left her job at the Oddfellows' Hall and joined Mr. Arthur Coote, the Methodist choir director and church organist, for tea in his salon next door – every afternoon for two hours during the months of January through April. Tongues wagged without charity. On his sixty-fifth birthday Arthur Coote retired, and at the May-the-first dinner to honour his twelve years of faithful service, he delivered a touching valediction, concluding his remarks with the announcement of his engagement to "the lady who has been the subject of your most heartfelt concern these past months, dear Mrs. Burgher." In the respectful silence that attended his sitting down, a teacup shrieked.

When Granny explained that she could not be married in the Methodist Church, Arthur said with a patient smile, "Well, then, how about the Anglican? I was raised C. of E. and didn't terribly mind it." When she quietly let him know that she meant no church of any kind, he paused just slightly, as if he'd lost his cue for a second, and said cheerily, "Then it will be the judge's chambers for us, luv; just like my first time."

Though she didn't know him well then, she knew enough to realize how difficult a decision he had just made, for while he was no religious zealot, Arthur Coote had given many years of faithful service to his church, and he continued to be loyal to it – in spite of everything – until his death. Oddly enough, she felt even then that it was his own passionate commitment to certain ideals and principles which enabled him to understand so adroitly and without explanation her own position on the issue. At any rate he accepted her wishes as worthy of his own unquestioned support, and once he made up his mind, he was not one to glance back with a moment's regret. Although he loved to regale her with tales of his legendary and shady past on the frontier, he was not one to dwell there. Those events, sad or comic, had been completed, lived-through, like the scenes in a play writing themselves so naturally they were now freed up to be re-enacted, shuffled, mocked, or adored – by the survivors – as objects of wonder. Often she found herself wondering what he dreamt about in his deep unhaunted sleep, or if he dreamt at all. "I certainly *do* dream," he'd proclaim, feigning umbrage. "Why, last night I dreamt of sweet LuLu Sweet," and then he'd wink his all-purpose wink.

With her and later on with Eddie, Arthur was lively and fully at ease, jubilantly talkative, and thoughtful, ever alert to the tones under and between their words. With strangers he was still diffident despite his years on the stage, and with those he knew casually – like his acquaintances in the Church and town – he was courtly and reserved. It was only when he got *en rôle*, as he was when she first saw him at the Christmas concert, that the hobgoblins and trolls and minor demons were allowed into the light, and only when there was enough music to animate and camouflage. The sparkle in his eye came from something so clear and aboriginal in his childhood, it was unquenchable. He reminded her of someone she'd known almost fifty years ago.

"Just because we're gonna get 'hitched' in the judge's broom closet doesn't mean we can't do this thing in style," Arthur said. And he meant it.

On the first Saturday of June, as many of the labouring men traipsed home from the sheds and docks through the afternoon sun, and most of their women gathered on street corners or under the awnings of the shops on main street and all of the children roamed loose about the alleys and vacant lots – a buggy was observed conspicuously decamping from the livery behind the Queen's Hotel and heading, without shame, up Michigan towards St. Clair, where it turned and in a sedate jog moved towards Sarnia. Everyone who looked, and there were few able to resist, recognized the vehicle at once. It was the butcher's cart: actually a regular two-wheeled touring buggy of vintage descent with scuffed leather seats and applewood doors and a garish tin box improvised behind the passengers section just big enough to hold 'on ice' a morning's delivery of steaks and roasts. Bobbin, the buckskin mare, was in her accustomed pace, a pertness in the arch of the mane and the carriage of the tail. Someone had tossed a sprig of lilac over her withers.

In the buggy where the butcher's boy ought to have been sat three odd figures: an old woman dressed simply in blue with no bonnet to shield her silver locks or dampen the audacity of the single plum-blossom adorning them; a very old gentleman dolled up in his Sunday suit with boots polished and shining like sin and a gray top-hat to crown his snowy hair; and between them, a small boy with eyes bigger than his face, the mare's rein curled in the glee of his grip. Many of the bystanders stood open-mouthed, some waved reflexively, a few waved anyway, but if the occupants were aware of such accolades, they acknowledged them only with their eyes. Likewise, when several young defenders of the public faith offered them a choice of catcalls, they responded to none, choosing silence and the dignity of their own company. As the wedding-carriage made the turn towards Bayview Park and the county seat beyond, three smudged urchins raced up behind it, caterwauling and hurling ill-rhymed taunts. Bobbin kept to her course and soon the boys fell back, winded and unrepentant. One of them, half-heartedly, flung a stone.

Arthur turned around, doffed his hat, and said without raising his voice, "Thank you, ladies and gentleman, for those good wishes". And the carriage rocked with laughter.

Granny and Eddie moved from the cottage near the Lane to Arthur's house on St. Clair Street near the geographical centre of the village. Arthur put a fresh coat of whitewash on the siding and managed to get one of the shutters to hang straight before losing heart. The only hammers he could use without injury were part of a piano. Granny got busy right away planting perennials and a bulb garden and vegetable patch in the rich soil of the yard. Often the three of them ate lunch or supper on a checkered cloth spread under the giant hickory tree where gray-squirrels convened and robins made their seasonal stand. Inside, the house was warm and cozy, with Arthur's piano to brighten the evening gloom of winter and his stage-trunk crammed with the props and memorabilia of a lifetime. Arthur insisted that his wife would not work, as his savings and small pension would carry them comfortably as far as they could ever wish to go, but Granny decided to keep on working her two days a week at The Queen's, partly because Eddie was doing well enough at school to be a candidate for high school and perhaps even university where extra money would be needed, partly because she still enjoyed working somewhere, and mostly because Duckface Malloney needed her. With the decline of his business in the 1890's Malloney had seen the bustling, polyglot clientele of the boom years turn into a trickle of tired drummers and advance men. The aged chorus had longago deserted the lobby in favour of the barbershop and the livery stable near the racetrack. Just after the new century dawned and the last Grand Trunk car-man was removed to the Sarnia shops, Malloney had a slight stroke that left him with a shuffle and blurred speech. The only person he would speak directly to was "Mrs. Burgher", as he still called her. Granny relayed his weekly instructions to the rest of the bewildered staff. When Duckface was removed to Sunset Glades in 1908, Granny's life of formal labour came to an end. So did The Queen's.

Arthur Coote was born in England in 1835 and raised very much to be an Englishman all his life, a not-inconsiderable challenge for his parents who emigrated to Montreal when little Arthur was only nine. To this day he retained much of the tripping cadence of his upper-middle-class upbringing in London and all of the courtly manners. His father was a furrier, his mother a lady of the lesser aristocracy who, if she had not had the misfortune of being overbred, would have spent her life on the illegitimate stage of music-hall and melodeon. Even in colonial, bourgeois Montreal she managed to find music teachers for her only son. And a boarding school that ranked good manners above mere academic attainments. He was such a deft *improvisateur* at the piano that the amateur theatrical groups among the better class vied for his services as accompanist to their farces and burlesques. At eighteen he entered McGill to prepare for law or commerce or some useful adjunct profession his father could deploy in the fur trade. In 1858 at the age of twenty-three, he left his father's second-best desk and headed for Chicago, and thence to the gold fields of the Fraser Valley in New Caledonia, whenever that was.

"I wanted to get away, anywhere that wasn't my family and their transplanted version of what life was. More truthfully, I still had a lot of the old Nick in me, I was young and I was frisky. But I'll tell you, luv, I didn't last two weeks in the mining camps along the Fraser where we froze at night and burned all day and nine out of ten 'panners' hailed from 'Californy' and spoke no English. I was very bashful in those days and though I wasn't afraid, I didn't know how to go about obtaining the least bit of information useful in becoming a successful millionaire in the gold business. I broke my left thumb driving in my first claimstake, and I was so worried I wouldn't be able to play the piano again I ran all the way to New Westminster, got a splint put on it by a horse-doctor, and resumed running till I hit Victoria and the Pacific Ocean."

Once there he got a job in a bank counting other people's gold. To his surprise and delight, this frontier town – deliberately concocted to stand as a cultural redoubt against a riptide of Yankee pollutants – was alive with theatrical and musical enterprise. "I started out playing in the local orchestras and bands brought in to support the professional troupes from California. When the Chapman family started their stock company and built the Colonial Theatre, I joined them, playing violin, squeeze-box and piano, and getting a chance to act in bit parts. We even travelled back to New Westminster and followed the gold fields as far north as the Caribou County. But when we got back to Victoria, the company folded, the winter set in, most of the Yankees went back to sunnier climates for the season, and I slipped back into the safer world of gentleman's theatricals, where I was often asked to sing as well as play. As no gentlewoman would ever be seen on a stage, the younger men like myself played the female parts. I discovered that I enjoyed these excursions; I did not creep out of my shyness, I burst out of it with a patter-song or a frenzied rhetorical flourish in one of the melodramas, or in the wee voice of the female I found way inside me. Occasionally several of the 'commercial' actresses would be asked to join us and that was great because then we could act out the tragedies, even some Shakespeare. Naturally such fallen women were excluded from the respectable dances and balls that always followed the play."

But when the good weather brought a new crop of American speculators and entrepreneurs, Arthur was drawn back into the greasier, tinsel world of the troupes. In 1861 he joined for a spell the John S. Potter Dramatic Troupe, quitting his job so he could travel with them to the Lyceum in San Francisco. "And there I fell madly in love with our resident *ingénue*, Miss Lulu Sweet, seventeen-years-old with a figure like Aphrodite's daughter and the lilt of a Siren. We billed her as 'Juvenile Actress, Songstress and Danseuse', and she was all of those and more." "Do go on," Granny prompted. "When I asked her to marry me, I was thunderstruck when she said yes, and we eloped with half the San Francisco police force on our trail, but not before we'd tasted enough bliss to make our trespass unforgivable."

"How long did it last?"

"Longer than you might imagine. About two months, the first month being a disaster and the second a total disaster. The only thing sweet about Lulu was her voice. I think."

The bank, short on men of probity, gave him his job back, and for a while he drifted again into the 'English set' of Victoria society where his soaring tenor voice and his engaging piano were in steady demand. By the mid 1860's, though, the Colonial Theatre had become a music-hall – American style with minstrel shows, olios and seedy burlesques – and Arthur regaled Eddie and Granny with stories of his sneaking out of his respectable boarding house, incognito, and joining the banal drollery of the 'box-house'. Vaudeville sketches and routines were added to the minstrels in the late 1860's and Arthur's versatile pianoforte was judged one of the wonders of the age. "Once I even put on a blackface when one of the regulars took ill, and I forgot to wash it off before coming down to breakfast at Mrs. Tiffen's; well, she went white and green and raspberry, and before I could interpret her gasps and think up a plausible excuse – like having fallen down in the mud of Governor Street so perfectly flat that only the front of my face was besmirched – one of the young rams around the table quipped, 'Why don't you-all sing us a chorus of Massa's in de col' co'l ground?'"

Arthur was quick at arithmetic and helped Eddie almost every night during the long winters. Granny and Arthur took turns reading aloud to him. Between or after, there was music and treble singing and the sizzle of the coal-fire. Many hours were passed in silent reading, Arthur in his chair, Granny in the rocker, Eddie curled on the chesterfield. Arthur loved romance novels and devoured the latest works of W. D. Lighthall and Sir Gilbert Parker and a newcomer from the States named Zane Grey. Sometimes he would go on at length about a book like Lighthall's *The Young Seigneur* or *Nation-Making*, amplifying its idealism and its plea for a belief in essential goodness till his eyes glistened and even little Eddie stopped his reading to watch. Later on, when Eddie brought some of his high-school chums to the house, Granny would use her special way to cajole Arthur out of his reserve and soon he would begin with a song at the piano, perhaps a vaudeville classic like:

> I saw Esau kissing Kate
> And in fact we all saw three
> For I saw Esau, he saw me
> And she saw I saw Esau

then, warming up, burst fully into the role as the Lord High Executioner, at which point the lads would join in and whole scenes would be spun out, impromptu and cavalier and self-engaging, and the mood set for one or more of Arthur's true-life tales. When he was finished and Granny served the tea or mulberry wine, Arthur reverted instantly to his courtly, gentle self.

Arthur subscribed to all the papers and read them avidly. He regularly tried to engage Granny in political discussion, which turned easily into harmless jousts of words. He never did learn how she could dismantle one of his arguments, ardently developed from the latest hard-data and editorial disquisition, without recourse to similar foundations of fact and opinion. He tried to catch her reading anything but the local pages of *The Observer* but never did.

"How can you be so critical of the Tories when you haven't looked at one blessed statement they've made since Laurier got in?"

"I've known about Tories for a long time, since I was a child. I don't need to hear their latest lines."

"No wonder they don't consider giving women the vote."

"I ain't heard no one proposin' it."

"Well then, if you don't approve of Tory policies, then you must be a Grit, deep down."

"Worse than the Tories by half, they are."

"But in Canada you have to be one or the other. If you're not a Liberal then you've got to be a Conservative. Red or blue, it's an axiom."

"I'd put the axe to both of 'em."

"Don't be impertinent, Granny Coote."

Though he personally admired Laurier and his optimism about the Dominion's place in the twentieth century, Arthur was a worshipper of the late Sir John A. Macdonald and his 'national policy'.

"The greatest man North America has ever produced, and that includes Lincoln. The epitome of the nineteenth century. Out in British Columbia where he was hated and loved, we called him the Old War Horse. He brought us the railroad and saved us from the Visigoths of California. He had a dream bigger than all of us."

"Never cared much for the man," Granny said as gently as she could.

Arthur peered out of his reveries long enough to say, "Oh, why is that?"

"He was a Scotchman through and through." And I know, she wanted to say aloud, I met the gentleman once with his promises down.

Arthur seemed more puzzled than hurt by this odd remark. Finally he winked omnivorously and said, "With a Frenchman's liver, eh?"

"Don't be impertinent."

Granny told Arthur only those few facts of her own life which she felt he could withstand. How much he guessed or she gave away, she never knew. The great advantage, she thought, of *not* having shared the same past at our advanced age is that we can choose to reinvent those parts that please us most or offer the best chance for hope or are necessary to our mutual living, here and now. What we dream in private must remain mostly our own; there is not time nor words enough to begin the whole retelling, and that is a blessing in itself. On his side, Arthur tried many devices to get her talking, particularly about the 'pioneer days' as he called them. One day he left *The Observer* open at the local page where she would be sure to see the lead story; it was a feature interview with one Bessie Sycamore: Pioneer of Warwick Township. Through a series of adroit questions, the cub reporter was able to elicit from ninety-year-old Bessie the fact that she had borne fifteen children in a log cabin snug in the back-bush, eight of whom, she was proud to say, lived to adulthood. Moreover, she seemed to have spent six happy, unscathed decades cooking for the survivors and caring for two husbands, thirty-one grandchildren and uncounted great-grandchildren. Apparently she was now distressed because just this year for the first time she had been unable to bake her two dozen blueberry pies for the church bazaar. Arthritis, you know. And the secret of her long life? Hard work and prayer twice a day.

When Arthur came in from the shed, Granny gave him such a look of malevolence he thought he must have inadvertently poisoned her tea. But later, alone, she realized that the article had dismayed her as much as it had angered her. *Did* such people exist? Were there ever *lives* like that? Was it possible to watch seven children perish – who had ripped their way out of your flesh and seized the air you offered them in hope and trust – could anyone suffer that and still go on baking blueberry pies as if God and not the world mattered? Someone, she thought bitterly, has a lot to answer for.

"You might say I squandered my youth leading a double life," Arthur said, recovering from his nap and trusting that she was awake in the chair next to him. "I couldn't stay away from the minstrels or the 'Free and Easies' as we called them back then. When Charles and Ellen Kean came to Victoria, I was in the front row of the Theatre Royal, I could hear the echo of the illustrious Edmund Kean himself, I vowed ever after to hold my appetites in check and feed only on a steady diet of *Hamlet* and *Richelieu*. I offered my services to one of the Anglican churches and rediscovered the organ. Still, I'm ashamed to admit I was not only present in 1875 when Charles McDonald's 'Occidentals' performed *Black-Eyed Susan* and pranced about the stage like trained bears, I was in the wings supplying some of the traitorous music. Nevertheless, that night marked a turning point in my life, for I saw a side of the theatre, and of theatrics, I had refused to acknowledge before. This American impresario had gathered together from each of the tribes of British Columbia nine native people whom he billed as 'the Occidentals' and described on his posters as 'four squaws and five men…the best specimens of the children of the forest'. Besides a repertoire of hideous farces in which he'd trained them to mime a grotesque self-parody, these wretches performed nightly an Indian War Dance, contorted their bodies into 'sixteen different pyramids' and concluded the evening's spectacle with the Indian Feast of Fire. You won't believe this but this so-called aboriginal ceremony consisted, as the playbill proclaimed in bold type, of 'eating fire, drinking burning naptha, devouring burning torches, breathing smoke and fire, and pulling long poles from their mouths'. And this travesty was put on at the Theatre Royal before a cheering Governor Douglas and all the local, highborn pooh-bahs."

Arthur sighed deeply. Granny shifted in her chair, audibly.

"Later on I heard that this monstrous troupe was feted in Philadelphia and Washington during the 1876 celebrations, and then went abroad to the Crystal Palace in England to be gawked at by thousands of foreigners. In Paris they were booed off the stage because they failed to closely resemble the inhabitants of the Punjab. Shortly after that night, a new customer came into our bank, and a few months later I was engaged."

As Arthur was fond of saying in jest, it was the longest engagement in recorded matrimonial history – eleven years and twenty-nine days. Helen Driscoll had come out to Victoria with her father, a Methodist preacher, and although the old man liked Arthur a great deal, he forbade his daughter to marry an Anglican, even a lapsed one. In desperation Arthur embraced the Methodist faith but apparently after too much doubt and reflection. When the old bigot finally died in 1887, they married. By this time Arthur was a full-fledged communicant and part-time organist of his bride's church. When a position as full-time organist back in Helen's hometown became available, the newlyweds returned east to London, Ontario. A year later internal politics and factional rivalries in the London parish prompted Arthur and Helen to accept the offer of the Point Edward Methodists, who were more than happy to have in their midst a musician of Arthur Coote's standing.

"But you still love the old ditties and the drumrolls," Granny said. "How did you hide them all those years?"

"I only disguised them a little," he laughed. "I don't think there was a soul who didn't notice."

She waited a while until some tone in the shuttered room had imperceptibly shifted, then she said, "Why did you really give it up?"

He let the question get comfortable before responding. "I wanted something… *authentic* in my life."

Granny murmured reassurance.

"I wanted, after a lot of wandering about, to come home."

They listened to the tic toc of the rocker through the room.

"I'm still here," Granny said.

53

1

When Eddie went off to Victoria College in Toronto to study philosophy and literature in the mellow autumn of 1910, the house was a lot quieter. And they were getting old, of course – Arthur and Granny – overtaken now by sudden naps, drifting into snoozes in the sunlight through the window, into dozes later denied, into lapses of thought or purpose, bickering pleasantly over the imperfections of memory. Whatever the season, Granny went out every day to check the mail for letters from Eddie, to buy the few groceries they pretended to need each day, to nod hello to the few souls she still knew who also could get up and about, and to listen from shy corners to the buzz of gossip among the young who barely remembered her – touched by their enthusiasm and by their sense of having inherited this time and place whole and without obligation. In the winter she pulled Eddie's sled to Redmond's – where Sandy now presided – or even up to the coal dock for a bushel of coke. Sometimes she would stand on the wharf and look north at the Great Lake and just wonder, till the chill took her and a brisk walk home warmed her up again. Arthur's gout kept him indoors much of the time, though he always came out once a day in the growing seasons to offer editorial comment on the flowers or vegetables or the trimming of the hedges Before he would be allowed to go back inside, they would promenade arm-in-arm around the perimeter of their land, admiring the view over the marsh clear to the River before turning homeward. Once, Granny overheard young Ethel Carpenter, who assumed all old people were deaf, whisper loudly to her husband: "Now ain't they a cute pair!" Granny winced, then smiled inwardly all the way to the stoop.

Eddie wrote them every week while he was in college. In the summers he worked for the Sarnia newspaper, *The Observer*, and lived at home. He had many friends, in Toronto and here in Lambton. Eddie assumed there was good in the world and spent much of his time searching it out, though Granny could see that the books he studied and the sights he'd seen in the big city had left him with little doubt of the magnitude of his quest. But he was not one to flinch from its pain, she could see that plainly. He had courage, and a winning heart. Friends flocked to him, and many of them, she thought, would remain steadfast in the causes he had persuaded them foolishly to undertake with him. Already he was talking about graduate studies, of being a professor or lawyer or someone who could move the earth an inch or two just by being in it. Arthur and Granny would sit at the kitchen table in the lamplight and jointly compose letters to him, Arthur's English-schoolboy 'hand' flowing across the white page carrying thought and feeling and happening into elegance and some kind of permanence he only vaguely comprehended. She was the one – always – to read back what they had written in a sober cadence that made Arthur laugh till she swatted him with the letter and started over, daring him to intercede. When the return letter arrived faithfully within the week, they sat on the chesterfield taking turns presenting it, re-enacting the best moments many times, constructing lovingly in their minds the unfolding biography and pageant of their grandson's life. You won't believe me, Cap Dowling, Granny said to him one day, but I am happy.

Arthur died at 1 a.m. in the morning of April 3, 1912, a month shy of his seventy-seventh birthday. Granny was beside him on the chesterfield where he'd been resting, close to the stove. His recurrent pleurisy had turned to pneumonia. He died peacefully in an interval between dreams. Just before he closed his eyes for the last time around midnight, he smiled wanly at the companion of his latter years and asked her to hold his hand. When she did she found his grip resolute. He was too weak to say anything more but as the lids came down, she saw something in the eyes she interpreted as 'forgive me' before it was extinguished by a twinkle. About one o'clock his breathing stopped. She permitted his hand to grow cold in hers.

Of all the deaths and departures she had endured in her seven decades of living, Arthur's was the most simple and most touching. For the first time in her life Granny found she could mourn with a pure and biding sadness, a sadness uncomplicated by guilt, remorse, rage, helplessness. Arthur lived a long and eventful time on earth, taking little and giving much. Near the end he could talk of heaven as if he believed it was waiting for him. He was one of the lucky ones.

Eddie felt terrible about having to go straight back to college to write his exams, but he was reassured by the steady look Granny gave him that said, 'You *have* to; I'll be all right'. Though not unexpected, Arthur's death had dealt Eddie a sideways blow. He was bearing up well, but when he came home again for the summer, she would have to keep a close watch on him.

Arthur's funeral was attended by most of the village and the outpouring of sorrow was largely genuine. Granny noted that many of the young people, students and choir members under Arthur, who came over to offer their condolences did not seem at all sure exactly who she was, other than Granny Coote. It was an odd sensation and one that disquieted her more than the tedious eulogy by the recently arrived Methodist minister. Arthur's tombstone stood in a perpetually sunny spot on the south-west side of the little cemetery. Granny noted how much it had filled with graves since the lonely day when Cap was put under the horse-chestnut in the north-east corner. She recognized too many of the names cut in stone. After the interment, she stood apart with Eddie and gazed at the ground that now possessed her husband – body and spirit – thinking that this was a fitting spot for him and most of all for her. I'll be laid right here, Arthur, she whispered to him, not a yard away. In the meantime, you behave yourself.

As they turned to leave, Granny took a step towards Cap's grave, acknowledged it, then swept her eyes across the plain tablet a few feet to the south of it. The strange syllables of Bradley's name hovered on her lips. She moved into the silence and dropped the flowers she had been holding. She felt Eddie's stare, and for a moment dared not turn to face him. In the carriage all the way back to the reception hall, she waited for his question. If he asks, she thought, I'll have to tell him. I have no choice.

Eddie said goodbye at the station, clinging to her as he used to with the blind trust of the child he no longer was.

2

It was good to hear Arthur's piano played again. Though it had little of Arthur's sprightly thunder in it, Eddie's performance was vigorous and high-spirited. Quite often his journalist friends would come down to take him out for the evening – usually dancing at Lake Chipican – and linger for an hour or so to sing along with him, and flirt with Granny in what they took to be an outrageous manner. "Isn't a gal at Chipican could hold a candle to you, Gran," one of them invariably proclaimed as he whirled her about carefully to a musical flourish from Eddie. "You must've been a ballerina," they'd tease, "A dance-hall girl in Dawson City!", "Come on with us, Gran, we won't tell them how young you are."

One of them, Ralph Sifton, had an automobile which he lent to Eddie on occasion so that he could take her for drives in the country on Sunday afternoons. She was amazed not only by the mechanical noise-maker they were miraculously seated upon but by the way in which the countryside it roared through had changed since she had grown up in it. She realized, too, how long it had been since she had driven out here on a cutter with Lucien Burgher. The bush was gone. A few strands of timber had been overlooked and left to brood over the wide spaces between them, rolling with wheat and oats and neatly fenced pastureland. Here and there secondary scrub growth nudged upward through swail or lowland; the primary forest, born in the slow surge of millennial time, would not come again. On the way home she had a hard time swallowing.

In the spring of 1914 Eddie graduated with honours from the University of Toronto. He desperately wanted her to come to the convocation and even arranged for Ralph Sifton to accompany her on the train. But she took ill a few days before the event – the doctor diagnosed it as severe grippe – and she had to send Ralph off alone. She was furious with herself. Even now nearing seventy-four, she was rarely sick except for her rheumatism, and that was never disabling. When Eddie came home, though, there was no hint of disappointment in his face. He modelled his cap and gown for her, he hung his framed baccalaureate next to the tintype of Arthur at the piano of the Theatre Royal, and then brought out the photographs Ralph had taken of the ceremony with *The Observer's* best camera. He escorted her to supper at the Colonial Hotel in Sarnia – still bustling with its own celebrations as the nation's newest city – and told her of his plans.

Using the money Arthur had set aside for him in his will, Eddie said he was going to return to Toronto in July to begin studying for his master's degree in comparative literature. That would take him about eighteen months, after which he would look for a job teaching in one of the small Maritime colleges or right here in Ontario where there was talk of expanding the university in London. He hoped to continue his studies, but for the near future he wanted to find a place where he could be useful and self-supporting, a small town preferably where he could put down roots and where he could bring his granny to live out her days with him.

"You can't say no, Gran. Arthur would have wanted it to be that way."

What could she say?

Eddie began to write to her as soon as he had returned to school, every two weeks as he had done since Arthur's death. But Arthur was no longer here to write out the words for her or tease and cajole in his special way so that what she ended up saying to Eddie was always lively, witty and charged with good humour. But seated alone at their table with her own thoughts and the elusive words to pin them on, with a shaky pen unaccustomed to writing of any kind let alone the free-fall of her inner speech, she found she could not in any way recapture the verve of those joint letters. Moreover, she had little to narrate in the way of current events; indeed, as she told him in one letter that first winter, "the word 'current' and your granny aren't to be seen in the same dictionary." She had lots of thoughts – she'd never been short on that score – but discovered that it took so long to scratch and blot them on paper they soon tumbled over one another and came up nonsense. "Try to picture yourself talking to someone," Eddie wrote back, "Arthur or me or a friend on the street corner." She occasionally had some success when Cap was in the room visiting, until he started to chip in too many of his own silly ideas. Gradually the task got easier, and though her replies were stilted and not newsy enough, she did manage her four pages a month.

In fact, during the unusual quiet of the summer of 1914, she came to the realization that what remained of her life was in Eddie's hands. Less and less did she attend to the daily traffic of human affairs she had spent a lifetime observing and recording. The great events of the world beyond her own township – elections and reciprocity fights and skirmishes in Africa and the Sea of Japan, which had never been able to hold her attention for long – now receded almost completely from the foreground of her existence. She lived for Eddie's letters and for the essence of him they conveyed minute by minute for her appraisal and concern. We have lived past our three-score-and-ten, old man, she said to Arthur who had been called in at the last second to help with the wording of a sentence. And we haven't got a lot to show for it. We tried. I know I did. I bore four children. I stayed put for seventy years, hoping to have planted here in this barren place something permanent, some memorial to my much-vaunted suffering. Nothing took hold. Nothing but Eddie out of all that. Eddie was a gift of the near-sighted gods, an oversight perhaps in the frenzy of their careless blundering – but we took him and fostered him, and let him be. Already I am learning to live through his eyes. May he prosper, may he love and marry and father a dozen children, each of them obsessed with living; may the roots of that tree be numerous and strong and deep as the underground rivers that feed them.

There, Arthur. Now, if only you could write that down for me.

In October Eddie wrote to say that he had decided to 'join up', that he hoped to complete his course work before he was sent overseas, that he would start in on his dissertation as soon as he got back, and that in any case he would come home for a few days before leaving. She wrote and begged him not to come home. But this time he could not bring himself to do what she wished.

54

1

Granny Coote sat at the window of her new house and kept a faithful watch on the workmen across the street. Mr. Stadler had brought along two helpers to assist him in unloading the rough slabs of limestone he would smooth and shape into a memorial pillar over the weeks to come. Sunny Denfield had shown her the drawings – deft pencil sketches on brown paper – and so she was able to speculate not unpleasantly about how these raw-cut stones might be teased into the elegant promise she'd seen on paper. The stones were very heavy. They had to be eased down ramps from the back of the truck – as dented and dusty as the old man's face – and then skidded over to a spot near the site itself. The young men appeared to be sons or nephews of the builder; they were as lithe and wiry as he, and moved with animal ease. Their skin was tanned and roughened, the mark of men who spend much of their life outdoors. The old man, who came almost every day, was a delight to watch: he hopped about like a rabbit on a griddle, firing off instructions (in a strange, jabbering tongue) that were respectfully ignored, lending a hand when it was least required, then unexpectedly lapsing into a state of deep repose from which he observed and blessed the intricate actions of his son (surely he must be Stadler's father) as if from a dream. When they sat down on one of the stone for a brief rest, the old fellow seemed to dominate the conversation, speaking in a low voice and gesturing as if he were telling long, thoroughly-weathered stories. There is something very familiar about the Stadler family, Granny thought, but then I've lived so long and seen so much around these parts, everything looks familiar to me.

2

Eddie began writing to her as soon as the troops reached Valcartier camp for the second phase of their training. Eddie had joined up in the new year when recruiting for the Second Canadian Division began in earnest. Five of his college friends joined with him as part of one of the university companies who would form replacements for Princess Patricia's Canadian Light Infantry already overseas and in combat. Such students were given permission to carry on with their studies during the local training period, which ended in March, after which they entrained for Valcartier. Granny knew Ralph Sifton well and though she had not met them, she felt she knew the other four because they had been part of Eddie's conversation for two or three summers. As she read over each name of 'the Vic platoon' in Eddie's letter, a picture of past exploits – college-boy derring do and hijinks and irresistible good humour – instantly formed in her mind. Besides young Ralph from Sarnia (studying law as his father had), the platoon included Cliff Strangways from British Columbia (graduate history); Sandy Lecker from Waterloo County (biological science), the first of his family ever to attend university; Bart Ramsay (graduate philosophy) whose Toronto family had enough money to protect him from the temptations of academia, but couldn't; and Henry Potter, raw-boned prairie lad who was studying French in hopes of joining the foreign service and seeing parts of the world that weren't flat. Although they didn't all get into the same platoon, they were part of a single company, an inseparable fraternity.

In April Eddie started writing once a week, his letter arriving on Tuesday morning where she was waiting in the Post Office on Michigan Ave. to pick it up. She never opened one before she got back home, nodding obscurely to friendly or anxious faces on the street and once there making herself a cup of tea to sip on as she read the words aloud at first, then silently – many times.

"Valcartier is a pleasant surprise considering the rumours we were foolish enough to believe in advance. It's a hug complex of barracks, drilling grounds, rifle ranges and mock battlefields – all cut right out of primeval bush. I get the strangest sensation firing my Ross .303 at a painted target two hundred yards across a scraped pasture and looking up at the evergreens behind them which roll unbroken and impassive for a thousand miles north of us, north of anywhere. Do you know what I mean?

Yes, Eddie, I do, though I haven't got the words you have to describe it.

"Bart, our city-boy, went for a stroll in the woods last night, as if he were off to High Park in pursuit of pretty girls – of which there are none, pretty or girlish, within twenty miles – and promptly got himself lost. The Vic-platoon volunteered for the search party, and it was Cliff, who grew up in the Kootenays, who found him on the second tallest branch of a spruce tree, where he claimed a black bear had driven him out of spite. Cliff is of the opinion that it was a sasquatch, abetted by the shadows and on overheated imagination."

Granny found it a daunting task to respond to these weekly outpourings – four or five pages of elegant script capturing a side of Eddie she knew she would not see if he were at home – closer, safer. But there was nothing else to do but sit at the kitchen table in the afternoon sun or the evening lamplight and try to make the pen say the thousand things racing through her. By the time the Second Division was ready to embark for England in May of 1915, she was able to write several pages of stilted prose, sweating laboriously over it for two days. In part Eddie made it a bit easier by asking questions about his chums in the village or about local events she herself had long ago excluded from her sphere of concern: "Who's joined up lately? Did they finally get Hitch? Or

Sandy Redmond? Who's to replace MacPherson on the council? Will you be sure to clip the theatre items from *The Observer?*" And so on. Though replying to these and making an occasional comment herself helped to fill up some of the weekly quota of two pages, she was not pleased with the results. Her first letters were choppy, disconnected pieces; she felt she was not conveying anything of herself in them, and every instinct she possessed told her that Eddie was waiting out there, and listening with his heart for some force behind her words more tender and more compelling than the voices he was hearing daily inside him and all around. I can't do it, Eddie, she thought sadly. I never learned. I'm too old, too stubborn, too stupid.

In desperation, as he prepared to sail for England and foreign battlefields thousands of miles away, she began to tell about a few of the simple follies that peppered the everyday life of the village and upon which she had begun to cast an ironic eye. To her surprise she found the effort much easier than she thought it would be – closing her eyes and recapitulating a scene or a conversation overheard and pressing Eddie's face as close to her own as she dare. "You remember old Ollie Jensen who used to be reeve, and was always suspected of treating his horses worse than his wife? Well, he enters his prize pacer in the May Day races down at the track, and when his driver shows up drunk, he decides to hop on the sulky himself. But Bomber, his gelding, sees his chance to get even for past whippings and indignities, and just as the horses come up to the starting line, Bomber breaks, rears up and stops as still as a stone right in front of the steward's stand. Well, you can imagine the cries of encouragement and helpful advice that started raining down from the bleachers. Ollie himself goes puffy and red in the face, like someone was pumping air into a tomato, and lashes the gelding's well-padded rump with his whip, which makes the creature jump an inch straight up in the air but not a fingernail forward towards the other pacers now disappearing around the first turn. 'Try sweet-talking, Ollie,' somebody shouts from the cheap seats, and Ollie pops out of his seat like a plucked radish and stomps towards Bomber's front end to whack him with the butt of his whip. But the victim, with better timing than he ever showed in a race, steps smartly into his hobbles and sprints off towards his companions. Ollie then breaks the whip over his knee and has to be helped off the track by his wife to avoid being run down by the approaching stampede. You never saw a happier horse in your life, running as free as a bluebird alongside of the others without the burdensome drone of a driver. He finished in a dead-heat with his old rival."

"The fellows want to hear more of your stories about the village. I assure them you're not making them up, but they're not inclined to believe me. Bart wants to know if Bomber had to share the purse with his master?"

Granny found herself in turn asking more and more about the fellows. "How did Bart make out with the nurses at the camp dance? Was Henry too shy to ask anyone?" "Bart naturally appropriated the prettiest girl among the two dozen allotted to our battalion and danced with her the whole evening. Unfortunately for the course of true romance, she was the worst dancer, stomping on his feet so often he had to be carried to the barracks and soaked up to his ankles in ice for three days. He claims he purloined a kiss behind the packing cases. As you surmised, Henry was too shy to ask for a dance, so Cliff did it for him. I don't think Henry had ever seen anything but a square dance (*you* remember them, I reckon), but he adapted remarkably well. I danced with a girl from London and one from Fredericton. How odd to be holding, as closely and intimately as sweethearts, two complete strangers from different parts of the continent coming together in a Quebec bush-camp for the sole purpose, we hear, of shooting to death a million Germans."

"You asked about young Redmond, the third generation of his family to embrace the grocery trade. Well, he did join up last week, and the talk around town is that circumstances forced him to do so. It seems that Grandma Quilty caught young Red with his thumb on the meat-scales, and thinking she had her umbrella in her hand, she started to whip him with it and call for the constable. It turns out she was carrying a large bunch of beets just plucked out of the vegetable hamper. She whapped him with seven or eight death-blows so hard that the beet-juice bled all over his face and ran down his white shirt, and he was laughing and yelling at the same time when his mother comes scuttling out of the storeroom and sees him tipped backwards on the butcher's block covered in gore, and she thinks he's dead and faints into her husband's arms. You can imagine the variations of *that* tale going around for the third time! The army will be a relief for young Red. By-the-by, did Sandy's father manage to get his corn in alone?"

"We are to complete our basic training here in Shorncliffe in the picturesque county of Kent. What a relief after the stories being told about First Division's autumn and winter in the rains and muck of Salisbury Plain. Here it is dry and warm, we are surrounded by tropical green and curious, anachronistic villages with quaint names like Dibgate, Otterpool and New Inn Green (very old). Our own bell-tents are pitched on St. Martin's Plain. Among the trees and shrubbery on every side we can see church steeples shining in the sun, and hear medieval bells tolling the hours. Ralph sprained his ankle during a bayonet drill. He didn't take kindly to suggestions that he engage the services of his prominent daddy in a lawsuit against the inventor of the Ross Rifle. By the way, Cliff has just learned of the death of his grandfather, and is feeling very remorseful about not going to see him before embarkation: it seems Cliff is interested in the history of the region and had promised that he would record the old tales his grandfather often told about the pioneer days in New Westminster. I told Cliff about Arthur, and it turns out that his grandfather knew Arthur quite well. This was confirmed recently by Cliff's mother. Cliff would like to hear from you about any of those great yarns Arthur used to tell us. He won't believe my versions, and I don't blame him. Henry is terribly homesick. Any advice?"

So it was that Granny came to add or interpolate into her letters whole paragraphs addressed directly to individual members of the Vic-platoon. "This is for Henry only" she would print in caps, teasingly, for she knew they sat around and read her letter together and likewise began to pen postscripts of increasing length to Eddie's own accounts. She found herself spending entire days in composing responses, part of the time spent in reflection on past events in reference to the questions and requests raised for her. Cliff could not get enough detail about Arthur's days in the theatre of the 1860's, and she found herself rummaging through Arthur's trunk, sometimes parting with a cherished playbill – the names receding but still legible – for the boy's sake, though she was quite certain nothing would ever fully assuage the sense of regret he was suffering so far away. Minor detail elicited from Cliff's mother would be duly relayed back to Granny and in some cases half-told stories from each side were dove-tailed to make a complete one, so that Arthur himself, through the eyes of the deceased Mr. Strangways, was enabled to speak to her with fresh and vicarious verve. When Sandy Lecker casually asked about farming techniques in the pioneer days, she found herself talking about events and impression she had not even dreamt about in more than twenty years. Sandy was a farm-boy and he was willing to brave the gentle derision of the others.

"Ralph and I took our furlough and went by train over to Salisbury and thence by car towards Stonehenge. The cathedral is as magnificent as the pictures we've seen of it, but no picture can replicate the awe we felt standing in the nave and looking heavenward, and feeling the incredible stillness created by the thousands of vaulting line so cunningly crafted they appear as natural as rivulets in the stone walls of a vast cavern. Next day we stood together on the English grass more than two thousand years old and stared without comprehension of any kind at the primitive, Druidic tablets aimed with imperfect magnificence at the stars. It was only when we passed by the old barracks and drilling ground on the road north that we came to realize we were preparing for war. The charred mud and filth of the rotting barracks looked to us very much like the trenches in Belgium we've been hearing about since the day of our arrival. Nevertheless, the peacefulness out here in the English countryside is real, and is as deep as the stones of Tintern Abbey, where we hope to go if we're not sent across the Channel."

But they were on their way to France on the seventeenth of September and thereafter not a single reference was ever made to that pastoral quietude. In his last letter before leaving Shorncliffe, Ralph typically made light of the impending event: "We went on manoeuvres yesterday for the sole purpose of proving that Sir Sam Hughes' secretary was right after all, that the 'MacAdam shovel' which bears her name (and a number of unofficial ones provided free of charge) will not only defy German bullets but dig a six-foot trench with the aid of the human hand. Sir Sam steadfastly refuses to believe reports, spread by the envious Brits, that the shield won't stop a B-B at thirty yards and, lacking a handle, the spade is useless as a delving device. Bart suggests the whole thing is a Canadian plot to have the Kaiser's army laugh itself to death."

Several of the boys now wrote to her separately as well as collectively in the packet-sized letters that left the postmistress puzzled and not-a-little suspicious. Granny in turn continued to compose equally impressive omnibus editions in addition to the smaller, private confidences to 'her boys'.

"There are no words to describe the battleground," Eddie wrote. "Nothing could have been done to prepare us for it. Our training over here was cut short when we were sent directly to the front as part of the newly organized Canadian Corps (chalk up one for the colonies!). They tell us we're in Flanders near the Belgian village of Vierstraat, south of Ypres. Some of the ground we occupy has changed hands several times already and the devastation here is complete. I expected to see battered houses and charred barns and rotting orchards, but there are no such human signposts anywhere. Between our trenches and the German's a few hundred yards away, and behind us for over a mile, there is not one distinguishing landmark; the outbuildings have been flattened, pulverized by repeated shelling and then tramped upon by marching feet so thoroughly into the mud there is not the slightest hint of a farm ever having been. Occasionally you step on something firm underfoot, and if it isn't a corpse, it's likely to be the submerged stump of a tree, blasted and then buried, with its roots still gripping something grim that lurks below us everywhere. As we approach our front-line position or as we're returning to billets for our stint in reserve, we can see the shattered orchards or half-burned rooves of hay barns, enough to remind us of what we must have ruined. As I peer ahead of me over the sandbag parapet, searching for prey with my sniper's eye, I cannot see any sign of where the ground itself was – the ruts, craters, stinkponds, the gouged and shredded turf are an alien landscape, bearing no resemblance to any of those earthly contours we have inherited and cherished for centuries. It is moon-ground, the erg-desert of my nightmares. Sorry to be so depressing, but I do need someone to unburden this on; among the fellows I have to be careful about each word, each gesture, each well-intended jibe: the feelings we have for one another are as fragile as they are deep; that is one thing I am learning about the war, even before we've gone into battle."

"Tell me your feelings, Eddie, all of them. Let me know how the boys are *really* doing, I can't trust the stories they invent to make me feel less anxious. Let me know what they need to hear."

"Some of the Canadians were involved a few days ago in the fighting around Loos, part of a larger offensive at Artois and Champagne – a fiasco, we suspect, from the endless lines of walking wounded filing past us with their faces gray as paste, the whites of their eyes the brightest colour visible against the backdrop of mud, the wan uniforms, the darkening bandages, the dirt-streaked faces – they remind me of blackface minstrels minus the smiles, music and hypocrisy. While rumours fly of our imminent involvement, Ralph and I go off on 'borrowed' bicycles all the way up to Ypes. It's a six-hundred-year-old country town, walled and sedate, its ornate churches and stately guild-hall a distillation of human civility. Ralph and I stood a few feet apart and stared at the partial ruins of the latter building, thinking of the handiwork and masonry and dogged imagination it took to create it hundreds of years ago in spite of the clerical armies of Europe who rolled back and forth across this very territory in their petty attempts at ravaging it. 'I wish we had gone AWOL and up to London to see the Abbey', I said to Ralph. He didn't say anything to me because by that time we were both weeping silently. When we got back, though, we were delighted to find that Henry's wound was only superficial, and he was returned to us in swaddling clothes. Please tell Sandy and Henry as much as you can about the old days on the farm: it's the only subject left which they can still argue about. Write soon."

"They always used axes to cut down the big trees because usually only one man started the process, or the bush was too thick to wield a two-man saw, or you couldn't control the drop-spot as easily. Then the hundreds of small branches had to be trimmed quickly with an expert axe-hand so that only the trunk remained. You must remember that in Lambton County we are talking about pines and plane trees and walnut that soared a hundred and fifty feet in the air and often ran six or eight feet across at the bole. It took a trained ox-team to move these trunks and get them into a pile where they could be burned. Only the best-looking limbs were sawn up for cordwood. Everything else was burned into powdery ash."

"When we were returning from our six-day stint in billets we marched by a mud-pasture where the Brits were practising manoeuvres with the latest 'engine of Armageddon' as our padre so quaintly calls the 'land-cruiser' or 'tank'. Our entire company stopped on the off-beat to watch, and laugh. Your boys decided to have a contest to see who could find the best comparison to describe these monstrosities, and you have been selected to be the judge. So here they are, starting with my own: 'armadilloes with indigestion', 'wood-burning locomotives run off the rails and floundering in the gumbo-beds below the elevator' (your grandson), 'mammoths coming out of the glacial muck and frightened by the sun' (our historian, Cliff), 'Henry Ford's rejects' (Bart, who likes autos), 'dinosaurs on a toot' (Henry, who's seen 'em), 'maggots with armour' (Sandy, who's been too long on the farm) – love, Ralph."

"In those days every field was outlined by bush, not as it is now with stump or snake fences and friendly little patches of forest for shade. We had homely and domestic names for each one as we cleared them: Pine Field, Orchard Field, Back Willow, or simply North Field, South Field. When we looked up, we never had any doubt where we were."

"Gran: we've discovered a virtue in the rain and mud that permeates our daily routine: only humans can live in it. Really. The rats, without barns or granaries, have retreated to the billet areas behind us. The field mice can find neither fields nor fodder, and their burrows are washed out faster than they can tunnel them. No birds fly overhead, except the tidy cormorants, because there is no tree to light on, no grass for a nest, no water that is not stinking. Even the earthworms have drowned. We are the only living things for miles. But enough of my dark philosophizing – Bart tells me to inform you that we also have mechanized ravens here, called aeroplanes, but they don't talk dirty like Mrs. Finch's crow and aren't half as much fun. The German version is called a Fokker, and Bart says it occasionally gets garbled in the translation."

"Mrs. Finch's crow has learned a new trick. He hops along the clothes-line behind the missus and picks off the pegs as she pins them, then slips into the apple tree before she can figure out what ill-wind keeps blowing her sheets away. I'm tempted to tell her, but the crow is known to have a vengeful streak in him."

"We've begun a series of what are called 'night-raids', our first real action in the two months we've been here. We blacken our faces and hands with burnt cork, and then when the moon goes under, our platoon slips silently over the parapet and pads through the muck of no-man's-land with only the point of a dark ridge to our north to act as a guide. The idea is to drop into the German's foremost trench, yell and stab and create havoc for ten mad minutes, then retreat in the darkness before they can warm up their field guns or counter-attack. This manoeuvre is designed to keep the enemy perpetually scared – as if that were a difficult objective to obtain. Our group went 'over the top' last week, and we got all the way to the Bosch trenches without incident; I heard Cliff Strangways give the attack cry and we leaped blindly into the gap at our feet. It was eerie beyond description, like jumping off the edge of the world, we didn't know whether we'd land on a soldier's stomach or a keg of Bavarian beer or a parked bayonet. We sang out our banshee howls and jumped, swivelling our spear-guns like the Turkish infidel and waiting for the wince of human flesh at the end of the blow. Nothing happened. We landed askew in the dark, shouting and stabbing, but no one shouted back. Our sergeant barked a 'cease attack' that brought us all to a quivering halt. No sound of the dying or the terrified. Cautiously a torch was turned on and we gazed in horror at the sight around us. An hour before, during one of the periodic artillery duels staged by mutual consent, one of our batteries must have misfired several 'short' rounds meant for the front-line ridge beyond. Those shells had made a perfect, if unintentional, strike on this isolated part of the trench. Thirty or forty corpses, still warm and oozing, stared out at us with death's eyes. We had been told in the silly propaganda paper circulating here that the Germans were troll-like creatures who devoured their own babies when angered, who drank blood for breakfast, and so on. But I can tell you, Gran, all of us have looked on the faces of our enemy: they are just men, who die as men everywhere in the futility of battle."

"Some of the logs, of course, would be used to make the settler's first home, there are still many standing to this day. Often that first winter only enough bush was cleared for the cabin and an acre or two of fall wheat sown between the stumps. The ash from the burning was used as fertilizer, and for soap. We made our tables and chairs out of split logs. Our beds were cedar or spruce boughs on a frame of poles and cross-hatch of saplings. We burned wood for fuel- heat and cooking fire. We made flutes out of softwood sticks to make the music to carry us through the long winter. We walked over the snow – five-feet deep – on wooden snowshoes. Our world was made of wood. We loved and we hated it."

"Bart was killed in one of the raids two nights ago. We were almost back from a *mêlée* in the enemy trench when their artillery opened fire. We'd stayed a minute too long. I landed among some piles of equipment and slashed my way through it without encountering a soldier until the cry went up to retreat. Just as I dropped safely into our own trench, the first shell exploded, and Cliff and I heard Bart scream as if a cat had raked his flesh. Despite the noise and panic all around us, we heard it as clear as if he'd spoken to us across a quiet room. He'd fallen about ten yards away, and Cliff and I went out after him, shells breaking up everywhere. I was as scared as I'll ever get – that much I know. I had thought under these circumstances that I would think of my past life or my life to come or of you and Arthur shielding me against the wind along the river flats, but I thought of nothing, nothing – there was nothing in my brain but a gray numbness, the way death itself may be. We got Bart's body back into the trench, but he was already dead. We drew lots to see who should write home to his parents. Ralph lost."

"Please do not give me any of the details of the boys' deaths or injuries, Eddie. My heart recoils at the thought of what you must bear, alone. Tell Sandy he can prevent Trench Feet by taking grease from the cook's skillet and rubbing it all over the inside of his boots. The Indians, they tell me, used to have much success with the method."

The Vic-platoon saw little action as the winter dragged on in Flanders where record rainfalls turned the mud into a quagmire. "Henry says he may be the only one here who isn't affected by the muck and slime. He claims the gumbo south of Winnipeg is twice as sloppy and has four times the sticking power. Some of the fellows are suffering terribly from the grippe and dysentery and Trench Feet which can easily become gangrenous. They wish they could get into battle, which they think would be a form of relief. We try to assure them it is not so, though the wet and the waiting are hellish in themselves – with the din of distant siege-guns reminding us that some people out there are fighting and dying and maybe winning the war. Morale is high, I hasten to add, more likely because we feel a powerful camaraderie here that is more important than the so-called reasons we're given for our sacrifices – the defense of the Empire and the freedoms it stands for, as if the two notions were connected or even compatible. But we're here; most of us volunteered in one form or another, and here we're going to stay, together, to see this thing through. A strange rationale for fighting, isn't it? But what can you say in defense of General Haig who refers to our combat casualties as 'tolerable levels of wastage'. We had a good laugh about that one, the five of us."

Granny was now writing as many as four letters a week, occasionally more. No longer did her left hand balk at the glare of a page; it skittered across with a nervous energy of its own, sensitive now to every eddy of the mind and emotion that propelled it. The words flowed – now guarded, now brazen, delicate, all-thumbs, scrolled, jagged – they carried their share of the burden and in them she was able at last to see those reflections of herself she had not thought possible in seventy-six years of living. She began to compose with inordinate speed, with a soft fury of phrasing – the words tumbling out like crumpled butterfly wings, jelling in the cold squeeze of ink against the page, and glowing there as bright as icons at the fulcrum of a dream. She felt and she wrote. She thought and she wrote. She read and she wrote. Her room was full of voices and urgencies. The letters accumulated in huge piles in the corner beside the table. She reread them at intervals. She put a rubber band around Bart Ramsay's, and one day she sat down and began writing a letter to Mrs. Ramsay in Toronto, the first of many. By March she was so weary she often woke up in the dark with her head on the table and a sentence half-finished on a page she couldn't recall writing.

At the end of April the Canadian Corps, now three divisions strong, went into full-scale battle, and though Eddie's description of the combat and of trench-life itself became more circumspect – he had sensed the alarm perhaps in her letters – she was able to reconstruct the horrific events surrounding the St. Eloi craters and the subsequent battles of Mount Sorrel with enough clarity to comprehend their impact on him. On April the twenty-ninth he reported that they had slogged through slime up to their waists while under constant fire. "But we achieved our objectives, according to the

C.O. That is no news at all to Henry. He left us yesterday at five o'clock. I am to write soon to his father. He was the only child of a widower. What do I say?"

For ten full days there was no letter from Eddie or any of the remaining boys. The papers boasted of the recent successful offensives, and mentioned the spearhead towards Mount Sorrel. A few days later three letters arrived, one of them from Eddie. They were all lengthy. Sandy Lecker went on and on about tracing his family tree back through the Lowlands to the broken clans of 1845. Cliff Strangways had written out several comic songs his mother had found in grandpa's theatre-trunk – did she happen to know the music that might go with them? Eddie described the feelings he used to have when he first went skating on the pond-ice of Little Lake, and quoted from a poem by Wordsworth, the English fellow he was writing part of his thesis on. Eddie's words were more beautiful than the poet's. At the end of a long letter he said, "We've just come back from Sorrel. Ralph did not come back with us. I've written to his mother."

Granny could not write for a week. For a while she thought that her arthritis had decided to stall her efforts permanently. A second letter arrived from Eddie. Was she all right? Perhaps it would be better if he only wrote once a month or so, perhaps she should not hear, right off, about the fellows leaving them. He was sorry, terribly sorry for placing such a burden on her, he had no right to do so. She wrote him back that afternoon, taking the letter down to the post office herself.

Eddie, Cliff and Sandy all wrote cheering notes to her that week, each describing in his own way the arrival of the Dumbells' troupe for a weekend of performance before their fellow soldiers. "The spirit of 1860 and the old Colonial Theatre," Cliff enthused. "You should have been there to see it. Arthur should have been there to take a bow." Near the end of his letter Sandy let it be known that rumours were flying about a "big push to end the war" coming up soon, so that if they stopped writing suddenly, she was not, repeat *not*, to worry. Eddie's letter was forcibly cheerful and obsessively newsy. "Don't worry, Gran," it concluded, "we're certain it will be over soon."

She dropped the letter on the table and went immediately to Arthur's trunk. Under some posters and playbills she found what she was looking for: a vellum envelope. From it she drew a sheet of ordinary writing paper on which, in Bradley's crabbed hand, were written several stanzas of poetry. The title over them read: "Colloquy, for Sarah." When she had finished writing to Eddie, she copied the poem out in her own hand, then tucked the original in with the letter. This is all your father brought home to me from the wreckage of his life, she said to herself. It's time you knew the truth about that, and about the gifts you have to carry you into the future he refused to face. You have an obligation to live. Please, Eddie.

On the evening of July 1, 1916 Granny was wakened from a restless sleep by a thunderclap that brought her upright into the silence of her living room. She felt a stabbing at her heart as if an icicle had been plunged there by the Bogeyman. My heart, she thought right away, and braced herself for the next blow. Several peremptory 'pops' from the direction of Bayview Park broke the momentary quiet, and she peered in puzzlement at the night-sky visible from her window. Three skyrockets, celebrating the forty-ninth birthday of the Dominion, burst against the velvet backdrop, obliterating the stars and fanning out like irradiated metallic flowers.

55

1

Granny had not heard from Eddie – nor Cliff or Sandy – for more than a month. She knew why. The papers couldn't be avoided. News of the 'big push' to end the war and bring the boys home for Christmas was in the air, and some believed it. Without letters, the hours were empty, and would not be filled. Ralph's mother came to see her, and stayed the afternoon. She wrote a long letter to Henry's father and, reluctantly, put all of Henry's notes and cards in the envelope. Except one. Bart's parents wanted her to visit them in Toronto. She felt strangely touched by the gesture.

Just before midnight on the fourteenth of September, Granny came awake with a start. She was fully dressed, in her chair by the back window where she had been watching the sun set behind the great hickory tree. The stars shone in the moonless dark. Something had drawn her awake, something outside. She got up, shook the sleep out of her left arm, and went out into the back yard. It was so dark she could only make out the curve of the tree-top where it blackened the skein of stars above it. Wittingly she entered the arc of the shadow under the tree, let its dark radiance possess her. The North Star brightened just to the left of the point where Lake and River conjoined. Then it widened, like the lens of a prophet's eye. Somewhere five or six hours away to the east, the sun was rising over the Somme and the Ancre.

Zero hour for the move on the village of Courcelette was 6:20 A.M. The Canadian Corps was to attack with two divisions on a 2200-yard front. In a single bound they were to advance 1000 yards and strike at the defences in front of Courcelette: Candy Trench, the fortified ruins of a sugar factory, and 1500 yards of Sugar Trench. The siege-guns in Sausage Valley behind Pozieres opened up in a furious bombardment as mile upon mile of batteries of every calibre joined in. Then came the grinding mechanical roar of tanks entering combat for the first time. The front-line German trenches, blown apart by the artillery barrage, were taken in fifteen minutes. On the right, three assaulting battalions of the 4th Brigade were on their objectives by 7 A.M. On the left near Monquet Farm, the 8th Brigade had done its duty with despatch. General Turner directed the 4th and 6th Brigades to establish posts on the south side of Courcelette.

...Eddie was sitting on his heels in the trench, a piece of paper that might have been a page from a letter tucked into the pocket over his heart. The five or six recruits squatting near him were not looking in his direction, yet the angle and arrangement of their figures took as their fulcrum the solemn calm of their corporal's face. Shreds of the night's shadows washed about their feet, more comforting than the yawn of light at the parapet's edge. Eddie glanced at his watch, then touched with a reassuring eye each member of his platoon. A few yards away to his left Cliff Strangways stood smoking a tailor-made. He risked a glance at Eddie. To Cliff's right Sandy Lecker checked and re-checked the bolt on his Lee-Enfield, the clicking noise jarring stomachs all the way down the mile-long trench. Reaching for his cigarettes, Cliff accidentally grazed the back of Sandy's hand, and the silence of the early morning resumed. Then the ground trembled as if there were anguish inside it, and the bastinado of cannonfire roared once before it deafened them all. The seventeen-year-old huddled next to Eddie was sobbing, his trousers wet and steaming. No one looked. The veterans counted the seconds by distinguishing the howitzer's screech from the whump of eighteen-pounders or the popping of trench mortars. The thunder ceased on some anonymous command. In its wake: the livid scream of silence in the heart's hollow. A minute later the first wave went over the top. Rifles cracked, cries schismed, smoke and cordite careened on the imperceptible breeze. Eddie counted to twenty and rose to his feet. He couldn't feel them. He put an arm on the boy beside him. He saw the sergeant's battle-cry before its tremor struck him. Eddie's lips were moving. He may have been shouting 'go', but the word *no* sallied in his head. He leapt up and over. The sunlight grooved him with all its strength. He released the boy, and watched him fall away, bowels blown out.

The second Canadian assault of that day was carried out in broad daylight. After ten minutes of 'smart bayonet fighting', the 22nd and 25th Battalions advanced right through the village. The 26th Battalion was left to mop up. However, in front of Courcelette, the Canadians came under severe German counter-attacks, suffering numerous casualties. There was also trouble on the right. The Princess Pats lost their bearings over the broken ground, where every distinguishing landmark had been obliterated. They struggled forward through shell-holes while being raked by repeated rifle and machine-gun fire.

...Within a minute the second wave had overtaken the first one. Eddie tripped on a body and went down, instinctively thrusting his rifle upwards at an angle as his elbows hit the muck. His face pitched into a patch of slime. He tasted urine and shit. His eyes burned. He could see nothing but a blurred echo of sun behind a shroud of smoke, like a Turner sunset. Then shadows jerking forward, lumpish puppets unstrung, running on their own courage. When he got up, there was blood smudged on his right sleeve. Not his own. He ran forward, dodging the bodies tipped and askew everywhere. Some seemed to be crying out, but he could hear no human sound whatsoever, not even his own frantic breathing. The crack of rifle and machine-gun was so continuous it was a single blank roar; only the quaking of the earth under the earth told him the big guns were mailing their javelins to the enemy's throat. He could sense comrades running beside him, faceless, trusting in kinship, in collective valour, in the numbers of death's lottery. No one was ahead. Through the smear of air before him he could make out the chasm of the German trench, the cordite puffs from their rifles drifting as wispy as pipe-smoke. Eddie dropped to his elbows, aimed vaguely and began firing. Something heavy and unprepared flopped on his legs. He twisted around, keeping low, and rolled the wounded soldier as tenderly as he could into a small depression. A bullet had ripped the right arm almost completely away from the shoulder. Muscle, bone and blood gaped at the sudden air. Cliff tried to speak but shock still gripped him. In a moment pain would annihilate speech. Eddie tore off a shirt-sleeve, already bloodied, and strapped the limb to the torso. Cliff was blinking as if he were staring down an eclipse. "It's okay, old chap, you're gonna get a pass home. Lie low and wait for a stretcher." Either Cliff smiled or the pain creased his lower face, but Eddie was already up and plunging ahead towards the ragged outrunners of his platoon no more than thirty yards from the enemy trench. Suddenly the ground jumped under him and a vertical wall of granite straightened him to his full height, flattened him and rolled on. He felt the ooze from his punctured eardrum as he scrambled to his knees, dizzy and sick. He had dropped his rifle somewhere. A shell. Trench mortars. From the German second-line behind the village. He was facing west. The morning sun warmed the skin on his exposed back. Cliff was gone. Where he had lain, the shell had made a crater, unblemished by blood, pus or excrement.

Six of the mechanized behemoths, now simply called 'tanks' by the infantry-men, were assigned to the Canadian Corps. The new weapon in its maiden gambit failed to carry out any of its objectives. All six were out of action before the first phase of the battle ended at 11 A.M. Several broke down, their 105-horsepower Daimler engines glowing as red as an overheated Dodo's heart and coughing black exhaust. Two got stuck permanently in the mud – one 'male' (with two six-pounders and four Hotchkiss machine-guns) and one 'female' (machine-guns only, five Vickers and one Hotchkiss), though it seems no attempt was made during the unexpected pairing to consummate the relationship. The sixth flipped over in a bomb-crater where it was dispatched like a capsized tortoise. Before dark on the 15th September, however, the 4th Canadian Mounted Rifles, with heavy losses due to German barrages and enfilading fire from the direction of Monquet Farm, captured parts of the Fabeck Graben Trench. Shortly thereafter the 49th took some chalk pits beyond. The infantry continued to beat off repeated counter-attacks from the north and east of Courcelette.

...The barbed wire and breastworks of Fabeck Graben were now visible through the pall of smoke that clung to the windless air. This time the Germans were ready. The ground Eddie was running over had no flat plane on it anywhere. Where the noon-hour artillery duel had accidentally focussed, it was an oozing rubble. Sandy had momentarily disappeared behind a hummock of dirt on top of which the trunk of a corpse lay preposterously – which side it had belonged to was impossible to say. Eddie could hear, with his good ear, pounding feet everywhere, yet he seemed to be alone. Ahead, the terrain levelled somewhat, pools of liquid phosphorous under the haze. He waited, crouched – the animal panic in him stunting, then stirring. Sandy's familiar figure uncurled in the light and charged across the open ground. A tear-gas shell burst behind him like a smashed sunflower. The ground bevelled and shivered. Eddie couldn't hear the shrieks of Sandy's platoon behind him, protesting dismemberment. He sprinted forward, dropped, fired with a keen-crazed instinct, rose and charged. As he dropped again, another shell exploded to his left. For a second he could see nothing. The searing pain in his eyes drove him to his knees, his arms flapping like a grounded gull's wings. He felt the din of battle and dying in the tremble of his skin, through the sting of his ruptured eardrum, along the taut veins of his strummed throat, in the tuning fork of his long leg-bones. The epileptic stutter of mortar shells, the screech of shrapnel, the wail of the maimed, the hiss of gas, the bark of futile commands, the ululation of the terror-struck – he heard each one as though he had ears and a heart that had survived dumbfounding.

The thirty-foot rolls of barbed wire glinted darkly just ahead. To the left some of his comrades had found breaks in the wire and their bayonets flashed silver and then red. Eddie sighted and fired, a green coat stiffened in the act of straightening, and folded. Dead ahead Sandy was running alone towards the bristling parapet, zigzagging like a soccer player, dancing wildly amidst the bullets, his rifle floating in his hand as if he were carrying a flag on the end of it. Then, aiming his body like a missile, he dropped the rifle, flew over the remaining terrain with the grace of a five-minute miler, and while the astonished enemy gaped in disbelief, sailed into the barbed wire as if he had not seen it or else disdained its petty intercession. As a result he lifted, flattened and hung there, stunned. Slowly, with some regret, a machine-gun barrel swivelled around, locked into place and chattered. Eddie saw the steel-jacket bullets rip out of Sandy's back, the helmet snap off and clatter to the ground, the head loll giddily from side to side saying no, no, no. But the body remained on the wire.

What was left of Eddie's platoon came up behind him. Their sergeant and company captain were dead. The soldiers raised their rifles and fired at the nameless targets. Bolts jammed. Barrels blushed and seized. Cartridge chambers exploded, blinding. Eddie took the rife from the corpse beside him, a scarlet welt where the face should have been. He inched forward. The dirt sizzled in front, this side, that side. Bullets hummed in there like maddened worms. When they didn't, you were dead. Eddie continued to crawl forward, alone now, close enough to throw his grenade. It landed short. The barbed wire unsprung, jangling. But nothing they could do over the next two hours, *nothing* could stop the Germans – standing in the ruins of Fabeck Graben on balustrades of their own dead – from blasting to shreds, one bullet at a time, the pinioned flesh-and-bones of Sandy Lecker, the farmboy from Waterloo County.

The Princess Pats, says one semi-official account, fought with magnificent valour, but their right suffered most severely. Scattered groups forced their way into Fabeck Graben here and there to the western side of Courcelette, where the 25th Battalion was pressing stubbornly forward. The men of the 49th reached the trench in time to relieve the situation and assist in the consolidation there, it being impossible in the face of enemy fire – both artillery and machine-gun – to advance farther. Down the line, one of the attacking companies ran into a terrific barrage, almost half its members being wiped out. The attack continued, however, and in spite of all obstacles the Germans in Fabeck Graben were routed. Throughout the entire line, despite some reverses here and there, the success was magnificent and quite deserving of the congratulations of the commander-in-chief.

...Eddie was alone. In the din and pall he recognized no one. There were no units, no officers, no direction. Twice out of the mist of smoke and steam of opened flesh, greenish limbs had blundered into the rage of light around him, and he had fired or stabbed, stepped over the crumpled baggage and tried to find a place to run towards. Once, he had stood up stock-still and tried to squeeze his eyes shut against his own death, but the cordite tears in them flushed them wide and searing with absolute sight. Everywhere he put his foot down, it skidded on blood, rubbed against bone, slithered on living intestine.

Through a fissure in the maelstrom, his glance caught the blank bulls-eye of a machine-gun. He felt himself launched towards it. It stuttered, and jammed. His rifle jumped and the youth behind the gun gasped as the bullet sliced through his throat and cut off his cry. Eddie turned in time to see the wayward shell – it could have been from either side – complete its mile-long random arc no more than a handspan from his next step.

Eddie was flung sunward with the slow-motion ease of a levitation dream, blood stretched to the fingertips, toes, the whites of the eyes. The joints unhinged. The bones disengaged – legs, arms, scapula, skull spun out of the disintegrated skin towards the compass-points of some unimagined gravity. The centrifuge of the heart at last gives way and releases with it from time's cradle these fragments: snatches of a Celtic lullaby; a telltale bubble of healing laughter; the perfect stanza of an unfinished poem; phrases of affection shaped but not uttered; three flawless lines from 'Tintern Abbey'; cherished moments of child-bravery, fright, longing, devotion, steadfastness, the courage-to-be; memories as green as the hours that nurtured them one by one in all the afternoons and evenings and mornings it takes to bring the man out of the boy; dreams of generation wherein the future is scanned with the past's prophecy; and dreams that run deeper than memory, that feed in the shrubbery of our chromosomes and sip the cryptic ink of that gene where the myths of the species itself are made memorial.

The Battle of the Somme began on July 1, 1916 and ended on November 28 of that year. The Germans lost 582,919 men. The Allied Forces counted 623,907 casualties. Of these, Canadian losses were 24,029 killed, wounded, and maimed.

Every one of them was Eddie.

2

Granny came out of the house into the austere light of the September morning. She might have been on her way to tend the chrysanthemums or the cucumber beds or the tomatoes that had survived the first frost. She carried her trowel but no hamper. Her left hand was tightened into a fist, and her walk a little less spontaneous than usual. She moved slowly but without hesitation towards the big tree at the end of the property. The wind which had risen with the sun filled the yellowing leaves with sibilant motion. She stood under its shade, the breeze from the Lake on her face, and tried to imagine what this place – the knoll east of the marshes below and the great hickory above – was like when Southener's forefathers had first come upon it, seeing it surely – as Lily had so long ago – from the water's edge staring eastward into the rising sun. Were they drawn to its sibylline whispers? Its promise of shade and renewal? Its bounteous strength bridging four seasons? The sweet nub of its fruit under Carcajou's tongue in the long hallucinatory nights? Even now with the magic of the talisman gone, she recalled the words Southener had spoken to her, in trust, more than sixty-five years before: "I received this magic stone on a sacred ground, long known as such by generation upon generation of tribes who have dwelt in these woods and waters and passed on, as we all do. The days of its guardianship are almost over; there is little magic left in the forests and the streams, older now than our legends. So when you have no more use for the stone's powers, I ask that you return it to the sacred grove whence it came, to the gods of that place who lent their spirit to it."

She opened her left hand. The jasper amulet lay in the palm as cold as when she had removed it a minute ago from the leather sachet she had carried out of the bush in another century. Only two of the treasures now remained there: the Testament with Papa's inscription inside the cover and the cameo pendant bearing the face of the woman who may have been her grandmother. Transferring the stone to her right hand, she dug a small hole in the ground between the two largest roots of the tree. She placed the jasper in the hole and for several minutes watched it carefully; then she brushed the soil over it. Under that seal of earth lay the dead amulet, Lil Corcoran, Lady Fairchild, Lily Ramsbottom, Lily Marshall, Cora Burgher, Granny Coote and what remained of whoever she was now.

Mrs. Carpenter, who had just heard the terrible news, came through the hedge and spotted Granny coming towards her from the garden.

"Oh Cora, we just heard. It's all over town. You poor, dear thing." She was wringing her apron and putting on the bravest face she could muster. "What *can* we do to help?"

Granny opened her mouth to reply but nothing came out – not a vowel, not a spent breath. From that day forward not a single intelligible word passed her lips.

PART FOUR

The Return

56

1

The work of the monument proceeded apace. Sam Stadler brought his sons along only on those days when there was lifting or manoeuvring to be done. Otherwise he laboured alone under the vigilant supervision of the old man now rumoured to be his uncle. When the grand-nephews were about, the old fellow gambolled and chided and gabbled and offered copious instruction. When they were not, he sat on one of the unprepared stone slabs and rarely took his eyes off the movements of the artisan's hands. Neither did Granny from her own watchtower across the street.

The monument was to consist of a double-pedastalled base of polished alabaster sandstone guarded by eight newel-posts linked with black iron chain. Surmounting this elegant base was a cube of rough-cut limestone with projecting cornice. On each facet of this cube was set a smooth tablet in which Sam Stadler had patiently inscribed the scroll of the dead. Normally these tablets would have been prepared in a workshop and transported to the site for installation, but Sam Stadler was no ordinary builder of memorials-in-stone. Every cut and gesture of his craft was executed on the grounds in the open air. When it rained, as it did often that April and May of 1922, he drew a tarpaulin over the unfinished pieces and sat in his truck smoking and smiling at respectable intervals as the old fellow chattered beside him. Sometimes if the rain were warm and misty, they sat silently in its midst, the droplets beading on the brims of their crumpled fedoras, cigarettes cupped lovingly in hand. Often several hours would pass before they moved – to return to the task or climb contentedly into the battered truck to go home, wherever that was.

On sunny days Sam Stadler sat on a stool and chipped into stone the strangers' names written on the sheet of paper spread out before him on the ground. Though hammer and chisel and file were his instruments, the play of his fingers across the grooved tablet reminded Granny of a pianist's fingers, Arthur's fingers – with their supple strength, their gentle probing, their easy precision, their effortless acceptance of art's tyranny. Letter by letter she watched him chisel into continuance the names of the children of the village, and something in the tenderness of his gestures and in the deep resignation behind the quick smile he gave to the curious attending silently from the sidewalk, told her that to him these were more than yet another set of sad anonyms. He was, she thought, a calligrapher spelling out the letters of his first born in the reverence and awe and regret we feel for all things cherished and mortal.

On top of the pedestal and memorial facets was to be erected a twenty-foot obelisk of cut limestone interspersed with inscribed tablets to record the names of the battles wherein the sons and fathers had fallen or whatever cause had driven them hence: Ypres, St. Eloi, Vimy, Passchendaele, Hill Seventy – names that would enter the village vernacular like the names of those diseases which had struck and departed without cause or care: diphtheria, typhus, small pox, Spanish influenza. They would be forever the whispered words of quarantine, of taboos only partially exorcized, of cold subcutaneous fear. The obelisk was constructed in five-foot sections to be fitted in place at the end of the work. On top of the last section a stone bust of the unknown soldier was to be erected. It was uncrated from a box delivered from the freight-sheds. Somewhere, Granny thought, there was a factory that turned these out from a single mold and shipped them to the hinterland. Against the wishes of Sam Stadler and of Reeve Denfield, the council had insisted on this necessary fillip, perhaps to offset the uncompromising idiosyncrasy of the rest of the piece, perhaps to ensure, for some, the military character of the memorial which the words alone, in their ambiguous solitude, could not do. "It's ugly and says nothing," was all Sunny said to her about the figure, and she nodded in agreement.

What was especially charming during the construction was the way in which people came to observe, almost always alone (even the children), posted in silence on the nearby walk, watching for long moments when you were certain they had not breathed and waiting as a faithful terrier does for recognition – usually just a tip of the mason's hat or a wink (for the kids) or a cornerwise smile for the regulars. Granny observed many of these brief exchanges, no two of them quite the same though generated from similar sources and needs, and she marvelled once again how much could be conveyed without the sweet contamination of language. One day just after the base was completed, Granny walked across the street with a thermos of tea. She stood and watched the three men sweating in the smooth sun, aware of the old fellow's stare. When the men had finished the task they were engrossed in, Sam Stadler acknowledged her presence with a grin.

"You been keepin' a good eye on us for some time now," he said pleasantly. "Denfield tells me it was your house they took down to make room for this."

Granny nodded and pointed to her lips.

"It's okay," Sam Stadler said. "I know." He turned to his sons. "I'm Sam and this here's Harry and Pat, my boys. The old wood-grouse there in the corner is my Uncle Jack but everybody calls him Old Jack for short."

Old Jack murmured an indistinct but not unfriendly greeting and kept his owl's eye fixed upon her in happy puzzlement. "He don't talk neither," Sam said and laughed good-naturedly as his sons and uncle joined in. "But that's never stopped him from gettin' his point across."

"If that's hot tea you got in there," Old Jack said with a superfluous wink in the direction of the boys, "we'd sure like some."

Sam Stadler spread the tea-towel in which he had wrapped their lunch over one of the slabs of stone."If you'd like to sit for a while, please do," he said. Granny sat down in the sun.

A little while later the boys drove off in the truck, and Old Jack, after some strenuous bantering over lunch, ambled to the back of the lot and fell asleep under the hickory tree. Sam Stadler picked up several chisels and awls, sat on his stool before one of the partly finished memorial tablets, and began chipping out the letters of a name. The sun warmed his fingers and mellowed the stone that gave way smoothly under their insistence. The shadow of his face fell over the name. When he sat back to roll himself a smoke, Granny read the letters he had just etched there: EDWARD ARTHUR BURGHER. Sam Stadler lit his cigarette, turned towards her, caught his smile in time, and said quietly, "You knew him."

After a deep draught of smoke he went on. "I didn't know him, of course, or any of these others. But four of my sons were there, and only two come home." She reached out and placed a hand over his. He didn't move. Not an eyelash.

Old Jack was holding forth over the lunch hour, ostensibly for the benefit of his grand-nephews slouched in the grass but more likely for the edification of his favourite nephew and anyone else near enough to be moved by his sad tale. Granny picked at one of the muffins she had brought over an listened politely.

"The younger generation's got no idea, not an inkling, of what life was like fifty or sixty years back. No sense of tradition, no respect for their elders. It's the cities and the wars and the ruination of Mother Earth herself. When I was a boy we lived in huts and we moved from place to place in the woods, following the deer and small game even we children were taught to trap and shoot. In them days we treasured every word that dropped from the lips of our elders. My father was a giant, a king, a great hunter, he was permitted to talk with the gods." He glanced towards Harry and discovered him in the midst of a yawn, which he chose to ignore. "Our history was passed down to us through the lips of our grandfathers. The lore of our people was passed along from hand to hand, and Mother Nature was the consort of our gods. We would've been ashamed to wear clothes not made from the skin of our brothers in the forest." Pat was dusting off his overalls in a badly timed gesture. Old Jack ventured a quick glower and then resumed his monologue.

Afterwards Sam Stadler told her: "We've got some Indian blood in us from way back, and the old fellow likes to have his dreams." Then perhaps as if he had gone further than he intended, he added, "Some of the things he talks about were true."

Towards the end of April with only the base completed and part of the memorial section, the town council proudly announced that the Governor-General, Lord Byng, and his wife, Baroness Byng, would take time out of their busy schedule to visit the Point and consecrate a cornerstone of the cenotaph. Sam Stadler was hastily contracted to make a suitably engraved tablet, which became the first stone to be set in place upon the pedestal. The whole town went into a flutter of anticipation. And even though their Excellencies would spend less than an hour in the village – the rest of their hectic day to be apportioned among the various functions devised by the Sarnia-city elite – the visit was generally held to be a matter of civic pride, and not-a-little boasting here and there. The veterans were to escort Lord Byng of Vimy from Bayview Park to the site of the cenotaph where patriotic speeches would be delivered, a bouquet of flowers presented to the Baroness by Harry Hitchcock's little girl, Susie, and a blessing uttered over the sacred cornerstone.

Granny heard the blare of bugles bent by the wind, and the tramp of military boots on pavement. The shadows of the restless throng around the site (some of them crowded back onto her lawn) flickered on the far wall. She heard the sparrow-chatter of children and the ooh's and aah's of their elders as the royal train approached. Although the words of the speeches – by Deputy Reeve Hitchcock and the Commanding Officer himself – were inaudible, Granny knew what platitudes they would employ, what pauses would be made so that the visiting press could capture each cliché intact and uncorrupted by novelty. Somewhere in the middle of an invocation or doxology by one of the innumerable local reverends, Granny drifted far enough into unconsciousness to enter the world of her own thought. She was thinking of Eddie and the time just after Arthur died when they went for a Sunday drive in Ralph's father's automobile, down into Moore Township.

2

Eddie was being especially cheerful, regaling her with stories of Bart's outrageous behavior last semester and showing off his driving prowess whenever the road widened sufficiently. They were taking the gravel highway that hugged the River south all the way to the county's end. The water lolled by them, midsummer blue. Iron-clad lake-steamers churned upstream or coasted down, no more than a hundred feet away. They looked for a schooner's sail but did not see one. To the east of the road the farms ran back from the riverfront for several miles, all neatly fenced; the forest was shaved clean around them except for a few anomalous spinneys, wispy on the far horizon. Wheat and oats and corn and green fallow gave proof of unremitting labour, steady progress and certain prosperity. Whatever the people in these clapboard or brick houses with the tall barns believed in, it was beneficent. They stopped for tea in Courtright. When Granny asked the elderly proprietress if she knew where 'Millar's Corners' might be, Eddie was surprised but asked no questions. Instead, he listened carefully as the woman, after recovering from her own surprise, gave them brief instructions.

"Do you know if there are any of the Partridge family still livin' in this area?" Granny asked as they were about to leave.

The woman peered at her as if she were a ghost likely to tell indecent stories on its return. Then she smiled dubiously. "I'm a Partridge. By marriage."

Eddie's cheeriness was replaced by respectful silence. Two concessions south of Courtright he turned east. The rectangular farms continued on either side. They passed a sugar bush. In one of the pastures Holsteins grazed as if in a dream of themselves. Metal mailboxes greeted the road at every gate. The houses, tidy and spare, were set back from the gates at a daunting distance, and spaced evenly apart every half mile or so. The heat shimmered, untouched, in the vacancy between. A boy, no more than ten, sat on a split-rail with his bare legs tucked under and stared at their passing. Nothing else moved.

The first time they went right past the sign and Eddie stopped the car about a mile to the east of it. He shut off the engine, and they sat in the sharpened silence of the afternoon heat and just listened for a long while. A song sparrow, two meadowlarks and a chorale of grasshoppers identified themselves. Eddie touched the back of Granny's hand on the seat beside him. "I think we passed it back there," he said.

Engrimed with seasons of dust and grit, the sign had been kicked over into a shallow ditch, and, unheeded by anyone anymore, had not been re-erected. If Millar's Corners had had hopes of expanding beyond a postal drop and a family's ambition, they had not been seriously entertained for many decades. Nevertheless, the castaway sign did mark one of the oldest crossroads in the township, and the sideroad that ran south of it was itself of ancient origin.

"Well," Eddie said, pointing to the mailboxes as they passed by, "*some* of the Millars stuck around."

"They were like that," Granny said, but did not elaborate.

Nothing was recognizable. Not a single memory could be reconstructed from these ruins, so complete was the transformation. The sickly clumps of trees were all second growth. The road itself was as straight as the ruler used to draw all the lines and sideroads on the flat map of the county. She scanned the names on mailboxes, and gave up. She tried to imagine a small girl walking along the shoulder, with a few curves secretly added, all the way home from the big cabin of the Millars. She counted trees, steps, invisible minutes.

"Stop here, Eddie."

He shut off the engine but did not follow her as she waded across the grassy ditch, slipped through a rail fence and walked towards a brick farmhouse situated on a slight rise to the east. Somewhere behind it, a creek lapped against low stones. She went up into the shade on the north side of the house, newly built, she could see, on some old site. A barn rose proudly on her left and she walked past it, measuring something in her mind, sealing her eyes now and then, ears alert for the sound of water. She did not go right up to the creek, knowing it would not resemble anything she would remember, but stood thirty or forty feet from it, listening to the timbre of its midsummer lament with the zeal of an adjudicator. Then she turned and stared at the knoll on which the house stood.

Sometime later a voice said: "You all right, missus?"

Granny looked up to see a red-cheeked farmer smiling uncertainly at her. "Where that new house of yours is," she said," was there every anyone buried there?"

"You sure you're all right?"

"I used to live here, a long while back."

"We been here an awful long time ourselves," he said. "And yes, there was a couple of gravestones just about where our kitchen would be now. I remember them still bein' there when I was a kid and we had the old house further down the lane. Relatives of yours?"

"What happened to them?"

"Well now, I couldn't tell you exactly when, but they was dug up an' moved off here about 1880 or so, when the township started to collect all those kind of graves an' put them in proper cemeteries. You know."

"Where did they take them?"

"More than likely up to the public cemetery near Corunna. Just off the highway."

"Do you remember the names on them?"

He paused. "That's a long ways back, but I do remember because when the county men came to fetch them, they couldn't read a word on either of the stones. The names weren't scraped on there too good, you see, an' by the time they got here there wasn't a letter you could recognize. So they took the bodies up to Corunna an' buried 'em all with the others that didn't have names." Unable to read the look on her face, he added, "They're real nice graves up there."

When Granny came back across the field towards the car, Eddie waved to her.

3

Work had started again on the monument. The immanence of the royal visitation had begun to fade and wax fantastical. Sam Stadler took up his tasks as if nothing much had happened. He was pleased when Granny herself returned in a few days, with tea and Mrs. Savage's muffins.

Old Jack was at the boys again, sensing a coeval and possibly sympathetic ear nearby and wishing she could speak on his behalf as eloquently as her eyes intimated she wished to.

"You can't change your blood, you know. Blood is kin and those bonds are unbreakable. They're written on the inside of your bones. So a person can put on all the fancy clothes he likes, he can cut his hair like a dude's and sprinkle perfume all over his shaved face and he can talk like all the White Mens talk, but he can't change what's buried in his blood and bones and what he's got an obligation to pass along to his sons. The White Mens killed the woods and the deer went with it; the White Mens brought us smallpox and rifles and cannon and now we take them up and get ourselves blown to bits in a White Mens' war, and I say we're getting what we deserve, it's our own punishment for pretending to be White Mens and putting up these false idols –"

"That's enough, old man," Sam Stadler said sharply, jarring the two boys awake.

Uncle Jack snapped something back at him. It was not English. Sam Stadler returned the compliment in kind. The argument may well have continued had not Granny got up from her place, walked between the two men, both of them now standing, and placed her hand on the old fellow's shoulder. He stayed bone-still as she scrutinized every line in his face, every crevice of light in his expressive, aged eyes. Then his jaw began to drop as he heard her straining towards speech, a throttled gargle bulging up and jamming its coherence against her teeth, her stubborn tongue.

"Waupoore." The double-syllable entered the air, released from its dumbfounding. The old man reeled back as if struck by his mother's fist; he sat down on a stone slab and tried to catch his breath. He looked to Sam Stadler for help, but Sam was peering in disbelief at the old woman, at the contortions of her mouth out of which no subsequent word could be uttered to qualify or explain. The hoarse expulsion of enjambed sounds from her throat had reduced both boys to a silent stare as they sat fixed to the ground. After a minute or so, the rattle eased and Sam Stadler took Granny's arm in a reassuring grip.

Uncle Jack had recovered. In the language that was not English he cried, "Yes, I'm Waupoore, the Rabbit!" He was hopping up and down and looking beseechingly at Sam Stadler and then at Granny, and finally at the boys who were staring with detached fascination at the scene.

Sam Stadler sat beside Granny while she sipped her tea and they both waited for Rabbit to settle down long enough for her to write on the pad in front of her these words: Rabbit, Birdsky, Michael Corcoran, Lil, Old Samuels. Rabbit seized on them singly, holding up his hand to slow their effect, and after each he gave out a wincing smile as, somewhere within, a bulb of memory burst into dim bloom. As Granny watched him, she remembered the shy dance he had perfected for the world, amazed at how little it had diminished with age and heartbreak.

"You're Lil," he said. "Oh, how I worshipped the ground you walked on."

Yes, I was Lil – once.

While Sam Stadler measured with his jeweller's squint the wedges of stone to fit the tapering column and cut them with his watchmaker's touch, while he whetted and polished the flat tablets on which the names of the battlegrounds appeared one letter at a time as if some mist-of-dawn were lifting to reveal the spellbound runes of a legendless people, while Sam Stadler's sturdy sons erected the scaffolding from which the separate parts of the obelisk would be successively fitted into place and he was free to sip tea in the shade of the great hickory and saviour the blue wind over the far bay – Granny gathered the pieces of Rabbit's story.

When Birdsky realized that Papa had left for good, she took up with a former lover, a Chippewa man who persuaded her, when the squatters' camp broke up, to come to the Muncey Reserve near London, where it was rumoured there was plenty of land and lots of work in the bush. Old Samuels and his family went north to the Sarnia Reserve, and Rabbit never saw them again. Old Samuels was very sick with a cough which he blamed entirely on the inferior quality of the 'White Mens' black tobacco. Soon after they settled at Muncey, Birdsky's man died under a felled tree, and within a month she married an Oneida named Doxtader. Rabbit took his name but resisted for a long time the imposition of 'Jack' which his step-father demanded when they moved to London and entered the white man's domain. Since his native name covered both cottontails and jackrabbits, Birdsky always laughed and said that 'Jack' was at least half-rabbit.

For many years they lived in the nether-world below the white man's, completely cut off from the Reserve and its native traditions, attenuated though they might be. They drifted. Of the numerous brothers and sisters born after him, only one boy survived, Joe, ten years his junior. With Rabbit and Joe and their sisters, Birdsky returned to Muncey after her husband died. They made a great effort to recapture whatever it was they thought they had lost. But too much had passed by them. Joe, black-haired and brown-skinned, his full-blooded hatchet-face the envy of Rabbit with his suspiciously brown hair and light skin, was wretchedly discontent. Though he retained some of the Ojibwa language his mother had preserved for him, the English words were more tailored to his lips and more native to his deepest feelings. Joe left the Reserve when we was sixteen and never returned. He married a white woman and got a job as a bricklayer. Sam was their firstborn. When he was only two or three, about 1880, Birdsky died, and for a time Rabbit clung to the Reserve where he had no relatives and few friends. Finally he was persuaded to live in London, first with one of his sisters and finally with his brother Joe. After a while he even got used to being called Uncle Jack by his nephews and nieces. He embarrassed himself by telling stories better in English than he had rehearsed them in Ojibwa in his head, though only Birdsky who never left his right shoulder really noticed, and she adored him too much to scold. Young Sam was good with his hands. He made bows and arrows under his uncle's tutelage, he carved out the emblems of Michebou, the Great Hare. He had a good ear and Rabbit whispered into it enough of the sacred words to keep his spirit afloat until it could be claimed. Later when Sam got back from the war in South Africa, he took up the craft of masonry and tombstone sculpture. He drew white men's angels on their monuments. He changed his name to Stadler. When Rabbit's brother Joe died, it hurt Rabbit very much. It hurt even worse to have to move in with Sam and be treated as if he mattered.

One day towards the middle of June, Sam and his sons hoisted the last section of the obelisk into place and fitted the bust of the unknown soldier on top of it. It had rained all morning, keeping the curious villagers at bay. When the weather unexpectedly brightened in mid-afternoon, Sam got up from his nap under the hickory and signalled for the work to begin immediately. Thus it was that Granny was the only observer that day when the monument was completed. While his boys dismantled the rough scaffolding which still marred any appropriate view of the finished object, Sam and Granny walked across the street and stood in the yard of her new house. He did not speak, and there was no need. They were both looking west, and waiting. Young Pat pulled the last timber away from the base and dragged it to the edge of the lot. He peered over at them, grinning. Harry was on the other side. Rabbit was still asleep in the shade.

The four o'clock sun was just visible above the roof of the hickory, burning down over its steaming green and striking with glorious force the upthrust altars of the village memorial, its elegant pedestals as pure and sudden as Athenian light, the limestone obelisk with the weight of the village dead on its facades soared aloft into the vivid air as if it had been carved whole from a pictographic-cliff high above Superior and anchored to the granite of the earth.

"I wanted to see it from here, with the trees behind it and the sun along the solstice line. It will be beautiful in the mornings as well. The shadow of the column will fall along the trunk of the tree."

Granny wanted to touch his arm but she dare not.

"Uncle Jack thinks we've sold out our heritage," Sam Stadler said in a voice that was clearly meant to have her remain within the ambience of the wonder they were sharing. "But that happened a long time ago, before Rabbit himself was born. When I came here, I knew right away this place had once been a magic ground. I felt the ghosts all around me. When I was a boy, Rabbit told me that magic was the hardest thing in the world to kill. Well, the old ways are gone for good. But that don't mean we have to forget them, do we?"

4

That night when Granny woke from a dream she didn't care to recall, she went over to her chair by the window and stared into the darkness until she was safely awake. Darkness as she knew was never an absolute quality, and soon the play of shadow on shadow arrested her deliberate misattention. The stars were etched like Braille on the infinite black, and somewhere behind her a low moon began to scatter a random light. Across the road the pillar of the monument glowed as if it had absorbed the sun all day and was now relinquishing it, like radium. The words inscribed there were more visible now that they were filled with night-shadow, and she strained to be able to read them, to be able to read one of them. Suddenly the whole facade of the memorial tablet went dark, as if a bat's wing had flicked over it. The slow light leaked back. She chanced a quick look to the right and left but nothing moved in the blackness behind. No wind touched the young leaves high in the hickory. But somewhere she could hear singing, not a human voice but one very like it, a horn simulating a perfect soprano so real you could almost whisper the near-words it devised to tantalize and tempt the forsaken. This time the shadow that flickered across the scroll of the dead was as diaphanous as an angel's wing, you could blow your breath through it. It dissolved, then came again, not actually touching the face of the stone but brushing it with the urgency of the singing that rose and fell in time with it. The singing stopped. The veil, which could have been a wing or a scarf, was, it was now clear, a sleeve with an arm in it and a tiny white hand unfolding out of it and fluttering. Granny followed the arm to the edge of the column where it ceased, though a spill of flaxen hair – unripened hair, a little girl's hair – fell absently over the sleeved limb now stretching, as if on tiptoe, towards the engraved sad letters. The fingers paused, then began tracing their way over one of the names in a fevered, amateur way – as a blind child might finger the face of a smiling stranger.

No, no, she heard the cry deep in her, and rose up with its surge. She struck her head sharply on the sash and fell back into the chair. When the dizziness subsided, she looked out again. The moon was down. Nothing moved, or shone.

Silly, silly woman. You must stop this. You must stop these foolish tears. The old ways are gone for good.

57

It's goin' to look beautiful for the opening ceremonies, now isn't it," Sunny Denfield said. Granny tilted her head slightly in agreement. "By then the sod'll be somewhat stitched together, an' your delphinium an' poppies'll be in their glory back there."

She accepted the compliment, knowing it was well-meant, and she was, she had to admit, secretly pleased that most of the flower-beds she had planted for Arthur had been left in their natural state, at least until next year. All the hedges except the one adjoining the Carpenter property had been dug up and the whole area around the monument turned into lawn and park. By autumn both monument and greenery would have taken hold, and who would there be to remember that they did not always belong to this place?

"We've set the date," he said. She held her teacup rigid. "The first of July at eleven o'clock."

She swallowed her tea but did not look up.

"For Dominion Day," he explained hastily. *And butchery along the Somme.*

She flashed him an ironic smile he pretended to miss.

"The unanimous choice of the council, though I suspect we didn't all vote for the same reasons. The vets will form up at Bayview, they'll be led by our own small drum-and-bugle corps down St. Clair to the monument. We've covered the Honour Roll with a flag, as you can see, and at precisely 11 A.M. I'll unveil the memorial plaque an' the first wreath of remembrance'll be laid."

He paused. She was listening intently.

"Could I have a bit more tea?"

She reached for the pot, stopped and peered over at him with a gesture which clearly said, 'Tell me what's really on your mind, I can take it'.

"The council – recognizin' all you've done an' meant to this community for sixty years, an' seein' that you're now a deed-holdin' landowner," – he was unable to complete the smile here – "would like you to lay the wreath. It was unanimous. Even Hitch. The rightness of the choice was self-evident. They – that is, I don't see how anyone else could possibly do." Finally he turned to face her. The burn-scar on his left cheek glowed softly in the muted sunlight of the room. Unconsciously he drew his fingers over its numbness.

"Look, Cora, I know how much we're askin' of you. And I have a pretty fair idea of what you think of the War an' politicians an' pooh-bahs. But that part of it's over, you see. We let Lord Byng an' his Lady an' his entourage of party hacks come here an' have their say back in April. You can't keep them away from a thing like this. So we invited the whole shebang includin' a brass band. They come an' they said their piece an' they went. Not a one of them will ever remember again where Point Edward is without checkin' a map first. What we're plannin' for July is goin' to be our own. Sure, we couldn't say no to the local M.P. an' his cell-mate from the Legislature, but that's all. Not even His Worship from the City will be here. Just us. The people who suffered an' the people who sacrificed. The people who wanted this monument built, an' know, each one of them, what it means."

The flies along the window-ledge buzzed in the local sun.

"I think you know, Cora, that in some ways you've been almost a mother to me. Sometimes Prudie gets annoyed with me comin' over here so much, and I'm at a loss to give her an explanation she can believe." He paused, drew a deep breath, and said more quickly, "This monument'll mean different things to different people, but let me tell you what I think, an' what I believe many others in the village think deep down inside. This monument isn't a memorial to war or the so-called triumph of good over evil. There's nothin' glorious about war whether you win or lose. We know that for ourselves. There's not a man between twenty-five an' forty in this town who isn't limpin' or half blind or wakin' up screamin' in the middle of the night from the shrapnel that ain't come out yet or the nightmares of shell-shock. An' the women know even better than we do – they suffered here at home for four years, they looked into the grim faces of the bereaved, an' most of them felt that pain themselves before it was over." He swallowed hard. "No one felt it deeper than you did."

She tried to deny it but her eyes failed her.

"I'll tell you what I think that monument means to most of us when we walk past it by ourselves, when we're sure no one is watchin' or listenin'. You've seen them already, haven't you, from this window? To them it's not a fancy pillar to the glorious dead. It's a memorial to those of our own who left us for a cause we thought to be right. They died, and I know that some of them found courage before they died and others didn't. That don't matter. They were ours, they left us, and if we don't remember them no one else will, no one but us will really care. We want our grandchildren to know, years an' years from now, whenever they see this column an' the names on it, that once there was a village here, with people who were brave an' foolish an' caring. This is goin' to be a monument to ourselves as a village, what we been through in the past, how much we can be together in the future. This is only *one* of the wars we've already been through. Who knows that better than you?" He got up and stood at the window looking across to the cenotaph and the ancient tree behind it.

"So you see why it has to be you to lay the wreath."

When he found the courage to face her, she gave a reluctant consent. "The council also asked me to give the dedication address," he said. "I agreed, of course. And I will. But I'd like you to write out the words for me."

Granny made no attempt to brush away the tears that would do as they pleased anyway. When Sunny started towards her, she held up her hand, and smiled. As he watched in a sort of anguished awe, she got up, joints creaking a bit, went over to Arthur's trunk on top of which she kept her writing tablet, and wrote something on it in slow, stiff surges. He waited as she brought the paper across to him.

It read: 'Not necessary, you already have'.

Sunny Denfield wrote out for her a detailed description of the ceremonies and her small role in them. "By the way, my cousin Ruth-Anne is comin' down for the occasion. She hasn't had any luck in tracin' her mother's relatives, but I guess she's heard so much about this fabulous town lately, she decided she had to come an' see it for herself. I'm delighted. I haven't seen her in eight years. We ain't been much of a family, I guess, and I'm anxious to make amends. I think you'll like her."

As he was about to leave, Granny wrote on her pad: 'I wish to give you a gift, something personal, for all you have done'. While he was energetically refusing such undeserved kindness, she reached into Arthur's trunk and brought out a leather pouch. She loosened the drawstring and he saw two objects inside: a pendant with what appeared to be a cameo portrait of some kind and a calf-bound book, perhaps a miniature Bible. He could tell from the way she fingered them that these objects were heirlooms of great value. Again he demurred, but she held out the book until he took it, gently, into his hands. On her tablet she wrote: 'This belonged to my father and he got it from his mother. He inscribed it for me and asked me to keep it until I could pass it along to my own children'.

58

1

Three days before the ceremony Prudie Denfield came over. She insisted on showing Granny how to use the new-fangled gas range in the kitchen, and after a brief one-sided tea, the two women went through the dusty trunks in the uninhabited bedroom until a presentable dress was unearthed. It was the black one she had worn to Arthur's funeral. How thin she had become since that time, ten years ago almost to the month. I thought I'd be with you long before now, she said quietly to him when Prudie's back was turned. But then I never was lucky at planning anything for long.

Prudie fussed over her, pinning the dress with elaborate care for the alterations she was threatening to carry out. She even promised to bring over a boxful of vintage hats – representing all sizes and generations – from which a choice eventually could be made. Before she left, she sat Granny down in her padded rocker and began brushing her hair with long, rhythmic, drowsing strokes. When her eyes opened, the room was dark. She let her dream continue. She was dreaming of Bradley and the night he came back from the dead...

Bradley had no sooner stepped into Hap Withers' cottage that night when he staggered and collapsed on the linoleum. The swaddled child struck the floor before she could catch it, and began crying. Holding it in her arms, she forced the door shut with her body, already soaked from the wind-driven, icy rain pouring in on them. She stripped off the wet rags and wrapped the baby in an old quilt, its cries shuddering through her, its tiny face wizening as if it were trying to squeeze all the blood out with whatever pain or terror was twisting inside. Bradley groaned and heaved onto his side. Something black and oily dripped from his mouth. The baby shrieked. She hurried back to the kitchen, but the stove was cold. She lay the baby down on her bed and returned to the front room. Somehow with the child wailing and the storm lashing about the eaves and sills, she managed to haul Bradley's unconscious form onto Hap's bed. She could not get more than his jacket off because each time she pulled at his clothes he jerked back as if he'd been jabbed by a cattle-prod. She pulled the large comforter over him, tucked it firmly in all around, and went back for the baby. Covering it with her own coat, she ran into the fury of the storm towards Peg's house, just across the tracks.

Despite her good marriage and religious conversion, Peg Potts Granger was still an Alleywoman. She asked no questions; the desperation in Lily's face was all the testimony she required. Two of her boys were dispatched to rouse the doctor in Sarnia. She herself took charge of the baby, and while Lily – Peg called her Mrs. Burgher because she could not bring herself to call her mother's lifelong friend 'Cora' even though most of the village had grown accustomed to the change – while Lily stood shivering in uncharacteristic helplessness, Peg dug out an old bottle, warmed some milk and soon had the baby's wailing damped down for the night. "Go back to Bradley, missus. I won't say a word till you tell me. The baby'll be here when you're ready for him."

After satisfying herself that Bradley was still breathing, Lily went into the kitchen and got a roaring fire started. Then she walked grimly back to her son. She was not even sure just how she had come to recognize him, something in the eyes perhaps that no metamorphosis however savage could disguise. The once-thin, ascetic face was monstrously bloated, his skin had the pallor and touch of gray-white mushrooms too long in the rain. The top of the head was bald but not smooth – as if the hair had been pulled out in frenzied tufts. What hair remained – on the sides and back of the head – was a weathered, colourless fungus no amount of scrubbing would ever make blond again, or curly. As she pulled away the vest and shirt, she saw that the body flesh was similarly puffed and shapeless. Under her touch, it oozed. As she drew his trousers down, she caught sight of the swollen, lopsided protuberance stretching out below his right ribs – like a blooded liverwort. His breathing came in short, gasping seizures followed by a death-like quiescence – equally frightening.

It was dawn when the rain stopped and Dr. Dollard arrived, white-haired and exhausted after a night in the township. He accepted Lily's offer of a cup of hot coffee and a biscuit, and they sat in a grateful silence for a while – though there was much that lay between them. Finally he said to Lily in a grave tone: "I'm afraid he's come home to die."

"How much time?" Lily said.

"A few days, a week. No one can say for sure. He's slipping in and out of hepatic coma, and it appears from his breathing as if pneumonia's setting in. His liver's finished."

"Drink?"

"I'm afraid so."

"Did you recognize him?"

"To be honest, no. I've seen a lot but I didn't think a young man could change that much in so short a time. I'm sorry, Mrs. Burgher."

"What do I do?"

"Keep him warm or cool as his temperature varies, get some liquid into him if you can. I must warn you, he may go into *delirium tremens* if the pneumonia don't work fast enough. If he does, get some help quick. And call me."

"Thank you."

At the door he said, "You take care, Lily."

Bradley had his first seizure before noon. Asleep on the chesterfield, Lily was brought upright by some loud muttering from the bedroom. When she went in, he was still unconscious and shouting violently at some antagonist in his dream and thrashing his arms about as if warding off savage blows. The comforter was knocked askew, and suddenly both of his knees shot up, flinging it to the floor. With a fierce cry he rose up and began flailing at his invisible assailants; she could distinguish only 'no, no, no' as he fell back in a crumpled ball, knees up and against the belly like a monstrous foetus. Then everything began to quiver, then tremble, then quake – skin, puffed flesh, the elastic bone, the pale lids of the eyes. She heard the scraping of his clenched teeth and the embowelled groan trapped behind it. The force of it unbent his body and popped his eyes wide open.

Hap Withers, bless him, promised to stay close, but Lily assured him there was no need. She was not frightened. After one of his brief seizures, Bradley was calm and perfectly lucid, as if some kind of exorcism had occurred without his blessing. Although his voice was thin and without colour, it was one she remembered, and from the ruined housing of that flesh it was Bradley's eyes that looked at her. On these occasions he was usually able to speak for half an hour or so before he tired and slipped into a sleep which was both shallow and fathomless. In the seven days that he lived – during which she left his side for brief moments only, trying to sleep when he did, eating with him, suffering with him as she had so many times before when the fever and the fever-dream chose to strike – they never really had a conversation. If he were quiet but alert, she would speak for a while, telling him what she thought he ought to know or just letting him hear the strength of her voice. He would dip his chin slightly or move his eyes in a certain way to let her know she was to continue, and sometimes, though rarely, he would murmur in assent or acceptance. At other times she would find him awake and before she could utter his name, he would begin talking in his whispered monotone. When this happened, she had to sit close to him to catch every word; if she moved an inch to loosen the crick in her neck, his eyes would widen with a childish terror and he would start to speed up his speech towards a frantic blur until she moved in close enough, once more. At times she felt he was talking right past her to some more unconvinced ear beyond this room – the words, the jumble of ideas, the arcane references, the assumed knowledge – all tending to puzzle and estrange. Yet even when the flow of his talk became trancelike or confessional, she had only to turn her head to one side before he seized upon the gesture as a betrayal. Every word that he uttered during the last week of his life was something he needed to say, and, in a way she never fully understood, something he needed to say to her or in her presence. Though all of it was obviously not meant for her, every word and every deed behind it required a sanction only she could give. She made it her business to cherish each syllable.

2

When Bradley and Paul Chambers made good their escape to Toronto in June of 1882, they knew precisely what they wanted and where to find it. They set themselves up in a bachelor quarters on King Street, close to the city's centre and some distance from the academic community they had vowed to repudiate. Though there were no salons in which they could instantly expose their superior talents, they knew which coffee-houses and taverns to frequent and which clubs to infiltrate to promote the cause they were now celebrating with selfless gratuity – art for its own sake, beauty because it is beautiful, the ideal of the mind transcendent and nudging towards cosmic conscious-ness. Or something like that. Bradley lugged his satchel of poems everywhere there was a potential audience and Paul Chambers his sheaf of political pamphlets. They badgered the journalists and cub reporters in the beverage rooms along King and Bay, they tried to impress the cognoscenti of Canada First who loitered about the coffee houses around Yonge and Adelaide, they even costumed themselves as gentlemen and passed undiscovered amongst a gathering of the literati at the Grange, a cabal whose bourgeois decadence they took pleasure in disparaging. They spent not a little of their time in haberdasheries searching for clothing appropriate to the Wildean image they had preserved intact from their encounter with the great man. They shunned black. When the University term began in September, they took a cab up to College Street and stood in the sunshine of the walkway below the Main Building, dazzling in their improvised Pre-Raphaelite finery, purveying disdain to the wretched freshmen by their mere presence. Paul's father, ever gullible, believed his son had settled in to school and continued to send money until the Dean's letter at Christmastime disabused him. Paul was summoned home, and for a few black days Bradley sat in the rooming house, out of money, and wondered when the walls would crash mercifully in upon him. Several times he started to write a letter home, the words tangling and seizing in his remorse. He could find no words to describe the aloneness deep within, impermeable to love or loathing alike. His poems seemed trivial, a mocking impertinence in the face of his suffering.

Paul Chambers arrived on New Year's day, in time to pay the rent and nurse his friend through a bout of pneumonia. He had succeeded in convincing his father that he needed merely to 'sow his oats' for a few months more, to 'get Europe out of his system' and then he would settle down. He even made flagrant promises to consider engagement to a plain young woman of resistible virtue who lived just down the street. He kissed her once on the front porch. The upshot was a guaranteed monthly income for as long as he needed it, the sum total to be deducted from his considerable inheri-tance if he turned out to be a bad investment. Paul grinned and said, "Now we can begin to live, you and I. We shall make things happen."

Bradley continued to have some success in getting his poems published in Goldwyn Smith's journals and elsewhere in underground circulars. Paul managed a few biting letters-to-the-editor in the *Mail* and one in the *Globe*. What happened, of more sig-nificance, was their meeting up with the Crawfords sometime late in January. Sarah

Crawford was a journalist of sorts, who wrote and sold fleeting pieces for the papers and did copy-editing when she needed to eat. "We met in a coffee-house, she was sitting alone in a dusky corner of the room; she was elfin and spare, with porcelain skin and starveling eyes; she exuded a brittle, painful beauty. When she spoke to me I fell madly in love. She knew who I was, we talked, I returned to my den and began pouring out breathless anapests to love and beauty and faithfulness – every one dedicated to the goddess Sarah."

They met again, and one day Sarah led Bradley and Paul back to her lodgings not far from their own. She wanted them to meet her cousin, a 'real poet'. Whatever they had prepared themselves for, the bard they were introduced to when they entered the drafty second-storey walkup over a wholesaler's depot was not one of the imagined possibilities. First of all, it was a woman, who also bore an odd name: Isabella Valancy Crawford. She did not resemble any picture of a poetess they were ready to accept. She was a plain woman in her early thirties, though her age was hard to determine because she was consumptively pale with luminous dark eyes that were simultaneously child-like and agedly wise, releasing only half the pain they were feeding upon. The rest lay hidden below a brave smile, waiting, as they were soon to learn, to be ambushed by words. Her speech was courteous but up-country Irish, unadorned by wit or felicity of phrase. Though she appeared to listen politely to the young men and her cousin while they postured and pamphleteered through the long evening hours in a room with the fire dead, the coal run out, the lamps sweating – she had little stamina for argument, lapsing into a trance interrupted only by a requisite smile now and again. She found no passion to respond to the great debates the young lions arranged on their tri-weekly visits throughout the winter.

Sarah lived with Isabella and the latter's mother in three rooms above the hubbub of a warehouse quiet only on Sundays. They were bitterly poor, lighting a fire in the morning and again in the evening though the winter was severe. The two young women wrote occasionally for the newspapers, but Isabella spent most of her time composing stories and poems. "I would come in with Sarah late on a wintry day; the room would be filled with the lurid light of sunless snow, the fire perished in its grate. Isabella would not immediately turn to greet us; she was always seated in a hard-backed rocker, facing at a quarter-angle the window which overlooked the frozen gardens to the south. She appeared to be gazing *through* the landscape, catching it with an odd perspective, you could still see the surprise in her whole face as she swung slowly round to acknowledge our presence. Sometimes I would ask Sarah to stay downstairs while I slipped unnoticed into the room to watch her there by the window, her hands gripping one another across her lap as if it was their task to hold back the petty anguish of daily existence while her eyes were freed to interrogate the bleak details of the universe out there. Once Paul said to me, 'She has a haunted look about her,' but I said, 'Yes, though it appears to me that when she stares outward at the world *she's* attempting to haunt *it*.'"

They read aloud their polemics – Emersonian Platonism, domesticated Darwin, *ars gratia artis* – and their poems. Isabella listened carefully, as a starved sparrow leans towards the dawn-light, but never made a comment of any kind. Nor did she offer to read her own verse, though Sarah showed them a stack of completed work almost a foot high. In the meantime Sarah was persuaded to return on occasion to Bradley's place where they made love. Sarah's eyes shone with gratitude and unappeased desire; he felt the glow of the halo everywhere on her skin. Holding his breath, he measured the dithy-rambics of her heart as she cadenced towards climax. They decided that she, not her cousin, ought to have been the poetess. She had the gift of gratuitous pleasure, she worshipped the beauty in the world as she did in herself.

One day in early April when Isabella and her mother were out for the afternoon, Sarah and Bradley made love on the cold floor, and afterwards, over coffee, Sarah suggested that Bradley take a look at Isabella's poems. "She's a great poet, I'm sure of it; she's sold many of her stories, but only a few of her poems. Maybe you could help." At first Bradley refused to violate Isabella's privacy, but at last he was persuaded to do so with a view to being of some assistance. Inside, he was trembling with anticipation. What kind of poetry would he find uttered by such an ungainly, plain-spoken, suffering creature? What he found – as he read page after page for more than two hours – amazed and appalled him. The effort was prodigious, thousands of striding epic lines; the great themes challenged – good and evil, love and hate, the primitive and the urbane; a compulsive energy of conviction and quest. But all this potential glory was disfigured by clumsy rhythms and preposterous images. Here the sweep of myth and idea was contaminated by the characters devised to speak for them – primordial savages, unschooled lumberjacks, backwoods damsels. And the scenery! Wild waterfalls, ugly pine-forests, rock-battered torrents, gaudy sunsets. The result was not beauty – of theme or cadence or delicacy of image. Bradley felt a cold pocket where his heart should have been. The poetasters of Canada First had written of the native maple with mock-eloquence and unimpaired metre in a pathetic attempt to graft beauty onto a colonial landscape, but this was infinitely more dangerous; here the ugly potence of raw landscape and its aboriginal scatology were released outright to mix, as they might, with the quintessentials of civility.

So, when Paul suggested a week later that their journey towards cosmic consciousness was in danger of being derailed by the impedimentum of phenomena – that is, getting bogged down in everyday obligations – Bradley agreed. A day later they were in Montreal, unencumbered by goodbyes of any kind. However, they did not find in the first city of the country that large, free air they wished to breathe. Here there was even more politics, in two languages, and even more obsession with the local and the transitory. They survived only till the summer of 1883 when Paul persuaded Bradley that only in England itself could they be free to worship the beautiful, in London where the great Wilde held court and where the accents of Swinburne and Rosetti echoed at matins and vespers. They decided to 'rough it' in true vagabond style, booking passage on a freighter. But when Bradley became ill, they both moved up to the officer's deck, at great expense. However, money was not a problem, then or ever. Paul was devoted to him. He sat by his cot and read aloud to Bradley some of his own verse, and though it failed to cure the flu, it gave both of them a bit of the courage they were afraid to admit the absence of. "You are a genius," Paul announced as the train pulled into Victoria

Station. "I am content to be the genie." He was true to his word. The loyalty he had longed to give to his family or even to his own bright hopes – and found he could not – was transferred to his friend without regret. They took up lodgings on the south bank, in Shakespeare's territory, but soon moved up to Chelsea to a flat they labelled a garret but might have served a duke's younger son. And while Bradley began once again to write poem after poem, Paul set about penetrating the literary chambers of the world's most cultured city.

Within months, using his connections with the few influential Canadians he met in London, Paul had insinuated Madame Wilde's salon, and though they were successful in meeting such rising luminaries as Whistler, Frank Miles and Byrne-Jones, they were never lucky enough to catch the Great Aesthete himself at home. But Wilde was everywhere – in the witticisms and putdowns that circulated secondhand but undiluted through salon and soiree. That winter was a harsh one and Bradley was sick most of the time. He wrote nothing. Paul remained at his side, reading constantly to him. By April the roses were in bud and Bradley began writing again. He had the outlines of an epic poem in his head. Paul foraged daily in the British Museum for books on ancient mythologies. By October he had the first of twelve sections completed. Paul decided that Oscar Wilde himself should see this paean to the Beautiful. The epic would bear the weight of this title: *The Ruin of Arcady.*

"We waited outside the Cafe Royal where we knew Whistler and Wilde spent most of their afternoons. It was pouring rain. We tried waiting in the main room but it was choked with smoke and a burly postilion stood guard at the door to the side-chamber where Wilde's silken accents mingled with the American's broadcloth twang." They had been waiting in the cold drizzle for two hours before the two men emerged, Wilde easily recognizable in his Eskimo coat, bare head cocked to one side as if just delivering or recovering from a verbal sally, brown shoulder-length curls as impudent as the womanly lips set for a snarl. 'I'm Chambers,' Paul said, 'I've written often to you.' He glanced at Whistler who chose not to remember their having met. Wilde scoured Paul's face, annoyed then faintly bemused at what he was seeing. "He waved us in under an awning farther up the street. 'We're the Canadians,' Paul persisted. 'We heard you speak in Toronto.' Wilde and Whistler exchanged glances and signals. Wilde then peered at me, who had said nothing to this point, and I saw a click of recognition as quick as a camera's shutter before it was extinguished by his perpetual ironic glint. I stared at him, trying to connect the beaver coat and the elegant epigrams of his published remarks. 'I see you're appraising my Canadian fur,' he said. 'It was given me by one of your Esquimaux during an uncharacteristic heat-wave, an act of foolish magnanimity I am certain he has had reason to regret many times since.' Whistler chuckled asthmatically. Encouraged, Wilde continued, this time looking at Paul. 'Odd country, though. I'm told, and have firsthand experience to prove so, that whereas other dominions have prevailing winds, Canada has a prevailing season: winter.' Paul managed a laugh of sorts, despite his chattering teeth, and said bluntly, 'Did you receive the outline of Mr. Marshall's epic I sent you in August?' 'So this is the tongueless Philomel, then?' he said to me. 'I'm no nightingale, but I am a poet, sir,' I said. He smiled, and for a moment seemed undecided how to extricate himself from the situation, the cold rain, the pestilence of minor bards. 'Ah yes, the young colonial with the epic grasp. I do remember,' he lied without a faltering blink. 'Well, my advice to you gentlemen is exactly the same as I gave to Mr. Whistler here when he arrived fresh from Atlantica: stay here long enough to learn how to speak English, then go back home and bedazzle your poor relations.' Whistler was still chortling when they turned the corner and headed for Tite Street."

Paul viewed the disaster as a minor setback. He said he had a good chance of meeting Swinburne who was, after all, the greatest practising poet in all of England. What had Wilde ever *written*? He took Bradley out for a night on the town. They brought a couple of sweet-faced whores home with them, but Bradley was too drunk to perform so Paul had to do double-duty. When Paul woke up late the next morning, the women were gone and the flat was in such a mess he almost did not see the suicide note on the table. It simply informed him that Bradley had decided to take the only path now open to him. He thanked his friend for his devotion and begged him – as a dying man's wish – not to inform anyone of his death, not Sarah and especially not his mother. But Paul knew Bradley better than he had suspected. He went immediately, instinctively, to the spot along the river below the Tower Bridge where he was certain the suicide attempt would take place. He found Bradley's clothing in a neat pile on the ancient wharf, the blurred shadow of the fabled bridge falling across it. He peered out into the water where a cold mist was rapidly descending and saw Bradley's head slowly disappear under the brown surface. He screamed, too late. For five minutes he watched the widening circle where Bradley had gone under until the mist sank over it. He picked up the clothing and returned to the flat. For three days he scanned the papers for accounts of the drowning. There were many each day. He visited the morgue and stared wretchedly at the puffed cadavers under dripping tap-water. Finally, he sat down and wrote Sarah. He had to tell someone. The burden was too great, too unfair.

"I heard Paul's cry but it made no impression on me. Wilde's remarks had served an inadvertently merciful purpose. They cut away with their cruel clarity the festering scab I had allowed to grow over the remorse and self-loathing I had felt unceasingly since the moment that crockery jar smashed on the bedroom floor and I fled like a thief into the night with the money you had laboured for and shored up against a future you expected we would share. My life was a sham. With Paul's cry ringing in my ears, I opened my mouth and swallowed death. I felt the fierce current pull my feet from the bottom and draw me into its horizontal rush to the estuary. I fancied I saw through the murk and haze the shadow of those twin towers and their eight-hundred-year-old stones. I waited for my breath to collapse so the Thames could enter my lungs. But it didn't. Though my arms remained motionless, my feet and legs were pumping steadily enough to force my face through the surface. I could not stop them. The will to live remained in them, out of reach of my despair, and gradually that determination eased upward until at last my arms began rocking as smooth as oars and I found myself not only afloat but aimed for a blunt headland on my left. I flopped down on the grass there like a beached whale – exhausted. I was miles from my entry point, out in the countryside somewhere. I could smell the mist sweet on the autumn grasses. I drifted into unconsciousness. When I woke I was in a fisherman's cottage with my head bandaged. The old woman said I'd struck a rock coming ashore. They'd seen me and arrived just as I collapsed. Three days had passed. I was too weak to hold a soupspoon. I was, alas, alive."

It was almost ten days later when Bradley walked into the Chelsea flat and surprised Paul as he was packing books into a large crate. After reunion and explanations, Paul remembered with horror that he had written Sarah. Bradley said it was better she think him dead. Paul then swore he would not tell her under any circumstances of the resurrection.

The next seven years were spent in the same flat and only the outlines of what happened need be told, shameful as they were, in Bradley's opinion. Paul's father continued to send his son money, mainly to keep him from coming home and disgracing everyone (his spies had given him too accurate a report of his son's activities, though they did not bother to mention the name of his 'live-in male lover'). Paul took a mistress and spent much of his time at her apartments in Paddington. Bradley went back to *The Ruins of Arcady* more convinced than ever by his brush with death that he was destined to suffer and create something of value. Paul remained his staunchest supporter. He got involved in politics, gathered some influence around him and promoted his friend's 'genius' unflaggingly. Bradley wrote and suffered, fell ill, wrote and drank. By 1890, the year that Wilde published *The Picture of Dorian Gray in Lippincott's Magazine*, Bradley was alternating bouts of alcoholism with bouts of illness and debauchery. Paul's mistress abandoned him for a Lord of the Realm, and he began bringing home a miscellany of tarts and cast-offs. Somehow in the brief interludes *The Ruins of Arcady* was completed. Wilde was now famous again, and what-is-more his latest companion was none other than Robert Baldwin Ross, teenage son of Canada's former attorney-general and patron of the Chamber's law firm. Robbie Ross was wined and dined, and at last agreed to present Bradley's magnum opus to Wilde. Bradley did not touch a drink for more than a month. He slept beside the fireplace, shivering, all during the month of February, 1891 while they waited anxiously for a response. Robbie Ross came around to their flat to inform them that they both were invited to a soirée at the Tite Street house on the fifteenth of March. Wilde had read the poem, all ten thousand lines of it.

"Young Robbie met us at the door, flushed with excitement. 'Oscar' was in the drawing room with 'Jimmy' Whistler and his new friend 'Bosie' Douglas and several other regulars, but first we had to be given the grand tour of Number 16 Tite Street. I was far too anxious to pay close attention to details – but I remember thinking how odd Robbie Ross's flat cadences sounded among the sophistication of Moorish casements, ceilings bedewed with pressed peacock plumage, the works of Whistler and Manet hanging everywhere, and walls decorated with a Pointillist's palette. As if to underline my thought, Robbie paused before a Constable-like painting of the Scottish countryside in the hallway just outside the drawing room and said, 'This is one of Oscar's favourite pieces, by Homer Watson – from Ontario. Oscar met him in Toronto'. He paused again and looking at me said, 'Oscar has a way of attracting people'."

"Oscar was seated on a throne-shaped, white wicker chair, delicately latticed and coifed with ostrich feathers not too distant from the moulting season. Around him everything was white – the eggshell walls, the ivory casements, the bleached wool of the sofa and settee – or its opposite among the decorated paraphernalia – black walnut, blue crystal, imperial crimson, chinese jade, polished onyx. The effect was of a brilliant chill, an exquisite tastefulness purged of feeling and the lesser niceties. The sun had not quite gone down yet, so the natural light still streamed in through the capacious windows unencumbered by curtains. The room, like the man himself, seemed an awesome combination of the austere Grecian and the sumptuality of Rome."

"Wilde was ornately polite to the guests, waving us with a plump sigh of his hands towards two cushions set out near the throne. He began immediately to regale his audience with drolleries from his visit to America, making certain to include us in the amusement by tilting his brow in our direction in the most confidential manner he could muster. Whistler and Bosie, a blonde leonine figure with a touch of Adonis in the face, mounted a mock counter-attack to accelerate the repartee, and as the banished shadows poured out of their burrows and worm-casts to engulf the ersatz aesthetic of the room, I never took my eyes off Wilde's face. Shorn of ambient light and the corona of the beautified room itself, his features – mercurial, wit-quick, tightened by tenderness, ransomed by inexhaustible humour – lapsed into shadow. Though the elegance of phrase and the swift épée-cut of his wit continued unabated, under lamplight I began to notice that the mobile lips, hedged by shadow, now seemed bloated; the cheeks more rounded, their translucent skin pulled by the jaw's swerve across rancid flesh; the impudent tumble of his Byronic curls now coiled and sensitive and raven. I turned my gaze at last to the manilla folder beside his chair, where my poem lay, my last bid on the future."

"Without preface, Wilde reached down and took up into his flaccid grasp *The Ruins of Arcady*. At that precise moment I became aware of the odour of incense; only one lamp burned in a far corner. Wilde did not acknowledge the ripple of chatelaine laughter as he flipped the folder open to the title page. I watched his face; the smile was gangrenous."

"I have read this epicurean saga with great care and much expense of time and spirit, not to speak of sweat. About the monumental text itself I can find nothing to say, which in its own way might be the highest form of perverse praise possible in these dreadful pedestrian days. Nonetheless, I do have some personal advice for you which I hope you will take to heart."

"It was suddenly still and silent; the air was perfumed with belladonna as the room readied itself for a proclamation from the messiah of the Beautiful. "My suggestion is that you should concern yourself with writing about...*bricks*. A word, wouldn't you agree, that has a certain granite ring about it, that conjures up – if that isn't too cogent a phrase – wonderfully rustic images. And think of the bucolic possibilities for rhyme: sticks, ricks, picks, ticks, hicks, not to mention the myriad *cricks* which I am assured decorate your unlettered landscape in America."

"Naturally there was appreciative laughter, and for a moment, despite the terror just below my throat, even I was willing to believe for a few seconds that these remarks were just a preliminary but necessary part to the game. But soon Wilde began quizzing Robbie Ross about life as it was presently lived in the backwoods of Ontario, tossing severe glances in the direction of Bosie – now slumped in a comatose embrace with a startled young man who professed to be a playwright but was at the moment beginning to doubt the authenticity of his muse. The shadows deepened and exposed. The conversations continued, desultory and fragmenting. I was numb, beyond panic. I closed my eyes. Wilde's voice carried on through its own fatigue. He was arguing with Whistler in a whining, strident tone that said 'we've been over this ground before, why are we doing it again, why can't we let the damn thing lie, what is left to be gained – not pride or point or jot of mother wit, we are tangled in the wearisome toil of language itself'. In rumpled corners I heard the slithering contact of septic flesh."

"Somehow I managed to reach over and retrieve my manuscript – the labour of eight years – and held it in my hands as if I were gazing at my own corpse not quite confined. Wilde's hand was on my shoulder. He swung his tall, sad face down to mine, and said for my ears only in the voice he might have used when talking to himself in a dream, 'Go home, lad. Your people are merely crazy; here they all claim to be sane. If you must grow roses for the world's consumption, start by digging in your own shit.' For a moment no hint of mockery creased his gaze. Then as if he sensed he might have been overheard and realized how much might have been revealed under the mask, he flicked open the high-speed shutter of his eyes just as a purpled lip pursed around the barb of his blackened tooth: 'I speak metaphorically of course,' he said with a fatigued glance at the revived Bosie."

"Somehow I found the courage to say goodbye to Paul Chambers, whose devotion to a cause and selfless loyalty to his friend's was a galling contrast to my own wasted existence. There was no one I had not let down. Everyone who had dared to love me I allowed to suffer with callous indifference as I pursued some demon disguised as an angel. He pressed some money on me and saw me off at the quayside. He said tearfully that he himself could never go home; I told him I had no other choice. When Landsend was no longer visible and I had not yet taken my first drink, I walked out onto the stern-deck and sitting on a canvas stool I opened the folder containing my epic to Eternal Beauty. There was a heartening breeze from the west, and one by one I lifted up each of those thousand misbegotten pages and let them blow into the wayward swells where they hung for a moment like swan's feathers before melting into the universality of the sea. I did not weep for a single page."

"When I finally got off the train in Toronto, after a typically rough March crossing, I was too sick to take another drink. I staggered into the station and fell onto a bench, trying to breathe. With the few dollars remaining, I planned to buy a ticket on the Grand Trunk express for Point Edward. Above me a calendar, with a fresh page turned, told me it was April1, 1891. My birthday. I was twenty-seven years old."

"A cabbie came over when he heard me coughing, and asked if there was any place in the city he could take me. I started to tell him I was going on to Lambton County when I was wracked by a coughing spell that left me dizzy and helpless. I could hardly hang on to his arm as he lifted me into the coach. I whispered an address to him, the only one I could remember. When we came to the wholesaler's on King Street, the old fellow kindly went upstairs to see if anyone there still knew me. When he returned, Sarah Crawford was running ahead of him."

"Isabella had died four years before but Sarah had stayed on, living with a succession of distant cousins eager to try out the big city. Her beauty had deepened, and sick as I was, I was terrified by those eyes where I saw undiminished the love she had long ago squandered on some evanescent ideal. However, I was too weak to make any protests as she took me in that weekend, cared for me, talked to me, veiled whatever disenchantment she must have felt, and finally got me into a profound, restorative sleep. By Sunday afternoon I was sitting up, taking soup and eager for the taste of news, some sign that the world had kept going in spite of my personal apostasy. Of course, nothing I thought or felt or said during those hours made any real sense – I was a man benumbed, hollowed out, incapable of coherent speech. That Sarah was ready to bless it with comprehension was a miracle I only dimly realized the danger of. Some thread of decency, voiceless but pressing, was telling me I must escape before it was too late, that I had no right to put another life at risk. The last thing a condemned man wants is salvation when he's already resigned himself to something less painful. But sometime later in the evening I felt her warmth unbending beside me; her flesh, never ample, descended like a comforter over my everywhere-aching; her breath, her murmuring, her cry of completion spun transcendent through my desperate dreaming. Before I woke to regret her absence, I dreamt that Isabella was across the room from me, seated in her straight-backed chair, her hands steadfast in their clasp against reality, the eyes in quest of the myths locked in the landscape's obscure angularity, the courage-to-be and of being-in-verse still shining out of the unshadowed face not yet ready to acknowledge the stopped heart. Even then I knew, as I did later when I read her poems again, that she had always been right. So had Wilde."

"I left next morning while Sarah was at work, leaving her a jumbled excuse of a letter. I still had some of Paul's money left, but I never got to the station. I was hale enough to reach The Tankard, the old haunt, and promptly got drunk with two journalists I recalled having despised. I remained drunk for a year. I was a beggar, a skid-row bum. I had hit bottom."

"I knew that Sarah would try to find me, so I arranged for my 'pals' to intercept her and tell her that I had gone home, and when I was recovered would return to Toronto. Under no circumstances was she to contact me first. With that good deed completed, I could settle down to destroying myself in earnest."

"It was August of this year – sixteen months later – when I woke up in a hospital and lay there helplessly while doctors and nurses forcibly revived me. I'd had my third bout of the D.T.'s, and the next one, the doctor reassured me, would be the last. Penniless, dried out and looking fifty years old, I tottered out into the midsummer heat of downtown Toronto. Sarah was waiting at the gate. Someone had been suborned. She too looked much older, much wearier. I was unable to offer resistance anyway, and allowed myself to be escorted home. Eddie was waiting for me. My son. Seven months old. Whole. He smiled at me as if it were the natural thing to do to your enemy."

"It was hard but I didn't take another drink. I knew full well that I couldn't build another life for myself. There was nothing left. But I thought I could perhaps borrow whatever of me remained in Sarah and the boy, and hang on as long as I could. I owed the world something. As soon as I was better, I planned to bring Sarah and Eddie here for a while. At long last I realized what I could never admit all those years, whether I was up or down: that it was you I must see – not to reconcile or expiate, but merely to release. Though less merciful, love is more binding than death."

"Suddenly a few weeks ago, I began writing poems, scraps of verse, lines only but powerful ones, expunging ones, untranslatable, with images so stark they seemed to have been drawn with the ink of dreams. Every one of them was about Sarah. I finished only one. It's in my satchel; I want you to have it. It's not much, but it's all that's left of me. I read it to Sarah in the evening before she died."

3

Granny woke up with the sun on her back, streaming through the kitchen window and the open doorway behind her. Stiffly she rose and went in to put the kettle on. She fidgeted with the new-fangled gas range until it popped into flame. Well, well, she thought, that wasn't too difficult, was it? Maybe I'll even get used to it.

At least you came home, Brad. That's something.

59

1

Knowing she would not sleep much the night before the ceremony, Granny switched off the electric lights in the front room, lit the coal-oil lamp and placed it on the table beside Arthur's trunk. She sat down and began leafing through the memorabilia of a lifetime. Each of the playbills recalled the story Arthur had associated with it, something bizarre in event or character, something that always ended with a chuckle or a wink in her direction that said 'the world's a funny place if you don't die laughing'. The lingering twilight – they were just past the high solstice – had just succumbed to the deep darkness of the summer night when she reached into Bradley's satchel and drew out the loose scraps of paper on which he had scrawled his last words. Among their blotted, unfinished number she found the copy of his poem to Sarah, the one she had made before sending the original off to Eddie. Had he read it before he died? Did it make any difference?

She stared at the five stanzas – not quite filling a single page with lines that touched neither margin. So this is it, she thought, this is what all the pain of birth and loss and absence and wishing-to-be has come down to? A few lines of shrunken verse. This is where all the joy of foolish affection and helpless love and desire under the dark has finally landed? In this let's-pretend house confected out of pity, with a worn-out skin-and-bones scarecrow of a crone who can't even say hello or goodbye or it's time to go. All that energy of genesis, all that procreative hope, all that suffering smothered in the mouth and held in and mined against the future. For this. For nothing.

After Mama's death Old Samuels, wise in his blindness, had said to her, "We must listen to the good gods and keep them on our side; they will help those who listen for them. But we must also help the gods. Sometimes the demons are strong and the good gods go into hiding." Well, she had done her share of listening and she had tried her best to help. So had the others. Old Samuels assured her she was one of those chosen to hear their special music and dance it for the world's sake. Well, she had danced in her time, but not enough perhaps, perhaps without the purity of purpose the music needed to prevail.

A series of images passed before her eyes. Maman LaRouche kneading fat buttocks of dough before the outdoor oven and sliding them into its wombing heat where they would pop into being like fairy-tale babies, and Maman LaRouche lying ever so quietly in her bed of ice afraid of waking the robins before spring arrived, and the Frenchman dead with the clench of a curse unuttered against the malign spirits of that place he could never recognize as home and knowing with his last breath his children would scatter before his flesh was cold and not a kinsman left even to tend a grave or whisper a purgatorial prayer, and her own Mama rocking to the rhythms of the brushstrokes through her hair as the sun mellowed in the little room she was preparing to enter alone, and Papa's voice above the embers telling of ocean voyages and rescue at sea and brave departures and love broken by effort and fatigue and failure against the deities of the bush and Papa's arm about her at last shepherding her into sleep, and Old Samuels' pipesmoke and the words that came through it and lifted some feeling/some hope that floated in her all the years and even now, and the dances she did to resurrect the twinkle in the old sagamore's eye, and the mask of Southener's face in the stillest of dawns and the sad auguries breaking there like raw light through ancient mist, and the graveyard of the lost and the dispossessed not a mile away where some of the benevolent spirits still crouched in anxious wait and where the wind-tossed grasses took root in that more ample quietude, and Aunt Bridie at twenty wrapped in her mother's shawl against the sea-wind, standing alone on the foredeck and staring ahead where some land was supposed to be in which even orphans could find love, and Uncle Chester among the workshop shavings coaxing wood into toy shapes his son would never see, and Tom dancing at the Great Western Ball happy and handsome and unaware that across the room an eye had caught him in its prophecy, and Tom's arms and Tom's laugh and Tom's touch in the near-dark and the mutual yearning that gave them Robbie and Brad and sent them off to cultivate the minor gods of this ground they hoped at last to be able to call home – but you left me, Tom, you left me and I don't know why and I never will and I've missed you every day since, even those days when I refused to say your name aloud and banished your treachery from all thought, and I think of you haunting some barren-ground above Superior with a ghost who can't find his way back, just as Uncle Chester lies among Baptists and do-gooders in a town he never saw and would have hated, as Aunt Bridie lies caged in some Yankee mausoleum with her emigré soul battering forever at the cold bars, as Solomon lies in his underwater coffin staring up at the chilling sun, as Mama and the La Rouches lie unvisited under nameless markers in a stranger's cemetery even the bees are ashamed to attend, as Lucien lies reclaimed by the territory he spent a lifetime fleeing from, as Sophie lies in the grief of the deep, cool earth and dreams of fire and air, as Robbie lies in his soldier's tomb at Batoche where the curious come to cluck and wonder, as Papa lies in a Negro churchyard worshipped in anonymity by puzzled blacks, as Eddie lies nowhere and everywhere in the charnel-house of Europe.

You, Eddie, you were the reason for it all, the reason the world held out to us in derision. You came like a son of Lazarus, conceived in a moment of miraculous randomness. You had the mark of redemption on you from the beginning. You redeemed the wastrel who fathered you and passed along to you the gift of speech and its poetries. You brought me back to the best part of myself, you reminded me that the benevolent gods Old Samuels talked about – always under siege – could in the midst of their powerlessness make subversive music, you showed me again what I had always known: that belief is a hard flame to extinguish; you brought me back to the words Cap had nourished me with before he could die, you brought me to Arthur and together we pledged allegiance to the future you promised just by your being.

It had come to naught. There was no meaning after all in events, in words, in the sufferings of the human heart. They were random and terrible. Cap was right: history is a fiction, a weak disguise for our disordered desires.

She was looking at Bradley's poem. Though she knew it by heart, she went through the motions of reading it.

COLLOQUY, FOR SARAH

MAN:

> December's grasped my soul,
> stark, leaf-bereft of
> all but spite
> at autumn's fall –
> from the infidel dark
> I curse you'
> for having loved.
>
>
> Alone, in your grave
> you sing with the
> strength for two
> of olives and January
> light

WOMAN:

> Across the winter's
> width a cruising wind,
> brute sun, a
> lecherous petal
> licking light.
> In your distress
> you rake the
> bruised map

GUTTERIDGE / *Lily's Story*

of my face with a
treacherous kiss
I draw down
towards the dappled
acre of my
          tenderness.
We go under
and wait.

Not enough to keep Eddie alive, she thought. But it was, without question, beautiful.

Just before she drifted into a clear, dreamless sleep, a single image asserted itself – without preface or prologue: she was five years old, she was in the woods, she was watching a tiny head squeeze out of some fleshly crevice like a water-logged chestnut, until its gleaming skull burst forth in a halo of blood whose petals spun at her feet, whose medallions dripped from the slow leafage. As the scene faded, she distinctly heard the sound of Rabbit's boyish laugh.

2

When she woke it was mid-morning, and she felt surprisingly rested. Moments later Prudie Denfield arrived, all smiles and about to make a to-do over getting her 'frumped up' for the grand occasion. Prudie noted with some satisfaction that Granny had been using the gas range. Prudie heated lots of water and helped her bathe and powder her wrinkles and ease her angles into the deceiving curves of the dress. A scarecrow in a tux is still a scarecrow, she thought, suddenly wishing she could speak – to murmur all the pleasantries and reassuring simplicities of woman's casual conversation. Prudie, bless her, gabbed on as if Granny were holding up her end of the bargain. There was perhaps something odd in that effusiveness, some special feeling of affection behind it that was not carried at all in the words or even the tone. Also, she caught Prudie more than once staring at her when she thought she was unnoticed, with a sort of wondering appraisal, the way one searches the face and gestures of a person you've just been told is a friend you haven't seen for thirty years. When she was caught out, Prudie blushed briefly, then began to talk with even greater urgency about the trivia of dress and protocol. Something strange was afoot.

About ten o'clock, an hour before the ceremony, as Prudie was putting the final touches on her stitchery, Granny saw three figures coming along the sidewalk towards her house. Prudie spotted them, too, and dropped her pins, said, "Oh my, Cora, it's time for me to go and get ready. I'll just let myself out the back way." And she did.

Sunny Denfield turned into her yard, resplendent in his uniform. Beside him, keeping pace, was a young woman of medium height whose brown hair, straight nose and curious dark eyes suggested close kinship with the Reeve. Ruth-Anne, she thought, the cousin from Toronto. The tailored clothing and confident bearing at once bespoke a woman from the city, with breeding and inherited urbanity. Between them, and struggling to keep pace with a sort of dancing skip-and-a-jump, was a waif of a creature, blond as a Viking water-sprite, with freckles as big as her blue eyes, in a flounced yellow dress as bold as a butterfly wing, out of which the narrow, tapered little-girl limbs sashayed with all the awkward grace of an apprentice ballerina.

Granny let them in, unable to take her eyes off the little girl. When she finally met Sunny Denfield's gaze, she knew something had happened since his last visit three days before, something more profound and unsettling than the arrival of a cousin and her daughter. He was in turn staring at her in a way which suggested that some long-suspected truth had been confirmed, though not unattended by surprise. The young woman was also staring at her with a mixture of curiosity and awe. The little girl hopped up and down on the spot between them. She couldn't have been more than six years of age.

These exchanges took seconds only, and Sunny said, "Mornin'. I brought you someone I know you've been anxious to meet."

She nodded to indicate that she knew who they were and was happy to receive them. When Sunny paused mysteriously, like a bad tragedian before a soliloquy, his cousin made as if to speak on her own behalf and he cut in quickly. "I'd like you to meet my first cousin, Ruth-Anne MacEnroe. Ruth-Anne, this is Mrs. Coote, my longtime friend, an' your long-lost grandmother."

Ruth-Anne opened her mouth to speak, but could not. What she had already seen, whatever form it had taken, had confirmed the impossible, and she let several unladylike tears escape through her astonished smile.

Sunny pressed ahead. He put his hand on the little girl's shoulder and she looked up at the old woman. "An' this is –" he said, his own voice on the verge of breaking... *Victoria*, Granny said to herself in a rush before Sunny said, "Victoria, your great granddaughter."

At fifteen minutes before eleven, just as the first strains of the drum-and-bugle corps were carried southward on the soft breeze of that special day, four figures emerged from the new house and crossed the street to join the host of villagers already assembled before the monument.

3

Over the next two weeks, and before Ruth-Anne and Victoria had to return to Toronto, the stories on both sides were gradually and lovingly told. Granny wrote out her responses to the questions of her granddaughter and her 'foster nephew' – as Sunny now called himself – in a cramped hand that only gradually began to flow and curve with the urgency and excitement of the impossible narrative.

When Mrs. Edgeworth in the spring of 1861 had written down 'Lily Fairchild' on a calling card and given it to the government man who had come to repossess the Prince's daughter, no one had any idea of the consequences of the act. Apparently the card accompanied the child, whom Lily had secretly named Victoria, to her new home in Toronto with Olive and Parker Macdonnell. Macdonnell was a busy minister in the

Baldwin-LaFontaine cabinet and thus left the raising of their adopted daughter mainly to his wife. The little girl was christened Grace and a year later, as often happens in such cases, a natural daughter was born to the Macdonnells, and called Faith. Faith and Grace were raised together, without prejudice. Both married, Faith to a barrister named Harvey Denfield and Grace to an entrepreneur named Bramwell Beattie. Just before she died in 1890, Olive Macdonnell summoned Grace to her bedside and told her that she was an adopted child, and that even though she had promised on her husband's grave not to break her vow of silence, she felt compelled to do so now that she faced her own death. She gave to Grace, who was pregnant with Ruth-Anne at the time, the note revealing her true mother's name – Lily Fairchild. She added that she had been able to discover only two other facts about her identity: she had aristocratic – perhaps even royal – blood in her veins and her mother came from Lambton County, probably Sarnia. While Grace was shocked by the revelation, her life was too crowded with feeling and activity to do much about it. For a long time, watching over her own daughter and her orphling nephew, Sunny, kept her thoughts entirely away from her royal lineage, but as she neared the end of her own life, just as her stepmother had done, she called her daughter to her and passed along the only scraps of information in her possession. Ruth-Anne has asked for Sunny's help in tracing any existing Fairchilds in the County. Mitch Strong, the postmaster, and a librarian friend of his in Sarnia, got hold of several old directories and gazetteers, and Sunny himself searched the registry records. No Fairchild of any sort had ever lived in Lambton. There were, of course, a thousand Lilys. The search came to an abrupt end.

Then only three days before the memorial ceremony, Granny had given Sunny Denfield a gift, a Testament with an inscription made by her father: 'To my dearest princess, the Lady Fairchild'. Excited but hardly knowing what to make of the discovery, Sunny tried to think of someone still alive who might have known Granny Coote or Cora Burgher in the distant past. Prudie suggested Duckface Malloney down at the Sunset Glades in Sarnia. Sunny went to see him and after several hours of frustrating interrogation, he learned conclusively that Cora had once been Mrs. Lily Marshall and before that Miss Lily Ramsbottom, and what-is-more she had lived on a farm near Sarnia about the time of the strange events of 1861. He didn't know why or how yet, but he knew. When Ruth-Anne arrived and he took a good long look at his 'niece', he had no more doubt. After all, blood was blood.

4

Reeve Denfield was about to speak. Moments before, the MLA for Lambton West, awed by the monumental stillness and the hushed crowd, had spoken briefly and from the heart, his prepared speech untouched in his pocket. Granny stood with the wreath in her hand, haloed by the perfume of uprooted flowers, and listened.

The Reeve spoke quietly with a gentle earnestness, the way people do in the sunshine after Sunday service. He reminded them of the things that had gone before: the days when the Attawandarons had roamed freely over territory still unmapped, when the land they were now standing on had been some sort of sacred grave or shaman's ground where prayers and incantations and holy relics had been offered in a language now lost to time and history. He recalled the days when the village site was a mere ordnance ground before the great railroad adventure began. He talked of the coming of the Grand Trunk and the first labourers who hacked a right-of-way through the bush, laid their cross-ties, slept in shacks and stayed on to found a community. He spoke of high hopes, the building of churches and schools, the passion for politics and nation-making, the movement towards villagehood. His tone darkened as he recalled the treacheries of railroad amalgamation, tunnel-construction, the removal of the car-shops. Many in the audience would remember the wagons with their human cargo moving sadly through the secretive mists of early morning, and the vacant neighbourhoods and boarded-up churches. The Reeve went on to talk about the long recovery, the heroic contributions of specific citizens, the struggles against annexation, the new pride of place at last gathering momentum as they faced the second decade of a new century. Sunny's voice continued on as she had heard it so many times over the years and he spoke those sentiments about the War and what it meant in the way he had inadvertently rehearsed them for her.

She too would remember all of these things. But what she would remember most, in whatever years remained to her, was placing around the neck of the little girl now clutching her hand the silver pendant and its cameo sketch of one said to have been a grandmother of her own blood in a far country. Something squeezed her hand. She glanced down. The cameo was turning tenderly on the child's tiny fingers, and as the sunlight struck the ivory profile there from a momentary quartering angle, you might have taken it for a replica of her own. The child's touch then trembled on the silhouette, circled some memory hidden there, and took possession.

Bibliography

Abels, Jules. *Man on Fire: John Brown and the Cause of Liberty.* New York: Macmillan, 1971.

Adventures on the Great Lakes. Coles Canadiana Reprint, Toronto: 1980.

Beasley, David H. *The Canadian Don Quixote: The Life and Works of Major John Richardson, Canada's First Novelist.* Erin, Ontario: The Porcupine's Quill, 1977.

Canada in the Great World War, 7 vols. Toronto: United Publishers, 1920.

Careless, J. M. S. *The Pioneers: An Illustrated History of Early Settlement in Canada.* Toronto: McClelland and Stewart, 1968.

Careless, J. M. S. *The Union of Canadas. 1841-1857,* Toronto: McClelland and Stewart, 1968.

Cellem, Robert. *Visit of HRH The Prince of Wales to the British American Provinces and the United States in the Year 1860.* Toronto: Henry Rowsell, 1861.

Chapman, L.J. and Putnam, D.F. *The Physiography of Southern Ontario,* 2nd ed. Toronto: University of Toronto Press, 1966.

Copleston, Frederick, S. J. *A History of Philosophy: Fitche to Nietzsche,* (vol. 7). Westminster, Maryland: Newman Press, 1965.

County of Lambton Gazetteer and General Business Directory for 1864-65. Ingersoll: Sutherland Brothers, 1864.

Craig, G.M. *Upper Canada: The Formative Years.* Toronto: McClelland and Stewart, 1963.

Creighton, D. G. *John A. Macdonald: The Young Politician.* Toronto: Macmillan, 1952.

Creighton, D. G. *John A. Macdonald: The Old Chieftain.* Toronto: Macmillan, 1955.

Currie, A.W. *The Grand Trunk Railway of Canada.* Toronto: University of Toronto Press, 1957.

Drew, Benjamin. *The Narratives of Fugitive Slaves in Canada.* Boston: John P. Jewitt, 1956.

Edwards, Murray D. *A Stage in Our Past.* Toronto: University of Toronto Press, 1968.

Elford, Jean Turnbull. *A History of Lambton County.* Sarnia: Lambton County Historical Society, 1967.

Evans, Chad. *Frontier Theatre.* Victoria: Sono Nis Press, 1983.

Fowke, Edith. *The Penguin Book of Canadian Folk Songs.* London: Penguin, 1973.

Goodspeed, D.J. *The Road Past Vimy: The Canadian Corps, 1914-1918.* Toronto: Macmillan, 1969.

Guillet, Edwin C. *Early Life in Upper Canada.* Toronto: University of Toronto Press, 1933.

Henry, J. T. *Early and Later History of Petroleum.* New York: Augustus Kelley, 1970.

Higgins, Frank G. *A Physical and Cultural Atlas of Lambton County.* Sarnia: Lambton Historical Society, 1969.

Hill, Daniel G. *The Freedom-Seekers: Blacks in Early Canada.* Toronto: Book Society, 1981.

Howard, John Kinsey. *Strange Empire: The Story of Louis Riel.* Toronto: Swan Publishing, 1965.

Illustrated London, Ontario, Canada, 2nd ed. London, Ontario: London Printing Company, 1900.

Judd, Denis. *Edward VII: A Pictorial Bibliography.* London: Macdonald and Jane's, 1975.

Jury, Elsie McLeod. *The Neutral Indians of South-Western Ontario.* London, Ontario: The University of Western Ontario, 1974.

Landon, Fred. *Western Ontario and the American Frontier.* Toronto: McClelland and Stewart, 1967.

Lauriston, Victor. *Lambton's Hundred Years: 1849-1949.* Sarnia: Corporation for the City of Sarnia, 1949.

Lauriston, Victor. *Romantic Kent.* Chatham: Corporation for the County of Kent, 1952.

The London Free Press: 1849-1922. Canadian Microfilms.

The London Advertiser: 1863-1922. Canadian Microfilms.

McGuffey's Fourth Eclectic Reader. New York: Van Antwerp Bragg, 1979.

Miller, Orlo. *The Point: The History of the Village of Point Edward.* Point Edward: Corporation for the Village of Point Edward, 1978.

Morley, Sheridan. *Oscar Wilde.* London: Wiedenfeld and Nicolson, 1976.

Morton, W. L. *The Critical Years: 1857-1873, The Union of British North America.* Toronto: McClelland and Stewart, 1964.

Morton, W. L. *The Kingdom of Canada*, 2nd ed. Toronto: McClelland and Stewart, 1969.

Mulvaney, Charles P. *The History of the North-West Rebellion.* Toronto: A. H. Hovey, 1885.

Nicholson, G. W. L. *Canadian Expeditionary Force, 1914-1919.* Ottawa: Queen's Printer, 1962.

Nock, O. S. *Railways of Canada.* London: Adam and Charles Black, 1973.

O'Brien, Kevin. *Oscar Wilde in Canada.* Toronto: Personal Library, 1982.

Pen Pictures of Early Pioneer Life in Upper Canada by 'A Canuck'. Toronto: William Briggs, 1905.

Pettigrew, Eileen. *The Silent Enemy: Canada and the Deadly Flu of 1918*. Saskatoon: Western Producer Prairie Books, 1983.

Phelps, Edward and Whipp, Charles. *Petrolia: 1866-1966*. Petrolia: The Petrolia Advertiser-Topic, 1966.

Phillips, C. E. *The Development of Education in Canada*. Toronto: Gage, 1957.

Richardson, John. "A Trip to Walpole Island and Port Sarnia" in *Tecumseh and Richardson*. A. H. U. Colquhoun, ed., Toronto: Ontario Book Company, 1924.

The Sarnia Observer: 1853-1922. Canadian Microfilms.

Siebert, William H. *The Underground Railroad from Slavery to Freedom*. New York: Arno Press, 1968.

Smith, W. H. *Canada: Past, Present and Future*, 2 vols. Toronto: Thomas MacLear, 1850.

Smith's Canadian Gazetteer: 1846. Toronto: William H. Smith, 1846.

Stamp, Robert M. *The Schools of Ontario 1876-1976*. Toronto: University of Toronto Press, 1982.

Stanley, George F. *Canada's Soldiers 1604-1954*. Toronto: Macmillan, 1954.

Stevens, G. R. *Canadian National Railways: Sixty Years of Trial and Error* (vol. 1). Toronto: Clarke Irwin, 1960.

Still, William. *The Underground Railroad*. New York: Arno Press, 1968.

Thomson, Colin. *Blacks in Deep Snow: Black Pioneers in Canada*. Toronto: J. M. Dent, 1979.

The Tour of HRH The Prince of Wales Through British America and the United States. Montreal: John Lovell, 1860.

Trading and Shipping on the Great Lakes. Coles Canadiana Reprint, Toronto: 1980.

Waite, P. B. *Arduous Destiny: Canada, 1874-1896*. Toronto: McClelland and Stewart, 1971.

Walsh, Henry H. *The Christian Church in Canada*. Toronto: Ryerson Press, 1966.

Wilgus, W. J. *The Railway Interrelations of the United States and Canada*. Toronto: Ryerson Press, 1937.

ISBN: 978-1-77084-388-2